YEARS OF GRACE

Years of Grace

BY

Margaret Ayer Barnes

Cherokee Publishing Company
Atlanta, Georgia
1990

Library of Congress Cataloging-in-Publication Data

Barnes, Margaret Ayer, 1886-1967.
    Years of grace / by Margaret Ayer Barnes.
       p.   cm.
    Reprint. Originally published : Boston : Houghton Mifflin, 1930.
    ISBN 0-87797-179-X : $24.95
    I. Title.
    PS3503.A61565Y4   1990
    813'.52--dc20   90-45838
                                                CIP

This book is printed on acid-free paper which conforms to the American National Standard Z39.48-1984 *Permanence of Paper for Printed Library Materials.* Paper that conforms to this standard's requirements for pH, alkaline reserve and freedom from groundwood is anticipated to last several hundred years without significant deterioration under normal library use and storage conditions.

Manufactured in the United States of America

ISBN: 978-0-87797-179-5 Hardcover
ISBN: 978-0-87797-360-7 Paper

Published by arrangement with Houghton Mifflin Co.

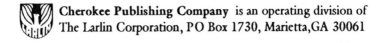 Cherokee Publishing Company is an operating division of The Larlin Corporation, PO Box 1730, Marietta, GA 30061

FOR

C. B.

WHO LISTENED TO IT

CONTENTS

PART I

YEARS OF GRACE

. .

PART I
ANDRÉ

YEARS OF GRACE

. .

PART I

ANDRÉ

CHAPTER I

I

LITTLE Jane Ward sat at her father's left hand at the family
breakfast table, her sleek, brown pigtailed head bent discreetly over her plate. She was washing down great mouthfuls of bacon and eggs with gulps of too hot cocoa. She did
not have to look at the great black clock, surmounted by the
bronze bird, that had stood on the dining-room mantelpiece
ever since she could remember, to know that it was twenty
minutes after eight. If she hurried with her breakfast she
could get off for school before Flora and Muriel called to walk
up with her. If she could escape them she could meet André,
loitering nonchalantly near the Water Works Tower, and
walk up with him. She could walk up with him anyway, of
course, but, with Flora and Muriel fluttering and giggling at
her elbow, it would not be quite the same.

Her father was buried behind the far-flung pages of the
'Chicago Tribune.' Her mother sat behind the coffee tray,
immaculately clad in a crisp white dressing-sack, her pretty,
proud little head held high above the silver urn, her eyes
wandering competently over the breakfast table. Her sister,
Isabel, was not yet down. Her sister Isabel was nineteen.
Grown up. Her school days behind her. A young lady.

About to become a débutante. Old enough to loiter, unrebuked, in bed, after a late party, until her father had left for the office and Jane was well on her way to school.

'Jane,' said her mother tranquilly, 'don't take such large mouthfuls.' Jane was not grown up. Jane was still fourteen. Young enough to be rebuked for almost anything, including table manners.

'What's the hurry, Kid?' said her father cheerfully, lowering the margins of the paper. He was nearly always cheerful. His brown eyes twinkled as they rested on Jane. They usually did.

'I want to get off to school early,' said Jane plausibly. 'I want to meet Agnes.'

'Agnes!' exclaimed her mother with a little fretful shrug. 'Always, Agnes!'

That was all, but it was quite enough. Jane knew very well that her mother did not approve of Agnes Johnson. And Jane knew why. With the crystal clarity of fourteen-year-old perception, Jane knew why all too well. It was because Agnes lived west of Lincoln Park and her father was a newspaper reporter and her mother worked in an office. Her mother was somebody's secretary. There was something unforgivable in that.

Her mother did approve, now, of Flora Furness and Muriel Lester. She approved of them wholeheartedly. They lived just around the corner, Flora on Rush Street, in a big brown stone house with lilac bushes in the yard, and Muriel on Huron, in a grey stone fortress, built by Richardson, the great Eastern architect. Muriel gave a party every Christmas vacation. A dancing party, with white crash laid down over the parlor carpet and an orchestra, hidden in palms, beneath the stairs. Flora's house was very large and lovely. It had belonged to her grandfather. It had a big ballroom, tucked away under its mansard roof and there was a tiger-skin rug in the front hall and gold furniture in the drawing-room and a conservatory, opening off the library, with hanging Boston ferns and a real orange tree and two grey parrots in a gilded cage.

Her mother liked Jane to walk to school with Flora and Muriel. She liked her to have them over to play. She had always liked it, from the days of their first paper dolls. There were things that were wrong with Flora and Muriel, too. But they were subtle things that didn't seem to make much difference. Nevertheless they caused comment. Comment, at least, from her mother and Isabel. Jane had sensed them always, without exactly understanding.

There was something wrong with Flora's mother, who was perhaps the prettiest, and certainly the most fashionable lady that Jane had ever seen. She was always going out to parties, sweeping out of her front door in rustling draperies, slipping through the crowd of staring children on the sidewalk, wafting a kiss to Flora, and vanishing into the depths of her little blue brougham that waited at the curb. She had a pug for a lap dog and drove out every spring and summer afternoon in a dark blue victoria, with two men up, behind a pair of spanking bays, with a little tiptilted sunshade of black lace held over her tiny flowered toque of violets. She had always the pug with her, and never Flora, and sometimes a gentleman called Mr. Bert Lancaster, who led cotillions and danced with Isabel occasionally at parties and skated with her sometimes on the Superior Street rink, and made her very happy when he did.

There was something wrong with all Muriel's family, though her eldest sister, Edith, had been the belle of last winter and her second sister, Rosalie, was going to be the belle of this and had been with Isabel at Farmington and was one of Isabel's dearest friends. This wrong was easier to fathom. It was because their name was Lester, though every one knew that it had once been Leischer, and their grandfather, old Solomon Lester, made no bones about it at all, but was just frankly Hebraic, so every one said who had met him in New York.

Jane knew all this and had always known it. She could not have said how. She was acutely conscious of everything that her mother approved or disapproved. And now that Isabel had come home from Farmington and was frankly recognized as some one to be listened to, Jane was acutely conscious of her opinions, too. It never occurred to her to agree or disagree with them, consciously. There they were. Opinions. Jane bumped into them, tangible obstacles in her path, things to be recognized, and accepted or evaded, as the exigencies of the situation demanded. Just now she didn't bother at all about Agnes. Jane was very fond of Agnes, but Agnes was, for the moment, a pretext.

'May I be excused?' she asked meekly.

'Use your finger bowl,' said her mother abstractedly.

'What's the rush, Kid?' asked her father again. 'Done your algebra?'

Her algebra was Jane's *bête noire*. She never told her teacher how much her father helped her. She nodded, rising.

'Understand that last quadratic equation?'

Jane nodded again and kissed her mother good-bye.

'Keep that frock clean,' said her mother. 'Don't climb on fences.'

Jane kissed her father. His face was lean and hard and smelled of shaving-soap. His cheeks were always very smooth in the morning.

'Good-bye, Kid. I see in the paper that the Gilbert and Sullivan operas are coming. We'll have to see "The Mikado."'

Jane flushed with pleasure. Even André was forgotten. Jane had only been to the theatre four times before in all her life. Once when she was very young to see Elsie Leslie in 'Little Lord Fauntleroy' and twice to see Joseph Jefferson in 'Rip van Winkle' and once last year to hear Calvé in 'Carmen,' with all the family, because there was an extra seat, on Thanksgiving afternoon.

'Really, Papa? Honestly?' Her face was shining. Then she heard the doorbell ring. Her heart sank, in spite of her glowing prospects. That was Flora and Muriel at the front door, of course. Minnie, the waitress, went to open it. There was a shuffle, a whispered joke, and a giggle in the hall. It was certainly Flora and Muriel. Jane walked slowly out of the room.

'I wish that child would drop Agnes Johnson,' she heard her mother say and caught the irritated rustle of her father's paper in reply.

'Just a jiffy!' she called, and raced upstairs, two steps at a time, for her home work.

'Don't wake Isabel!' called her mother.

When Jane came downstairs again her father was struggling into his coat in the front hall. Flora and Muriel sat mutely on the bench beneath the hatrack, school books in hand. Minnie handed her her lunch for recess. A little wicker basket with a leather strap, containing two jelly sandwiches, Jane knew, and a piece of cake and her favorite banana.

Flora and Muriel rose to meet her. Her father was humming, gaily, regarding the children before him with a benevolent smile. As they reached the front door he broke into jocular song.

> 'Three little maids from school are we,
> Pert as a school girl well can be,
> Filled to the brim with girlish glee,
> Three little maids from school!'

Flora and Muriel were regarding him dispassionately. Jane was just a little bit ashamed of him. In the presence of her contemporaries, Jane felt almost grown up. Her father opened the door for them with mock ceremony.

> 'Everything is a source of fun.
> Nobody's safe for we care for none.'

He tweaked her pigtails affectionately.

> 'Life is a joke that's just begun!
> Three little maids from school!'

They were out and had run down the steps before he could go any further. Jane's sense of embarrassment had deepened. Flora was fifteen and was already talking of putting up her golden curls. Muriel had a real suit, with a skirt and Eton jacket, and her dresses reached almost to her boot tops. It was too bad of her father. The song wasn't so very funny, after all. Nor so very true.

Life didn't seem at all a joke to Jane as she skipped down Pine Street, that crisp October morning, arm in arm with her friends. She was wondering whether André would be waiting under the Water Works Tower. And whether Flora and Muriel would try to tease them if he were. And what he would think, if they did. And what her mother would say if she knew that André was waiting almost every morning, when she reached Chicago Avenue, waiting to walk up the Drive with her carrying her school books. Funny French André, whom Flora and Muriel always laughed at, a little, and of whom her mother and Isabel didn't at all approve, because he was French and a Roman Catholic and went to church in the Holy Name Cathedral and lived in a little flat in the Saint James Apartments and had an English mother who wore a funny-looking feather boa and a French father who was a consul, whatever that was, and spoke broken English and didn't know many people.

Muriel was talking of Rosalie's coming-out party. There was to be a reception and a dinner and a dance and Muriel was going to sit up for it and have a new pink muslin dress, ordered from Hollander's in New York.

Isabel was going to have a reception, too, but no dinner, as far as Jane knew, and certainly no dance. Jane's clothes were all made on the third floor by Miss McKelvey, who came twice every year, spring and fall, for two weeks, taking possession of the sewing machine in the playroom and turning out an incredible number of frocks and reefers and white percale petticoats with eyelet embroidery. She made lots of Isabel's dresses, too, and some of Jane's mother's. And doll clothes, on the side, for Jane, though Jane was too old for that, now. She hadn't looked at her doll for nearly two years. That wonderful French doll with real hair and eyes that opened and shut, that her mother had brought her from Paris on the memorable occasion, five years before, of her trip abroad.

Jane had always loved Miss McKelvey from the days that she used to ride on her knees when she wound the bobbins. And she always liked her new clothes. It was only when Flora and Muriel talked of theirs that it occurred to her to disparage them. Flora and Muriel had lovely things. Dresses from New York and coats made at real tailors'. But Jane didn't want them, really. At least she wouldn't have wanted them if Flora and Muriel had only let her alone. She hadn't wanted them, at all, until she had met André. Now she couldn't help wondering what André would think if he could see her at a real dance, some evening, in a pink muslin dress from Hollander's. Of course she and André didn't go to dances. But there would be the Christmas parties and if she *had* a pink muslin, just hanging idle in the closet, perhaps she could wear it to dancing school or even to supper, some Saturday night at André's, if he ever asked her again and her mother would let her go.

Not that a mere pink muslin could ever make Jane look like Muriel. Jane knew that all too well. Or like Flora. She hadn't any curls, to begin with, and she simply couldn't look stylish. The way Isabel did, for instance, in any old rag. Isabel was just as pretty as Muriel's sisters, no matter what she wore.

There was André, school books in hand, loitering under the Water Works Tower. He grinned a little sheepishly as the trio approached him. Flora and Muriel were pinching her elbows.

'Don't be *silly!*' she implored.

'*He's* silly!' tittered Flora.

'No, he's not!' she declared hotly.

They only giggled.

'Well, anyway, he's sissy,' said Muriel accusingly. 'Why doesn't he play with the other boys?'

By this time they had reached him.

'Hello,' said André.

'Hello,' said Jane.

He took her school books. Flora shook her curls at him. They shone like burnished gold against the rough chinchilla cloth of her navy blue reefer. Muriel rolled her great blue eyes under her wide hat brim. Her eyelashes were very long and curly and her cheeks were rose red in the sharp lake breeze. André grinned. He dropped into step at Jane's elbow. They walked half a block in silence. Almost in silence. Jane could hear Muriel's stifled giggles. Then Flora leaned mockingly forward. She looked across Muriel's mirthful countenance to Jane's disdainful one and then on, to André's cold young profile.

'I'll race you to the corner, Muriel,' she said wickedly. Muriel dropped Jane's elbow.

'Two's company!' she heard Muriel cry as they set off in a rush. Jane felt a little foolish. Then André glanced shyly down at her. He met her eyes and smiled. She looked hurriedly away, but she knew, instantly, that everything was all right. Let them be silly. It didn't matter. And she *did* want to talk to André. André talked of things she liked. André had seen lots of plays, here and in New York and in Paris. And André had lived abroad. He had been born in Fontainebleau and he had visited in London and he had crossed the ocean three times since his father had come to America. André had read everything and he had a little puppet theatre and an awfully good stamp collection and a work shop in his bedroom where he modelled in clay and made some very clever things, book-ends and paper-weights and statues, that his father had cast, sometimes, for his mother to keep. André went to a class every Saturday morning at the Art Institute. A life class, so Flora and Muriel had said with a telling titter. Jane devoutly hoped her mother wouldn't hear of that.

André was sixteen and he wasn't going to college. Not to Harvard or Yale or Princeton, at least, where the other boys were going. He wasn't even going to boarding school. He was just going to go on studying in Chicago and taking courses at the Art Institute until he went back to Paris. He was going back, when he was nineteen, to study at the Sorbonne, whatever that was, and try to get in the Beaux Arts. He was putting on a play called 'Camille,' now, in his puppet theatre. He wanted Jane to help him. That was what he was talking about.

He talked so long and so interestingly that they were actually in front of the school before Jane realized it. There was Agnes, sitting on the front steps. She waved cheerfully at André, her funny freckled face wreathed in smiles. Agnes liked André and Agnes was never silly. She knew just how

Jane felt about him and still she didn't think that there was anything to laugh at. Out of the corner of her eye Jane could see Flora and Muriel up at the front window, pointing André out to some other girls. He saw them, too, of course, but he didn't seem to care. André never did care if people thought things. Jane always did. She wished he'd leave her at the corner every morning, half a block from the school, but she didn't want to tell him so. For most of all she cared what André thought. She knew André awfully well, of course, but not well enough to tell him a thing like that.

The first bell rang while he was talking with Agnes. Jane slipped her arm through hers and turned toward the door.

'See you after lunch,' said André, cap in hand. 'If you could manage to come over about half-past two we could paint the first set. Mother told me to ask you to tea.'

Jane only smiled and nodded, but she walked into the study hall in a thrill of anticipation. Tea with André. His mother had asked her. She wouldn't tell her mother. She would just go. Jane's eyes were dancing behind her lowered eyelids as ancient Miss Milgrim read the Beatitudes and the Lord's Prayer over the bowed heads of the assembled school. She was almost laughing aloud as she rose for the morning hymn. Her thin little voice shrilled up to Heaven's gates in purely secular ecstasy.

> 'Rejoice, ye pure in heart!
> Rejoice, give thanks and sing!
> Your glorious banner raise on high
> The cross of Christ, your King!'

She was going to tea with André.

> 'Rejoice! Rejoice! Rejoice, give thanks and sing!'

André was waiting for her on the steps of the Saint James Apartments at half-past two. He wore a funny navy-blue béret on his sleek black hair and he was spinning a top. No other Chicago boy of sixteen ever spun a top and Jane had never seen any other béret. That was the kind of thing that André did that made Flora and Muriel think that he was sissy. Jane wished he wouldn't. She liked to spin tops herself and the béret was most becoming. Still, there was no sense in wilfully laying yourself open to mockery. Flora and Muriel had no idea how nice André really was.

They went upstairs in the elevator and André's mother opened the front door. André's mother had only one servant and that one was often out. The children entered the little crowded living-room. There were lots of books in it, filling the walls from floor to ceiling. Not nice volumes in neat, uniform sets of sombre leather, as in Jane's own father's library or in Flora's grandfather's, but all sorts and sizes of books in all kinds of variegated bindings, some quite dilapidated, set haphazard on the shelves. There were some sets, of course. A long line of bound 'Punch,' for instance, and many more 'Arabian Nights' than Jane had ever known there were, and a red row of nearly thirty volumes by Guy de Maupassant. Jane had never heard of *him*.

André's mother had been reading in the big green Morris chair in the bay window that looked down Rush Street, all the way to the river. The book still lay in the chair seat. It was a French book, called 'Madame Bovary.' André's mother saw Jane looking at it.

'You'll like that book, Jane,' she said, 'when you're older.'

That was the way André's family always spoke of books. Just as if they were people living in the world with you, nice friendly people, whom you were bound to meet some day and get on famously with when you finally knew them.

Jane followed André into his little bedroom. His paints were all set out on a table with some sheets of Bristol board.

'I saw Bernhardt do "Camille" in Paris, last summer,' said

André eagerly. 'And I remember all her sets. We can make ours just the same.'

Jane sat down beside André at the little table, feeling a little flushed and excited to think that this was really André's very own room. She had been in it several times before, of course, but it made her feel that funny way inside every time. André was very near her, just across the paint water. He went on talking about Sarah Bernhardt most enthusiastically, but there was something about his very enthusiasm that made Jane think that perhaps he was feeling funny too. Terribly happy and excited and just a little nervous, as she was herself. But then they fell to discussing colours and later to painting and André grew lost in his work, as he always did, and Jane applauded him and was very much interested and greatly surprised when André's mother stood in the doorway and said it was half-past four and time for tea.

Jane had never known any one who had tea, regularly, every day, like breakfast, lunch, and dinner, except André's family. Jane's mother had it on Wednesdays, when lots of ladies came to call, and now that Isabel was home from school, she had it on Sundays, too, for hordes of young men in frock coats, who came early and lingered late. The last of them usually stayed to supper and hymn-singing around the Steinway upright in the parlor.

But those teas were parties, with candy and three kinds of cake and funny fishy little sandwiches that Minnie made meticulously in the pantry. The tea-table was always set with the silver tray and the silver tea-set and lots of little Dresden plates and embroidered napkins and Jane's mother and Isabel were always all dressed up in their best bib and tucker, sitting primly behind the tea-kettle, never dreaming of eating anything until the doorbell rang.

André's tea was very different. His mother presided non-

chalantly from the depths of the Morris armchair over a gold
and white china tea-set and there was nothing to eat except
very thin slices of bread and butter and a plate of sponge cake,
untidily torn to pieces. That sponge cake, André's mother explained as Jane's eyes widened at the sight of it, was a
spécialité de la maison. It seemed you couldn't cut it without
spoiling it. A funny kind of cake, Jane thought, to serve for
tea. But very good.

André's father came in just before the bread and butter was
finished. Mr. Duroy was a little grey-haired Frenchman, with
wise brown eyes that glittered behind his *pince-nez* eyeglasses.
The glasses balanced precariously on his aquiline nose and he
was continually taking them off and waving them about as he
talked. They were fastened to his coat lapel with a narrow
black ribbon, which made him look very unlike other men.
A shred of scarlet silk was always run through his buttonhole.
Jane never knew why.

He talked a great deal and so did André's mother. But not
at all as Jane's family did. Never about people. People you
knew, at least. This afternoon he was talking very excitedly
about something called the Dual Alliance and a Frenchman
named Alexandre Ribot who was Président du Conseil, whatever that might be, and seemed to be doing something important about France and Russia. Mr. Duroy had a great
deal to say about Mr. Ribot, though he didn't seem to know
him. The only people that Jane could ever remember hearing her family talk about whom they did not know were
Benjamin Harrison and Grover Cleveland. And these gentlemen never provoked her mother and Isabel to utterance. Her
father occasionally made statements about them that always
passed unchallenged, André's mother, now, had views of her
own on Mr. Ribot.

Jane and André didn't talk at all, but before she knew it

the clock struck six and Jane realized that she should have gone home long ago. She rose a little shyly. Jane never knew just how to leave a party.

'I must lend you "Camille," ' said André and plucked the book, in a yellow paper cover, from off the bookshelves. 'La Dame aux Camellias' was printed on the outside. 'Mother is going to help me do a good translation. See if you don't like it.'

Jane privately hoped that she knew enough French to read it, with a dictionary.

'André will walk home with you,' said André's mother.

And indeed it was very dark. Jane didn't know what her mother would say, if she were home. Of course she might be out with Isabel. They were very busy these days with parties and dressmakers.

The street lamps were flickering on their tall standards as they stepped out on Chicago Avenue. The drugstore windows across the street in the Kinzie flats glittered with yellow light. Great green and red and blue urns of coloured water glowed behind the glass.

'Pure colour,' said André. 'Pure as light.'

He took her arm as they crossed the car tracks. Jane held her elbow very stiff and straight but she felt a little thrill run right up her arm from where his fingers rested on her coat sleeve. He was looking at her face and he was very near her, but Jane didn't turn her head. When they reached the further curbstone he dropped her arm, at once. Jane felt awfully happy.

'I'll try to find those pictures of Bernhardt for you,' said André. 'They're around somewhere in an old copy of "Le Théâtre." If you *could* copy them for the puppet ——'

'I'd love to,' said Jane. 'I can make her hair of ravelled yarn.'

'Golden brown,' said André, 'and very frizzy. She has beautiful hair.'

They walked in silence for a few minutes. Pine Street was very empty and very quiet. A hansom cab went by, the horse's feet clapping sharply on the cedar block pavement. A belated errand boy whizzed past on a bicycle. He trilled his bell shrilly for the Superior Street corner. Jane was thinking how dark and straight her pigtails were. Her hair was so fine that it didn't show for much, except just after a shampoo. She wished, terribly, that she had Flora's red-gold tresses. Or Muriel's seven black finger curls. Or this Bernhardt's golden-brown frizz, that she had never seen and André so admired.

He took her arm again for the next crossing.

'I know you'll copy her beautifully,' he said. And Jane felt happy once more. Warm and glowing, deep down inside.

When they reached her house André lingered a moment on the pavement, under the big bare elm tree.

'I — I had a lovely time,' said Jane.

'You'll read the play?' said André. 'And come again to-morrow?'

Jane nodded. There was a little pause. André moved about a bit. The street was very dark. The street lights were on the corners.

'Will you — will you dance the Hallowe'en cotillion with me at dancing-school?' said André.

Jane's heart leaped up in ecstasy.

'Oh,' she said softly, 'I — I'd love to.'

'All right,' said André. 'That's fine.' He lingered a moment longer. 'Well — good-night,' he said, taking off the béret.

Jane ran up the front steps and rang a peal of triumph on

the doorbell. She skipped up and down in the vestibule waiting for the door to open. Unconsciously she hummed a fragment of her father's morning song.

'Life is a joke that's just begun!' she carolled, as Minnie stood on the threshold. The words, at the moment, had for her no meaning. She was just singing.

II

Jane had no time to read 'La Dame aux Camellias' that night. Her home work was very long. She looked it over, translating a line here and there, hoping in vain for pictures, before she went to bed. She left it on her table next morning when she started out for school.

André had the copy of 'Le Théâtre' under his arm when she met him under the Water Works Tower. They sat down on a green bench in the little public park to inspect it. Flora and Muriel went on ahead. There were four pictures of Bernhardt. Three of her as Camille and one in a play called 'Phèdre.' In 'Phèdre' she wore a Greek costume and a chiffon veil was over her frizzy hair. But in 'Camille' Jane could see clearly just how lovely it was. There was one of her dying, on a kind of sofa, with her curls straying out all over the pillows. No wonder that André thought it was beautiful. Jane thought she could copy the costumes. André remembered all the colours.

She told Agnes about the play at recess and Agnes was very much thrilled. She took special pains with her French that morning and learned one extra irregular verb. She hoped it would appear in 'Camille,' in one of its most unusual tenses. She decided, quite firmly, to work hard on the grammar that winter and really learn to speak the language. Perhaps when she and André had done Camille he might ask her to do Phèdre, too. She talked about that possibility very seriously with Agnes after school. So long and so seriously that she was just a little late in getting home for luncheon.

Her mother and Isabel were already seated at the dining-room table. The homely odour of fried ham greeted her nostrils as soon as she entered the room. She flung her books on a chair. She was pleasantly hungry.

'Gosh, I had fun in school to-day,' she said.

Then she noticed that something was wrong. She would have noticed it sooner if she hadn't been thinking so intently of the joys in store for her.

'You're very late,' said Isabel.

Jane sat down and unfolded her napkin. Minnie passed the ham. No one said anything more for a moment. The silence was very forbidding.

'Jane,' said her mother presently, 'where did you get the book that I found on your table this morning?'

Jane dropped her knife and fork. She was extremely surprised.

'Wha — what book?' she asked, instinctively playing for time.

'That French book,' said her mother, and her tone spoke volumes.

Jane stared at her in silence.

'Where *on earth* did you find it?' asked Isabel.

Jane's great brown eyes turned on her sister.

'Answer Mother, Jane.' The tone brooked no delay. Jane's eyes returned to the head of the table.

'From — from André,' she said. Her voice, in her own ears, sounded strangely husky.

'*André!*' said her mother, staring at Isabel. '*That* explains it.'

'You don't mean to say,' said Isabel, 'that *André* gave you that book?'

'Yes,' said Jane with difficulty.

'What *for?*' said her mother. The last word was really almost a shriek.

'To — to read,' said Jane.

Isabel and her mother exchanged a glance of horror.

'Well — honestly ——' said Isabel.

'Have you read it?' asked her mother.

'No,' said Jane. Her ear caught their little gasps of relief. She didn't understand at all. She only knew that she and André and their perfect plan were in some dreadful danger. She must try to explain.

'He's going to give it in his theatre, Mamma,' she went on hurriedly. 'He wants me to help him. He wants me to make the costumes. We're going ——'

Her mother and Isabel exchanged another glance of horror.

'What's the *matter?*' cried Jane, her nerves breaking under the strain. 'What's *happened?*'

Her mother smiled at her very kindly.

'Nothing has happened, Jane. I'm very glad you haven't read the book. It's not at all a nice book for a child to read. But we'll just return it to André to-day. You needn't think anything more about it.'

'But Mamma!' cried Jane. 'You — you can't do that! Why — why we've made all our plans — I was going over there this afternoon — we've almost finished the first set — he ——'

'It doesn't make any difference *what* you've done, Jane,' said her mother firmly, 'or what you've planned. It's not a nice book for a little girl to read and ——'

'Have *you* read it?' asked Jane rudely. And she meant to be rude. She knew her mother couldn't read French. Isabel herself couldn't read it, half as well as Jane could.

'You don't have to *read* books, Jane,' said her mother with dignity, 'to know that they shouldn't be read. This book is very unpleasant.'

'Why, it's notorious!' said Isabel.

'Isabel!' said her mother.

Jane felt very confused.

'If you haven't read it, Mamma,' she said reasonably, 'don't you think that perhaps you've made a mistake? André's mother saw him give it to me. She's going to help us with the play.'

She saw at once that she hadn't helped her cause at all.

'Honestly!' said Isabel again. 'Those frogs!'

'French people,' said her mother, once more with dignity, 'don't feel about these things the way we do. They have very different ideas of right and wrong.'

'André's mother is English.' said Jane sullenly.

'She married a Frenchman,' said Isabel, as if that settled it.

'We won't discuss it further,' said Jane's mother. 'Eat your lunch.'

'*Mamma!*' cried Jane in desperation. 'You don't understand. I — I can't go back on André! I can't ——'

'Jane,' said her mother. 'You will eat your lunch. And then you will call up André and tell him that you can't have anything to do with the play and that you can't go over there this afternoon. I'll send Minnie over with the book. I don't want you to go over to André's any more at all. You've been seeing far too much of him lately. Any boy that would give a little girl a book like that ——'

But Jane had sprung to her feet.

'I *won't* eat my lunch!' she cried. 'And I *won't* call up André! I think you're too mean! You don't understand! You don't understand *any*thing!' Her voice was breaking. She *wouldn't* cry before them! She rushed from the room.

'It's a long time,' she heard her mother say, as she reached the door, 'since Jane has had a tantrum.'

She stumbled up the stairs. She gained the refuge of her bedroom and banged the door. The book was gone. She couldn't go to André's. She couldn't help him with that play. She flung herself on her bed in stormy tears.

It wasn't very long before the door opened and Isabel entered, without a knock. Jane lay very still and tried to hush her sobs.

'Don't be silly, Kid,' said Isabel. She sat down on the bed.

'Don't talk to me,' said Jane.

'Stop crying,' said Isabel reasonably, 'and be sensible.'

There was a little pause.

'That's a dreadful play, Jane,' said Isabel.

Jane didn't reply.

'Sarah Bernhardt does it,' said Isabel. 'She's an awful woman.'

Jane lay very still.

'When she was here,' said Isabel, 'none of us girls were allowed to see her. She's not nice.'

Jane sat up. André's reverent accents still rang in her ears.

'She has beautiful hair,' thought Jane. 'Golden brown — and frizzy.'

'What do you mean by "not nice"?' she inquired indignantly.

Isabel's face looked a little queer. She was watching her younger sister rather curiously.

'Immoral,' said Isabel finally.

'I don't believe it,' said Jane, after a moment.

'Oh, yes, she is,' said Isabel easily. 'Every one knows that.'

Jane stared, unconvinced. Isabel was still looking at her in that funny way.

'Don't you know what I mean?' said Isabel.

There was an awful pause. Jane wasn't sure that she did. But it sounded dreadful.

'I — don't — believe — it,' said Jane slowly. 'André said ——'

'French people are different,' said Isabel. 'They don't mind things like that.'

'They're *not* different!' said Jane. But of course she knew that they were. Not different like that, though. Whatever it was, if it were true, André *couldn't* know it.

'Now, don't be silly, Jane,' said Isabel once more. 'Minnie's keeping your lunch. Go down and eat it and then telephone André and tell him.'

'I *can't* tell him!' wailed Jane.

'Well — you can tell him something,' said Isabel plausibly. 'You can tell him that Mamma doesn't want you to stay indoors on such a bright afternoon.'

'Do you want me to *lie* to him?' said Jane.

'Well, Jane!' Isabel was actually laughing. 'You wouldn't tell him the truth, would you?'

'I won't lie to André,' said Jane. 'Besides, Mamma ——'

'Oh, Mamma'll get over it. She won't care what you say as long as you don't go.'

The door opened again. Jane's mother stood on the threshold.

'Don't be silly, Jane,' she said.

Jane wiped her eyes.

'Go down and eat your lunch!' She patted Jane very nicely on the shoulder. They all turned toward the door.

'Isabel,' said her mother, halfway down the hall, 'I can't find that book *any*where. I left it on my desk.'

'Oh!' said Isabel, and her voice sounded a bit confused. 'It's in my room. I started to bring it downstairs for you.'

Jane looked through Isabel's door. There was the little

yellow volume on the sofa, with Jane's own French dictionary beside it. Jane despised Isabel, for a moment. Her mother picked up the volume gingerly as if it burned her fingers.

'I never expected to see,' she said, 'a paper-covered French book in this house.'

'*All* French books have paper covers,' Jane began. André had told her that. But of course it was no use. She didn't go on with it. Instead she went downstairs and tried to eat her lunch at the pantry table beneath the telephone, thinking of what she had better say to André.

The telephone was very new. It had only been put in that autumn and Jane usually thought it was lots of fun to use it. But she didn't think so now. When she had eaten her ham and one preserved peach she stood before it quite a little time in silence before she gave André's number.

He answered the call himself. She knew his voice immediately. His funny telephone voice, trickling so miraculously into her ear, when he was four long city blocks away.

'Hello, Jane,' he said.

She didn't waste any time on preliminaries.

'I can't come over,' she said miserably.

'Why not?' said André.

Jane gulped a little before she could reply.

'Mamma — Mamma ——' she began weakly. How *could* she tell him?

'I don't hear you,' said André.

'Mamma,' said Jane desperately. She *couldn't* tell him. 'Mamma wants me to play out of doors — it's such a nice day.'

'Oh,' said André. He sounded very sorry. 'Well — perhaps we could take a walk by the lake.'

Jane fell a prey to panic. This was what always happened when you lied.

'I — I can't,' she said very quickly. 'I — I'm going over to Flora's.'

'Oh,' said André. And his voice sounded just a little queer.

'We — are going to play in her yard,' said Jane.

'I see,' said André.

'I — I'll see you to-morrow,' said Jane.

He didn't answer.

'Won't I?' asked Jane pitifully.

'Oh, yes,' said André. 'Yes. I — I'll be waiting.'

'Well, good-bye,' said Jane.

'Good-bye,' said André. 'I'm awfully sorry.'

Jane hung up the receiver. She felt perfectly miserable. She had lied to André. She despised Isabel, yet she'd taken her advice. And he hadn't believed her. He hadn't believed her at all. He had known she was lying. Jane was plunged in despair. Well — at least she could go over to Flora's. She could make that lie come true.

Flora's front door was opened by Flora's butler. Jane always felt a little uneasy with butlers but she knew this one very well. He had been with the Furnesses for years. Not like Muriel's butlers who changed every month or so. He smiled reassuringly down at Jane.

'Miss Flora is upstairs,' he said. All Flora's servants called her 'Miss Flora.' It was very impressive. At home every one said just 'Jane.'

Jane walked very softly down Flora's hall, skirting the black walnut furniture with care. The floor was very slippery and the tiger skin rug before the fireplace snarled with its *papier maché* jaws and glared with its yellow glass eyes in a very realistic manner.

At the foot of the stairs she met Flora's mother. She was beautifully dressed in a dark green velvet gown, with leg-of-mutton sleeves of lighter green taffeta, and her little blond

head was held very high and topped with a tortoise-shell
comb, tipped sideways in her hair. She was running down
the stairs very quickly, with her little tan pug behind her, and
her cheeks were very pink and her eyes were very bright, and
when she saw Jane she stopped and laughed as if she were
just so happy she had to laugh at every one.

'Hello, little Jane!' she said.

At the sound of her voice some one came out of the drawing-room. It was Mr. Bert Lancaster. He looked very tall
and handsome, Jane thought. She didn't wonder that Isabel
liked to dance with him. His moustache was beautiful and
he had a black pearl in his necktie. He walked at once up to
Flora's mother. He took her hand as if he liked to hold it.
Flora's mother looked happier than ever.

'This is little Jane Ward,' she said.

'Hello, little Jane Ward,' laughed Mr. Bert Lancaster. He,
too, looked as if he were so happy that he had to laugh at
every one.

Flora's mother stooped over and kissed Jane's cheek. Her
face felt very smooth and soft and it smelled of flowers. Mr.
Bert Lancaster was watching her. Then she picked up the
pug and held it tenderly in her arms and kissed the top of its
little tan head and looked up at Mr. Lancaster over its black
muzzle. They turned away from Jane toward the drawing-
room door.

'I told you not to come 'til four,' said Flora's mother, still
smiling up at Mr. Lancaster over the pug. Jane couldn't hear
his reply.

'Silly!' said Flora's mother, as he held the brocade portières
aside for her at the drawing-room door. She passed through
them, looking over her shoulder at Mr. Lancaster. He followed her rustling train. Jane ran upstairs to Flora's bedroom.

Flora's bedroom was beautiful. All blue and white, with white-painted furniture and a little brass bed and real silver brushes and mirrors on her little dressing-table. Jane had no dressing-table. She kept a wooden brush and a celluloid comb and a steel nail file in her upper bureau drawer. Flora had two heart-shaped silver picture frames, too. In one was her mother, smiling over a feather fan in a lovely light evening gown, with pearls on her throat and long white gloves running up her arms to her great puffy sleeves. In the other frame was Flora's father. He looked a little silly in that silver heart. Fat-faced and bald-headed and solemn. It was a very good picture, though. That was just the way he always looked, on the rare occasions when Jane ran into him in Flora's hall.

Flora wasn't doing much of anything. Jane explained that she had come to play in the yard. Flora said that was fine. Muriel was coming over and they could go out to the playhouse.

The playhouse was a tiny structure, out near the stable, the scene of all their childish frolics. They didn't use it to play in now, of course, but Flora sometimes made candy on the little cooking-stove and she and Jane and Muriel always liked to talk there undisturbed.

'We'll make fudge,' said Flora.

'Mamma wants me to be out-of-doors,' said Jane, still trying to make that lie come true.

'We'll leave the windows open,' said Flora.

Jane decided that would be true enough. They ran down the back stairs and got some things from the cook and went out the side door by the lilac bushes. Muriel was just coming around the corner.

Jane began to feel much better as soon as she measured out the chocolate and sugar. She thought she could explain to André to-morrow morning. She thought he would understand. Mothers were mothers. You weren't responsible for what they thought or what they made you do.

Flora's fire began to burn almost immediately. The scent of cooking chocolate permeated the air. Muriel's pink muslin had come from Hollander's. It had real lace on the bertha. She was going to have some high-heeled slippers.

'Hello!' said Flora suddenly. 'There's André.'

There was André, indeed, loitering a little aimlessly by the iron fence. Muriel immediately began to giggle. Jane rushed to the playhouse door.

'Yoo-hoo, André!' she called ecstatically. 'Come on over!'

He vaulted the fence at a bound. Jane ran out to meet him.

'Oh, André,' she said, 'I'm terribly glad you came!'

He looked pleased, but he didn't say anything.

'We're making candy,' said Jane.

'André! Do you like fudge?' shrieked Flora from the doorway.

'You bet,' said André. Muriel went right on giggling. Jane walked with André into the playhouse. How good the chocolate smelled! Jane felt *she* liked fudge, as never before.

She told him all about it, an hour later. He was walking home with her down Erie Street, in the last red rays of the October sun. It was awfully hard to lead up to it. Suddenly she took the plunge.

'I — I'm afraid I can't do "Camille" with you, André,' she said.

He stopped quite still on the pavement.

'Why not?' he asked.

Jane felt her cheeks growing very hot and red.

'Mamma — Mamma doesn't want me to,' she said.

'Why not?' asked André again.

Jane looked miserably away from him.

'She — she doesn't like the play.'

André looked extremely astonished.

'Why,' he said finally, 'she — she *must* like it. Every one likes "Camille."'

'Mamma doesn't,' said Jane. There it was. That was all there was to say.

'Do you mean to tell me,' said André hotly, 'that she won't *let* you do it?'

Jane nodded unhappily. André looked extremely puzzled.

'Well, then,' he said finally, 'I guess you can't.'

Jane's heart leaped up with gratitude. He *did* understand. Mothers were mothers. But there was still the lie.

'André ——' said Jane, and stopped.

'Yes?' said André. It was terribly difficult.

'André,' said Jane again and her voice was very low. She couldn't look at him. 'I — I didn't tell you the truth, over the telephone.'

André didn't say anything.

'Mamma *didn't* say I had to play out-of-doors this afternoon. I — I was scared to tell you what she really said.'

'Why?' said André very seriously.

Jane felt her eyes fill with tears.

'Because,' said Jane, and her lips were trembling, 'I didn't know what you'd think of me.'

André saw the tears. He looked awfully embarrassed and terribly kind.

'That's all right, Jane,' said André. She was smiling straight up at him through the tears. 'I guess you know I'll always think one thing of you.'

Jane was consumed in a flame of grateful happiness.

'Oh, André!' she breathed.

'Never mind "Camille,"' said André, as they began walking again. 'We can do something else.'

Jane became suddenly conscious of the windows of her house. They stared down on Pine Street.

'Perhaps — perhaps,' she said guiltily, 'you hadn't better come any further.'

André flushed right up to the edge of his béret. But he never stopped smiling.

'Oh — all right,' he said.

'See you to-morrow!' said Jane.

He waved his cap at her. Jane ran across the street and up the block. At her front steps she paused to look after him. He waved again. She felt terribly happy. She didn't mind about 'Camille,' now. No one could help mothers. And they would do something else.

CHAPTER II

I

'I DON'T see why you want to go to college,' said Muriel, 'at all.'

Jane was taking lunch with Muriel. And Jane was very different. Her sleek brown pigtails had vanished, turned up in a knot on her neck beneath a big black hair ribbon. Her skirts were down to her boot tops and her dresses, though they were still made by Miss McKelvey, had a subtly young-ladyfied air. Jane was sixteen. It was September. Jane would be seventeen in May.

Muriel was sixteen, too, of course, and the seven black finger curls had been twisted into two, that hung down her back under a black hair ribbon, just like Jane's, and she wore a thick, cloudy bang on her white forehead and her eyes were bigger and bluer than ever and her eyelashes longer and even more curly. She looked just like a postcard that André had sent Jane from the Tate Gallery in London last summer. 'A typical Pre-Raphaelite,' he had written across it. Muriel looked almost as old as her second sister, Rosalie, thought Jane admiringly. It was the being pretty that did it. Being pretty made Muriel look old and Rosalie look young. Rosalie was twenty-one and about to become engaged, so Isabel said, to Freddy Waters.

Edith, the eldest, had married and was living in Cleveland, but had come back to her mother's house to have her first baby. Jane privately sympathized with Muriel about it. It was awfully embarrassing to have Edith around, looking so large and queer, with great dark shadows under her big black eyes and grey hollows in her waxen cheeks, when only

last Christmas she was the prettiest bride Chicago had ever
seen, floating up Saint James's aisle on old Solomon Lester's
arm, in a cloud of tulle and yards and yards of stiff gored
satin, with a waist so tiny that she looked as if she'd break in
two in the middle. Flora and Jane had been very much
thrilled by the wedding. They had sat together in the sixth
pew on the bride's side, because Muriel was a flower girl.

Jane's mother and Isabel had thought it was awfully funny
to import old Solomon Lester to stand by his granddaughter's
side in that Episcopal chancel, when every one knew that
back in New York he was a pillar of the synagogue. Of course
Edith had been on the altar guild for years, and she had no
brother and her father was dead. Nevertheless, Jane's mother and Isabel had thought it would have been better taste
to have had a house wedding.

There she sat, at any rate, in a cerise silk tea-gown, at her
mother's right hand, languidly sipping her tea with lemon
and looking quite as uncomfortable as she made every one
else feel. It was awfully hard on Rosalie, Isabel told Jane, to
have her always in evidence when Freddy Waters came to
call. And Isabel thought it was perfectly disgusting of her to
go about to parties. She had a long story that Jane had never
thought so terribly funny about her almost pulling the horse
off his feet when she stepped into a hansom, right in front of
Bert Lancaster, on her way home from one of Flora's mother's
receptions.

Mrs. Lester, however, sitting comfortably behind her silver
tea-tray, seemed sublimely unconscious that there was anything embarrassing in her presence. Isabel said that she
positively encouraged Edith to go about everywhere and was
continually seen in public, brazenly knitting on the most un-
mistakable garments, and talking of the baby in the most
extraordinary way, as if it *could* be talked about — as if it were

really there. She didn't do this in front of Jane and Flora and Muriel of course. Jane's mother said it was the Jew coming out. They were very queer about family life.

Jane didn't exactly see why you *couldn't* talk about a baby before it was born, but obviously you didn't, and it certainly made her feel very uncomfortable to look at Edith. There was something in the expression of Mrs. Lester's big brown eyes, however, as they rested on her first-born, that brought a lump into Jane's throat. Something anxious and worried and somehow proud and tender, all mixed up. Fat, funny Mrs. Lester, who was almost as large as Edith this minute! Her napkin was always slipping off her lap and she had three double chins that cascaded down from her tiny mouth to her broad lace collar. It would seem awfully funny, Jane thought, if you were having a baby yourself, to know you must never mention it, when it would be all you would think about, all those long months.

'I don't know why you don't want to go to Farmington next year, Jane,' continued Muriel, 'with Flora and me.'

Jane knew very well. She was very fond of Flora and Muriel — why, she had known them in her perambulator! But she wanted to go to Bryn Mawr, just the same, with Agnes, and live for four years with her in Pembroke Hall in one of those double suites that looked so enchanting in the catalogue and study more French and English and, yes, get away from her family and postpone the awful day when she would have to stop being shy and make a début and go to dances with a lot of young men whom she didn't know and compete with Flora and Muriel on their own field, which could never be hers, in a dreadful artificial race, over hurdles of cotillion partners, with an altar at the end of it and bride-grooms given away in order of excellence, like first, second, and third prizes in a public competition. Jane always thought

of bridegrooms like that. That was just the way her mother
and Isabel talked about them. Like something the panting
bride took home and unwrapped and appraised at her
leisure. Her mother and Isabel always weighed all bridegrooms' qualities minutely in the balance and usually found
them wanting. Jane knew all about bridegrooms.

Edith's, now, had been rich and of very good family — for
there *were* very good families in Cleveland, who had moved
there, years ago, from the East. But he looked very frail —
Jane's mother thought almost consumptive — and Edith
didn't need the money and would certainly miss living in a
large city and find it hard to get on without her mother, who
had always been so indulgent. Even Freddy Waters, who
was not a bridegroom yet, but, according to Isabel, soon
would be, had been scrupulously balanced on jeweller's
scales. Jane, facing Rosalie's unconscious face across the
luncheon table, knew perfectly well that Freddy was awfully
clever and a divine dancer, but hadn't a cent to bless himself
with and had thrown himself at the feet of every rich girl in
Chicago for the last seven years. Jane's indifferent mind was
crowded with snapshot biographies like that of every actual
and potential bridegroom in town. And she *did* want to go to
Bryn Mawr and get away from the family and live with Agnes
and study some more French and English. It seemed a great
deal simpler.

She had taken her preliminaries last spring and passed
them well enough and Agnes had reserved a double suite in
Pembroke Hall and her father had said explosively on one
memorable occasion, 'Oh, hell! Let the kid go!' But her
mother and Isabel had never consented.

It was partly because of Agnes, of course, whom her mother and Isabel had never grown to like, though she was
turning out to be awfully clever and had passed her pre-

liminaries with an amazing number of high credits and might be the Middle-Western Scholar and could write essays that Miss Milgrim thought were very unusual. Agnes had actually taken a job last summer, on her father's paper, though she was only seventeen. Jane thought it was very wonderful of her, but it seemed to be the last nail in her coffin as far as her mother and Isabel were concerned.

'A young girl in a *newspaper* office!' Mrs. Ward had said. Considering the tone in which it was uttered, the comment had sufficed.

'I don't know what I'll do without Muriel for a year,' Mrs. Lester was saying, 'now Edith is gone.' Her eyes lingered pensively on Rosalie as if she sensed an approaching farewell. Her three dark-haired daughters were very dear to Mrs. Lester.

'And Flora's mother has only Flora,' said Jane sympathetically.

A little gleam of cynicism shone in Edith's melancholy eye.

'I dare say she'll be glad to have her out of the way.'

'Flora's getting old enough to notice,' sighed Mrs. Lester.

'Freddy saw her lunching alone with him at the Richelieu last Wednesday,' said Rosalie. And added with perverse pleasure, 'They were having champagne.'

Mrs. Lester clucked her dismay. But it was no news to Jane. She had heard Isabel telling all about it at the dinner table on Thursday night.

'Bert Lancaster ought to be ashamed of himself,' said Mrs. Lester.

'*She's* old enough to know better,' said Rosalie pertly. 'How old *is* she, Mother?'

'She was married,' said Mrs. Lester dreamily, 'the year that Edith had scarlet fever. I couldn't go to the wedding. That makes her about thirty-eight.'

'She doesn't look it,' said Edith. 'She's an amazing woman.'

'Bert's thirty-five,' said Rosalie meditatively. 'He told me so himself.'

'I admire her husband,' said Mrs. Lester, 'for the way he takes it.'

'Mother!' said Rosalie and Edith at once. And Rosalie continued, 'How *can* you admire him! He's a perfect dodo!'

'He has been very much tried,' said Mrs. Lester, 'these last three years.'

'He might die,' commented Edith hopefully. 'He's awfully old.'

'He's not sixty,' said Mrs. Lester. 'He'll have to die soon to do any good.'

'Mother!' said Rosalie again. 'Bert's simply mad about her.'

'Now,' said Mrs. Lester, with meaning. 'Men are all alike,' she sighed irrelevantly, as she rose from the table. 'Except yours, Edie.' She put her arm around Edith as they passed through the door.

The Lesters' living-room was awfully like the Lesters. Mrs. Lester liked comfort and the girls liked gaiety. The entire house was both comfortable and gay. It was also untidy, for Mrs. Lester was a terrible housekeeper. Her servants never stayed a minute and never seemed to pick up anything while they were there. Jane's mother said she didn't wonder, with the demands that were made upon them. The Lesters had lots of company and meals at all hours, and the girls, so Jane's mother said, had never been taught to do for themselves. Jane had often seen Muriel step out of a lovely new dress and leave it lying on her bedroom floor, and her upper bureau drawer was a sight. There was hair in her comb and soiled handkerchiefs everywhere. Jane had been taught to be very careful about combs and soiled handkerchiefs.

Jane liked their living-room, however. The walls were covered with emerald-green silk and hung with oil paintings in great gold frames. The paintings were mostly landscapes, but there was a copy of a Murillo Madonna over the fireplace. Jane's mother and Isabel thought it was awfully funny that the Lesters' hearth should be dominated by the Christchild. The furniture was rosewood, upholstered in bright green brocade and there was a grand piano in the corner. Muriel's music was always scattered all over it, gay popular tunes that Jane loved to hear her rattle off when she had Flora and Jane and some boys in for a chafing-dish supper after their evening dancing-class. This afternoon Rosalie's embroidery was strewn all over the rosewood sofa, and the morning paper, with the social column turned out and a copy of 'Town Topics' and one of the 'Club Fellow' lay on the floor by Edith's easy chair, and Mrs. Lester's compromising knitting was on the marble-topped table. All but two balls of blue and white worsted that had rolled under the sofa. A little fire was smouldering on the hearth and Jane thought that all the untidy litter made the large, luxurious room look very homelike and comfortable as if people lived in it and loved it. But Jane picked up the two balls of worsted and wound up the yarn.

Muriel sat down at the piano and began to play 'Ta-ra-ra-ra Boom-de-ay,' singing, as her hands rattled over the keys,

> 'A sweet Tuxedo girl you see,
> Queen of swell so-ci-e-ty,
> Fond of fun as fond can be,
> When it's on the strict Q.T.!'

Edith and Rosalie and Jane all joined uproariously in the chorus.

> 'Ta-ra-ra-ra Boom-de-ay! Ta-ra-ra-ra Boom-de-ay!
> Ta-ra-ra-ra Boom-de-ay! Ta-ra-ra-ra Boom-de-ay!'

'That song,' said Mrs. Lester comfortably, as she picked up her knitting, 'will always make me think of the World's Fair.' The celebrated Columbian Exposition had been running all summer down in Jackson Park. Muriel slipped easily into 'After the Ball,' the great band hit of the season. She sang the popular parody with pathos, as she played,

> 'After the Fair is over, what will Chicago do
> With all those empty houses, run up with sticks and glue?
> I'd rather live in Brooklyn (somebody'd know me there)
> Than to live in Chicago, after — the — Fair.'

'We ought to go out there again some night for dinner,' said Rosalie, 'before it gets too cold.'

Muriel stopped playing.

'Let's go this week,' she said. 'Let's go to-morrow night.'

'Let's have a party,' said Rosalie.

'Whom do you want to ask?' asked Mrs. Lester. 'Besides Freddy.'

This was just like the Lesters. No sooner said than done.

'I don't care,' said Rosalie. 'Let Muriel have some kids. It's her last fling. School begins next week.'

'Flora,' said Muriel promptly, 'and Jane, of course, and Teddy Stanley — he's just crazy about Flora — and Bob Withers for me and — when does André get home, Jane?'

'I don't know,' said Jane. And she really didn't. He hadn't said in his last letter from Paris. Jane hadn't seen André for three months.

'He's got to be back for school,' said Muriel. 'I'll give him a ring.'

'You're not going, are you, Edith?' said Rosalie hopefully. Edith looked a little undecided. 'It's a tiring trip.'

Edith was still looking undecided when the Lesters' new butler appeared in the door.

'Miss Jane Ward?' he asked hesitatingly. He hadn't been

there long enough to know Jane's name. 'You're wanted on the telephone, miss.'

Jane got up in astonishment. She was very seldom wanted on the telephone anywhere. A call in some one else's house was very exciting. Muriel went with her out into the back hall.

'Hello,' said Jane.

It was André's voice. She knew it immediately. It wasn't quite the same, though. A little huskier and deeper. It made Jane feel very queer to hear it. André really sounded like a man.

'Yes. It's me,' she said ungrammatically.

'Who is it?' asked Muriel.

'I called up your house,' said André. 'They said you were over at Muriel's.'

'Yes. I am,' said Jane rather unnecessarily.

'I — I want to see you,' said André.

'Who is it?' asked Muriel, again.

'When did you get back?' said Jane politely.

'This noon,' said André.

'Well,' said Jane, 'why don't you come over?'

'Over to Muriel's?' inquired André. His voice seemed a little doubtful.

'Oh, no,' said Jane quickly. 'Over to my house. I'll go home.'

'All right,' said André. 'How — how are you?'

'Oh, I'm fine,' said Jane.

'Well,' said André, 'I'll be right over.'

'All right,' said Jane. She hung up the receiver.

'Who was it?' asked Muriel.

Jane turned to face her. She was laughing a little. She didn't know why.

'It was André,' she said.

Muriel began to giggle.

'I thought you didn't know when he was coming home.'

'I didn't,' said Jane, and started for the door into the front hall.

'Where are you going?' asked Muriel.

'Home,' said Jane. 'He's coming over.'

Muriel seemed to think that was natural enough.

'Ask him to come to-morrow,' she said.

Jane was putting on her hat.

'All right,' she said. She was at the front door before she remembered her manners. She went straight back into the living-room, and shook hands with Mrs. Lester.

'I had a lovely time, Mrs. Lester,' said Jane. Mrs. Lester looked a little bewildered, but Jane didn't stop to explain. It certainly wasn't necessary. As soon as she reached the hall she heard Muriel giggling about it in the living-room.

'Is Isabel in?' asked Jane, as soon as Minnie opened the front door.

'No,' said Minnie.

'Is Mamma?' asked Jane.

'No,' said Minnie again.

'Minnie,' said Jane confidentially, 'I'm going to have a caller.'

Minnie looked very much surprised.

'It's André,' said Jane. 'When he comes just take him into the library and say you will tell me. And, Minnie,' said Jane almost pleadingly, '*don't* call up the stairs.'

This display of formality Jane felt she owed to André's changed voice. She had been thinking of it ever since she had heard it. André must be very different. André had been away three months. André must have met lots of other girls, English ones and French ones, too, over in Europe. Still — he had telephoned her just as soon as he had arrived. Jane still laughed a little, excitedly all to herself, when she thought of that.

She ran up the stairs and hurried into her bedroom. She took off her little sailor hat and went up to her bureau and began to do over her hair. She parted it very neatly and pulled it down over her forehead in front and pinned up the braid under the black hair ribbon and wished, terribly, that she had a curly bang like Muriel's. Then she pulled her belt two holes tighter over her white shirt waist and looked critically at her figure in the mirror. Her waist was all right. It was really just as small as Muriel's. It was smaller than Flora's. The door-bell rang just as she arrived at that comforting decision. She took a clean handkerchief out of her upper bureau-drawer and put three drops of German cologne on it and tucked it in her belt.

Minnie appeared at the door. She was smiling all over.

'He's come,' she said. 'He looks awful big.'

Jane ran down the stairs feeling very much excited. She glanced at herself once more in the mirror under the hat-rack and then passed on to the library door. André was standing on the hearth rug. He *did* look awfully big, and somehow broader about the shoulders. His coat sleeves were just a little short for his arms. As soon as he saw Jane he broke into a beaming smile.

'Hello, Jane,' he said.

Jane was smiling, too, all over. She walked quickly over to him and held out her hand. His closed completely over it. He didn't let it go immediately.

'I'm awfully glad to see you,' he said.

His voice was certainly very different. And his cheeks, though just as red, looked just a little darker and harder. Jane realized, with a sudden blush, that André had begun to shave. She almost felt as if she oughtn't to have noticed a thing like that.

'Won't you sit down?' said Jane politely.

'Won't you?' said André with a smile.

Jane suddenly realized that she hadn't. They both laughed, then, and sat down side by side on the sofa near the hearth.

'I think we might have the fire,' said Jane a little doubtfully. Isabel had it, always, when she had callers. 'It's not very cold, but it makes the room look nicer.'

André jumped up again and struck a match and lit the paper under the birch logs.

'I love this room, anyway,' said André. 'It looks just like you.'

Jane flushed with pleasure. She loved the room, too, but she thought it looked just like her father. It was very different from the yellow drawing-room across the hall. It was quite small and the walls were covered with black-walnut book-cases with glass doors, behind which the leather-covered volumes of her father's library glowed in subdued splendour. Over the bookcases were four steel engravings, one of George Washington and one of Thomas Jefferson and one of Daniel Webster and one of Abraham Lincoln — the four greatest Americans, her father always said. On the mantelpiece was a mahogany bust of William Shakespeare. 'The Bard of Avon' was carved in a ribbon scroll on its little pedestal. The sofa by the fire was covered in dark brown velvet and there were two big leather chairs and a revolving one, that Jane used to like to swing on when she was little, behind the big green baize-topped desk of black walnut. Near the desk was a globe on a black-walnut standard, with a barometer hanging over it. That was all there was in the room except a big branching rubber tree in the one west window. Just now the September sun was slanting obliquely in across Pine

Street, striking the glass bookcase doors, making them look just a little dusty, and the firelight was dancing on the shiny surfaces of polished walnut, here and there, in the darker corners, and shining on the big brass humidor on the desk that held her father's cigars.

André sat down again beside her on the sofa.

'What happened to you this summer?' asked André. 'You look awfully grown-up.'

'It's my hair,' said Jane, referring to the knot on her neck. 'Nothing happened to any of us except the World's Fair.'

'I must go right down there,' said André. 'I never really saw it before we sailed in June.'

'Muriel wants you to go to-morrow night,' said Jane, and unfolded the plan. André was delighted. He could go, of course.

'And what have you been doing all summer?' asked Jane, when they had exhausted the subject of Muriel's party. She had a most delightful sensation of being a real young lady. Leading the conversation, like a hostess, with ease and distinction from one subject to another. But it seemed a little strange to be talking to André like this, quite seriously on the library sofa instead of up on the playroom window seat or out in the side yard beneath the willow tree.

His face lit up at the question.

'Oh, Jane!' he said. 'It's been great. You would have just loved it. I couldn't tell you in my letters. I — I hated to come back, really, except — except ——' His voice broke a little and sounded young and trembly. He didn't look at her. 'Except for you.'

That made him seem like the same old André. Jane felt that happy feeling again, deep down inside. But she didn't know just what to say to him.

'Tell me what it was like,' she ventured, after a little pause.

He began then, in a great rush, just as he always did when he wanted to share things with her. Jane's eyes grew big and round as she listened, and they never left his face. It sounded just like books. Different books, and all of them nice ones. June in London lodgings. That was like 'Punch' and Dickens and Thackeray. And July in his grandfather's house in Bath. That was like Jane Austen. And August and September in Paris, working with his clay in an artist's studio, living with his father in a garret bedroom on the rue de l'Université, eating at little iron tables on the sidewalks of cafés, and drinking at them too, red wine in carafes, as every one did in France, why — that was just like 'Trilby.' The book that Rosalie had lent to Isabel and Jane had read, knowing perfectly well that she shouldn't, that it wasn't at all the kind of book her mother would wish her to read.

'A *real* artist, André?' she asked. 'In a *real* studio?'

'You bet he was. A friend of Rodin's. He wouldn't have let me mess around except that he had always known my father. I learned a lot from him. More than in any regular class. I — I did a study of your hands, Jane. I brought it back to show you.'

Jane stared entranced. Why, this was *just* like 'Trilby.' Trilby's beautiful bare foot — and Little Billee.

'André! I'll love to see it.'

'It's pretty good,' he said. His eyes were on her hands, clasped tight in ecstasy. 'I remembered just how they were.' He looked up laughing. 'But you can't have it.'

'Oh!' she said fervently, 'I — I don't want it! I want you to keep it. I just want to see it ——'

'Who lit the fire, Minnie?' said her mother's voice. Jane hadn't heard the door-bell. Her mother stood in the doorway. André sprang to his feet.

'It's André, Mamma.'

Her little look of annoyance over the fire faded instantly into one of surprise. She held out her hand and smiled up at André exactly as if he were one of Isabel's callers.

'Why, you've grown up,' she said.

André smiled and blushed and Jane suddenly realized that he towered over both of them.

'You're quite a young gentleman,' said her mother, still smiling. 'Have you had a nice summer?'

'He's been working in a studio in Paris,' said Jane. And realized instantly that it was the wrong thing to say. It didn't please her mother.

'Oh,' she said, 'in a Paris studio?'

'Yes,' said André confidingly. 'It was lots of fun.' That was the one stupid thing about André. He never seemed to sense what people were thinking. Was it because he never, never cared?

'Was it, indeed?' said her mother and her tone seemed somehow to terminate André's call.

Jane walked to the door with him.

'I'll call up Muriel,' said André, 'and see you to-morrow night.'

'Yes,' said Jane.

'I *am* glad to be back,' said André.

'Are you?' said Jane a little wistfully. 'I'm glad you're glad.'

Muriel telephoned to her after dinner. André was coming and so were Bob and Teddy. Flora was delighted with the plan. She was all alone in the big brown stone house. Her father had gone to New York for a board meeting and her mother had gone away rather suddenly to spend three days with her sister in Galena, who wasn't very well. Rosalie wanted Isabel to come, too. She'd get another man.

'She said to tell Isabel,' said Muriel, giggling over the wire. 'that she knew who.'

Jane knew who, too. She must mean Robin Bridges, Isabel's latest beau. She ran back to the parlor to tell the family all about it. Isabel looked very pleased.

'That's nice of Lily Furness to go up to stay with that unattractive sister,' said Jane's mother.

'And in Galena, too,' said Isabel.

'Lily Furness has her nice side,' said Jane's mother.

Jane went upstairs to see if her foulard frock needed pressing. It seemed to bring the party nearer to be doing something about it.

II

Jane woke next morning in a state of great excitement. For a minute she couldn't quite recollect, as she lay in her big walnut bed with the early sunshine streaming in her east window, just what was going to happen that was so very nice. She felt strangely entangled by dreams that she couldn't remember. Happy dreams, though, and vivid, but lost even as she tried to clutch after them. Then she knew. André was back. André still — liked her. She was going to see André that evening at Muriel's party.

Jane sprang from her bed and ran to the window. It was a lovely day. The sky was bright and blue above the willow tree. The tree itself was waving, silvery green, in the soft September breeze. There would be a moon that evening. She had looked it up in the weather report in the paper, the night before.

André would like the World's Fair. He would like those vast white buildings standing stark in the moonbeams. And the twinkling lights on restless, moving water. And the terrace at the restaurant. And the music. And the crowds. It would be fun to see him see it.

Soon after breakfast she was called to the telephone. At the sound of Muriel's voice Jane was awfully afraid that something dreadful had happened. But no, the party was getting better and better. Flora had called up Muriel to say that her father had come home from New York unexpectedly that morning. As his wife was in Galena he wanted to join the party. He had asked if Mrs. Lester would let him take them all down to the fair grounds in the tally-ho.

The tally-ho! Even Muriel had thought that that would be magnificent. The Furnesses' coach and four was quite the most splendid vehicle that Jane and Muriel had ever seen. They weren't asked to ride on it very often. Mr. Furness had bought it only that summer and Flora herself seldom went on the elegant parties that he drove up the lake to the end of the pavement, or down to Washington Park, with the clatter of prancing hoofs and the jingle of chain harness and the toot of the triumphant horn. Mr. Furness was quite a judge of horse-flesh. He always sat on the box seat, very plump and straight, his short arms stiffly outstretched to hold the four yellow reins, his whip cocked at the proper horse show angle, and his high hat cocked too, just a little bit, over his fat puffy face and great pale eyes. It was always fun to stand in the yard with Flora to watch his parties start out from under the *porte-cochère*. Tall, frock-coated, high-hatted gentlemen helping beautiful billowing ladies to climb up the little steps to the top of the coach in their voluminous silken flounces. Beautiful billowing ladies, blushing at the display of slender ankles. Flora's mother was always the most beautiful and billowing and blushing of all.

And this afternoon he was coming to pick them all up at five o'clock and Jane and Isabel must be ready at the window, for Flora's father never liked to be kept waiting, holding his pawing horses, at any one's door. Jane assured Muriel earnestly that she would be on the front steps. Of course she would. She didn't even want to miss seeing the coach swing around the corner, clattering and jingling and tooting — the Furnesses' new coach — to pick her up to drive all the way down to Jackson Park with André, to show him the World's Fair.

At four o'clock Jane began very seriously dressing for the party. She solemnly considered the possibility of borrowing Isabel's curling tongs, but the sight of her sister, standing nervously in petticoat and combing jacket, heating the tongs in question for her own use at the gas jet beside her rosewood bureau, dissuaded her from the thought. Isabel didn't like to be bothered when she was dressing.

'I wish you wouldn't talk to me,' she said irritably, when her mother came in, conversationally minded, and sat sociably down on the sofa. Mrs. Ward rose obediently and almost ran into Jane at the door. They walked together down the hall. All the family had learned it was better never to disturb Isabel. But her voice floated out to them, down the passage.

'Shall I wear the blue or the green?' she called abstractedly. Jane's mother turned back, with interest.

'The green, I think, dear.'

Jane went into her own bedroom. She wouldn't borrow the curling tongs. She would rough up her hair by running her comb through it the wrong way. That, after all, would be safer. Jane had never used curling tongs. It would be better not to experiment for such an important party.

At a quarter to five Jane came out of her front door and looked anxiously up the street. It was perfectly empty, save for one yellow ice-wagon that was waiting, halfway down the block. The big white horses stood patiently, their noses in feed-bags. Their flanks were just a little yellow, as if the paint from the wagon had run into them. The iceman was a long time delivering the ice. Jane knew him well. He was a friend of Minnie's.

Jane sat down on the top step, carefully turning up the skirt of her blue foulard frock so that she wouldn't soil it. The mellow afternoon sunlight slanted down the quiet street. The grass plots looked yellow-green behind their iron palings. The elm trees were just a little brown and rusty with the decline of summer, but they still hung plume-like and ponderous, almost meeting over the cedar block pavement. The big red brick and brown stone houses stood tranquilly in their wide yards. Down at the corner was a grey brick block of five high-stooped residences. Jane's mother had thought it was dreadful when they were built, five years before.

'Eye-sores!' she had said. She declared they spoiled the street. She thought it would be horrible to live in them and share a party wall with a neighbor. 'Dark as a pocket,' was her phrase. Jane's father had advanced the theory that, with the rise of real estate values, they'd live to see the yards built up all around them.

'You might as well say,' Jane's mother had said incredulously, 'that we'll all be living in flats before we die — one on top of the other like sardines in a box.'

They had all laughed at that. Jane didn't know any one who lived in a flat except André.

The iceman came out of the house down the street, suggestively wiping his mouth with the back of his hand. He hung up the ice tongs at the back of the wagon, then stepped around to take off the horses' nose-bags and climbed up over the wheel to the driver's seat.

'Gittap!' he said. His voice echoed down the quiet block. The horses lumbered awkwardly into motion. Jane waved at him as he went by.

Suddenly the coach swung around the corner, a warning fanfare sounding on the horn.

'Isabel!' screamed Jane. It seemed terribly important not

to keep Mr. Furness waiting a single second. Isabel appeared at the door. She looked very blond and pretty in her bright green dress. She had borrowed their mother's black silk cape. She shaded her eyes against the western sun and waved cheerfully to Rosalie as the coach drew up at the door.

The groom sprang down with incredible alacrity and took up his position at the bridle of the prancing roan leaders. The horses arched their pretty necks and pawed the cedar pavement. The chain harness jingled and the smart red rosettes on their bridles fluttered with their restless motion. Jane and Isabel ran down the steps.

The coach was a chaos of festive colour and movement. Mrs. Lester had her purple parasol and Muriel her bright red frock and Flora her pale blue one. Rosalie looked lovely in rose-coloured taffeta, sitting with Mr. Furness on the box seat, but leaning back to talk to Freddy Waters, on the row behind her. Jane realized with relief that Edith had not come. But Bob and Teddy were there, and Robin Bridges for Isabel. André was on the back seat, close by the little platform where the groom stood up to blow the horn. Jane scrambled up over the back wheel to sit beside him, while Robin was helping Isabel up the little steps.

'Where's Jane?' said Mrs. Lester, bewildered.

'I'm here!' piped Jane, brushing the dust off her flounces.

Mr. Furness waved his whip and flicked it over the shoulders of the leaders. The little groom sprang back, under peril of instant dissolution. The horses plunged and started. The groom climbed up behind Jane and André. In a minute they were trotting smartly down Pine Street and the wind was blowing freshly in Jane's face, blowing her hair across her pink cheeks as she laughed up at André, terribly happy to be driving like this, right under the boughs of the elm trees, high up in the air, almost on a level with the second stories of the houses, laughing at André, with a whole evening before her that was going to be such fun.

The sun had long been set when they reached the fair grounds. They all climbed down from the coach and strolled in the gathering twilight past the glimmering, glamorous buildings, through the jostling, pleasure-bent crowd until they reached the restaurant.

'Let's eat on the terrace,' said Rosalie. The September night was very mild. Mr. Furness found a waiter who made one long table out of five so all twelve of them could sit together. Jane sat between André and Freddy Waters. Freddy didn't speak to her once, all through the meal, he was so busy talking to Rosalie on his other side and answering the sallies of Isabel from across the table. André didn't say much, either.

'Is this like Paris?' Jane asked him. She meant the terrace and the candlelit tables and the sky overhead, with just the largest stars gleaming faintly through the yellow glow of the fair grounds.

'Something,' said André. 'Paris is really just like itself.' Jane felt a little disappointed. She had hoped so much that it was.

The moon came up before the meal was over, a little lopsided, just past the full, enormous and very clear, out of the waters of the lake. It made a silver path from the horizon to the very foot of the terrace.

'There's nothing like that in Paris,' said André solemnly. Jane felt a little better about Chicago. When dinner was over they started for the Midway. The crowds were dreadful there, but Jane loved the side shows. Rosalie had her fortune told and so did Isabel and so did Muriel. But Mr. Furness didn't want Flora to touch the dirty gypsy and Jane didn't want to hear *her* fortune with André there and Muriel at hand to giggle. Muriel had even giggled at Freddy Waters when the gypsy found a blond young man in Rosalie's pink palm.

Then they went to the Streets of Cairo and rode riotously on camels. Mrs. Lester sat on a green bench beside Mr. Furness and laughed herself into hysteria as the girls climbed timorously up on the leather saddles, clutching at petticoats in a vain attempt to cover protruding ankles, when the dreadful animals lurched clumsily to their feet and rocked away. It was like nothing else than an earthquake, Jane decided, as she clung desperately to the awkward humps.

Later Mrs. Lester shepherded them safely past the hoochee-couchee dances and the perils of the Dahomey Village to the more adequately clothed Esquimos, who tactfully volunteered upon question, as a tribute to the Chicago climate, that they felt the cold more on the Midway than in Labrador. The Ferris wheel loomed up before them in the night. They must all go up in that, Rosalie decided.

Jane stepped into one of the swinging cars in front of André. She had never been up in the Ferris wheel before. The compartments looked as small as bird cages when dangling in mid-air. Jane was surprised to see that they were really almost as big as street cars. She sat down with André in a corner seat. The car swayed slightly as the wheel started. They moved up and out, then stopped again while other cars were loading. They swung slowly around the huge circumference, starting and stopping at regular intervals. The ground fell away beneath them and Jane lost all sense of movement. The car seemed suspended motionless in mid-air, with the ground sliding sideways beneath it and the great steel trusses of the wheel revolving slowly past the window. It paused a moment as they reached the top of the circle. The lights of the fair grounds glittered brightly below them. Long lines of yellow street lamps radiated out in the darkness.

The illuminated cable-cars on Cottage Grove Avenue crawled like mechanical toys. The glow of the city was visible at the north but the stars overhead were lost in the radiance of the myriad gas-lamps of the Midway. The silver moon looked incredibly remote, hung halfway up the eastern sky.

Jane drew in her breath with a little gasp of delight. Why — flying must be like this! They started slowly down again around the great wheel. The car swung out over the circle's edge. It seemed horribly unsupported, hanging dizzily over an abyss. Jane shut her eyes quickly and groped for André's hand. She felt a distinct shock of surprise when his fingers closed on hers.

'I — I'm giddy,' she said faintly.

André took her hand in both his own.

'Keep your eyes shut,' he said practically. He moved a little nearer on the seat and his arm rested against her shoulder. 'All right, now?' he asked.

'Yes,' said Jane faintly, still not daring to look. André continued to hold her hand in his. The starting and stopping went on disquietingly.

'Aren't we nearly there?' asked Jane.

'We go around twice,' said André. 'The second time without stopping.'

'Can't I get out?' asked Jane.

'No,' said André, 'but it's all right now. You can look.'

She did, and removed her hand from his as they moved slowly by the crowded landing platform and out and up once more into the heavenly vault.

'Shut your eyes again,' said André very capably as they began the descent. He took her hand as if a precedent had been established. Jane felt his fingers close reassuringly about her own. She was roused a moment later by a giggle from Muriel. She pulled her hand away and forgot to be dizzy in the heat

of her indignation. Muriel was outrageous. The car stopped
at the landing stage. Every one crowded out.

They strolled back, now, for a look at the Court of Honour before picking up the coach at the gates. Mrs. Lester was
tired and walked very slowly at Mr. Furness's side. No one
said much of anything. Even Rosalie and Isabel were silent.
The lights from the Japanese tea-house on the Wooded Island
glimmered across the pond. A few scattered gondolas were
drifting softly in the moonlight. Jane watched their graceful
motion.

'Have you ever been in Venice?' she asked.

'No,' said André.

'I went there on my wedding trip,' said Mrs. Lester.

'That's what I mean to do,' said André.

Jane walked along in silence, looking very straight before
her. She was a little startled by her own thoughts.

The Court of Honour was ablaze with light and crowded
with people. The strains of a Strauss waltz, rising and falling
with the light September breeze, fell faintly on their ears.
John Philip Sousa was conducting his orchestra in the open
air band stand.

'I'd like to see the MacMonnies fountain,' said André.

'Well — there it is,' said Mrs. Lester wearily. She didn't
look as if she wanted so see much of anything any more. The
party strolled over to the Grand Basin and leaned against the
parapet of stucco. Mrs. Lester sank on a green bench. Mac-
Monnies's medieval barge, propelled by Arts and Sciences,
with the figure of Time at the helm, rose sharply up before
them in the moonlight, amid its misty jets of water. André
stood silent at Jane's side, looking at it intently.

'I like it,' he said.

Flora was leaning a little wearily against the parapet beside
her father. Isabel and Robin and Rosalie and Freddy and

Muriel and the two other boys were laughing together, facing the band stand, a few feet away. The Strauss waltz was over, but Sousa was still leading his band. Suddenly he raised his arm. The high, shrill notes of a cornet solo rose above the orchestral accompaniment. The sweet, sentimental strains soared over the heads of the restless, moving crowd. Freddy Waters began very softly to sing. His eyes were fixed a little mockingly on Rosalie's pretty, laughing face. It was De Koven's love song.

> 'Oh, promise me that some day you and I
> Will take our love together to some sky ——'

Jane was looking at André's stern young profile. He was still quite intent on the fountain. Freddy Waters continued to sing:

> 'Where we can be alone and faith renew ——'

Suddenly Flora gave a little startled cry.

'Why, there's Mamma!' She pointed in the direction from which they had come. Jane turned quickly, in surprise, to look.

There, gliding from the darkness into light, beneath the little bridge across the lagoon, was a single gondola. The romantic figure of the gondolier stood stark in the moonlight. The light from a lamp on the parapet fell clearly on the faces of his passengers. Jane recognized them in an instant. They were Mr. Bert Lancaster and Flora's mother. Flora's mother, looking more beautiful than Jane had ever seen her, with a long black lace veil about her head, hiding her golden hair, framing the oval of her lovely face. A veil of mystery and romance.

It was over in a moment. The gondola turned, on a deft stroke of the oar, and the hood hid its passengers. Mrs. Lester had risen to her feet at Flora's cry. She stood there, now, at Mr. Furness's side, still staring at the unconscious back of the gondolier. Suddenly she threw a quick glance at Mr. Furness. Jane's eyes followed hers. Flora's father was looking after the gondola, too, and his great pale eyes were almost starting out of his head. His lips were trembling under his grey moustache and his face looked queer and wooden, as if all expression had been wiped out of it. Mrs. Lester looked quickly at Flora, Jane, and André. André's eyes had never left the fountain. Mrs. Lester put her arm around Flora.

'It *did* look like your mother, didn't it, dear?' said Mrs. Lester kindly. 'But of course it couldn't have been, as she's in Galena.'

Mr. Furness stirred at that.

'We — we'd best be going home,' he muttered thickly.

Mrs. Lester threw him a strangely admiring glance.

'Yes. That's best,' she said simply. None of the others had seen it. They moved slowly off toward the entrance gates.

Jane thought it was all very funny. Mrs. Lester and Mr. Furness looked so very queer. And of course that *was* Flora's mother. She had seen her quite distinctly. Suddenly she realized that Mrs. Lester was beside her.

'Wait a minute, Jane,' she said kindly. 'Your frock's unbuttoned.'

Jane paused, blushing, and Mrs. Lester's fat friendly fingers fumbled up and down her back.

'That wasn't Flora's mother, Jane,' she said, as she stood behind her. 'It *did* look very like her. But it wasn't. Flora was mistaken.'

Jane didn't reply. This was funnier and funnier. Why did Mrs. Lester care so much? People often saw Flora's mother out with Mr. Bert Lancaster. Freddy Waters had seen them last week, lunching at the Richelieu.

'Jane ——' said Mrs. Lester, and stopped.

'Yes,' said Jane, twisting about to look at her.

'I don't like to tell a little girl not to — to tell her mother anything,' said Mrs. Lester hesitatingly, 'but I wouldn't — I wouldn't mention Flora's mistake at home. Not even to Isabel.'

Jane looked at her wonderingly.

'It — it might make trouble,' said Mrs. Lester falteringly.

Jane understood that, though she didn't understand why. Jane knew all about things that made trouble. Things that were never forgotten and always discussed. Funny little things. Like André's Paris studio.

'I won't mention it, Mrs. Lester,' she said firmly.

Mrs. Lester looked incredibly grateful.

'Good little Jane,' she said; 'I don't like to give you a secret.'

Jane privately thought that it wasn't her first. She couldn't remember a time when there weren't things she knew it was wiser not to say to her mother and Isabel. She smiled brightly at Mrs. Lester.

'I don't mind,' she said.

The drive home was just a little cold and very strange and silent. Jane found herself, rather unexpectedly, on the box seat with Mr. Furness. Mrs. Lester had André in the row behind. The others sat back of them, singing a little just at first, reminiscent strains of 'Oh, Promise Me,' then lapsing into silence. Mr. Furness never spoke once, all the way home. He drove very fast, flicking his horses with his whip, until they broke their trot and cantered for a step or two, then pulling them in again, with a great tug of the reins. The leaders reared once, near the Rush Street Bridge, and Jane very nearly screamed.

'I had a lovely time, Mr. Furness,' she said, as they drew up in front of the house on Pine Street. He didn't seem to hear her.

'Good-night, Mrs. Lester,' said Jane politely. 'I had a lovely time.'

Mrs. Lester held her hand a moment and patted it.

'You're a good little girl, Jane. I'm sure you can be trusted.'

'Oh, yes, Mrs. Lester,' said Jane. And then, 'Good-night, André.'

'Good-night,' said André. 'I'll call you up in the morning.'

'Why does Mrs. Lester think you can be trusted?' said Isabel curiously, as she was fishing in her bag for the door-key.

'I don't know,' said Jane. 'I can't imagine.'

Isabel opened the door. As they walked down the hall their mother called over the bannisters.

'Was it fun, girls?' She was sitting up for them in her lavender wrapper. She followed Isabel into her bedroom to talk it all over. Isabel seemed to have lots to say.

'I never saw Freddy so gone on any one as he is on Rosalie. I think he's really in love with her. Of course, I don't say he would be if she didn't have money, but ——' Jane's mother closed Isabel's door.

Jane went into her own room alone. She could hear their whispering voices, broken by low laughter, long after her light was out. It was funny, Jane thought, but it was perfectly true. Telling lies made you trustworthy.

CHAPTER III

I

'I DON'T know why you want to go,' said Jane's mother, 'anyway.'

'Just to the Thomas concert,' said Isabel.

'And down in the street cars,' said Jane's mother, 'in your
pretty frock.'

'Well — I do,' said Jane.

It was a party of Agnes's that was under discussion. Agnes
had asked her, yesterday in school, to come up to dinner that
evening and go down to the Auditorium later to the Thomas
concert. Agnes's mother was going to work that night. She
couldn't use her seat. Agnes's father would take them. Jane's
mother and Isabel had argued about it all last evening and
now they were beginning all over again at the breakfast table.

'Oh, let her go,' said Jane's father. 'It can't hurt her.'

Jane smiled at him gratefully. Mrs. Ward sighed and
poured herself a second cup of coffee.

'You don't make it any easier, John,' she said, 'to control
the children.'

'Papa, can I go?' asked Jane, appealing directly to the
higher court, a little impertinently.

'Of course she can go, can't she, Lizzie?' said her father,
smiling disarmingly over the morning 'Tribune.'

'Oh — I suppose so,' said Mrs. Ward, with a resigned shrug.
'We won't have much more of it. Agnes goes to Bryn Mawr in
the fall.'

Jane's eyes met her father's with a little gleam of understanding. But there was no use in opening the college issue,
just then. It was late April, and Jane was almost ready for

her final examinations. She was going to take them, anyway. Miss Milgrim insisted on that. She rose from the table
to telephone to Agnes.

'I'm coming up early,' she said, 'and I'm going to bring my
Virgil. We can read over that passage.' Jane loved Latin,
but she wasn't nearly as good at it as Agnes. She wasn't
nearly as good as Agnes at anything. Agnes was terribly
bright. Agnes was going abroad that summer, to tutor a little
girl. She was going to England and Germany and Switzerland. Both she and Jane were awfully excited about it.
Agnes was eighteen.

Jane left the house quite early with her Virgil. She walked
up the Drive and west through the Park to Center Street. It
was a beautiful, breezy day, with a wind off the lake. The elm
trees were in tiny feathery leaf. The yellow forsythia was in
bloom. The heart-shaped leaves of the lilacs were very soft
and small. They hadn't begun to bud yet. Jane left the Park
and crossed the Clark Street car-tracks and wondered, as she
did so, why they formed such a social Rubicon. Her mother
and Isabel never had any opinion of any one who lived west of
Clark Street. It was the worst thing they had to say of Agnes.

Agnes lived in a little brown wooden house in a street of
other little brown and grey wooden houses. Some of them had
quite large yards and here and there was a newly planted
garden. The street was lined with cottonwood trees. Their
flickering leaves looked very bright and sticky in the April
sunshine. The wooden sidewalk was covered, here and there,
with a dust of cottonwood seed. Agnes's street was very like
the country.

Agnes's house had a little front porch and Agnes was sitting
on it in an old maple rocking chair. Agnes was reading a
French book. Jane knew what it was, 'Extracts Selected and
Edited from Voltaire's Prose,' by Cohn and Woodward.

Agnes was reading it quite easily, without a dictionary. Agnes was going to take some advanced standing examinations in French in the fall. She closed the book with a bang as Jane came up the front steps. Jane sat down on the top one.

'This is lovely,' said Jane. 'Like summer.' It really was. The sun fell hot and bright on the wooden steps. Agnes's father had put out some crocuses along the little path that led to the gate. Some little boys were playing baseball in the empty lot across the street. Agnes's next-door neighbor was hanging out the wash — great wet flapping sheets that waved like banners in the spring breeze. Behind her a row of children's dresses, pink and green and yellow and blue and four pair of men's white underdrawers danced a fantastic ballet on a second clothes-line.

'I like your street, Agnes,' said Jane.

Then they buckled down to the Æneid. They were reading the end of Book IV. The part about Dido's funeral pyre. Agnes could read it so well that it almost made Jane cry, at the end.

'Vixi et quem dederat cursum fortuna peregi,
Et nunc magna mei sub terras ibit imago.'

Agnes crooned the sonorous lines, then translated slowly.

'I have lived and accomplished the task that destiny gave me and now I shall pass beneath the earth no common shade.'

'That's beautiful,' said Jane. 'Nice and proud. That's the way you ought to feel if you were dying. Not snivelling, you know, or frightened, or crying over spilled milk.'

'It didn't do her much good,' said Agnes, turning over a page or two. 'The next book begins "In the mean time Æneas unwaveringly pursued his way across the waters." He didn't turn back, you know, though he saw the light from the flames.'

'I don't care,' said Jane stoutly, 'what Æneas did. He was

a poor thing anyway. But Dido died like a lady. A gallant lady. I hope I'll never cry over spilled milk, Agnes.'

'I don't believe you will,' said Agnes. Her funny freckled face was bent very admiringly on Jane. 'You're as gallant as any one I know. Always running uphill. I bet I see you in Bryn Mawr in October. I bet you get there.'

Jane was suddenly electrified to see André turn the corner and come walking up the street. He waved his cap to the two girls.

'Agnes!' said Jane. 'Did you ask André?'

'This afternoon,' said Agnes. 'Dad telephoned that he couldn't go with us. He was kept at the newspaper.'

'But who *is* going with us?' asked Jane.

'André,' said Agnes.

'Just you — and me — and André?' asked Jane again.

'Yes,' said Agnes. 'And we have to cook our own dinner first. Mother's down at the office.'

André turned in at the gate. Agnes sprang up to meet him. Jane sat very soberly on the top step, pricking a brown paint blister with her finger nail, her eyes on the worn porch floor. Her mother wouldn't like this, thought Jane. Her going with André and Agnes, alone, to the Thomas concert. Jane didn't like it, herself. Jane knew perfectly well she ought to have some older person with her when she went out in the evening. She felt very much troubled.

'Hello, Jane,' said André. 'Can't you smile?'

Jane tried to.

'Can you scramble eggs, André?' asked Agnes.

'Just watch me!' said André. 'If you've got some ham I can make eggs Benedictine.'

'If we haven't,' said Agnes, 'we can get it at the grocery.'

They all went into the house. Agnes's house always looked just a little mussy. Not mussy like the Lesters', because people lived all over it, but mussy in quite another way, as if nobody lived in it quite enough. The living-room was often dusty and the chairs and sofas weren't pushed around quite right. They looked as if the people they belonged to never had time to sit down on them. The dining-room had a funny unused look. The fernery needed water and the dishes were piled a little askew in the golden-oak built-in sideboard. André and Agnes and Jane were going to eat in the kitchen. The kitchen was the nicest room in the house.

It was quite large and the stove was always beautifully polished. There were two rocking-chairs in it, near the window that looked over the yard. The curtains were made of blue and white gingham and a blue-and-white tablecloth covered the kitchen table. Mrs. Johnson's mending basket stood on one corner. Agnes pitched it off onto one of the rocking chairs.

'Set the table, Jane,' said Agnes. She was peering into the icebox. 'André,' she said solemnly, 'there *is* ham.'

André tied a dishcloth around his waist and began to call for eggs and butter and lemon. He was going to make Hollandaise sauce. He picked up an egg-beater and poured his ingredients into a big yellow bowl. Jane was devoutly thankful that Flora and Muriel couldn't see him. Agnes was taking the vegetable salad out of the icebox. André had views on salad dressing. Jane set the table very neatly and arranged the snow pudding on a plate. She went out on the back porch and picked six tiny leaves of Virginia creeper to trim the eggs Benedictine. There wasn't any parsley. André was mixing the salad dressing when she came in again. Agnes had put the coffee on the stove. Jane couldn't cook, at all. Agnes could do everything and André was certainly displaying latent talents that she had never suspected.

'*This* is like Paris,' he said to her with a grin. She had so

often asked him if things were. But she would never have
thought of putting that question in regard to the Johnsons'
kitchen. 'This is just like the studio, except that there's running water and a better stove.'

They all sat down together. The blue-and-white tablecloth looked very gay. The vegetable salad was used as a
centre piece, a heaping pyramid of red beets and green beans
and écru cauliflower, piled on crisp lettuce leaves. The eggs
Benedictine were perfectly delicious. Agnes's coffee was awfully good.

Jane felt her spirits rising in spite of her conscience. She
knew that her mother wouldn't even approve of this meal
alone in the house with just André and Agnes. She wouldn't
like their eating in the kitchen and she'd think it was terribly
funny that André could cook. But Jane really couldn't feel
that there was anything to disapprove of in all that. Going
downtown alone, at night, with just another girl and boy —
that was different. Still, Jane's spirits *were* rising. It was certainly lots of fun.

Jane washed the dishes, later, and Agnes wiped them.
They wouldn't let André help them, so he sat in one of the
rockers and made funny suggestions, and, after asking Agnes's
permission, smoked two cigarettes. André had begun to
smoke with his father last summer in Paris. He didn't do it
very often and it always made Jane feel very queer to see him.
It brought home to her, terribly vividly, that they were all
growing up.

André *was* grown up, thought Jane, as she listened to him
bantering Agnes. He really looked just like a young man, as
he sat smoking in that rocking chair. An experienced young
man. Not a boy at all. André was nineteen. He was going
back to Paris in June to stay — Jane couldn't bear to think of
it — really forever. To go to the Sorbonne and work at the

Beaux Arts and learn how to be a sculptor. It would take him years and years.

And Agnes was going, too. Going to Europe to tutor a little girl and then to Bryn Mawr for four long winters. Things would never be the same again. It made Jane feel very sad to think of that.

And she, Jane, would just have to stay in Chicago and go to Farmington for a year with Flora and Muriel, and come home and live with the family and go out like Isabel and never get away at all. Never get out in the world to see all the beautiful things that she'd read of in books and André had told her about. Just stay in Chicago — and grow up — and grow old — like her mother or even Mrs. Lester. Flora's mother hadn't grown old, like that, of course. But Jane knew very well that she could never grow up to be like Flora's mother. Flora herself might. Or maybe Muriel. But never Jane. There were tears in her eyes as she hung up the last damp dishcloth.

'What's the matter, Jane?' asked André, in the hall. Agnes had run upstairs to get her hat and coat. 'You're awfully serious to-night.'

'I was just thinking how old we all were,' said Jane, mustering up a smile. 'And how soon it would be all over — good times like this I mean — with Agnes in college and you ——' She broke off abruptly. She was terribly afraid that she was going to cry.

André caught up her hand, suddenly, in the darkness. Jane gave a little gasp of astonishment. Almost of fright.

'I'll never be very far away from you, Jane,' said André solemnly, 'wherever I am.'

Jane knew what he meant. It was dear of him to say it. She loved to think that he would take her with him, to all those lovely places that she might never see.

'And I'll come back, Jane,' said André, still more solemnly. That was even more comforting.

'Will you, really?' she breathed. His face was very near her.

'Of course I will,' he said, almost roughly. 'Don't you know I will?'

He dropped her hand again, as Agnes ran down the stairs.

Agnes went out in the kitchen to lock the back door. André turned out the lights. Agnes locked the front door as they stood on the porch together. It all seemed very simple — not to have anything more to bother about than just what was in this little brown house. Jane thought of the fuss there always was at home when any one left for a party, with Minnie racing up and down stairs on forgotten errands, and some one at the front window, watching for the cab, and her mother in the hall giving last counsel and directions.

'Have you got your key, dear? I'll be sitting up for you. Try not to muss that nice frock. If you have anything good to eat, remember what it was. Haven't you got your *party shoes?* Minnie! Run upstairs and bring down Jane's party shoes. Nod to the cabman, Isabel. She'll be out in a minute!'

Jane thought it would be very restful to go out like this, just locking the door and leaving, with no questions asked. She walked soberly down the street between André and Agnes. Agnes's arm was linked in hers. The lamps were lighted, now, in all the little houses. You could see them on tables, with families grouped around them. No one pulled down window shades, much, on Agnes's street. At home it was a solemn ritual of the twilight. Here you could see fathers with newspapers and mothers with mending and children bothering them, in almost every house. It was fun to peek in at them and think of all those different lives.

At the Clark Street corner they waited for the cable-car. Jane began to feel very conscience-stricken again. The car rumbled up and stopped and they all climbed up in the grip car in front. It was such a lovely evening it was fun to ride in the open air. Jane still liked to look down the crack where the levers were and watch the grip pick up the cable. She had loved to do it as a little girl.

The car went on down Clark Street. It looked awfully dark and not very respectable. The light from the cable car flashed in the spring puddles along the road. The stores were all dark except the saloons and drug stores on the corners, and an occasional café in the centre of a block. Down near the river they passed a cheap burlesque house. 'Ten, Twenty, Thirty,' it said, over the door. Jane could read the sign quite clearly in the flaring gas lights. And underneath there was a poster of eight kicking ladies in tights and ballet skirts. 'The Original Black Crook Chorus,' was the legend above them. And below in great red letters with exclamation points, 'GIRLS!!! GIRLS!!! GIRLS!!!' A dismal-looking crowd was gathering about the entrance. Jane felt more conscience-stricken than ever. The cable car plunged into the La Salle Street tunnel under the river.

The crowds on the other side were much less dismal and the lights were brighter and there were many more of them. The theatre-goers were gathering around the scattered play-houses. They looked very cheerful and gay. There was something sinister about it all, however. The city seemed very dark and dangerous to Jane, though André and Agnes were chattering gaily on, as if nothing out of the usual were transpiring.

They got off the car where it turned at the corner of Monroe Street and started to walk south on Dearborn. Jane slipped her arm through André's. She really had to. She felt too queer and unprotected in that dim, nocturnal thoroughfare. After a few blocks they turned east again and very soon the familiar entrance of the Auditorium loomed up in the dark like an old friend.

André and Agnes pushed casually through the concert crowd and ran up the great staircase. Agnes had good seats, in the front row of the balcony. Jane always thought the music sounded better there than downstairs. She wondered, though, if any of her mother's friends would see her, perched up alone with André and Agnes. They would think it was very queer.

The orchestra was already assembled on the enormous stage. Theodore Thomas made his entrance as they took their seats. The first bars of the Third Symphony diverted Jane's mind from all temporal troubles. They wafted her away from the world of her mother and Isabel, and even from that of André and Agnes, on waves of purest sound to an ethereal region where the problem of chaperonage didn't matter. Jane leaned forward in her seat, intent on the music, watching the little waving arms of Theodore Thomas pulling that mysterious magic out of strings and keys. The Eroica Symphony — how beautifully named!

The second movement made her think of Dido — the throbbing Marche Funèbre for all gallant souls. She whispered as much to Agnes and fell to listening with closed eyes, dreaming of the deserted queen and the flames of the funeral pyre and Æneas's white-sailed ships turned toward the promised land across the tossing seas. 'I shall pass beneath the earth no common shade,' she whispered softly. A proud thought. A self-respecting thought. Something to live and die for. Something much better than just keeping a restive Æneas, tied to your apron-strings.

She came out of her trance at the applause of the intermission. André was wild with enthusiasm. Agnes was talking of the German music she hoped to hear that summer.

'While you drink beer, Agnes!' cried André cheerfully. 'And eat sausage. Beer and sausage do a lot for a symphony!'

The last half of the program was all Wagner. It was over all too soon. André and Agnes and Jane descended the stairs very slowly. Jane was beginning to think once more of the Clark Street cable car.

'I'll take you home in a four-wheeler,' said André magnificently, as they stood at the entrance. 'Jane looks tired.'

Jane smiled at him gratefully. André always understood. He hailed a disreputable vehicle. They all climbed in. It smelled dreadfully of the stable. André lowered the windows. They rattled quickly north up Wabash Avenue and over the Rush Street bridge and down Ohio Street, then turned into Pine. Nice familiar streets, safe ones, that Jane had known from her babyhood. Jane slipped quickly out of the cab at her door.

'Don't come up the steps with me, André,' she said. 'I'm all right.'

She opened the door with her latchkey. It was not late, barely half-past ten. Her mother came out of the library. She looked quite pleased.

'I didn't think,' she said, 'that Mr. Johnson would have the sense to bring you home in a cab.'

Jane made no comment. It was really a backhanded compliment for André, if her mother only knew it. And this time her mother was right, though there was no use in saying so. Jane knew perfectly well that a girl of almost seventeen shouldn't go downtown alone with a couple of contemporaries to a Thomas concert in a Clark Street car.

II

'Don't get oil on that coat!' called Jane's mother from the dining-room window. Jane was oiling her bicycle under the willow tree.

'Don't worry!' retorted Jane with a grin. The coat was made of tan covert cloth with large leg-of-mutton sleeves. It had just come home from the tailor's and Jane thought quite as well of it as her mother did. It looked very pretty with her blue serge skirt and white shirtwaist and small blue sailor. She had laid it very carefully on the grass before getting out her oil can.

It was late June and school was over. Jane had just been thinking, under the willow tree, how strange it was that school, incredibly, was over forever. The Commencement Exercises had been very impressive. Jane and Agnes and Flora and Muriel had sat in a row on a temporary platform at the end of the study hall with seven other classmates, all dressed in white muslin and carrying beautiful bouquets of roses. A clergyman had prayed over them and a professor from Northwestern University had delivered an address on 'Success in Life,' and Miss Milgrim had made a little speech about the Class of '94 and all it had done for the school and had handed each of them a little parchment diploma tied with blue and yellow ribbon. Blue and yellow were the school colors.

Ten days before that Jane had taken her Bryn Mawr examinations. Only last week she had heard that she had passed them. Her mother had received that information with a tolerant smile. But her father had been very much pleased. He had given her a little green enamel pin shaped like a four-leaved clover, for luck, with a real pearl, like a dew drop, in the centre. She was wearing it now, at the collar of her shirt-waist.

Jane felt a little sad when she thought of that important entity, the Class of '94, already irrevocably scattered. Agnes had sailed for England and the day after school closed Flora and her mother had left for Bar Harbor. The Lesters were

packing up for the White Mountains. Edith was going to join
them there later with her beautiful little boy.

Jane would see Flora and Muriel, of course, in September,
but Agnes was gone for a year and, what was much worse,
André was leaving for France next week.

Jane was waiting for him now, in the afternoon sunshine,
under the willow tree. She was going on a supper picnic with
his father and mother up the lake shore beyond the City Lim-
its. Jane was oiling her Columbia Safety in preparation for
the fête. Suddenly she saw him, pedaling down Pine Street,
a big picnic box strapped to his handlebars.

'Yoo-hoo,' she called.

He waved his cap and turned to bump up over the curb
stone, then dismounted at the gate.

'Ready?' he asked.

Jane picked up her coat and wheeled her bicycle down
the path.

'Just,' she said.

André held her coat for her.

'Isn't this new?' he inquired.

She nodded, smiling under her tiny hat brim.

'It's awfully good-looking.'

Jane mounted her wheel.

'Where are your father and mother?'

André pointed.

'Here they come,' he said. 'Aren't they sweet?'

Jane's glance followed his finger. Half a block away Mr.
and Mrs. Duroy were approaching down Pine Street. They
were mounted on a tandem bicycle. Mrs. Duroy's tall figure
rose above the handlebars with a certain angular ease. Her
long brown skirts flapped gaily against her mudguard and her
sailor hat was rakishly askew. Mr. Duroy, behind her, was
riding the bumps of the cedar-block pavement with Gallic

grace. He wore a grey tweed suit with knickerbockers and he
looked very plump and elderly and debonair. When he saw
Jane he waved his tweed cap and tried to kiss his hand and
his eyeglasses fell off promptly. The wheel wobbled perilously as he recaptured them.

'Don't be so gallant!' said Mrs. Duroy. 'Hello, Jane.'

Jane and André bumped down over the curb and swung
into line with them. Jane's mother was waving from the parlor window. She was laughing, a little, at Mr. and Mrs.
Duroy, but she looked very good-natured. As if she weren't
thinking anything worse about Mr. Duroy than that he was
French.

Jane and André sailed easily ahead of the tandem.

'They *are* sweet,' said Jane. 'They have so much fun together.'

'They always do,' said André. And added simply, 'They're
so much in love.'

That was a strange comment, thought Jane, to make on a
pair of parents. She would never have thought of saying it
about *her* father and mother. Nor about Flora's mother and
Mr. Furness. To be sure Mrs. Lester often spoke very tenderly to Edith and Rosalie and Muriel of their father. But
that was different. He was dead. Now that she came to think
of it, it was obviously quite true of Mr. and Mrs. Duroy.
He never looked at her, queer as she sometimes looked, without a little beam of admiration in his wise brown eyes. Even
when they argued, as they often did, and he disagreed with
her utterly, he greeted the sallies that routed him with a whimsical air of flattering applause. Very different from her
father's 'Oh, all *right*, Lizzie!' that terminated so many domestic discussions. Funny, when she thought of it, she could
hardly remember Flora's mother ever speaking to Mr. Furness at all, *really* speaking to him, even to argue. Marriage

was a strange thing. It began, she supposed, as André said, by being so much in love and it ended —— ?

André's thoughts must have followed hers.

'They're lucky, I suppose,' he said. 'All marriages aren't like that.'

Jane didn't reply.

'But they could be,' said André, 'if people cared enough.'

Jane went on pedaling in silence.

'I don't see how it comes,' said André, 'that change — in the way you feel — toward the girl you want to — marry.'

Jane still felt that really she had nothing to say. André had never talked just like this before. Of how people felt. Real people — not people in books. It was part of growing up, she supposed.

The lake was very bright and blue as they bowled along up the Drive. The Park was lovely in fresh June leaf. North of the Park the city stopped abruptly. The yards grew larger and the big brick and frame houses further apart and the pavement very much more bumpy. For some time they had to follow the car-tracks, jolting off the cobblestones at intervals, to let the horse-cars jingle by. Soon they turned off toward the east again.

The road here was so sandy that they had to push the bicycles and there were no more houses. Just clumps of willow trees and groves of scrub-oak and stone pine, with wild flowers underfoot. They heard the lake before they saw it. The sound of little waves, breaking and pausing and breaking again, on the long hard beaches. They found an oak wood, crowning a tiny sand dune. The ground was blue with wild geranium and a few late violets, purple and yellow dogtooth, stunted by the cool lake breeze, still lingered in the damper places. Beyond the trees was the great stretch of yellow sand and the stainless wash of blue that was the lake.

Mr. Duroy stretched himself beneath an oak and took out a long black cigar. Mrs. Duroy began unpacking the picnic basket at once. She had brought a little brass kettle, with an alcohol lamp, in which to boil water for tea.

'Don't be so restless, *m'amie*,' said Mr. Duroy lazily. 'The sun is still high.'

'It's six o'clock,' said Mrs. Duroy capably, as she laid the tablecloth. Jane was getting out the sandwiches. André was walking over the sand to fill the kettle in the little breakers.

'She must be practical,' said Mr. Duroy to Jane. 'It's her British blood. Thank God I'm a Celt. What is time on a night like this?' His brown eyes twinkled as he watched Jane arranging the sandwiches in neat little piles on the paper plates. 'But you, too, little Jane, are practical.'

'Oh, no!' said Jane earnestly. 'Really, I'm not.'

'Why, then,' continued Mr. Duroy lazily, 'do you arrange the sandwiches?'

Jane could easily answer that.

'Oh,' she said again, 'I just do what's expected of me.'

'That's a bad habit,' said Mr. Duroy seriously. 'Especially for youth. You must stop that in time, or you'll never get anywhere.'

Jane looked at him, a little perplexed. André came back with the kettle.

'What must Jane stop?' he asked.

'Doing what's expected of her,' said Mr. Duroy promptly.

'You're right,' said André. 'The unexpected is what's fun.'

Mr. Duroy nodded at him approvingly.

It was all very well, thought Jane, for them to talk like that. Their lives were full of funny surprises. In three weeks they'd all be in Paris, where anything might happen. But the unexpected was never allowed to happen to her. If it ever did, thought Jane, she'd embrace it with joy. She'd fight for it, against the world, and hug it to her heart.

When the water was boiling they all began to eat their supper. The sun sank down behind the oak trees in a saffron sky and a silver glow hung over the eastern horizon. Almost immediately the great golden disk of the moon came up out of the lake. It rose, incredibly quickly, balanced a moment on the water's edge, then floated, free, in the clear evening air. The sky was still quite blue. Jane could see Venus, through the tree trunks, low in the west, paled to a yellow candle in the afterglow. The colour faded quickly out of the world. The lake grew grey and the path of the moon more silvery. When Venus vanished in the sunset mists Jane could count seven stars, high overhead, piercing the pale sky.

Mr. Duroy lit his second cigar. André produced his cigarette. Mrs. Duroy lay flat on her back, her hands under her head, gazing spellbound at the moon.

'It is a night for a serenade,' said Mr. Duroy. And no one contradicted him.

'Sing, André,' said his mother after a brief pause. 'Sing, or your father will!'

André smiled a little self-consciously at Jane.

'Do, André,' she said.

He was sitting cross-legged on the grass beside her. His strong, capable hands, sculptor's hands, she'd heard his mother say, were crossed between his knees. His cigarette trailed negligently from his slender fingers. Without moving, his eyes upon her face, he suddenly began to sing. His light, young tenor soared softly up in the words of the old nursery rhyme.

> *'Au clair de la lune,*
> *Mon ami Pierrot,*
> *Prête-moi ta plume,*
> *Pour écrire un mot,*

Ma chandelle est morte,
Je n'ai plus de feu,
Ouvre-moi ta porte
Pour l'amour de Dieu!'

It *was* a serenade. Why, it was — it was a love song. Jane had never heard that note of tender entreaty in André's voice before. Her eyes fell quickly before his own. His mother was looking at him a little anxiously.

'*Magnifique!*' said Mr. Duroy. 'It is a splendid old song. And it always makes me think of rocking you to sleep.' He cast away his cigar. 'You inspire me to emulation!'

'Georges!' said André's mother warningly.

'Mine,' said Mr. Duroy imperturbably, 'is a more modern ballad. In tune with the age. And very appropriate to the lady of my dreams.' In his booming bass, humming as he started like a great bumble bee, trilling his *r*'s as he continued, he slipped into the familiar cadence of 'Daisy Bell':

'Daisy, Daisy, give me your answer do!
I'm half crazy, all for the love of you!
It won't be a stylish marriage.
I can't afford a carriage.
But you'll look sweet
Upon the seat
Of a bicycle built for two!'

His voice was shaken with mock emotion. André's mother and Jane were both laughing uproariously. André, however, sat very still, just smiling a little, his eyes on Jane's face. Suddenly he sprang to his feet.

'Come walk on the beach,' he said.

Jane looked up at him questioningly. Then quickly at Mrs. Duroy. Her eyes were fastened on André and they had again that faintly worried look. André's glance followed her own.

'It's all right, isn't it, Mother?' he said.

'Yes,' she said slowly. 'Quite all right, of course. But don't stay long. We must be starting home.'

Jane rose to her feet and set off with André across the beach. They plodded silently down to the water where the sand was dark and firm and the little waves broke softly on the shingle.

'Jane,' said André almost immediately, 'do you realize that I'm — leaving you — next week?'

'Yes,' said Jane softly.

There was a little pause.

'Jane,' said André again, 'I can't go without — without talking to you.'

'Talking to me?' repeated Jane stupidly.

'Telling you,' said André. He was walking quickly along the beach, not looking at her. Jane was hurrying a little to keep up with him.

'Telling me?' she said.

Suddenly he stopped. He stood looking down at her in the moonlight.

'Telling you,' he said. 'Though of course you know. Telling you that I — love you.'

Jane felt her heart jump, as if it skipped a beat. She felt terribly excited. And terribly happy.

'Oh, André!' she said.

'I — love you ——,' said André again.

She was staring up at him. His face looked very stern.

'Oh, *do* you?' she cried. 'Do you, really?'

'Don't you know?' said André.

Jane suddenly began to tremble, tremble uncontrollably, all over. She put out her hands to him, quickly. He clasped them in his own. Suddenly he seemed to realize how she was shaking.

'Jane!' he said, and his voice was suddenly tremulous.

For a moment they stood staring into each other's eyes. Then ——

'Jane!' he said again, and took her in his arms.

'My love,' said André.

Jane clung to him desperately. Why, this — this was terrible. She was utterly shattered.

'Jane,' said André again, 'look at me.'

Obediently she raised her eyes to his.

'You're crying!' said André. Jane hadn't known it.

'Jane — you *do* love me,' said André.

Jane only wept the more.

'Kiss me,' said André.

She raised her lips to his. The ground fell away from under her feet. The world was no more. Nothing existed but just — herself and — André.

'My love,' he said again.

She opened her eyes, then, upon his face. And there was the moon and the lake and the beach. The world hadn't vanished, after all.

'André!' she said desperately, 'What will we *do?*'

'You'll marry me,' said André.

She pushed away his arms.

'André — I can't. We're too young.'

'You're seventeen,' said André.

'Last month,' said Jane.

'I don't care,' said André. 'You'll marry me.'

'André — I can't.' The world was back indeed. Jane was thinking desperately of her mother — and Isabel — and, yes, even of her father. 'They'll never let me.'

'I'll talk to them to-morrow. I'll tell Father to-night.'

'And your mother, André. They'll never let *you!*'

'Oh, yes, they will,' said André. 'When I tell them.'

'Marry you,' said Jane wonderingly. 'Marry you — now?'

'If you will,' said André.

'I — I couldn't — now.' The thought of temporizing brought a little hope. 'I *am* too young.'

'Well — later, then,' said André confidently. 'In the fall. When your family are used to it. I'll come back and get you ——'

Suddenly just his saying it seemed to make it true.

'Oh, André,' breathed Jane. 'I — I can't believe it.'

'What?' said André.

'That we're — engaged.'

'You bet we are,' said André.

'André!' It was his mother's voice. 'You must bring Jane back. We're leaving, now.'

'Kiss me, again,' said André. He took her once more in his arms. This second kiss was not quite so wildly unexpected. And his mother was calling.

'André!'

'Yes, Mother! We're coming.' They turned back across the beach.

'I have you, now,' said André. 'I *have* you.'

Jane didn't deny it. She clung to his arm until they were very near the oak grove.

The supper was all packed away. Mr. Duroy still sat beneath his tree but Mrs. Duroy was erect by the tandem. She looked at André still a little anxiously, Jane thought.

They pushed their wheels in silence back to the car tracks.

'Stay with us, children,' said André's mother. 'It's very late.' They peddled slowly home. The park was filled with bicycles. Their myriad lamps glittered like fireflies in its bosky alleys. Jane kept glancing at André's face in the moonlight. It was very stern again. But beautiful, Jane thought. He threw her a smile, now and then. A happy, confident smile. Mr. and Mrs. Duroy went with them to her house. André, however, walked into the yard. She went to the side door because she had her bicycle. Mr. and Mrs. Duroy were waiting at the curb. As Jane was getting out her key, he pulled her quickly into the vestibule.

'Good-night,' said André, taking her in his arms.

'Good-night,' she breathed, against his lips.

'I'll come — to-morrow afternoon — to see your father.'

'Oh, André,' she whispered fearfully.

'You're mine,' said André, 'and I'll never give you up.'

Jane unlocked the door.

'Good-night,' she said again, and smiled up at him. He blew her a little kiss. She slipped into the hall. He vanished, down the path. Jane closed the door and stood a moment, quite still, leaning against the panels. 'I'm his,' she thought. 'He'll never give me up.' It was very late. The family were all in bed. Jane turned out the back hall light. 'He loves me,' she thought, as she crept up the stairs. 'André loves me.' She paused a moment by her mother's door. She tapped gently on the wooden panels.

'I'm in,' said Jane. A sleepy murmur was the only reply. Then, 'Did you turn out the light?'

'Yes,' said Jane and went on down the hall. 'He loves me,' she thought, as she opened her bedroom door. 'André loves me.'

III

Jane came downstairs, next morning, a little late to break-fast. The family were all at the table. Isabel was talking of Robin Bridges. He had invited her to go to the theatre with Rosalie and Freddy Waters. As Rosalie and Freddy were engaged, Isabel thought it would be quite proper for the four of them to go alone. But her mother was standing firm.

'No,' she said. 'Not without a married couple.'

Jane slipped silently into her seat and unfolded her napkin. It seemed very strange to hear her mother and Isabel, arguing just as usual, and to see her father buried, as always, in the morning 'Tribune,' and to realize that for them this golden morning was just like any other. For her it opened a new era. Jane felt a little guilty as she hugged her happy secret to her heart. And very much frightened. And terribly excited.

Just after breakfast the telephone rang. Jane rushed to the pantry to answer it. Yes, it was André. His voice sounded just a little confused, but cheerful, too.

'Hello,' he said. 'How — how are you?'

'Oh — I'm fine,' said Jane. Her heart was beating fast.

'Happy?' said André.

'Oh — yes,' breathed Jane. That was all. It seemed to satisfy André.

'When does your father come home?' asked André.

'Half-past five,' said Jane.

'Mother thinks,' said André, 'that I — I oughtn't to see you again, until I speak to him.'

'What else does she think?' asked Jane anxiously.

'Well,' said André, and his voice sounded just a little rueful. 'She — she thinks it's all right — now.'

'What did your father say?' asked Jane.

André's voice seemed to hesitate.

'He — he was awfully surprised,' he said. 'Much more surprised than Mother. But they — they understood — after I talked to them.'

'André,' said Jane miserably, 'they don't like it.'

'Oh, yes — they do,' said André uncertainly. 'At least ——' Then with increasing confidence, 'They like *you*, Jane. It's — it's just what they think ——' He stopped.

'We're young,' said Jane.

'Yes,' said André.

'Well — we are,' said Jane.

'Anyway,' said André cheerfully, 'Father said of course I must tell your father.'

There was a little pause.

'It's really all right,' said André.

Jane wished she could be sure of that.

'Well — good-bye,' said Jane. 'I'll see you this afternoon.'

A funny little sound clicked in Jane's ear.

'That was a kiss,' said André. 'Good-bye — dear.'

Jane hung up the receiver and pressed her forehead weakly against the mouthpiece. Dear André — darling André. She was terribly frightened. Yet radiantly happy, through and through. She could hear his voice still, with that funny little break at the end. 'Good-bye — dear.' He *did* love her. She had said she would marry him. Marry — André. But they were *much* too young. Her mother ——

Jane walked slowly up the stairs to her own bedroom and closed the door. She sat down at the window and looked out at the willow tree. It seemed only yesterday that she and André had climbed it. The remnants of their tree house — a few weatherbeaten planks — were still visible in its middle branches. She was going to marry André. She was going to be his wife.

At five o'clock Jane took up her stand in the parlor window to wait for her father. Isabel was out playing tennis, thank goodness, on the Superior Street courts. Her mother was in the kitchen superintending the solemn rites of the June jelly-making. You could smell the cooking currants all over the house. Presently Jane saw her father come around the corner. In a moment he passed the parlor window. Jane leaned against the screen and watched him up the steps. He was whistling 'The Bowery' and looked a little warm but very

nice and carefree. Jane felt guilty again. She heard his key
in the door.

Jane heard the door open and close and her father's quick
step in the hall. She heard the click of his sailor hat as he
dropped it on the bench beneath the hat-rack. Then his
footsteps receded toward his library and were lost. Silence
and the smell of cooking currants dominated the house once
more.

She ought to go in, thought Jane, and — and talk to him.
She ought to break the ice for André. It would be terrible for
André. She walked slowly toward the parlor door. At the
entrance to the library she paused. Her father was seated at
his desk, running through the afternoon mail.

'Come in, Kid,' he said.

Jane entered slowly. Her father went on opening letters.
Jane stood beside the globe and looked down at him.

'What's the matter, Kid?' asked her father. 'You look as
sober as a judge.'

'Nothing,' said Jane.

Her father threw some mail in the waste basket. Then he
looked up again with a smile.

'Any one dead?' he inquired cheerfully.

'No,' said Jane.

'What's the trouble?' he asked. 'Been worrying about Bryn
Mawr?'

'No,' said Jane. Bryn Mawr, indeed!

'Well — don't,' said her father. 'I'll see you get there.'

'Papa ——' began Jane desperately, and stopped.

'Yes,' said her father.

'Papa,' said Jane again, 'I — I want you to help me.'

'All right,' said her father. 'I will.'

'I — I hope you will,' said Jane a little desperately, then
went on in a rush. 'I — I want you to understand. I want you

to remember that I — I'm not a — a child, any more. I want you to be good to André. I want ——'

'Good to *André?*' repeated her father. He looked very much astonished.

'Yes — good to André,' said Jane. And then the doorbell rang. She rushed incontinently from the room and halfway up the stair. Minnie was coming out of the pantry. Jane sat down, just above the first landing. Minnie opened the front door. Jane could see André quite distinctly, from the dark of the staircase. He couldn't see her.

'Is Mr. Ward in?' he asked. His voice sounded very brave and steady to Jane.

'Yes,' said Minnie and led him to the library door.

'Mr. Ward?' Jane heard him say, on the threshold. And then her father's voice. 'Come in, André.' She heard her father's footsteps. André vanished into the library. An unknown hand closed the door.

Jane sat quite still, crouched down beside the bannisters. She couldn't hear a thing. Not even the sound of muffled voices. It was dark on the staircase. The afternoon sunshine came slanting in, below, through the ground-glass panels of the front door. Little motes were dancing in it, up and down the hall. Jane clasped her hands and really prayed for André. She was praying to her father, she thought, though, not to God. Praying to her father, through that closed library door, to understand, to realize, to be good to André. The minutes slowly passed. It was so quiet she could hear the clock tick in the dining room.

Presently her mother came out through the pantry door. She had on a long white apron, stained with currant juice, and her hair was ruffled. She looked very flushed and pretty after an afternoon in the hot kitchen. But not very neat. She noticed André's hat on the hat-rack, immediately.

'Who is here, Minnie?' she called over her shoulder.

'Mr. André,' said Minnie from the pantry.

'Where is he?' asked her mother.

'He asked for Mr. Ward,' said Minnie.

'For *Mr. Ward?*' said Jane's mother incredulously. Then after a pregnant pause, 'Where is he, now?'

'They're both in the library,' said Minnie.

Then Jane's mother perceived Jane. She looked her up and down as she sat crouched on the staircase.

'What does André want of your father?' she said.

Jane didn't reply.

'Jane!' said Jane's mother.

Jane stared at her in silence.

'What does this mean?' said Jane's mother.

'Oh, Mamma!' pleaded Jane, suddenly finding her voice. 'Please — please don't — spoil it. Let him talk to Papa! Oh, Mamma ——'

Without another word, regardless alike of Jane's imploring entreaties and her own currant-stained apron, Mrs. Ward opened the library door. She closed it after her. Jane sat quite still, for several minutes, in horror. Then she heard her mother's voice raised in incredulous indignation behind the closed door.

'I never heard anything so ridiculous in all my life! John, you haven't been *listening* to them? André — it — it's perfectly absurd ——'

Jane waited to hear no more. She flung herself hotly down the stairs and burst in at the library door.

Her father was sitting very quietly in a leather armchair and André was erect at his side. Her mother stood in the centre of the room, her flushed, indignant face turned toward the men before her. She looked quickly at Jane.

'Jane, leave the room,' she said.

'I won't,' said Jane. And closed the door behind her. Her father held out his hand.

'Come here, Kid,' he said. Jane rushed to his side. She looked quickly up at André. She hoped her heart was in her eyes. André smiled steadily down at her. He looked shaken, however.

'Jane ——' began her mother again.

'Lizzie,' said her father, and there was a note in his voice Jane had never heard before. 'Leave this to me.'

Her mother, with compressed lips, sank down in the other armchair. Her father pressed Jane's hand very kindly.

'Kid,' he said gently. 'You know this won't do.'

'*What* won't do?' cried Jane in desperation.

Her father still held her hand.

'You —you and André can't — get married.'

'Why not?' flashed Jane.

'Because you're *children*,' said her father. It was terribly true.

'I don't care!' said Jane.

'Well, I do,' said her father. 'And so does your mother. And so do André's parents. He very honestly told me that. And so does André, really. André doesn't want to persuade you to do anything that isn't right — that won't bring you happiness ——'

Happiness! Jane threw a tearful glance at André. He looked very proud and stern, standing there before her father. He gave her a tremulous smile.

'Papa,' said Jane, 'I know I'd be happy with André ——'

'Don't *talk* like that!' cried her mother sharply. But her father silenced her.

'You think so now, Kid,' he said kindly. 'But you can't tell. You don't know anything about it, either of you. André's nineteen years old. He's got five or six years of education ahead of him, on his own say-so, before he can be any kind of a sculptor. You were seventeen last month. You've known André for four years and you've never said three words to any other boy. You *can't* know your own mind and he can't know his, either. Five or six years from now, you might both understand what you were talking about. André's going to France next week, to live. He's a Frenchman and that's where he belongs. You've got to stay here with your mother and me and grow up into a woman before you talk about marrying any one.'

'I — I don't have to — marry him,' said Jane faintly. 'I just want to — to promise that I will when we're old enough. I just want ——'

'Jane,' said her mother very reasonably, 'we'll cross that bridge when we come to it. We don't have to think of that now.'

'I just — want to — wait for him,' faltered Jane. Then, with a flash of spirit, 'You can't help my waiting!'

'Of course not,' said her father pacifically. 'But no promises, André, on either side.'

'And no letters,' put in her mother. Jane's father shook his head at her, but she insisted. 'No, John. No letters until Jane's twenty-one. You must promise that, André. I won't have her tied down to any understanding.'

'I guess that's right, André,' said Jane's father soberly. 'You'd better promise.'

Jane and André exchanged a glance of despair. There was a brief pause.

'How about it, my boy?' said Jane's father.

'I — I promise,' said Andrè huskily.

Jane's mother gave a sigh of relief. She had the situation in hand now.

'I think you had better go, André,' she said very kindly.

'Can I see Jane again?' André asked.

'I think you'd better not,' said Jane's mother. 'It would only be painful.'

'Then I'd like — I'd like ——' said André steadily, 'to say good-bye to her now.'

'Of course,' said Jane's father, very promptly rising. 'Come, Lizzie.'

Jane's mother looked very reluctant to leave the room.

'I don't like this,' she said.

'Mrs. Ward,' said André, 'you can trust me.'

Jane's father threw him an admiring glance. He fairly pushed her mother from the room. He closed the door behind them. Jane turned to gaze at André.

'André,' she said breathlessly, 'what — what can we do?'

'We can wait,' said André. 'And we can think of each other.'

'André,' said Jane earnestly, 'did — did your father and mother talk like that, too?'

'They didn't talk like that — but they thought the same things. I — I could see them thinking.'

'They didn't — like it?'

'They like you,' said André. 'Father said you were a girl in a thousand.'

'Well, then ——?' said Jane.

'Mother thought I was much too young and she thought I ought to be able to support a wife before I asked a girl to marry me. She thought it was pretty rotten — my asking you. And Father — well, Father had always expected me to marry in France, of course. And we're — we're all Catholics. That doesn't mean much to me, but it does to him. But when I told them how — how I felt about you — well, they said — all right —— I could try my luck with your father. I — didn't have much. Though he was awfully decent. I haven't a leg to stand on, of course. I *can't* support you and I — I've *got* to go to France — you — you — understand that, Jane — I've *got* to go — to study, you know, if I'm ever going to amount to anything. Father and Mother both said that. I couldn't do *anything* here. I — I guess I don't sound like much of a son-in-law ——'

'But, André,' said Jane, 'do you mean — do you mean that there's nothing, absolutely nothing, that we can do?'

'Well,' said André, 'what is there?' What was there, indeed?

'I — I *shouldn't* have asked you,' said André.

'Oh, André!' cried Jane. 'You must *never* think that!'

'Why not?' said André.

'You made me so happy,' said Jane simply.

André took a quick step toward her. Then he stopped. He remembered.

'Oh, Jane!' he said, and dropped down on the sofa. 'Jane — my love!' He buried his face in his hands.

Jane sank down on her knees beside him. She pulled his hands away from his face. André was crying. She took him in her arms.

'André,' she said breathlessly, 'André!' She looked eagerly up at him.

'I — I promised your mother,' he said huskily.

'I didn't promise *any* one!' cried Jane desperately. 'André — you must kiss me good-bye!'

He took her in his arms. His lips met hers. The world was lost again. But this time Jane knew that it was really there, pressing close about them, menacing them, parting them, saying they were — young. She slipped from his embrace. She rose to her feet. André stood up, too, and held out his hands. She seized them in her own. He stooped to kiss her fingers.

'Good-bye,' he said.

'André,' she said, 'I'll always ——'

He managed a wavering smile.

'No promises,' he said. 'Just thoughts.'

'*All* my thoughts!' said Jane. He stumbled toward the door. On the threshold he turned again.

'Good-bye,' he said.

'André!' cried Jane. 'I — I can't bear it!' She heard her father's voice in the hall.

'I'm sorry, André. You — you've behaved so well, both of you.' Their steps died down the passage. Jane heard the front door open and close. She rushed to the window. André was walking, furiously fast, up Pine Street. At the corner he turned to look back. She waved wildly. She kissed her hand. He smiled again, very bravely. Then turned and vanished. Jane flung herself face downward on the sofa. The mark of André's elbow was still on the pillow. She buried her face in it passionately. She heard her father enter the room. He walked slowly over to the sofa.

'Little Jane,' he said, 'don't cry like that.'

Jane only buried her face the deeper. There was a little pause.

'Kid,' said her father, 'you're so young that you don't know that you'll get over it. You get over everything.'

Jane thought that was a horrible philosophy. She heard her father moving about a little helplessly. Then he bent over and touched her shoulder.

'I'll see you go to Bryn Mawr,' he said, 'with Agnes.'

'Oh, let me alone!' cried Jane. 'Just — let — me — alone!' She heard her father turn and walk quietly out of the room. Jane put both her arms tightly around André's pillow. She was sobbing as if her heart would break. She thought it *was* breaking.

CHAPTER IV

I

THE October sun was shining brightly down on the Bryn Mawr maples when Jane and her father first walked under the arch of Pembroke Hall, where Agnes was awaiting them. Jane thought Bryn Mawr was very beautiful. Much more beautiful than the pictures. The most beautiful place, indeed, that she had ever seen.

'Let's look it over, Jane,' said Mr. Ward, 'before we go in.' They strolled on, arm in arm, down the gravel walk beyond.

The campus stretched fresh and green before them. On one hand it terminated in a group of grey stone buildings, hung with English ivy. On the other it extended past a row of breeze blown maples to an abrupt decline, where the ground dropped off down a grassy hillside. In that direction you could see the rolling Pennsylvania country for miles and miles. Jane had never lived among hills. She thought the view was very lovely.

They passed some groups of girls, walking in twos and threes on the gravel path. They were laughing and chattering together and they paid no attention whatever to Jane and her father. Other girls were sitting, here and there, under the maples. Four or five ran out of a building, that Jane knew from the pictures must be Merion, and almost bumped into them. They were dressed in bright red gym suits, with red corduroy skirts, and they carried hockey sticks. They cantered across the campus toward the hillside, making a bright patch of colour against the green as they ran.

Pembroke Hall, as they returned to it, looked very big and important. Jane drew a little nearer to her father as they entered the front door. It seemed quite deserted for a moment. Then a coloured maid, in a neat black dress and apron, came out from a little room under the stairs. She said she would tell the warden. 'The warden' sounded a bit forbidding, Jane thought. Rather like a prison. But when she appeared she proved to be a nice-looking girl with dark brown hair, not much older than Isabel. She shook hands with Jane's father and told them how to find Jane's room. It was on the second story, in the middle of the corridor.

Jane and Jane's father walked alone up the wooden stairs. In the upper hall they met some more girls, laughing and shouting, hanging about the open doors of bedrooms. Inside the rooms was confusion twice confounded. Open trunks and scattered books and dishes and clothing flung on chairs. An odour of cooking chocolate permeated the air.

Agnes was waiting for them in the three-room suite. It looked very small to Jane, but otherwise just as it had in the catalogue. There was a little study with an open fireplace and a window-seat that commanded the campus, and two tiny bedrooms, opening off it. Agnes's trunk was already unpacked. Agnes had come yesterday, straight from the steamer. She had already been out, exploring the country. A great vase of Michaelmas daisies was on the study table.

'Well, girls,' said Jane's father, 'this is great.'

It *was* great, thought Jane. It was much nicer than she had ever imagined. She didn't feel shy any longer, now she had seen Agnes.

Agnes had taken her advanced standing examination in French that morning. It was easy, she said. Much easier than entrance.

Jane sat down on the window seat and gazed out over the campus. It looked very tranquil and pleasant. Yet exciting, too, with all those different girls, that seemed so much at home, walking about as if they owned the place. No one seemed to be watching them, as in school. No one was telling them what to do. As Jane looked six girls came out from under the arch. They were carrying a picnic basket and a steamer rug and several cushions and they wore green gym suits and corduroy skirts, just like the red ones Jane had seen before. They hung about under a big cherry tree under the window for a minute and they were all singing. Jane could catch the words by leaning out, around the ivy.

'Once there dwelt captiously a stern papa.
Likewise with him sojourned, daughter and ma.
Daughter's minority tritely was spent,
To a prep boarding school, glumly she went.
One day the crisis came, outcome of years,
Father and mother firm, daughter in tears,
With stern progenitors, hotly she pled,
Lined up her arguments, this is what she said:
"I don't want to go to Vassar, I can't bear to think of Smith."'

They were strolling off across the campus, now, but Jane could still hear the words of the song.

'"I've no earthly use for Radcliffe, Wellesley's charms are merest myth,
Only spooks go to Ann Arbor, Leland Stanford's much too far."'

Their fresh young voices rose in a final wail in the middle distance.

'"I don't want to go to col — lege, if — I can't — go — to — Bryn — Mawr!"'

'That's a nice song,' said Jane excitedly.

'They sing all the time,' said Agnes. 'The Seniors sing on the steps of Taylor Hall after dinner.'

'I'm going to love this,' said Jane.

Her father looked very much pleased.

'I hope you do, Kid,' he said heartily. 'And I'm sure you will. Jane's had a pretty poor summer, Agnes.'

Agnes knew all about Jane's summer. Jane had written her about André, just as soon as she could bear to put it down on paper. Agnes had sent her an awfully nice letter. She looked very sympathetic now.

'You must look out for her, Agnes,' said Jane's father.

'I don't think she'll need much looking out for,' said Agnes. 'This is Jane's kind of place.'

Jane was sure it was, even at the long Freshman supper table in Pembroke, which was very terrifying. Jane sat between her father and Agnes. On Agnes's other side was the warden and beyond her father sat a little dark-eyed Freshman from Gloversville, New York. Her name was Marion Park. She talked very politely to Jane's father throughout the meal.

'That's a bright kid,' Jane's father said, as they left the table. 'I bet she'll amount to something some day.' Jane felt that she and Agnes would like Marion Park.

The Seniors were singing on Taylor steps just as Agnes had prophesied. Jane and her father and Agnes strolled up and down in the gathering twilight and listened to them. There were lots of girls about, more than a hundred, Jane thought, all in light summer dresses, walking up and down under the maple trees, occasionally lining up in a great semi-circle before the steps, joining the Seniors in a song. Some of the songs were awfully funny.

'If your cranium — **is** a vacuum — and you'd like to learn
How an intellect — you can cultivate — from the smallest germ,
On the management — of the universe — if your hopes you stake,
Or a treatise — on the ineffable — you propose to make,
If you contemplate — making politics — your exclusive aim,
And are looking for — some coadjutor — in your little game,
And in short if there — should be anything — that you fail to know,
To the Sophomore — to the Sophomore — go — go — go!'

Jane's father thought the songs were awfully funny, too.

He laughed quite as much over them as Jane and Agnes did.

'Bright girls,' he said. 'Nice bright girls.'

That was just what they were, thought Jane. And her kind. Like Agnes. Not at all like Flora and Muriel, whom she loved of course and who had written to her only last week from Farmington, but who she didn't feel would fit into Bryn Mawr very well. They were just — different.

Agnes came into her bedroom that night in her cotton crêpe kimono, just before she turned out the light. Jane was sitting up in her little wooden bed.

'Open the window, Agnes,' said Jane. 'I like this place. I'm going to like it a lot.'

Agnes opened the window in silence. Dear old Agnes — it was fun to be rooming with her! But Jane hadn't forgotten. She hadn't forgotten one bit. She sat there in her high-necked, long-sleeved nightgown, with her hair braided tightly in two straight pigtails, looking very like the little Jane that used to run up Pine Street to meet André under the Water Works Tower. She hadn't forgotten, but she wasn't the same little Jane, in spite of appearances. She was beginning to learn that the world was wide.

'Since I can't marry André,' she said solemnly, 'I'd rather be here than anywhere else.'

II

'It's funny,' said Jane to Agnes. 'All the years you're trying to get into college you think it's the work that counts. When you get there you see it's the people.'

Jane and Agnes were sitting on their window-seat, looking out over the gnarled branches of the cherry tree. It was an afternoon in late January. The sun was sinking behind the stripped boughs of the maples and the campus was covered with snow. Jane and Agnes had just finished their midyear examinations. They had taken Minor Latin that morning. And English two days ago. And Biology the day before that. They were pretty sure that they had passed them all. Now they had five days of vacation before the second semester began.

'The work counts a lot,' said Agnes.

Jane wondered if the work counted more for Agnes than it did for her. Agnes was continuing to be terribly bright. She expected to take a job, when she graduated, and she was hoping to write, on the side. Agnes was writing now, all the time. Stories that she sometimes sent to magazines. Jane thought they were awfully good, though the editors always sent them back with rejection slips. Agnes was never discouraged. She just went on writing.

Jane never did much of anything, except just enough work to keep up in her courses. She loved the General English and she liked Horace and she found the Biology awfully interesting. She didn't think, though, that she was going to enjoy cutting up rabbits, much, next semester. Angleworms were different. They seemed born to suffer. On fish hooks and in robins' beaks if not in laboratories. Little soft furry rabbits — that was different.

Jane liked all her work and she liked her professors, much better than any of the teachers that she had ever had at Miss Milgrim's. Still — she never applied herself like Agnes. It was too much fun to take long rambling walks over the wooded countryside with friendly classmates, and make tea in the dormitory, and get up hall plays, and sit up half the night on somebody's window-seat, talking about — well, almost anything. Beowulf or the Freshman show, or whether there really was an omniscient God that heard your prayers, or the funny thing that had happened in the Livy lecture when —— Sometimes Jane thought, very solemnly, that she would never really be serious. Serious as a young woman ought to be who had the advantage of a college education and lived in a world where there was so much to be done.

President M. Carey Thomas always had a great deal to say to the students about the advantage of a college education and she was always calling their attention to the opportunities for women's work that were opening up in the world. Jane felt a little guilty when she listened to her.

President M. Carey Thomas spoke to the students every day in chapel, after the morning hymn and the reading from the Bible and the Quaker prayer. Jane always went to chapel for she simply loved to hear her. She loved to look at her, too. President Thomas was very beautiful. She stood up behind the reading desk in her black silk gown with the blue velvet Ph.D. stripes on its floating sleeves and her little black mortar board on her dark auburn hair. Her face was very tranquil and serene. The auburn hair was curly and rippled smoothly back from her forehead. Her mouth was firm and her chin was proud and her dark brown eyes could look very wise and persuasive. When she laughed, as she often did, there were funny friendly little lines about them in the corners.

'How lovely she looks!' Jane always thought. It was strange that Miss Thomas's beauty always made Jane think, for a passing moment, of Flora's mother. Flora's mother — who was so beautiful too, in such a different way. Beautiful with hair of burnished gold tightly coiffed on her distinguished little head, and gowns of rippling silk and wraps of clinging velvet, and pink cheeks with dimples, and eyes that danced and smiled, but could look very wistful, too, and romantic and sometimes very sad, like windows through which you could see down into her very soul. Miss Thomas's eyes were like windows, too, but the soul inside was very different.

Flora's mother's soul was like a rose-lit room, a little intimate interior where gay and charming and tender things were bound to happen. Miss Thomas's soul was like a vast arena, a battleground, Jane sometimes thought, where strangely impersonal wars were waged with a curiously personal ardour. Moreover, Miss Thomas could shut her windows. Flora's mother's were always wide open. Inviting, unprotected. You could see exactly what went on inside. But Miss Thomas could draw down the blinds, and sometimes did, when things displeased her. Then her face grew very cold and austere, but no less beautiful. A wise, wilful face, that made you understand just how she had accomplished so much, and feel that it was terribly important to do just what she wished you to do and help her make the world the place she thought it ought to be.

Jane came to know Miss Thomas's face very well and she never tired of looking at it. She came to know her views very well, too, and it always made her feel a little unworthy to hear them. Miss Thomas spoke to the students of women's rights and women's suffrage and women's work for temperance. She spoke to them of education and economic independence and their duty, as educated women, to make their contribution to the world of knowledge. She spoke with eloquence and conviction and a curiously childlike and disarming enthusiasm. Jane always felt very conscience-stricken because she knew, in her heart, that she would never do anything about all of this, that the seed was falling, as far as she was concerned, on barren ground.

Miss Thomas read from the Bible, too. Always very beautiful passages that she read very beautifully. Sometimes the echo of them lingered in Jane's mind, long after Miss Thomas had closed the book and the Quaker prayer had been said, and Miss Thomas was talking on quite mundane topics.

'She speaks with the tongue of men and angels,' Jane often thought, as she listened and looked at the upturned faces of the students all around her. 'Doth it profit her nothing?' The adolescent audience seemed dreadfully unworthy of the eloquence. Jane couldn't believe that her generation would ever grow up to be great and forceful and wise, like the generation that had preceded them. But Miss Thomas's confidence in the power of youth seemed to remain unshaken. She was never tired of directing it. Agnes said that was why she was a great college president.

'She works,' said Agnes, 'to make what she believes in come true. You can't do more than that.'

That was what Agnes did, in her small way, and Marion Park, too, who had turned out to be quite as nice as she looked. But did Jane? Jane often wondered. She couldn't see her life as a crusade — grievous as the wrongs might be in a world that needed them righted. Listening to Agnes and Marion Park, Jane often felt just as frivolous as Flora and Muriel.

At home, in the Christmas holidays, however, listening once more to her mother and Isabel, going out to parties where she tried not to be shy, missing André so dreadfully at every turn that nothing else seemed really to count at all, Jane had realized, of course, that she was all on Miss Thomas's side. Life must be more important than this, she thought. There must be things for even a woman to do that would be interesting and significant. She had only to look at Flora and Muriel, comparing their dance programs in a dressing-room door, to feel just a little smug and condescending. But back at Bryn Mawr, among the people who had definite plans for concrete accomplishment, she felt again very trivial and purposeless. She didn't really worry a bit as to whether or no she ever voted and she didn't want to work for her living and,

really, she only cared about pleasing André and growing up
into the kind of a girl he'd like to be with and talk to and love
and marry. It was very confusing. At home she felt like an
infant Susan B. Anthony. She had aired her views on women's rights with unaccustomed vigor, at the breakfast table.
Isabel had derided her.

'I hope you're satisfied, John,' her mother had said. 'She's
a dreadful little blue-stocking already.'

But her father had only laughed.

'The blue will come out in the wash,' he had prophesied
cheerfully. 'I doubt if it's a fast colour.'

Jane doubted it, too, as she sat on the window-seat with
Agnes. Agnes had the Latin examination paper in her hand.

'We might go over it with the trot,' she said, 'and see what
we got wrong.'

'Oh, Agnes!' said Jane. 'It's a lovely day. Let's go for a
sleigh ride. We'll have time before supper. You go and get
Marion and I'll call up the livery stable and order a cutter.'

III

'Next year,' said Agnes lazily, stretching her long limbs beneath the budding cherry tree, 'I'm going to begin Greek.'

Jane thought she would like to begin Greek, too. It made
her feel awfully illiterate to have to skip the quotations she
bumped into in English and French books. But she knew she
would never have the stamina to do it. The alphabet was too
discouraging.

'Agnes,' she said, 'it makes me tired to listen to you. I'm
going to take French and Philosophy and English.'

'I'm going to take an elective in Narrative Writing,' said
Agnes. 'I'm going to learn to write if it kills me.'

Jane contemplated the white froth of the cherry blossoms
against the stainless sky.

'This place is heaven,' she said.

The captain of the Freshman basket-ball team sauntered up to them across the green lawn.

'I wish you two would get out and practise with the team,' she said.

'Well — we won't,' said Agnes obligingly.

'We're intellectuals,' explained Jane sweetly. 'Sit down, Mugsy, and look at the cherry blossoms.'

Mugsy dropped down cross-legged on the grass.

'You'd be good, if you'd try,' she said persuasively.

Agnes shook her head.

'Our arms and legs don't work,' she said cheerfully.

'Only our brains,' said Jane.

'Oh — honestly!' said Mugsy.

'But they work very well,' said Agnes.

'Agnes's do,' said Jane. 'You know she's got two scholarships. They'll be announced to-morrow.'

Mugsy looked pleasantly impressed.

'Just the same,' she said, 'it wouldn't hurt you to get out and hustle for the class.'

'We never hustle,' said Jane. 'We achieve our ends with quiet dignity ——'

Mugsy arose in wrath.

'You make me sick,' she said, with perfect amity, and strolled off across the campus.

'This place is *so* nice,' said Jane, returning to the contemplation of the cherry blossoms. 'You can insult your dearest friends with perfect impunity.'

'There's Marion,' said Agnes.

Marion approached, Livy in hand. She waved two letters at Jane.

'Mail for me?' said Jane. Marion tossed the envelopes into Jane's lap and passed on, toward Taylor Hall. The letters were from her mother and Isabel. Jane opened Isabel's with a faint frown. Letters from home were not very inspiriting. Except her father's. Her eyes ran down the closely written pages.

'Good gracious!' she said.

'What's the matter?' asked Agnes.

'Great heavens!' said Jane.

'What's happened?' asked Agnes.

'Isabel's engaged!' said Jane, and turned the page. 'Oh, mercy! It's a secret! Don't you write home about it, Aggie!'

'Who's the man?' asked Agnes.

'I haven't come to him yet, but I gather he's a god.' Jane turned another page. 'She's awfully happy. He sounds perfectly wonderful.'

'Who *is* it?' asked Agnes.

Jane turned another page.

'Oh — for heaven's sake!' she said. 'It's Robin Bridges.'

'Robin Bridges?' questioned Agnes. Agnes didn't know many people.

'Oh, yes. You know. The fat boy. He's been underfoot for *years*. Small eyes and spectacles. Too many teeth. Nice and jolly, though. He plays a good tennis game.'

'When are they going to be married?' asked Agnes.

'She doesn't say, but she wants me to be maid of honour.' Jane's eyes continued to peruse the letter. 'Rosalie's going to be bride's matron. Just us two. A yellow wedding. Oh — here she says — this autumn. September. She does sound happy.' Jane's voice was just a little wistful.

'How old is Isabel?' asked Agnes. Perhaps her thoughts were following Jane's.

'Oh — awfully old,' said Jane. 'Twenty-three, last January.' She opened her mother's letter. 'Let's see how Mamma takes it.' She continued to read in silence.

'Well — how does she?' asked Agnes.

'She thinks it's grand,' said Jane. 'She says he's a dear boy. Boy! Why, Agnes, he's all of thirty! As if I didn't know Robin! She says it's very suitable. She says Papa went to Harvard with his father. She says Isabel has a beautiful sapphire. She says the engagement's going to be announced May first. She says they've begun on the trousseau already and she's going to take Isabel to New York to get her underclothes.'

'How romantic,' commented Agnes. 'There's a postscript on your lap.'

Jane picked up the second sheet. She read it very slowly.

'She says it's going to be very hard to give up her dear daughter and she says —— Oh, Agnes, she says — she says — that — that they want me home next winter because they'll be all alone.'

'Don't you listen to them!' cried Agnes excitedly.

Jane looked very much disturbed.

'It's awfully hard not to listen to Mamma,' she said.

'Don't you do it!' said Agnes. 'You got here, now you just stay!'

'Papa got me here,' said Jane.

'Well, he'll keep you here, if you put it up to him,' said Agnes.

Jane thought perhaps he would.

'Don't you let them put it over on you!' said Agnes.

'It must be awfully hard,' said Jane, 'to give up your children.'

'Don't talk like that!' said Agnes. 'Why do people have children?'

'I suppose,' said Jane soberly, 'because they love each other.'

'Well — we don't ask to be born, do we?' said Agnes. 'Just you stand firm, Jane.'

Jane looked a little doubtful.

'You gave up André,' said Agnes. 'I should hope that was enough.'

A little spasm of pain passed over Jane's sober face.

'This — this isn't like giving up André,' she said quietly.

'No,' said Agnes, 'but it's one more thing. You've got to do what you want to some of the time.'

Jane wondered if you ever really did. Life seemed terribly complicated. She rose to her feet.

'Come walk with me to the Pike,' she said. 'I want to wire Isabel.'

Agnes rose in her turn.

'Jane,' she said, 'don't tell me you've given up already!'

'No,' said Jane very seriously. 'No. I haven't. But families are difficult. I never know — *what* to do.'

She didn't know any better that night, as she lay wide awake in her little wooden bed. Miss Thomas would say — take your education. Her mother would say — honour your parents. Jane thought she honoured her parents and she knew she didn't want an education, really. Not enough to fight for it. What she wanted was liberty. But was even liberty worth the fighting for? Jane hated to fight. But perhaps, her father —— ? He was something to tie to. Jane honoured *him*. She honoured him more than any one, really. Except André. Her father would see her through. He liked people to be free. Her father —— Anyway there were two more months to this semester. Jane fell asleep at last with a final thought for Isabel. Isabel — who had a beautiful sapphire — and was happy with Robin — fat funny Robin — with spectacles — who was suitable — and thirty — so he could marry Isabel — when he wanted to — without any one making a fuss ——

IV

'It's grand,' said Agnes, 'to think you're really here. I can't get used to it.'

'I felt like a dog to leave them,' said Jane.

They were sitting out under the maple row in the bright October sunshine. The leaves overhead were incredibly golden. The October sky looked very high and hard and blue. A stiff west wind was blowing and the leaves were fluttering down all around them in the gale. Golden maple leaves twisting and twirling and drifting in every direction. The tops of the trees were already bare.

'That's nonsense,' said Agnes. 'You have to live your own life.'

You did, of course, but just the same Jane had felt it was almost impossible to take the train to Bryn Mawr the week after Isabel's wedding. Her mother had been very sweet about that wedding and very sorry to lose Isabel. Her father had been very sorry, too. He had come out of Isabel's bedroom, when he went up to say good-bye to her after the reception, choking and blowing his nose. He had squeezed Jane's hand very hard on the staircase, where she stood watching Isabel throw her bouquet. Under the awning, a few minutes later, in the midst of the laughing, jostling crowd, waiting for Isabel and Robin to rush madly in a shower of rice from the front door to the shelter of the expectant brougham, Jane knew just how he had felt. Her own eyes were full of tears as she saw the brougham, absurdly festooned with bows of satin ribbon, disappear down Pine Street. Incredible to think that Isabel was *married*. That she had left home forever.

That very evening, over the haphazard supper, mainly compounded of leftover sandwiches and remnants of caterer's cake, Mrs. Ward had begun on Bryn Mawr.

'How you can think of leaving your father and me at a moment like this ——' she said.

'I thought it was decided, Lizzie,' Jane's father interrupted.

Jane bit into an anchovy sandwich in silence, then discarded it in favour of a macaroon.

'How you can want to waste any more time in that ridiculous college,' said Mrs. Ward, 'instead of coming home and making a début with the girls your own age, friends you've had all your life ——'

'Minnie,' said Mr. Ward, 'do you think you could get me a cup of coffee? Lizzie — do we have to go over all this again?'

'Flora and Muriel will be grown up and *married* before you come home,' prophesied Mrs. Ward gloomily. 'You'll come out with a lot of girls you don't know — years younger than yourself ——'

'Flora and Muriel,' said Jane indifferently, 'aren't coming out this year, after all. They're going back to Farmington.' Muriel had told her yesterday. She hadn't thought to mention it at home.

'Flora and Muriel,' said her mother incredulously, 'are going back to Farmington?'

Jane nodded and passed her father the cream.

'Why?' asked her mother.

'Muriel wants to be with Flora,' said Jane, 'and Flora's mother doesn't feel up to a début this winter. You know she — she hasn't been very well.'

Jane didn't want to say quite all that Muriel had told her about Flora's mother. In a moment, however, she observed that discretion was not necessary.

'I shouldn't think she would be,' said her mother tartly. 'I always knew how it would end. Lily Furness is a little fool and always has been.' She looked eagerly over at Jane's father. 'I don't blame Bert Lancaster for getting tired of it.

He's been dancing attendance, now, for four years and more, and what does he get out of it? I shouldn't think she *would* feel very well, and I'm not at all surprised that she doesn't want Flora on her hands. She's got all she can do to hold Bert enough to keep up appearances. Why her husband didn't put a stop to it long ago, before it got to *this* pass —— '

'Lizzie!' said Jane's father with a glance at Jane. 'Minnie, I'd like another cup of coffee.'

Jane felt she had unconsciously dragged a very effective herring across the scent. Her mother had forgotten Bryn Mawr. Her thoughts were busily employed on more congenial topics.

'So Lily Furness doesn't want Flora home this winter,' she said dreamily. 'Well — I don't wonder. A great girl of nineteen in the drawing-room doesn't make it any easier to keep up the illusion.'

'Pass me a lady-finger,' said Jane's father.

There was a moment's pause.

'Well,' said Jane's mother at last, 'if Flora and Muriel aren't going to come out I suppose you might just as well be in Bryn Mawr as anywhere else for one more year.'

Jane could hardly believe her ears. She threw a startled glance at her father. He was draining his coffee cup with a slightly sardonic smile.

'But — leaving you and father,' began Jane conscientiously.

'You don't think very much of your father and me,' said Mrs. Ward, with a sigh. She rose from the table. 'This house is a sight,' she said. 'Minnie, get the dead flowers out of the way to-night. The men will come to pack the wedding presents in the morning.' She moved toward the door. 'If there's any punch left, keep it on ice.' She paused on the threshold to look back at Jane's father. Her face suddenly softened and looked a little wistful. 'Didn't Isabel look lovely?' she said.

'She did, indeed,' said Jane's father, rising in his turn.

'Robin's a sweet boy,' said Jane's mother. 'I hope ——' She paused inarticulately and looked up a little helplessly in her husband's face.

'I hope it, too, Lizzie,' he said very tenderly. Incredibly, he kissed her. Jane, staring at them in amazement, felt her eyes fill suddenly with tears. That was when she had felt like a dog to leave them.

'My Gawd!' said Agnes. And Agnes never swore. She was staring at the letter held open in her hand. Jane had just brought it upstairs, as she came in for tea. Marion was kneeling on the window-seat, looking out at the afternoon sunshine slanting palely over the March campus.

'What is it?' cried Jane. She paused, tea-kettle in hand, at the door.

'Scribner's — has — taken — my — story!' said Agnes solemnly.

Jane dropped the tea-kettle.

'Agnes!' she cried.

'They've sent me a check for one — hundred — and — fifty — dollars!' said Agnes. 'Jane! It can't be true! I must have died and gone to heaven.'

'Let me see it!' cried Jane.

There it was — the little green slip. One hundred and fifty dollars.

Jane and Marion could hardly believe their eyes. They all had tea together. They had tea together almost every afternoon, but this was a festival. They made a laurel wreath out of a strand of potted ivy and crowned Agnes's triumphant head. Jane began to quote Byron. They had just reached the Romantic Poets in General English.

> '"Oh, talk not to me of a name great in story,
> The days of our youth are the days of our glory,
> And the myrtle and ivy of sweet two-and-twenty
> Are worth all your laurels, though ever so plenty!"

There's your ivy, darling, we haven't any myrtle, but ——'

'Don't you believe it,' said Agnes. 'Byron was wrong. He was a funny man, anyway. I'd give up anything — anything in the world — just to write.'

'Maybe you won't *have* to give up anything,' said Jane. 'You write awfully well, now. Maybe you'll have your cake and eat it, too. Byron did,' she added very wisely. 'All the cake there was.'

'I'm not a bit like Byron,' said Agnes very seriously. 'I'm not at all romantic. I just want to accomplish.'

Marion nodded her head soberly as if she understood. There it was, again. Accomplishment. That thing for which Jane could never muster up any enthusiasm. Jane just wanted to live along and be happy. Live along with nice funny people who were doing interesting things and told you about them. Like Agnes and Marion. And André, who had always told her so much. Nice funny people who thought you were nice and funny, too.

Jane liked her work, though. Jane liked it awfully. She could really read French, now, almost as well as English, and she had loved the lectures on Shakespeare and she was thrilled by the Romantic Poets. She always did a lot of outside reading and she had learned pages of poetry by heart. Nevertheless she never got very good marks. Not marks like Agnes and Marion. It was because she couldn't be bothered with learning grammar and dates and irrelevant facts that didn't interest her. She had missed that entire question in the English midyears paper on the clauses of Shakespeare's will. Why should any one remember the clauses of Shakespeare's will? Jane couldn't be bothered with them. Not when she could curl up on the Pembroke window-seat and learn 'Romeo and Juliet' by heart. Jane thought 'Romeo and Juliet' was the most beautiful thing that she had ever read. She loved to repeat it aloud when she was alone in her bed at night or striding over the Bryn Mawr countryside with Agnes and Marion.

> 'What lady's that, which doth enrich the hand of yonder knight?'
> 'I know not, sir.'
> 'O, she doth teach the torches to burn bright!
> It seems she hangs upon the cheek of night
> Like a rich jewel in an Ethiop's ear.'

Lovely sounds — lovely phrases!

> 'He jests at scars that never felt a wound!
> But soft! What light through yonder window breaks?
> It is the east and Juliet is the sun!'

What fun to know lines like that! To have them always with you, like toys in your pocket, to play with when you were lonely.

> 'It was the lark, the herald of the morn,
> No nightingale. Look, love, what envious streaks
> Do lace the severing clouds in yonder east.
> Night's candles are burnt out, and jocund day
> Stands tiptoe on the misty mountain tops.
> I must be gone and live, or stay and die.'

Who would learn the clauses of Shakespeare's will? Agnes and Marion had, however.

Philosophy was simpler. Philosophy was very easy to learn. It was all about just what you'd thought yourself, one time or another, after you'd begun to grow up. It was strange to think that every one had always thought about the same things,

down the ages. God and man and the world. Herself and
Sophocles. Agnes and Plato. And felt the same things, too.
Romeo and Juliet. 'He jests at scars that never felt a wound.'
That was what Isabel had done, when André went to France.
Maybe, now she had Robin, she understood.

'Let's go for a walk,' said Agnes.

Jane jumped to her feet. There would be mud underfoot
but all the brooks would be running fast and the stripped tree
branches would be tossing in the mad March wind, and the
sun would be bright, and the sky would be blue, and perhaps
they would find the first hepatica.

They would go for a walk.

VI

The Commencement procession was forming in front of the
gymnasium. The day was hot and sultry, with the promise of
rain in the air. Jane and Agnes and Marion were all Sophomore marshals. They were dressed in crisp white shirt-waists
and long duck skirts and they had on their caps and gowns.
They each held a little white baton, with a white and yellow
bow on it, sacred insignia of office. The Seniors were in cap
and gown, too, and all of the faculty. The staid professors
looked strangely picturesque, standing about on the thick
green turf, with their brilliant hoods of red and blue and
purple silk. One scarlet gown from the University of London
made a splash of vivid colour against the emerald lawn. The
Seniors' hoods were all white and yellow, trimmed with rabbit fur. President Thomas was talking to the commencement
speaker. Some college trustees were clustered in a little group
around her. Funny old men, thought Jane! They looked
very flushed and hot in their black frock coats under academic
dress. Some of them were fanning themselves with their
mortar boards.

Jane was busy getting the Seniors into line. She knew nearly all of them well. She couldn't imagine how the college was going to get along next year without the Class of '96. She couldn't imagine, either, how she was going to get along without the college. It was settled, now. She was not coming back.

Her father had done his best for her. They had talked about nothing else all Easter vacation. Except Isabel's baby, which was coming in July. Her mother was determined that she should 'come out' with Flora and Muriel. Nothing else mattered. Her father had championed her cause whole-heartedly. But Jane had detected in his final surrender a certain note of relief.

'Two years,' he said, 'has been a long time to live without you, Kid. In this big house.'

The procession was taking form and substance at last. The trustees had lined up at its head. Miss Thomas had fallen in behind them with the speaker. Jane slipped into her place with Agnes just behind the wardens and in front of the Seniors. The procession began to move slowly along the gravel walk.

The day was really terribly hot and the air was lifeless. The maple trees in the distance looked very round and symmetrical, almost like toy trees. Their boughs were thick with leaves. The shadows beneath them were round and symmetrical, too, and very dark. The air was sweet with the odour of newly cut grass.

The procession wound deliberately across the lawn. The black-gowned figures looked very dignified and austere in the summer sun. The bits of silken colour flashed and shimmered, here and there, with the movement of their wearers. The campus seemed strangely empty, with all its inhabitants gathered into this little procession. Jane suddenly remembered her Keats.

'What little town by river or seashore,
  Or mountain built with peaceful citadel,
  Is emptied of this folk, this pious morn?'

The morn *was* pious and the great, grey, ivied buildings quite deserted. The sky overhead was softly blue. Beyond the maple row, however, great puffy white and silver thunderheads were rolling up in the west. It would surely rain before nightfall.

The procession turned into Taylor Hall. It shuffled down the tiled corridor, past the great bust of Juno at the head of the passage, and slowly ascended the stairs. The chapel was decorated with the Commencement daisy chain. It was very hot and very full of people. Fathers and mothers and sisters and brothers, all fanning themselves and craning their necks to look at the Seniors as they passed by. The faculty took their places on the platform. The Seniors filled the first six rows of chairs. Jane stood in line with the other marshals, facing the audience. The Head Marshal raised her baton. Every one sat down at once. The visiting clergyman rose to make his prayer.

Jane didn't listen much. She felt very hot and very, very sleepy. She had been up at dawn and out in the fields at six picking the daisies for the chain. It had been hard to get up but it was lots of fun to pick the daisies. The day had been cool, then, and the meadows were wet with dew. Jane had loved wading about in the long damp grass with Agnes and Marion, plucking great armfuls of the white and yellow flowers. They had gathered thousands in less than two hours. Whole fields were white with them. Great green fields, sloping up against the morning sky, with big white patches of dazzling daisies, shining in the morning sun. They picked until their fingers were red and sore.

"The meanest flower that grows,"' said Agnes, struggling

with a fibrous stem, 'in the words of the worthy Wordsworth.'

'Worthy, but wordy,' said Jane. She had found the 'Pre-lude' rather long. 'You could make an epigram out of that.' Agnes had done so at once.

> 'Wordsworth was a worthy man.
> He wrote as much as poet can.
> But if you try to read him through
> You'll find him rather wordy, too.'

Jane and Marion had both laughed uproariously. It made Jane laugh, now, sleepy as she was and right in the middle of the prayer, just to think of it. Agnes was terribly funny. It made Jane feel very sad to think that she would never laugh again like that, over nothing at all, with Agnes and Marion. She was going out into a world where, she was quite certain, nothing would ever seem as irresistibly funny as everything did at Bryn Mawr. She was going out to grow up and live at home and come out with Flora and Muriel and be a good daughter to her father and mother and a sister to Isabel and a sister-in-law to Robin and an aunt, grotesquely enough, to Isabel's baby. She thought she would much rather stay on in Pembroke and just be a Bryn Mawr Junior with no entangling alliances, whatever.

The prayer was over and the Commencement speaker was rising to his feet. Jane stifled a yawn. The heat was really terrific. Every window was open and Jane could see far out over the campus and the maple row to the rolling Pennsylvania hills beneath the thunder heads. What a lovely place to have to leave for Pine Street. She would carry it with her, though, back to the flat, sandy shores of Lake Michigan. She would remember, always, this paradise of flowering shrub and tree, of sweet green spaces and grey ivied walls. The memory would be a sanctuary. She was momentarily grateful to the wordy Wordsworth for an unforgettable fragment.

'They flash upon that inward eye
Which is the bliss of solitude.
And then my heart with pleasure fills,
And dances with the daffodils.'

Jane knew all about the inward eye. But she thanked the
poet for the phrase. If her education had done nothing else
for her, Jane reflected, it had provided her with an apt quotation for every romantic emotion.

The Commencement exercises dragged wearily on. Jane
couldn't remember, when she tried to concentrate, just what
the speaker had said his subject was. He seemed to be talking
about Opportunity. Jane didn't hear him define it. He had a
lot to say, somewhere toward the end, about Preparation for
Wifehood and Motherhood. That wouldn't please Miss
Thomas. She took those states of grace decidedly for granted.
He sat down at last and Miss Thomas arose in his place.
Jane listened dreamily. Not to the words but to the familiar cadence of that admired voice. She might never hear it
again, like this from a rostrum. Miss Thomas was very brief.
The dreary routine of giving out degrees began. The Seniors
advanced to the platform, six at a time, received their parch-
ments and descended. Miss Thomas's voice went steadily on.
'By the authority vested in the trustees of Bryn Mawr College
by the State of Pennsylvania and by them vested in me,' and
so forth and so on, for each little group, ending up with the
presentation of the parchment and the final impressive phrase
'I admit you to the degree of Bachelor of Arts of Bryn Mawr
College and to all rights, dignities, and privileges thereto
appertaining.' Rights, dignities, and privileges that would
never be Jane's. It was over at last.

The procession reformed and moved slowly out of the chapel.
On the stairs of Taylor Jane became suddenly conscious of
the change in the weather. The wind was up and great drops

of rain were pattering down on Taylor steps. The air felt clean and cold. The caterer's men were hurriedly dragging the tables set for the Commencement luncheon into the shelter of Pembroke. It couldn't be out on the campus, after all. And Jane couldn't take that last walk she had planned with Agnes and Marion, under the maple trees and down into the hollow. The procession had broken and scattered. Students and faculty, alike, were scurrying, with gowns upturned over silken hoods, to the protection of Pembroke Arch. Jane and Agnes ran there, hand in hand. There was nothing to do, now, but snatch a hurried luncheon and run back to her room to change for the train. Agnes was going to New York at three o'clock. She had taken a job with 'Scribner's Magazine' for the summer. Jane was leaving for the West a little later. Her last glimpse of the campus would be in the rain.

PART II
STEPHEN

PART II

STEPHEN

CHAPTER I

'You'll need,' said Jane's mother reflectively, 'at least four new evening dresses. The blue can be made over in the house.' She was standing in the doorway of Jane's closet, regarding Jane's depleted wardrobe with an appraising eye.

Jane, darning a stocking by the window overlooking the willow tree, was conscious of a certain sense of unwonted importance. Four new evening dresses. Nothing like that, of course, had ever occurred to her before.

'The pink,' continued her mother, turning to look at her earnestly, 'will be home in time for Flora's dance. You will need three others.' She gave a little sigh as she spoke. 'Things aren't as simple as they were when Isabel came out.'

'Here's Isabel now,' said Jane.

Her mother hurried to the window. There was Isabel, indeed, pushing the baby carriage up the side path.

'She's getting nice and thin again,' said Jane's mother, 'now she's stopped nursing the baby.'

Isabel saw them and waved cheerfully over the hood of the carriage. Jane thought she had never looked so pretty.

'I like her fat,' she said.

Isabel stooped to lift up the soft armful of afghans that was her son. His head wobbled alarmingly in his big blue bonnet and came safely to rest on Isabel's shoulder. She picked up a bottle and a bundle of blankets with her free hand and turned toward the side door.

'It's a great deal for Isabel to do,' said Jane's mother, 'to take care of that great child all by herself.'

'I think she likes it,' said Jane. 'I'd like it if he were mine.' Her nephew always appealed to her as an animated doll. She loved to go over to Isabel's little apartment in the Kinzie flats and watch her bathe and dress him.

Isabel's voice floated up the stairs.

'Aren't you ready?' she asked.

'You're early,' said Jane's mother.

'I know. I brought the baby over so he could have his nap.' Isabel appeared in the doorway. 'Jane ought to be there before it begins.'

They were all going over to Muriel's reception. Jane and Flora were going to pour tea.

'She will be,' said Jane's mother. 'Let me have him.'

Jane's mother sat down in the chair by the window with her grandson in her arms. She began unwrapping the afghans.

'Isabel,' she said, 'you don't keep this child warm enough.'

Isabel exchanged a covert glance with Jane. Jane knew just how she felt. He was Isabel's baby.

'Oh — he's all right,' Isabel said. 'Put him on the bed and let him kick.'

'Shut the window, Jane,' said Jane's mother, 'so there won't be a draught.'

Jane obeyed in silence.

'You ought to be getting dressed, Mother,' said Isabel.

'Give me that bottle,' said Mrs. Ward. 'I'll put it on ice.' She left the room, bottle in hand.

'Tell Minnie she has to watch him while we're out,' called Isabel. Then privately to Jane, 'Honestly — Mother gets on my nerves.'

'She's crazy about the baby,' said Jane.

'She gets on Robin's nerves, too, sometimes,' said Isabel, and opened the window.

It was curious, thought Jane, to see Robin and the baby insidiously wedging their way in between her mother and Isabel. They had always been so close before.

'Do you like my dress?' asked Isabel.

It was very pretty. Jane recognized it at once. The blue and yellow stripe made over from the trousseau.

'It's just as good as new,' said Jane.

'No, it's not,' said Isabel. Her pretty face was clouded. 'And it's *much* too tight. But it has to do.' Then irrelevantly, 'Robin got a raise last week.'

'That's good,' said Jane. 'Unbutton my waist, will you?' Isabel's fingers busied themselves with hooks and eyes.

'What do you know about Muriel?' she asked.

'Muriel?' said Jane, surprised. She wasn't conscious of anything.

'Muriel and Bert,' said Isabel. 'Bert Lancaster.'

'Bert *Lancaster?*' echoed Jane. 'What about them?'

'Rosalie says he's crazy about her.'

'Isabel!' cried Jane. 'That old man!'

'He's not forty,' said Isabel. 'I don't believe he's more than thirty-eight.'

Jane slipped out of her skirt and turned toward her closet door.

'He sends her flowers,' said Isabel, 'three times a week.'

'Every one,' said Jane, 'sends Muriel flowers.'

'He's over there,' said Isabel, '*all* the time.'

'Great for Muriel,' said Jane laconically. Then, emerging from the closet, 'Here's my new dress.'

'It's lovely,' said Isabel. Jane thought it was too. Pink taffeta with écru lace revers over the enormous sleeves. 'You'll look sweet.'

Jane walked over to the walnut bureau and began to take down her hair.

'Mrs. Lester.' said Isabel, 'doesn't like it a bit.'

'Why, she hasn't seen it!' cried Jane indignantly. No one could help liking that pink taffeta dress. It was ordered for Muriel's début.

'Not the dress, goose!' laughed Isabel. 'Bert.'

'Oh!' said Jane, immensely relieved.

'Rosalie says she can't do a thing with Muriel,' said Isabel. 'Of course she never could.'

'Do you think I ought to curl my hair?' asked Jane anxiously. 'I suppose I could learn ——'

Isabel regarded her very seriously, her head on one side.

'N-no,' she said slowly. 'I like it straight. 'You've got a certain style, Jane, all your own.'

That was the first time that Jane had ever heard that. She flushed with pleasure.

'I shouldn't think she *would* like it,' resumed Isabel. 'Robin says Bert's been awfully fast.'.

'Ready, Jane?' It was her mother's voice. Mrs. Ward stood in the doorway. She looked very pretty in her violet gown with her little black lace shoulder cape and violet bonnet. 'Who opened the window?' Mrs. Ward promptly shut it and walked over to the bed to feel the baby's feet solicitously, with a reproving glance at Isabel.

'Hook me up,' said Jane, backing down on her sister just in time to prevent an outburst of protest.

'What were you saying,' asked Mrs. Ward, 'that Robin said about Bert?' The baby was forgotten. Isabel faced her mother over Jane's shoulder with a kindling eye. Jane could see her in the mirror.

'Robin says,' she began eagerly, 'that Bert has always gone an awful pace. And Rosalie says that Freddy thinks it's dreadful of her mother to let Muriel have anything to do with him.'

'It would certainly be very awkward,' mused Jane's mother, 'if it should come to anything. Considering Muriel's friendship with Flora.'

'I don't think Flora has ever noticed a thing,' said Isabel. 'Do you, Jane?'

'Did she ever mention it?' asked Jane's mother.

'No,' said Jane, and took her new hat out of the hat-box.

'Lily Furness is a fool,' said Mrs. Ward, 'but in a way she's clever. I dare say she'd be very careful.'

'She's not very careful now,' said Isabel. 'She looks like the wrath of heaven.'

'I don't understand,' said Mrs. Ward with dignity, 'why she hasn't more pride.'

'You never see him there any more,' said Isabel. 'You *don't* ever see him, do you, Jane?'

Jane was putting on her hat before the mirror. It was a very pretty hat with a big pink taffeta bow standing high in the back. Jane adjusted her white face veil, making little mouths at herself in the glass as she drew it down tightly over her chin.

'Why, no,' she said slowly, 'I — I haven't — lately.'

'It would be sad,' said Jane's mother, shaking her head, 'if it weren't so silly.'

'It's certainly silly,' said Isabel, laughing. 'Giving yourself away like that over a man who's running around after your daughter's best friend ——'

Jane turned suddenly to face them. Her eyes were snapping with anger.

'I don't think it's silly at all,' she said abruptly. 'If it's true, I think it's tragic. I *like* Flora's mother. She's always been lovely to me. And she's always been perfectly beautiful. She is still. If — if Bert Lancaster ever — ever loved her and

—and got over it, I think he's the one that's silly. Chasing after Muriel Lester who's young enough to be his own daughter! I think it's dreadful for people to get over loving ——'

'Has it ever occurred to you,' said Jane's mother icily, 'that Flora's mother is a married woman?'

Jane felt suddenly deflated. And a little unequal to coping with the complications the situation presented. But she stood by her guns.

'I don't care if she is,' she said stoutly. 'She's no more married now than she was when it began. Anyway, I think it's her own business.' She caught up her wrap from the bed and stooped to kiss the baby. 'Isabel, he *is* cute. I'm ready, now.'

'You look very well,' said her mother.

In the hall they met Minnie, coming up all smiles to play nursemaid. Isabel lingered to speak to her for a moment. Mrs. Ward was on the stairs.

'You can open the east window,' Jane heard Isabel murmur. Then her mother's voice rang out from the lower hall.

'Come on, girls! The cab's at the door.'

II

The November air felt very cool and bracing as they stood on the front steps. It was very luxurious, Jane thought, to be driving over to Muriel's in a cab when it was only four blocks away. Everything at home seemed luxurious, after Bryn Mawr. It really wasn't nearly as bad as she had thought it was going to be. It was fun to be with her father again. He had given her a new desk and a bookcase to hold all her Bryn Mawr books. Her mother had had her room repapered. It was very exciting to buy all the new clothes and to feel herself, for once, the central figure on the little family stage. Even Isabel seemed to think that nothing was too good for her. Hats and frocks and shoes and stockings were arriving every day, regardless of expense. Jane was a little appalled at the outlay, but every one else seemed to take it completely for granted. Jane was a débutante. She had to have things. Her mother had even ordered her some new calling cards, though the old ones were not half used up. 'Miss Ward,' they said, with the 'Jane' left off. Jane couldn't quite think of herself as 'Miss Ward.' She was, of course, now Isabel was married.

The cab turned the corner that always made her remember André's last smile. She could still see his tall, slender figure, walking, furiously fast, up Pine Street. But she had grown accustomed, now, to missing André. The first fall days, that always made her feel that school should be beginning, had brought him to mind at every turn. She had planned to go to see his mother just as soon as she was sure that she was back from her summer in France. Mrs. Duroy would tell her all about him.

She had mentioned that projected visit a little diffidently to her father. She had not seen Mrs. Duroy since the night of the bicycle picnic. Two years ago and more. Her father had looked at her very kindly.

'They've gone, Jane,' he said gently.

'Gone?' she had echoed faintly.

'He was called back to Europe. Stationed in Prague, now, I think. They left last winter, soon after Christmas.'

So that was that.

'Papa,' Jane had said, rather hesitantly, 'do — do you know anything about André?'

'Not a thing, Kid. Haven't heard of him since he left.'

'I — I wish I could have seen his mother,' Jane had said miserably, 'before she went away.' Her father patted her hand. There was nothing to say. Prague. Jane wasn't even quite sure what country it was in. She kept thinking of André in Prague. Or Paris.

She kept thinking, too, of Agnes and Marion, and of what they were doing, each hour of the day, on the green October campus. It was very easy to imagine that, for the Bryn Mawr days were marked off meticulously hour by hour, with a fixed, unchanging programme. A quarter to nine — chapel was assembling. Miss Thomas was entering the rostrum. The choir was tuning up. The Quaker prayer was begun. Ten minutes past nine — Agnes was settling down for her Greek lecture. Ten — Marion was entering Major Latin. Twelve — the English professor was ascending the stairs. One — Pembroke dining-room was a babel of tongues. Four — Agnes was getting out the tea-kettle. Five — they were running down the Gulf Road for a brisk walk before supper. Jane could almost hear Taylor clock striking off the hours.

It was nearly four now. Nearly five in Bryn Mawr. Agnes and Marion were washing up the tea-things that very minute. They were laughing about something, of course. Something funny that Agnes would have said. Jane forgot them, however, at the sight of Muriel's awning. It was her first big party. Next week she would have an awning of her own.

The doorman, resplendent in maroon broadcloth and brass buttons, flung open the cab door with a flourish. Jane followed her mother and Isabel up the red velvet carpet. She remembered, just in time, to pick up her pink taffeta train.

The Lesters' big house was in very festive array. There were palms from the florist's and flowers everywhere. Great gold and russet bunches of chrysanthemums and roses of every kind and colour. The front hall smelled faintly like a greenhouse. A line of caterer's men bowed them up the stairs. They were very early, which was quite as it should be. Jane's place was awaiting her behind the great silver tea-kettle in the dining-room.

Jane flung off her wrap in the lacy splendour of the Lesters' guest-room. A waiting-maid seized it as it fell. She folded it meticulously and laid it on the bed. Jane looked in the long glass. So, she had a style of her own, she thought. Isabel had said so, and Isabel knew. Jane couldn't see it, however. But her gown was very pretty and her waist was very small and her cheeks were pink with excitement behind her sheer white face veil. She ran down the stairs ahead of her mother.

The four Lesters were standing ceremoniously at the parlour door. The room seemed very bare and strangely neat, with all the furniture pushed back against the walls, and all the ornaments removed to make way for the magnificent flowers. Mrs. Lester looked perfectly enormous in purple satin. Muriel, at her side, incredibly angelic, in white lace. Her hair was a black cloud. Her eyes were very bright and blue, dancing with pleasure. She carried a great bunch of white sweet peas. She flung her arms around Jane excitedly. Edith, imported from Cleveland, was next in line. Jane hadn't seen her for nearly three years. She looked a lot older, Jane thought, and rather tired. Rosalie was chattering to the last guest, a funny old lady in a satin cape. Freddy Waters and the Cleveland brother-in-law were talking together near the front window. With their sleek blond heads and their black frock coats and their dove-coloured neckties they looked as much alike as the two Dromios.

Jane passed down the line and stood a moment, uncertainly, in the empty room. She didn't know the old lady and she never knew what to say to Freddy Waters. She hadn't seen the Cleveland brother-in-law since his wedding day, four years before. She wandered a bit uneasily toward the dining-room door. There was Flora behind the chocolate pot. Flora, very fair and frail, looking like a little Dresden shepherdess in pale blue silk. Jane took her place at the other end of the table. An obsequious caterer's man hovered behind her chair. Or perhaps he was the new butler. Jane couldn't remember. Some people that she didn't know were standing around the table, plates in hand. She was too far away from Flora to talk. She could hardly see her over the great orchid centre-piece.

Somebody asked for some tea. Jane poured it out in silence. More people were coming into the room. Jane didn't know any of them. Lots of them wanted tea. Jane was kept quite busy. She could hear Flora chattering away at her end of the table. Flora knew ever so many people. Some men came in. Quite old ones. They gravitated around Flora. She seemed to have lots to talk about. One grey-bearded gentleman was a trifle deaf. He was asking Flora a question.

'Jane Ward,' she heard Flora say. 'Jane Ward. Mrs. John Ward's daughter.'

'John Ward's daughter?' Jane heard him reply. 'Didn't know there was another.' He was staring at her over the orchids. 'Pretty little filly.'

Jane felt unaccountably exhilarated. She looked up at an old lady who was asking for tea, with a ravishing smile.

'Doesn't Muriel look lovely?' she said politely. The old lady must at least know Muriel.

'Muriel who?' said the old lady. But Jane was not discouraged. She went on smiling and trying to talk. Pretty little filly, he had said.

Freddy Waters came in with three young men. He brought them up to Jane.

'They want tea,' he said, and introduced them.

Jane realized at once that she had been so excited that she hadn't heard their names. But she smiled very steadfastly,

Pretty little filly. Very soon the young men were laughing. One of them pretended that the massive hot-water kettle was too heavy for her to lift. He filled the empty teapot himself. Jane thought he was awfully attractive. She felt her cheeks growing hot in the crowded room. She hoped they were growing pinker. More young men came in. Her unknown swains introduced them. Jane didn't hear their names, either. One of them brought her some pink punch.

'There's a stick in it,' he said, smiling.

Jane felt quite daring, drinking it. She glanced across at Flora. Flora was drinking it too. She was surrounded by young men. The old ones had all gone. Two elderly ladies were waiting for their chocolate, a bit impatiently. They got it, finally, from the caterer's man.

The room was very hot, and very, very noisy. Jane had to scream to be heard. It was easier to talk when you screamed, she discovered, much easier than in a silent room. When you screamed, things seemed funny.

Presently there was a little disturbance at the dining-room door. Lots of young men came in, and then Muriel. Muriel looked flushed and terribly excited. Her cheeks were rose pink. She was waving her sweet peas and laughing at every one. Close behind her was Mr. Bert Lancaster. He looked old, Jane thought, among all those gay young people, but awfully handsome. His moustache was just right. It was waxed, the least little bit, at the ends. There was a white sweet pea in his buttonhole.

He cleared the way for Muriel to the tea-table. The crowd was thinning out. Muriel patted Jane's shoulder.

'Tired, darling?' she asked. Mr. Lancaster offered her a cup of tea. She shook her head. 'I want something cold.'

One of the young men sprang to get some punch. When he came back with it, Mr. Lancaster took the glass cup out of his hand and gave it to Muriel himself. The young man glared resentfully. Muriel smiled up into the eyes of Mr. Lancaster and drank the punch with little gasps of delight.

'I *was* so thirsty,' she said. 'I'm awfully hot.'

Mr. Lancaster took her arm very gently, just above the elbow. He steered her through what was left of the crowd to the bay window at the end of the room. He opened the sash a little. Muriel stood leaning against the red velvet window curtains, fanning herself with her sweet peas. Mr. Lancaster was bending over her, his eyes upon her face.

'May I have a cup of tea, Jane?' said somebody softly. Jane started and looked up. It was Flora's mother. She had on a tiny black bonnet with one pink rose and a perky little black velvet bow that stood up behind. Her face was framed in the black lace ruff of her little cape. It looked very pale against that background and when she raised her veil, Jane thought her lips were white. In a moment, though, she was laughing with one of the young men. Her laugh was very low and silvery and her eyes were very bright. Her black dotted veil was tucked coquettishly up over her little nose. The young man seemed enslaved at once. Flora's mother looked up into his eyes and laughed again. The young man was immensely flattered. Jane was staring up at them, just as she had stared, a moment before, at Mr. Bert Lancaster and Muriel.

'Do you know this dear child?' said Flora's mother. She introduced the young man. Jane smiled very dutifully, but she couldn't compete with Mrs. Furness. The young man returned to his devotion. Flora's mother put her teacup down. The tea was untasted. Two more young men were talking to her now. She turned to leave the room and all three went with her.

Jane's eyes returned to Muriel. She was still standing with Mr. Lancaster by the window. He was talking to her, very earnestly, but Muriel's eyes were wandering brightly over the crowd. She was not bothering much to listen to him. Jane returned to her tea-pouring.

Suddenly she saw Rosalie enter the room. She walked straight over to Muriel and she looked very much provoked. She said something sharply and Muriel turned away with her toward the door. Mr. Lancaster followed.

'You've got to stay in line with Mamma,' said Rosalie angrily, as they passed Jane's elbow. 'I've been looking all over for you.'

They walked toward the door together. Mr. Lancaster was strolling behind them pulling his moustache and smiling. On the threshold they almost ran into Flora's mother. She spoke at once to Mr. Lancaster and smiled, very prettily, up into his face. He answered rather briefly, and, after a moment, Flora's mother turned away with her three young men. Mr. Lancaster followed Muriel into the parlour.

Jane heard an excited whisper in her ear.

'Did you see that?' It was Isabel. Jane thoroughly despised her. She felt terribly sorry for Flora's mother and she hated Mr. Bert Lancaster. But, most of all, she despised herself for having seen it. She had seen it all, she had stared at it, just like Isabel. It quite spoiled the end of the reception.

III

Jane stood in Flora's bedroom, smoothing her hair before the long mirror, while Flora's maid sewed up the torn net flounces of her pink dancing-frock. Lots of other girls were there, too, repairing the ravages of the evening. Muriel, at her elbow, was busy changing her flowers. She had carried a big bunch of gardenias all the first part of the party and, now that they were bruised and brown, she was replacing them with a second corsage of white violets. Jane knew that Bert

Lancaster sent white violets, sometimes. Muriel looked very
pretty. She had on a dress of bright blue satin that exactly
matched her eyes and she had a snood of blue velvet ribbon in
her hair.

It had been a beautiful evening. Flora's dance had been a
great success. They had just come up from supper and the
cotillion was going to begin immediately. You could hear the
orchestra faintly, from the ballroom upstairs. It was playing
a waltz. Muriel began to sing the air, very softly:

> 'Casey would waltz with a strawberry blonde,
>   And the band played on.
> He'd glide 'cross the floor with the girl he adored,
>   And the band played on——'

Jane's feet were twitching to the rhythm. She could hardly
stand still long enough for the maid to take the last hurried
stitches.

'Ready, Muriel?' she said.

Muriel pitched the gardenias into the waste-basket and
skewered the violets more securely to her whalebones.

Jane paused to pat Flora's mother's pug. He was a very old
dog, now, and he was lying in his little blue-and-white basket
on the sofa where the maid could keep him company. His
name was Folly. It didn't seem very appropriate as he
wheezed and snuffled over her caress. He wore a tan blanket
for his rheumatism and he looked just like a little pop-eyed
old man in a light overcoat.

'There!' said Muriel. 'Come on.'

They ran lightly up the stairs together to the third floor. The
arched entrance to the ballroom directly faced the staircase.
The ballroom stretched across the front of the house. Its
six tall windows pierced the mansard roof. The orchestra was
bowered in palms on a little platform at the end of the room.
The walls were hung with smilax. The floor was quite empty,

for the moment. It was ringed with gold caterer's chairs and in one corner there was a long table festooned with cotillion favours. Hoops and staffs and wreaths and hats of coloured paper. There was a great crowd of young men around the door and five or six girls. Among them Flora, queen of the ball, shimmering in white taffeta, a great sheaf of pink roses in her arms. Mrs. Furness was standing beside her. She didn't look like a mother at all, Jane thought, in that violet velvet gown, with its long, slinky train. Her golden hair was just as bright as Flora's, and her willowy waist as slender. She was smiling and shaking her head at one of the young men over a spangled violet fan. Mr. Furness, looking very plump in his evening dress and just a little choked in his high stiff collar, was opening the windows to cool off the room before the dancing began again. He had quite a little struggle with one of them. His bald head was shining in the light of the crystal chandelier. Several young men ran over to help him. The cold night breeze swept over the floor.

Many more girls had come in, now, and the band was slipping into a polka. Flora's mother caught up her train over her long gloved arm and glided out on the floor in the arms of one of the young men. Her great puffy violet velvet sleeves accentuated the slimness of her figure. She was a beautiful dancer. In a moment two other couples had joined them. Muriel pranced past with an impetuous partner. Jane found an arm around her waist. She picked up her train and began polka-ing with ardour. The floor was crowded all too soon.

The music stopped at the note of an imperious whistle. Mr. Bert Lancaster was standing in the doorway. Mr. Bert Lancaster always led cotillions.

'Take seats!' he shouted.

There was a mad rush for partners and a madder rush for the little gold chairs. Jane had promised this cotillion weeks

ago. Miraculously, her partner found her in the confusion of
the room. They ran for the coveted places near the favour
table. Mr. Bert Lancaster advanced slowly to the centre of
the floor. It was clearing rapidly. Mr. Lancaster stood waiting, whistle in hand, under the crystal chandelier. He had a
lieutenant at his elbow. Jane had met him at supper. He
was Stephen Carver, Flora's cousin from Boston. He knew all
about cotillions, Flora had said. He was a very slim young
man with frank blue eyes and curly blond hair and a budding
moustache that didn't show for much, just yet. He had just
come to Chicago to live, and he didn't know many people.
Jane thought he was very good-looking. Flora said he was
nice. Every one was seated, now. Mr. Lancaster blew his
whistle.

The band immediately struck up 'El Capitan' and Mr.
Lancaster began running very swiftly around the circle,
counting off couples as he ran. Sixteen of them rose to dance.
They led off in a romping gallop. A little group of dowagers
had gathered behind the favour table, Jane's mother among
them. The whistle blew imperiously. The dancers raced for
favours. The first girl on the floor was Flora. She was holding
a great hoop of paper flowers over her head. An eager young
man dragged Mrs. Furness, lightly protesting, from the group
of dowagers. She caught up her train and whirled off in his
arms. Jane caught the gleam of disapproval in her mother's
eye. The floor was crowded now. The whistle blew again.
The girls formed in a great circle, with hoops upraised, the
men in another around them. Mr. Lancaster was miraculously agile and very active, coat-tails flying, in the centre.
Stephen Carver had joined the line of men. Both circles began revolving rapidly in opposite directions. The whistle
blew. The men took partners. The dancing started once
more.

Jane sat very excitedly on the edge of her gold chair, her
eyes bright with pleasure. She didn't bother to talk to her
partner. Cotillions were fun.

'Wait for me!' a young man called, waving his white-gloved
hand. He returned at once with a crêpe-paper boa. Jane
flung it around her neck and sprang into his arms. Halfway
round the room the whistle parted them. Jane joined the great
crowd of girls at one end of the floor. The whistle blew
and the men came racing, slipping, sliding down upon them.
Jane found herself in the arms of Stephen Carver. She looked
up in his face and laughed.

'You're the girl I met at supper,' he said. He was really
very handsome. And he danced divinely.

'You met lots of girls at supper,' said Jane, laughing.

'I remember *you*,' said Stephen. Jane felt pleasantly elated.
He *was* nice, just as Flora said. The whistle blew.

'Refavour!' shouted the commanding voice of Mr. Bert
Lancaster.

'Don't let's,' said Stephen. This seemed strangely anar-
chistic. Jane was a little doubtful. But Stephen's arm continued to hold her firmly, steering her steadily away from the favour table to the empty end of the room. Jane was afraid she
was being conspicuous. But she loved to waltz. In a moment
whirling couples were all around them. The whistle blew
and they were inevitably parted. In the serpentine line of
girls, however, he incredibly found her again.

'You're a beautiful dancer,' he said.

'Our steps go well together,' said Jane simply.

'You bet they do,' said Stephen, and his arm tightened
slightly. Jane was almost glad when the whistle sounded and
he returned her to her chair. Of course he was Flora's
cousin. But she had only just met him.

Mr. Bert Lancaster was really outdoing himself. The danc-

ing waxed fast and furious. Soon the girls looked a little di-
shevelled and the young men very hot indeed. The chairs
were heaped with the débris of favours. The crowd around
the punch-bowl in the hall grew thicker. In spite of Mr.
Furness's open windows the room was very warm.

Flora was on the floor every minute. Her mother was constantly whirling past. Jane caught a glimpse of Mr. Lancaster
dancing with Muriel. Muriel had on a red paper sunbonnet.
Her hair was loosened around her flushed face and she was
leaning back to look up at Mr. Lancaster as they waltzed.
Her gloved hand, outstretched in his, held her swirling blue
train. Mr. Lancaster seemed to have forgotten all about the
whistle. Stephen Carver blew his and the couples all parted,
a little hesitantly. Mr. Lancaster remembered, then. He led
a grand right and left with abandon and ended it just where
he could catch up Muriel at the end of the line. They raced
off together in a rollicking two-step.

Mrs. Furness began to look just a little tired. Faint shadows
showed beneath her eyes and in the hollows of her cheeks. She
sat with the dowagers, now, smiling over her spangled fan,
springing up to offer great armfuls of favours to insistent
young men as they bore down on the table.

Jane danced and danced until her pink-slippered feet were
weary. It must be growing late, she thought. She hated to
have the party over. The favour table was nearly depleted.
Some of the dowagers were already gone. She kept meeting
Stephen Carver in the cotillion figures. He had favoured her
four times. Suddenly she found herself hand in hand with
him in a circle of six that should have been four. He dropped
out at once, taking her with him.

'That's a leading from the Lord,' he said. 'Let's go and get
some punch.'

They slipped out into the hall together.

'What's your name?' he said. 'Do you know, I can't remember it!'

'Jane Ward,' said Jane.

'You look like a Jane,' he said.

She laughed at that.

'It's a very plain name,' she said. 'I was named for my grandmother.'

'Not plain,' he answered. 'Simple. Like your hair. Like your face, too.'

They had reached the punch table. He handed her her glass.

'Come and drink it on the sofa,' he said.

They walked across the hall and sat down together.

'I'm going to like Chicago,' said Stephen. 'I didn't think I would.'

Jane thought that was just the way she had felt, when she first came home from Bryn Mawr.

'Are you lonely?' she asked.

'Not very,' said Stephen. 'Just bored. I live in Miss Miller's boarding-house.'

Every one knew Miss Miller. Lots of young men boarded with her.

'That's just around the corner from me,' said Jane.

'May I come to see you?' asked Stephen.

'Of course,' said Jane.

'May I come Sunday?' Sunday was day after to-morrow.

'Of course,' said Jane again.

'Flora told me about you,' said Stephen. 'You're a great friend of hers, aren't you?'

'Yes,' said Jane. She had finished her punch. The music sounded very alluring. Jane began to think of her deserted partner. 'We'd better go back,' she said.

Stephen rose a little reluctantly. The whole room was

up, when they returned, twisting about in an intricate basket.

'That's the next to the last figure,' said Stephen. 'There's just one more for Flora.'

They mingled with the dancers as the basket broke into couples. Jane had seen her mother watching her as she came in from the hall. Her eye was very indulgent. The whistle blew. Every one sat down. Jane's partner greeted her with enthusiasm.

'Look what's coming,' he said.

Mr. Bert Lancaster was dragging a gold chair out into the centre of the ballroom floor. In one hand he held a silver mirror and a red paper rose.

'All men up!' he shouted.

A regiment of black-garbed figures sprang to the command. The gaily dressed girls, left on the golden chairs, looked like a flower border around the room. 'Of course,' said Jane to herself, 'wall flowers!' She had never thought of it before.

Mr. Lancaster was running down the room toward Flora's seat. Muriel was sitting beside her. Jane could see her smiling steadily at Mr. Lancaster as he approached. She had taken off the sunbonnet, now, and her curly hair was ruffled all over her head. The blue snood had slipped rakishly askew. Flora was putting down her roses on the empty seat at her side. Mr. Lancaster made a little gesture. Both girls half rose. Flora sank back in her seat at once, but Muriel stood up, still smiling steadily. Mr. Lancaster paused an instant. Muriel laughed, a little wickedly. Every one could see that she was laughing at Mr. Lancaster. Her blue eyes were dancing straight into his.

Suddenly Mr. Lancaster seized her hand and began running with her down the room. Flora looked very much astonished. She picked up her roses again. Muriel was laughing still and her hair was flying. She was trying to tuck it under the snood with one hand as she ran. Mr. Lancaster almost hurled her into the little gold chair and gave her the red rose and the silver mirror. His face looked very queer. He blew his whistle and the band began playing 'After the Ball.'

The long line of men filed by, one by one, each pausing to peer over Muriel's shoulder in the silver mirror. Muriel was laughing all the time. She shook her head at every face in the glass. Stephen Carver was the last to go by. His hand was outstretched to help her to her feet. She shook her head at him. He looked very much astonished. Every one was watching rather breathlessly. The men in front of Muriel were a little nonplussed.

Suddenly she threw the rose right over their heads, straight into the hands of Mr. Bert Lancaster. He almost dropped it, he was so surprised. Then he suddenly made a dash for Muriel. The music swirled up in a triumphant wave. Muriel and Mr. Lancaster began dancing. For a moment they were the only couple on the floor.

Then the other men began to favour. Four slid at once to Flora's feet. Stephen Carver catapulted himself at Jane. Every one was dancing at once, almost immediately. Round and round the room they went, swooping and swirling with the lilting strains of the waltz. Stephen was looking down all the time at Jane's brown head. She could feel his eyes on her. She could feel them so hard that she didn't look up.

The music rose and fell, in surging waves of sound. Some of the men began to sing, sentimentally. The light voices of girls joined airily in the chorus. The tender words rose mockingly, liltingly, above the strains of the band.

> 'After the ball is over, after the break of morn,
> After the dancers' leaving, after the stars are gone ——'

The verse was a little ridiculous, Jane reflected. Not up to the music.

> 'Many a heart is aching, if you could read them all,
> Many the hopes that have vanished — after — the — ball!'

The words *were* silly. Unreal, like all poor poetry. Stephen was a marvellous dancer. Dancing was heaven, thought Jane.

But the party was over. The waltz changed insensibly into the familiar cadence of 'Home, Sweet Home.' Every one kept on dancing. When the band finally stopped, it was greeted with a burst of applause. A little staccato rattle of clapping hands.

Flora was standing at the ballroom door with Mr. and Mrs. Furness. She looked excited and happy as she shook hands with the departing guests. But her mother's face was very cold and proud. A little bright spot of color burned in either cheek. She held her little blonde head very high. Mr. Furness looked more sleepy than anything else.

Mr. Lancaster passed from the room at Muriel's elbow. Flora's mother hardly spoke to either of them. Muriel kissed Flora. Jane's mother turned up at her side as she was talking to Stephen in the hall.

"Til Sunday, then,' he said, as he turned away.

'Flora's cousin,' said Mrs. Ward, as they went down the stairs, 'is very attractive.'

'Isn't he?' said Jane indifferently.

'He comes from a very good Boston family,' said Mrs. Ward, 'on his father's side.'

They had reached the entrance to the dressing-room. The dressing-room was very crowded. Mrs. Ward had nothing more to say until the doorman had shut the cab door upon them.

'Did you see,' she asked, then, at once, 'what Bert Lancaster did?'

'I thought Muriel did it,' said Jane.

'It was disgraceful of both of them,' said Mrs. Ward.

'Muriel's like that sometimes,' said Jane very wisely.

'Lily Furness looked as if she were through with him forever,' said her mother.

Jane stifled a yawn. She felt suddenly very sleepy.

'But I don't suppose she is,' said Mrs. Ward.

IV

The Christmas tree spread its green boughs in the darkest corner of the library. The little pink wax angel at its top almost touched the ceiling. The little pink wax angel had always crowned the Christmas tree. Jane could remember the time when she had thought it was very wonderful of Santa Claus to remember to bring it back every year.

Mr. Ward sat comfortably in his leather armchair. He was smoking a new Christmas cigar. Mrs. Ward was watching the Christmas candles a little anxiously. She was always afraid of fire. Isabel was sitting on the floor under the tree trying to keep the baby from snatching the low-hung ornaments. The baby could creep, now, and he was very inquisitive. Robin Bridges was standing beside them, watching his son with a proud proprietary twinkle in his small blue eyes. His gold-bowed spectacles glittered in the candlelight. Around his neck was a welter of Christmas socks and ties. He was really a dear, thought Jane.

The room was a chaos of tissue paper and scarlet ribbon. Jane had a new gold bracelet. She was awfully pleased with it. Agnes had sent her a book of poetry. It was called 'Barrack Room Ballads.' It was written by Rudyard Kipling. Jane had never heard of him. She had dipped into them and she thought they were very good. She had never read anything just like them.

Christmas morning was fun. This year it was more fun than ever because there was Isabel's baby. He was called John Ward after his grandfather. Jane's father had been very pleased about that.

Christmas morning was gay. The doorbell kept ringing and Minnie kept bringing in intriguing little packages. Several potted plants had come for Mrs. Ward. They stood on the window seat, underneath the holly wreath. But Mrs. Ward was more interested in her family than in her presents.

'Look out, Isabel!' she said. 'Don't let him suck that cornucopia!'

Isabel exchanged a silent glance with Robin. Suddenly Minnie appeared once more on the threshold. She held a long florist's box in her arms.

'For Miss Jane,' she said.

'Somebody loves you!' cried Isabel.

Jane jumped up, flushing with pleasure. People didn't send her flowers very often. Not as they did Flora and Muriel, who had always a bunch of violets on their coat collars. Jane opened the box. Twelve beautiful dark red roses. Jane buried her nose in their dusky petals.

'Who sent them?' cried Isabel.

Jane looked at the card.

'Stephen Carver,' she said. She was very much surprised. She had only seen Stephen Carver twice since Flora's dance, two weeks ago.

'How nice of him,' remarked her mother. 'A young man like that, in a boarding-house.'

'He can afford it,' said Isabel. 'Rosalie says his father is the president of the Bay State Trust Company.'

No one could ever tell Jane's mother anything about any one's father.

'It was said at the time,' she remarked thoughtfully, 'that Lily Furness's sister-in-law married very well.'

Jane took the roses out of the box. Their stems were very long and impressive.

'Get a vase, Minnie,' said Mrs. Ward.

The doorbell rang again. Minnie hurried to answer it. A sound of stifled laughter arose in the hall.

'Don't announce us, Minnie. We want to surprise them,' said a tittering voice. The library door was flung open and Muriel stood on the threshold. She was dressed in a bright red broadcloth suit, trimmed with black astrakhan fur. Her hands were tightly clasped in a little black muff. A great bunch of white violets was pinned to her shoulder. Behind her loomed the tall figure of Mr. Bert Lancaster.

'Come in!' cried Isabel, scrambling to her feet. Mrs. Ward began to pick up the tissue paper.

Muriel just stood in the doorway and laughed. Her cheeks were bright red from the frosty December air. Her eyes were very starry.

'Merry Christmas!' she said. 'Do you know why we've come?'

Mrs. Ward stopped picking up the paper. Every one stared at Muriel.

'We're engaged!' cried Muriel. She took Mr. Bert Lancaster's hand and pulled him into the room.

Every one began talking at once. In the midst of the uproar Jane felt Muriel's arms around her neck and the cold pressure of her cheek against her own.

'Isn't it exciting?' said Muriel. She was sitting on the edge of the sofa now, smiling up at all of them. Mr. Lancaster stood looking down at her. He looked just a little embarrassed, Jane thought, but awfully handsome, with his overcoat thrown open over his red muffler and his tall silk hat in his hand. Jane stared at him incredulously. She couldn't believe that Muriel was going to — marry him. It made Jane

feel very queer to think that any one just her age was really
going to marry any one. And Mr. Bert Lancaster. He was
older than Robin. He was older than Freddy Waters. He
was almost old enough to be Muriel's father.

'Look at my ring,' said Muriel, pulling her hand out of the
little black muff. It was the largest solitaire that Jane had
ever seen.

'Oh — Muriel!' said Isabel reverently.

'We've got to go,' said Muriel, jumping up. 'We just
came for a minute. We've got to go and tell Flora.'

Jane saw her mother and Isabel exchange a covert glance.

'We'll be married Easter Week,' said Muriel. 'Of course,
Jane, darling, I want you for a bridesmaid. Rosalie's going to
be matron of honour.' She was out in the hall already. She
was hanging on Mr. Lancaster's arm. Jane and Isabel and
Robin trouped with them to the front door. It was barely
closed before Jane heard her mother's voice upraised in
shocked surprise in the library.

'Well — it's happened,' she said.

They all went back to the tree.

'Mrs. Lester did all she could,' said Isabel.

'And she's going over, now, to tell Flora.' For a moment
Jane's mother's eyes met Isabel's.

'Do you suppose,' said Isabel at last, 'that Muriel really
knows?'

'Every one knows,' said Mrs. Ward. There was a brief
pause.

'Oh, well,' said Mrs. Ward, 'we must let bygones be bygones.'

'Just the same ——' said Isabel. Then, 'I suppose Flora
will be a bridesmaid.'

'Lily Furness,' said Mrs. Ward very firmly, 'is just reap-
ing what she sowed.'

Jane was glad to hear the doorbell ring again. In a moment Minnie appeared on the threshold.

'Mr. Carver,' she said, 'for Miss Jane.' Stephen Carver's tall blond head was visible over her shoulder. Mrs. Ward made another dive at the tissue paper.

'This room is a sight,' she murmured hurriedly.

'Merry Christmas!' said Jane.

Stephen Carver advanced into the library a little shyly. He had never met Isabel. In shaking hands he almost stepped on the baby. Robin snatched his son from the path of danger.

'Isn't this nice?' said Stephen. 'I didn't think I was going to see a Christmas tree.'

'Your roses were beautiful,' said Jane. Stephen looked very much pleased.

'Sit down, Mr. Carver,' said Jane's mother.

'Have a cigarette,' said Robin.

'Christmas at Miss Miller's must be rather dreary,' said Isabel.

Jane's father was looking at Stephen rather steadily behind a cloud of cigar smoke. He looked pleased at what he saw, however, and a little amused. Stephen turned to Jane.

'I — I hope you don't mind my dropping in like this,' he said, 'on a family party.' His smile was still a little shy. Jane beamed at him reassuringly.

'Why don't you stay to luncheon?' said Mrs. Ward very cordially. 'Since you're just at that boarding-house.'

Stephen's face lit up.

'I'd love to,' he said. 'If — If ——'

Jane's eyes began to twinkle.

'Don't hesitate,' she said mockingly. 'We have plum pudding on Christmas with brandy sauce.'

'I wasn't hesitating!' said Stephen indignantly. Then

added humbly, 'I was just thinking — do — do you really want me?'

'Of course we do,' said Jane's mother.

Stephen's eyes questioned Jane's a little uncertainly. He wasn't speaking to her mother. Jane felt a pleasing sense of power. Her father looked even more amused.

'Why, of course, stay,' said Jane loftily.

Stephen looked extremely delighted. Jane's sense of power increased. She glanced at him rather archly. She felt just like Flora and Muriel.

'Run and tell Minnie to put on another place, Jane,' said Mrs. Ward. And Jane felt just like Jane again. She was glad Stephen had come, however. It would keep her mother and Isabel from talking. She felt very badly about Muriel's engagement.

CHAPTER II

'THERE!' said Isabel, with a last reassuring pat at Jane's blue muslin train. 'You look lovely.'

Jane tried to peer through the bevy of bridesmaids into the tall mirror that was hung on the dim brown walls of the vestibule of Saint James's Church. They all looked lovely, she thought. They were carrying great shower bouquets of pink sweet peas over their muslin flounces and they wore broad-brimmed hats of pale blue straw. Rosalie looked loveliest of all, and as young as any one. No one would ever have guessed, thought Jane, that Rosalie was twenty-five, or that she was going to have a baby before the summer was over. Jane would never have known about the baby if Isabel hadn't told her.

Isabel had dropped in at the improvised dressing-room for a private view of Muriel's wedding dress. Muriel hadn't come yet. When Jane peeked through the curtains she could see the late afternoon sunshine slanting in at the west door of the church and the wedding guests entering by twos and threes, hushing their laughter as they crossed the vestibule, waiting in silence for the frock-coated, boutonnièred ushers to take them in charge at the inner door. The organ was playing the 'Barcarolle' from 'The Tales of Hoffmann.' Jane could hear it quite distinctly.

Isabel's eyes were wandering over the bridesmaids.

'Where's Flora?' she asked.

'She's not here yet,' said Jane.

'Was her luncheon for Muriel fun to-day?' asked Isabel.

'Yes,' said Jane.

'Was Mrs. Furness there?' Isabel lowered her voice.

'No,' said Jane. She had been sorry not to see Flora's mother. Jane had hardly had a glimpse of her all spring. She had carried Flora off to St. Augustine immediately after Christmas and when they returned in February she had left town again at once, to visit her sister-in-law, Stephen Carver's mother, in Boston. Stephen had said she had been very gay there. She looked tired, Jane had thought, when she came home.

'I *do* wonder ——' began Isabel.

Her voice was a mere murmur. Jane moved away from her a little impatiently. She knew very well what Isabel wondered. Isabel and her mother had been wondering it all week. So had lots of other people, to judge from the wealth of opinion that they had managed to quote on the question. Would Flora's mother come to Muriel's wedding? Would she walk up the aisle at her husband's side and take her place in the pew reserved for Flora's family to see Muriel marry Mr. Bert Lancaster? Isabel had been inclined to think that she would never have the nerve to do it. Jane's mother had declared that you could always do what you had to do, and that she would be very much surprised if Lily Furness didn't carry it all off beautifully.

For Jane this continued speculation had quite spoiled the wedding. Other things had spoiled it, too, of course. The parties before it hadn't been so very gay. The ushers were all old men, for one thing, not one under thirty-five. And for another, Mrs. Lester, who was usually so jolly and easy-going, had never succeeded in looking really happy about it. She never seemed to achieve with Mr. Bert Lancaster the comfortable maternal approach that she had with Freddy Waters and her son-in-law from Cleveland. Freddy Waters was in the wedding party. All the ushers but one were married. No, the parties hadn't been so very gay.

'Here's Muriel now!' cried Isabel eagerly. The brides-maids all turned from the mirror. Here was Muriel indeed, a transfigured, preoccupied Muriel, trailing great lengths of stiff white satin, her cloudy hair hidden beneath the formal folds of her mother's lace wedding veil.

'Look out for my train!' was the first thing that Jane heard her say. She was speaking to the maid who was carrying it very carefully over the red velvet carpet.

Mrs. Lester and Edith and Edith's husband followed her into the dressing-room. Edith's husband was going to give Muriel away. Old Solomon Lester was too infirm, now, to make the trip from New York to his granddaughter's wedding. Jane's mother and Isabel had thought his recent stroke a merciful intervention of Providence. It would be a relief, they said, to have *one* Lester wedding that was free from the taint of the synagogue.

Mrs. Lester stood silently by Muriel's elbow, adjusting the wreath of orange blossoms that held the veil in place. Mrs. Lester was growing old, thought Jane. She had on a beautiful gown of wine-colored silk, but her face looked very worn and tired.

The bridesmaids made an aisle so that Muriel could look in the mirror. She stood quite still and straight, smiling into the glass. Edith and Rosalie and the maid began to arrange the long folds of the satin train. Muriel's gloved hands were clasped on a white vellum prayer book. The third finger of the left glove was slit, so that Mr. Lancaster could slip on her wedding ring.

Jane felt very solemn as she looked at her. She thought of all the years that she had known Muriel. She couldn't remem-ber the time, really, before she had known her. In a way this was worse than Isabel's wedding. Isabel had been twenty-three. Her big sister. And Jane had loved Robin. Muriel was — just Muriel. A kid, really, like Jane herself. And yet she was getting married. To Mr. Bert Lancaster. It all seemed very sad and terribly irrevocable. It would be dreadful to be getting married, thought Jane.

Muriel turned from the mirror.

'See my pearls, girls,' she said brightly. 'Aren't they lovely? Bert sent them this morning.'

Jane winked away her tears. The bridesmaids circled about the pearls with little cries of admiration.

'I must go,' said Isabel. She kissed Muriel and turned toward the curtain. Flora was just coming in. Jane caught a glimpse of Mr. Furness standing alone in the outer vestibule beyond. Isabel joined him.

'How lovely Flora looks!' said Isabel brightly. 'What a beautiful day for a wedding!' They turned toward the church door in the slanting sunshine. Jane wasn't deceived for a moment by Isabel's airy inconsequence. Jane knew that before Isabel sank decorously on her knees beside her mother in the third left-hand pew, she would whisper that Mrs. Furness hadn't come.

Edith was kissing Muriel, when Jane turned around.

'Come, Mother,' she said.

Mrs. Lester took Muriel in her arms. Mrs. Lester was frankly crying.

'Don't muss her veil!' cried Rosalie.

Mrs. Lester relinquished her daughter. Rosalie rearranged Muriel's draperies. The Cleveland brother-in-law offered his arm.

'How's your nerve?' he asked cheerfully.

'Fine!' said Muriel. Her eyes were dancing behind the folds of white lace. Her cheeks were very pink.

'Come, Mother,' said Edith again. They turned toward the church door.

Jane fell into line with Flora. They were to be the first pair of bridesmaids. The ushers were lining up in the vestibule. The one in front of Jane was quite bald. He had one absurd long brown lock of hair, combed carefully over the thin place on top of his head. Flora nodded at it and nudged Jane's arm and giggled. The organ throbbed forth a solemn premonitory strain. The ushers began to move slowly through the inner door. The first notes of the Lohengrin wedding march swelled out over the heads of the congregation.

Jane and Flora walked very slowly, keeping their distance carefully from the ushers in front of them. Jane held her head very high and her shower bouquet very stiffly so her hands wouldn't tremble. The church looked very dark, after the afternoon sunshine, and the aisle very long indeed. Over the heads of the ushers Jane could see the green palms and the white Easter lilies and the twinkling candles of the altar. They seemed very far away.

The pews were crowded with people, all rustling and moving and craning their necks to look at the wedding party as it went by. Jane suddenly remembered the Commencement procession in the Bryn Mawr chapel. She turned her head very slightly, half expecting to see Agnes's funny freckled face under a black mortarboard at her side. But no. There was Flora's pure pale profile beneath the blue straw hat-brim. Her lips were curved, just the least little bit, in a self-conscious smile. Her step was a trifle unsteady. Jane felt her own smile growing set and strained and her own knees wobbling disconcertingly. It was hard to walk so slowly, with so many people staring.

Suddenly she noticed Mr. Bert Lancaster. He was standing with the best man at the left hand of old Dr. Winter, the clergyman, on the chancel steps. He looked very calm and handsome, just as he always did. Just as Jane had seen him

look at innumerable other weddings, that were not his own.
The ushers were forming in two rows along the chancel steps.
Jane and Flora passed them slowly, separated and took their
places at the head of the line. Jane could see Muriel now.
Her head was bowed under the white lace veil. At the chancel
steps she raised it suddenly and smiled at Mr. Bert Lancaster.
Mr. Lancaster wheeled to face the clergyman. Jane could see
both their faces now, upturned toward the altar. They were
so near her that it seemed indecent to look at them, at such a
moment. Jane turned away her eyes.

The organ sobbed and throbbed and sank into silence. The
voice of the clergyman could be distinctly heard.

'Dearly beloved brethren, we are met together in the sight
of God and this company to join together this man and this
woman in the holy estate of matrimony ——'

'This woman,' thought Jane. Muriel *was* a woman, of
course, not a kid any longer. Muriel was twenty. Jane would
be twenty, herself, next month. Flora was twenty-one. They
were grown up, all of them. Capable of entering the holy
estate of matrimony, if, and when, they chose. Mrs. Lester
had hated this marriage. But she hadn't stopped it. She
couldn't stop Muriel. Nevertheless, Jane knew that if Muriel
had been *her* mother's child something would have been done.
Still — Jane wondered. Muriel was — Muriel. Greek would
have met Greek. Jane's mother, at any rate, Jane knew very
well, would always prevent Jane from doing anything that she
didn't think was wise. But who, Jane wondered, was the best
judge of wisdom? Didn't you know yourself, really, better
than any one, what you really wanted, what was the real right
thing for you?

André — Jane knew, now, of course, that the family
couldn't have let her marry him at seventeen. She couldn't
even imagine, now, what their life would have been together,

what *her* life would have been without all those other experiences that had crowded into it since she had closed the door on that early romance. Bryn Mawr and all the things she had learned there. Agnes and Marion and, yes, Miss Thomas, with her flaming torch of enlightenment, and that gay, carefree life in Pembroke Hall. The beauty of the Bryn Mawr countryside. This last year, too, with its funny frivolities, its social amenities, its growing friendships with people that Jane knew, really, in her heart of hearts, were awfully unlike herself. All those experiences were part of her, now. Inalienable. Not ever to be ignored, or belittled, or set lightly aside.

But, nevertheless, there was the memory of that incredible joy of companionship that she had known with André. That identity of interest, that tremulous sense of intimacy, that glorious dawning of emotion.

The sound of Muriel's voice roused her from revery.

'I, Muriel, take thee, Albert, for my wedded husband, to have and to hold from this day forward ——'

'From this day forward' — solemn, irrevocable words. How could Muriel say them? Some marriages lasted for fifty years. How could *any one* say them? How could she have been so sure, so very sure, with André? She hadn't thought about the fifty years at all. Jane felt quite certain it was just because she had been seventeen. She hadn't reflected. She hadn't considered. She would never feel like that, thought Jane with a little shiver, about any one ever again.

The ring was being slipped on Muriel's finger. Mr. Lancaster's firm voice rang out in those irrelevant words about his worldly goods. Jane had always considered them a blot on the wedding service. The clergyman was uttering his last solemn adjuration.

'Those whom God hath joined together, let no man put asunder.'

The organ was tuning up with the first shrill pipes of the Mendelssohn wedding march. Muriel, her veil thrown back from her lovely flushed face, had turned, on Mr. Lancaster's arm, to walk down the aisle. Rosalie and the best man had fallen in behind them. Jane and Flora turned smartly to move in their turn. The organ pealed joyously on. High up above their heads the chimes in the steeple were ringing. The march down the aisle was executed much more quickly. Jane kept recognizing the faces turned up to her, from the aisle seats of pews. She smiled and nodded gaily as she went. The recessional had taken on a very festal air. All sense of solemnity was lost.

Jane caught a glimpse of Stephen Carver, staring at her face from his seat beside Mr. Furness. She almost laughed, he looked so very serious. He smiled back, just as he passed from her field of vision. The church doors were open. The vestibule was a confusion of bridesmaids. Great crowds of people were pressing against the awning to see the wedding party come out. Jane jumped into a waiting hansom with Flora. They must hurry over to the reception. Jane wanted, awfully, to give Muriel a great hug for luck. She wanted to stand in line and laugh and be gay and talk to all the people. Weddings were fun, always, if you could just forget the ceremony. Jane felt she *had* forgotten it. And Flora was chattering gaily about the bridesmaids' dresses. Flora was so glad they were blue. She was going to take out the yoke and turn hers into an evening gown. The cab drew up at Muriel's door. There was another crowd around this second awning. Jane and Flora ran quickly, hand in hand, up over the red carpet.

Muriel and Mr. Lancaster were standing, side by side, under a great bell of smilax. No one had come, yet, but the ushers and bridesmaids. Jane flung her arms around Muriel in a great rush of feeling. Muriel looked perfectly lovely. Jane

almost kissed Mr. Lancaster in the strength of her enthusiasm.
But not quite.

II

Jane woke next morning a little weary from the festivities
of the wedding. The reception had ended in a buffet supper
for the nearest friends of the family. Later there had been
dancing. Mr. and Mrs. Albert Lancaster had left about half-
past nine in the evening. It had all been over by ten.

Isabel and Robin had strolled down Huron Street with Mr.
and Mrs. Ward and Jane. The April night was pleasantly
warm. They had parted from Mr. Furness and Flora under
the awning.

'I really admire Mr. Furness,' Isabel had commented as
soon as they were out of hearing, 'for the way he stuck it out
all evening.'

'He had to — for Flora,' Mrs. Ward had said.

'Just the same,' said Isabel, 'he behaved beautifully with
Bert.'

'He always has,' said Mrs. Ward; then added meditatively,
'and you must remember that Bert Lancaster's marriage may
simplify things in the end.'

Jane had thought silently of Flora's mother. She had
thought of her more than once during the party. She couldn't
help wondering what Mrs. Furness was finding to do, all alone
at home all evening with Folly, the pug, in that big brown-
stone house. She wondered again, as she was dressing for
breakfast.

Jane sauntered downstairs, humming the first piping bars
of the Mendelssohn wedding march. Muriel and Bert were
well on their way to the Canadian Rockies, by now. As soon
as she entered the dining-room, she saw that something dreadful had happened.

Her father was standing at the window, his back to the table, gazing out at the bright amber branches of the budding willow tree. Her mother was in her accustomed place behind the coffee urn, but her chair was pushed back, her napkin was on the table, and her eyes were fixed questioningly on her husband's motionless figure. Her face had a curiously shocked expression. Jane paused a moment, fearfully, on the threshold.

'What's — what's the matter?' she asked.

Her mother turned slowly to look at her. The colour had quite gone out of her face.

'Lily Furness has killed herself,' she said.

'Wh — what?' said Jane. She couldn't take it in, just at first. She leaned a little helplessly against the door jamb.

'She killed herself last night — after supper,' said Mrs. Ward excitedly. 'She turned on the gas in the bathroom. Mr. Furness found her there when he came home.'

Jane walked weakly over to the breakfast table and sat down in her chair.

'*Killed* herself?' she asked stupidly. 'Flora's mother is *dead?*' It was the first death that Jane had ever known.

'They couldn't bring her 'round,' said Mrs. Ward. 'They had to break down the door. They worked over her for hours. They didn't give her up until long after midnight. Stephen Carver telephoned this morning.'

'How — perfectly — terrible!' said Jane, through stiff lips. Words seemed dreadfully inadequate.

Mr. Ward turned suddenly from his contemplation of the willow tree.

'Eat some breakfast, Kid,' he said gently. He walked over to Jane and put his hand on her shoulder.

'What will Flora *do?*' cried Jane. Her eyes filled suddenly with tears.

'Lily Furness should have thought of that,' said Mrs. Ward. Jane's father looked at his wife very soberly.

'Will you give me a cup of coffee, Lizzie?' he said. He sat down quietly at his end of the table.

'I — I want to go over to Flora,' said Jane suddenly. 'She'll be all alone — with Muriel gone.' A sudden memory of whom Muriel had gone with froze the words on her lips.

'Eat your breakfast first, Kid,' said her father. Her mother handed him his coffee cup. 'Ring for Minnie, Lizzie,' he said.

Minnie came in very promptly with the steaming cereal. Her face looked shocked, too, but discreetly curious and very subtly, delicately pleased. Jane felt that Minnie was enjoying disaster. She choked down a few spoonfuls of oatmeal and bolted a cup of scalding coffee.

'I'm going, now,' she said. She rose as she spoke.

'Jane' — her mother's voice was just a little doubtful — 'I don't quite like your going over there, so soon — all alone ——'

'I *want* to go,' said Jane. 'I want to be with Flora.'

'I think you had better wait,' said Mrs. Ward, 'until I can go with you.'

Jane stood irresolutely beside her chair.

'Let her go, Lizzie,' said Mr. Ward. 'She may be able to do something for that poor child.'

Jane's mother's face was still a little doubtful, but she made no further objection as Jane turned toward the door.

'How Lily Furness could do this to Muriel ——' Jane heard her say, very solemnly. 'It will *kill* Mrs. Lester.'

'I think the honours are still Muriel's,' said Mr. Ward gravely. 'She did a good deal to Lily Furness first.'

Jane walked very slowly and soberly down Pine Street in the brilliant April sunshine. The grass plots were already green and there was an emerald mist on the plume-like boughs of the elm trees. The streets were quite deserted, save for a milk wagon or two and an occasional bicycle. Jane saw the first robin, prospecting for worms, under Flora's budding lilac bushes.

The shades were all drawn down in the big brown-stone house. Halfway up the front steps, Jane stopped in dismay. She hadn't expected to see the great bow of purple silk and the huge bunch of violets on the doorbell. She didn't quite know whether to ring it or not. As she stood hesitantly in the vestibule, the door was opened silently. The Furnesses' elderly butler stood gravely on the threshold. His face looked very old and grey and tired and his eyes were sunken. Jane suddenly realized that he had been crying. As she stepped into the silent hall she felt her own eyes fill quickly with tears.

The house was very dark, because of the drawn window shades. A great vase of Easter lilies stood on the hall table. Their pure, penetrating perfume suddenly recalled the church chancel of yesterday.

'May — may I see Miss Flora?' asked Jane.

Suddenly she heard a masculine step behind the drawing-room portières. The tall, slim figure of Stephen Carver was framed in their green folds. His eager young face looked strangely serious. His manner was curiously hushed and formal. Nevertheless, his eyes lit up when he saw Jane.

'Jane!' he said softly. 'How like you to come!' He walked quickly over to her side.

'How is Flora?' asked Jane. 'Can I see her?'

'She's in her room,' said Stephen. 'I haven't seen her, myself, since — last night.'

'Is — is she — terribly broken up?' asked Jane.

Stephen nodded gravely.

'And Mr. Furness?' questioned Jane. She hoped very much that she would not have to meet Mr. Furness.

'He's with — Aunt Lily,' said Stephen. 'He's been there right along. I don't think he's slept at all.' There was a little pause. 'I just came over to answer the telephone,' said Stephen.

'Do you think,' said Jane hesitantly, 'that I could go upstairs?'

'I'll take you up,' said Stephen.

Side by side they mounted the staircase in silence. In the upper hall Jane was vaguely conscious of a faint, penetrating odour. It was almost imperceptible, but Jane recognized it at once. The great round red gas tanks on Division Street smelled that way, sometimes, when you bicycled past them.

The door to Flora's mother's room was closed. As they went by, Jane stumbled over something in the darkness — something small and soft and living. Jane knew, instantly, before she looked, that it was Folly, the pug, lying on the hall carpet, his little wrinkled muzzle pressed tightly against the crack of the door.

'Oh — Stephen!' she said faintly. Folly seemed terribly pathetic. It was incredible to think that little, old, rheumatic Folly was living, when Flora's mother — Flora's brilliant, young, gay mother — was dead. Irrevocably dead.

Stephen pressed Jane's hand in the darkness. Then she saw the bathroom door. There was a Chinese screen drawn around it, but Jane could see the splintered panels over the top. In the hushed order of that silent corridor, those broken, battered bits of wood assaulted the eye with the brutality of a blow.

Stephen paused before Flora's door. Jane tapped lightly.

'Flora,' she said, 'it's Jane.'

'Come in, Jane,' said Flora's tearful voice. Jane opened the door and closed it again upon Stephen Carver.

Flora was sitting up in her little brass bed, surrounded with pillows. She looked incredibly childlike and appealing, with her long yellow hair falling around her little tear-blanched face and the great tear-stained circles under her wide blue eyes. She held out her arms to Jane. Jane hugged her passionately.

'Flora,' she said, 'do you know how I loved your mother?' Jane was a little shocked to observe how easily she had slipped into the past tense. Flora's mother seemed dreadfully dead, already.

'Every one loved her,' said Flora brokenly.

'Every one,' thought Jane, 'but one. And that one ——' Jane found herself wondering, with the horrible curiosity of Isabel, if Flora knew.

'She never came to, at all,' said Flora presently. 'Her — her heart had stopped. I — I don't see how it could have happened. She was locked in the bathroom. She — she must have fainted.'

Jane's horrible curiosity was satisfied.

She sat quite still on the bed, holding Flora's hand in hers. There did not seem to be much to say. The old heart-shaped picture frame had been moved from the dressing-table to the bed ·stand. Within its silver circumference Flora's mother smiled radiantly over her feather fan. Alone on the dressing-table Mr. Furness stared solemnly from *his* silver heart. He looked as out of place there as ever. Jane's mind wandered, uncontrollably, to Flora's mother's problem. She felt she understood perfectly. Flora's mother's heart was just another silver frame. Fat, puffy Mr. Furness, with his pale, popping eyes, and grey moustache, had never really belonged there. Life was dreadful, thought Jane.

There was a gentle tap on the door. The discreet voice of a maid was heard.

'Miss Flora — Mrs. Lester has called.'

Flora looked doubtfully at Jane.

'Shall I tell her to come up?' she asked.

Jane nodded. Mrs. Lester could always be counted on.

The maid departed with the message. Presently there was a second tap at the door. Jane rose as Mrs. Lester entered the room. Mrs. Lester's enormous bulk was shimmering in dull black taffeta. Under her little black bonnet, her face looked terribly old and yellow and shocked and sad. Her kind dark eyes were weary and bloodshot. Their whites were ivory yellow. Jane realized, suddenly, how grey Mrs. Lester's black hair had grown during this last year. In her arms she held a bunch of white roses and a big cardboard dress box.

'Flora, dear,' she said very gently, 'I've come to do anything I can for you.' She laid the roses down on the bed. Flora picked them up and buried her face in them and suddenly began to cry.

'Flora, dear,' said Mrs. Lester again, 'you'll need help. You and your dear father are very much alone.' She sat down in an armchair that Jane had drawn forward and began to open the dress box. 'I've brought you the little black frock, dear,' she said, her hands busy with the wrappings, 'that Rosalie wore last year for Freddy's father. I think it will just about fit you. You can wear it until your new things come home. You must let Rosalie shop for you, Flora. You must let every one help you.'

Flora continued to cry, silently, into the roses. She didn't look at the black frock at all. Jane had forgotten all about mourning.

'You'd better get up, dear,' continued Mrs. Lester steadily; 'you'll feel better if you're doing something.'

'There's — nothing — to do,' sobbed Flora.

'There's lots to do for your poor father,' said Mrs. Lester sadly.

'Papa doesn't — want me!' faltered Flora. 'He — he's with Mamma. He's locked the door. He doesn't want me at all.'

A sudden spasm of pain seemed to pass over Mrs. Lester's face. The absurd little mouth above its double chins quivered, uncontrollably. Mrs. Lester took her handkerchief out of her little silver chatelaine. She wiped her eyes, quite frankly.

'He *will* want you, Flora,' she said. 'Come, dear, get up now. The thing to do is always to keep busy.'

Flora obediently slipped from beneath the bedclothes. She looked very slim and frail in her long white nightgown.

'We'll stay with you, dear,' said Mrs. Lester kindly, 'while you dress.'

Flora moved silently about the room, collecting her underclothes. The blue muslin bridesmaid's dress still lay in a heap on a chair. Jane rose to pick it up. She smoothed its crumpled folds and hung it up, very carefully, in Flora's closet. Flora sat down before her mirror to comb her yellow hair. She was looking much better already. Mrs. Lester was right. The thing to do was to keep busy.

'I — I somehow forgot about Muriel,' said Flora presently, with a wan little smile. 'Of course you haven't heard from them yet, Mrs. Lester?'

Mrs. Lester had risen and was shaking out Rosalie's black gown. She looked a little startled.

'No, dear,' she said. 'No — I haven't.'

'Of course,' said Flora, 'they're still on the train.'

A forgotten fragment of something rose up in Jane's mind. Something very far away and almost forgotten. What was it? Oh — of course! 'In the mean time Æneas unwaveringly pursued his way across the waters.' Faithless Æneas! Why hadn't she thought of it before? It was just like Dido. Dido, who had loved and lost and died a gallant lady. Why did books seem so different from life?

When Flora's curls were coiled in place she rose and took the black dress from Mrs. Lester's hands. Mrs. Lester hooked it up the back for her.

'It fits you beautifully,' she said.

Flora looked very white and thin in the sepulchral folds. And strangely older. She moved to the bed to pick up the white roses. As she did so another discreet tap sounded at the door.

'Mrs. Ward, Miss Flora,' said the voice of the maid.

'I — I'll come down,' said Flora. They moved silently together out of the room. Jane didn't look at the bathroom door again. Folly was still keeping his vigil. They stepped around him and went down the staircase.

Mrs. Ward was waiting in the green-and-gold drawing-room. She was standing up in the centre of the room, under the crystal chandelier. Stephen Carver was nowhere to be seen. Mrs. Ward took Flora in her arms and kissed her very kindly. She smiled then, gravely, at Mrs. Lester. Jane caught the faint glint of appraisal in her eye. Mrs. Lester looked terribly sad and broken and somehow unprotected. Jane was sorry she did.

'Flora, dear,' began Mrs. Ward, taking a little package from under her arm, 'I've brought you the crêpe veil I wore for my own dear mother. A young girl like you will only need crêpe for the funeral ——' Mrs. Ward drew the veil from its wrappings. It was very long and black and crinkly and it smelled faintly of dye. Mrs. Ward sat down on a little gold sofa. The veil trailed over the skirt of her light grey street dress. Flora looked at it in silence. Mrs. Lester sank wearily down in a gilt *bergère*. Mrs. Ward looked up at Flora as if she didn't know just what to say to her. Then she patted the sofa seat beside her.

'Come and sit down, dear,' said Mrs. Ward. 'I want to talk to you about your dear mother.'

Flora sank obediently on the green brocade cushions. She turned her big blue eyes silently on Mrs. Ward.

'Flora,' said Mrs. Ward very solemnly, 'this is a very terrible thing. I don't know what you've been thinking, but I just want to tell you that I have always felt that we should never judge others. We must keep our charity. You must remember always only the best in your mother. You must try to forget everything else. You may be very sure that every one else will forget it too ——'

A sudden noise in the hall made Jane turn suddenly to stare at the door. Mr. Furness stood there, between the green brocade portières. His puffy face was livid and swollen and his pale blue eyes looked very, very angry. His mouth was trembling under his grey moustache. He was positively glaring at Mrs. Ward and Mrs. Lester and Jane.

'Stop talking about my wife!' he said suddenly. His angry voice rang out in the silent room. 'Stop talking about her at least until you are out of this house!'

Mrs. Ward rose slowly to her feet, staring at Mr. Furness's distorted face.

'I want to speak to my daughter,' said Mr. Furness. 'I want to speak to her alone.' He advanced belligerently into the room. Mrs. Ward began to move with dignity toward the door. The black crêpe veil fell at her feet. Mr. Furness pointed to it contemptuously.

'Take those trappings with you,' he said.

Mrs. Ward stooped, without a word, and picked up the veil. Two little spots of colour were flaming in her cheeks. She walked with composure from the room, however, her head

held high. She never even glanced at Mr. Furness or at
Flora. Flora, who was standing in terrified silence by the
sofa, a little black streak in the gold-and-green splendour of
the room.

Mrs. Lester rose hesitatingly, and moved unsteadily to Mr.
Furness's elbow. He glared at her in silence. He might never
have seen her before. Mrs. Lester put out her hand and gently
touched his arm. Her face was working strangely. Jane saw
her try to speak, then shake her head, and stand staring at Mr.
Furness while great tears gathered in her dark eyes and rolled,
unheeded, down her fat, sagging cheeks. Mr. Furness just
kept on glaring, like a crazy man. Mrs. Lester dropped his
arm, after a minute, and followed Jane's mother out into the
hall. She hadn't uttered a word. Jane scurried after them.
She suddenly realized that she was crying. Jane's mother was
standing beside Mrs. Lester and Stephen Carver near the
front door. Stephen looked awfully concerned. Mrs. Ward
was talking very excitedly.

'I don't blame him,' she was saying, 'I don't blame him a
particle. He was like one distraught. And I don't wonder —
with all the disgrace!'

Jane suddenly realized that Stephen Carver had seen her
tears. He was looking down at her very tenderly. Mrs. Lester
was getting her mother to the door.

'Jane — don't!' said Stephen. His arm was half around her.
He looked very understanding.

'It's just that Mamma —' faltered Jane, 'Mamma shouldn't
talk so.'

'It *is* a disgrace,' said Stephen solemnly.

Jane felt terribly shocked. He didn't understand at all, after
all.

'Oh — no!' she said faintly. 'It's just — tragedy.' Stephen
still stared at her, quite uncomprehending. 'Never — disgrace,' said Jane. 'She loved him.'

Stephen was looking at her as if he found her words quite unintelligible. Jane slipped through the front door. Her mother, on the steps, was still talking volubly to Mrs. Lester.

'I don't think he knew what he was saying or to whom he was speaking,' she said eagerly. 'But how he'll explain it to Flora ——'

Jane silently followed them down to the sidewalk. She felt strangely calmed and exalted. A finished life was a very solemn, very splendid thing. She didn't care what her mother said, now. Death had an unassailable dignity.

'And it's not only the disgrace,' her mother was murmuring earnestly. 'The whole thing seems so terribly sordid — turning on the gas like that — in a bathroom — like any woman of the streets. Lily Furness had always so much pride.'

'I have lived and accomplished the task that Destiny gave me,' thought Jane very solemnly, 'and now I shall pass beneath the earth no common shade.'

CHAPTER III

I

JANE sat beside Flora on the little rosewood sofa in Mrs. Furness's bedroom. They were listing the contents of the bureau drawers. That morning they had gone through the closets. Mrs. Furness's wardrobe was heaped in four great piles on the big rosewood bed. Dresses that Flora wished to keep for herself. Dresses that her aunt Mrs. Carver might care to wear in Boston. A few darker, soberer dresses that Flora thought might be suitable for her mother's sister in Galena. And a very few much older, shabbier ones that Flora was planning to send to the Salvation Army. It had been a very hard morning for Flora. It had been a very hard one for Jane. Jane could remember just how Mrs. Furness had looked in nearly every gown that they had examined. She could see her dancing at Flora's début in the violet velvet. She knew just how the black lace ruff of the little silk shoulder cape had framed her white face, while Mr. Bert Lancaster was talking to Muriel in the dining-room at the coming-out tea.

Muriel and Mr. Bert Lancaster were still in the Canadian Rockies. Muriel had written at once to Flora. Jane had seen the letter. Muriel wasn't much of a letter writer, but you could read between the inarticulate, straggling lines that she was really awfully sorry. Muriel wrote just the way she did when she was a little girl at Miss Milgrim's. It made both Jane and Flora think of their school compositions to read her round childlike hand.

The western sun was slanting in the bedroom windows. Their task was nearly finished. Flora was keeping all the underclothes. And the jewellery, of course. She had given

Jane a little gold pin, set with turquoises in the form of forget-me-nots. Jane had often seen Mrs. Furness wear it, nestling in a tulle bow on her bare shoulder.

The room was quite dismantled. The window curtains were down and the carpet was up and all the little ornaments were put away. Mr. Furness was going to close the house next week. He was going to take Flora around the world. They were going to be gone for a year. Mr. Furness said he might never open the brown-stone house again.

'I'm awfully tired,' said Flora suddenly. She *looked* tired, and very white in the sable folds of her crisp new mourning.

'Go and lie down,' said Jane brightly. 'We've almost finished. There's just the desk.'

'Papa is going to do the desk, himself,' said Flora. 'He told me not to touch it.'

'Then we're through,' said Jane.

The sound of the doorbell rang through the silent house.

'That's Stephen,' said Flora. 'I forgot all about him. He said he would drop in on his way home from the bank for a cup of tea.'

'Never mind Stephen,' said Jane. 'You go and rest.'

'Stephen's been awfully good to us,' said Flora.

'He'd want you to rest,' said Jane. 'I'll go down and explain to him. I'll give him tea.'

'I wish you would,' said Flora. She looked unspeakably weary. Jane kissed her pale cheek and turned toward the door. 'Don't stay in here alone,' she said, pausing on the threshold.

'I won't,' said Flora. She followed Jane into the hall.

Jane ran lightly down the staircase. She looked a fright, she thought, after a day spent poking into shelves and boxes. Her hair was very mussy and, when she closed one eye, she could see a streak of soot on one side of her nose. She paused

by the walnut hat-rack to remove it with her handkerchief.
Then passed in through the drawing-room door.

Stephen Carver was standing at the open front window,
looking out at the flowering lilacs. Their sweet, passionless
perfume pervaded the room. The gold-and-green furniture
was all in linen covers. The rugs were up and the crystal
chandelier was swathed in a great canvas bag. It all looked
very cool and clean and unlived-in. Stephen turned at the
sound of her step.

'Hello, Jane,' he said. He looked awfully pleased.

'Flora's too tired to come down,' said Jane. 'We — we've
been working all day long.'

Stephen nodded gravely. He knew what they had been
doing.

'Ring for tea,' said Jane. 'Flora said I was to give it to you.'

Stephen pulled the beaded bellrope by the white marble
fireplace. Jane sat down on the linen-covered *bergère*.

'You look tired, too,' said Stephen sympathetically.

Stephen was nice, thought Jane. She had come to feel very
near to Stephen in the last sad weeks. He had been very
sweet with Flora.

'I *am* tired,' said Jane.

The butler brought in the tea. The big silver tea-set was
down at the bank. The little china service on the old tin tray
looked very strange in the Furnesses' drawing-room.

'I'll never see a china tea-set,' thought Jane suddenly,
'without thinking of André's mother.'

She made Stephen's tea in silence. She was much too tired
to talk. She didn't *have* to talk to Stephen. She knew him
awfully well.

Stephen didn't seem to have much to say, himself. He sat
across the swept and garnished hearth and drank his tea
without uttering a word.

'I'm glad Flora's going away,' said Jane presently. 'It will be good for her.'

'You'll be going away, yourself, soon,' said Stephen.

Jane's face lit up at the thought. Her father was taking a three months' holiday that summer. Such a thing hadn't occurred since he had gone abroad with Jane's mother eleven years before. They were going to make the grand tour of the West. They were going first to Yellowstone Park. Jane was thrilled over the plan.

'Yes,' she said simply. 'It will be good for me. I'm awfully glad to go.'

'Are you, really?' said Stephen. He put his teacup down as he spoke.

'Of course,' said Jane. 'I've never seen a mountain.'

There was a little pause.

'I hate to have you go,' said Stephen, breaking it.

Jane was a little surprised at just the way he said it. She looked over at him rather questioningly. Stephen was sitting, elbows on knees, his head bent to look at his clasped hands.

'Oh, you won't be lonely,' said Jane lightly. 'You know lots of people now. Chicago is fun in summer.'

'Lots of people won't do,' said Stephen. He was still looking at his hands. Jane knew just how he felt. Very few people 'did,' of course, when you came down to it. Stephen must miss his friends in Boston. Suddenly he looked up at her.

'No one will do — but you — Jane,' he said hesitatingly. 'Surely, you know that.'

The note in his voice was suddenly very alarming. Jane felt a little frightened. Stephen stood up. He walked quickly over to the *bergère* and stood looking down at her.

'Jane,' he said, 'you know how I feel about you.'

Jane was shrinking back into one corner of the great armchair, staring up into his suddenly ardent face.

'No — no, I don't,' she said defensively.

'I love you,' said Stephen. He said the three words very quickly, with a funny little gasp at the end. His face was flushed.

Jane's hands flew up as if she could tangibly put the three words away from her.

'No, you don't, Stephen!' she cried quickly. 'No, you don't!'

'Oh, yes, I do,' said Stephen.

Jane looked up at him very solemnly. Her hands dropped limply in her lap.

'I love you — terribly,' said Stephen. 'I've loved you from the night we first met, here in this house.'

'Oh, no!' said Jane again, piteously. 'That — that isn't possible.'

'I've never loved any one else,' said Stephen, 'like this.'

'But you *will!*' cried Jane hopefully. 'Oh, Stephen, you will!'

Stephen continued to look down at her, very queerly.

'Do you mean,' he said stiffly, at last — 'do you mean — there's no hope for me?'

Jane felt terribly overcome with a sense of helpless guilt. She — she ought to have known this was coming. Clever girls did. Flora and Muriel always had.

'Do you mean,' said Stephen, a little hoarsely, 'that you — that you can't care for me — at all?'

Jane shook her head, very slowly. She felt dreadfully sorry for him.

'No — I can't,' she said simply. 'Not that way.'

Stephen looked very much discouraged.

'I thought,' he said sadly, 'I thought — these last weeks——'

Jane rose suddenly to her feet. She stepped right up to Stephen and took his hands in hers.

'Stephen,' she said, 'you've been darling to Flora. And darling to me. I — I'm terribly fond of you. But I don't love you. I don't love you at all.'

'How do you know?' asked Stephen, eagerly. He was holding her hands now, close against his breast. 'How do you know — if you're terribly fond of me?'

'I know,' said Jane. She dropped her eyes as she felt them fill with tears. She could see the moonlit beach that minute. She could feel the shattering sense of André's nearness.

'Jane ——' pleaded Stephen. 'You can't be sure.'

'I'm very sure,' said Jane. She withdrew her hands from his.

'I'll never give you up,' said Stephen. Jane shuddered, faintly, at his ill-chosen words. She could feel André's lips on hers in the dim-lit side vestibule. 'You're mine,' he'd said; 'I'll never give you up.'

'Don't — don't talk like that,' said Jane sharply. She turned toward the door. 'I'm going home now. You must let me go, Stephen. I — I don't want to hear you.'

He looked terribly sorry and just a little hurt, but Jane didn't care. She *couldn't* care for any one now, in the sudden surge of memories that had overwhelmed her. André. André Duroy. She would never care like that for any one again. She wasn't even sure that she would care like that for André, now, if she could see him. But Jane knew. Jane knew all too well.

'I don't love you, Stephen,' she said, with dignity, on the threshold. He just stared dumbly, despairingly, at her from the empty hearthstone. Jane turned and left the room.

II

'He's crazy about you,' said Muriel lightly. 'It's ridiculous for you to say you haven't noticed it. Isn't he crazy about her, Isabel?'

Muriel was sitting on Jane's window-seat, looking out into the lemon-coloured leaves of the October willow. Isabel was perched on Jane's bed. Little John Ward was standing in a baby pen in the centre of the room. Jane was sitting on the floor beside him. She had only been back three weeks from the West and a walking John Ward was still a provocative novelty.

'You never can tell with men,' said Isabel warily.

'I can tell,' said Muriel, shaking her black curls very sagely. 'Last night at the Saddle and Cycle he never took his eyes off her.'

'Eyes aren't everything,' said Isabel. 'How about it, Jane?'

Jane looked up from the baby. She met their eager glances very coolly.

'Muriel's a bride,' she said calmly. 'She's not responsible for her views on sentiment.'

'Stephen's a lover!' retorted Muriel. 'He's not responsible for his. He looked at you across the table, Jane, as if he'd like to *eat* you.'

'How cannibalistic of him!' smiled Jane, cheerfully. 'Somehow that picture doesn't lead me on.'

'You're a perfect *idiot*,' said Muriel, 'if you don't accept him.' Again she glanced at the bedstead for support. 'Isn't she, Isabel?'

Isabel became suddenly practical.

'What's wrong with him, Jane?' she asked earnestly. 'He's young' — her voice faltered a moment, with a glance at Muriel, over that qualification. She went hurriedly on, 'And good-looking and he has plenty of money and a very good family and he's your best friend's cousin. I'd say he was made to order, if you asked me.'

'Why don't you fancy him, Jane? You *know* he's in love with you,' said Muriel accusingly. 'You ought to have seen her last night, Isabel. You wouldn't have known our Jane. She just wiped her feet on him.'

'Who does Jane wipe her feet on?' questioned Mrs. Ward's voice. Jane's mother stood, smiling, on the threshold.

'Stephen Carver,' said Muriel promptly, ignoring Jane's warning eyebrow.

Mrs. Ward looked very much pleased.

'She's a very foolish girl if she does,' she said advancing into the room. She cast an apprehensive glance at the baby. 'Isabel, are you sure that there isn't a draught on that floor?' Isabel moved a trifle restlessly on the bedstead. She didn't stoop to reply. 'Stephen Carver,' went on Mrs. Ward, 'is a very charming young fellow. If Jane is wiping her feet on him she may find out when it's too late that he's not the stuff of which doormats are made.'

'Oh — I think he likes it,' said Muriel. 'He *does* like it, doesn't he, Jane?'

Jane couldn't help smiling a trifle self-consciously. Stephen *did* like to have her notice him anyway at all. He had been terribly glad to see her when she came back from the West. And she had been — not *terribly*, but really *very* glad to see him. He had given her a whirl at all the early autumn parties. Last night at the Saddle and Cycle Club — well — Jane knew very well that she shouldn't have acted just the way she did, since she didn't love Stephen at all and wanted, so terribly, to make it perfectly clear to him that she never could.

'You'd like it, wouldn't you, Mrs. Ward?' asked Muriel impishly.

Mrs. Ward looked a trifle disconcerted. She exchanged with Isabel a slightly embarrassed glance. Jane was more amused than anything, to see Muriel beating her mother and Isabel at their own game. Muriel would like nothing better than to go out onto Pine Street that very afternoon and say with conviction, 'Mrs. Ward is setting her cap for Stephen Carver.'

'Every mother,' said Mrs. Ward a trifle sententiously, 'would like her daughter's happiness.'

Isabel rose from the bed.

'I've got to go, Jane,' she said. 'Hand me Jacky.'

Jane picked up her nephew over the railing of the pen. His little arms twined confidently around her neck. His fat little diapered figure felt very firm and solid in her arms. It would be fun to have a baby, all your own, thought Jane. It would be fun to have a home of your own like Isabel and Muriel. However, there was more to marriage, Jane reflected very sagely, than a home and a baby. And she didn't love Stephen. She didn't love him at all.

Isabel took Jacky.

'I'll walk along with you, Isabel,' said Muriel. 'Good-bye, Jane. Don't come down.'

Mrs. Ward turned to Jane as soon as the other two girls were out of hearing. She still looked pleased, and a little excited.

'What's this, Jane,' she said, 'about Stephen Carver?'

'Just Muriel's nonsense,' said Jane.

'Is he really in love with you?' said Mrs. Ward.

'Oh, Mamma!' protested Jane very lightly. 'You know Muriel.'

Mrs. Ward was looking at her very attentively.

'Has he asked you to marry him?' she said.

Jane hesitated for an almost imperceptible instant.

'Not — not this fall,' she said.

'Last winter?' said Mrs. Ward very quickly.

Jane hesitated no longer.

'Of course not, Mamma. I hardly knew him last winter.'

Mrs. Ward looked rather puzzled. Jane felt very triumphant and only a little untruthful. May was not winter.

'He's a very dear boy,' said Mrs. Ward impressively. 'I like Stephen Carver.'

Jane made no comment. She began to fold up the baby pen.

'Your father admires him, too,' said Mrs. Ward.

'How about Isabel?' asked Jane sweetly. 'And Robin? And the baby?'

Mrs. Ward laughed in spite of herself.

'They *do* all like him,' she said.

Families were terrible, thought Jane. But her eyes were twinkling.

'So if I did, too,' she said brightly, 'it would make it unanimous.'

'Do you?' said Mrs. Ward.

'Mamma,' said Jane, 'you are really shameless.'

She walked out of the room with the baby pen. She was going to put it away in the back hall.

III

'Marion,' said Agnes confidently, 'is surely going to get the European fellowship.'

'Why not you, Agnes?' asked Jane.

They were sitting side by side on the brown velvet sofa in Mr. Ward's little library. Agnes was having tea with Jane. She was spending the Christmas holidays in Chicago.

'I haven't a chance,' said Agnes. 'Marion's had wonderful marks these last two years.'

Jane thought of the little dark-eyed Freshman she had met

that first night in Pembroke Hall and of her father's sapient comment, 'I bet she'll amount to something some day.' Marion amounted to a great deal already.

'And I don't want it,' said Agnes. 'I don't want to study any more. I only want to write. I'm going to live in New York next winter. I'm going to look for a job on a newspaper.'

Agnes seemed terribly capable and confident and self-sufficient. Jane couldn't imagine how she would set about finding that job, but she knew that she would get it. Jane tried to think of herself, turning up alone in New York, looking for a living wage and a good boarding-house. It *wasn't* thinkable.

'What have you been doing, Jane?' said Agnes. 'What are *you* going to do?'

Jane couldn't think of any adequate answer to those incisive questions. She wasn't going to do anything. She hadn't done anything, in the Bryn Mawr idiom, since she had left Bryn Mawr.

'I don't know,' she said slowly. 'I — I've just been home.' Then she added honestly, 'I've liked it a lot.'

Agnes's friendly, freckled face was just a little incredulous.

'You *can't* like it, Jane,' she said. 'Not really.'

'Oh, yes, I do,' said Jane. She felt terribly unworthy.

'You're too good for a life like this,' said Agnes. 'And much too clever.'

Jane didn't deny the soft impeachment.

'You can be clever anywhere,' she said.

Agnes looked a little uncomprehending.

'You can think about people,' said Jane. 'You can learn about life.'

'If you don't look out, Jane,' said Agnes very seriously,

'you'll marry one of these days — marry a cotillion partner — and never do anything again as long as you live.'

'I'd like to marry,' said Jane honestly.

'So would I,' said Agnes with equal candour. 'I expect to, some day. But not a cotillion partner.'

'There are all kinds of cotillion partners,' said Jane, defensively. The Bryn Mawr point of view seemed just a little restricted.

Agnes drank her tea for a moment in silence. Then silently stirred the sugar in the cup.

'Jane,' she said presently, her eyes on the teaspoon, 'Jane — have you ever heard from André?'

Jane felt a sudden shock at the name.

'No, Agnes,' she said very gently. 'I never have.'

There was a little pause.

'Agnes,' said Jane, a trifle tremulously, 'have — have you?'

'No,' said Agnes.

Silence fell on the room, once more.

'You'll be twenty-one in May,' said Agnes. 'I bet he writes.'

'He — he's probably forgotten all about me,' said Jane. 'You know, Agnes, we *were* just children.'

'It was very clever of your mother,' said Agnes, 'not to allow any letters.'

Jane felt a little stir of loyalty in her perplexed heart.

'It was probably very wise of her,' she said.

'Possibly,' said Agnes.

'I — I'll never see him again, I suppose,' said Jane. 'He'll always live in Paris.'

Agnes continued to stir her tea.

'It would be dreadful,' said Jane, 'if I were still in love with him.'

'I suppose it might be,' said Agnes at last. 'Four years is a long time.'

'He must be very different,' said Jane. 'I'm very different myself.'

'Of course,' said Agnes meditatively, 'you've both met a lot of people.'

Jane heard the doorbell ring. She almost hoped that this conversation would be interrupted. It was too disturbing.

'And done a lot of things,' she said cheerfully. 'Think what André's life must have been, Agnes. I can't even imagine it.'

Minnie stood at the library door. Before she could speak, however, Jane heard Stephen's cheerful tones in the hall.

'Hi! Jane! Where are you?'

'Here in the library,' called Jane. 'Come in, Stephen.'

Stephen stood in the doorway, overcoat thrown open, hat in hand.

'I just stopped in,' he said, 'to see if you'd go skating this evening.' Then he saw Agnes.

'Miss Johnson, Mr. Carver,' said Jane promptly. 'Sit down and have some tea, Stephen. Agnes Johnson was my Bryn Mawr roommate.'

Stephen seated himself in a leather armchair. He looked very young and charming and debonair, with his blond hair just a little ruffled from his soft felt hat and his cheeks bright red from the December wind. Jane really felt quite proud of him. She looked over at Agnes with a mischievous smile. She was a little dismayed at the expression of Agnes's funny, freckled face. 'Cotillion partner!' was written all over it.

'I've just been telling Jane,' said Agnes, a trifle severely, 'that she ought to be doing something with her life.'

Stephen looked extremely astonished.

'Why — isn't she?' he asked.

'Nothing important,' said Agnes.

'Must Jane do something important?' asked Stephen. Jane handed him his tea.

'She could,' said Agnes firmly, 'if she would.'

'I never have liked,' said Stephen dreamily, 'important women.'

Jane began to feel a trifle amused. She didn't know that Stephen had it in him. Agnes didn't reply. Jane knew that Agnes always felt above a cheap retort. Stephen was left a little up in the air with his last remark. It began to sound ruder than it was, in the silence.

'Agnes,' said Jane lightly, 'is a serious-minded woman.'

'I can see that,' said Stephen. He tried to muster an admiring smile, but, under Agnes's dispassionate eye, it didn't quite come off.

'Life is real and life is earnest,' explained Jane sweetly, 'and the grave is not its goal.'

Stephen grinned at her very appreciatively. He was grateful for her levity. But Agnes was quite disgusted. She rose abruptly.

'I must go,' she said.

The front door opened and closed.

'Don't go, Agnes,' said Jane. 'Here's Papa. He'll want to see you.'

Mr. Ward appeared in the library door. His hands were full of newspapers and illustrated weeklies.

'Why, Agnes!' he said. He shook hands warmly. He was very glad to see her. 'How's the busy little brain working?'

'One hundred per cent,' grinned Agnes. 'But we miss Jane.'

'I missed her myself,' said Mr. Ward heartily, 'for two long years.' He walked across the room and put his papers down on the desk.

'What does Bryn Mawr think about Spain, Agnes?' he asked. 'Are we going to have war?' Mr. Ward was very much interested in Cuba. He was always talking of intervention.

'War?' said Agnes vaguely. 'What war?'

'Ever hear of "Cuba libre"?' questioned Mr. Ward with a smile.

'Oh, yes,' said Agnes. 'But I can't say I've thought much about it.'

'Did you read the President's message to Congress?' Mr. Ward had read it, himself, to Jane.

Agnes shook her head.

'What's the matter with Miss Thomas?' said Mr. Ward. 'I thought you women's rights girls would be getting up a battery!'

Agnes laughed.

'In the cloister,' she said, 'our wars are of the spirit. But I must go.' Mr. Ward walked with her to the door. He came back into the library, chuckling.

'Agnes is a great kid,' he said. 'Bright girl, Stephen. You ought to know her. Keep you jumping to get ahead of her.'

Stephen looked as if he wouldn't care very much for that form of exercise.

'Will you come skating?' he said.

'Yes,' said Jane, 'I'd love to.'

'Eight o'clock?' said Stephen.

'Yes,' said Jane.

'Good-evening, sir,' said Stephen meticulously to Jane's father.

'Good-night,' said Mr. Ward. He was looking at Stephen with that air of faint amusement, with which he always looked at him. Stephen went out into the hall.

'That's a nice boy, Jane,' said Mr. Ward. Jane nodded. Her father walked around the desk and put his arms around her. He twisted her about, so that he could look into her face.

'But don't get too fond of him,' said Mr. Ward.

'I won't,' said Jane, promptly.

Mr. Ward was looking down at her very tenderly.

'Don't get too fond of any one, Kid,' he said, 'just yet.'

IV

Jane was waiting with her skates in the hall, when Stephen rang the doorbell. She opened the door herself. He smiled down at her.

'Prompt lady!' he said. He tucked her skates under his arm.

Jane ran down the front steps. The December night felt very fresh and cold. Pine Street was buried in snow. The tall arc lamp on the corner threw a flickering light, pale lavender in colour, and strange gigantic shadows of the elm boughs on the immaculate scene. They walked along briskly, single file, in the path shovelled out of the drifts. The December stars were glittering overhead. The noises of the city were muffled by the snow fall. Jane could hear sleigh bells, dimly, in the distance. When they reached the corner the sound of the band at the Superior Street rink fell gaily on her ears. It was playing 'There'll be a Hot Time in the Old Town Tonight.' The path was wider, now. Stephen fell into step beside her. Jane began softly to sing:

> 'When you hear dem bells go ding, ling, ling,
> All join 'round and sweetly you must sing,
> And when the verse am through, in the chorus all join in,
> There'll be a hot time in the old town tonight — my baby ——' [1]

Jane was skipping in time to the tune.

'Oh, Stephen,' she said, 'it's a marvellous night! I'm so glad you asked me!'

'I'm glad you're glad,' said Stephen cheerfully. 'I love to see you love things.'

'I *do* love them,' said Jane seriously. 'Ever so many.'

'I know you do,' said Stephen. 'That's one of the nicest

[1] Copyright, 1924, by Edward B. Marks Music Co.

things about you.' Jane skipped a moment in silence. 'What did Agnes Johnson mean,' said Stephen a little irrelevantly, about your doing something with your life?'

'She thinks I should,' said Jane.

'Well,' said Stephen, 'aren't you?'

'Why, no,' said Jane. 'Not really. I'm just letting it happen.'

'Isn't it all right?' said Stephen. 'Your life?'

'Oh, yes,' said Jane. 'But of course I don't feel really settled.'

'Why not?' asked Stephen a little uneasily.

'Well — a girl doesn't, you know, until ——' Jane didn't quite want to finish that sentence. 'I mean I can't go on this way forever — just living with Mamma and Papa — I mean — I probably won't ——' Jane abandoned that sentence also.

'No,' said Stephen very gravely, 'I suppose not.'

They walked a few minutes in silence.

'Do you know,' said Stephen confidentially, 'I really hate college women?'

Jane twinkled up at him.

'I'm a college woman,' she said.

'You?' Stephen burst out laughing.

'I'm a fighting feminist,' said Jane.

'Yes, you are!' said Stephen.

'Really I am,' said Jane. 'I just haven't the courage of my convictions.'

'I like you cowardly,' said Stephen.

'It has its advantages,' said Jane. 'She who thinks and runs away, lives to think another day. I shall probably do a great deal more thinking than Agnes, before our lives are over. Agnes acts.'

'She doesn't act like you,' said Stephen. They had reached the rink now. It was circled by a high hedge of cut evergreens, bound closely together, their trunks thrust down in the snowdrifts.

'I don't act at all,' said Jane. 'I just drift.'

They turned in at the gate. The music of the band was loud in their ears. The rink was not crowded yet. Just a few isolated couples were swerving about in the lamplight. Jane dropped on the wooden bench. Stephen knelt to put on her skates. Jane leaned her head back against the evergreens. They smelled faintly of snow and very strongly of pine needles, like a Christmas tree. Winter was lovely, thought Jane.

She sprang up, as soon as her skates were on. She glided out on the rink, and began to skate slowly, with long rhythmic strides, in tune with the band. She was halfway round before Stephen caught up with her. He held out his hands. Jane crossed her wrists and took them. She could feel his strong, warm grasp through their woollen gloves. Stephen was a beautiful skater. They glided on in perfect unison. Skating was even more fun than dancing, thought Jane, because you did it out-of-doors. You did it under the stars, with Orion and Sirius and the Dipper shining over your head, and the frosty winter wind in your nostrils.

'I never knew a girl,' said Stephen, 'that skated as well as you. You'd love the river skating, near Boston.'

Jane knew she would.

'I'd like to take you out,' said Stephen, 'for a day of it, with just a picnic lunch by a bonfire.'

Jane knew she would like a picnic lunch by a bonfire.

'There are lots of things,' said Stephen, 'that I'd like to do with you.'

'Aren't some of them in Chicago?' laughed Jane.

'I can't think of a place,' said Stephen, 'where some of them wouldn't be.'

'Let's try a figure eight,' said Jane. 'Let's try one backward.'

They swerved and swooped for some minutes in silence. Stephen ended up facing her, still skating easily, her hands held in his. He looked happily down at her, never missing a stride, never losing a beat of the band.

'Why, look who's here!' cried a laughing voice. It was Muriel, standing at the bench side with Mr. Bert Lancaster. Stephen had almost run into them. He didn't look too pleased.

'Let's go four abreast,' said Muriel. The glint in her eye made Jane remember the days when Muriel used to giggle. She extended a hand obediently to Mr. Bert Lancaster.

Mr. Bert Lancaster was a good skater too, but the party of four was not a great success. Muriel couldn't quite keep up. Every now and then she lost a step and stumbled. Twice round the rink they halted. Stephen edged, perceptibly, away from Muriel. Mr. Lancaster extended his hands once more to Jane. But Jane really felt that she hadn't come out that perfect December night to skate with Mr. Bert Lancaster. She glided easily away from him.

'Stephen?' she said. His hands met hers in a moment. Muriel's eyes held again that giggling glint. But Jane didn't care. She didn't care at all. She struck out, easily, with Stephen. She felt very much cheered and very confidential.

'I don't like Bert Lancaster,' she said. 'I don't like him at all. Don't let him get me!'

'You bet I won't,' said Stephen. Stephen was terribly nice. And always to be counted on. They skated on in silence. The rink was crowded, now. Muriel and Mr. Lancaster were soon lost. The band was playing 'Just One Girl.' Jane thought really she could skate all night with Stephen.

'Are you cold?' he asked presently. Jane suddenly realized that she was. Her feet were like cakes of ice.

'What time is it?' she inquired. Stephen released one hand and looked at his watch.

'Not ten,' he said.

'We'd better go back,' said Jane. 'The band stops at ten. I *am* a little chilly.'

They glided slowly up to the wooden bench. Stephen knelt at her feet once more. Side by side they mounted the wooden steps and turned into Pine Street.

'Are you hungry?' said Jane. 'Would you like some crackers and cheese? Mamma said she'd leave some beer on ice.'

'I'm ravenous,' said Stephen, smiling.

They walked along in silence.

'Jane,' said Stephen presently, 'did you really mean that about your life? That you didn't feel settled?'

'Why, yes,' said Jane. 'In a way I meant it.'

'You — you're not thinking of doing anything else are you?' asked Stephen anxiously. 'Going away, I mean, or — or anything?'

'What else could I do?' said Jane simply.

Stephen looked down at her in silence. His face was very eloquent.

'I couldn't do anything,' said Jane promptly, answering her own question.

Stephen didn't speak again until she handed him her doorkey.

'Sooner or later you'll do it, Jane,' he said, then, very soberly.

Mrs. Ward was waiting up in the library. The beer was on ice, she said. Did Stephen like Edam cheese? There was cake in the cakebox.

'You know where everything is, Jane,' she remarked tactfully. 'I'm going upstairs, now. I have letters to write.'

Jane led the way to the pantry. There was the beer, two beaded bottles, and the crackers, and the cake, and a round, red, Edam cheese.

'Let's take them in by the dining-room fire,' said Jane.

Stephen carried the tray. Jane lit two candles on the dining-room table. The fire had sunk to a rose-red glow. But the room was very warm. The candle flames were reflected in the polished walnut and in the two tall tumblers. The Edam cheese looked very bright and gay.

Jane sat down in her father's chair and leaned her elbows on the table. She felt her cheeks burning, after the winter cold. Stephen's were very red and his blue eyes were bright. He drew up a chair very near her.

'Not much beer,' said Jane. 'I don't like it.'

He poured her half a glass, then filled his own. Jane dug out a spoonful of cheese. Stephen drained his beer in silence. Jane crunched a cracker.

'You're not so very ravenous,' said Jane at length, 'after all.'

'No,' said Stephen, 'I'm not. I came in under false pretences.'

Jane looked up at him quickly.

'I came, Jane,' said Stephen, 'to — to talk to you again.'

'To — talk to me?' said Jane faintly.

'To talk to you about — us,' said Stephen.

'I don't think you'd better,' said Jane.

'Jane,' said Stephen, 'I'm not getting over you — I'm not getting over you at all. I — I care more than ever.'

'Oh, Stephen,' said Jane pitifully, 'don't say that.'

'Do you want me to get over you?' asked Stephen.

Jane pondered a moment, in silence. Life would seem strangely empty without Stephen.

'N — no,' she said honestly. 'I — I don't think I do.'

'Well, then,' said Stephen eagerly, 'don't you think that you — you're beginning to care?'

'I don't know,' said Jane.

'Jane,' said Stephen very persuasively, 'you can't go on like this forever. You said yourself you didn't feel settled. You — you'll have to marry some time. Wouldn't you — *couldn't* you —?' He paused, his eyes on hers.

'Stephen,' said Jane very miserably, 'I don't know.'

'You *would* know,' cried Stephen earnestly, 'if you'd just let me teach you.'

'Teach me what?' said Jane.

'Teach you what it's like — to love,' said Stephen simply.

'Teach me,' thought Jane. There was a moment of silence.

'Love isn't taught,' said Jane finally.

Stephen's eyes had never left hers.

'Jane,' he said solemnly, 'you don't know.'

Jane shook her head. She couldn't explain. But she knew. Love was no hothouse flower, forced to reluctant bud. Love was a weed that flashed unexpectedly into bloom on the roadside. Love was not fanned to flame. Love was a leaping fire, sprung from a casual spark, a fire that wouldn't be smothered, a fire that ——

'Stephen,' said Jane, 'I'm sure I don't love you. I'll never marry you unless I do.'

'But you think,' said Stephen still eagerly, 'you think perhaps you might ——'

'I don't know,' said Jane.

Stephen stood up abruptly.

'I'll ask you and ask you,' said Stephen, 'until some day ——'

Jane rose and put out her hand.

'I wish I *could* love you,' said Jane. 'I'd like to.'

'Just keep on feeling that way,' said Stephen hopefully. 'You didn't talk like this last May.'

'Good-night,' said Jane.

'Good-night,' said Stephen.

Jane stood quite quietly by the candlelit table until she heard the front door open and close. Then she blew out the candles. She turned out the hall light and tiptoed very silently upstairs in the darkness. Nevertheless, she heard her mother's door open expectantly. Mrs. Ward's eyes wandered critically over her.

'We had a grand time,' said Jane very firmly. 'The ice was quite cut up, but Muriel and Bert were there.' She walked on to her bedroom. At the door she turned. She abandoned herself to fiction. 'Stephen taught Muriel the figure eight. I'm quite getting to like Bert Lancaster.' She heard her mother's door close softly. Jane turned up her light. She laughed a little excitedly, to herself. It was nice to be loved. It was nice to be loved by Stephen.

CHAPTER IV

I

'THIS,' said Mr. Ward, 'means war.' He looked very seriously across the dining-room table at his wife and daughter. On the shining damask cloth at his elbow several copies of the evening papers flaunted their thick black headlines. Jane could see them from where she sat. 'U.S. BATTLESHIP MAINE BLOWN UP IN HAVANA HARBOR.' 'THREE HUNDRED AND FIVE MEN KILLED OR INJURED.' 'PRESIDENT MCKINLEY DEMANDS INQUIRY.'

Jane looked at her father very solemnly.

'War,' thought Jane. It was somehow unthinkable. War couldn't be visualized in that quiet candlelit room. No one said anything more. The hoarse, raucous voices of newsboys, crying the last extras on the disaster, punctuated the silence. Jane could hear them blocks away, echoing across the silent city. Newsboys were crying extras like that, thought Jane, in every large city in the world. In New York and London and Berlin and Paris — Paris where André might hear them — newsboys were shouting 'U.S. BATTLESHIP MAINE BLOWN UP IN HAVANA HARBOR.' War with Spain. War — after, her father had just said, thirty-three long years of peace.

'I think,' said Mrs. Ward finally, 'that some one will do something. There will never be another war between civilized people.'

'The Spaniards aren't civilized,' said Mr. Ward. 'Their Cuban atrocities have proved that.'

'They're a very powerful nation,' said Mrs. Ward.

'They're a very tricky one,' said her husband. 'But we'll free Cuba if it takes every young man in America.'

'I hope,' said Mrs. Ward severely, 'you won't talk that way to Robin. I think a married man, with a child, should not be encouraged to think that his duty lies away from his home.'

'Robin,' said Mr. Ward calmly, 'is the best judge of his own duty.'

'John,' said Mrs. Ward excitedly, 'Isabel isn't strong. If she were left with that baby ——'

'Isabel,' said Mr. Ward, 'will have to take her chance with the rest of us.' Then he paused a moment and considered his wife's worried face. 'We're a long way from enlistments yet, Lizzie.'

'And of course,' said Mrs. Ward hopefully, 'the bachelors will all go first.'

'The bachelors,' thought Jane. Would she live to see young men marching out heroically behind the colours to fight the Spaniards — to kill — and be killed — over Cuba — which meant nothing to them — and less to her. Would she live to see — perhaps — Stephen ——

'No one will go for months,' said Mr. Ward. 'Congress will talk about this inquiry 'til there isn't an insurrectionist alive in Cuba.'

Jane sincerely hoped that Congress would. She didn't care at all about the insurrectionists. She was going over to Muriel's that evening to play egg football, around the dining-room table. Muriel loved egg football. Stephen and Jane thought it was very funny to see her pretty face grow red and distended in her frantic efforts to blow the eggshell over the line. Jane's mother and Isabel thought that she ought to give it up now. They said it wasn't quite prudent, with the baby coming. Jane had no opinion on that. It would be an amusing party. Jane rose from her chair.

'Can Minnie walk over with me?' she said. The February night was mild.

Mrs. Ward nodded. The cries of the newsboys had died down in the distance. Mr. Ward had picked up his papers. The game of egg football seemed much nearer than war.

II

'It's only a question of days, now,' said Mr. Ward. 'There can be only one outcome.'

'We're awfully unready,' said Robin.

'Roosevelt was right,' said Stephen. 'He's been right all along. We ought to have been preparing. We ought to have been preparing for years.'

'He's done wonders with the Navy Department,' said Mr. Ward. 'He's got Dewey in Hongkong. He's had his eye on Manila from the start.'

'He should never have left his desk,' said Mr. Bert Lancaster. 'His place is in Washington. This stunt of rushing down to San Antonio to get up a regiment of cowboys is all nonsense. You can't make a soldier out of a cowpuncher in ten minutes.'

'You can make a campaign out of him,' said Freddy Waters very wisely. 'There's more than one kind of campaign. Teddy Roosevelt keeps his eye on the ball. He never passes up a chance to play to the grandstand.'

'Teddy Roosevelt,' said Mr. Ward slowly, 'is all right.'

Jane sat in solemn silence. So did all the other women. That February evening seemed very long ago, when the newsboys were crying extras on the Maine and the game of egg football had seemed nearer than war.

It was mid-April, now. They were all sitting out on the Wards' front steps, enjoying the early twilight of the first warm evening. The Wards had sat out on their front steps on spring and summer evenings ever since Jane could remember. Minnie always carried out the small hall-rug and an armchair for her mother, immediately after dinner. The neighbours drifted in, by twos and threes, dropped down on the rug and talked and laughed and watched the night creep over Pine Street. Sometimes they sang, after darkness fell. The Wards' front steps were quite an institution.

Pine Street looked just the same, reflected Jane, as it always had, on April evenings. The budding elm boughs met over the cedar block pavement. The arc light on the corner contended in vain with lingering daylight. The empty lawns looked very tranquil and, in the clear grey atmosphere of gathering dusk, poignantly green. Bicycles passed in groups of two and three. Other front steps, further down the block, were adorned with rugs and dotted with chattering people. Nothing was changed.

Nothing was changed on Pine Street. But in Washington, Jane knew, garrulous Congressmen were discussing ultimatums, friendly ambassadors were shaking their heads over declined overtures of intervention, weary statesmen were drawing up documents, and President McKinley was sitting with poised pen. In Chickamauga troops were concentrating. The regular army was in motion. Regiments were entrained for New Orleans and Mobile and Tampa. Twenty thousand men were moving over the rails. Down in San Antonio, Leonard Wood was organizing the First United States Volunteer Cavalry, Roosevelt's Rough Riders, and Roosevelt himself was cutting through the red tape of the Navy Department to join the plainsmen and adventurers and young soldiers of fortune from the Eastern colleges who had answered his first call. Across the wide Pacific seas Dewey was lingering, with his tiny fleet, in neutral waters. Off Key West the North Atlantic Squadron was riding at anchor. Jane could fairly see them across the tranquil green lawns of Pine Street, battleships and monitors and cruisers, talking with Captain

Sampson's flagship in flashing points of fire. All waiting for the stroke of the President's pen.

They were waiting for it on Pine Street, too. Horribly waiting. Jane's father had been waiting for it for weeks, and Robin had been waiting, and Bert Lancaster and Freddy Waters, too, for all their scoffing. Stephen had been waiting. Jane knew that. Stephen had been waiting in a queer inarticulate suspense that held for Jane a note of tacit doom. Jane had never been able to phrase the question that would terminate it. It had trembled, countless times, on her lips, during the last two months. But it had never been asked. Jane didn't want to know, beyond the possibility of doubt, just what it would do to her to face the startling realization that Stephen was going to go to war.

Last week he had shown her a clipping, cut from the morning 'Tribune.' A copy of Alger's letter to the State Governors.

The President desires to raise —— volunteers in your territory to form part of a regiment of mounted riflemen to be commanded by Leonard Wood, Colonel; Theodore Roosevelt, Lieutenant-Colonel. He desires that the men selected should be young, sound, good shots and good riders, and that you expedite, by all means in your power, the enrollment of these men.

[Signed]   R. A. ALGER,
Secretary of War

Jane had made no comment.

'It would be fun,' said Stephen, 'to go.'

'Fun!' thought Jane.

'I'm pretty bored with the bank, you know,' said Stephen. 'I've nothing else to do here, unless ——'

The sentence was left unfinished. Jane had tried to look very non-committal. In the perplexities surrounding her Jane clung firmly to one assuaging certainty. She wasn't going to be railroaded into marrying Stephen to keep him from going to war.

But — if he went, thought Jane in the gathering dusk of Pine Street? If the dreadful moment came, when, like a girl in a book, she had to dismiss him to follow the flag to death or glory ——

The notes of the first hurdy-gurdy of the season tuned up on the corner. Jane could see the little street organ, dimly, in the light of the arc lamp. A tiny object that must be the monkey was crawling around the musician's feet. Jane loved hurdy-gurdies. They meant the coming of spring on Pine Street. They meant it much more than the first robin. Jane had loved to dance to them when she was little. To follow the monkey and slip her allowance in pennies into its cold, damp little claw. She always laughed, still, at a monkey, snatching off its little red cap with a spasmodic gesture and blinking its thanks for a coin.

This was a very up-to-date hurdy-gurdy. The tune was a new one, but already familiar. Freddy Waters never missed an opportunity to sing.

> 'Good-bye, Dollie, I must leave you,
> Though it breaks my heart to go.
> Something tells me I am wanted
> At the front to fight the foe ——'

Jane moved a trifle uneasily. She wished that Freddy wouldn't sing the silly words quite so sarcastically. You couldn't laugh away war — not even with the most banal of love songs. She was glad when the hurdy-gurdy slipped into the safer strains of 'Cavalleria Rusticana.'

'Well — we must go,' said Muriel. Muriel was beginning

to take care of herself at last. She rose to her feet a little clumsily. Incredible, thought Jane, to think of Muriel with a baby. It was coming in August. Mr. Bert Lancaster steadied her arm. How awful, thought Jane, to have Mr. Lancaster for your baby's father. It didn't seem possible that he could have had anything to do with Muriel's baby. Jane resented his protective air.

'We'll walk along with you,' said Rosalie. Her little girl was almost a year old now. And Isabel's boy would be two in July. All three of them, thought Jane, with babies. Babies mysteriously produced and brought into the world — with fathers. They were all growing old.

Isabel rose to her feet. She was still humming, half unconsciously, the chorus of 'Dollie Grey.'

'Come, Robin,' she said.

Jane's mother rose in her turn.

'It's growing very chilly,' she remarked, with a little shiver.

Mr. Ward tossed his half-finished cigar over the balustrade. It fell on the black turf in a shower of sparks, then glowed, incandescently, for a moment in the darkness.

'Good-night,' said Robin. He slipped his arm through Isabel's. They wandered off together up Pine Street. Mr. Ward rose from his seat on the steps with a heavy sigh.

'It's only a question of days,' he repeated.

Stephen was standing up, now, at Jane's feet.

'Good-night,' he said.

The question trembled once more on Jane's lips and once more remained unspoken.

'Good-night,' said Jane.

Stephen turned and went down the steps. Jane watched his slender figure disappearing down the darkened street. Under the arc light she could see it again quite clearly. Beyond it he vanished instantly into the night. Jane turned to her father.

'Are — are you sure, Papa?' she asked. Mr. Ward nodded gravely. He picked up her mother's chair. Jane stooped to gather up the little rug. Mrs. Ward had already opened the front door. Several blocks away Jane could still hear the hurdy-gurdy.

'Something tells me I am wanted
At the front to fight the foe ——'

The mock pathos of the jingling tune held a dreadful irony. Jane had suddenly a desperate sense of a trap, closing in upon her. Life shouldn't be like this. Life shouldn't force your hand. In moments of decision you should always be calm, untrammelled by circumstance.

'Come, Kid,' said Mr. Ward. He was standing by the open door. Jane followed him slowly into the front hall.

Life wasn't fair, thought Jane.

III

'Miss Jane,' said Minnie, 'Mr. Carver has called.'

'Mr. Carver?' questioned Jane. It was only four o'clock on a week-day afternoon. Why wasn't Stephen at the bank?

'Tell him that I'll come down,' said Jane.

Minnie departed in silence. Jane turned slowly toward the bureau, but merely from force of habit. What was Stephen doing on Pine Street at this hour? She rearranged her hair absentmindedly. Stephen never left the bank until five. Jane picked up her mirror and gazed very thoughtfully at the knot at the back of her neck. She didn't see it at all. What did Stephen want of her? Facing the glass once more she plumped up the sleeves of her plaid silk waist with care. Day before yesterday the United States had declared war.

Jane walked very slowly down the stairs.

'Stephen?' she called questioningly.

'Here, Jane,' he answered. His voice came from the library. Jane entered the room.

Stephen was standing very straight and tall by the smouldering fire. He grinned as she entered. Nevertheless he looked a little solemn.

'What are you doing here in office hours?' smiled Jane. 'Come to sell me a bond?'

'No,' said Stephen simply. 'I haven't.'

Jane dropped down on the sofa by the fire. She gazed up at Stephen in silence.

'I've come to sell you,' said Stephen, 'this idea of going to war.'

Jane's heart gave a great jump beneath her plaid silk bodice. The unspoken question was answered.

'I'm going to join the Rough Riders,' said Stephen firmly. 'I made up my mind this morning. There's no excuse for my sticking around here a minute longer.'

'When — when are you going?' said Jane faintly.

'Right away,' said Stephen. 'I spoke to my boss this afternoon. I'll write to Father to-night.'

'Oh — Stephen!' said Jane again still more faintly.

'I want to go,' said Stephen. 'It's not so often that you want to do what you ought.'

That was true enough, thought Jane. But who could want to go to war?

'Lots of Harvard men have joined up,' said Stephen, 'because of Roosevelt — some men I know in Boston are going. They wrote me last week. I'm all signed up with them. We're going to meet in San Antonio.'

'When?' asked Jane.

'As soon as they can make it,' said Stephen. 'One of them has to tie up his business. Another one's married.'

'How — how long do you think?' asked Jane.

'Oh — we ought to be down there in two weeks,' said Stephen.

Jane sat in silence on the sofa. Two weeks.

'It will be fun,' said Stephen. 'Roosevelt's got a great crowd down there.'

Jane still sat in silence.

'Don't look so solemn, Jane,' said Stephen.

'I feel solemn,' said Jane.

'You wouldn't want me not to go,' said Stephen.

'Yes, I would,' said Jane promptly.

Stephen looked very much pleased. And a little amused.

'When it comes to the point,' said Jane, 'I guess I'm not much of a patriot.'

'Oh, yes,' said Stephen persuasively, 'you want to win the war.'

Jane felt a refreshing flash of levity.

'Do you expect to win it?' she asked lightly.

Stephen flushed a bit.

'Don't mock me, Jane,' he said seriously. Then a little hesitantly. 'I'm awfully glad you're sorry.'

'Of course I'm sorry,' said Jane. 'But I don't know that you ought to be glad about it.'

'Just the same, I am,' said Stephen a little tremulously.

Silence fell on the room once more.

'Jane ——' said Stephen presently and paused. He was still standing on the hearth rug. He was looking down at Jane very steadily.

'Yes,' said Jane nervously. Her eyes were on the fire.

'Don't you think — don't you think,' said Stephen almost humorously, 'that it's just about time for me to ask you again?'

It was very disarming. Jane couldn't help twinkling up at him.

'There's no time like the present,' she said.

'Jane!' In a moment he was beside her on the sofa. 'Jane — does that mean ——' He had her hands in his.

'It doesn't mean anything,' said Jane hastily.

'I don't believe you,' said Stephen. He was very close to her. His eyes were gazing eagerly into hers. His lips were twisted in a funny little excited smile.

'I don't believe you at all,' said Stephen. 'Jane ——' And suddenly he kissed her. His moustache felt rough and bristly against her lips.

'Oh!' said Jane, drawing back. Her heart was beating fast. That kiss was strangely exciting.

'Darling!' said Stephen. His arms were around her now. Jane's hands were pressed against the tweed lapels of his coat.

'Kiss me again!' said Stephen.

'I — I didn't kiss you!' cried Jane in protest. 'I — I didn't at all!'

'But you will,' said Stephen. His face was flushed and eager. His eyes were gazing ardently into her own. Jane stared into them, fascinated. She could see the little yellow specks that seemed to float on the blue iris. She had never noticed them before.

'You will!' he declared again. And again his lips met hers. This — this was dreadful, thought Jane. She — she shouldn't allow it. He pressed his cheek to hers. It felt very hard and just a little rough, against her own.

'Stephen,' said Jane weakly. 'Really — you mustn't.'

'Why not?' said Stephen. 'I love you.'

Jane felt herself relaxing in his arms.

'You know I love you,' said Stephen.

'Well,' said Jane faintly, her head on his shoulder, 'don't — don't kiss me again — anyway.'

Stephen laughed aloud at that. A happy, confident laugh.

'You darling!' he said. Then very happily, 'I — I'm so glad you told me, Jane, before I went.'

Before he went, thought Jane desperately! Of course — he was going. She had forgotten that. But she *hadn't* told him. It was all wrong, somehow. Jane looked despairingly up into his face.

'Stephen,' she said pitifully, 'I — I don't know, *yet*, if I love you.'

'Of course you do,' said Stephen promptly. Jane wondered, in silence.

'Jane,' said Stephen presently, 'it — it's going to be terribly hard to leave you.'

Jane did not speak. She felt all torn up inside. His tremulous voice was very moving.

'Jane,' said Stephen very quietly, 'you — you wouldn't marry me — before I went?'

Jane gave a great start. She slipped from his embrace.

'Oh — *no!*' cried Jane.

'I — I was afraid you wouldn't,' said Stephen humbly.

'Oh — I couldn't!' said Jane. 'I — I couldn't — marry — any one.'

Stephen was smiling at her very tenderly.

'I don't want you to marry any one but me,' he said cheerfully.

The levity in his tone was very reassuring.

'Stephen,' said Jane, 'you *are* a dear.'

Stephen looked absurdly pleased. It was fun to please Stephen so easily.

'What sort of ring shall I get you?' he asked.

That, again, seemed oddly terrifying.

'Oh ——' said Jane evasively. 'I — I don't care. Don't — don't *get* a ring just yet.'

'Of course I will,' said Stephen. 'I'll get it to-morrow.'

Jane heard the doorbell ring — three brief peremptory peals.

'That's Mamma!' said Jane. Then in a sudden panic. 'Oh, Stephen, please — please go. I don't want to tell her.'

'We needn't tell her,' said Stephen calmly.

'She'd guess!' cried Jane. 'You don't know Mamma!' She heard Minnie's step in the hall. 'Oh, Stephen! Please go!'

'All right,' said Stephen. He rose a bit uncertainly.

'Come back!' said Jane wildly. 'Come back after dinner! But now — I — I *can't* talk to Mamma. I — I want to think.' She heard the front door open. She rose to her feet.

'Kiss me,' said Stephen. He took her in his arms. Jane slipped quickly out of them. She fairly pushed him to the door. She heard him meet her mother in the hall.

'Why Stephen!' Her mother's voice was pleased and, mercifully, unsuspecting. Stephen's answer was inaudible. Jane turned to poke the fire. Her mother entered the room.

'What was Stephen doing here at this hour?' she asked pleasantly.

'He came to talk about the war,' said Jane, turning over the bits of charred birch very carefully

'The war?' said Mrs. Ward.

'He thinks he'll enlist,' said.Jane.

'Oh — I think that's a mistake,' said Mrs. Ward earnestly.

'Well — maybe **he** won't,' said Jane casually, still busy with the fire.

Mrs. Ward walked over to the desk. She laid some letters down before her husband's chair.

'You're a funny girl, Jane,' she said. 'Don't you care at all if he does?'

'Oh, yes,' said Jane. 'I care — of course. But it's for him to decide.' She turned to face her mother. 'Is that the mail?' she asked.

'Yes,' said her mother. She was watching Jane very closely. Jane went over to the desk.

'Anything for me?' she asked.

'I didn't notice,' said Mrs. Ward. There was a faint suggestion of irritation in her tone. Jane picked up the letters. She felt her air of indifference was just a little elaborate. Her mother left the room, however, without further parley.

Jane stood quietly, leaning against her father's desk, absently holding the letters in her hand. What had she done, thought Jane? How had it happened? Was she glad or sorry? She could hardly believe it, now Stephen had left the room. A moment ago she had been in his arms, on that sofa. He had — kissed her. Three times. She had let him do it. She had sat with him, on that sofa that always, always, made her think of André, of that dreadful moment when André had left her — she had sat there and let him kiss her —— But Stephen was going to war. She would have time. She wouldn't tell a soul. Not a soul — except her father. She would think it all over. She would tell Stephen to-night, that, at best, it must be just an understanding —— Suddenly Jane's eye fell on the French stamp of the topmost letter in her hand. A — French — stamp! Jane gazed at it, in horror. Yes — 'Miss Jane Ward' — in handwriting that, though changed, was unmistakably André's. She would be twenty-one next week. He had written! Of course he had written. She had always *known* he would write! And she — faithless — within the hour had let Stephen Carver kiss her. Had let Stephen think that —— Jane dropped the other letters on the desk. Holding André's close above her heart she rushed frantically out of the room and up the stairs and gained the sanctuary of her own bedroom. Softly she locked the door. Then sank into the chair by the window overlooking the amber willow tree. André had written. He had not forgotten. André was going to come.

Jane slowly drew the letter from the thin-papered envelope. It looked strangely foreign. The very writing, faintly blotted on that sheer French paper, had a subtly alien air. But it was undeniably André's own. Yes — at the end of the twelfth closely written sheet, there was his name, 'Your André.' Her André! Jane turned to the first page and began to read.

'DEAR JANE, I hardly know what to say to you, or how to say it. But of course I want to write. I want to write, even though I have no idea, now, what sort of a person you may have grown up to be, how you may have changed from the child that I loved.'

Loved, thought Jane with a faint chill of foreboding? And child?

'We were both children, of course. We see that now. And in the four years that have passed you have grown up into a woman. I have a strange sense of embarrassment in writing to you. For I have grown up, too, Jane, and I am not at all sure that you will welcome my letter. Perhaps you do not even remember that I was to have written it.'

Remember, thought Jane! What had she ever forgotten?

'When I left you that day on Pine Street — that day which, now, perhaps, you may not even care to recall — I thought my heart was breaking. I thought your heart was breaking too. But I was nineteen, Jane, and of course, I have learned that hearts are of tougher fibre than I thought.

'I was miserable all summer long. Miserable all winter, too, though I was working very hard over my modelling. I thought of nothing but you and counted the days until I could see you. Actually counted them, Jane, on a calendar I made, crossing one off every evening.'

Darling André, thought Jane!

'But I was nineteen, Jane. And life is life. I began, almost against my will, to be interested in all sorts of things. The Sorbonne and the studio and lots of other pure frivolities, though I was dreadfully ashamed of that, at first. Then I began to see, of course, that we would both have to go on living and growing up and changing into the kind of people that we were meant to be, and when the four years were over, we would meet and see each other again and know, instantly, if we still cared. I couldn't imagine not caring about you. But what the four years would do to you, I couldn't imagine either. I was awfully afraid of them.

'Mother wrote me about you, of course, as long as Father was in Chicago. I knew that you went to Bryn Mawr with Agnes and I was terribly glad. I knew you wanted to go and, besides that, it seemed, somehow, to put off life for you, to keep you safe in an environment that I could imagine, to shut out the world. I never heard anything about you, after that. I thought of writing Agnes, but I never did. Mother didn't think it was quite on the level, after my promise to your father, to write Agnes letters that were really for you.

'And then, Jane, I entered the Beaux Arts and my work began to get me. I began to care terribly about it. I always had, of course, but this was very different. I was thrilled over what I was doing. I was thrilled all the time, day and night. I am still. I can't think of any time, during the last three years, when I haven't been terribly excited and happy to be working with my clay. I hope I can make you understand that — how much it has come to mean to me.

'For, Jane, I have just been told that I am to be awarded the Prix de Rome. It means three years' work in Italy. It means a chance for accomplishment that I have never known before. It means living for three years with the other students in bachelor quarters in the Villa Medici. I'll live like a monk, there, in a little white cell, working night and day to get all I can out of the opportunity the three years give me.

'Jane — I did mean to try to get to the States this summer. To work my way over on some boat just as soon as my courses were over and I'd finished a fountain I'm doing. I meant to spend next winter in Chicago. I thought I'd take a studio there and try to get a job at the Art Institute. I did mean to, I mean, if you, by any chance, still wanted me to come. I meant to write you a letter at this time, saying I would come like a shot if you would tell me to. But, Jane, surely you see that this is a chance that I can't let slip. I've *got* to take advantage of it. Next spring, if you want me, I'll come without fail. I'll leave Rome for a month or two — I'll manage it somehow — I'll come and we can see each other. Just as I write the words, Jane, I feel all the old emotion. Do you, I wonder, feel it, too? I feel so very strange with you. What have the four years done to you? *Are* you the same Jane? You can't be, of course. But are you a little like the girl that ——'

The sentence was not finished. Jane sat with burning cheeks, gazing at the closely written paper. How *could* he write like that — as if he still cared —— when he was taking this Prix de Rome? The Prix de Rome? What was the Prix de Rome? Jane didn't know and felt she didn't care. What was *any* prize, *any* reward, *any* opportunity compared with love? Love, such as she and André had known? He had forgotten. She must face that fact. He *must* have forgotten. If he had remembered, nothing would have counted, counted for one moment, against the joy of reunion. 'Next spring, if you want me, I'll come without fail!' Pallid words! Insulting words. Really insulting, from André to her. What had the four years done to *her?* What had they done to *him?* Jane turned again to the letter.

'Write me, dear Jane, that you understand. And tell me that you will want to see me, next spring, only half as much as I want to see you.

'Your
'ANDRÉ'

' "Her — André"!' Jane's cheeks flushed again at the irony of the phrase. But there was still a postscript.

'I think you'd like my fountain. It's the best thing I've done. I wish I could show it to you. It's a study of Narcissus, gazing at his own reflection in the water. There's a nymph behind him, a deserted nymph, standing with arms out-stretched, ignored, forgotten, as he stares, infatuated, in the crystal pool. There's something of you in the nymph, Jane. There's something of you in all my nymphs and Eves and saints and Madonnas. Something you brought into my life. Romance, I guess it is. Nothing more tangible.

'ANDRÉ'

Something of her in the deserted nymph! Something of him, thought Jane, with unwonted irony, in the fatuous Narcissus! And for this André she had been keeping herself for the last four years! This André who would rather go to

Italy and take his Prix de Rome than cross the ocean to see the girl that —— For this André she had been steeling her heart against Stephen. Stephen who loved her and wanted her and was going to war, still wanting her more than life itself. Stephen who had been her very slave for the last eighteen months, who had loved her from the moment that he set eyes on her in Flora's little ballroom.

Jane rose and went to her desk. She pulled out her best notepaper and seated herself squarely before her little blotter. When you killed things, thought Jane grimly, you killed them quickly.

'DEAR ANDRÉ,' she wrote, 'I loved your letter. And of course I remember everything. Quite as much, I am sure, as you do yourself. I understand perfectly about the Prix de Rome and I hope very much you will come to Chicago next spring. I should love to see you and I should love to have you meet the man I am going to marry. His name is Stephen Carver and he is going to war, immediately, to fight the Spaniards. I shall marry him before he goes.

'As you say, we were both children, four years ago.' Jane paused a moment, trying vainly to blink away her tears. It had been just a dream, she knew, but the end of even a dream was very dreadful. 'Like you I was awfully upset, at first, but as you say, life is life. I loved my years at Bryn Mawr with Agnes. Soon after I came home I met Stephen. He has just persuaded me to marry him. Of course I am terribly happy.' Jane paused to wipe her eyes, then added, as an afterthought. 'Except for the war.' That seemed to dispose of everything she thought. Just one more word was needed. She wrote it — 'JANE.'

She mailed the note before dressing for dinner. When she came up to her room again André's letter was still lying on her desk. She made a sudden movement as if to tear it into a hundred pieces. Then checked herself and slowly put it back in its envelope. André might be incredibly different. André might have forgotten. She would pluck him from her heart. But the André that he used to be was still the lover of her childhood. Jane felt an odd sense of outrage at the thought of denying the past. She slipped the letter into a desk drawer.

Jane turned slowly toward her closet door. She would wear her prettiest dress for Stephen. She would tell him at once that she would marry him. She would try to make up to him for the way she had treated him. What if Stephen, discouraged, had forsaken her? Jane felt an overwhelming sense of gratitude for Stephen's faithfulness. She had never appreciated it before. Of course she loved him. She loved him and she would marry him. It was perfectly terrible that he was going to war.

IV

Jane stood before her mirror, gazing incredulously through her snowy veil at the slim white reflection that was herself. Fancy dress, it seemed to her, this paraphernalia of bridal finery. Isabel stood at her side, holding her shower bouquet of lilies of the valley. Her mother was leaning against the bureau, looking her up and down and softly crying. Isabel's eyes were full of tears. Minnie, standing admiringly at the bedroom door, was pressing a mussy handkerchief to trembling lips.

After the past two weeks, however, Jane was quite accustomed to being cried over. She was a hero's bride, dedicated to a romantic destiny that had not left a dry eye in her little circle. Even Muriel had cried, and Mrs. Lester, of course, and Rosalie. Jane wondered if Agnes and Marion had wept a little in Bryn Mawr and Flora and Mr. Furness in London. Flora had cabled and Agnes and Marion had written her lovely letters. Jane had glimpsed in Agnes's a tacit attempt to retract that unfortunate, unspoken verdict of 'cotillion partner,' that Jane had read, last December, in her candid eyes. It was quite all right with Jane. 'Cotillion partners' didn't go to war. Agnes must understand, now.

Her mother had cried almost continuously ever since Jane had told her of the engagement. She had cried most terribly during that one awful interview with Stephen when she tried to persuade him that if he married Jane he shouldn't enlist. Mr. Ward had cried, too, but only once and very furtively, making no capital out of his tears. And yesterday, when Stephen's family arrived from Boston, Stephen's mother, in the railroad station, had cried most of all.

Jane had been terribly afraid to meet Stephen's family. They had been very much surprised at the news of the engagement. But when they came, they proved to be very nice. They really didn't seem to bother about Jane at all. They were mainly preoccupied with Stephen's enlistment. The wedding was, in their eyes, a mere preliminary, a curtain raiser, to the great drama of the war. Jane was the leading lady, to be sure, but she played a conventional rôle. The hero's bride again, dedicated, this time, to the romantic destiny of making Stephen happy for a week before he went away to fight the Spaniards. Jane, facing the disquieting group of future relatives-in-law, was profoundly relieved that nothing more complicated was required of her.

There were six of them and all very friendly, indeed. Except for their short, clipped accent and a certain funny something that they did, or rather did not do, to their r's, they might have been born and bred on Pine Street. Stephen's mother, whom Jane had, of course, dreaded the most of all, proved to have a very reassuring resemblance to her brother, Mr. Furness. She was short and plump, with the same pale,

protruding eyes and iron grey hair. Like Mr. Furness she had
very little to say. This deficiency was more than made up
for by the fact that Stephen's father had a great deal. Mr.
Alden Carver was a very impressive gentleman. He was
grey-haired, too, and he had a close-clipped grey Vandyke
beard and moustache, and shrewd light-blue eyes that peered
out from under his grey eyebrows with an uncanny resemblance to Stephen's. His cheeks looked very soft and pink
above the close-clipped grey beard. His collar and cuffs were
very white and glossy and his grey sack suit was in perfect
press. Jane thought him a very dapper old gentleman.

Alden Carver, Junior, looked just like his mother. He was
four years older than Stephen and he had never married. He
had told Jane, immediately, on the platform of the train shed,
with the air of placing himself for her, once for all, that he
was in the Class of '88, at Harvard. Jane had received that
biographical item with a very polite little smile. It didn't
help her much, however, in her estimate of her new brother-
in-law.

Stephen's sister, Silly, was easier to talk to. She talked a
great deal herself and always amusingly, about horses and
dogs and sailboats. Silly's real name was Cicily, after
Stephen's mother. She was older than Stephen, but younger
than Alden. Silly was thirty-one and Jane had never met any
other girl just like her. Silly, it seemed, kept a cocker-spaniel
kennel and hunted with the Myopia hounds and sailed a catboat at the Seaconsit races. Jane had thought she was perfectly stunning when she saw her get off the train in her blue
serge suit and crisp white shirt waist and small black sailor.
A perfect Gibson girl. Slim and distinguished. But that night
at dinner on Pine Street she had not looked nearly as well in
evening dress. Somehow lank and mannish, in spite of blue
taffeta, long-limbed and angular, and, yes, distinctly, old.

She didn't seem like a sister at all to Stephen. More like an aunt.

Stephen had an aunt, who had come too, with his uncle who was his father's brother. The Stephen Carver for whom Stephen had been named. He was nice, Jane thought. He was a college professor in Cambridge. He lived on Brattle Street, Alden said, and his field was Restoration Drama. Jane knew all about Restoration Drama and she knew all about college professors. It made her remember Bryn Mawr very vividly, just to see his wrinkled brown tweed suit and gold-bowed spectacles. His dinner coat was just a little shiny. Jane knew she would like her Uncle Stephen. He got on famously with her father. It seemed that they had been at Harvard together. That fact seemed to help the bridal dinner a great deal.

Uncle Stephen's wife was Aunt Marie. She looked like the wives of all college professors, thought Jane. Nice and bright and friendly and not too careful about how she did her hair. She was 'Nielson's daughter,' Alden had said, adding as Jane stared up at him uncomprehendingly, 'the great Nielson.' Considering the tone in which those three words were uttered, Jane didn't dare to inquire further. She smiled, very politely. Then she met her father's quizzical gaze from across the room. He saw her difficulty immediately.

'Geology,' he had breathed, over the heads of their guests. And then Jane remembered. Six fat volumes, bound in brown cloth, in her father's library. Nielson's 'Ice Age.' She had never read them but she 'placed' Aunt Marie, at once.

The bridal dinner, Jane had thought, had proved just a trifle disappointing. It was to be a very small house wedding, so only the two families were there. You couldn't, somehow, be awfully gay with just two families that had never seen each other until that afternoon. Mr. Alden Carver, however,

talked very steadily and informingly, to Jane's mother and
Mr. Ward chatted very pleasantly with Mrs. Carver about
how much every one in the West had come to think of Stephen.
Jane, herself, had sat in frozen silence between Stephen and
his father, watching Isabel trying to talk to Alden about the
last Yale-Harvard football game, which she hadn't seen, and
Robin's cheerful attempts to interest Aunt Marie in anecdotes
of his career in Cambridge. Jane couldn't think of a single
thing to say, even to Stephen, in such a solemn setting. Not
on the very last night before they were to be married.
Stephen was silent, too. He had held her hand very tightly,
under the tablecloth, and had smiled, encouragingly, every
time she glanced at him. It wasn't until the guests were all
leaving to walk over to their rooms in the Virginia Hotel,
three blocks away, that Jane had a moment alone with
him.

They were standing in the hall together, at the foot of the
staircase. Stephen's mother and sister and aunt were upstairs in the guest-room, putting on their party coats. Jane's
mother had gone up with them. The other men were all
talking to Isabel at the front door.

'Don't let them worry you,' said Stephen very tenderly.
'You won't have to live with them.'

'They don't worry me,' said Jane promptly. 'I like them.
I like your uncle a lot.'

Stephen looked very much pleased.

'Uncle Stephen's all right,' he said warmly. 'They're all
all right, really, but I thought they seemed a little fishy this
evening. A little of Alden will go a long way, of course.'

'Your mother,' said Jane hesitantly, 'was very sweet to
me.'

'Mother's a dear,' said Stephen, 'when you get to know her.
She's awfully domestic and rather shy.'

Jane would never have thought of that for herself. Shyness, she reflected, was a very endearing trait in a mother-in-law.

'I know I'll love her,' said Jane. As she spoke Mrs. Carver and her mother appeared at the top of the stairs. They all trooped together to the front door. Stephen lingered a moment to say good-bye to her in the vestibule. Jane smiled up at him, very calmly.

'Jane,' said Stephen a little wistfully, 'do you really love me?'

'Of course I do,' said Jane simply. That point, she felt, was settled at last. She was never going to worry about it any more. Stephen took her in his arms.

'Are you happy, Jane?' he asked.

'Except for the war,' said Jane. He kissed her very gently, very unalarmingly. It was peaceful, thought Jane, to have all her dreadful indecision over forever.

But now, as Jane stood facing her slim white reflection in her mirror, she really couldn't realize that she was getting married. Where were the thoughts, she wondered, that she had always imagined such a portentous occasion would engender? Where were the thoughts, for instance, that she had had at Muriel's wedding? Jane felt she should have reserved them for her own. She stretched out her hand for her shower bouquet.

'Well, I'm ready,' she said.

Isabel kissed her tenderly and turned to run downstairs to say that Jane was coming. Mrs. Ward, still crying, took her in her arms.

'Mamma,' said Jane smiling, 'it isn't a funeral.'

Mrs. Ward tried to dry her tears.

'I want Minnie to see the ceremony,' said Jane.

They all left the room together. At the head of the stairs

Mr. Ward was waiting. He watched Jane's approach down the darkened corridor with a very tender smile. She slipped her hand through his arm. Jane's mother went down the stairs, followed by Minnie.

'Kid,' said Mr. Ward, 'you look perfectly lovely.'

Jane smiled up at him through the tulle.

'Kid,' said Mr. Ward again, 'it will be a naval war. I doubt if the land forces ever reach Cuba. Cervera will blockade the ports.'

Jane smiled again, this time a little tremulously. She was trying to forget the war.

The little stringed orchestra under the stairs struck up the Lohengrin wedding march. Jane was glad she wasn't going to be married to those doomful premonitory notes of an organ. The violins made even Lohengrin sound gay. She walked slowly down the stairs on her father's arm.

The little library seemed very full of people. Mrs. Ward had thought the ceremony should be in the yellow parlour. But Jane had never liked the parlour. She had declared in favour of her father's room. Old Dr. Winter from Saint James's was standing in snowy vestments in front of the mantelpiece. A little aisle led straight from the door to the hearth. The empty fireplace was filled with smilax. Two great vases of white roses were placed on the mantelpiece. The flowers met over the bald wooden head of the bust of Shakespeare. Jane's mother had wanted to take it down for the ceremony. But Jane had thought that Shakespeare was a very appropriate genius to preside over a wedding. Shakespeare had known all about weddings. 'Romeo and Juliet.' Jane remembered the friar's solemn words as she stepped over the threshold and met 'The Bard of Avon's' wise mahogany eye.

'So smile the heavens upon this holy act
That after hours with sorrow chide us not.'

The library, filled with softly smiling, softly stirring people, was very little like a friar's cell. Still Jane had an almost irresistible impulse to jar the solemnity of the occasion by greeting old Dr. Winter with Juliet's sprightly opening line,

'Good even to my ghostly confessor!'

What would he do, thought Jane, if she did? What would Stephen? Stephen would think she was mad. Stephen had never even read 'Romeo and Juliet.' He had told her so, months ago, and she had marvelled, at the time, that a Harvard degree could crown an education so singularly deficient!

Stephen was standing with Alden, embowered in smilax, at the left hand of the clergyman, both fearfully correct in new frock coats and boutonnières of lilies of the valley. Stephen looked very charming and serious and distinctly nervous. Jane smiled reassuringly up at him, as she relinquished her father's arm. The music died away into silence.

'Dearly beloved brethren,' began Dr. Winter.

Jane looked up, very calmly, at Stephen's set young profile. How young he was, she thought! How terribly young to be going to war! Her fingers tightened slightly on his broadcloth sleeve. He looked down at her and smiled reassuringly in his turn. She stared up into his eyes. She was marrying Stephen. Her father's voice aroused her. It was very clear and firm.

'I do,' he said. Jane could hear him behind her, stepping back beside her mother. Then Dr. Winter took up his part, again, sonorously. Presently there was a barely perceptible pause in the familiar cadence of the ritual.

'I, Stephen, take thee, Jane,' said Stephen hastily.

Jane felt herself smiling. She was sorry for Stephen. When her turn came she was quite collected.

'I, Jane, take thee, Stephen, for my wedded husband,' the

words were devoid of meaning. She could have said them all, unprompted by the clergyman. She had an odd sensation of playing a rôle. Dr. Winter was blessing the ring. They were putting it on her finger. Stephen was speaking again.

'With this ring I thee wed ——' It stuck a bit, over the last knuckle. Stephen was still nervous. Dr. Winter had resumed. Suddenly the stringed orchestra swelled out into Mendelssohn. Jane's main feeling was that it had all been over in a moment — this ceremony that every one had been talking about for two weeks. Why — it was nothing. Stephen stooped to kiss her — a self-conscious little kiss — barely brushing her cheek. He became entangled in the tulle veil. Jane laughed up at him. She felt her mother's arms about her. Then she was looking up into her father's eyes.

'Kid, be happy,' he said, as he kissed her.

Every one was around her then. Stephen's mother was crying. Mr. Carver's beard felt very bristly. Muriel's cheek smelled of French toilet water. Freddy Waters's hair of bay rum. Rosalie was saying 'What a lovely dress!' Alden surprisingly kissed her. Silly was laughing at Stephen.

'Your form's not up to par in the ring,' she was crying. 'All right in the paddock, old boy, but you fell down in the show! Jane's the prize entry. She gets the blue ribbon!'

'Come cut the cake!' cried Isabel. Every one was kissed by now.

'Carry my train!' cried Jane to Stephen. She felt very light-hearted. He picked it up, laughing. He looked awfully happy. They led the crowd to the dining-room. Minnie handed Jane the knife, festooned with white satin. Jane dug into the bride's cake, just under the sugar cupid. Every one was applauding. The orchestra in the hall was playing 'The Stars and Stripes Forever.' The groom's cake was decorated with a little silken flag.

Jane sank down in her mother's armchair at one end of the room. Stephen was standing beside her. People began to bring them food. Dr. Winter, with vestments removed, showed up to wish them happiness. She must go upstairs, soon, and change her dress. They were taking a six o'clock train. They were going up to The Dells, in northern Wisconsin. They had only a week before Stephen left for San Antonio. People were singing now. Alden had started 'Fair Harvard.' All the men, old and young, knew the words. The male chorus swelled out very bravely, the orchestra accompanying softly:

'Fair Harvard, thy sons to thy jubilee throng,
And with blessings surrender thee o'er,
By these festival rites from the age that is past
To the age that is waiting before——'

Uncle Stephen, red-faced and white-headed, arm in arm with her father, was singing loudest of all and a little off key. It made Jane feel just a little chokey to look at them. All Harvard men, she thought, every one except Freddy. Even Mr. Bert Lancaster. Freddy went to Yale. He was singing, though, very generously. The words were lovely, thought Jane, just as lovely as the air.

The song over, Stephen's father raised his champagne glass.

'A toast to the bride!' he cried. Every one drank it, cheering. When it was over Stephen crashed his goblet to the floor. Applause greeted the gallant gesture. Jane saw her mother, however, noting with gratitude that it was only a caterer's class.

'I must go up,' said Jane. Stephen squeezed her hand.

'I'll go with you,' said Isabel. Hand in hand they ran up the stairs. Minnie was waiting in Jane's bedroom. The packed suitcase was lying on the bed.

'Stephen's magnificent,' laughed Isabel, as she unhooked the wedding dress. Jane was removing the veil.

'I don't believe the Rough Riders will ever see action,' said Isabel. 'Robin says it will be a short war.'

'Alden thinks,' said Jane doubtfully, 'that it will last forever. He says the Spanish fleet may bombard Boston.'

'That's nonsense,' said Isabel promptly.

Jane stepped out of her wedding dress.

'Sit down,' said Minnie gruffly. 'I'll take off your slippers and stockings.' Jane sank down on the chair overlooking the willow tree. She had never been waited on like that before.

'Mr. Carver says,' said Jane, 'that lots of Bostonians have taken their securities out of the Bay State Trust Company and put them in banks in Worcester.'

'They're crazy,' said Isabel. Some one downstairs had ineptly started the orchestra on 'Dollie Grey.' Every one was singing it.

'Papa thinks they are,' said Jane. Minnie handed her her waist and skirt. Isabel busied herself with hooks once more. Mrs. Ward appeared in the doorway.

'Nearly ready, Jane?' she asked.

Jane picked up her hat from the bed. It was a pretty hat, with a wreath of bachelor's buttons around it.

'In a minute,' said Jane, facing the mirror again. 'It was a lovely wedding, Mamma.'

'I thought so,' said Mrs. Ward a little tremulously. Jane heard tears in her voice. Jane was determined to fight off sentiment.

'Mamma,' she said quickly, 'I'll be back in a week.'

That simple statement didn't seem to make things any better.

'Jane dear,' said Mrs. Ward, 'I can't bear it ——'

Mr. Ward appeared in the doorway.

'Mrs. Carver, your husband is waiting for you,' he said. Jane was very grateful for his twinkle.

'It won't be the last time he'll wait for me!' she laughed. She caught up her coat and kissed Isabel.

'I'll take down the suitcase,' said Isabel. She left the room. Mrs. Ward took Jane in her arms.

'My child ——' she began, with emotion. Jane stopped her with a kiss.

'Good-bye, Minnie,' she said lightly. At the door her father slipped his arm around her. She stood looking up at him. Her — father. Jane was suddenly overcome with a sense of what she was doing. She was leaving home — forever.

'Papa,' she said brokenly, 'Papa, you've always ——' She couldn't say it.

Mr. Ward patted her back.

'Good luck, Kid,' he said huskily. She gave him a tremendous hug.

'Don't forget to throw your bouquet,' said Mrs. Ward solemnly, through her tears. Jane snatched it up from the bed.

Stephen was waiting in the upper hall. Jane took his arm. There was no time to speak to him. Every one was pressing around the foot of the staircase. Alden was leading the band. As Stephen appeared it struck up 'Hail, the Conquering Hero Comes.'

'Oh, good Lord!' muttered Stephen disgustedly. 'That's just like Alden!' They started down the stairs. From the first landing Jane pitched her bouquet straight into the virgin arms of Silly, the only maiden present. Stephen gripped her elbow. A shower of rice and confetti rose from the little crowd below. They dashed madly down and through the press of people. The front door was open, Robin standing guard. The mild May air was very refreshing, after the crowded rooms. Jane took a great breath of it as they rushed down the steps, past the crowd by the awning. The wedding guests came running after them. Rice still flew. Jane gained the shelter of the waiting brougham. Stephen flung himself after her and banged the door. The brougham started smartly into motion. Jane was looking out of the little back window at Isabel and Robin and Rosalie and Freddy, on the curb. Silly suddenly appeared to wave the lilies of the valley with one long, thin arm, above their heads. The brougham turned into Erie Street.

'Jane!' said Stephen, and suddenly his arms were around her. 'Jane,' he said again, very solemnly, 'we're — married.' Jane felt again that frightful fear of sentiment. Couldn't — couldn't people take weddings — calmly? She smiled, a little shakily, into Stephen's eyes. Suddenly his arms grew strong and strangely urgent. He pulled her to him roughly, abruptly.

'Stephen!' cried Jane, in consternation. His eyes were smiling, excitedly, straight into her own. Jane fell a sudden prey to panic. 'Stephen,' she said quickly — 'don't — please — don't!'

His face changed then, perplexedly. It grew strangely wistful.

'I — I won't, Jane,' he said very gently. His arms relaxed their hold.

Jane felt suddenly contrite. And somehow — inadequate. She felt she was failing Stephen. Stephen, whom she had married, who would have only a week with her, who was going to war. Deliberately she put her arms around him.

'Stephen, truly I love you,' she said. Stephen's lips met hers. Dear Stephen! She *did* love him. She *would* love him. She had married him. That point was settled. The brougham rolled on up Erie Street.

V

The midsummer willow stood motionless in the late August sunshine, not a grey-green leaf stirring, and Jane was sitting at her window looking out at it and thinking of Stephen, when André's second letter arrived.

Minnie brought it up to her, immediately after the postman's ring. No one could do too much for Jane now. Jane saw the Italian stamp, the strange transparent paper, before she took it from Minnie's considerate hand. She had a queer revulsion of feeling the moment she recognized it. An impulse to cast it from her, unread. Jane didn't want to hear from André. She didn't want to hear anything he might have to say.

When Minnie had left the room, however, she opened it, very thoughtfully. After all — it couldn't make any difference. She was glad to see that it was very brief.

'DEAR JANE,

'I was terribly surprised and terribly shocked at the news your letter contained. Why, I don't know. I was always afraid, all these past four years, that I would hear that you were going to marry. I hadn't counted, though, on just what the sight of my name on an envelope, in your handwriting, would do to me. I haven't felt ready to answer until just now.

'I hope, awfully, that you will be very happy. That you're happy now. But I won't plan to come to the States. I know I don't want to meet your husband next spring and I think I don't want to meet you, Jane, ever again. You mean a very special thing to me. No one will ever take your place. But I won't come to Chicago. Feeling as I do, I should really have nothing to say to you. "*Il faut qu'une porte soit ouverte ou fermée.*"

ANDRÉ'

Well, thought Jane, that was that. But why did he have to write just as he did? Jane frowned over her instant recognition of the pluck the brief note had given to her heart strings. It was unforgettable, like everything else about André.

Jane put it away with his other letter in her desk drawer. She was terribly glad that she would not have to see him. She didn't want to see André, ever again. He — he shouldn't have mentioned it, of course, but he was quite right about doors.

A great deal of water had run under the bridge since the April afternoon when his first letter had arrived. Stephen, an authentic hero, had charged up San Juan Hill, following the waving sombrero of Theodore Roosevelt. He was recovering from malarial fever, now, down at Montauk Point. The war was over. Cuba was free. The United States owned the Philippine Islands. Boston had not been bombarded. And Jane had known, for more than three months, that she was going to have a baby in February.

PART III
JIMMY

PART III

JIMMY

CHAPTER I

I

Jane Carver opened the screened door that led from the living-room of her father-in-law's house at Gull Rocks, Seaconsit, to the verandah that commanded a view of the sea. She closed it quietly behind her and walked quickly over to the wooden steps that led down to the grassy terrace.

Fifteen years of matrimony had not impaired the lightness of Jane's step. Her fine straight hair was still untouched with grey, her waist was still slender, and her eyes were still bright. They gleamed, now, with a spark of irritation. Had Mrs. Ward and Isabel been present they would have recognized, immediately, the storm signal. 'Tantrum' would have been their verdict.

Jane stood still, for a moment, by a porch pillar and looked up at the vast assuaging reaches of blue sky beyond the green festoons and orange flowers of the trumpet vine. The sky was delightfully impersonal, thought Jane. Its very impersonality was vaguely comforting. With an acute sense of peril, momentarily escaped, Jane drew in a great breath of the warm sea-scented air. She was feeling better, already, just because of the sky and the sunshine and the soft sea-breeze and the tender waving tendrils of the trumpet vine.

If she had stayed in that living-room another minute, Jane knew she would have been rude to her mother-in-law. And Jane had never been that. Not really. Not once in fifteen years. But if she had listened once more to Mrs. Carver's gentle expression of the pious hope, already reiterated three times since luncheon, that the good weather that they were now enjoying did not mean that it was going to rain during Stephen's vacation, Jane knew her record would have been broken.

It was terrible, thought Jane, it was really terrible, what it did to her to listen to Stephen's family talk about Stephen. And incomprehensible. For Jane loved Stephen. They were very happy together. Yet, somehow, when his mother —— Oh, well, there was no use going into it. She had been knitting quietly by the living-room fire when Aunt Marie had observed that it was a pleasant afternoon for the race and Uncle Stephen had remarked that there was not much wind and Mrs. Carver had opened her mouth to reply. The pious hope had cast its shadow before. Jane had known what was coming. She had sprung to her feet and made good her escape.

It all seemed rather silly, now, as she looked back on it. Jane opened her knitting-bag and sat down on the top step in the sunshine.

A sunshot August haze hung over the familiar view of lawn and beach and bay. The Seaconsit harbour was filled with flitting sails. The Saturday afternoon race would begin in half an hour. Her father-in-law's launch was riding at anchor, ready to follow the contestants around the course, and Jane could see her father-in-law, dapper in blue coat and white flannels, standing at the end of the pier, binoculars in hand. He was watching Alden and Silly, rounding the first flag in their catboat, already manœuvring for position, half an hour ahead of the starting gun.

Mrs. Carver was watching them, too, Jane knew, from a living-room window, but without binoculars. On racing afternoons the binoculars became the passionate personal property of Mr. Carver. No one else would have thought of touching them.

Jane picked up her worsted and began to knit. She was making a blue sweater for her fourteen-year-old daughter, copying the shoulder pattern from the printed directions on the Mothers' Page of 'The Woman's Home Magazine.' She spread the periodical on the porch floor beside her and bent placidly over her work. The sweater would be becoming to Cicily. When this one was finished, she would knit another for Jenny and a third for little Steve, much as he disliked being dressed to match his sisters. All three children were very blond. Like the Carvers, thought Jane, with a little sigh. When she looked up she could see her son's yellow head bent over his pad and paint-box on the beach at the foot of the lawn and the stiff white contour of his trained nurse's figure, stretched in the shadow of a rock at his side. Her daughters were nowhere to be seen. They were out in their Aunt Silly's kennels, perhaps, playing with the cocker-spaniel puppy that she had given them.

It was very peaceful, alone on the verandah. And very quiet. Jane could hear the faint eternal ripple of the little lapping waves on the beach beyond the lawn, the insistent put-put of an unseen motor-boat in the harbour and the mechanical tap of a woodpecker in the oak tree near the garden. The click of her own knitting-needles was the only other sound that broke the sunny silence.

It was pleasant to be alone. At Gull Rocks, Jane perversely reflected, one seldom was. The Carvers, as a family, were animated by the clan spirit. They did things, if at all, in concert. They even did nothing in concert. They abhorred solitude as nature does a vacuum.

Jane's fingers were busy and her eyes were occupied, but her mind was not concerned with the work in hand. Quite

mechanicallyshe purled and plained and tossed the blue wool
over her amber needles. She was thinking wise, thirty-six-
year-old thoughts about the relative-in-law complex. 'The
relative-in-law complex' was the phrase that Jane herself had
coined to account for the obvious injustice of her thoughts
about Carvers. She was privately rather proud of it. The
Freudian vocabulary was not yet a commonplace in the
Western hemisphere, but Jane knew all about complexes and
was vaguely comforted to feel herself in the grip of one that
was undoubtedly authentic. There was nothing you could do
about a complex. There it was — like the shape of your nose.
You had no moral responsibility for it and it innocently explained all the baser emotional reactions, of which, alone
with your conscience, you were somehow subtly ashamed.

Jane was decidedly relieved to feel able to evade all moral
responsibility for the emotions aroused in her breast by the
constant society of Carvers. For, from any point of view but
that of the enlightened Freudian, she could not but feel that
they were distinctly unworthy. Even ridiculous. For years
she had struggled against them. But emotions were strangely
invincible. Ephemeral, however. That was a comfort. It was
only when visiting at Gull Rocks, Seaconsit, that Jane fell
a prey to the baser variety of which she was subtly ashamed.
Safe at home with Stephen, in her little Colonial cottage in
the suburbs of Chicago, Jane could always look back on the
complications presented by life at Gull Rocks with a tolerant
smile. Seen from that secure perspective, the congenital
peculiarities of Carvers seemed always harmless, at times
picturesque, and often pathetic. For ten months of the year
they figured in her life as mere alien phenomena at which she
marvelled detachedly, with easy amusement. In July and
August they reared their sinister heads as dragons in her path.

Jane had spent July and August at Gull Rocks, Seaconsit,

every summer but two since the birth of her first baby. The year that Steve was born, Stephen had gone East alone with their two little daughters. And the year after that Stephen had incredibly taken a three months' vacation from the bank to make the grand tour of Europe, leaving the three children at home in the Colonial cottage in Mrs. Ward's care. Twelve Julys and twelve Augusts at Gull Rocks, Seaconsit! When Jane put it like that, she really felt that she had joined the Holy Fellowship of Martyrs. Stephen didn't know what it was like — how could he, being born a Carver? — marooned alone with the children at Gull Rocks summer after summer, while he held down his job at the bank at home and only came on to join them for a three weeks' holiday. Stephen wanted his children brought up with some idea of the New England tradition. That was only natural, of course, still ——

However, Stephen was coming, that very afternoon, on the six o'clock train, for the three weeks' holiday. Jane was very glad of that. Stephen's coming would make everything much better. Gull Rocks was almost fun, when Stephen was there. They would swim with the children and Stephen would teach little Steve to sail and ——

Jane heard the screened door open behind her and the brisk, decided step of Aunt Marie crossing the piazza. She did not raise her head from her knitting.

'I've come out to keep you company,' said Aunt Marie pleasantly.

Jane made no comment. She was counting stitches again, softly, under her breath. She heard the Nantucket hammock at the corner of the verandah creak faintly under her aunt's substantial weight.

'Have you read the August "Atlantic"?' asked Aunt Marie presently.

Jane shook her head in silence. She could hear the pages of the magazine flutter faintly in her aunt's deliberate fingers.

'There's a very good article in it,' continued Aunt Marie, in her pleasant practical New England voice, 'by Cassandra Frothingham Perkins, on "The Decline of Culture."'

'Twenty-three, twenty-four,' whispered Jane defensively. Then 'Has it declined?' she asked. The innocence in her tone was not entirely ingenuous.

'Well, *hasn't* it?' returned Aunt Marie very practically, as before. Then, after a pause, 'You know who Cassandra Frothingham Perkins *is*, don't you?'

'One of the Concord Perkinses,' said Jane, as glibly as a child responding with '1492' or '1066' to the question of a history teacher. She had not spent twelve summers at Gull Rocks, Seaconsit, in vain.

'She's the daughter,' said Aunt Marie, 'of Samuel Wendell Perkins, who wrote the Perkins biography of Emerson and "Literary Rambles in Old Concord." The "Atlantic" publishes a lot of her stuff.'

'I've read it,' said Jane briefly. Who cared, she thought perversely, if culture *had* declined? But the question was purely rhetorical. For obviously Cassandra Frothingham Perkins did. And Aunt Marie Carver. All the Carvers, in fact. Nevertheless, the decline of culture was not a burning issue with Jane.

She bent her head again over the knitting directions in 'The Woman's Home Magazine' and her eye caught a flamboyant headline on the opposite page. 'How Can We Keep Our Charm?' by Viola Vivasour. And below in explanatory vein, 'Fifteen minutes a day devoted to Miss Vivasour's simple formula of face creams solves woman's eternal problem.' But Aunt Marie was again speaking.

'Cassandra's made a little schedule,' she said. 'She claims

that fifteen minutes a day, spent reading the *best* books — and she adds a little list of one hundred ——'

How much less important, thought Jane wickedly, the decline of culture than that of charm! Not, however, in the Carvers' circle. There the significance of a five-foot bookshelf would always rise above that of a good cosmetic. The society of her relatives-in-law made Jane feel wantonly frivolous. She would just as soon read one article, she thought, or follow one recipe, as the other. Both equally absurd. Prepared for different publics — that was all.

Jane heard the screened door open once more behind her and the heavy, slightly hesitant step of her mother-in-law crossing the piazza. She did not turn her head. Her hands still busy with her knitting, she gazed steadily out over the close-clipped lawn, pierced here and there with outcrops of granite rock, stretching smooth and green and freshly watered, three hundred feet before her, to where the coarser growth of beach grass, rooted in sandy soil, met the yellow line of beach that fringed the blue expanse of sea. Jane loved the beach grass. It continued to exist in a state of nature, rooted in primeval sand, defeating the best efforts of the impeccable Portuguese gardener to impose on it an alien culture. There it was. The Carvers could do nothing about it. Jane wondered if her Aunt Marie had ever reflected that her Western niece-in-law was rather like the beach grass.

Mrs. Carver's footsteps paused at her side.

'Dexter doesn't think he can get me any lobster to-day, Jane.' Mrs. Carver's voice was grave and just a trifle anxious. 'Do you think Stephen would prefer bluefish or mackerel?'

'I don't know,' said Jane.

'He's so fond of sea food,' said Mrs. Carver.

Jane felt again that absurd surge of irritation. Stephen would never know *what* fish he was eating. Why fuss about it?

'I wanted to give him an old-fashioned shore dinner.'

The wistful note in the worried voice suddenly touched Jane's heart. She looked up and met her mother-in-law's anxious gaze. The fat, elderly face was creased in lines of vivid disappointment. Old age was pathetic, thought Jane, secure in the citadel of her thirty-six summers. Mothers were pathetic.

'I think he'd *love* mackerel,' she said warmly.

Mrs. Carver's face brightened.

'I shall keep on trying for the lobster,' she said solemnly, 'until the last minute.'

Suddenly Jane loved her mother-in-law. She loved her for the solemnity. It was touching and disarming. Why didn't she always say the things that Mrs. Carver liked to hear? It was so easy to say them. She really *must* reform.

'Is that little Steve on the beach?' said Mrs. Carver.

'Yes,' said Jane.

'Don't you think the sun is too hot for him?' asked Mrs. Carver.

'No,' said Jane.

'The glare's very bright on those rocks,' said Mrs. Carver, 'and Miss Parrot never seems to notice ——'

'The doctor said the sun was good for him,' said Jane tartly. Her moment of reform was short-lived.

'We can't be too careful,' said Mrs. Carver.

They couldn't be, of course. Why was she so perverse? Poor little Steve, pulled down, still, from his scarlet fever in June, still watched by his nurse, still worrying them all with that heart that wasn't quite right yet, but would be, so the doctor said, by next spring!

'I think he ought to come into the shade,' said Mrs. Carver.

Jane rose abruptly and picked up the megaphone behind the hammock.

'Yoo-hoo!' she called. 'Miss Parrot!' The white cap turned promptly in response to her call. 'Bring Steve up, please!'

She sank on the steps again and picked up her knitting. She could see Miss Parrot's slender starched figure rise from behind her rock. It assumed a slightly admonitory angle. Steve's yellow head was raised from the sands in obvious protest.

'She doesn't know how to manage children,' said Mrs. Carver.

Steve, pad and paint-box in hand, was wading through the beach grass, now, beside his nurse. His thin little voice could be heard, raised in inarticulate argument. Miss Parrot walked steadily on. Steve, reaching the smooth green turf of the lawn, paused to scratch a mosquito bite on his brown little knee.

'Why doesn't she wait for him?' said Mrs. Carver.

'Oh, he's all right,' said Jane. 'He loves Miss Parrot.'

Mrs. Carver watched her grandson's approach in silence.

'I don't want to come up, Mumsy!' he cried. 'I was painting the harbour.'

'Don't run, dear,' said Mrs. Carver.

'You can finish your painting to-morrow,' said Jane.

'The light will be different, Mumsy!' His tanned little nine-year-old countenance was eager with protest.

'Mrs. Carver thinks the sun is too hot on the beach, Miss Parrot,' said Jane.

The trained nurse turned her pretty, pleasant face upon them with a tolerant smile.

'All righty!' she said. 'Come on, Stevey, we'll paint in the garden.'

'I don't want to,' said Steve. He glared crossly at his grandmother.

Miss Parrot smiled again, throwing a glance of frank, professional understanding at the adults on the verandah.

'Oh, yes, you do,' she said easily. 'If Grandma wants you to. Grandma's the doctor!'

She disappeared around the corner of the house. Steve trailed aggrievedly after her. When he was irritated, reflected Jane, his little nine-year-old figure took on exactly the angle of that of her preposterous father-in-law. Mrs. Carver's lips were slightly compressed. Jane knew what was coming.

'I don't like that woman's tone,' said Mrs. Carver.

'She's a very good heart nurse,' said Jane.

'She has no proper deference,' said Mrs. Carver.

Jane's lips, in their turn, were slightly compressed at the familiar phrase. Proper deference! That commodity that the Carvers sought in vain, throughout the world, looking for it, Jane thought, with the most pathetic optimism, in the most unlikely places. In the manners of Irish housemaids, on the lips of trained nurses, and in the emotional reactions of modern grandchildren. They never lost their simple faith that they ought to find it. That it was somehow owing to them. Was it, thought Jane curiously, because they were all over sixty? Or because they were Carvers? Stephen was a Carver, yet proper deference meant nothing in his life.

'Here comes Alden!' said Mrs. Carver suddenly. 'Marie, are you ready?'

The figure of Mr. Carver had indeed deserted the pier and advanced to the beach grass. He was waving peremptorily. Aunt Marie rose from the Nantucket hammock a trifle hastily.

'I'll get my sneakers,' she said, and vanished into the house.

'Now, where is your Uncle Stephen?' said Mrs. Carver. 'Jane, you'll need your hat.' She was hurriedly swathing her own with a purple face veil.

'Didn't you hear the horn?' called Mr. Carver. 'I blew it twice.'

'We didn't, dear,' said Mrs. Carver. 'The wind's off shore.'

'Jane, not much time,' said Mr. Carver. He took out his watch as he spoke. 'It's twenty minutes to three. Where are your rubber shoes?'

'I'll get them,' said Jane. 'They're in my room.'

'Call your Uncle Stephen,' said Mrs. Carver. 'He's working in the study.'

'I can't see why you can't all be ready at the proper time,' Jane heard her father-in-law observe as she crossed the porch. 'I only keep up the launch for the pleasure of the family.' The screened door banged behind her. She crossed the living-room with an air of extreme deliberation. What a ridiculous old man Mr. Carver was! Domestic dictator! Why didn't they all revolt? Why hadn't they all revolted, years ago, long before she came into the family?

Jane paused before the living-room chimney-piece to kick, vindictively, a smouldering log back into the ashes and place the screen before the dying fire. Always this fuss about nothing, every Wednesday and Saturday afternoon, at twenty minutes to three! That launch! The Whim! Ironic name! It ought to be called The Duty, The Responsibility, The Obligation. Or perhaps, like a British dreadnought, The Invincible. It *was* invincible, when manned by Mr. Carver. Those Wednesday and Saturday races! That sacred necessity of following them, twice every week, out of the harbour and into the bay, around the three buoys and home. Watching those ridiculous catboats with Alden and Silly at the helm of one, appraising the wind, discussing the course, commending the seamanship. No one cared to go — except Mr. Carver. Take to-day when Mrs. Carver wanted to telephone for lobsters and Aunt Marie to read the 'Atlantic' and Uncle Stephen to work in the study and she just to be let alone for a quiet afternoon, to finish Cicily's sweater and think of Stephen's arrival. No one *ever* cared to go, really—except the children. And they couldn't because they made Mrs. Carver nervous, climbing around the boat, and Mr. Carver irritated, ever since little Steve had dropped the compass and broken the glass and spilled the alcohol all over the varnished table in the cabin.

'I only keep up the launch,' thought Jane in resentful retrospect, as she crossed the hall, 'for the pleasure of the family.' What bunk! It was really Mrs. Carver's fault, of course. She should have taken him in hand just as soon as she married him. Her weakness was his strength. She'd made him what he was to-day and the rising generations had to suffer for her folly. Stephen might have been like that if he had married a woman like his own mother. There was lots of 'Carver' in Stephen. Jane knew she had been good for him. All the Wards had been good for him. Her father in one way, and her mother, and even Isabel, in quite another. The West had been good for him. Jane paused at the living-room door.

'Uncle Stephen?' she said.

The elderly professor was seated at his brother's mahogany secretary, bent over a little pile of manuscript. He did not hear her.

'Uncle Stephen!' said Jane again.

Her uncle raised his shiny bald head abruptly. His big blue eyes looked mildly up at her over his gold-rimmed spectacles. His face was very fat and round and pink and his head was very spherical and almost hairless. In spite of his white moustache, Jane always thought he looked just like a good-natured baby. Uncle Stephen was always good-natured and Jane was very fond of him. He didn't seem at all like a Carver. Was that perhaps because of Aunt Marie, the indomitable daughter of 'the great Nielson,' with whom he had been united in matrimony for more than forty years? Aunt Marie seemed so much more like a Carver than Uncle Stephen himself. There was a subtle warning in that thought, reflected Jane. In patiently eradicating, throughout a long lifetime, the more disagreeable traits of a husband, did a wife herself acquire them?

But Uncle Stephen's pleasant pink old face had assumed a guilty expression.

'Good Lord, Janie!' he said regretfully. 'Is it twenty minutes to three?'

'You bet it is,' said Jane briefly. And her eyes met those of her uncle in a twinkle of understanding. Jane never discussed Carvers with Carvers, but she knew just how Uncle Stephen felt about The Whim. Fumbling a little in his haste, he began to put away his manuscripts in a shabby brown brief case.

'I wanted to finish these notes,' he said helplessly, 'but ——'

'What are you doing?' asked Jane. The activities of Uncle Stephen at Gull Rocks were always refreshing. Jane thought scholarship a trifle amusing. Impersonal, however, and assuaging, like the blue sky. Uncle Stephen's conversation could always be counted on to rise above the domestic plane.

'A monograph,' he said meekly, 'on the Letters of William Wycherley, for the Modern Language Society. His correspondence with Alexander Pope.'

'I thought Wycherley wrote plays,' said Jane vaguely. In spite of the early exhortations of Miss Thomas, the details of a Bryn Mawr education were fast fading from her memory.

'He did, my dear,' said Uncle Stephen. 'Good plays and bad poems and very bad letters.'

'Then why write monographs on them?' asked Jane.

'They are interesting,' said Uncle Stephen, rising from his chair, 'because they stimulated Pope to reply.'

'Then why not write on Pope's answers?'

'That has been done, my dear.'

Jane felt that the mysteries of scholarship were beyond her.

'Pope was very fond of him,' said Uncle Stephen, as they turned toward the door. 'He said "the love of some things rewards itself, as of Virtue and of Mr. Wycherley."'

As she mounted the stairs in search of her rubber shoes, Jane wished that she were a scholar. Scholarship would be a resource at Gull Rocks. She wished that she were capable of generating a passionate interest in the thoughts of Alexander Pope on Virtue and Mr. Wycherley. She wished that she were capable of generating a passionate interest in almost anything that would serve to pass the time. On the landing she met Miss Parrot.

'Mrs. Carver,' said the trained nurse. Her voice was pleasant but a trifle cool.

'Yes,' said Jane.

'I wanted to speak to you again about Steve's diet,' said Miss Parrot. 'His grandmother *will* keep on giving him too much sugar. He had three tablespoons on his raspberries at luncheon. I *can't* convince her it won't build him up ——'

'I'll speak to her,' said Jane. She turned to mount the stairs.

'And Mrs. Carver ——'

'Yes,' said Jane, pausing again on the third step above the landing.

'I'll have to speak to you again about my supper tray. The desserts — last night the cook sent me up only three prunes. I thought you'd like to know.'

'Oh, I *love* to know!' thought Jane. But — 'I'm sorry, Miss Parrot,' she said. 'I'll see about it.'

'And Mrs. Carver — Madam Carver spoke to me again about using the back stairs. I'm not a servant, Mrs. Carver.'

'You're a guest, Miss Parrot,' said Jane, 'as I am myself. You'll have to use whatever stairs Madam Carver asks you to.'

Miss Parrot's pretty lips were firmly compressed. Jane looked at her in silence. She was a very good heart nurse. Jane fell a prey to inner panic.

'Please be patient, Miss Parrot,' she said weakly. 'It won't be for long now.'

'I shall use the front stairs,' said Miss Parrot firmly. And turned to descend them.

Jane mounted to her room in silence. At thirty-six life was terrible, she thought, as she pulled on her rubber shoes. It had no dignity. It wasn't at all what you expected, when you were young. Youth wasn't dignified, of course, but it was simple, it was joyous, it was expectant. In youth life seemed — important. The things you thought about *were* important, no matter how inadequately you thought about them. But later you found yourself involved in a labyrinth of trifles. Worrying, ridiculous trifles. Things that didn't matter, yet had to be coped with. And you'd lost that sustaining sense that, at any moment, something different might be going to happen. At thirty-six you found yourself a buffer state between the older generation and the younger. You had to keep your son's trained nurse and you had to keep the peace with your mother-in-law. Did Miss Parrot think she liked to live with Mrs. Carver? Did Mrs. Carver think she liked to live with Miss Parrot? If she could live with both of them, Jane thought, they might at least succeed in living with each other for two brief months ——

'Jane!' It was the voice of her mother-in-law, raised in

anxious protest from the terrace below her window. 'What *are* you doing, dear? The launch is *waiting!*'

Jane snatched up a hat and ran from her room. She dashed down the stairs. Oh, well! Stephen was coming that evening. They would go home in three weeks. Miss Parrot *was* a good heart nurse. She took all the responsibility. And Steve was much better. Gull Rocks had done a lot for him. The sun and the sea air. Her mother-in-law was pathetic. She couldn't really help Mr. Carver. And Stephen was coming.

Jane banged the screened door and overtook Mrs. Carver on the path to the pier. She slipped her hand through her plump arm.

'I'm sorry,' she said. 'I was talking to Miss Parrot.'

'What about?' asked Mrs. Carver.

'She was telling me she didn't like prunes,' said Jane, laughing.

'Did she think that you cared?' inquired Mrs. Carver with acerbity.

'Yes. But she was wrong!' Jane dropped her mother-in-law's arm and stooped to pluck a handful of sweet fern from among the beach grass. The grey-green petals, wrenched from the fibrous stem, exhaled a pungent perfume. Jane buried her nose in them. They were very sweet and warm from the sun. She ran lightly ahead of her mother-in-law out onto the pier.

Mr. Carver was standing on the float, his watch in his hand. He looked severely at her from under his straw hat-brim.

'Quickly, now,' said Mr. Carver.

Jane sprang from the float to the boat. Aunt Marie was seated in a canvas deck chair. Her ankles looked thick and her small, wide feet very flat and stubby in her white sneakers. She had brought the August 'Atlantic' with her. Jane knew she wouldn't be allowed to read it. Uncle Stephen was sitting

on the little varnished bench along the rail. He looked more
like a baby than ever, thought Jane, in his round canvas
boating hat. A semicircle of pink scalp showed under its
floppy brim in the rear. Mr. Carver was carefully handing
his wife up over the little landing-ladder. Her feet fumbled
on the rubber treads and she clung a trifle nervously to his
blue serge sleeve.

'We may be in time yet,' said Mr. Carver quite happily.
Then, with severity, 'The starting gun is late.' His tone im-
plied that starting guns were not what they used to be. In the
days when *he* was president of the Seaconsit Yacht Club ——

Jane, perched on the rail, her rubber-shod feet upon the
varnished bench, suddenly realized that she was laughing
aloud. Carvers *were* pathetic. They were all over sixty. They
didn't know how funny they were. Jane felt distinctly sorry
for them. To a discerning daughter-in-law they didn't really
matter.

One white-clad sailor was pulling up the ladder. Another
was standing by to push off the launch. Mr. Carver had taken
his seat at the wheel. His shrivelled little New England face,
with its grey Vandyke beard, was turned sideways and up-
ward, estimating the weather.

'Not much wind,' he said.

The whir of the gasoline engine increased in volume, then
quieted suddenly to a steady purr. The water widened between the launch and the pier. Jane turned to watch the catboats, veering and tacking now, around the first buoy. Suddenly she heard the gun. Mr. Carver rose from his seat, still
holding the wheel, to observe the start. Alden and Silly were
well in the rear. That was too bad, thought Jane. She had
long ago decided that, all things considered, it was preferable
to listen to Alden talking all evening of how he had won a race
than of how he had lost one.

II

'If the wind hadn't dropped at the second buoy,' said Alden, 'we should have come in third.'

'You made a mistake,' said Mr. Carver, 'splitting tacks on the second leg.'

'We only missed that puff by four seconds,' said Silly.

'But you missed it,' said Mr. Carver.

'That was a matter of luck,' said Alden.

'Exactly,' said Mr. Carver. 'I'm talking of the science of seamanship.'

Jane, busy again with her knitting before the living-room fire, was not bothering to listen. It was just the same sort of talk she had heard at Gull Rocks every Wednesday and Saturday evening of July and August for the last twelve years. Sometimes she listened. Sometimes she even joined in the argument. But to-night she was watching Stephen over her amber knitting-needles in silence.

Stephen, settled in a chintz-covered armchair, with his daughter Cicily on a stool at his feet, was following the conversation of the assembled Carvers with interest. He was sailing the race over again with Alden and Silly. Jane knew he knew every rock in the harbour, every trick of the summer breeze that blew over the blue waters of the bay. In spite of the animation of his face, he seemed tired and very much in need of his holiday. Surrounded by the tanned yachtsmen he looked strangely white. The flesh under his eyes was just a little puffy and there was a new drawn line that Jane had never seen before around one corner of his mouth. Stephen had been very busy working over that bank merger. It had been a hot summer in the West.

Stephen didn't have much fun, thought Jane. With a sudden pang she realized that he looked his forty-four years. His curly, blond hair had receded over his temples and was

streaked with grey above the ears. The temples were rather
shiny and the hair was growing perilously thin — considering
Uncle Stephen and the forces of heredity — in a small circular
area at the top of his head. His grey sack suit was just a little
wrinkled after a hot afternoon in a New England train. Yes
— Stephen looked just like what he was — the forty-four-
year-old first vice-president of the Midland Loan and Trust
Company, badly in need of his summer vacation.

Men drew the short straw in the lottery of life, reflected
Jane, as she looked at him. Men like Stephen, at least. Miss
Thomas had claimed it was a man-made world. If so, men had
certainly made it with a curious disregard of their own comfort and convenience. How terrible to have to be the first vice-
president of a bank and work eight hours a day for forty years
at a mahogany desk in the executive offices of the Midland
Loan and Trust Company and never have more than a three
weeks' holiday! Why did men do it? When the world was so
wide and so full of a number of things and they didn't really
have to marry to — to enjoy themselves.

Wives didn't appreciate husbands. Ridiculous for her to
carry on so about just having to live in idleness with the
Carvers — who were, after all, quite harmless — at Gull
Rocks — which was, after all, very pretty — for two brief
months every summer, while Stephen ——

'It wasn't luck,' said Mr. Carver, 'that you had to con-
cede the right of way to the Uncateena. If you hadn't been on
the port tack, she would have had to give you room around
the mark.'

'We shouldn't have been on the port tack,' said Alden
stubbornly, 'if the wind hadn't shifted.'

'I think the winds are so uncertain this time of year,' put in
Mrs. Carver pacifically.

It was really pretty terrible to have to listen to them,

thought Jane. Day in and day out. Perhaps it was worse than being the first vice-president of a bank. Men never had to listen to what bored them. Or did they? A sudden recollection of Stephen's patient face across the candlelight at her father's dinner-table rose in Jane's mind. Stephen, listening to her mother and Isabel. Robin, listening to her mother and Isabel. Her father, listening to her mother and Isabel. The patient 'Oh, all *right*, Lizzie!' that had terminated, since her earliest memory, so many of the Wards' domestic discussions.

Perhaps people were all bored most of the time after they were thirty-six, thought Jane. Perhaps being bored was just a part of growing up and growing old. The excitement went out of things. Life no longer had a surprise up its sleeve. But still, after you were thirty-six, you went on living for another thirty-six years or so. Living and thinking about annoying trifles.

Why had Stephen, at twenty-two, wanted to be a banker? Why had Stephen, at twenty-nine, wanted, so desperately, to marry her? Why did he want, now, after fifteen years, to go on working at that mahogany desk, to protect the interests of the Midland Loan and Trust Company and support his wife and three children? Why did he want to waste the pathetic brevity of his three weeks' holiday at Gull Rocks every summer, when the world was full of beautiful, bewildering places that he would never see and life might be full of strange exotic experiences that he would never know? What kept men faithful, throughout a long lifetime, to the banks and the wives they had embraced in early manhood? The sense of duty? The force of habit? The hands of their children, perhaps.

Jane looked at her fourteen-year-old daughter. Her young tanned face alight with enthusiasm, Cicily was sailing the race over, too, but rather with her father in a phantom catboat than with her aunt and uncle in the prosaic vessel now riding at its moorings beyond the pier. Cicily adored Stephen. And Stephen adored Cicily. In his eyes she could do no wrong. She could not even sit up too late. Jane knew she should have been in bed an hour ago. The other children had gone upstairs at eight.

'Cicily,' she said, 'it's ten o'clock.'

'But to-night's Saturday,' said Stephen quickly. It was a family joke. Whatever night it was was always his excuse for letting Cicily sit up ten minutes longer.

'Yes, to-night's Saturday, Mumsy!' echoed the child. 'And it's Daddy's first evening.'

Jane smiled indulgently. It was very difficult not to smile indulgently at Cicily and Stephen.

'You heard your mother,' said Mr. Carver with severity.

The child rose reluctantly from her stool. She looked reproachfully at Jane, with Stephen's eyes and Stephen's smile. 'Why stir up Grandfather?' her glance said, plainer than words. She looked a trifle mutinous and very pretty, with her cheeks flushed in the firelight and her crisply curly fair hair a little loosened from the bow at her neck.

'Good-night,' said Stephen, as she kissed his bald spot.

'Good-night,' said Jane, as her lips met her daughter's smooth cheek. As she stooped for the caress, the child's fair hair streamed over her mother's shoulder.

'Mélisande!' laughed Stephen.

'I want to put it up,' said Cicily. 'I'm fourteen and a half.'

'Picnic to-morrow!' said Stephen, as his daughter turned toward the door. Her face lit up as she threw him a smile over her smocked shoulder. 'That child's growing up,' said Stephen, as she vanished into the hall.

III

Jane sat at her dressing-table, brushing the long straight strands of her brown hair, looking critically at her reflection in the glass as she did so. For more than a year, now, Jane had been endeavouring to think of herself as 'middle-aged.' On the momentous occasion of her thirty-fifth birthday she had said firmly to Stephen, 'Middle-age is from thirty-five to fifty.' But curiously enough, in spite of that stoical statement, Jane had continued, incorrigibly, to think of herself as 'young.' In this soft light, thought Jane dispassionately, in her new pink dressing-gown, she really did not look old. And she was prettier at thirty-six than she had been at twenty. No, not that, exactly. The freshness was gone. But prettier *for* thirty-six than she had been *for* twenty. At twenty every one was pretty, and most girls had been, after all, much prettier than she. But at thirty-six — Jane smiled engagingly at her reflection — she held her own with her contemporaries.

At thirty-six the trick was not so much to look pretty as to look young. Beauty helped, of course, but not as much as youth. And she was still slim and agile and not grey and — but what difference did it make, anyway? It didn't make any difference at all, thought Jane solemnly, unless, like Flora, you were still unmarried, or, like Muriel, though married, you went on collecting infatuated young men.

What use had Jane, in the Colonial cottage in the Chicago suburb, for youth or beauty or any other intriguing quality? Looking young didn't help you to preside over the third-grade mothers' meeting in the Lakewood Progressive School. Looking beautiful didn't help you to keep your cook through a suburban winter. There was Stephen, of course. But wasn't it Stephen's most endearing quality — or was it his most irritating? — that for ten years or more Stephen had never really thought about how she looked at all? To Stephen Jane looked like Jane. That was enough for him.

The attitude was endearing, of course, when you looked a fright. When you were having a baby, or trying to get thin after nursing one, or hadn't been able to afford a new evening gown, or suddenly realized that you looked a freak in the one you *had* afforded. In crises of that nature it was always very comforting to reflect that Stephen would never notice. But in other crises — when the baby was a year old and you weighed a hundred and thirty pounds again and you had bought a snappy little hat that — or even when you were sitting in front of your dressing-table in a soft light and a new pink dressing-gown, waiting for Stephen to stop gossiping with his mother and come up to join you — it *was* irritating to reflect that, no matter what you did, to Stephen you would always look exactly as you always had. That you would look like Jane.

Jane put down her hairbrush with a sigh of resignation and selected a new pink hair-ribbon from her dressing-table drawer. She tied it carefully in a bow above her pompadour and, picking up a hand glass, turned to admire the effect in the mirror. She wished her hair were curly. Suddenly the frivolity of that immemorial wish and the sight of the flat satin hair-ribbon and the long strands of straight hair made Jane think of André. Of André and of being fourteen. Of Flora's red-gold tresses and Muriel's seven dark finger curls. Of André's resolute young face and the shy, unspoken admiration in his eloquent young eyes. Funny that just the sight of a hair-ribbon should make her feel his presence so vividly. Should so recall that funny little warm, happy feeling, deep down inside, that was so integral a part of being fourteen and loving André and never feeling quite sure of how he felt about her in return.

Andrè. André was a bridegroom now. Four months a bridegroom. Jane wished she had written to him, as she al-

most had, that day last spring when she had found his picture
in the May copy of 'Town and Country' in Muriel's living-
room. But it had seemed absurd to break a silence of fifteen
years' duration just because she had seen a snapshot, from
the camera of the Associated Press, of André, with averted
head and raised silk hat, resplendent in bridal finery, hasten-
ing through the classic portico of the Madeleine with a vision
in floating tulle on his arm. A vision reported to be, in the
legend beneath the snapshot, Mademoiselle Cyprienne
Pyramel-Gramont, daughter of the Comte et Comtesse Jean
Pyramel-Gramont. 'Noted Sculptor Weds' had been the
caption.

André *was* a noted sculptor. One of France's most distinguished sons. Eight years ago, on the occasion of her memorable trip abroad with Stephen, Jane had come suddenly on
his 'Adam' in the corridors of the Tate Gallery. Stephen had
called her attention to it. He had noticed it because it was
double-starred in Baedeker. 'This can't be *your* Duroy,' he
had said.

Later his 'Eve' had met Jane's eye with an enigmatic smile
over her yet untasted apple, in the entrance of the Luxembourg. An Eve still innocent, but subtly provocative. Jane had
regarded her with wistful interest. What had André said in
the postscript of his long explanatory letter — Jane had never
forgotten — 'There is something of you in all my nymphs and
Eves and saints and Madonnas?' And what was Stephen saying at the moment? 'Golly, she smiles like you, Jane! He
never got over you!'

'Well, why should he?' she had retorted lightly. But her
mind was still busy with the postscript. 'Something you
brought into my life. Romance, I guess. Nothing more
tangible.'

She had brought romance into André's life, as they walked

up the Lake Shore Drive together, with their schoolbooks under their arms. He was achieving its fulfilment, now with this French Cyprienne, in exotic settings that Jane could not even imagine. André was thirty-eight. Yet André was a bridegroom, while she, Jane, was a settled suburban house-wife and the middle-aged mother of a fourteen-year-old daughter and an eleven-year-old daughter and a nine-year-old son. Jane felt devoutly grateful that the Atlantic rolled between them. That André would never see her again. That he would think of her, always, as she looked in a hair-ribbon, while Cyprienne had babies and grew old and came to look only like Cyprienne. But Cyprienne wouldn't grow so *very* old, thought Jane almost resentfully, while André lived to see her. Cyprienne, under the floating tulle, hadn't looked a day over eighteen. Four years older than Cicily, perhaps, and be-witchingly pretty. Sixteen-year-old André, a middle-aged Frenchman with a child bride!

Jane shivered as she thought of it. Men should marry when they were young. André should have married when he loved her. But if he had he would never have become one of France's most distinguished sons. Chicago would have stifled him. André might have been a banker by this time, thought Jane, if he had taken her on at nineteen. And he had had the sense to foresee it. His abrupt departure from her life had been much in the romantic tradition established by Romeo in the balcony window. His alternatives had been the same. 'I must be gone and live, or stay and die!'

But *she* had married young. And Stephen had been young when she married him. They had had together those ridicu-lous, unthinking, heart-breaking years of almost adolescent domesticity, with two babies in the sand pile and another in the perambulator and a contagious disease sign often on the front door and a didy always on the clothesline! They'd had all that. But had they really had romance? Romance, such as she'd known with André? Stephen had had it, perhaps, in the first years of their marriage. But — had she? Hadn't she always been rather afraid of romance, all those young years when it might have been hers for the taking? Did a woman ever really value romance until she felt it slipping away from her? Wasn't that the surest sign of all of being middle-aged? You might be still slim and agile and not grey, but when you felt that wistful, almost desperate impulse to live your life to the full before it was over, didn't it really mean that it *was* over, that youth, at any rate, was over, that it was too late to recapture the glamour that you saw only in retrospect ——

But this was ridiculous, thought Jane. Life wasn't over at thirty-six. She loved Stephen and Stephen loved her. He had never looked at another woman. Anything they wanted was theirs for the taking. Their personal relationship was only what they made it. She must say to Stephen, 'Look at me, Stephen! *Really* look at me! You haven't for ten years!' And he would laugh — of course he always laughed at her —— That was Stephen's step on the stair.

Jane looked quickly about the bedroom. Yes, it was very neat. Mrs. Carver was an excellent housekeeper and Jane herself was always tidy. Her underclothes were meticulously folded on a chair by the dressing-table and the linen sheets of the twin four-poster mahogany beds were turned smoothly down over the rose-coloured comforters. Stephen's clean blue pajamas were folded on his pillow.

As he opened the door, Jane rose from her mirror to meet him. He stood a moment on the threshold, smiling content-edly around the lamplit room. Dear old Stephen — even in the soft light he still looked white and jaded. Jane walked slowly over to him.

'Glad to be here?' she smiled up into his eyes.

'You bet!' said Stephen fervently.

'I'm glad you've come,' said Jane.

Stephen closed the door.

'How's it been?' said Stephen. 'Family been bothering you?'

'Oh, no,' said Jane.

Stephen slipped off his grey sack coat and hung it carefully over the back of a chair.

'It's a pretty good old place,' said Stephen. He walked over to the window in his shirt-sleeves and peered out into the darkness beyond the screen.

'Smell that sea-breeze,' said Stephen. He snuffed the briny air luxuriously for a moment in silence.

'Put out the lamp,' said Stephen. 'The moon's just rising over the bay.'

Smiling a little, Jane pushed the button and walked blindly over to him in the darkness. She slipped her arm though his. The brown film of screen had grown suddenly transparent. The lawn and beach and harbour were flooded with silver light. The waning moon swung low in the eastern sky. Jane gazed in silence as small objects on the lawn slowly took form and substance in the unearthly radiance. The outcrops of granite rock cast clear-cut shadows on the greyish grass. The weather beaten outline of a clump of stunted cedars at the foot of the pier stood out in black silhouette against the silver waters of the harbour. The slender mast of the catboat rocked uneasily at its moorings. A lighthouse winked, deliberately, far out in the bay. One white flash and two red. Jane could hear the little harbour waves, quite distinctly, as they rippled on the shingle. Then the faint moaning of the bell-buoy that marked the hidden reef beyond the point. Jane pressed her cheek gently against Stephen's arm.

'I'm *very* glad you've come,' she said.

Stephen turned his head abruptly. Her voice seemed to rouse him from revery.

'I guess it was time,' he said cheerfully. 'Mother seems a bit on edge.'

Jane dropped his arm. She moved away from him in the square of moonlight that fell through the casement.

'What about?' she asked.

'Oh — nothing much,' said Stephen still cheerfully. Then, after a moment, 'Don't you think, Jane, you could persuade Miss Parrot to use the back stairs?'

Jane moved in silence back to her dressing-table. She switched on the light abruptly and sat down on her chair.

'I've said all I could,' said Jane. 'You know how Miss Parrot is. She's an awfully good heart nurse. I don't want to rock the boat.'

Stephen untied his necktie and removed his collar in silence. He walked slowly across the room to place them on top of his chest of drawers. Jane watched him in her mirror. Suddenly she caught the gleam of irritation in her own eyes. She gazed steadily at her reflection until it faded into a twinkle of amusement.

'Stephen,' she said resolutely, wheeling round in her chair, 'don't talk about Miss Parrot.'

'All right,' said Stephen, 'I won't.' He was unbuttoning his waistcoat a trifle absent-mindedly. 'How's the weather been? Good sailing breeze, all month?' As he spoke he turned to smile at her. Jane regarded him steadily. Poor old Stephen — he looked very tired. As for herself, from the nature of his smile Jane knew what *she* looked like. There was absolutely nothing to be done about it. She looked like Jane.

IV

'I'd go, if I were you,' said Silly.

'It's only for a week, of course,' said Jane.

'The children will be all right with Miss Parrot,' said Silly.

'Oh, yes,' said Jane. 'It's just moving them back West.'

'Stephen can do that,' said Silly.

They were lying side by side in the shadow of a rock on the sands of Pine Island. Two weeks of Stephen's precious holiday had already passed. The litter of a picnic luncheon defiled the beach at their feet. A few yards away little Steve, in his scarlet bathing-suit, was digging a canal in the wet brown sand where the waves were breaking. Cicily and Jenny were tossing a baseball back and forth, a little farther down the beach. Stephen and Alden, leaning back against a boulder, were enjoying their after-luncheon cigarettes and discussing the hilarities of the twenty-fifth reunion of the Class of '88, which Alden had superintended at Cambridge the preceding June.

'And on Sunday,' said Alden, with a reminiscent chuckle, 'we had an excursion by steamer to Gloucester. Some excursion! More liquid in the bar than in the bay!'

'I'd go,' repeated Silly. 'I'd do whatever I wanted to, whenever I could.'

On Silly's lips the simple statement took on a wistful significance. Jane's absent eyes had been fixed on her unconscious children. She turned, now, to contemplate her sister-in-law. Silly's long angular frame was carelessly clothed in a weather-beaten brown tweed skirt and sun-streaked tan sweater. A dilapidated brown felt hat of Alden's was pulled well down over her forehead to protect her eyes from the glare. Her clean white sport shirt was buttoned mannishly about her neck, and a diamond horseshoe pin, which had been Mr. Carver's generous gesture on the occasion of her forty-fifth birthday, was negligently thrust through her orange tie. It twinkled, inappropriately, in the brilliant sunshine. She lay flat on her back on the beach, gazing up at the silver clouds that floated in the stainless August sky. A queer weather-beaten figure curiously akin to the rocks and the sands and the clumps of stunted pine trees that gave the island its name. A pathetic figure and, strangely enough, it seemed to Jane, a beautiful one at the moment. The rough outline of tweed and worsted could not conceal the Diana-like grace of Silly's lank body, nor mar the delicacy of her slender ankles nor the strength of her slim wrists nor the angular beauty of her long, lean hands. Jane peeped under the turned-down hat-brim. Silly might boast the body of a goddess, but her face was un-compromisingly that of a forty-six-year-old New England spinster. Plain, tanned, and austere, it was set in its familiar lines of controlled resignation.

When had Silly ever done what *she* wanted to, thought Jane? Never since Jane had known her. For the last fifteen years, as all the Carvers knew quite well, Silly had wanted to do only one thing. To break away from the family and the place at Gull Rocks and the house on Beacon Street and buy a little stone-strewn farm at Topsfield, Massachusetts, and keep cocker-spaniel kennels there with Susan Frothingham. Susan was now forty-eight. For the last fifteen years *she* had wanted to break away from the Frothinghams on Arlington Street and live with Silly on a Topsfield hilltop. Jane saw no charms in Susan. A fat, uninteresting New England old maid, if there ever was one. Still — if Silly liked her and she liked Silly — it was dreadful what life did to single women. What families did to single women. Well-to-do families, throwing destitute middle-aged daughters an occasional diamond horse-shoe, but denying them the right to independence. The right to life, liberty, and the pursuit of happiness.

'If you want to go to New York to see Agnes,' pursued Silly, still gazing at the silver cloud, 'I think you ought to go.'

'Your mother won't like to have Stephen take the children back West alone,' said Jane.

'I'm tired of seeing the men in this family considered!' said Silly with sudden violence. 'I'd like to see one of the women get her innings for a change.'

'Oh, I never consider Stephen much,' said Jane honestly. 'And I get plenty of innings.'

'Well, this is an outing,' smiled Silly. 'How long since you've seen Agnes?'

'Oh, mercy!' said Jane. 'Ever so long! Seven years. Not since she married. The last time I saw her was when she came West for her father's funeral.'

'I think you ought to go,' repeated Silly. 'Mother won't care as long as you're going to meet Flora.'

That was probably true, thought Jane. The bond between Mrs. Carver and her brother was a very close one. Flora and Mr. Furness were on the water now, returning from a summer in England. Whatever Mrs. Carver might think of the folly of a headstrong daughter-in-law who deserted her husband and children to spend a week in New York for the purpose of seeing an old Bryn Mawr classmate, she would consider it a very suitable attention for Stephen's wife to meet his uncle and cousin on the dock at Hoboken, bearing appropriate greetings from the Boston connection.

Not that Jane cared particularly about meeting Flora. She had seen her in Chicago at Easter and would see her again there in two weeks at the very latest. But the Furnesses' arrival *did* make a plausible pretext for a trip to New York, and Jane *did* care, terribly, about being with Agnes again for a few days and seeing her five-year-old daughter and meeting the gentleman whom Jane had always privately characterized as 'that dreadful husband.'

In Jane's opinion, Agnes had ruined her life by marrying Jimmy Trent. She never understood how it could have happened. Level-headed Agnes, at the great age of thirty-one, with a reputation really established as a writer of short stories, with one good novel published and a better one half-finished, had succumbed to the incomprehensible charm of a ne'er-do-well journalist, hanging about the outskirts of the newspaper world of New York, three years younger than Agnes and perfectly incapable of holding down a lucrative job for more than two months at a time. When Jane considered Agnes as she had been in college, the marriage was really incredible. Agnes, on a Bryn Mawr window-seat, the level head triumphantly crowned with a wreath of potted ivy, saying seriously, 'I'm not at all romantic. I just want to accomplish.'

One moment of romance had ruined for Agnes ten years of accomplishment. The baby had come at once, of course, and the second novel had never been finished. After a year or two of living in boarding-houses and trying to subsist on Jimmy's non-existent income, Agnes had abandoned her writing and had taken a job in the advertising department of Macy's. It was a good job, she had written Jane very cheerfully, at the time. She liked advertising. On the whole, she liked it better than writing. They had taken a nice little flat in Greenwich Village and little Agnes was established in a play school at the age of three and Jimmy did a little writing, now and then, mainly musical criticism, and worked with his fiddle, which amused him awfully, and took her to hear a lot of good music, of which he was very fond.

Jane's lip curled as she remembered that letter. She had had another last week. It was this second letter that had determined her to go to New York.

'I wish I could see you,' Agnes had written. 'Jimmy may go West for a few months. He's had a temporary position offered him on the Chicago "Daily News." I hope he takes it. I'd like him to see Chicago. Of course I have to stick at Macy's.'

Jane read between the lines just what Agnes really wanted. She wanted Jane to meet Jimmy and like Jimmy and make things pleasant for him in Chicago, so that he would hold down this new job and make life a little easier for them all, financially speaking, when he returned to the Greenwich Village flat. Jane didn't relish the task. She knew perfectly well what she would think of Jimmy and what Stephen would think of Jimmy and what her mother and Isabel and even her father would think of Jimmy, when he showed up in the West. But Agnes was Agnes. And Agnes's husband was Agnes's husband. Jane would do what she could for him. But she would like to go to New York and look over the field.

'Stephen!' called Silly suddenly. 'Don't *you* think Jane ought to go to New York?'

'Sure I do,' said Stephen amicably. 'I'm going to make her go. Of course, I've never seen the fatal charm in Agnes ——'

'But you're a perfect husband!' cried Jane, sitting up in the sunshine. 'It's time we set sail for home. Come on, girls!'

Cicily and Jenny turned at her call. Jenny threw the baseball, with unerring aim, straight into the group around the picnic basket. It landed with a plop, right in the centre of her father's waistcoat. Cicily and Jenny and little Steve all burst into laughter as he collapsed in mock agony under the force of the blow. Jenny came running up in hilarious apology. An Alice in Wonderland child, with straight fair hair strained back from a round comb on her forehead, and a plain practical little face that was her Aunt Silly's all over again. She had none of Cicily's blonde beauty.

'Come help us pack up,' said Jane. 'We must leave a clean

beach.' She was picking up eggshells as she spoke. Silly's
support had strengthened her determination. She would go
to New York. Suddenly she realized that she was humming
aloud. The refrain of an old Bryn Mawr song, 'Once there
dwelt captiously a stern papa!' Good gracious! She hadn't
thought of it for nearly twenty years! It would be fun to see
Agnes again.

CHAPTER II

I

NEVERTHELESS, seven days later, as Jane stood on the platform of the Bay State Limited in the Boston South Station, waving good-bye to Stephen and the children and Miss Parrot, she felt her eyes fill suddenly with tears. She was always absurd over partings. That very morning, on the front porch at Gull Rocks, when she was saying good-bye to Mr. and Mrs. Carver and Uncle Stephen and Aunt Marie, she had felt a sudden surge of emotion. They were all over sixty. She wouldn't see them for another ten months. They had been awfully good to her. The congenital peculiarities of Carvers already seemed harmless. Jane had embraced her relatives-in-law with ardour.

And now, at the sight of the little smiling, waving group on the dingy platform, Jane had an almost irresistible impulse to jump off the New York train and return to the West with her family at half-after two that afternoon.

'Mumsy!' shouted Cicily, hanging on Stephen's arm. 'Can I order the meals 'til you get home?'

'Don't you let her!' cried Jenny, tripping over the cocker-spaniel puppy's leash in her excitement. 'She'd forget and we'd starve!'

'Now, don't worry about anything, Mrs. Carver,' called Miss Parrot, almost losing her balance as little Steve tugged at her hand. He was on his knees on the platform, peering under the train.

'I want to see the air brakes!' he cried.

'Have a whirl with Agnes,' smiled Stephen. 'Don't let that husband cramp your style!'

'I won't,' said Jane. 'But I know I'll hate him.'

The train jerked into motion. Jane pushed by the porter to the step of the car.

'Kiss me again, Stephen!' she cried. Stephen jumped to the step beside her. She raised her lips to his. Suddenly he realized that she was crying.

'Good-bye, goose!' he said tenderly. As the train gathered speed, he swung back on the platform.

'Don't worry!' called Miss Parrot again, dragging little Steve to his feet. The children were all waving wildly. Stephen threw a last kiss.

The porter led Jane firmly back into the vestibule and closed the train doors. She couldn't see the family any longer. She hoped Miss Parrot would hold little Steve's hand until they were out of the trainshed. It would be just like him to run out on the tracks. But she would, of course. She was very responsible.

Jane made her way slowly back through the narrow Pullman corridor to her seat in the parlour car. She was really off. She had not been in New York since she came home from Europe, eight years before. It *would* be fun to see Agnes again. The children would be perfectly safe with Miss Parrot. And she would be home in a week.

II

The heat of the September day still pervaded the city streets as Jane descended from the top of the Fifth Avenue bus and turned, a trifle uncertainly, under the arch, to walk south and west across Washington Square. Jane had had very little experience in looking after herself and she always felt a trifle uncertain when wandering alone in strange places. Earlier that very afternoon, in emerging from the Bay State Limited, she had found the congested turmoil of the Grand Central

Station a little overwhelming. It had seemed quite an adventure to choose a black porter and follow him as he threaded his way through the crowded concourse and out past the swinging doors through the traffic of Forty-Second Street to the lobby of the Belmont Hotel.

Jane had felt just a little queer, as she stood alone at the desk, her luggage at her feet, signing the register and asking for a single room and bath for the night. It was perfectly ridiculous — she was thirty-six years old — but Jane really couldn't remember ever having spent a night alone at a hotel before. She was very glad that Flora and Mr. Furness would join her at noon next day and greatly relieved to discover that a letter from Agnes was waiting for her, confirming her invitation to dinner and containing explicit directions as to how to reach the Greenwich Village flat.

'Come at six,' Agnes had written. 'I get out of Macy's at five-thirty and I'll be there before you.'

She was perhaps a trifle early, reflected Jane, as she paused in the path to reassure herself as to just which direction *was* west. She had allowed too much time for the bus ride through the afternoon traffic. She had been glad to get out of her hotel bedroom. Once her bag was unpacked, there was nothing to do there but stare through the dingy lace curtain, which had seemed at once curiously starched and soiled, at the taxis and street-cars that congested Forty-Second Street and the crowds of suburbanites who were pouring into the entrance of the Grand Central Station. She had watched the station clock for fifteen minutes and when the hands pointed to five she had left the room.

Washington Square, thought Jane, gazing curiously about her, wasn't all it was cracked up to be. It didn't look like the cradle from which a city's aristocracy had sprung. There was a nice old row of red-brick houses at the north end, but many of them seemed rather gone to seed and dilapidated, and the grass in the Square was worn down to hard-caked mud and the elm trees were leafless, and the shirt-sleeved men and shawled women on the benches and the dirty little dark-eyed children who were playing marbles and hopscotch on the path were the kind that you would only see 'west of Clark Street' at home.

Jane left the Square at the southwest corner and, referring once more to the written directions that Agnes had given her, plunged into the congestion of the city streets. This was a funny place to choose to live in, thought Jane, as she pushed through a group of pale-faced little girls, skipping rope on the sidewalk. It was a funny place to choose in which to bring up a child. A group of shabby young men, hanging about the entrance of a corner saloon, commented favourably on her appearance as she approached them. Jane held her chin high and passed on in disdain. The green baize door swung open to admit an elderly hobo and Jane caught a whiff, across the stale heat of the pavement, of the acrid damp odour of beer. She thought the disreputable bar looked rather cool and dark and inviting from the glare of the city street. She could quite understand why the group of shabby young men liked to linger there.

At the next corner she stood amazed and delighted at the sight that met her eye. A curving vista of narrow street, flanked by tall red-brick houses trellised with iron fire escapes. The fire escapes were festooned with varicoloured washing and all the windows were wide open and the window-sills were hung with bedding. From nearly every window a dark-haired woman and a couple of children were hanging out, leaning on the bedding and gazing down at the street beneath them. The street itself was crowded with push carts and fruit stands. Great piles of golden oranges and yellow bananas were displayed for sale. Clothing hung fluttering from improvised frame scaffolds. A fish vendor was crying his wares at her elbow. The front steps of all the houses were crowded with people laughing and talking together and shouting to the purchasers that clustered about the open-air booths. The dingy store on the corner had a sign in its dirty window, 'Ice — kindling — coal and charcoal.' A little olive-faced girl came out of it balancing an old peach basket on her head. It contained a melting lump of ice. She skipped gaily down the street and vanished into a basement entrance. The store on the opposite corner had a foreign sign in the doorway. 'Ravioli. Qui si vende Pasta Caruso. Specialità in Pasta Fresca.' Jane was suddenly enchanted with Greenwich Village. Still — it *was* a funny place to choose in which to bring up a child.

Presently she came to Agnes's corner. Charlton Street was quite broad and paved with cobblestones. A car-track ran down the centre of the street. The houses on both sides were built of red brick, with white frame doorways. Nice white-panelled front doors with fanlights above them and brass knobs and knockers, some brightly polished. The windows were all square-paned and many of the houses had green window-boxes. The plants in them were drab and shrivelled, however, in the city heat. Jane did not see a single flower.

Agnes's house was in the centre of the block. It looked just like all the others. There was a sign in the downstairs front window, 'Furnished Room. Gents Preferred.' Jane mounted the front steps and regarded the empty hole, where a doorbell had once hung, for a moment in perplexity. Then she pushed open the front door. She found herself in a small white-panelled vestibule, carpeted with yellow linoleum. Three mail-boxes met her eye and on the middle one a card, 'Mr. and Mrs. James Trent.' She pushed the electric bell beneath

the mail-box and, after a minute or two in which absolutely
nothing happened, she opened the inner door. The odour of
cooking cabbage instantly assailed her nostrils. The entrance
to the first apartment was on her left hand. A white-panelled
door, soiled with countless finger-prints. A straight, steep
staircase, with uncarpeted wooden treads, led to the upper
floors. Jane slowly ascended the stairs into comparative darkness. The odour of cooking cabbage grew fainter. At the
front end of the upper corridor was a second white-panelled
door. Jane knocked at it tentatively. She heard, immediately,
the sound of masculine footsteps and the airy notes of a
masculine whistle, a fragment of 'La Donna e mobile' from
'Rigoletto.' The door was suddenly opened by a young man.
He stood smiling at her on the threshold. A rather charming
young man, with tousled dark hair and an open collar, who
looked, Jane thought from the dusk of the corridor, with his
quizzical eyebrows and his pointed ears and his ironical
smile, exactly like a faun.

'Come in,' he said pleasantly.

'I — I'm looking for Mrs. James Trent,' said Jane.

'Come in,' the young man repeated. Jane stepped, a little
hesitantly, over the threshold. 'You must be Jane.' His smile
deepened into a grin of appreciation. 'You don't look at all
as I thought you would. Come in and sit down. Agnes will
be home any minute.' Then, as she continued to stare at him
in perplexity, 'I'm Jimmy.'

Jane's eyes widened with astonishment. This boy, Jimmy
— Agnes's husband? He did not look a day over twenty-five.
Jane knew he was thirty-four, however.

'Oh — how do you do?' she said. 'Yes — I'm Jane.'

Agnes's living-room was pleasantly old-fashioned. The
ceiling was high and was decorated with a rococo design in
plaster that looked, Jane thought, like the top of a wedding

cake. A charming Victorian mantel of white marble dominated one end of the room. It was adorned with a bas-relief
of cupids holding horns of plenty in their chubby arms. The
cupids were dusty and the hearth was discoloured and the
fireplace was filled with sheets of musical manuscript, torn in
twain. Two tall chintz-hung windows looked over Charlton
Street and a battered davenport sofa was placed beneath
them. The sofa was strewn with other sheets of music, and a
violin lay on a pile of disordered cushions in one corner. The
top of the mantelpiece was piled with books, and a high white
bookcase, filled with heterogeneous volumes, occupied one
end of the room. A small gate-legged table, covered with a
clean linen cloth, stood near the hearth, with an armchair on
one side of it and a child's Shaker rocker on the other.
Through the half-open folding-doors across from the fireplace
Jane caught a glimpse of a little room that was evidently a
nursery. The floor was strewn with toys and a white iron
crib stood near the window.

'Sit down,' said Jimmy, throwing an armful of music from
the sofa to the floor. 'Hot as hell, isn't it?'

'I'm afraid I'm very early,' said Jane, sitting down in the
armchair.

'No. Agnes is late,' said Jimmy. He was standing before
the Victorian mantel, still regarding her with an appreciative
grin. 'You look as cool as a cucumber in that blue silk.
Maybe I ought to put on my coat.'

'Oh, no,' said Jane politely. She hadn't noticed his shirt-
sleeves until that moment.

'Well, anyway, a necktie,' persisted Jimmy engagingly,
fingering his open collar.

'You look very nice and Byronic as you are,' smiled Jane.

'I know I do,' said Jimmy rather surprisingly. 'I get away
with a lot of that Byron stuff. But just the same I think I owe

that French frock a cravat.' He walked across the room as he spoke and, opening a door, disappeared into the inner recesses of the apartment.

Jane, left to herself, began to inspect the room once more without rising from her chair. Her eyes wandered to the high bookcase. She recognized some old Bryn Mawr books that had adorned, for two years, the walls of her Pembroke study. The two small blue volumes of Palgrave's 'Golden Treasury.' The green Globe editions of Wordsworth and Shakespeare. The Buxton Forman Keats and Shelley. The Mermaid Series of Elizabethan dramatists. And the long dark red line of Matthew Arnold and Pater.

The sound of running water from the interior of the apartment distracted her attention. Jimmy was a great surprise. She had never thought that he would be like that. She glanced at the sheets of music on the sofa. The one on top of the pile was half-filled with pencilled notations. He must have been writing music. Evidently he was a composer on the side. Agnes had never mentioned that.

The door to the inner rooms opened suddenly and Jimmy reappeared, freshly washed and brushed, his collar rebuttoned, and a soft blue necktie bringing out the colour in his smiling eyes. He picked up his coat from the back of the sofa and put it on with a sigh.

'What men do for women!' he murmured as he adjusted his collar.

'What women do for men!' laughed Jane. 'This dress *is* French, but it's fearfully hot.'

'I bet you didn't put it on for me!' grinned Jimmy. Jane's blush acknowledged the home thrust. 'You just wanted to show Agnes how well you'd withstood the assaults of time.'

Jane *had* thought Agnes might think the dress was pretty. Not that Agnes ever noticed clothes, of course.

'You must have been an infant prodigy,' went on Jimmy. He was sitting on the sofa now, his elbows on his knees, his eyes fixed flatteringly on her face.

'Why?' asked Jane unguardedly.

'To have been Agnes's classmate,' said Jimmy promptly.

Jane frowned. She didn't like that. She didn't like it at all. That was no way for Agnes's husband to speak of Agnes.

'I wish she'd come home,' she said with severity.

'Do you?' smiled Jimmy. 'Well, she will soon. She stops at the Play School every evening to bring home the child. It began again last week, thank God! Another day of vacation and I should have committed infanticide.'

Jane did not reply to this sally. She continued to look, very seriously, at Jimmy. But he rattled on, ignoring her silence.

'A Play School is a wonderful invention. It takes children off their parents' hands for nine hours a day. I call it immoral — but very convenient. So much immorality *is* merely convenience, isn't it? We resort to it, *faute de mieux*. Saloons and play schools and brothels — they're all cheap compromises, forced on us by civilization. In an ideal Utopia I suppose we'd all drink and love and bring up our children at home. Do it and like it — though that seems rather a contradiction in terms. Progressive education is really only one of many symptoms of decadence. It's a sign of the fall of the empire.' He paused abruptly and looked charmingly over at Jane, as if waiting for her applause. Jane felt an inexplicable impulse not to applaud him.

'That's all **very** clever,' she said quickly. 'But of course it isn't true.'

Jimmy burst into amiable laughter.

'So you are a pricker of bubbles, are you, Jane?' he asked amusedly. 'You certainly don't look it. Are you a defender

of the truth and no lover of dialectic for dialectic's sake? Do
beautiful rainbow-coloured bubbles, all made up of watery
ideas and soapy vocabulary, floating airily, without foundation, in the void, mean nothing in your life?'

'Very little,' said Jane severely. 'I'm a very practical
person.'

'I seem to be a creature of one idea this afternoon,' said
Jimmy lightly, 'but I can only repeat — you don't look it!
The picture you present, as you sit in that armchair, Jane, is
far from practical ——'

As he spoke, Jane heard with relief the sound of a latch-
key in the outer door.

'That's Agnes!' she cried, springing to her feet.

'It must be,' said Jimmy, rising reluctantly to his.

The door opened quickly, and Agnes, hand in hand with
her five-year-old daughter, stood beaming on the threshold.
Just the same old Agnes, with her funny freckled face and her
clever cheerful smile! No — somehow a slightly plumper,
rather more solid Agnes, with a certain maturity of gesture
and authority of eye! Jane clasped her in her arms. It was
not until the embrace was over that she noticed how grey
Agnes's hair had grown. It showed quite plainly under her
broad hat-brim. Jane sank on her knees before the child.
She looked a little pale and peaked, Jane thought, but she
was Agnes all over again — the little Agnes that Jane had
known in the first grades of Miss Milgrim's School! How
preposterous — how ridiculous — to see that little Agnes
once more in the flesh! How absurdly touching! Jane clasped
the child gently in her arms.

'Agnes!' she cried. 'She's precious! She's just like you!'

'Unfortunately,' remarked Agnes with mock cynicism.
'When she might have favoured her fascinating father! Whatever you may say against Jimmy, Jane, you have to admit he

has looks. In six years of matrimony they've never palled on me.'

'Don't talk like that, Agnes,' remonstrated Jimmy promptly. 'You make me feel superficial. I've much more than looks. I've all the social graces. I've been exhibiting them for Jane's benefit for the last twenty minutes and I leave it to her if my face is my fortune! I've many more important assets.'

'How about it, Jane?' said Agnes, smiling. 'Did he make the grade?' Behind the smile Jane detected a gleam of real concern in Agnes's glance. She suddenly recalled that winter afternoon, sixteen years ago, when she had first displayed Stephen to Agnes in Mr. Ward's library on Pine Street. Handsome young Stephen, flushed from the winter cold! She remembered her own dismay at the unspoken verdict of 'cotillion partner' in Agnes's honest eyes.

'Y-yes,' she said slowly, with a twinkle, rising to her feet, still holding the child's hand in hers. 'I think he did — for a first impression.'

'If anything,' said Jimmy engagingly, 'I improve on acquaintance. I'm an acquired taste, like ripe olives. I feel that's been said before. Let's say I'm a bad habit, like nicotine or alcohol. Once you take me up, you'll find it hard to get on without me.'

'Don't be ridiculous!' said Agnes. She threw a glance at Jane to see how she was taking his banter.

'I was just warning her,' said Jimmy.

'Jane never needs much warning,' said Agnes.

'Now, that's just the sort of thing she's always said of you,' sighed Jimmy plaintively. 'It gave me such a false impression. I've never been attracted by the type of woman who doesn't need to be warned against a handsome man ——'

'Agnes,' interrupted Jane, 'is he always like this?'

'Always,' said Agnes, with great good cheer. She looked

distinctly relieved by Jane's frivolous question. She knew now that Jane was taking Jimmy in the right spirit. 'Sometimes he's worse.' She placed her hand affectionately on Jimmy's shoulder. 'How did the music go to-day, old top?'

'Oh — rotten!' said Jimmy lightly. 'My rondo's a flop.'

'He's writing a concerto for the violin,' explained Agnes, with a glance at the music on the sofa.

'Really?' cried Jane, honestly impressed. Then, turning to Jimmy, 'Aren't you excited about it?'

He met her shining eyes with an ironical smile.

'Well,' he said calmly, 'I've lost my first fine careless rapture. I've been writing it for ten years.'

'Some of it's very good,' said Agnes.

'And some of it isn't,' pursued Jimmy cheerfully.

'I want him to finish it,' said Agnes.

'And I'm eager to please,' said Jimmy. 'So I sit here, day after day, pouring my full heart in profuse strains of unpremeditated art, while Agnes supports me in the style to which I was never accustomed before she laid me on the lap of luxury. I don't get much done, however.'

His voice sounded a little discouraged, Jane thought, in spite of his levity. Agnes changed the subject abruptly.

'We're dining out at a restaurant,' she said. 'I won't cook dinner in hot weather.'

'She's a swell cook, you know,' said Jimmy to Jane.

'I've known it for twenty years,' said Jane to Jimmy.

'Come with me while I clean the child,' said Agnes. She opened the door through which Jimmy had vanished in quest of his necktie. It led into a narrow dark corridor. Agnes pushed open another door and Jane found herself in a bedroom. A very dark bedroom, with one corner window opening on a dingy airshaft.

'No electricity,' said Agnes. 'It's a curse.' She struck a

match and lit a flaring gas-jet beside a maple bureau. The bureau and two iron beds completely filled the room. One bed was neatly made and covered with a cotton counterpane. The other was in complete disorder.

'Jimmy never gets up until after I've gone in the morning,' said Agnes apologetically, 'so he never gets his bed made until I come home at night.' As she spoke she picked up a pair of pajamas from the floor and hung them on a peg behind the door. A couple of discarded neckties were strewn on top of the bureau. Agnes added them to a long row of other neckties that hung from the brass gas-bracket. Then she tossed off her hat, without even a glance at the mirror, and opening a bureau drawer, took out a clean blue romper for the child. Jane suddenly realized that Agnes looked tired. Her hair was really very grey.

'I'll make the bed,' said Jane.

'Oh — do you want to?' asked Agnes. Jane nodded. 'Well, it would save time.' She vanished into the bathroom with her daughter.

Jane walked very soberly over to the bed and pulled off the sheets and turned the mattress. She heard once more the sound of running water. This bedroom was not fit to live in, thought Jane. A black hole of Calcutta. How could Agnes put up with it? How could Agnes put up with a husband who didn't get out of bed in the morning until after she had gone down to her office to earn his living? Jane tucked the bottom sheet firmly under the mattress. She'd like to take Jimmy by the ear, she thought, and make him make his own bed, while Agnes sat in a rocking-chair and watched him do it. Jane was thoroughly shocked by Agnes's revelation. Lots of wives, of course, lay serenely in bed every morning until long after the bread-winner had departed for his day's work. But that seemed different, somehow. Why did it? If Jimmy had

nothing in life to get up for, there was, of course, no real reason
for his getting up. Still ——— Jane smoothed the blankets and
turned to pick up the counterpane from the window-sill.
Wasn't Jimmy acting just the way she had always wished
that Stephen sometimes would? Stephen thought the world
would come to an end if he did not catch the eight o'clock
train every morning at the Lakewood Station. Jane had been
mocking that delusion of Stephen's for the last fifteen years.

Agnes reëntered the room with a clean blue-rompered
daughter at her side. Jane smoothed the counterpane over
the pillow. Agnes walked over to the bureau and, still without glancing in the mirror, ran a comb casually through her
low pompadour. Agnes did her hair just the way she always
had since the day that she first put it up — a big figure eight
twisted halfway up her head in the back. She had always run
a comb through it just like that, without a thought for a
looking-glass.

'Come on,' said Agnes.

Jimmy rose from the sofa as they entered the living-room.

'Where are we going?' he asked. 'Tony's?'

'I thought so,' said Agnes. Then, turning to Jane, 'Or do
you hate Italian food?'

The night was so hot that Jane thought that she would
hate food of any nationality.

'I love it,' she said falsely.

They all walked down the corridor and the uncarpeted
stairs into the odour of cooking cabbage and out into the comparative freshness of the sultry street.

'Tony's is just around the corner,' said Agnes. She slipped
one arm through Jane's and the other through Jimmy's.
Little Agnes skipped on ahead of them. She seemed to know
the way to Tony's quite as well as her parents did. Jane
threw a glance past Agnes's clever, contented face to Jimmy's

faun-like countenance. It was clever, too, but it wasn't very contented, Jane thought. In the grey September twilight Jimmy looked older than he had in the softer light of the chintz-hung living-room. Suddenly he met her eyes and smiled.

'This is swell!' he said cheerfully. 'But an embarrassment of riches! Taking two beautiful women out to dinner at Tony's the same night!' And suddenly he began softly, ridiculously, to sing.

'How happy could I be with either,
Were t'other dear charmer away!'

A wrinkled old woman, pulling a little wagon full of kindling, turned to smile toothlessly up at him at the sound of his artless tenor. He grinned at her pleasantly and resumed his song. Jimmy might be irritating, thought Jane, and of course he was a worthless husband, but he *had* charm.

III

The waiter's hand, which touched Jane's accidentally as he placed her *demi-tasse* before her, felt damp and warmly clammy. His collar was wilted and great drops of perspiration beaded his swarthy brow. Throughout the meal Jane had seen him surreptitiously mopping it with the wrinkled napkin that hung over his arm. 'Tony's' was hot and very crowded. Vaguely conscious of having eaten too much garlic in the salad and too much cheese in the spaghetti and of having drunk rather more Chianti than was perhaps quite wise on such a warm evening, Jane was half-listening to Jimmy, who was conversing most intelligently on modern American music, and half-reflecting that little Agnes, who had eaten quite as much garlic and cheese as she had herself, should have been in bed hours ago and would certainly be sick when once she was. The child was half-asleep in her chair.

Agnes was arguing with Jimmy, also most intelligently, on modern American music and every one else within hearing at the little candlelit tables seemed to be arguing also. Across the room four dark-eyed, oily-headed, hairy-wristed young men were certainly arguing very vociferously in Italian on some unknown subject, and, just beyond them, a middle-aged woman with short grey hair and a green smock was arguing in tense undertones with her adolescent escort as to whether or no he should order another apricot brandy, and at the round table in the middle of the room an uproarious group of young men and women were shouting their arguments on the relative merits of Matisse and Picasso, two painters, apparently, of whom, until that moment, Jane had never even heard.

In spite of the heat and the garlic and the cheese and the arguments, and, possibly, Jane thought, partly because of the Chianti, she had enjoyed the evening very much indeed. It was fun to be with Agnes again and fun, after two months at Gull Rocks, to be chattering carelessly with contemporaries whose intellectual slant on life was the same as her own. Moreover, Jane, in the course of the evening, had become comfortingly reassured about Jimmy. Why, she almost understood, already, why Agnes had married him. He was certainly amusing and seemed also to be intelligent, and he was very much sweeter with Agnes and his little daughter than Jane had expected him to be after his cavalier references to them in his initial advances toward her. He did not seem at all like Agnes's husband, of course. He did not seem like any one's husband. More like some young relative — a brother or a cousin or even a nephew — whose attitude toward his family was marked by humorous detachment, affectionate and appreciative, but distinctly irresponsible.

His attitude toward Jane had been marked by a mocking,

but flattering, attention and a rapidly increasing sense of intimacy. There was something in his manner, not at all unpleasant, that seemed subtly to suggest that he was always remembering that Jane was a woman and never allowing her to forget that he was a man. Jane could not think of any other American husband who was just like him. Bert Lancaster, of course, was always woman-conscious, but in a slimy, satyrish sort of way that bore no resemblance to Jimmy's cool recognition of a world in which you felt he thanked God that there were two sexes. There was a friendly matter-of-factness about Jimmy's frank admiration that made Jane feel very sure that they would get on well together. She was glad that he was coming to Chicago.

He *was* coming, almost immediately, to take up a friend's job as musical critic on the 'Daily News,' while that friend spent the winter in Munich. He was bringing his fiddle and the unfinished concerto and he expected to get a great deal of work done in some boarding-house bedroom, with no woman around to distract him. Agnes hoped that he would. She hoped to do some writing herself, in the evenings after little Agnes was in bed. Not the novel, of course — she would never finish that now; but she had plots for a couple of short stories that she thought she could sell and — Jane would laugh at her, she knew — an idea for a play about newspaper life that had never been done before.

Jane did not laugh at her. She had no high hopes for Jimmy's concerto, but she longed to see Agnes take up writing again. She thought that Jimmy would like Chicago. She would introduce him to all Agnes's old friends and Stephen would put him up at the clubs ——

'He hadn't better do that,' Jimmy had interrupted lightly. 'At the only club I ever belonged to I was kicked out for non-payment of dues. I shouldn't advise a conservative banker to back me at another ——'

Jane had laughed at his nonsense, wondering, however, just how much Stephen would have laughed had he been present that evening. Jimmy did not seem just Stephen's kind. Something told her that Jimmy would not take the importance of bank mergers very seriously, and that to Stephen a man without visible means of support, who had spent ten years of his life writing a concerto for the violin, would seem rather one of the broader jokes — unless he seemed just an object of charity, in which case Stephen would be very kind and considerate and helpful, of course, but possibly not entirely understanding.

'Agnes,' said Jane suddenly, in the midst of the argument on modern American music, 'you ought to put that child to bed.'

'I know I ought,' said Agnes, rising regretfully from her chair, 'but it's such fun to be with you again, Jane, and Jimmy's always so pyrotechnic in the presence of a third person! When I get arguing with him, I never want to stop!'

'Not only,' said Jimmy mockingly, 'in the presence of a third person. Night after night, Jane, while Agnes is arguing with me, the child falls asleep on the hearth rug.' He, too, was rising regretfully to his feet. He picked up his drowsy daughter.

'Can I get a taxi down here?' asked Jane.

'Jimmy'll cruise out and find one,' said Agnes.

He left the restaurant with the child on his shoulder. Agnes sank back into her chair. Suddenly she leaned forward across the candlelight.

'If I *could* write a play, Jane,' she said earnestly, 'a good bad play, such as managers have confidence in, it might run for a season. If it did, I'd make fifty thousand dollars.'

'Oh, Agnes!' said Jane reproachfully. 'Don't talk like that! You never used to. Why do you want to write a bad play —

just for a manager? Write a good one if it never gets on. I bet you could. You have lots of ideas — you always had ——'

'Exactly,' said Agnes, briefly. 'I've always had more ideas than cash.' Her face clouded a little under Jane's incredulous stare, then lightened suddenly with conviction. 'If you think there's an idea in my head that I wouldn't sacrifice for a dollar, you're very much mistaken. Jane — you *have* to have money to be happy. If I could make fifty thousand dollars, I'd put every cent of it in trust for little Agnes. It would clothe her and educate her and take care of her as long as she lived. I'd never have to worry about the future again. I wouldn't feel anxious and driven any longer and I'd stop nagging Jimmy the way I *have* nagged him ever since Agnes was born, and if I stopped nagging him, we'd have time to talk together the way we used to — to *be* together the way we used to —— Jimmy's adorable when he isn't nagged — I adore him when I'm nagging him. But I just can't help it. I'm growing cross and nervous and old before my time and ——'

'Taxi waiting!' said Jimmy, at Jane's elbow. He looked a little curiously, Jane thought, at Agnes's excited face. But he asked no questions.

Agnes rose from the table without speaking. Her hands were trembling a little as she picked up her daughter's hat from the back of her chair. Jane followed her out onto the sidewalk in silence. She was almost trembling herself from the contagion of Agnes's excitement. Or was it from the disconcerting glimpse she had had of Agnes's private life through the rent that Agnes had torn in the curtain that hides the private lives of all married couples from the eyes of the world. She was acutely conscious of the intimacy of the moment that had just passed between them. And terribly sorry for Agnes. And for Jimmy. And terribly thankful, in the dark of the uptown bound taxi, for a husband like Stephen, who was a banker and caught the eight o'clock train every morning and didn't write concertos and lie in bed and goad her into nagging him until ——

Jane was so preoccupied with thoughts of husbands and marriage, and what life did to girls who were once young and full of promise and sat on Bryn Mawr window-seats confidently assuming that the world was their oyster, that she almost forgot to feel queer as she passed through the lobby of the Belmont Hotel alone at midnight. But not quite.

IV

'I thought you'd be more enthusiastic,' said Flora.

'I *am* enthusiastic,' protested Jane. 'It's just that I'm not used to the idea yet ——'

They were sitting on the edge of Flora's bed at the Belmont. The room was crowded with gaping trunks and strewn with the silk and satin confusion of Flora's new winter wardrobe, fresh from the fingers of the Paris dressmakers. Flora, very *chic* and fair in a new sheath dress of black chiffon, was fastening on her slender wrist the first diamond wrist watch that Jane had ever seen. She was wearing the first slit skirt that Jane had ever seen, also. Jane could not keep her eyes off the unseemly exposure of Flora's slender black legs. Flora had said they were wearing dresses like that in the streets of Paris.

'Be that as it may,' thought Jane, 'in the streets of Chicago that skirt will look very queer.'

But Flora was only superficially preoccupied with slit skirts and wrist watches. She had been unfolding to Jane her plans for the winter. Jane wondered what her mother and Isabel would think of them. For those plans were very surprising. Flora, incredibly, was going to open a shop. A hat shop. And, of all places, in the old brown-stone stable in the back yard on Rush Street.

'Lots of women are doing it in London,' said Flora. 'I've got the duckiest French models and a very clever French *vendeuse* to help me. We're going to make hats on the head, you know, just the way they do in Paris. I'm going to turn the coach-house into a show-room and make fitting-rooms out of the stalls. The workshop will be in the hayloft. Papa sold the Daimler last spring, and he thinks it would really be more convenient to use cabs this winter than buy a new one. I'm going to have a black-and-gold sign made to put over the door — "Chez Flora," in a facsimile of my own handwriting. And copy it for the tags inside the hats. That lid of yours is a fright, Jane. It looks almost like Silly's. I bet you bought it in Boston. You must be my first customer.'

The hat did *not* look like Silly's, thought Jane indignantly. Then, as she recovered from the passing insult, 'Do you expect to make much money?' Jane had been thinking rather wistfully of money and of the difficulty of making it, since her dinner last night with Agnes.

'Oh, I don't know,' said Flora easily. 'I guess so. My expenses will be quite heavy. If I do I'll give it away, of course.'

'To whom?' asked Jane. She was wondering already whether if she and Flora could get up a little trust fund for Agnes's daughter, Agnes would consent to accept it.

'Oh — to some charity. I haven't thought which. My goodness, Jane, I don't have to worry about that! The poor we have always with us. Mrs. Lester would be glad to grab it for her crippled children.'

'I see,' said Jane doubtfully. She was not at all sure that she did. She could not help feeling that Flora must have some very special reason for wanting to do anything so unusual and so unusually unpleasant as running a hat shop. Of course, if it were for charity ——

'I do think,' said Flora with conviction, 'that a really *chic* hat shop is needed in Chicago. But the main thing is — it will give me something to do.'

Across the brass hotel bedstead Jane looked at Flora. Her red-gold hair was just as shiny as ever, her figure was as slender and her eyes as brightly blue. She had never lost that look of the Dresden-china shepherdess. Was it just because Flora had never really done *anything* that she still seemed as delicate and fragile and fair as a precious piece of porcelain? Things had always been done *to* Flora. From the hour of her mother's dreadful dishonoured death, her life had been swallowed up by her ageing father. He had carried her around an empty world, trying to fill its emptiness with her Dresden-china prettiness. She had summered in England and France and Germany and Switzerland. She had wintered in Italy and Egypt and India and Spain. She had opened and closed the brown-stone house on Rush Street for innumerable brief Chicago seasons. But she had never settled down — never really belonged anywhere, since the winter of Muriel's marriage. There had been, of course, that incident in Cairo, eleven years ago, with that young Englishman with the unbelievably British name. Inigo Fellowes — that was it! Jane had had a letter from Flora — such a happy letter — confiding the secret of her engagement. And three weeks later a second letter, saying that Mr. Furness had been ill in Shepheard's Hotel and that Flora had been very much worried about him, and that the engagement was broken and that Flora was going to take her father to the South of France for the spring. Jenny had been born two days after the arrival of the second letter. Jane had been too preoccupied to think much about it. She did not see Flora again for two years, and

Flora had never mentioned Inigo's name. And now Mr. Furness was seventy-nine years old and really too feeble to travel any longer. And Flora was thirty-seven and was going to open a hat shop in the brown-stone stable in the back yard.

Jane thought she would much rather be as grey and as tired as Agnes and work in Macy's advertising department and sleep in a black hole of Calcutta and nag a worthless husband and worry about a baby's future than open a hat shop to give herself employment.

But she only answered: 'Yes, of course it will, Flora. And I'd love to buy a hat. So will Isabel, I know. And Muriel and Rosalie.' She thought her encouragement sounded a trifle hollow, however, and changed the subject brightly. 'Did you have fun this summer?'

'Yes,' said Flora absently. 'We motored in Ireland. How was Gull Rocks? Pretty dull?' Then, without waiting for an answer, 'Oh, Jane! Whom do you think I saw in London, just before I sailed?'

Jane couldn't imagine.

'André Duroy!' cried Flora. 'After all these years! In a picture gallery in New Bond Street. He recognized me. I should never have known him. He asked after you, Jane. I told him all about your children.'

Jane sat a moment in silence.

'What — what was he like?' she ventured.

'Oh — funny,' said Flora. 'He's gone frog. He had a little black beard and a wife who couldn't speak English.'

'Nice-looking?' said Jane, after a pause.

'The beard or the wife?' questioned Flora.

'The wife,' said Jane.

'Oh, very pretty,' said Flora. 'A mere child.'

Jane sat another moment in silence. She couldn't think of

any other question to ask and Flora evidently considered the subject finished.

'Let's get some theatre tickets,' said Flora. 'I'd like a gay evening.'

'So would I,' said Jane. She sprang up from the bed. 'I'm here for a time and I mean to have it!'

Flora took down the telephone receiver and called the ticket broker.

'We'll make Papa stand us to a magnificent dinner,' she said.

Jane did not answer. So André had gone frog and had a little black beard. It seemed only yesterday to Jane that she had noticed that André had begun to shave. And Cyprienne couldn't speak English. She wondered if Flora had told him that Cicily was fourteen. Somehow she hoped that she hadn't.

'Well — I guess this is good-bye,' said Agnes.

'I hate to say it,' said Jane.

They were sitting on two high stools in a Broadway Huyler's and had just finished a luncheon composed of a sandwich and a soda. Jane was going back to Chicago on the Twentieth Century Limited next day and that evening she and Flora and Mr. Furness were having a last whirl at the theatre.

Jane had had a gay week in New York. She had seen six plays in seven days and all the picture exhibitions up and down Fifth Avenue and had gone twice to the Metropolitan, and had bought a new dress at Hollander's and a boxful of toys for the children at Schwartz's, and had dined once again with Agnes and had had her and Jimmy to dine at the Belmont one evening before a symphony concert.

This, of course, was Agnes's noon hour. She had to be back at Macy's in ten minutes. Jane seized the soda check and slipped regretfully from her stool.

'It has certainly been great to see you,' she sighed.

'And you'll take care of Jimmy in the corn belt,' said Agnes a little wistfully.

'Of course I will,' said Jane, pushing the check through the cashier's cage. 'I think he's a darling. When will he show up?'

'Oh — right away,' said Agnes. 'He would have loved to go with you, Jane, but he has to pay his own expenses, so the Twentieth Century seemed foolish. He'll loiter out on some milk train in a day or two and show up in Lakewood looking hungry for a square meal.'

'Well, he'll get one!' Jane pocketed her change.

'And now, darling' — Agnes looked steadily in Jane's shining eyes — 'you *are* a darling, you know, Jane — wish me luck on the play!'

'You know I do,' said Jane. 'I hope it's bad enough to run forever.'

'It won't be my fault if it isn't,' said Agnes. She put one arm around Jane's waist. Jane looked tenderly at her funny freckled face.

'Agnes,' said Jane. 'You're the most gallant person I ever knew.'

Agnes smiled in defensive mockery.

'No,' said Agnes. 'You've forgotten. Dido was that.'

'Dido?' questioned Jane. Then she remembered. The memory of Agnes's little front porch, 'west of Clark Street,' rose before her. The Æneid and André and the Thomas Concert.

'No,' she said earnestly, 'you beat Dido. I'm going to see that the Eroica Symphony is played at *your* funeral pyre.'

'Jimmy might whistle it,' suggested Agnes. Her lips met Jane's cheek.

'Duty calls!' she said. 'Good-bye, old speed!'

Jane watched her solid, slightly shabby figure disappear in the Broadway traffic. To Jane it looked very heroic. She was conscious, curiously enough, of a slight sense of envy. Agnes's life, at least, was still an adventure. She was fighting odds and overcoming difficulties. She was struggling with life and love. Goodness! Jane jumped — that taxi had almost exterminated her! If it had, thought Jane, as she pushed her way through the hurrying crowd of Broadway pedestrians, Agnes would have rated that best of epitaphs — 'I have lived and accomplished the task that Destiny gave me, and now I shall pass beneath the earth no common shade.'

VI

Jane sat beside Flora in their compartment on the Twentieth Century, watching Flora and Mr. Furness play cribbage. She was thinking how much Mr. Furness looked like her mother-in-law and how much he looked a venerable codfish and how much more feeble he had grown during his summer months abroad. His hands trembled terribly when he dealt the cards and fumbled as he fixed the little pegs in the holes in the cribbage board. The train had just passed Spuyten Duyvil and the Hudson stretched glittering, a river of steel, in the hazy September sunshine outside the window.

It was warm in the compartment, in spite of the whirring electric fan, and Jane was not particularly interested in cribbage. She thought she would go back to the observation car and read a magazine. She said as much and Flora looked up patiently from the cribbage board. Flora was not particularly interested in cribbage either, but Mr. Furness loved it. Jane could remember him playing it with Flora's mother in the green-and-gold parlour of the Rush Street house. She could remember just how the rings had looked on Flora's mother's lovely listless hands as she moved the cribbage pegs. One of those rings, a sapphire between two diamonds, was on Flora's hand that minute. And Flora's hand was just as lovely and just as listless. Mr. Furness should have taken up solitaire early in life, thought Jane brutally.

She walked through the plush and varnished comfort of the Twentieth Century thinking idly that Flora's life was terrible. Nothing ever happened in it. She wondered in how many trains, bound for what exotic destinations, Flora had played cribbage with Mr. Furness. Of course, on the Twentieth Century Limited, just passing through Spuyten Duyvil, you would not expect anything very surprising to happen in any case, but on those trains *de luxe, en route* for Calcutta and Luxor and Moscow, had not Flora ever felt —— Jane passed from the narrow corridor to the observation compartment and saw Jimmy Trent, stretched comfortably in an armchair, scanning the columns of the 'Evening World.'

He saw her instantly and cast aside the paper.

'I was wondering when you would show up,' he said casually. Then, rising to his feet, 'I saw you get aboard and took an upper on the same section. I was just about to page the train for you.'

Jane stared at him in astonishment. She could not believe her eyes.

'Did—did Agnes know you were coming?' she asked stupidly.

'Oh, yes,' said Jimmy. 'I had lunch with her. I only decided to come this morning.'

'Oh!' said Jane. Then after a tiny pause, 'I thought ——'

'I've no doubt,' said Jimmy cheerfully, 'that you shared all those thrifty thoughts of Agnes's about that milk train. But I say anything that's worth doing at all is worth doing well. And I haven't been out of New York City for six years.'

'Oh!' said Jane again.

Jimmy continued to contemplate her with a sunny smile.

'I took this train,' he said presently, 'because I thought we'd have fun on it together. Don't you think it's time we began? We've lost almost an hour already.'

'What — what do you want to do?' asked Jane, again rather stupidly. She felt totally unequal to coping with Jimmy.

'I want to talk to you,' said Jimmy disarmingly. 'There's nothing in all the world as much fun as talk. When you're talking, that is, with the right person.'

Jane, still staring up at him, felt her features harden defensively.

Jimmy burst into gentle laughter.

'Jane,' he said, 'you look like a startled faun! You needn't. Would it have been more discreet of me to use the plural? Should I have said "the right people"? I don't like that phrase. It has an unfortunate social significance.'

Jane began to feel a little foolish. She laughed in spite of herself. Her laughter seemed to cheer Jimmy immensely.

'Curious, isn't it,' he went on airily, 'that "talking with the right people" means something so very different from "talking with the right person"? You *are* an awfully right person, Jane. No doubt you're of the right people, too, but don't let's dwell on that aspect of your many charms. Do you want to stand here in the train aisle all afternoon?'

Having once laughed, Jane found it perfectly impossible to recapture her critical attitude.

'Where shall we go?' she asked.

'How about the back platform?' said Jimmy promptly. 'Or will the dust spoil that pretty dress?'

'Mercy, no,' said Jane. 'Nothing could spoil it.'

The back platform was rather sunny and quite deserted. Jimmy opened one of the little folding chairs and brushed off the green carpet-cloth seat and placed it in the shade for Jane. He opened another for himself and sat down beside her. Jane looked out over the sparkling river.

'Isn't the Hudson beautiful?' she said.

'Don't let's talk about the Hudson,' said Jimmy.

Jane couldn't keep from smiling as she met his twinkling eyes.

'What shall we talk about?' she said.

'I'll give you your choice of two subjects,' said Jimmy promptly. 'You or me!'

'In that case I think I'll choose you,' said Jane.

'All right,' said Jimmy. 'Shall I begin or do you, too, find the topic stimulating?'

'I think I'd like to hear what you have to say for it,' said Jane.

'It's my favourite theme,' smiled Jimmy. 'I'll begin at the beginning. I was born in East St. Louis and I was raised in a tent.'

'A tent!' cried Jane. Vague visions of circuses rose in her mind.

'Not the kind you're thinking of,' said Jimmy. 'A revivalist's tent. I'm the proverbial minister's son. My father was a Methodist preacher.'

Jane looked up at him with wide eyes of astonishment.

'My mother,' went on Jimmy brightly, 'was a brewer's daughter. Not the kind of a brewer who draws dividends from the company, but the kind who brews beer. My grandfather — so I'm told — used to hang over the vats in person and in shirt-sleeves and my mother used to bring him his lunch at the noon hour in a tin pail. My father was an itinerant revivalist. When my mother met him, he was running a camp meeting in town, crusading against the Demon Rum. She met him in a soft-drink parlour and promptly got religion and signed the pledge. After that my grandfather had to eat a cold lunch and carry his own pail when he went to work in the morning. Mother wouldn't have anything more to do with the brewery. Father told her it was the Devil's kitchen. That made quite a little trouble in the family, of course. My grandfather kicked my father out of the house a couple of times, but Mother was hell-bent to marry him, and so, of course, presently she ran off and did. That's how I came to be raised in a tent.'

'I don't believe a word of it,' said Jane. 'You're making it all up.'

'It's Gawd's truth,' said Jimmy, 'and you don't know the half of it! I'm just the kind of a young man that H. G. Wells writes novels about. I ought to get in touch with him. He'd pay me for the story of my life. I'd make him one of those wistful, thwarted, lower-middle-class heroes ——'

'I know you're lying,' said Jane cheerfully, 'but go on with the story.'

'You see,' said Jimmy triumphantly, 'it holds you! It would be worth good money to H. G. Wells. Well, I was raised in a tent, and before I was six I knew all about handing out tracts and passing the plate. All about hell-fire, too. I believed in a God who was an irascible old gentleman with belligerent grey whiskers and in a bright red Devil with a tail and a pitchfork. I thought Father was God's ablest lieutenant on earth and Mother was His most trusted hand-maiden. Mother loved music and she learned to play the melodeon at the camp meetings. By the time I was ten I was equally expert with the drum and the fiddle and the tambourine. We wandered up and down the Mississippi Valley with our tent, keeping up a guerilla warfare with the Devil, and, until I was fifteen, I really thought the chances were about a hundred to one that I'd burn through eternity for my sins.' There was a note of real emotion in his voice.

'Is this actually true?' asked Jane.

'You bet it is,' said Jimmy. 'But at fifteen I met a girl. I met her on the mourner's bench, singing "Hallelujah" with the rest of the saved. She fell off it pretty soon and I kept on seeing her. She was a bad egg, but she taught me more than you can learn at a camp meeting.

'By the time we moved on to the next town, I'd lost all real interest in fighting the Devil. I took a pot shot at him now and then, but most of the time I declared a neutrality. I didn't state my views to Father, of course, but he noticed a certain lassitude in my technique with the tracts and the plate. He began to row with me a good deal and ask me questions about what I was doing when I wasn't in the tent. I'd skip a prayer meeting whenever I could and hang around the soda fountains and cigar stores. I used to long to steal money from the offering and run off to a burlesque show, but I never had the nerve to do it. Long after I'd lost my faith in the Irascible Old Gentleman I used to feel a bolt would fall on me if I did a thing like that.

'When I was seventeen, I had my first real drink at a real bar, and when I came home Father smelled the whiskey on my breath. First he prayed over me and then he beat me. I snatched the cane away from him and broke it over my knee, and that night he prayed for me by name, in public, at the camp meeting. That finished religion for me. Mother tried to patch things up between us, but it was no use. After six months of family warfare she gave up. I travelled around with them after that in the position of Resident Atheist. I never went to any more prayer meetings, but I was useful

putting up and taking down the tent and doing odd jobs
backstage. Every now and then I'd consent to drop in and
play a violin solo while they were collecting the offering.

'I was just nineteen when my father died of pneumonia,
caught preaching in the rain. And my mother and I went
back to East St. Louis. Jane — your eyes are as big as
saucers!'

'Why wouldn't they be?' cried Jane breathlessly. 'It's perfectly thrilling.'

'It wasn't very thrilling while it was going on,' said Jimmy.
'My grandfather was dead, but my grandmother took us in
and my mother got me a job with my rich uncle. He lived
across the river in St. Louis and he was a fashionable druggist.
I worked in his shop for two years, making sodas and mixing
prescriptions. At first I liked it. I had money of my own for
the first time in my life and I didn't have to hear any preaching. I went to night school at a settlement and I read all the
books I could lay my hands on and pretty soon I turned
socialist. That got my uncle's goat right away. He was
making a pretty good thing off the drug business and the
established order was all right with him. He talked of Karl
Marx just the way my father had of the Devil, and I was too
young to have the sense to keep my face shut. I'd air my
views and he'd call me an anarchist and I'd say there were
worse things than anarchy. I used to like to get him on the
run. Pretty soon he really got to believe I had a bomb up
my sleeve, and he was afraid to let me mix prescriptions any
longer for fear I'd add a little strychnine to the cough-mixture
of a plutocratic customer. So he told Mother he guessed I
wasn't suited to the drug business.

'Mother thought I'd better learn to run an elevator, but I
didn't fancy a life in a cage and presently I got a job with my

fiddle in a theatre orchestra. That nearly finished Mother, of course. She thought the stage was the Devil's recruiting office. I lost the job pretty soon and got another through a man I knew at the settlement as a cub reporter on the "St. Louis Post-Dispatch." That didn't last long either, but it made Mother's last days happy to think I was through with the stage. She died when I was twenty-two and left me three thousand dollars saved from Father's life insurance. The day after the funeral I took the train to New York and signed up with a vaudeville circuit as a ragtime accompanist for a black-face comedian. I guess I lost forty jobs in the next six years on newspapers and in orchestra pits. But I learned a lot about music and more about slinging the English language. I was just twenty-eight when I met Agnes. I thought she was a card. She was the only woman I'd ever met who was as good as my mother and as clever as I was. She took a fancy to reform me, though I told her at the time I'd been immunized to salvation from early childhood. After that, of course, it was all over but the shouting.'

'It *is* like a novel,' said Jane breathlessly. 'It's *just* like a novel.'

'But how does it end?' asked Jimmy, a trifle gloomily.

'It ended when you married Agnes,' said Jane promptly.

'It isn't a fairy story,' said Jimmy gently. 'H. G. Wells's novels never end at the altar.'

Jane did not reply to that. She was watching the ruddy September sun sinking into the western haze behind Storm King. She was conscious of Jimmy's eyes, fixed thoughtfully on her face. They sat a long time in silence. Jane could see the dim outline of the Catskills, pale lavender against an orange sky, before he spoke again.

'And your novel, Jane?' he asked gently. 'Who wrote that?'

'Louisa M. Alcott,' said Jane promptly. 'There's nothing modern and morbid in *my* story.'

'Now it's my turn to be disbelieving,' said Jimmy.

'Do I look morbid?' said Jane, turning to smile serenely into his admiring eyes.

'You look modern,' said Jimmy. 'And you look very, very thoughtful. All people who think sooner or later go through hell.'

'Then my hell must be ahead of me,' said Jane steadfastly.

'You haven't even experienced a purgatory?' smiled Jimmy. 'Something you got in and got out of?'

'Not even a purgatory,' said Jane. 'I'm a very naïve person. I've never experienced much of anything.'

'Perhaps that will be your hell,' said Jimmy.

The door behind them opened suddenly and Flora stood on the platform.

'Oh, here you are, Jane!' she cried. 'Papa wants to dine early. He's pretty tired.' Then she recognized Jimmy. She had met him, of course, at that dinner at the Belmont. She looked very much astonished.

'Why — Mr. Trent ——' she said uncertainly.

'Jimmy decided to come West on the Century,' said Jane, rising from her chair.

'How nice!' said Flora, in her best Dresden shepherdess manner. Then to Jimmy with a smile, 'You'll dine with us, of course?'

'I'd love to,' said Jimmy.

They all walked together into the observation car. Flora looked distinctly cheered at the thought of a little male companionship other than Mr. Furness's. Jane was thinking of Jimmy's story. How fairy-like and fantastic it was compared to her own! By what different roads they had travelled to reach that intimate moment of companionship on the back platform of the Twentieth Century Limited. Having met at last, it seemed very strange to Jane that they could speak the same language. But yet they did. Jimmy, holding open a heavy train door to let her pass in front of him, smiled down into her eyes. She thanked him with an answering smile. Jane felt as if she had known Jimmy for years.

VII

The Twentieth Century was pulling slowly into the La Salle Street Station. Jane stood in the vestibule, knee-deep in luggage, looking eagerly for Stephen beyond the little crowd of porters that lined the greasy platform. Jimmy was at her elbow, but Flora and Mr. Furness were still sitting in the compartment. Mr. Furness found crowds very tiring.

The train came slowly to a standstill. Jane tumbled down the steps, stumbling over suitcases. She looked quickly down the long vista of the trainshed. The platform was crowded, now, with red caps galvanized into action and with travellers trying to sort out their bags from the heaps of luggage piled at each car entrance. No Stephen was to be seen. Jimmy was watching her with his ironical smile.

'He's forgotten you,' he said presently. 'He isn't here.'

'He always meets me,' said Jane. 'In fifteen years of matrimony he's met me every time I've come home.'

'What an idyll!' smiled Jimmy. It didn't seem impertinent because of the smile.

Suddenly Jane saw Stephen. She saw his grey Fedora hat towering over the heads of the crowd.

'Oh — Stephen!' she called, her voice lost in the uproar of the trainshed. He saw her waving arm, however. In a moment he was at her side. Jane cast herself into his arms. She knew Jimmy was watching them. She pressed her cheek against the rough tweed of Stephen's coat lapel, then turned her face to his. She felt a trifle histrionic, under Jimmy's ironical eye. Stephen kissed her cheek, very tranquilly.

'Hello, Jane!' he said cheerfully. 'Your train's an hour late. You can get a dollar back from the railroad.'

Jane wished his greeting had been a bit more idyllic. Jimmy was grinning now, quite frankly.

'Stephen,' said Jane, 'this is Jimmy — Jimmy Trent. He's been giving me a whirl all the way from New York.'

Stephen looked over at Jimmy. He seemed a little surprised, Jane thought, at what he saw. Or perhaps it was at what she had said. She remembered her last words on Jimmy in the Boston South Station, eight days before, 'I know I'll hate him.' Jimmy had stepped forward and extended his hand.

'How do you do, sir,' he said simply.

His ultimate monosyllable struck Jane's ear. She glanced from Jimmy to Stephen. Jimmy looked very casual and debonair. Stephen looked — well, Stephen looked just like what he was, the forty-four-year-old first vice-president of the Midland Loan and Trust Company. Jane felt again that curious little pang of pity. Stephen had once looked quite as casual and as debonair as Jimmy. He was only ten years older than Jimmy that minute. Yet Jimmy had called him 'sir.' And the worst of it was that it had sounded quite suitable.

Flora and Mr. Furness had descended from the train. They were greeting Stephen, now, very warmly. They all trooped down the platform together and into the station, and over to the ticket window to collect their dollars. Jimmy pocketed his and turned to Jane with a smile.

'Could you have lunch with me?' he said. 'Meet me somewhere at one and show me the town.'

'Oh, I couldn't,' said Jane. 'I have to go out to the country and have lunch with the children.'

'Have dinner with the children,' smiled Jimmy persuasively. 'I'm a dollar in pocket and I'd like to give you a time.'

'I couldn't,' said Jane firmly. 'But I'd like you to have lunch with Stephen. Stephen!' she called. He turned from the ticket window. 'Don't you want to lunch with Jimmy at the University Club? I'd like him to meet people.'

Once more, Stephen looked just a little surprised.

'I'd be glad to,' he said, 'if he can come early. I've a date to meet Bill Belmont there at noon. He's on from New York to put through that Morgan deal. If Jimmy doesn't mind talking of bond issues ——'

'I'm not awfully helpful on bond issues,' said Jimmy self-deprecatingly. 'And I'm afraid I couldn't get off at noon. I'll be busy with the boys at the "News." Thanks ever so much, though.'

They all turned away from the ticket window to the taxi entrance. Jane was solemnly reflecting that Jimmy was outrageous. She felt very thankful that Stephen had not heard him invite her to lunch. Suddenly she heard his voice at her ear.

'And when am I going to see you?' said Jimmy.

Jane hadn't forgiven him.

'You must come out to Lakewood sometime,' she said vaguely. 'For a night or a week-end.'

'Oh, I'll come out to Lakewood,' said Jimmy.

'When you're settled,' pursued Jane politely, 'let me know where I can reach you. Give me a ring when you find a good boarding-house.'

'Oh, I'll give you a ring,' said Jimmy.

By this time Stephen had hailed a taxi.

'I won't go with you to the other station,' he said. 'I've got to run into the Federal Building.' Jane stepped into the cab. 'Your mail's on your desk, dear. Don't pay the painter's bill 'til I talk to you about it.'

Jane nodded very brightly. She was once again conscious of Jimmy's ironical eye. This time she wouldn't stoop to be histrionic. She waved her hand casually as the taxi started. Jimmy and Stephen, standing bareheaded on the curbstone, both smiled and waved cheerfully in reply. Their waves and their smiles were very different, however, reflected Jane, as the taxi turned into the traffic at the station entrance.

CHAPTER III

I

'THEY say it wasn't a stroke,' said Isabel, 'but of course it was.'

'Mrs. Lester told me it was acute indigestion,' said Mrs. Ward.

'And Rosalie told *me* it was brain fatigue,' said Isabel.

'I don't know what Bert Lancaster's ever done to fatigue his brain,' said Mrs. Ward.

Jane laughed, in spite of her concern for Muriel. They were all sitting around the first October fire in Jane's little Lakewood living-room. Her mother and Isabel had motored out from town to take tea with her and they were all discussing, of course, Bert Lancaster's sudden seizure at the Commercial Club banquet the night before.

'It must have been awful,' said Isabel, 'falling over like that, right into his own champagne glass, in the middle of a speech.'

'They say he was forbidden champagne,' said Mrs. Ward. 'Dr. Bancroft's wife told me that the doctor had warned him last winter that he must give up alcohol.'

'Have some more tea, Isabel,' said Jane.

'I oughtn't to, but I will,' said Isabel. At forty-one Isabel was valiantly struggling against increasing pounds. 'No sugar, Jane.' She opened her purse and taking out a small bottle dropped three tablets of saccharine into her cup.

'Of course he's pretty young for a stroke,' said Mrs. Ward.

'He's fifty-five,' said Isabel. 'He was fifty-five the third of August.'

'It's frightful for Muriel,' said Jane.

'Oh, I don't know,' said Mrs. Ward. 'Perhaps it's providential. Of course if he's disabled ——'

'If he lives, he will be,' said Isabel. 'Sooner or later. If you have one stroke you *always* have another.'

'Well, he may *not* live,' said Mrs. Ward. 'He can't have any constitution to rely on after the life he's led.'

'What do you think Muriel would do, Jane?' asked Isabel. 'Do you think she'd really *marry* Cyril Fortune?'

'I don't know,' said Jane.

'She was off at the "Scandals" with him when it happened,' said Mrs. Ward. 'They paged her at the theatre.'

'You mark my words,' said Isabel, taking a piece of toast and scraping the buttered cinnamon off it, 'whenever Bert Lancaster dies, Muriel will marry the man of the moment the day after the funeral. Not that I think she's really in love with Cyril. I never thought she was in love with Sam or Binky or Roger or any of them.'

'Not even with Sam?' said Mrs. Ward.

'Not really,' said Isabel with conviction. 'Rosalie always said she wasn't. I think Muriel is really just in love with herself. It keeps up her self-confidence to have a young man sighing gustily around the home. But just the same, if Bert Lancaster dies to-night, I bet she marries Cyril Fortune before Christmas.'

'Nonsense!' said Mrs. Ward. 'Muriel would do everything decently. She'd stay in mourning for at least a year. She'd have to show the proper respect for her son's sake.'

'They've sent for young Albert,' said Isabel, 'to come home from Saint Paul's.'

'Well, I hope Muriel behaves herself while he's here,' said Mrs. Ward severely. 'He's fifteen and he's old enough to notice.'

'That's just exactly,' said Isabel dreamily, 'what you used to say of Flora.'

'Well, she *was* old enough to notice,' said Mrs. Ward, 'but I doubt if she ever did. Lily Furness had a curious magnetism. Somehow she always made you believe the best of her.'

'Flora simply adored her,' said Jane suddenly. 'I adored her, myself.'

'Just the same,' said Mrs. Ward, 'she had no principle.'

'You don't know,' said Jane. 'Perhaps she went through hell. You can't help it if you're not in love with your husband.'

'Every wife with principle,' said Mrs. Ward firmly, '*is* in love with her husband.'

'Mamma!' cried Isabel. 'Don't be ridiculous! How many wives are? But what I say is, even if you're not, you don't have to take a lover ——'

'No,' said Jane, 'of course you don't. But I can see how you might.'

'Don't talk like that!' said Mrs. Ward sharply. 'I don't know where you girls *get* your ideas! When I was your age I wouldn't even have said those words — "take a lover"! And you two sit there talking as if it were actually *done!*'

'But it *is* done, Mamma,' said Isabel. 'Not very often, of course, but sometimes. Lily Furness did it, even in your day. And you know, in your black heart, that you're wondering whether Muriel hasn't gone and done it in ours.'

'I am *not!*' said Mrs. Ward indignantly. 'I shouldn't think of making such an accusation against Muriel. All I say is, she isn't very discreet. She gets herself talked about. There's been a lot of gossip about Muriel. And every one knows that where there's so much smoke, there's bound to be some fire.'

'Well, what do you think you're saying now?' said Isabel. 'What are, or aren't you, accusing Muriel of this minute?'

Mrs. Ward looked slightly bewildered.

'I don't like the way young people speak out nowadays,' she said. 'And I don't like your attitude toward wrongdoing. You and Jane are both perfectly willing to condone whatever Muriel has done. At least, in my day, we all made Lily Furness feel she was a guilty woman. We took the marriage vows seriously.'

'I take the marriage vows seriously, Mamma,' said Jane gently. 'But I can understand the people who break them. At least,' she added doubtfully, 'I think I can. I think I can understand just how it might happen.'

'Any one could understand how it might happen in Muriel's case,' said Isabel. 'Bert's a perfect old rip. There's a certain poetic justice in the thought of him, standing in Mr. Furness's shoes ——'

Mrs. Ward rose with dignity from her chair.

'Come, Isabel,' she said, 'I'm going home. I'm not going to listen to you girls any longer. I only hope you don't talk like this before Robin and Stephen. It's a woman's duty to keep up her husband's standards.'

Jane and Isabel burst into laughter.

'Robin and Stephen!' exclaimed Isabel. 'Imagine either of them on the loose!'

'They keep up *our* standards,' said Jane, as she kissed her mother. Mrs. Ward still looked a trifle bewildered.

'Put on your heavy coat,' said Jane, as they all turned toward the door. 'Don't let her catch cold, Isabel.'

'I won't,' said Isabel. 'Mind that rug, Mamma. The floor is slippery.'

'You girls think I'm just an old lady,' said Mrs. Ward, as Jane opened the front door. 'I wish you'd both remember that I took care of myself for about forty-five years before you thought you were old enough to give me advice.' She climbed, a little clumsily, into the waiting motor.

'Give my love to Papa,' said Jane. 'And Isabel — when you telephone Rosalie, ask if there's anything I can do for Muriel.'

'I will,' said Isabel. 'There probably will be. Muriel never does anything for herself.'

The car crunched slowly around the gravel driveway. Jane watched it to the entrance. Curious, she thought, the gap between the points of view of different generations. The facts of life were always the same, but people thought about them so differently. New thoughts, reflected Jane, about the same old actions. Was it progress or merely change? Sex was a loaded pistol, thought Jane, thrust into the hand of humanity. Her mother's generation had carried it carefully, fearful of a sudden explosion. Her generation, and Isabel's, waved it nonchalantly about, but, after all, with all their carelessness, they didn't fire it off any oftener than their parents had. What if the next generation should take to shooting? Shooting straight regardless of their target. As Jane entered the front hall, the telephone was ringing.

She stood still, suddenly, on the doormat. That might be Jimmy, she thought instantly, and despised herself for the thought. Jane hated to think that she had been back in the Lakewood house for three weeks and that, in all that time, the telephone had never rung without awakening in her unwilling brain the thought that it might be Jimmy. For Jimmy had never telephoned. He had vanished completely out of her life that morning in the La Salle Street Station. At first she had been only relieved to find that the voice, whosever it was, trickling over the wire, was not his. Jane had been firmly determined to discipline Jimmy for that outrageous refusal to lunch with Stephen on the day of his arrival. But, as the days passed and she did not hear from him, her relief had been subtly tempered first with curiosity then with concern,

and, at last, with indignation. Jimmy ought to have telephoned. It was rude of him not to. She had really felt, after
those intimate hours on the back platform of the Twentieth
Century, that she meant something to Jimmy, that he really
liked her, that he was depending on her for support and di-
version during his visit to Chicago. And then — he had not
telephoned. By not telephoning he had made Jane feel rather
a fool. For Jimmy had meant something to *her*, she had really
liked *him*. Of course he was irritating and she had known he
was not to be counted on, but still — she *had* thought that she
had read an honest admiration in his ironic eyes, she *had* felt
that he was a very amusing person, she had even wondered
just what she had better do in case Jimmy's honest admiration became a trifle embarrassing. She had solemnly assured
herself, on her arrival at Lakewood, that if she were firm and
pleasantly disciplinary she could, of course, handle Jimmy,
who was a dear and Agnes's husband, but not very wise, perhaps, and obviously in the frame of mind in which he could
easily be led astray by the flutter of a petticoat. And then —
he had not telephoned.

'Mrs. Carver,' Miss Parrot's pleasant voice called down the
stairs, 'Mr. Carver wants you on the wire.'

Jane walked to the telephone in the pantry.

'Yes, dear?' she said.

'I can't get out for dinner this evening,' said Stephen.
'Muriel wants me to come up and talk business with her. It
seems Bert was just advising her about some investments
when he was stricken. She's got some bonds he wanted her to
sell immediately.'

'Of course go, dear,' said Jane quickly. Stephen would be
very helpful to Muriel. Every one turned to Stephen when in
trouble. And Muriel had no one to advise her except Freddy
Waters, her volatile brother-in-law. Unless you counted

Cyril Fortune, who was a young landscape gardener recently rumoured to have lost twenty thousand dollars in a flyer in oil. He wouldn't be much to lean on in a financial crisis.

'I'll be out on the ten-ten,' said Stephen. 'Don't be lonely.'

'I won't,' said Jane. 'I've got letters to write. Give my love to Muriel.'

As Jane turned from the telephone she heard the whirr of a motor. That would be the children coming home from school. The car called for them at the playground every afternoon at five. Jane was always afraid to let them walk home alone through the traffic. The country lane on which her house had been built, fourteen years before, had long since become a suburban highroad. As she entered the hall again, they burst in at the front door. The cocker-spaniel puppy tumbled down the stairs to meet them.

'Mumsy!' called Jenny. 'Oh, there you are! I've made the basket-ball team and I need some gym shoes!'

'I'm going to take my rabbits to school for the Animal Fair!' cried little Steve.

'Can I ask Jack and Belle to come out on Saturday?' said Cicily. Jack and Belle were Isabel's seventeen- and thirteen-year-old son and daughter. No week-end was complete without them.

'When can we get the gym shoes?' said Jenny.

'I need a cage for the rabbits,' said little Steve.

'I've got to have the gym shoes by Monday, Mumsy,' said Jenny.

'Do you think I could make a cage out of a peach crate?' said little Steve.

'Hush!' said Jane. 'Pick up your coat, Jenny, and hang it in the closet. Steve — your books don't belong on the floor.

Yes, Cicily, you can telephone Aunt Isabel to-night and ask them.'

'Mumsy, where can I find a peach crate?'

'Be quiet!' said Jane. 'Now go upstairs, all of you, and *wash!* If you get your home work done before supper, I'll read King Arthur stories to you to-night. Daddy's not coming home.'

The children clattered up the staircase. Jane walked into the living-room with a sigh. They were terribly noisy. They never seemed to behave like other people's children. She sat down at her desk and began to look over the afternoon mail. An invitation to dine in town with Muriel before an evening musical — that would be off, now, of course. A bill from the plumber for repairing the faucets in the maid's bathroom. A note from the chairman of the Miscellaneous Committee of the Chicago Chatter Club asking her to write a funny paper on 'The Hand that Rocks the Cradle' for the December meeting. A note from the chairman of the Literary Committee of the Lakewood Woman's Club, asking her to write a serious paper on 'Oriental Art' for the Spring Festival. A bill from the Russian Peasant Industries for smocking Cicily's and Jenny's new winter frocks. A notice from the Lakewood Village Council, announcing that Clean-Up Week began on Monday next. A note from Steve's teacher, suggesting that she see that he spend more time on his arithmetic. An advertisement of a Rummage Sale for the benefit of Saint George's Church. A bill from the Lakewood Gas and Coke Company for the new laundry stove. A notice that her report would be due as chairman of the Playground Committee at the annual meeting of the Village Improvement Society next Wednesday night.

Jane pushed the mail into a pigeon-hole. She felt she could not bear to cope with it. She felt she could not bear to cope with the winter that lay before her. Which was, of course, ridiculous. Jane knew that it would be just like all other winters — fun enough, when you came to live it. But always in October, reëstablished in Lakewood after the break of the Eastern summer, Jane wondered why she and Stephen chose to live just the way they did. Lakewood was good for the children, of course. No longer country, not much more rural than the Pine Street of her childhood, but better than Isabel's town apartment, nicer, even, than Muriel's smart city residence overlooking the lake.

Still — suburban life was pretty awful. Narrow, confining, in spite of the physical asset of its wider horizons. Jane rose from her desk and walked to a western window. The sun was setting over the Skokie Valley. An October sunset, red and cold, behind her copper oak woods, beyond the tanned haystacks in the distant meadows. A western sunset, violent and vivid, glorifying the flat swamps with golden light, setting the tranquil clouds in the wide, unbroken sky aflame with rosy fire. The Skokie always looked like that, on autumn evenings. It was lovely, too, on winter nights, a snowy plane beneath the sparkling stars. In the spring, when the Skokie overflowed its banks and the swamps were wet and the moonlight paled the pink blossoms of the apple tree at the foot of the garden, it was perhaps most lovely of all. Jane was lucky to live there — lucky to have that picture to look out on, always, outside her window. Still ——

Jane watched the burnished sun sink slowly beneath the flat horizon, the low clouds lose their colour and turn darkly purple, the high clouds flame with pink and pure translucent gold. Then they, too, faded into wisps of grey. The western sky was lemon-coloured now. A crescent moon was tangled in the oak boughs.

Jane turned back to her desk and stood looking at the il-

luminated quotation from Stevenson that hung over it in a
silver frame — the work of Jenny's hand in the sixth grade
of the Lakewood Progressive School, a gift of last Christmas.

'To make this earth, our hermitage,
A cheerful and a changeful page,
God's bright and intricate device
Of days and seasons doth suffice.'

'What a damn lie!' thought Jane, and turned at the sound
of a step in the doorway. Jimmy Trent, his hat in his hand,
his fiddle-case under his arm, stood smiling at her on the
threshold. The children had left the front door open, of
course. He had come in quietly ——

'Hello!' said Jimmy. 'How's every little thing?'

'Jimmy!' said Jane. 'Come in! Sit down. I'm awfully glad
to see you!'

'That's quite as it should be,' said Jimmy. 'May I stay to
dinner?'

'Of course,' said Jane. Then, before she could stop herself,
'Why didn't you telephone?'

'Why didn't you telephone *me*?' said Jimmy, tossing his hat
on a table and placing the fiddle-case beside it. 'You could
have, you know, at the "Daily News."'

Jane thought her reason for not telephoning Jimmy might
sound a little foolish. If you said you thought a man should
telephone you first, it really seemed as if you took the fact that
he had not telephoned quite seriously.

'Oh, I don't know,' said Jane; 'I've been busy.'

'So have I,' said Jimmy. 'Awfully busy. It's the first time
in six years that I've cut loose from a woman's apron strings in
a big city. I like Chicago.'

'Do you like your job?' said Jane severely. Jimmy looked
white, she thought, and just a little tired.

'My job?' said Jimmy. 'Oh, yes. I like my job. It isn't very arduous.'

'I hope you're working at it,' said Jane.

'Now, Jane,' said Jimmy sweetly, 'lay off salvation. I get enough of that at home.' He strolled over to the hearthrug and took his stand upon it, his back toward the smouldering fire. He was still smiling. 'I met Stephen at noon to-day. I met him, I regret to tell you, Jane, in the University Club bar. Every one was talking about this Lancaster's stroke. Stephen said he was going up to see Mrs. Lancaster this evening. So I thought I'd come out with my fiddle and offer you a little entertainment. I want to play you Debussy's "La Fille aux Cheveux de Laine."'

'How nice of you,' said Jane a little uncertainly.

'Like Debussy?' asked Jimmy.

'Yes,' said Jane.

'Me, too,' said Jimmy.

There was a moment of silence. Jane suddenly realized how dark the room had grown. She turned on a lamp and sat down in her chair by the fireside.

'This is nice,' said Jimmy. 'This is very nice.' He was looking interestedly around the chintz-hung living-room. The panelled walls, the books, the Steinway, the few good pieces of mahogany furniture all seemed to meet with his approval. 'It's just like you, Jane. Modern, but not morbid.' He sank into Stephen's armchair across the hearthrug and picked up the October 'Question Mark' from the table at his elbow. The 'Question Mark' was the monthly magazine of the Lakewood Progressive School. Jimmy idly scanned a photograph of the football squad for a moment in silence and dropped the 'Question Mark' back upon the table. His eye fell upon the copy of the King Arthur stories. 'Not at all morbid,' he repeated. His eyes were twinkling as they met Jane's.

'I must go up and dress for dinner,' said Jane, rising suddenly. 'Here's the newspaper if you'd like to read it until I
come down.'

'Are you glad I came?' The question arrested her abruptly
in the doorway. Curiously enough, Jane was not quite sure.
But ——

'Very glad,' said Jane evenly. She mounted the staircase
rather slowly. She *wasn't* quite sure about the gladness.
Nevertheless, she was inexplicably determined to look her
best that evening. She would put on that red Poiret tea-
gown she had so foolishly bought at a bargain sale last June.
She had often regretted that folly. What use had Jane at
Lakewood or Gull Rocks for a red Poiret tea-gown?

'Miss Parrot,' said Jane, pausing in the playroom doorway,
'I want Steve to wear his blue suit this evening. And tell
Cicily and Jenny, please, to put on their new yellow smocks.'
On entering her bedroom she rang for the waitress.

'Sarah,' she said, 'Mr. Carver will not be home for dinner,
but Mr. Trent will stay. We'll have cocktails. And some of
the good sauterne at table. And crême de menthe, please,
after the coffee. Be sure and see that the ice is cracked fine.
You can pound it in a towel. It ought to be almost pulverized.'

Jane walked slowly to her closet and took out the red tea-
gown. Jimmy was something different at Lakewood. Still,
she wasn't quite sure about the gladness. She wished that
Agnes were downstairs with him. When Jane realized how
much she wished that, she felt better about the gladness. She
was even willing to admit to herself how **very** glad she was.

II

'Let's play parchesi,' said little Steve.

'I have to telephone Aunt Isabel,' said Cicily.

'I haven't done my practising,' said Jenny.

They were all sitting around the living-room fire. Jane was presiding over the little silver coffee service on the table at her knee. Sarah was passing the crème de menthe. The little cut-glass goblets, filled with vivid green liquid, looked very festive and frivolous, on the small silver tray. Jimmy grasped his with a sigh of satisfaction. Miss Parrot took hers with the deprecatory gesture of every trained nurse accepting an alcoholic beverage. Jane sipped hers with the comforting realization that the ice was perfectly pulverized.

'Do you like parchesi?' said little Steve to Jimmy.

'I love it,' said Jimmy, 'but I hurt my finger yesterday and I'm afraid I couldn't throw the dice.'

'Anyway,' said Jenny, 'I have to practise.'

'Not to-night,' said Jimmy cheerfully. 'Day before yesterday I hurt my ear and sudden noises pain it dreadfully.'

Jenny and Cicily and Miss Parrot all laughed uproariously at his nonsense.

'Well,' said Cicily, 'I *do* have to telephone Aunt Isabel.'

'That's a fine idea,' said Jimmy approvingly. 'And Miss Parrot looks to me like a perfect parchesi fan. I think it would be very nice, Cicily, if Steve got the board all ready in another room so that, when you had finished telephoning your aunt, you and she and Jenny and Steve could all play parchesi together, while your mother sat here in the firelight and told me what to do for my finger and my ear.'

Miss Parrot, having finished her crème de menthe, rose with a smile. She was obviously quite captivated by Jimmy.

'Come up to the playroom, children,' she said. 'I'll play parchesi with you.'

'And *don't* I have to practise?' asked Jenny jubilantly.

'Not if Mr. Trent's ear is hurting him,' smiled Jane.

Jenny threw Jimmy a grateful smile. Steve dragged Miss Parrot from the room. Cicily followed with Jenny.

'I can't believe,' said Jimmy, as he lit a cigarette, 'that those great children are yours.'

'They are,' said Jane briefly.

'Cicily's a perfect heart-breaker,' said Jimmy.

'I'm afraid she will be,' said Jane.

'Why "afraid"?' asked Jimmy.

'I don't think breaking hearts is a very rewarding occupation,' said Jane.

'Oh — some one else can always mend them,' said Jimmy lightly. He twinkled across at her, through a blue streak of cigarette smoke. 'You know that, don't you, Jane?'

'I've never broken any hearts,' said Jane, smiling. 'So really I don't.'

'Well — experience is the best teacher,' said Jimmy affably.

Sarah reëntered the room to remove the coffee tray. She picked up the cups and the little cut-glass goblets with the silent efficiency of the perfect servant and retired noiselessly into the hall.

'It moves on greased wheels, doesn't it, Jane?' said Jimmy.

'What does?' asked Jane.

'Your life,' said Jimmy.

'Yes,' said Jane. 'But I grease them.'

'I suppose you do,' said Jimmy. 'But you don't mind it, do you?'

'I get awfully sick of it,' said Jane honestly.

Jimmy watched her for a moment in silence behind the cigarette smoke.

'Sick of what?' he said presently.

'Sick,' said Jane earnestly, 'of greasing wheels. Sick of running the house and bossing the servants and dressing the children. Sick of seeing that everything looks pretty and everything goes right. Sick of seeing that the living-room is dusted before ten every morning and that dinner is served on the stroke of seven every night. Sometimes I wonder what's the use of it all. Sometimes I wish that Stephen and I could just tear up our roots and buy a couple of knapsacks and put the children in a covered wagon and start out to see the world. Just wander, you know, for a year or two. Wander everywhere, before we're too old to do it. Not bother about anything. Not care. Not do anything we didn't really want to —— I suppose you think I'm crazy!' She broke off abruptly.

'Crazy?' said Jimmy. 'I think you're just right. There's a lot of the nomad in me, you know. I guess the tent got into my blood. If I'd been born a gypsy instead of a Methodist minister's son, I'd never have broken home ties. Golly!'—he waved his cigarette with enthusiasm — 'I'd like to go round the world. Round and round it in circles. Round it in every latitude. Let's do it, Jane! Let's surprise Stephen to-night! You leave a note on the pincushion and I'll send a wire to Agnes. "Gone — to points unknown!" We'll set out for the Golden Gate — I guess we can buy those knapsacks in the Northwestern Station — and sail for the South Sea Islands and drift over to Siam and Burma and India and on up to China — and by that time Stephen and Agnes will have divorced us and I'll make you an honest woman, Jane, in a little Chinese shrine with the temple bells ringing overhead, and we'll wander on, through Tibet and Afghanistan and Persia to Asia Minor, or maybe up to Russia, and then down through the civilized countries, which won't be so nice, but where the food will be much better, to Africa, Jane! To the Dark Continent. And maybe when we get there we'll stay — stay in the village of some cannibal king who never even heard of a musical critic or a suburban housewife, where concertos for the violin are unknown and living-rooms are never dusted! How about it, Jane?' He paused out of breath and looked engagingly over at her.

'It sounds very alluring,' said Jane, 'but a little uncomfortable.'

'Comfort!' scoffed Jimmy. 'You don't really care about
comfort!'

'Yes, I do!' cried Jane. 'When I haven't got it! And so do
you. I don't know you so awfully well, Jimmy, but I know
you well enough to know that. You care so much about comfort that you won't get up in the morning and make your own
bed for Agnes! You won't ride on a milk train instead of the
Twentieth Century! I don't think you'd be so good in a
jungle. When I go to a jungle, I think I'll take Stephen. He'd
be very capable there.'

'I'm sure,' said Jimmy cheerfully, 'he'd have sanitary
plumbing installed in a fortnight. Nevertheless, something
tells me that Stephen is no gypsy. If you ever see the Dark
Continent with Stephen, you'll see it in the discreet light shed
on it by Thomas Cook and Sons! But as for me, with or without Agnes, I'm going to see the world before I die.'

'Mumsy' — it was little Steve on the threshold — 'we want
to kiss you good-night.'

'Come in,' said Jane. 'Come in, all of you.' The three
children were lingering in the doorway.

'How'd the game come out, Steve?' asked Jimmy affably.

'Miss Parrot won,' said Steve gloomily. 'She always does.'

'I'm going to send you a set of loaded dice,' said Jimmy
benevolently. 'Come in, kids, and sit down.' He rose as he
spoke. 'I want to sing to you.' He had picked up his fiddle-case
and was removing the violin. Jane looked up in surprise.
Jimmy was a strange mixture of contradictions. The children
settled themselves delightedly on the floor near the fire.
Jimmy tucked his violin under his chin and tuned it airily as
he sauntered across the room.

'It's an old English ballad,' he said, 'and a particular favourite of mine. It appeals to your mother, too, who is really a gypsy at heart. Did you know that, children? There she sits by those polished brass andirons looking very pretty in a French tea-gown, but at heart she's dancing barefoot by a bonfire in a tattered red shawl — dancing in the dark of the moon to the tinkle of a tambourine. When she married your father, children, she jumped over a broomstick. But later he took up with the bond business. That's the way most of us get married. Did you know that, Cicily? But later we nearly all of us take up with something else and after that we only use broomsticks to sweep with.'

The children were staring at him in wide-eyed fascination. They were still staring when he began softly to sing:

'There were three gypsies a-come to my door,
And downstairs ran my lady, O!
One sang high and the other sang low,
And the other sang bonny, bonny Biscay, O!

'Then she pulled off her silk-finished gown
And put on hose of leather, O!
The ragged, ragged rags about our door —
She's gone with the raggle-taggle gypsies, O!'

Jimmy paused to smile mockingly at Jane, drawing his bow with a flourish across the strings of his violin.

'It was late last night when my lord came home,
Inquiring for his lady, O!
The servants said, on every hand,
She's gone with the raggle-taggle gypsies, O!

'Come saddle me my milk-white steed
And go and fetch my pony, O!
That I may ride and fetch my bride,
Who is gone with the raggle-taggle gypsies, O!

'Then he rode high, and he rode low,
He rode through wood and copses too,
Until he came to an open field
And there he spied his lady, O!

'What makes you leave your house and land
What makes you leave your money, O?
What makes you leave your new-wedded lord,
To go with the raggle-taggle gypsies, O?'

Again Jimmy paused to smile mockingly at Jane and again his bow swept over a string and a note of triumph quivered in the air.

'Oh, what care I for my house and land,
And what care I for my money, O?
What care I for my new-wedded lord,
I'm off with the raggle-taggle gypsies, O!'

His bow ran wildly, jubilantly over the high strings, then dropped to a sombre note of accusation.

'Last night you slept on a goose-feather bed,
With the sheet turned down so bravely, O!
But to-night you sleep in a cold open field,
Along with the raggle-taggle gypsies, O!'

Again the bow fluttered over the strings. The recreant lady's laughter seemed tinkling in the room.

'Oh, what care I for a goose-feather bed,
With the sheet turned down so bravely, O!
For to-night I shall sleep in a cold open field,
Along with the raggle-taggle gypsies, O!'

He dropped his bow abruptly. In the sudden silence Steve's voice rang out shrill with interest.

'And did she?'

'That lady did,' said Jimmy gravely. 'She had the courage of her convictions.'

'And she never went back?' pursued Steve eagerly.

'Oh — that I can't tell you,' said Jimmy gaily. 'The song doesn't say. I shouldn't be surprised if she did, though. Lots of ladies do.'

'Children — you must go to bed,' said Jane. 'It's very late.'

'I must go back to town,' said Jimmy. He was putting the violin away in its case.

'Must you?' said Jane. 'It's very early.'

'I think I must,' said Jimmy.

'But we haven't had any Debussy,' said Jane.

'We'll have him next time,' smiled Jimmy.

'We'll have Stephen next time, too,' said Jane.

'That will be delightful,' said Jimmy. The words might have seemed sarcastic if he had not been smiling so pleasantly. Suddenly, hat in hand, he crossed the room. He held out his hand to Jane. 'You must make Stephen like me,' he said disarmingly.

'He will,' said Jane. Looking up into Jimmy's charming faun-like face, Jane, at the moment, could not imagine any one not liking him.

'I hope he will, Jane,' said Jimmy. 'For I like you.'

'Stephen always likes people who like me,' said Jane loyally.

'Then that's just as it should be,' said Jimmy. 'When may I come again?'

'How about Tuesday?' said Jane. 'Come out to dinner. Take the five-fifty with Stephen.'

'I will,' said Jimmy. 'Good-night, kids! Now, all together, before I go! Do *you* like me? The answer is "yes"!'

In the resulting clamour Jimmy made his escape. He threw Jane one last smile from the threshold. As she heard the front door close behind him, Jane walked over to little Steve. For no reason whatever, she kissed him, very warmly.

'What are you smiling at, Mumsy?' said Jenny.

'Nothing,' said Jane. She ran her hand caressingly over Cicily's fair crinkly hair. She kissed Jenny's little freckled nose and pushed her toward the door.

'Go to bed, now, all of you,' said Jane. Left to herself, she picked up a book from the table and sat down in her chair to read it. She did not open it, however, but sat softly smiling, her eyes upon the fire. Stephen found her, sitting just like that, when he came home an hour later by the ten-ten.

'Bert's better,' he said from the doorway. 'And Muriel's in fine shape. She's taking everything very calmly. Young Albert gets home to-morrow!'

Jane realized that she had not once thought of Muriel since she had left the telephone after talking with Stephen five hours before. She felt suddenly conscious-stricken. She jumped up to help Stephen off with his coat.

'I'm glad,' she said. 'Did you fix everything up for her?' Even now, Jane felt she wasn't really thinking of Muriel. She did not give Stephen time to answer her question. 'Jimmy Trent was here for dinner,' she said.

'Jimmy Trent?'

'Yes. He came out unexpectedly. He brought his fiddle and sang to the children.'

'Can he sing?' Stephen was walking across the room to lock the glass doors that opened on the terrace.

'Yes. Quite nicely. He's very amusing. Stephen ——' Jane hesitated.

'Yes,' said Stephen, fumbling with a door-latch.

Jane did not answer. She had had it on the tip of her tongue to say 'Stephen, I think he's falling for me.' Then she remembered. She remembered the three weeks in which Jimmy had not telephoned. He was probably just getting a rise out of her that evening. Well — anyway, even so, he did not know that he had got it. That was a comfort. Of course he was not falling for her. He was Agnes's husband and, obviously, a very volatile young man.

'Yes?' said Stephen again, turning from the window.

'Oh — nothing,' said Jane. Stephen turned out the lights.

'If Bert lives,' said Jane, 'we ought to ask young Albert out here for the week-end. It would relieve Muriel, and Cicily would love to have him. Jack and Belle are coming.'

'All right,' said Stephen. Jane preceded him up the staircase. The spell invoked by Jimmy was already evaporating. She was glad that she had not said anything silly to Stephen. She was really a very silly woman, thought Jane, as she slipped out of the Poiret tea-gown. Jimmy did not mean anything by all that nonsense. It was just his line.

III

It happened just seven weeks later. It happened Thanksgiving afternoon, out beneath the apple tree beyond the little clump of evergreens at the foot of the garden. Jane was very much surprised when it did.

The seven weeks had been full of incident. She had been seeing Jimmy quite often, of course. He had come out perhaps once a week to dinner. She had lunched with him in town one day and gone with him to a concert that he had had to review for his paper. That was the only time, really, that they had been alone. He usually brought his fiddle when he came out to Lakewood and they had had lots of Debussy and a few more ballads. The children adored him, of course, and he had, somewhat to Jane's surprise, made rather a hit with Stephen. Jimmy had made rather a hit with every one, in fact. With her mother and Isabel and Flora and Muriel, who had had him to dinner just as soon as Bert was pronounced out of immediate danger, and declared him charming —

much too good, indeed, for Agnes. Mr. Ward had raised the
only dissenting voice. And all he had said was, after Jimmy
had spent an unusually scintillating evening at the Wards'
dinner-table, that Agnes deserved a better fate. Jane knew
that her father would think almost any fate unworthy of
Agnes. He had admired her since her first days at Miss Milgrim's School. When pressed by his indignant daughters for
further and more flattering comment, even Mr. Ward had admitted that Jimmy was very clever. He fitted delightfully in
Jane's most intimate circle. That was why she had asked him
out for Thanksgiving luncheon with the family.

Thanksgiving luncheon had been like all Thanksgiving
luncheons — not very brilliant. There had been too much
turkey and too many children to make for clever conversation
around the groaning board. Mr. Ward had sat on Jane's right
hand and Jimmy on her left. On either side of Stephen sat Mrs.
Ward and Isabel. Robin and Miss Parrot and the five children
filled up the centre of the table. They had eaten for nearly
two hours and then had sunk in recumbent attitudes around
the chintz-hung living-room. Suddenly, early in the afternoon, Jack Bridges had sprung to his feet and asked Cicily,
rather sheepishly, to go for a walk. She had deserted the
younger children immediately and, whistling to the cocker-
spaniel puppy, had started off with him across the terrace.
Jane had watched Jack help her, with adolescent gallantry, to
climb over the stile that led to the open meadows. She had
smiled, a trifle wistfully, over Cicily's budding coquetry.
Cicily could have cleared that stile at a bound. While she
was smiling, Jimmy had roused himself from lethargy. He too
had been watching the children.

' "The younger generation is knocking at the door," Jane,'
he had smiled. 'But they have the right idea. Come out and
walk five miles with me before sunset.'

She had gone for her hat and coat without a moment's hesitation. Every one was staying on for supper. The children were playing jack-straws, and Stephen was talking politics with Mr. Ward and Robin, and her mother and Isabel were discussing Bert Lancaster's paralysis, with an occasional digression on Flora's hat shop. She was not needed in the living-room and she would love a long walk.

They went out the terrace door and down the garden path and out into the fields in the opposite direction from the one which the children had taken. The November day was very cold and clear. The oak trees were already bare. The winter fields were brown. A high northwest wind was blowing across the Skokie Valley. It was difficult to talk in the teeth of the gale, and they had covered nearly two miles over the uneven stubble before they said much of anything. Then they paused in the shelter of a haystack.

'We must go back,' said Jane, trying to tuck her wind-blown pompadour under her felt hat-brim.

'Must we?' said Jimmy. 'This walk was just what I wanted.'

'I'm all out of breath,' said Jane. 'That last cornfield was rough going for an old lady.' She drew in a great gasp of the bracing autumn air.

'Was it?' said Jimmy. 'You don't look much older than Cicily this minute. Your cheeks are red and your eyes are bright and your mussy hair is pretty. That's the true test of age for a woman. She's young as long as she looks beguiling with mussy hair!'

'I look like a wild Indian,' said Jane, still struggling with the pompadour. 'You ought to look at Cicily when the wind gets romping with her head of excelsior.'

'That's Jack Bridges' privilege,' said Jimmy. 'I'm no cradle-snatcher.'

Jane left the haystack and started to walk back across the cornfield. It was easier to talk, now, with the wind at their backs. Nevertheless, they did not say anything for several minutes. Jane was hoping that Jack would bring Cicily home before dark. Jimmy broke the silence.

'Whose privilege was it, Jane, to look at you when you were Cicily's age?' he asked.

Jane started at the question. But she did not answer.

'I bet some one did,' said Jimmy. 'Who was he, Jane?'

'Oh,' said Jane vaguely, 'he — he was — just a boy.'

'A broth of a boy?' questioned Jimmy. 'Did you get much of a kick out of it?'

'Yes, I did,' said Jane simply.

Jimmy looked very much amused at her candour.

'We all do at that age,' he said cheerfully. 'I'll never forget the girl who fell off the mourners' bench.'

Jane felt very indignant at the tacit comparison.

'Oh!' she said quickly. 'He wasn't like that!'

'How do you know what she was like?' smiled Jimmy.

'I know she wasn't like André,' said Jane. The name had slipped out unconsciously.

'Do you mean that André never taught you anything you couldn't learn at a camp meeting?' queried Jimmy. 'Oh, Jane!'

'I mean that André wasn't like any one — any one else I've ever met,' said Jane.

'My God!' said Jimmy, addressing the empty November sky. 'She never got over him! I hope,' he continued severely, 'that you confessed him to Stephen.'

'Oh, I confessed him to Stephen,' said Jane.

Again Jimmy looked very much amused at her candour.

'Good girl!' he said approvingly. 'You must always confess them to Stephen.'

Jane thought that her mother would think that Jimmy was taking the marriage vows lightly. She almost thought so herself.

'There haven't been any others,' she said severely.

'Do you expect me to believe that?' said Jimmy.

'Not *really* any others,' said Jane.

'While there's life there's hope,' said Jimmy.

'I don't *want* any others,' said Jane indignantly.

'Oh, Jane!' said Jimmy.

'I don't,' protested Jane. 'I think clandestine love affairs would be horribly inconvenient.'

'There are higher things than convenience,' said Jimmy sublimely.

Jane ignored his comment.

'And I think,' she went on, 'they'd be dreadfully smirching and soiling. And too terrible to look back on when they were over. They *would* be over, you know. You get over loving any one ——'

'Oh!' said Jimmy. 'You've discovered *that*, have you?'

'No, I haven't!' said Jane quickly. 'I — I've just — observed it.'

Jimmy chuckled quietly to himself. They walked nearly half a mile in silence. As they entered the garden, he resumed the conversation.

'You *do* get over loving any one, Jane,' he said gently. 'But you don't always regret that love in retrospect.'

Jane thought that sounded very sweet and understanding.

'Perhaps not,' she said. By this time they had reached the apple tree.

Jimmy paused for a moment beside the clump of evergreens. Jane looked up at him with a smile. They had had a nice walk.

'Jane,' said Jimmy suddenly, 'are you really as innocent as you seem?'

Jane's eyes widened in astonishment. Jimmy's eyes were very bright. His breath was coming quickly and a funny excited little smile twisted the corners of his mouth.

'You're like a child, Jane,' said Jimmy. 'An inexperienced child!'

Jane still stared at him.

'Jane,' said Jimmy suddenly, 'I'm going to kiss you.' And he caught her suddenly in his arms and turned her face to his.

'Jimmy!' cried Jane in horror. 'Jimmy!' His lips stopped her words. He kissed her long and ardently. Jane struggled in his arms. His cheek scratched her face. She pulled herself from his embrace and stood staring at him in the garden path.

'Oh, Jimmy!' she cried again. 'How — how *could* you?'

Suddenly she remembered the house at the end of the garden. She glanced quickly, fearfully, at the white clapboard façade. The clump of evergreens hid the living-room windows. But was that Miss Parrot's white sleeve in the playroom bay above? Jane felt suddenly overwhelmed with a sense of humiliation. She had been kissed — kissed like a pretty chambermaid in her own garden. She had glanced at her own front windows, fearful of a spying servant's ironical eye.

'Jimmy,' she said, 'I wouldn't have *believed* it of you!' He was looking down at her, now, still breathing rather quickly. The excited little smile still twisted the corners of his mouth. He looked more like a faun than ever, thought Jane, with an unconscious shiver. 'Will you please go back to Chicago, now, at once?' she said with dignity. 'Will you please go back without coming into the house?'

Jimmy looked very much astonished.

'Why, Jane — Jane ——' he faltered. 'Do you really mind, so awfully?'

'I'm going in,' said Jane. 'And I don't want you to follow me.' She turned abruptly away from him and walked up the garden path to the terrace, trying to put her face in order. She opened the terrace door and entered the living-room. The family were all still lounging about the fire.

'Where's Jimmy?' asked Isabel.

'He's gone,' said Jane, turning her back on them to close the terrace door. 'He wasn't staying to supper. He had to get back to the "News."' Lies, she thought contemptuously, lies, forced on her by Jimmy, forced on her by her own damnable lack of foresight! She ought to have known what was coming. She ought to have prevented it. She turned from the door and faced the family tranquilly.

'What's up, Jane?' asked Robin. 'You look like an avenging angel. Your cheeks are as red as fire.'

'It's just the wind,' said Jane. More lies! 'There's a perfect tornado blowing.' She raised her hands to rearrange her pompadour. As she did so, she rubbed her fingers violently across her mouth. She could still feel Jimmy's lips there. She could feel his kiss, still vibrating through her entire body. Suddenly she caught her father's eye. Mr. Ward was sitting comfortably in Stephen's armchair beside the smouldering fire. Behind a cloud of cigar smoke he was watching his younger daughter very intently. Jane managed to achieve a smile. No one else was paying any attention to her whatever. Jane sat down on the sofa beside Isabel and tried to listen to what she had to say about the cubistic designs that Flora was painting on the wall of the old coach-house. Isabel thought they were very comic. Mrs. Ward thought they were hardly respectable. Mr. Ward continued to watch them all from behind the cloud of cigar smoke. Jane tried to look as if she had forgotten that kiss.

IV

Mrs. Lester's living-room was in festive array for a very gala occasion. The occasion was Mrs. Lester's seventy-fifth birthday. When Jane entered the room with Stephen and the children, she could not see her hostess, at first, in the crowd of people who were laughing and talking around the hearth beneath the Murillo Madonna. Mr. and Mrs. Ward were there, and Flora and Mr. Furness, and Isabel and Robin, and Rosalie and Freddy Waters, of course. Edith and her husband had come on from Cleveland for the celebration and Muriel had invited Cyril Fortune. Bert Lancaster was not yet out of his bed. Rosalie's daughter was in school in Paris and Edith's son was in Oxford, but young Albert was there, home from Saint Paul's for the Christmas vacation, so Isabel had brought Jack and Belle and Jane had brought Cicily and Jenny and little Steve. It was little Steve's first dinner-party. The children were to eat at a separate table in a corner of the dining-room.

Mrs. Lester was sitting in her wheel-chair on one corner of the hearthrug. Enormously fat and somewhat crippled with gout, she had not left her wheel-chair for years. She still gave parties, however, great gay parties, and was pushed to the head of her dining-room table to preside over them with all her old-time gaiety. Her three dark-haired daughters and their attendant husbands had never ceased to flutter about her. They weren't dark-haired any longer, of course. Edith was really white-headed, slim, worn, and distinguished at forty-three. Pretty Rosalie was growing grey, and even Muriel had one white Whistler lock, that she rather exploited, in the centre of her dark pompadour. Mrs. Lester herself, with her straight snow-white hair, her wrinkled, yellow face, and her great gaunt nose hooked over her ridiculous cascade of double chins, had come to look much more Jewish with advancing years. In spite of her invincible gaiety, her large dark eyes, with yellow whites, were shadowed with racial sadness. No eyes, thought Jane, were ever as beautiful as Jewish eyes. Mrs. Lester's had always touched her profoundly. They were twinkling now, up at Mr. Ward, as she sat enthroned on the hearthrug. An enormous bowl of seventy-five American beauties nodded over her snowy head. Jane kissed her with real emotion. Then turned to Muriel.

'How is Bert to-night?' she asked.

'Oh — Bert's fine,' said Muriel easily. 'He's going to sit up next week. They've given him exercises for his arm. They think he'll get some motion back.'

'I see,' said Isabel, at Muriel's elbow, 'you asked Cyril to fill his place.'

'Cyril's always helpful,' grinned Muriel shamelessly. 'He does what he can.'

'Who else is coming?' asked Isabel interestedly. 'You're still a man short.'

'Jimmy Trent,' said Muriel, smiling. 'I asked *him* for our Jane.'

Jane glanced casually at her father, then turned, to smell an American beauty, rather elaborately. She had not expected this. She had not seen Jimmy since she had turned away from him, five weeks before, under the apple tree in the Lakewood garden. He had telephoned three times, but Jane had not gone to the telephone. He had not written, for which fact Jane was devoutly thankful. She felt somehow very unequal to answering that unwritten letter and still more unequal to the melodramatic gesture of sending it back unread. She had known, of course, that she would have to meet Jimmy sometime, but she had not anticipated that meeting at Mrs. Lester's seventy-fifth birthday-party. She was wondering just how to handle it when Jimmy appeared at the living-room door.

Muriel moved quickly to meet him and Jane slipped quietly away from Mrs. Lester's side before he came up to present his compliments. She began talking to Freddy Waters in a great burst of gaiety. In a moment the butler appeared at the dining-room door. He announced dinner and moved to push Mrs. Lester's chair in to the table. Almost immediately Jane heard Jimmy's voice at her elbow.

'I found your name in my envelope in the dressing-room, Jane,' he said, 'and you can bet your life I was glad to see it there.' He offered his arm with a smile. His eyes, however, looked very serious. Freddy Waters had gone off in quest of Isabel. The dinner-party was passing into the dining-room, two by two.

Jane rested her finger-tips on Jimmy's black broadcloth sleeve. She felt there was nothing whatever to say to him. Jimmy looked anxiously down at her as they joined the little procession. Jane saw her father watching them as he offered his arm to Edith. Mr. Furness had gone in with Mrs. Lester.

'Can't you forgive me, Jane?' asked Jimmy earnestly, as they entered the dining-room.

'I don't know,' said Jane. 'I still don't understand at all how you could have done such a thing.'

'Don't you, Jane?' said Jimmy wistfully. 'Don't you, really?'

'I don't understand how you could have done it to me,' said Jane.

'I didn't know,' said Jimmy, pulling out her chair for her as they reached the table — 'I didn't know that you would take it quite so seriously.'

Jane seated herself in silence.

'I've taken it seriously myself,' said Jimmy, 'since I did it.' He sat down at her side.

'I'm very glad to hear it,' said Jane severely.

'And you'll forgive me?' said Jimmy.

'I don't know,' said Jane again. She turned to look into his contrite eyes. There was something irresistibly funny about a penitent faun. Jane could not help smiling. Jimmy drew a long breath at the sight of her smile.

'You *have* forgiven me!' he said triumphantly.

Jane saw her father looking at him from across the table. She wished that Jimmy had not spoken quite so loudly. Then despised herself for the wish.

'Don't let's talk about it any longer,' she said evenly. 'It happened, and I wish it hadn't. But it doesn't do any good to go on harping on it.'

'I don't want to harp on it!' cried Jimmy jubilantly. 'I don't want to harp on anything you don't want to hear.' He was looking at her now, with just the same old look of friendly admiration. 'Let's talk about the weather.'

They did, with mock solemnity. Then they talked of other things. Of Jimmy's reviews, which were making quite a sensation in the 'Daily News'; of Agnes's play, which was already half-written; of Cicily, shaking her dandelion head at Jack at the foot of the children's table; of Mrs. Lester, nodding her white one at Mr. Furness at the head of theirs; of the charms of fourteen and of the charms of seventy-five. Jane was quite sorry when Mrs. Lester turned the conversation at the beginning of the salad course and she had to begin to talk to Edith's husband of the charms of living in Cleveland — if there were any, which Jane very much doubted.

Later, when the men joined the women in the living-room, Jane was rather surprised to find herself talking to her father. He sat down beside her on the green brocade sofa with a sigh of satisfaction.

'I don't see enough of you, Kid,' he said cheerfully. 'Nor enough of Stephen. What with all the grandchildren, I

hardly spoke to either of you on Christmas Day. I'm going
to put in the evening catching up on what you've been doing.'

'I haven't been doing much,' said Jane. 'Just Christmas
shopping.'

'Many town parties?' asked Mr. Ward.

'None in the holidays,' said Jane. 'I'm too busy with the
children.'

'Much company in the country?'

'No one but the children's friends.'

'Jimmy been out often?'

Jane looked straight into her father's eyes.

'He hasn't been out since that luncheon on Thanksgiving
Day,' she said.

Mr. Ward settled back against the sofa cushions.

'What do you hear from Agnes, Kid?' he asked.

v

Motoring out to Lakewood when the party was over, tucked
in beside Stephen in the front seat of their little Overland,
with the children asleep in the tonneau behind them, Jane
felt very happy over the events of the evening. She would not
have believed it possible that she could have arrived so easily
at an understanding with Jimmy. He was obviously very
sorry and she had made her attitude quite clear. Jimmy
knew now that she was not to be kissed like a chambermaid,
caught in an upper corridor. Jimmy knew now that she was
not entertained by philandering. Jimmy knew now that she
was not that sort of wife to Stephen and that the idea of flirt-
ing with Agnes's husband was, to her, unthinkable. Jimmy
knew all those things, though they had not referred to his
mistake again after they left the table. Jane had hardly
spoken to Jimmy all the latter part of the evening. Jane had
talked to her father and Jimmy had hung devotedly over

Muriel. He had entered into open competition with Cyril Fortune for her favour and by the end of the party the blond young landscape-gardener was quite sunk in depression. Stephen had talked with his cousin Flora about her new hat shop. He had given her some splendid ideas about cost accounting. Flora had told Jane she was very grateful. Flora was not much of a bookkeeper.

How wise she had been, thought Jane, how very wise, not to have said anything to Stephen about that kiss. Not that wisdom had really entered into her decision to keep silent. In fact, all those weeks, when she had been wondering whether or no to talk to Stephen about it, she had felt that the wiser course would be to make a clean breast of the whole affair. And yet she hadn't. Partly, of course, because of what Stephen would think of Jimmy, but even more because of what Stephen would think of her. Jane thought very little of herself, as she reviewed the incident. Jimmy had been outrageous — Jimmy had been insulting. Yet Jane could not quite bring herself to tell the story to Stephen in the rôle of the betrayed damsel. Jane knew that she had been growing very fond of Jimmy. Jane knew that she had liked his flattering attention. And Jane knew that, though she had not expected his kiss and certainly had resented it, yet, after she had had it, she had not been able to get it out of her mind, out, indeed, of the very fibre of her being. That was the kind of thing a wife could not tell a husband — not a husband like Stephen, at least, who had never even glanced at another woman since the day he had married her. Stephen would never understand how she could have thought about that kiss, the way she had. And if she did not tell him that, she really would not be telling him anything. Half-truths had no place in conjugal confidence. Half-truths were cowardly, misleading. Half-truths were really lies. Whereas silence was — merely silence. No —

it was not the kiss half as much as the way she had felt about it.

What was a kiss, after all? Lots of women were kissed. Some of them had told her about it. Muriel was often kissed, and thought nothing of it. It was the thinking something of it that really counted. Jane had been awfully troubled.

But now, she felt, she had been very wise not to tell Stephen. The incident was over. It was forgiven and — well, if not yet forgotten, it soon would be. Jane hoped she was not going to spend the rest of her life remembering that Stephen's wife had been kissed by Agnes's husband and had liked it. Yes, *liked* it, in retrospect. Jimmy had learned his lesson. It would not happen again.

Jimmy had not even asked when he might come out to see her. When he had said good-night, he had left her to interpret the expression of his wistful eyes in silence. It was Stephen who had said in parting, 'How about dinner on Friday, Jimmy? It's fish night. You ought to taste Jane's receipt for planked whitefish!' Even then he had not responded with a questioning glance at her. She had slipped her arm through Stephen's and said serenely, 'Of course, Jimmy. Just a family party.' And he had accepted without undue rejoicing. No grateful, penitent glances. Nothing to shame her before Stephen's innocence.

Jimmy knew, now. There would be no more mistakes in the future. Jane snuggled down against Stephen's shoulder under the furry laprobe. He took his eyes from the road a moment to smile down into her face.

'Nice party, wasn't it?' said Stephen.

'I had a lovely time,' said Jane, smiling softly. She kept on smiling all the way to Lakewood. A sleepy, reassured, little smile.

CHAPTER IV

I

THE April sunshine was slanting in Jane's open bedroom window. The pale, profuse sunshine of early April, flickering through the bare boughs of the oak trees. The crocuses were blooming in the garden. The daffodils nodded their yellow heads in the bed beneath the evergreens. The apple tree was an emerald mist of tiny budding leaves.

Jane sat at the window, sewing a fresh lace collar in the neck of a new rose-coloured gown and talking to Miss Parrot. From her chair she could see Jenny, swooping luxuriously up and down in the swing beneath the apple tree, and hear Steve, concealed in the upper branches, clamouring vociferously for his turn.

'I really hate to leave him,' said Miss Parrot. 'But he'll be all right now, Mrs. Carver, if you just watch him a little. Don't let him race around too much this summer. And of course no competitive sports.'

Jane nodded, over her sewing. She was awfully glad, of course, that little Steve's heart was really so much better, but almost gladder, she thought with a smile, that she would no longer have to talk to Miss Parrot at table, three times a day, or listen to her unasked advice on little Steve's care. Of course, she had been wonderful. She was a very good heart nurse. Still, it had been irritating, having her around under foot all winter, a tacit critic of Jane's every action, an alien observer of her every thought. But it was over now. Little Steve had completely recovered. Dr. Bancroft had dismissed Miss Parrot. She was going in three days.

'You'll see that he takes his tonic,' said Miss Parrot.

'Of course,' said Jane, with a hint of irritation in her voice.

'Well, I hope Sarah remembers it when you're out,' said Miss Parrot, with a sigh of resignation.

Jane looked up from her sewing at Miss Parrot's starched, immaculate figure. She met her pleasant, impersonal eye. She wished dispassionately that she could push Miss Parrot out of her bedroom by main force. Suddenly Sarah appeared in the doorway.

'Mr. Trent to see you, madam,' she said impassively.

Jane jumped to her feet.

'Mr. Trent? Downstairs?' Jane glanced at the little French clock on the mantelpiece. It pointed exactly to three. Jimmy had said he was taking the three-nineteen. He was an hour ahead of time. She thrust her sewing into Miss Parrot's hand. 'Miss Parrot,' she said hastily, 'just baste this collar in for me, will you? As quickly as you can, please. I'm wearing it this afternoon. And, Sarah — I want tea in the living-room at four. We won't wait for Mr. Carver. Toast, please, and anchovy sandwiches, and some of that sponge cake we had at luncheon.' She was already slipping out of her morning gown. 'Tell Mr. Trent I will be down immediately.'

Sarah turned from the door. Jane sat down hastily at her dressing-table and began to take down her hair. Miss Parrot had seated herself at the window and was picking up Jane's thimble. Jane could catch her reflection in the slanting plane of the cheval glass, near the dressing-table. She was looking at Jane with a faint smile of cynical amusement. Her eye was no longer impersonal. Jane hated Miss Parrot, at the moment. She hated herself for that question she had never been able to answer — *had* that been Miss Parrot's white sleeve in the playroom bay window, that Thanksgiving afternoon when Jimmy —— She pushed in the last hairpin and rose to her feet.

'Ready, Miss Parrot?' she said evenly.

'Yes,' said Miss Parrot, handing her the gown. She lingered a moment, to put away the thimble and close the sewing box. Again she looked Jane over with that not impersonal eye. 'You look very pretty, Mrs. Carver,' she said.

Jane dabbed a little perfume on her cheeks and hurried from the room without answering. In the hall she stumbled over the children's cocker spaniel. It yelped sharply, then wagged its tail and started after her down the stairs. At the foot of them Jane saw Belle, just starting up for Cicily's room. She and Jack were coming out for the week-end. They must have been on the train with Jimmy. The child looked up at her with wide, round eyes of admiration. The eyes were so round and the admiration so apparent that Jane stopped and laughed down at her. Belle was really charming. She looked like an apple blossom.

'Hello, little Belle,' said Jane.

At the sound of her voice, Jimmy Trent came out of the living-room. He looked taller than he really was, beside the staring child. His eyes were very bright and blue and his necktie exactly matched them. He stood smiling up at her from the foot of the staircase. As Jane ran down the last steps, he took her hand and held it for a minute. Jane laughed up at him.

'You know little Belle Bridges,' she said, withdrawing her hand.

'Of course I do,' said Jimmy. 'Hello, little Belle Bridges!' He too smiled down at the child. Jane stooped over and kissed little Belle's cheek. It felt very smooth and cool, like the petal of an apple blossom. The little spaniel was jumping forgivingly about her feet. Jane picked it up and held it tenderly in her arms and kissed the top of its little black head and looked up at Jimmy over its long, floppy ears. Then they turned away from Belle toward the living-room door.

'I didn't expect you 'til four,' said Jane, smiling up at Jimmy over the spaniel.

He paused to let her precede him through the living-room door.

'I couldn't wait to play you my last cadenza,' said Jimmy. 'Jane, that concerto is finished. I couldn't wait an hour ——'

'Silly!' said Jane, looking over her shoulder at Jimmy, as they passed into the living-room. In a moment she heard little Belle, scrambling upstairs to Cicily's bedroom. 'But I can't wait myself to hear it. Oh, Jimmy, I can't believe — truly I can't believe — that you've really done it.'

'You know who made me,' said Jimmy. His eyes searched hers for a moment, before he turned to pick up his fiddle-case from the table. 'It's really your concerto.' He tucked his violin under his chin and tuned it airily as he strolled across the room, just as he had done on that first Lakewood evening. He took his stand on the hearthrug, bow in hand, and looked down at her. 'Your concerto, Jane,' he repeated. It seemed to Jane, at the moment, a very solemn dedication. She looked up at Jimmy very seriously as he raised his bow. She never took her eyes off his slender, swaying figure, until the last note had sounded.

'It's beautiful, Jimmy,' she said then, solemnly, 'it's very beautiful.'

'You know why, don't you?' said Jimmy, looking down at her from the hearthrug.

Just then Sarah came in with the tea.

II

'You wouldn't think it was so funny,' said Isabel scathingly, 'if you'd heard Muriel talking about it yesterday in Flora's hat shop. She didn't even stop when I came in.'

'I don't think it's funny,' said Jane loftily. 'I think it's ridiculous.'

'Muriel ought to be ashamed of herself,' said Mrs. Ward.

They were all sitting around the fire in Mr. Ward's library, waiting for Minnie to bring in the tea-tray.

'She said it was as plain as a pikestaff,' said Isabel. 'She said it right before me. She said that just as soon as she and Flora came in they saw you two sitting over at a corner table. She said that you had a quart of champagne, Jane, and that you said something and that Jimmy smiled and lifted his glass and looked at you and kissed the rim before he drank from it.'

'It was only a pint,' said Jane. 'We were drinking to the success of his concerto. He finished it last week.'

'It was very unfortunate,' said Mrs. Ward, 'that Muriel had to come in at just that moment.'

'It was very unfortunate,' said Isabel severely, 'that Jane had to be there at all. If you want to lunch with him, Jane, why can't you lunch at the Blackstone or the Casino as if you'd *like* to be seen, instead of sneaking off to a place like De Jonche's where no one you know *ever* goes ——'

'We *didn't* sneak,' said Jane hotly. 'And we go to De Jonche's because we both like snails. They have the best in town.'

'You *go?*' said Mrs. Ward. 'Had you been there before?'

'Often,' said Jane briefly.

'When I was your age,' said Mrs. Ward, 'it was as much as a young married woman's reputation was worth to be caught lunching with a man who was not her husband ——'

'Oh, nonsense, Mamma!' interrupted Isabel. 'Every one lunches with men, nowadays. It all depends on how you do it. Of course, as for Jimmy's kissing the rim of his champagne glass in a public restaurant ——' She stopped abruptly as Minnie came in with the tea-tray. Minnie loved family gossip, but she was never allowed to hear any. Minnie had been twenty-five years in Mrs. Ward's service, and in all those years Mrs. Ward had never failed to change the conversation from the personal plane whenever she entered the room.

'I wonder where your father is?' she said now, in a note of hollow inquiry, as Minnie, wheezing slightly, placed the heavy silver tray on the tea-table. Minnie, at fifty-three, was rather plump and puffy. She had recently developed a chronic asthma. But she never allowed any one else to wait on Mrs. Ward.

'Hello, Minnie!' said Jane.

Minnie smiled her acknowledgement of the greeting.

'How are the children, Mrs. Carver?' she asked. Then bending solicitously over Mrs. Ward. 'Don't you eat too much of that plum cake, Mrs. Ward. It's too rich for your blood pressure.' Her cap slightly askew on her iron-grey hair, she made a triumphant exit.

'Does Minnie think plum cake sends up blood pressure?' smiled Jane.

'She's really getting impossible,' said Isabel.

'Sometimes I think she takes more interest in my condition than you children do,' said Mrs. Ward. She poured out a cup of tea for Isabel.

'No sugar, Mamma,' said Isabel. Then, returning to the charge, 'Well, Jane, I think you ought to cut it out.'

'Cut *what* out?' said Jane angrily. 'Two lumps, Mamma.'

'Cut out those clubby little parties à *deux*, with a pint of champagne. When Muriel starts talking ——'

'*She's* a good one to talk,' said Mrs. Ward.

'Set a thief to catch a thief!' laughed Isabel.

'Oh, Isabel, *shut up!*' said Jane, in a sudden, snappish return to the vernacular of her childhood. She had not said 'shut up' to Isabel for more than twenty years. As the words left her lips, Mr. Ward entered the room. He came in just as he always did, and laid the evening paper on his desk and began to turn over the afternoon mail.

'Hello, Kid!' he said tranquilly. 'Why must Isabel shut up?'

'Because she's an ass!' said Jane, still rather snappishly. Mr. Ward raised a quizzical eyebrow.

'So are we all of us,' he said pleasantly, 'sometimes.' Then, running his paper-cutter through an envelope, 'What's Isabel been doing now?'

'Talking,' said Jane briefly. 'And listening. And repeating silly gossip.'

Mr. Ward looked as if he thought Isabel had merely been running true to form.

'That all?' he said, with a smile.

'I've been telling Jane,' said Isabel, 'that she's getting herself talked about.'

'Oh!' said Mr. Ward. 'Lizzie, could you make me a cup of weak tea?' He dropped his mail and sat down in his leather chair, lowering himself into it rather carefully, his hands on the arms. 'It's like summer out,' he said pleasantly. 'Makes me think of the old days when I used to walk home from the office. The Furnesses' lilacs are almost in bud.'

'They don't bud any more, Papa,' said Jane. 'The soot is killing them.'

'One does,' said Mr. Ward. 'Thank you, Lizzie. The one by the old playhouse.'

'It's terrible,' sighed Mrs. Ward, 'what's happening to the neighbourhood.'

Jane knew just what her mother thought about what was happening to the neighbourhood. She walked over to the window and stood staring across Pine Street at the new flat building that had gone up in the opposite yard the previous autumn.

'Boarding-houses,' said Mrs. Ward, 'and dressmakers and apartments —— ' Jane was no longer listening. She stood staring out of the window at the terra-cotta façade of the flat building, thinking furious thoughts about Isabel — and Muriel — and a world in which you could not phrase a funny little toast to a man's concerto, without —— Presently she heard her father get up and go out of the room. Jane glanced at her watch.

'I must go,' she said. 'I'm motoring out to Lakewood.'

'Are you picking up Stephen?' asked Mrs. Ward.

'No,' said Jane. 'He prefers the train.' She kissed her mother's cheek. 'Good-bye, Isabel,' she added coldly.

'Now, Jane — don't be a dumb-bell,' said Isabel cheerfully. 'You think over what I said.'

Jane left the room without stooping to further discord. In the hall she met her father. He was standing there, outside the library door, exactly as if he were waiting for some one. He slipped his arm through hers and walked to the front door. Jane opened it.

'Good-bye, Papa,' she said. There was a note of finality in her tone. He followed her out onto the front steps, however. He stood a moment on the top one, gently detaining her by his restraining arm.

'Kid,' said Mr. Ward, 'I know you're a grown woman, but you seem just like a child to me.'

Jane smiled, a little nervously. She did not speak.

'But you're a wise child, Kid,' went on Mr. Ward, 'and I wouldn't presume to dictate on your conduct.' He too smiled just a little nervously. Jane still stood silent. 'I'll only trespass on the parental prerogatives so far as to urge you,' said Mr. Ward, 'to avoid all appearance of evil. It's a wicked world.'

'Papa,' said Jane, 'I haven't been doing anything I shouldn't.'

'I'm sure you haven't,' said Mr. Ward quickly.

'It's just Muriel's nonsense. You know Muriel.'

'Yes, I know Muriel,' said Mr. Ward. 'That's why I urge you to avoid all appearance of evil.' He stood looking steadily at Jane. The nervousness had left his smile. His eyes looked worried, however. His eyes looked tired, Jane thought. His eyes looked old. They seemed a darker brown since his hair had turned so white. Jane kissed him, tenderly.

'I will, Papa,' she said. 'Don't worry.' Then she ran down the steps and jumped into the Overland. She glanced back to wave at her father. He was still standing on the top step, looking after her with that faintly troubled expression. Jane forgot him as she set the gears in motion. Her thoughts returned, angrily, to Isabel. That luncheon was perfectly harmless. Muriel, of course, was always malicious, but Isabel ought to have more *sense*.

III

Jane could not, however, keep her angry thoughts on Isabel. The April afternoon was very warm and fair. The elm trees were budding down the stretch of Pine Street. The bushes in the park around the Water Works Tower were already green. Jane saw the bench where she and André had sat to look at the pictures of Sarah Bernhardt. She remembered Muriel's adolescent giggle. Muriel was an idiot, even then.

The lake stretched, softly blue beyond the Oak Street breakers. A gaunt skyscraper or two loomed up on the filled-in land to the southeast. A whole section of the city had been created there since Jane's childhood. Created from garbage and tin cans and rags and old iron. Apartments were going up in the waste of empty land. Magnificent red-brick and grey-stone apartments, with liveried doormen and marble entrance halls and wrought-iron elevators, standing where once there had been only blue water. Blue water beyond the vacant lots where sweet clover and ragweed had bloomed. Jane felt like the first white child born west of the Alleghenies when she looked at them. She had seen Chicago change from a provincial town into the sixth largest city in the world.

She turned the car abruptly from the Drive at the Division Street corner. She was going to pick up Jimmy at his North State Street boarding-house and motor him out to Lakewood for the week-end. They would have lovely weather. One more hot day like this, thought Jane, and perhaps the apple tree would burst into bloom.

Jimmy was standing on the curbstone, his suitcase at his feet.

'Am I late?' asked Jane anxiously, as she brought the car to a standstill.

'No — I'm early,' said Jimmy. He opened the door of the motor and slipped into the seat beside her. 'I thought maybe you'd come sooner than you said.'

'I was having tea with Mamma,' said Jane, 'and talking to Isabel.' She set the gears in motion.

'What about?' asked Jimmy.

'Oh, nothing,' said Jane. 'Nothing much.' Suddenly she decided to tell him. 'Muriel told Isabel about seeing us at De Jonche's yesterday,' she said, her eyes on the street before her.

'What was there to tell?' asked Jimmy innocently.

'Oh — Muriel can always make a good story,' said Jane. There was a little pause. Jane knew Jimmy was looking at her profile.

'Well — do you care?' asked Jimmy presently.

'Oh, no,' said Jane falsely. 'No — not at all. Only ——' She stopped.

'Only what?' asked Jimmy gently.

'Only it seems too bad that people have to try to spoil lovely things. To — to smirch them, you know, with ugly gossip and false interpretations.' Again Jane stopped.

'They can't spoil them really, Jane,' said Jimmy very seriously. 'No one could ever spoil what happens between you and me but just ourselves.'

That was just like Jimmy, thought Jane, smiling softly at the North State Street traffic. It was just like Jimmy to understand. He had perfectly phrased the thought she had been groping for ever since her angry altercation with Isabel. As long as she and Jimmy kept their heads and — well — did not allow anything — anything silly to happen, there was nothing in their friendship to be ashamed of.

And it would so soon be over. Jimmy's job at the 'News' would be ended in a fortnight. His friend was on the water now, coming back from Munich. They had had a lovely winter — the loveliest winter, Jane thought, that she had ever known. Jimmy had written his reviews and had finished his concerto, and she — she had never been so happy, really, with Stephen and the children, never so contented at Lakewood, never so sure and satisfied, in her secret heart, that life was worth living, that it would always, somehow, be fun to live.

There had been, of course, Miss Parrot's cynical smile and Sarah's impassive silence and Muriel's malicious twinkle and her father's troubled eyes. And now there was Isabel's uncalled-for interference. It was, as her father had just said, a wicked world. But she and Jimmy had never exchanged a word that she could be sorry for. Never said anything, really, that Stephen might not have heard. Stephen, himself, had never been troubled. Stephen liked Jimmy. Stephen knew she was to be implicitly trusted.

And now Jimmy was going — going in two weeks — back
to New York to the Greenwich Village flat and the big and
little Agneses. And Jane — Jane would be left in Lakewood
to — to watch the spring come and buy the children's thin
clothes and clean the house and pack up for the Gull Rocks
summer. Jane sighed a little as she thought of the months before her. Just like all other spring months, of course. But she
would miss Jimmy dreadfully, and she would never see him
again, of course, just as she had this last lovely winter. He
would go back to New York and produce the concerto and
become suddenly distinguished. Suddenly distinguished,
really, a little bit because of her. Of course it was absurd of
Jimmy to call it her concerto, but Jane knew that she had
kept him working. Her encouragement and enthusiasm had
spurred him on. Yes, both she and Jimmy would always be a
little better for the winter's friendship, which no one but themselves could ever spoil. No one but themselves could ever
understand it, really — a simple friendship that had meant
so much to them, a joy of companionship ——

'A penny for your thoughts, Jane?' said Jimmy.

'I was just thinking of us,' said Jane, 'and of all that's
happened this winter.'

'Have you really liked it?' asked Jimmy.

'Oh, yes,' breathed Jane. Then, after a moment, 'It seems
so funny, now, to think I didn't think I would, when Agnes
first wrote me you were coming. I thought you'd be *terrible*,
Jimmy ——'

'I *am* terrible,' said Jimmy, with a smile.

'Oh, no, you're not,' said Jane very wisely.

'You don't know the half of it,' said Jimmy.

'Yes, I do,' said Jane. 'I know pretty nearly the whole of
it. I understand you perfectly.'

'Sure you do?' said Jimmy.

'I know you can do great things if you're prodded by a little encouragement ——'

'Say rather if I'm prodded by "the endearing elegance of female friendship,"' said Jimmy, still with the smile. 'It does more for a man than you know. There's a little lyric of A. E. Housman's, Jane — I wonder if you remember it? — it has always been a particular favourite of mine.' Still smiling into her appreciative eyes, he quoted lightly:

> 'Oh, when I was in love with you,
>   Then I was clean and brave,
> And miles around the wonder grew
>   How well did I behave.'

'Well,' laughed Jane a little confusedly, 'even so, what of it? As long as you *do* behave, you know.'

'There's a second verse,' said Jimmy warningly.

> 'And now the fancy passes by,
>   And nothing will remain,
> And miles around they'll say that I
>   Am quite myself again.'

Jane felt unaccountably disappointed in the second verse. She summoned up a laugh, however.

'I call that cynical,' she said. 'It won't be that way with you. As soon as you get to New York, Jimmy, you must show that concerto to Damrosch. I know he'll like it. And you must write something else. Something else immediately, while you're still in the mood for it.'

'Perhaps I won't be in the mood for it,' said Jimmy. 'I don't feel as if I'd be much in the mood for anything when I get back to New York.'

'You've been working awfully hard,' said Jane sympathetically. 'I liked what you wrote last week about Mischa Elman. You're right. No other living violinist has his combination of warmth and light — of feeling, yet detachment ——'

They talked of Mischa Elman's concert all the way to Lakewood. Stephen was waiting for dinner and reading a King Arthur story aloud to the children when they entered the living-room. He was glad to see Jimmy and glad, too, of the soft spring weather.

'We'll have eighteen holes of golf to-morrow morning, Jimmy,' he said cheerfully. 'Don't dress, Jane. I'm as hungry as a bear.'

But Jane thought she would just slip into the red Poiret tea-gown. It would not take a minute.

IV

That evening Jimmy played parchesi with the children. Jane sat at Steve's elbow and advised him on his moves. Stephen lounged in his armchair and read the 'Evening Post.' Stephen was no parchesi fan. He was glad to be relieved of a duty that had devolved upon him every evening since Miss Parrot's departure the week before. Jane thought the game was really quite amusing. They laughed a great deal over Steve's success with the dice. He sent Jimmy's foremost man home eight times in succession. It was half-past nine before the game was over.

When the children had gone upstairs, Stephen cast aside his paper with a yawn.

'I'm tired to-night,' he said. 'This first hot weather takes it out of you. I'm going up to bed.'

Jane caught a glint of elation in Jimmy's eye across Stephen's unconscious figure. Jane did not like that glint. Of course, Jimmy just wanted to sit and gossip by the fire as they had so often gossiped, but he should not have allowed himself to look elated. Curiously, at that moment, Jane thought of her father. 'Avoid all appearance of evil.' She thought also of Sarah, washing dishes in the pantry.

'I'm tired, too, Stephen,' she said evenly. 'I'd like to turn in early myself.'

The glint of elation in Jimmy's eyes turned quickly to a look of incredulity, then to one of mock consternation.

'See here,' he protested, '*I'm* not tired. I'm not tired at all. I was looking forward to a big evening.'

'Sorry,' smiled Jane. 'You're not going to get it.' She turned with Stephen toward the door.

'See here,' said Jimmy again, 'are you just going off to bed and leave me standing here on the hearthrug? I don't call it civil.'

'That's just what we're going to do,' smiled Jane. 'Good-night.'

'It's a sell,' said Jimmy. 'It's not ten o'clock yet. What will I do with myself? I can't go to sleep for hours. I'll be reduced to writing a letter to Agnes!'

The mention of Agnes's name instantly confirmed Jane's plan to go up with Stephen. He had already started for the stairs.

'That's a fine idea, Jimmy,' said Jane pleasantly. 'There's note-paper in the desk by the window. Give her my love and tell her I think the concerto is grand.'

Jimmy crossed the hearthrug and stood at her side for a moment in hesitant silence. He laid a restraining finger on her arm.

'Don't go up, Jane,' he said persuasively. 'I want to talk to you.'

'Can't you talk to me to-morrow?' asked Jane, a trifle uncertainly.

'Good-night, Jimmy,' called Stephen from the staircase. 'Remember, eighteen holes to-morrow morning!'

Jane turned to glance up at him. He was standing on the landing, looking down on them a little wearily. Jane suddenly thought their figures had assumed a rather intimate pose. She started away from Jimmy and walked out into the hall. She threw him a glance over her shoulder, however. He was gazing after her so wistfully that she could not help twinkling back at him.

'No, I'm going up,' she said pleasantly. 'Good-night, Jimmy.' She followed Stephen up the darkened staircase and into the mellow lamplight of their little blue bedroom. Stephen, with a familiar gesture, was already hanging his grey sack coat over the back of a chair. He looked up at Jane as she entered.

'You look very pretty to-night in that red thing,' he said.

Jane glanced at herself in the cheval glass — she *did* look pretty. Her eyes were still twinkling at the thought of deserted Jimmy and her lips were curved in a little involuntary smile. Stephen continued to look at her in silence.

'You'll miss Jimmy,' said Stephen, 'when he goes back East.'

Jane turned to stare at him. Stephen had never made any comment on Jimmy just like that, before. Could Stephen be really — troubled? He went on speaking very evenly.

'But you'll have more time,' he said. There was a little pause. 'I've been thinking, Jane,' he continued — what had Stephen been thinking? Jane thought breathlessly — 'I've been wondering if this wouldn't be a good spring to see about getting Steve's teeth straightened. If he wore braces at Gull Rocks this summer ——'

Jane turned from him in an absurd surge of irritation. Oh, yes — she would have plenty of time, now, to straighten Steve's teeth and plan for Gull Rocks and —— Stephen was unbuttoning his waistcoat.

'I think you'd better take him in to the dentist ——' he began.

'I'll take him in, Stephen,' said Jane snappishly. 'Of course I'll take him in. Why do you act as if you had to nag me ——' Her voice died down. Stephen had paused, in the act of untying his necktie, to look at her in amazement. Jane walked over to him and laid her hand on his arm. 'I'll take him in, dear,' she said. Her tone was a tacit apology. Stephen went on untying his necktie. Jane slipped out of the Poiret tea-gown. Jimmy, she supposed, was writing a letter to Agnes at the living-room desk downstairs.

v

Next morning Stephen had his eighteen holes of golf with Jimmy. The April day had dawned very bright and fair. The men came home from the links just a little late for luncheon with Jane and the children. It was nearly three before the meal was finished. While they were drinking their after-luncheon coffee, Mr. and Mrs. Ward turned up, rather unexpectedly. The day was so pleasant, Mrs. Ward remarked, that they had motored out to spend Sunday afternoon with the grandchildren. Mr. Ward had greeted Jimmy very affably, but Mrs. Ward looked distinctly affronted by his presence at Jane's fireside. When Stephen produced a cocktail for the men at tea-time, Jane saw her mother fasten a lynx eye on Jimmy, as he stood on the hearthrug, nonchalantly toying with his glass of amber liquid. Jane could not suppress a smile. She knew that her mother was determined that Jimmy should not kiss the rim of *that* glass unobserved. He made no attempt to do so, however. He had made no attempt, all day, to resume the conversation of which Jane had deprived him on the previous evening. Mr. and Mrs. Ward did not leave their grandchildren until after six o'clock. It was time to dress for dinner when they had gone.

Both men seemed silent, Jane thought, at table. Tired out,

perhaps, by their morning of golf in the open air. Cicily rather monopolized the conversation. She was chattering of the educational plans of the rising generation. In particular of the educational plans of Jack Bridges, on whom the family interest was centring that spring. At seventeen Jack was about to take his final entrance examination for Harvard. He was a clever boy, snub-nosed and twinkle-eyed like his father, with a strong natural bent for the physical sciences. Robin and Isabel were very proud of him. Cicily, herself, wanted to go to Rosemary next year with her cousin Belle. Jane had tried in vain to interest her in Bryn Mawr. She tried again, a little half-heartedly, this evening at the table.

'Why should I go to college, Mumsy?' said Cicily. 'And lock myself up on a campus for four years?'

Lock herself up on a campus, thought Jane. That was what college life meant to the rising generation. For her Bryn Mawr had spelled emancipation. Through Pembroke Arch she had achieved a world of unprecedented freedom. Under the Bryn Mawr maples she had escaped from family surveillance, from the 'opinions' of her mother and Isabel, from ideas with which she could never agree, from standards to which she could never conform. To Agnes and herself the routine existence in a Bryn Mawr dormitory had seemed a life of liberty, positively bordering upon licence. To Cicily it seemed ridiculous servitude.

'I don't want to go to college,' said Cicily. 'I want to room with Belle at boarding-school and come out when I'm eighteen.'

'Don't you want to *know* anything?' asked Stephen, rousing himself from his silence. The twinkle in his eyes robbed the question of all harshness.

'I don't want to know anything I can learn at Bryn Mawr,' said Cicily airily.

'That's a very silly thing to say,' said Jane.

'Oh, I don't know,' interposed Jimmy brightly. 'What use is knowledge to a girl with hair like Cicily's? Let her trust to instinct. I bet that takes her farther, Jane, than you'll care to see her go.'

'A little knowledge might hold her back,' said Jane.

'I don't want to be held back,' said Cicily promptly. 'I want to do everything and go everywhere.'

'Nevertheless, you want to know what you're doing and where you're going,' said Jane severely.

'I don't know that I do,' said Cicily. 'I like surprises.'

'The child's a hedonist, Jane,' said Jimmy. 'Let her alone. You'll never understand a hedonist. "Not the fruit of experience, but experience itself, is the end." Pater said that first, but it's very true. You'll never read Pater, Cicily, if you don't go to Bryn Mawr, and you probably wouldn't like him if you did. He doesn't speak the language of your generation. Nevertheless, he is your true prophet. I learned pages of Pater by heart, when I was at night school at the settlement. I thought he had the right idea. "A counted number of pulses only is given to us of a variegated, dramatic life. How shall we pass most swiftly from point to point and be present always at the focus where the greatest number of vital forces unite in their purest energy? To burn always with this hard, gem-like flame, to maintain this ecstasy, is success in life." That was my credo, Cicily, when I was not so much older than you are. Go on burning, my dear, burn like your golden hair, and never bother about the consequences.'

Cicily was staring at him with wide, non-comprehending eyes. Jane knew she had not understood a word of the Pater.

'That's very immoral doctrine,' she said.

'But didn't you think it was swell,' said Jimmy, 'when you first read it with Agnes at Bryn Mawr?'

'Yes, I did,' said Jane honestly. 'But I was too young to know what it meant.'

'The trouble with education is,' said Jimmy cheerfully, 'that we always read everything when we're too young to know what it means. And the trouble with life is that we're always too busy to re-read it later. There's more sense in books, Cicily, than you'd really believe. Though, of course, they don't teach you anything vital that you can't learn for yourself.'

Jane rose from the table.

'Go up and do your home work, Cicily,' she said cheerfully. 'And don't listen to Mr. Trent. You'll never learn the past participle of *moneo*, unless you apply yourself to Harkness's Latin Grammar.'

The children trooped upstairs to the playroom. Stephen picked up the Sunday paper. What with the golf all morning and the family all afternoon, he had not really assimilated the real estate columns. Jimmy wandered over to the glass doors that opened on the terrace.

'Come out in the garden, Maud,' he said lightly to Jane. 'The moon is full to-night.'

Jane looked at Stephen a little hesitantly.

'You come, too, Stephen,' she said.

Stephen looked up over the margin of the 'Morning Tribune.'

'Run along with Jimmy,' he said. Then, as his eyes returned to the real estate page, 'I think this Michigan Avenue Extension Bridge is really going through. That lot of your father's on Pine Street will be worth a fortune some day, Jane.'

Jane walked at Jimmy's side across the shaded terrace and down into the moonlit garden. They strolled the length of it in silence. The night was fresh and just a little cool. The moon was high in the eastern sky. It seemed racing rapidly through the ragged rents in the tattered clouds. There was no wind in the garden, however, The moon-blanched daffodils were motionless in their bed beneath the evergreens. The boughs of the apple tree did not stir. Only the cloud-shadows raced, as the moon was racing, across the expanse of lawn. Jimmy sat down on a green bench beneath the apple tree.

'Sit down, Jane,' he said. 'Are you cold?'

'No,' said Jane, sinking down on the bench beside him. 'I think the air is lovely.'

'Better put on my coat,' said Jimmy.

'No — I don't need it,' said Jane.

Jimmy took it off, however, and wrapped it about her shoulders. He turned the collar up, very carefully, around her bare throat. Jane could smell the faint distinctive odour of the tweed as he did so.

'I want you to be comfortable,' said Jimmy.

'I *am* comfortable,' smiled Jane.

'I want you to be comfortable,' continued Jimmy, ignoring her comment, 'because I'm going to talk to you for a long, long time. It will take a long, long time, even out here in the moonlight, to make you understand all that I have to say.'

Jane looked quickly up at him, disquieted by his words. Jimmy's face was very calm. He seemed, at the moment, a very tranquil faun. In one instant, however, by one sentence, he shattered the tranquillity of the moment.

'What do *you* think,' he said, 'is going to happen to you and me?'

Jane stared at him.

'To you — and me?' she faltered. He looked steadily down at her. 'Why, Jimmy' — she was conscious of smiling nervously — 'what — what *could* happen?'

He ignored her foolish question.

'I'm married to Agnes,' said Jimmy; 'you're married to Stephen. We've known each other just seven months and we're in love with each other. What's going to happen?'

Jane, in her utter astonishment, half-rose from the bench.

'We — we're *not* in love with each other,' she protested hotly.

'Jane' — said Jimmy sadly — 'don't waste time in prevarication. The night is all too short as it is.'

'I'm not in love with *you*,' said Jane, sinking back on the bench.

'Oh, yes, you are,' said Jimmy.

'I love Stephen,' said Jane, staring straight into his eyes.

'Yes,' said Jimmy; 'that makes it worse, for you're not in love with him. There's a great difference, you know, in those two states of mind, or rather of emotion. You're in love with me and I'm in love with you. I haven't been in love with Agnes for years. I don't even love her, any more. She's irritated me too often. I respect her — she amuses me — I'm grateful to her ——'

'Jimmy! Don't talk like that!' cried Jane sharply.

'But you love Stephen,' went on Jimmy imperturbably. 'Which complicates everything, for of course you'll want to consider him.'

'*Consider* him!' cried Jane. 'Of course I want to consider him!'

'Yes,' said Jimmy reasonably. 'That's what I said. That's what makes it so difficult.'

'Makes *what* so difficult?' cried Jane.

'My persuading you to come away with me,' said Jimmy calmly.

'Have you lost your mind?' demanded Jane.

'For you *are* going to come away with me, in the end, Jane,' said Jimmy. 'But I'll have to do an awful lot of talking first.'

'I'm not in love with you,' said Jane again. Meeting Jimmy's eyes, however, her glance fell before his gaze.

'No use in not facing it, Jane,' said Jimmy.

'I — I didn't even know you were in love with me,' said Jane. 'You — you've never made love to me except — except just that once ——'

'I've been making love to you, Jane,' said Jimmy, 'from the moment that you resented that kiss. Not before. I just kissed you for the fun of it, and you were quite right to resent it. But since then, Jane, I haven't thrown a glance or said a word that wasn't arrant love-making. Oh' — he stopped her indignant protest — 'I know you never recognized it. You're invincibly innocent. Any other woman would have known it at once, and would either have kicked me out or responded in kind. In either case I'd have tired of her in two months.'

'You're asking me to respond in kind, now,' said Jane tremulously. 'At least — at least I suppose you are.'

'You bet I am,' said Jimmy.

'So that you can tire of me in two months?' asked Jane.

'So that I can marry you,' said Jimmy promptly. 'I want you to come away with me, Jane, to-night, or to-morrow or next week Wednesday — any time you say. I want you to face the music. I want you to meet your fate. I want you to *live*, before you die. Did you know that you'd never lived, Jane? That's why you're so invincibly innocent. I want you to live, darling. I want to live with you.' His eager face was very close to hers. But still he had not so much as touched her hands. They were clasped very tightly together in her lap.

'Jimmy,' said Jane brokenly, 'please stop.'

'Why?' said Jimmy eagerly.

'Because it's no use,' said Jane. 'I won't deceive Stephen, or betray Agnes, or leave my children.'

'But you love me?' said Jimmy.

Jane's troubled eyes fell before his ardent glance.

'You love me?' he repeated a little huskily. 'Oh, Jane — my darling — say it!' His shaken accents tore at her heart-strings.

'Yes,' whispered Jane. 'I — I love you.' Her eyes were on the cloud-shadows racing across the lawn. She could hardly believe that she had uttered the sentence that rang in her ears. It had fluttered from her lips before she was aware. The words themselves gave actuality to the statement. Once said they were true. They trembled in the silent garden. Winged words, that could not be recalled.

'Jane!' breathed Jimmy. And still he did not touch her. Staring straight before her at the cloud-shadows, Jane was suddenly conscious of a dreadful, devastating wish that he would.

'Jane ——' said Jimmy falteringly. Suddenly he took her in his arms.

Jane felt herself lost in a maze of emotion.

'Jimmy,' said Jane, after a moment, 'this is terrible — this is perfectly terrible. I — I can't tell even you how I feel.' She slipped from his embrace.

'Even me?' smiled Jimmy. Until he repeated them, Jane had not realized the tender import of her words. He took her again in his arms.

'Jimmy — don't!' said Jane faintly. 'I'm sinking, Jimmy, I'm sinking into a pit that a moment before was unthink-able! Stop kissing me, Jimmy! For God's sake, stop kissing me! I want to think!'

'I don't want you to think,' said Jimmy. 'I just want you to feel.'

'But I — I *am* thinking!' said Jane pitifully.

'Don't do it!' said Jimmy.

But Jane steadfastly put away his arms.

'Jimmy,' she said desperately, 'we *must* think. We must think of every one. If I went away with you, we wouldn't achieve happiness.'

'Of course we would,' said Jimmy. 'We've only one life to live, Jane, and that life's half over. Let's make the most of it while it lasts.'

'But Stephen's life,' said Jane, 'and Agnes's ——'

'Don't think of them,' said Jimmy. 'Think only of us. Are our lives nothing?'

'I *can't* think only of us,' said Jane.

'You could if you came away with me,' said Jimmy. 'You *will* come, won't you, Jane?'

'No, Jimmy,' said Jane very sadly.

'Then I'll carry you off, darling,' said Jimmy, 'to some chimerical place. We'll jump over a broomstick together in the dark of the moon to the tinkle of a tambourine! Let's sail for the South Sea Islands, Jane, just as we planned that first evening. Let's go to Siam and Burma and on into India ——'

'Oh, Jimmy,' sighed Jane, 'you're so ridiculous — and so adorable.'

There was only one answer to that.

'You're adorable,' said Jimmy, as he kissed her. 'And ridiculous!'

'Jimmy,' said Jane, 'am I dreaming? I *must* be dreaming — though I never dreamed of you like this before.'

'Invincible innocent!' laughed Jimmy. 'You're going away with me! You're going to leave this garden forever. You'll never see that apple tree in bloom again ——'

'Never that apple tree?' said Jane.

'But you'll see other trees in bloom,' smiled Jimmy, 'in other gardens.'

'But not that one?' said Jane. 'Not that one with Jenny's

swing hanging from its branches and Steve's tree-house nailed to its trunk and the bare place beneath it where the grass never grew after we took up Cicily's first sandpile?'

'Don't think, darling!' said Jimmy quickly.

They sat a long time in silence.

'Cold, darling?' whispered Jimmy, as Jane stirred in his arms.

'No — not cold,' murmured Jane.

'Thinking?' whispered Jimmy.

'No — not thinking,' murmured Jane. 'Not thinking any more at all.'

'Coming?' smiled Jimmy.

'I — don't know,' said Jane. 'Don't ask me that or I'll begin thinking. Just hold me, Jimmy, hold me in your arms.'

VI

When Jane opened her eyes next morning, the cold light of the April dawn was breaking over the garden. She had come into the house with Jimmy some four hours before. They had turned out the lights in the living-room and crept silently up the stairs and exchanged one last kiss at the door of Jane's bedroom. She had opened the door with elaborate precaution and moved quietly into her room. Precautions, however, were unnecessary. Stephen was sound asleep on the sleeping-porch. Jane had slipped out of her clothes and into her nightgown in the darkness and had stood, for a moment, in her bedroom window gazing out at the silvery garden. She had raised her bare arms in the moonlight, as if to fold to her heart a phantom lover. She had smiled at their milky whiteness. Then she had jumped into bed and covered herself up and waited, a little fearfully, for besieging thoughts. They had not come, however. Defeated by victorious feeling, perhaps they lay in ambush. Jane wondered and, while wondering and feeling, fell serenely asleep.

She was wakened at dawn by the chirping of birds in the oak trees on the terrace. She opened her eyes in her familiar blue bedroom. She did not remember, for a moment, what had happened in the garden. Then the thoughts pounced on her. They *had* been in ambush. Serried ranks of thoughts, battalions of thoughts, little valiant warrior thoughts that rose up singly from the ranks and stabbed her mind before she was aware of their coming. She recalled the events of the evening with horror and incredulity. It could not have happened. If it had, she must have been mad. She was Jane Carver — Mrs. Stephen Carver — Stephen Carver's wife and the mother of his three children. She was Jane Ward — little Jane Ward — John Ward's daughter — who had been born on Pine Street and gone to Miss Milgrim's School with Agnes and to Bryn Mawr with Agnes. Little Jane Ward, who had loved André and grown up and married Stephen. She had been Stephen Carver's wife for nearly sixteen years. Yes, she must have been mad last night in the moonlit garden. Mad — to let Jimmy speak, to let him hold her in his arms. Mad to sit with him there — beneath the apple tree — how many hours? Four — five — six hours she had sat with Jimmy beneath the apple tree, deceiving Stephen and betraying Agnes and planning to abandon her children.

Had it really happened? Was it a dream? Something should be done about dreams like that. You should not even dream that you were deceiving your husband or betraying your friend or planning to abandon your children. But it was not a dream. If it were a dream, she would be lying beside Stephen in her bed on the sleeping-porch. No — it had happened. It had irrevocably happened. The long path into which she had turned at the moment that she had looked into Jimmy's eyes on the threshold of the Greenwich Village flat had come to its perhaps inevitable ending. She loved Jimmy. She had, incredibly, told him so. The telling had changed everything. It had changed Jimmy. It had changed herself, most of all. It had changed everything, Jane saw clearly in the light of the April dawn, but the most essential facts of the situation. You did not deceive your husband — you did not betray your friend — you did not abandon your children.

Yet she had promised Jimmy only four short hours ago, on the bench beneath the apple tree, to do all those things. She had promised him, just before parting. Jane closed her eyes to shut out the awful clarity of the April dawn, to shut out the familiar walls of the bedroom, to shut out the serried ranks of thoughts that clustered about her bed. It was no use — the thoughts were still there, crowding behind her eyelids. They would not be denied — battering, besieging thoughts. No feeling left, curiously enough, or almost none, to combat them. Only an incredulous bruised memory of feeling — feeling so briefly experienced, to be forever forsworn.

Of course she would forswear it. She *had* been mad in the garden. Moon-mad. Man-mad. She had been everything that was impossible and undefendable. She had not been Jane Carver or little Jane Ward. She had been some incredible changeling. But she was Jane Carver now, and Jane Ward, too. Little Jane Ward, who had been brought up on Pine Street by a Victorian family to try to be a good girl and mind her parents. Jane Carver, who had behind her the strength of fifteen incorruptible years of honest living as Stephen's wife. Of course she would forswear the feeling. She would tell Jimmy that morning.

Jimmy. At the memory of Jimmy the serried ranks of thoughts fell back a little. A sudden wave of emotion reminded her that feeling was not so easily forsworn. Jimmy's face in the moonlight — his eyes — his lips — his arms about her body. Suddenly Jane heard Stephen stirring on the sleeping-porch. It was seven o'clock, then. The day had begun. This day in which thoughts must give birth to action. This day in which feeling must be forsworn. Stephen, struggling into his bathrobe, appeared on tiptoe at the door to the sleeping-porch. He looked a little sleepy, but very cheerful.

'Hello,' he said, 'you awake? Why did you sleep in here?'

'I didn't want to wake you up,' said Jane. She was amazed at the casual tone she managed to achieve. 'I sat out very late with Jimmy in the garden.'

'I went up early,' said Stephen, 'just as soon as I finished with the paper. Coming down to breakfast?'

'No,' said Jane. 'Ask Sarah to bring up a tray.'

Jane felt she could not face a Lakewood family breakfast. Whatever life demanded of her on this dreadful day, it did not demand that she should sit behind her coffee tray, surrounded by her children, and pour out Jimmy's coffee under Stephen's unconscious eye. She would wait in her room until Stephen had gone to the train, until the children had left for school. Then she would go down and tell Jimmy that she had been mad in the garden.

Two hours later, Jane opened her bedroom door and walked down the staircase. No Jimmy in the hall. She entered the living-room and saw him standing by the terrace doors, gazing out at the apple tree. He wheeled quickly around at the sound of her step on the threshold. Jimmy looked tired. Jimmy looked worn. But Jimmy looked terribly happy. Jane smiled tremulously.

'Jimmy ——' she said, still standing in the doorway.

'Don't say it!' cried Jimmy. 'I know just how you feel. I know just how you've reacted. Don't say it, Jane! Give yourself time to — to get used to it.'

'I *am* used to it,' said Jane pitifully. 'I'm terribly used to it. I've been thinking for hours.'

'I know what you've been thinking!' cried Jimmy. He walked quickly over to her and caught her hand in his. 'It was inevitable, Jane, that you'd think those thoughts. Don't — don't let them trouble you, Jane. I knew how it would be.'

'You knew how it would be?' faltered Jane.

'I even knew you wouldn't come down to breakfast. In point of fact, I didn't come down to breakfast myself. In spite of all the many things I've done, Jane, in and out of camp meetings, I can't say that I ever planned to run off with the wife of a friend before. I didn't seem to care much about meeting Stephen myself, this morning. I didn't seem to care much about sharing his eggs and bacon.'

'You haven't had any breakfast?' said Jane stupidly. Jimmy shook his head. 'I'll ring for a tray.' She moved to the bell by the chimney-piece. Jimmy followed her across the room.

'But, Jane ——' he said.

'Yes,' said Jane, her hand on the bell-rope.

'Those thoughts, you know, aren't really — really important. I mean — they don't change anything.'

'They change everything,' said Jane dully. 'Sarah, a breakfast tray, here in the living-room, for Mr. Trent.'

'And one for Mrs. Carver,' said Jimmy, with an affable smile for the maid in the doorway. 'I'm sure you haven't eaten a bite this morning. I'm sure you just drained down a cup of black coffee.'

'That's just what I did,' said Jane, smiling wanly at Jimmy's omniscience.

'Two breakfast trays, Sarah,' grinned Jimmy in dismissal. Then, when the girl had gone: 'Sit down here, darling, on the sofa, with a pillow at your back. Put your feet up. There! Comfortable, now?'

'Very,' said Jane with another wan smile. 'Jimmy, you make it awfully hard for me to tell you.'

'Tell me what?' said Jimmy brightly. 'That you take it all back? Don't trouble to tell it, Jane. Just sit there and rest and wait for your breakfast. When you've eaten it, life will seem much rosier.' He stood looking down at her very cheerfully from the hearthrug. 'I wish I could sit down on the floor, Jane, and take your hands and tell you I adore you, but I really think I hadn't better do it until Sarah has come in with the breakfast trays.'

'You hadn't better ever do it,' said Jane.

'Nonsense,' said Jimmy. 'I'm going to do it innumerable mornings. In the South Sea Islands and Siam and Burma ——'

Jane couldn't help laughing.

'Jimmy,' she said, 'you're perfectly incorrigible. But I mean it. I really mean it. I'm terribly sorry — I know it's rough on you — but — but I made a dreadful mistake last night in the garden.'

'And now you've discovered that you don't love me,' smiled Jimmy. 'Well, presently you'll discover again that you do.'

'No, Jimmy.' Jane's voice was shrill with conviction.

'Here's Sarah,' murmured Jimmy, turning with nonchalance to fleck the ash of his cigarette in the empty grate. Sarah placed the breakfast trays on two small tables and retired noiselessly from the room.

'Now eat, Jane,' said Jimmy commandingly. 'I'm going to let you have all that breakfast before I even kiss you.'

Jane thought the breakfast would choke her. But somehow, under the stimulus of Jimmy's pleasant conversation, she

found she had consumed the entire contents of the tray.
Jimmy rang again for Sarah. When the trays were removed,
he stepped quickly over to her and sank on his knees by the
sofa.

'Darling!' said Jimmy, seizing her hands in his.

'Jimmy!' cried Jane in terror. 'Don't kiss me! Don't you
dare to kiss me! I'm not the woman I was last night in the
garden.' Her earnestness held him in check.

'Darling,' said Jimmy, still clinging firmly to her hands, 'I
know it's terribly hard for you. I know it's much worse for
you than it is for me. You'll have to face Stephen, whom you
love, and a scandal, which you'll hate. You'll have to leave
your children for a time — though, of course, you'll see them
afterwards. I love your children, Jane, and they like me.
They're great kids. But of course you'll have to leave
them. It's a terrible sacrifice — and what have I to offer
you?'

'Oh, Jimmy,' said Jane pitifully, 'don't say that! It isn't
that!'

'I know it isn't, but still I have to say it. I'm a total loss as a
husband, Jane. I'm a rolling stone and I'll never gather moss.
We'll wander about the world together and I'll write a little
music and look for pleasant little jobs that won't keep me too
long in any one place. You'll be awfully uncomfortable,
Jane, a great deal of the time. And maybe lonely ——'

'No, I wouldn't be lonely,' said Jane.

'I'm not so sure,' said Jimmy. 'I think there are lots of
raggle-taggle gypsies that you wouldn't find so very congenial
on closer acquaintance. They're rather sordid, you know,
and just a little promiscuous, in close quarters.'

'I wouldn't care,' said Jane eagerly; 'I wouldn't care,
Jimmy, as long as I had you.'

'Well, then,' smiled Jimmy, drawing a long breath, 'well,

then — if that's the way you feel, just why am I not to dare to kiss you?'

'Because I'm not going away with you, Jimmy.' Jane drew her hands from his. 'I'm not going to do it. This isn't just the silly reaction of a foolish woman to a moment's indiscretion. It's something much more serious. I'm in love with you, Jimmy, but I love you, too. I love you, just as I love Stephen and the children. I love you as I love Agnes. And that's one of the reasons why I won't let you do this thing. Can't I make you understand, Jimmy, what I mean? When you love people, you've *got* to be decent. You *want* to be decent. You want to be good. Just plain good — the way you were taught to be when you were a little child. Love's the greatest safeguard in life against evil. I won't do anything, Jimmy, if I can possibly help it, that will keep me from looking any one I love in the eye.' Her voice was trembling so that she could not keep it up a moment longer. She turned away from Jimmy to hide her tears. In a moment he had tucked a big clean handkerchief into her hand. She buried her face in the cool, smooth linen. Jimmy rose, a trifle unsteadily, to his feet.

'Jane,' he said, 'Jane — you almost shake me.'

Jane wept on in silence.

'See here,' said Jimmy presently; his voice had changed abruptly: 'This won't do, you know. For it really isn't true — it's very sweet, but it's silly — it's sentimental. It doesn't do anybody any good for a man and woman who are in love with each other to go on sordidly living with people they *don't* love. Stephen wouldn't want you to live with him under those circumstances. Agnes wouldn't want me to live with her. They're both exceptionally decent people.'

'So we're to profit by their decency?' said Jane coldly. 'To be, ourselves, indecent?'

'Darling,' said Jimmy, 'it isn't indecent to live with the man you love.'

Jane rose abruptly from the sofa.

'You're just confusing the issues, Jimmy,' she said sadly. 'But you can't change them. It isn't *right* for married people, happily married people, to leave their homes and children for their own individual pleasure.'

'But we're not happily married people,' said Jimmy.

'If we're not,' said Jane steadfastly, 'it's only our own fault. Neither Stephen nor Agnes has ever sinned against us. They love us and they trust us. They trusted us, once for all, with their life happiness. I couldn't feel decent, Jimmy, and betray that trust.'

'Jane,' said Jimmy, 'I don't understand you. With all your innocence you've always seemed so emancipated. Intellectually emancipated. You've always seemed to understand the complications of living. To sympathize with the people who were tangled up in them. You've always said ——'

'Oh, yes,' said Jane, 'I've done a lot of talking. It made me feel very sophisticated to air my broad-minded views. I was very smug about my tolerance. I used to say to Isabel that I could understand how anybody could do anything. I used to laugh at Mamma for her Victorian views. I used to think it was very smart to say that every Lakewood housewife was potentially a light lady. I used to think I believed it. I *did* believe it theoretically, Jimmy. But now — now when it comes to practice — I see there's a great difference.'

'But there *isn't* any difference, Jane,' said Jimmy. 'Not any essential difference. Just one of convention. You're a woman before you're a Lakewood housewife. "The Colonel's lady and Judy O'Grady are sisters under their skins!"'

'But they're *not*, Jimmy! That's just Kipling's revolt against Victorian prudery. I suppose *he* felt very sophisticated when he first got off that line! The complications of living seem very complicated when you look at them from a distance. When you're tangled up in them yourself, you know they're very simple. If you're really the Colonel's lady, Jimmy, no matter how little you may want to do it, you know exactly what you *ought* to do.' She turned away from him and stood staring out through the terrace doors at the April garden. For a long time there was silence in the room. Then ——

'I — I don't believe — you love me,' said Jimmy slowly.

Jane turned her white face from the April garden.

'Then you're wrong, Jimmy,' she said gently. 'You're very wrong. It's *killing* me to do this thing I'm doing. It's killing me to be with you, here in this room. Will you please go away — back to town, I mean — and — and don't come back until you've accepted my decision.'

'I'll never accept it,' said Jimmy grimly.

'Then don't come back,' said Jane.

Without another word he left the room. Jane opened the terrace doors and walked out into the garden. She walked on beyond the clump of evergreens and sat down on the bench beneath the apple tree. She had been sobbing a long time before she realized that she still held Jimmy's handkerchief in her hand. She buried her face in it until the sobs were stilled in a mute misery that Jane felt was going to last a lifetime. She sat more than an hour on that bench. When she returned to the house, Sarah told her that Mr. Trent had gone back to the city on the eleven-fifteen.

VII

Five days later, Jimmy returned to Lakewood. He turned up, early in the afternoon, and found Jane superintending the gardener, who was spading up the rose-bed in the garden.

She looked up from the roots of a Dorothy Perkins and saw him standing on the terrace. She was no longer surprised that she was so easily able to dissemble her emotion. Jane had had plenty of practice in the fine art of dissembling emotion during the last five days.

'I think you'd better order another load of black earth, Swanson,' she said casually and turned to walk over to the terrace.

Jimmy stood there, quite motionless, watching her approach through the sunny garden. His face was very serious and his smile was very grave. Jane ascended the terrace steps and held out her hand to him. He took it in silence and held it very tightly.

'You don't know what it does to me,' said Jimmy, 'to see you again.'

'Have you accepted my decision?' said Jane.

'No,' said Jimmy abruptly, 'of course not. Did you think I would?' He drew her hand through his arm and led her over to the corner of the terrace that was sheltered by the oak trees. The oak trees were just bursting into pink and wine-red buds. They did not give much shelter, but from that terrace corner you could not see the rose-bed.

'I asked you not to come back until you had,' said Jane, withdrawing her hand from the crook of his arm and sitting down on the brick parapet of the terrace.

'Jane, you're really invincible,' smiled Jimmy. 'Invincibly determined as well as invincibly innocent! Do you really mean to tell me that you haven't spent the last five days regretting that you sent me out of your life?'

'I don't think that there's anything to laugh at in this situation,' said Jane severely.

'Darling!' said Jimmy — in a moment he was all penitence and contrition — 'I'm not laughing. You know I'm not laughing. I'm preserving the light touch — something very different in situations of an emotional character. But I repeat my question — haven't you been awfully sorry?'

'Of course I've been sorry,' said Jane. 'I've been in hell.'

Jimmy looked down at her very tenderly.

'I've been there with you, Jane,' he said soberly. 'Don't you think it's time you let us both out?'

Jane shook her head.

'I guess we're there to stay, Jimmy,' she said. 'Do you know, as far as I'm concerned, I almost hope I *will* stay there. The one thing that I *couldn't* bear would be the thought that I could ever get over you.'

'Why?' said Jimmy.

'To feel the way I feel about you, Jimmy,' said Jane, 'and then to get over it, would be the most disillusioning of all human experiences. I'm going to keep faith, forever, with the feeling I have for you at this moment.'

Behind the tenderness in Jimmy's eyes glittered the ghost of his twinkle.

'Well, that's very sweet of you, darling,' he said. 'But don't you think that assurance, taken by itself, is just a little barren? It has a note of finality ——'

'It *is* final,' said Jane. 'That's all I have to say to you.'

'Well,' said Jimmy, drawing a long breath, 'I've a great deal more than that to say to you. Listen, you ridiculous child — if you think I'm going to let you ruin both our lives with a phrase ——'

'Jimmy,' said Jane, 'I *beg* of you not to go into this again. I've had — really I've had — a terrible five days. But I haven't changed my mind. I haven't changed it one iota. I'm glad you're going away. I hope I don't see you again for years. It just *kills* me to see you. It kills me to live with your

memory, but I wouldn't forget you for anything in the world.'
His eyes were very bright as he stood looking down at her.
Jane turned her head to gaze out over the flat, sunny Skokie
Valley. After a moment she spoke again. Her voice had
changed abruptly. It had grown dull and lifeless. 'When are
you going?' she asked.

'That depends upon you,' said Jimmy.

'If it depends upon me,' said Jane, still not turning her
head, 'you can't go too soon.'

'Jane,' said Jimmy, dropping quickly down beside her on
the parapet. 'You — you really *won't* come with me?'

'No,' said Jane.

'You don't *want* to live?'

'I'll live,' said Jane tonelessly, 'for Stephen and the children. That sounds very melodramatic, I know, but it's exactly
what I'm going to do. There's just one other thing I want to
say to you, Jimmy. I thought of it after you'd gone the other
day.' She turned her head to look into his eyes. 'I'm never
going to tell Stephen anything about this, and I hope you
won't tell Agnes. I couldn't decide, at first, just what I ought
to do about that. I couldn't decide whether it was courage or
cowardice that made me want not to tell. I couldn't decide
whether Stephen *ought* to know. You see' — she smiled a
little gravely — 'I really feel terribly about it, and I know, no
matter how dreadful the telling was, I'd feel better after I'd
told it. Confession is good for the soul. I wish I were a
Catholic, Jimmy. I wish I were a good Catholic and could
pour the whole story into the impersonal ear of a priest in the
confessional. But I'm not a Catholic and Stephen isn't a
priest. So I think I'll just have to live with a secret. I'll just
have to live with Stephen, knowing that I know, but he
doesn't, just what I did.'

Jimmy's sad little smile was very tender.

'You didn't do so awfully much, you know, Jane,' he said.

'But I felt everything,' said Jane soberly. 'I think it's not so much what you do that matters, as what you feel. What I felt is somehow what I can't tell Stephen. I've never had a secret before, Jimmy. I've never had anything I couldn't tell the world. I hope — I hope you'll feel that way about Agnes. For I really feel about Agnes just the way I do about Stephen.'

'I'm not going back to Agnes,' said Jimmy suddenly.

Jane stared at him in horror.

'You're not — going back — to Agnes?' she faltered.

'Did you think I could?' said Jimmy harshly.

'Why not?' asked Jane. Her eyes searched his. Suddenly her mouth began to tremble. 'Why not — if I can — stay with Stephen?'

'Oh — my darling!' breathed Jimmy.

'You *must* go back to her, Jimmy,' said Jane. 'Don't you see — if you don't, I'll have ruined her life just as if I'd gone away with you?'

'I can't go back to her,' said Jimmy. He stood up suddenly and took a few steps across the terrace, then turned to look at her again. 'No, Jane. If you won't come with me, I'm going without you. I'm going to see the world before I die. I'm going West — out to the coast — to sail on the first boat I can catch for the Orient. I don't know just how I'll manage it, but I'll work my way somehow.'

'But you'll come back?' said Jane. She rose as she spoke and walked anxiously over to him. 'You'll *have* to come back, you know.'

'Oh — I suppose one always comes back,' said Jimmy uncertainly. 'I'll probably die in East St. Louis.'

'But before you die,' urged Jane, attempting a shaky little smile, 'before you die, you *will* come back to Agnes?'

'Well — nothing's impossible,' said Jimmy. He looked moodily down at her. 'Except, apparently, one thing.'

'When are you leaving?' asked Jane.

'To-morrow, perhaps. It's Saturday, you know. I need my last pay-check.'

'Then this is good-bye?' They were strolling, now, side by side, back to the terrace doors.

'I guess it is, Jane. Considering how you feel.'

He opened the door for her and they crossed the living-room in silence. He picked up his hat from the hall table and stood looking down at her by the front door.

'Do you want me to kiss you good-bye?' said Jimmy.

Jane shook her head. Two great tears that were trembling on her lashes rolled down her cheeks. She ignored them proudly.

'Well — I'm going to do it anyway!' said Jimmy. He caught her roughly in his arms. In the ecstasy of that embrace, Jane knew that she was crying wildly. Suddenly, he put her from him. Without a word of farewell, he had opened the door and was gone. Jane leaned helplessly against its panels, exhausted by emotion. Suddenly she turned and ran rapidly up the stairs to the window on the landing. But she was too late. The gravel road was empty. Jimmy had disappeared around the bushes at the entrance of the drive.

CHAPTER V

I

JANE stood staring at the map of Europe that Stephen had tacked up on the living-room wall. She was staring at the little irregular row of red-and-blue thumbtacks that marked the battle-line in eastern France. She was staring at the holes in the canvas where the thumbtacks had once been and where they might be again to-morrow, as the fortunes of men and war wavered over the battle-fields. Over the battle-fields where men were fighting and dying while Jane stared at the map. She had been staring at it just like that for five days.

For more than three months that map had hung on the living-room wall and Jane had thought nothing of it. She had not shared Stephen's interest in the fluctuating battle-line. To Jane, preoccupied with desolate thoughts of Jimmy, the war had been merely an irrelevance. A quarrel of diplomats that was no concern of hers. The fantastic thought that German and French and English men were dying on those battle-fields, dying by scores of thousands, had never really captured her imagination. It was another European war. Incredible, of course, in this civilized age, but no nearer to Jane, emotionally speaking, than the War of the Roses, the Napoleonic campaigns, the French defeat of 1870. Even the thought that André, at the age of thirty-nine, might be drawn into the conflict had failed to arouse her. Jane was preoccupied with desolate thoughts of Jimmy.

He had left Chicago without trying again to speak to her. He had disappeared into silence. Silence that had lasted for two months. Then she had had a picture postcard with a

Chinese stamp upon it. A Chinese stamp and a picture of a little tower-like temple. Jimmy had written just four lines beneath it. 'Here's the Chinese shrine, Jane, where I'd have made you an honest woman. To-day the temple bells are tinkling out of tune.'

That was all. And again there had been silence. A curious silence in which the vast echoes of war could rumble without arresting her attention, but which could always be shattered by the postman's ring. Silence, in which Jane waited to hear again from Jimmy. Five days ago — it was the ninth of November — Jane had received his letter. At the sight of the New York stamp her heart had leapt up — was it with thankfulness or a strange, instinctive revulsion? Jimmy had returned to Agnes. Jane had opened the letter. She could not understand it. It was dated in Berlin, on the tenth day of August.

'I'm going to war, Jane. I've joined the German army. I joined it under the influence of a beer and a blond. I wasn't too drunk, though, to remember my old friends Karl Marx and Bach and Beethoven and Wagner, and just drunk enough to have let Martin Luther slip my mind.

'I've got a pull with a Prussian I roomed with when he was a cub reporter on the New York "Staats-Zeitung." He's an officer now, and he made me an aide because of my English. It was all awfully irregular, for the army here is highly organized. Nevertheless, he did it and I'm going to see action at once. If they set me to using my English, I'll probably be shot at dawn by the British. Anyway, I'm writing the Kaiser that, before I am, we've got to take Paris, because I've never seen it. I'd like to enter it in style the first time.

'I'm sending this letter through the lines in a spy's pocket. He's going to ramble around through Switzerland and Italy to Washington and hopes to come back with a blue-print or two, just in case we follow England into the war. He'll mail it in New York, if he ever gets there.

'And now, Jane, to be quite serious for a minute, do you know that I adore you? Do you know that I feel about you just as I did on the day that I left you? Do you know that I wish to God that I didn't? Darling — there's nothing much to say. If you had come away with me, I certainly should not be going to war. This quarrel's not of my making. If you had, we'd be safe in that cannibal village by this time, eating roasted missionary in an undusted living-room. But you wouldn't, and you were wrong, but I couldn't do anything about it. I can't do anything about it now, not even about the way I feel — so I'm going to war, because that, at least, will be something else again. I certainly don't want to be killed. Why, I don't know. If you won't marry me, there is nothing new under the sun — but there might be, under the sod, where proverbially there is neither marriage nor giving in marriage.

'I bet I live to sack Paris absent-mindedly, because I will be thinking of you.   Your

'JIMMY'

Jane stood staring at the map of Europe. Somewhere on that wavering battle-line, as she stood there, Jimmy was fighting in the quarrel that was not of his making, Jimmy was seeking 'something else again,' under a rain of shot and shell. How like Jimmy, how terribly like Jimmy, to go to war on that casual quest! To go to a war that had become a crusade in the minds of all civilized people in an attitude of ironic detachment. To become — of all things — a Prussian officer at a moment when a Prussian officer represented to the minds of his countrymen a symbol of all evil. How like Jimmy to become a Prussian officer because of a beer and a blond and

a few romantic thoughts on Karl Marx and Bach and Beethoven and Wagner! Jimmy — in a Prussian helmet, looking
like a caricature of the Crown Prince. No, not that — for
there would always be his quizzical eyebrows and his pointed
ears and his ironical smile, exactly like a faun's. A faun,
mocking himself, in a Prussian helmet — that would be how
Jimmy would look, even in the heat of battle. That would
be how Jimmy would look, if he lived to sack Paris. If he
lived to sack Paris absent-mindedly, because he would be
thinking of her.

If he lived! The thought of Jimmy's death was unthinkable.
Jimmy's death in a conflict about the issues of which he did
not care a damn. A conflict into which he had been driven
by her unkindness —— No, she would not think that. She
would never think that. She had done what she had to do.
She had never really regretted it. She would not regret it now.
Jimmy had been driven into that conflict by his own restless
spirit — by his ——

The ring of the doorbell roused Jane from revery. Not the
postman's ring, though, at two o'clock in the afternoon. Jane
returned to the map again. Sarah stood a moment on the
threshold, unnoticed.

'Mrs. Carver,' she said. 'Mrs. Carver, here's a telegram.'

Jane turned from the map and stared at her in silence. No,
she thought, dully, no, it would be a cable! She took the
yellow envelope from Sarah's hand. She opened it without
misgiving.

'Jane, dear, this may be a shock to you. Have just received
letter from Prussian officer in French prison camp that Jimmy
had joined the German army and was killed on the Marne.
Had had no word from him since he left Chicago. Jane, dear,
this seems for me the end of everything. Could you come to
me?   AGNES'

The yellow papers fluttered from Jane's fingers. The chintz-hung living-room turned black before her eyes. She caught herself, however, before falling, on the back of Stephen's armchair. She closed her eyes a moment and then dully opened them. The familiar living-room had returned. Suddenly she felt Sarah's hand upon her elbow, she heard Sarah's voice in her ear.

'Mrs. Carver — here — sit down a moment. I'll get a glass of water.'

Jane shook her head. She stooped suddenly down and picked up the yellow papers. She read the message through once more. All feeling seemed dead. She felt only the need for practical action.

'I'm all right, Sarah,' she said smoothly. 'I — I must talk to Mr. Carver.' She walked to the telephone in the pantry and gave Stephen's number. How strange, she thought, at such a moment to turn instinctively to Stephen!

'Mr. Carver,' she said to his secretary. 'Mrs. Carver speaking.'

'Yes, dear,' Stephen's familiar voice trickled over the wire.

'Stephen,' she said quickly, 'Stephen, I've just had a wire from Agnes. Jimmy was killed on the Marne.'

'On the Marne!' cried Stephen, in stupefaction.

'Yes,' said Jane dully, 'he's dead. He's been dead for two months.' Suddenly she heard her voice break into breathless sobbing. But still there was no feeling. 'Agnes wants me. Will you get me a compartment on the five-thirty, this afternoon? I've just time to pack and catch it.' She was still sobbing.

'Of course,' said Stephen. 'But Jane ——'

'I'll motor in,' said Jane, 'and pick you up at five o'clock at the office. Can you see me off?'

'Of course!' cried Stephen. 'But Jane ——'

Jane hung up the receiver. She had never told Stephen, she reflected weakly, that Jimmy was in the German army.

'Sarah!' she called sharply. 'Bring down my big black bag to my bedroom and order the motor for a quarter-past four.'

II

'He was killed instantly,' said Agnes. 'He was shot in the trenches. He was shot through the head. This German saw it happen.' She handed Jane a creased and wrinkled paper. It was the letter of the Prussian officer, written in perfect English, in a fine German hand, on a sheet of plain block paper. Jane took it in silence. She was sitting beside Agnes on the battered davenport sofa of the Greenwich Village flat. Little Agnes was playing in the nursery beyond the half-open folding doors. It was Saturday afternoon and Agnes had just come home from Macy's. She was still wearing her new black serge street coat. She had not even taken off her hat. The sheer black chiffon of the widow's veil, thrown carelessly over it, shadowed her weary eyes.

'He saw him buried,' went on Agnes tonelessly, though Jane was reading the letter. It was as if she could not make herself stop talking about it. 'He saw him buried next day. There can't be any mistake.'

Jane went on reading the letter in silence.

'It was nice of the French to let him mail that letter, wasn't it, Jane?' said Agnes. 'Otherwise I might never have known what happened. I might never have known that he had gone to war.'

Jane, having finished the letter, sat turning it over in her hands.

'Jane,' said Agnes suddenly, '*Why* did he do it? *Why* did he go to war?'

Jane still sat staring at the finished letter.

'I suppose,' she said a little huskily, 'I suppose he — he was just caught up in the general excitement.'

'But that wasn't like Jimmy,' said Agnes earnestly. 'General excitements always left Jimmy cold. There was nothing that Jimmy despised more than the mob spirit. Why, Jimmy was a pacifist — as much as he was *any*thing ——' Her voice trailed off into silence.

Jane looked slowly up at her. Agnes's sad, worn face was twitching and her throat was throbbing convulsively with the sobs she was trying to master. Jane took her hand in hers.

'Don't — don't think about that, Agnes,' she said simply. 'It won't do any good. You'll never know.'

'No,' said Agnes, 'I'll never know.' Then, after a pause, 'Jane, you saw what he said about Jimmy's concerto — that he had it with him at the front.'

'Yes,' said Jane.

'It — it must be lost,' said Agnes sadly. 'They fought over that trench for days after Jimmy — died. The dugouts must have been simply exterminated.'

'Yes,' said Jane.

'Jane,' said Agnes, 'did you ever hear the end of it? Did he play it for you?'

'Yes,' said Jane.

'Was it good?' asked Agnes eagerly. 'Was it really good?'

'I thought it was very beautiful,' said Jane.

Again they sat in silence.

'Jane,' said Agnes suddenly, 'isn't it dreadful to think there's nothing *left* of Jimmy? With all his cleverness and all his talent he left nothing behind him. The world is just the same as if he had never lived.'

'He left you,' said Jane tremulously. 'He left you and little Agnes.'

'Yes,' said Agnes, 'of course he left little Agnes. And he left me. You're right, Jane. He left me a very different woman than if he'd never loved me. You're very clever, Jane, darling, to think of that. A man *does* live in the change he made in the life of a woman who loved him ——'

'Yes,' said Jane.

Again there was silence. Again it was Agnes who broke it. And this time with a gallant attempt at a cheerful smile.

'I haven't thanked you, Jane, for all you did for Jimmy last winter. He simply loved Chicago. He was awfully happy there. He wrote me the gayest letters.'

'I'm glad he did,' said Jane.

'He was happy in his work and happy about the concerto. He seemed so *young*, Jane, and somehow care-free — just the way he did when I first knew him. He wrote me very often — and always such funny letters.'

'No one could be as funny as Jimmy,' said Jane.

'No,' said Agnes. 'He was always funny when he was happy. Do you know, Jane, I've always understood why he didn't come back to me? I understood it even at the time. The strongest thing in Jimmy's life was his sense of adventure. I think those months in Chicago must have seemed rather adventurous, after the years with me and little Agnes in this flat. That seems absurd to you and me, of course, for to us Chicago is just the town we grew up in — but to Jimmy I think it must have been rather a castle in Spain. He couldn't come back to humble domesticity just after it. He had to wander. To look for other castles, you know, in other countries. But he *would* have come back, Jane ——' Her voice trailed off a trifle wistfully.

'Of course he would have!' said Jane warmly.

'The thing that kills me,' said Agnes soberly, 'is that if he *had*, you know, our life might have been quite different. My play's doing awfully well, Jane. They're going to start a second company on the road. I'm going to take a chance, Jane, and resign from Macy's to write another. I think — I think that perhaps I can really make a lot of money. Enough to have changed everything for Jimmy ——'

'Agnes,' said Jane solemnly, 'you're perfectly wonderful.'

'No, I'm not,' said Agnes. 'I'm just a worker.'

'You're always right,' said Jane.

'But not wonderful,' smiled Agnes. 'Jimmy was wonderful. And always wrong. Oh, Jane!' Agnes's smile was very tremulous. 'Wouldn't you *know* that Jimmy would fight with the Germans and die a hero's death on the wrong side of the Marne? Jimmy was on the wrong side of every Marne from the day he was born!'

'But always wonderful,' smiled Jane. 'And always the hero.'

'To me,' said Agnes gently.

'To me, too,' said Jane.

PART IV
CICILY, JENNY, AND STEVE

PART IV

CICILY, JENNY, AND STEVE

CHAPTER I

I

'KARO,' said Isabel, 'is just as good as sugar. In cake you can't tell the difference.'

The morning sunshine was slanting in the wide dusty windows of the Chicago skyscraper. The big bare room was hung with Red Cross posters and filled with long deal tables and crowded with smartly dressed women. They sat, uncomfortably, on caterer's folding chairs around the tables, meticulously pressing small squares of cheesecloth into intricately mitred rectangles. Isabel was working the bandage roller at the head of the first table. Muriel, at her elbow, looked up from her gauze sponges.

'But is it fattening?' she asked.

'Everything good is fattening,' said Isabel with a little sigh of resignation.

Jane smiled as she heard her. She knew that Isabel, at forty-six, did not really care much any longer if everything good was. But Muriel, at forty-one, still cared a great deal. She was constantly repressing a slightly Semitic tendency toward rounded curves. She was still awfully pretty, Jane thought. Her blue eyes had never lost that trick of dancing. They were dancing now, as she responded lightly:

'The women of this country have done a great deal for Herbert Hoover. I think the least he can do for them is to offer a few reducing food substitutes.'

Isabel did not join in the laugh that went round the table. Jane knew that Isabel seriously deplored Muriel's tendency to be frivolous about the war. Jack had been nine months in training now at Camp Brant in Rockford. Albert was there, too, of course. The boys had left Harvard together as soon as war was declared and had joined the first R.O.T.C. at Fort Sheridan. They would undoubtedly be shipped to France before the summer was over.

Isabel and Robin took the war very seriously. They were terribly worried about Jack. As far as they were concerned, it was just Jack's war. Though he was still safely detailed to shoot machine guns over an Illinois prairie, Jane knew that Isabel was always thinking of him lying dead or wounded on a French battle-field. Every bandage she was rolling that morning in the big bare room on top of the Chicago sky-scraper was turned out with a sense of personal service for her son.

Muriel was worried about Albert, too, of course. But she took a vicarious pride in his military exploits. She loved to have him gracing her Chicago drawing-room on his brief leaves from Camp Brant, looking decorative and dedicated and dapper in his second lieutenant's uniform. Albert Lancaster was a very beautiful young man and he was very fond of his mother. In the presence of Muriel's other beautiful young men he always flirted with her, very flatteringly. Jane had sometimes felt that Muriel was just a little in love with him. She had said as much one day to Isabel at their mother's luncheon-table.

'Now, Jane,' Isabel had responded airily, 'don't suggest that Muriel is going to add incest to her list of crimes!'

Mrs. Ward had said they should not talk like that. With Bert in the helpless condition he was, it was very natural for Muriel to centre her affections on her only son.

'If she only did!' had been Isabel's telling comment.

Muriel had been very capable about the war, however, in spite of her frivolity. She had organized the Red Cross circle on top of the Chicago skyscraper. She had ordered the supplies and enrolled the workers and persuaded the owner of the skyscraper to give them the room rent free. She was a member of the countless Food Administration and National Council of Defence committees.

Nevertheless, Isabel deplored her frivolity. Muriel did not care. She just went on being frivolous. At the moment she was making airy little jokes about the sunny side of being a famine victim.

Jane soon ceased to listen. From her seat near the window she could look out over the roofs of the smaller office buildings toward the east, past the slender silhouette of the Montgomery Ward Tower, across the desert wastes of Grant Park, to the Illinois Central switchyards, where the miniature engines, dwarfed by distance, pulled their toy trains and belched their black smoke and puffed their white steam up into the serene face of the May sky. Beyond them stretched the sparkling blue plane that was the lake.

A lovely day, reflected Jane, idly. A lovely day, with a bright spring sun and a stiff east breeze to sweep the city clean. Her hands still busy mechanically folding her gauze sponges, she gazed up, blinking a little, at the golden orb that shone dazzlingly down on the city roofs above the gilded Diana that topped the Tower. What had that sun seen, she was thinking, since it had last sunk behind the murk of the stockyards, since she herself, staring from that same window, had watched its dying rays paint the Montgomery Ward Diana with rosy fire? The words of the Stevenson nursery rhyme she had so often repeated to the children, when they were little, came into her mind.

'The sun is not abed when I
At night upon my pillow lie,
But round the earth his way he takes
And morning after morning makes.'

One morning here on the Chicago lake front. A few hours
earlier a very different one on the battle-fields of France. The
battle-fields that would so soon swallow up Isabel's Jack and
Muriel's Albert. But the battle-fields that still, in May, 1918,
almost four years after Jimmy's death, achieved for Jane their
major significance as Jimmy's last resting-place.

Curious that Jimmy's death had never made her realize the
war. It had remained for her the supremely irrelevant accident that had killed him. An act of God, like a casual stroke
of lightning. Or perhaps an act of man, like the blow of a
death-dealing taxi, turning too quickly on a policeman's
whistle, to crush an absent-minded pedestrian under its indifferent wheels.

Jimmy had not died for Germany, in spite of his Prussian
helmet. He had not died for her, in spite of his love. He had
died — for fun, perhaps, as he had lived. Died true to his
creed embraced in night school, in a supreme desire 'to be
present always at the focus where the greatest number of vital
forces unite in their purest energy.' Jimmy had died for
Pater, as much as for anything! Strange end for a hedonist.

You grew accustomed to pain, thought Jane. You really
did. Even to pain like hers over Jimmy, that was so sharp, so
constant, so distinctly localized that she almost felt that it had
an organic focus in her heart. You grew wise and philosophi-
cal about it. You generalized. You struggled for resignation.

In her struggles for resignation, Jane knew that she was
sometimes guilty of the great injustice to Jimmy of wondering
if it weren't all better so. Better so, she tried to think she
meant, because of Agnes and little Agnes, who were living on

the proceeds of Agnes's third play so much more comfortably
with Jimmy's memory than they could ever have lived in his
restless, unhappy presence. Jane tried to think she meant
that, but really she knew she was thinking only of herself and
of the intolerable problems a future, with or without a living
Jimmy, had propounded.

For death had given her Jimmy. He had died loving her.
He had died with that love unsullied and unspoiled. Would
he have lived to love her always? Few men were capable of
that. Would *she* have lived to see him grow indifferent, remote, concerned, perhaps, oh, vitally concerned! with some
other woman? Now he was hers forever. The future held no
fears. Time, changing relationships, distance, estrangement
— all these were powerless. She could dismiss that fearful
question as to whether she had ever really, in her secret heart,
wanted Jimmy to go back to Agnes. She could dismiss her
vague forebodings on the world of women that waited for him
if he didn't. She could dismiss the thought of Stephen. You
could love the dead without disloyalty to the living.

Nevertheless, it was an act of treachery to Jimmy's memory
to allow herself to think, even for a moment, that he was better dead. Jimmy — dead. The thought was still incredible.
She had never lost the illusion of his laughing, living presence.
He was the constant companion of her reveries. He would be
laughing now, if he could read her thoughts. Laughing at her
involuntary sense of guilt. 'Invincible innocent!' would be
his ironical comment. You could not shock Jimmy. And he
always mocked you when you shocked yourself. Jimmy would
be the first to advance the consoling theory that he had made
everything much easier for every one by passing, so oppor-
tunely, out of the picture. He would have prided himself on
the felicitous gesture. He would have admired his romantic
rôle.

Yet Jimmy had not wanted to die. He had said as much, very definitely, in that last letter he had written her. Not that he hoped much from the future. But he had no fear of it. Jimmy accepted life on its face value. He lived for the moment.

Sudden death. At thirty-five. Before you knew the answer to any of life's riddles. Perhaps you never knew that, though. Perhaps there *was* no answer. Perhaps all lives, at any age, ended like Jimmy's on an unresolved chord. What difference did it make, anyway, once you were safely dead? It did not make any difference, if you had played the game and had done what you had to do and had never really regretted it.

But there was the pain at your heart that made you keep on thinking. Thinking, in spite of Stephen, whom you loved, and the children, whom you adored, and all the little practical things you had to do every day, like folding sponges for the Red Cross.

Why *couldn't* she feel the war more keenly? With the maps still hung on the living-room wall and Stephen immersed in Liberty Loan campaigns, and Jack and Albert always about the house on their leaves from Camp Brant, and Cicily and Jenny and Isabel's little Belle out every day in Red Cross uniforms, feeding hot dogs and coffee to the entrained doughboys at the canteens in the city switchyards?

They felt the war keenly enough — Cicily and Jenny and little Belle. They were all eager to go to France with the boys from Camp Brant. Cicily wanted to drive an ambulance. Under age, thank Heaven! She and Stephen would not have to face that problem. Uncle Sam, a less yielding relation than two indulgent parents, could be relied upon to keep the girls at home. Yes, ignoble but consoling thought, with little Steve still only fourteen the war could not touch her immediate family.

Isabel was talking of Crisco, now. She was saying it could never take the place of butter.

Jane rose from her seat abruptly. She had promised to meet Cicily at Marshall Field's at noon. They were going to look for a new evening gown. Jack and Albert were coming down for the next week-end. Cicily and Belle were planning a party.

II

'But you're *children*,' said Stephen.

'Oh, Dad,' said Cicily, with a tolerant smile, 'be your age!'

Jane looked from Stephen to her twinkling daughter. Stephen was sitting in his armchair in the Lakewood living-room. The 'Evening Post,' which had fallen from his hands a moment before at Cicily's astounding announcement, lay on the floor at his feet. He was gazing at Cicily with an expression of mingled incredulity and consternation.

Cicily, her hand thrust casually through Jack Bridges's arm, was standing on the hearthrug. She looked very cool and a little amused and not at all disheartened. She looked, indeed, just as she always did, like a yellow dandelion, with her tempestuous bobbed head of golden excelsior. The severity of her khaki uniform with its Red Cross insignia enhanced her flower-like charm. It was the common clay from which the flower had sprung. She looked as fresh as a dandelion, and as indifferent and as irresponsible. Jack Bridges was in khaki, too, with the crossed rifles of the infantryman on his collar and the gold bar of the second lieutenant on his shoulders. He had come down yesterday for that week-end's leave from Camp Brant at Rockford. He had just learned that he was sailing for France in six weeks, with the Eighty-Sixth Division.

Jack did not look at all disheartened, either, but not quite as cool as Cicily, nor nearly as indifferent nor as much amused. He looked just like Robin, Jane thought, with his pleasant snub-nosed smile and his friendly pale blue eyes. He was glancing at Stephen a trifle apologetically, but with no lack of self-confidence.

'How *could* I not have seen this was coming?' thought Jane.

'We're not children, Dad,' continued Cicily with a pleasant smile. 'I was nineteen in February and Jack will be twenty-two in July. We're both well out of the perambulator!'

'I know just how you feel, sir,' said Jack sympathetically, 'and I dare say, in a way, you're right. If it weren't for the war, I don't suppose we *would* be getting married. If it weren't for the war I'd be going to Tech all next winter and Cicily would be buzzing about the tea-fights at home. Still, she'd soon be marrying some one else, you know. I'd never have had the nerve to ask a girl like Cicily to wait for me. If it weren't for the war, I'd be just an "also ran"!'

'Wasn't fought in vain, was it, Jacky?' said Cicily, pinching his elbow.

He kissed her pink cheek, very coolly, under her parents' startled eyes.

'I wouldn't expect to keep Cicily waiting at the church very long, even in war-time,' said Jack — Jane caught the note of humility behind his levity — 'so we thought ——'

'Jack!' said Cicily. 'Don't put it like that! We don't think — we *know!* We're going to get married, Dad, on the last day of June and have a two weeks' honeymoon before he sails for France.'

'Cicily,' said Jane, 'you're much too young. You haven't had *any* experience. You can't know your own mind. The war has been fearfully upsetting, I know, for your generation. But you're still a child. Oh — I know you've been home a year from Rosemary! But what sort of a year has it been?

Just war work — and Jack. Not even a proper début. He was here every evening last summer when he was at Fort Sheridan in the R.O.T.C. And since he went to Rockford you've been getting letters and motoring up to see him and planning to get him down here on leave! You've never *looked* at another man ——' Why *hadn't* she seen this was coming? It was all so terribly clear in retrospect.

'You can't get married,' said Stephen firmly, 'before Jack goes to France.'

'You married Mumsy,' said Cicily sweetly, 'before you went to Cuba.'

'That was very different,' said Jane.

'Why was it different?' said Cicily.

'Because your father was twenty-nine years old,' said Jane decidedly, 'and I was twenty-one and I'd been home from college for two years and I'd known lots of men and ——'

'Well, I bet if you'd wanted to marry the first man you looked at you'd have done it!' said Cicily.

A sudden flood of memories swept over Jane. Her father's library on Pine Street. Her mother, shrill and effective. Her father, kind and competent. Herself and André, two shaken, irresolute children, standing mute before them, a world of young emotion lying shattered at their feet. But this generation was different. No trace even of anxiety in Cicily's amused smile.

'Anyway, I'm going to. We're not asking you, Mumsy, we're telling you! It's all settled. Belle's talking to Aunt Isabel this minute ——'

'Belle?' questioned Jane.

'Belle and Albert,' said Cicily. 'Albert Lancaster. He's told his mother. We're going to have a double wedding, here in the garden, the last day of June.'

'A double wedding!' cried Jane and Stephen at once.

'Yes,' said Cicily calmly. 'Do you think the roses will be out? We've planned for everything. Why, Jenny's known about it for two weeks. She's going to be bridesmaid for both of us. Just Jenny — but lots of ushers, with crossed swords, you know. Belle and I are going to cut the cakes with Albert's and Jack's sabres.'

'Cicily,' said Jane, 'this is perfectly preposterous! Aunt Isabel will never listen to you! Why, Belle's only eighteen! Albert's not yet twenty.'

'He will be in August,' said Cicily. 'I don't see why you carry on about it like this. I don't see why you don't think it's all very sweet and touching. Belle's been my best friend all my life and now I'm marrying her brother and she's marrying the son of one of *your* best friends and ——'

'In the first place,' said Stephen, 'you're all first cousins.'

'Albert isn't anybody's first cousin,' said Cicily pertly. 'So that lets Belle out. And as for Jack and me — that's all right. We looked it all up in Havelock Ellis. There's no danger in consanguinity if there isn't an hereditary taint in the family. We've been awfully eugenic, Mumsy! We've simply scoured the connection for an hereditary taint! And we haven't found a thing but Uncle Robin's short-sightedness. Of course I'd hate to have a short-sighted baby — but maybe I wouldn't as it's not in the common line. Anyway, there's no insanity, nor epilepsy, nor cancer, nor T.B., nor venereal disease ——'

'Cicily,' said Stephen a little hastily, 'you don't know what you're talking about ——'

Cicily dropped Jack's arm and sank down on the arm of her father's chair. She kissed the bald spot on top of his head very tenderly.

'Dad, dear,' she said very sweetly, 'perhaps we don't. Perhaps you didn't know just what *you* were talking about when you wanted to marry Mumsy. But still you did it. You did it and you went to war and it all came out all right. Can't you remember how you felt when you wanted to marry Mumsy ——?'

Across the dandelion head Stephen's eyes met Jane's.

'What are we going to do with them, Jane?' he said, with a smile that was half a sigh.

'Nothing,' said Jane very practically, 'at the moment. We'll talk it over with Isabel and Robin. And Muriel, of course. I don't suppose Bert understands much, any more, of what goes on around him, but Muriel's always decided ——'

Cicily jumped to her feet and threw her arms around Jane's neck.

'That's a good Mumsy!' she cried. Then, turning to Jack, 'Come out in the garden, old thing! The apple tree's still in bloom!' She seized his hand and turned toward the terrace doors.

'Cicily,' said Jane doubtfully, 'nothing is settled. I don't quite like ——'

Cicily burst into indulgent laughter.

'What do you think I am, Mumsy?' she inquired cheerfully. 'Sweet nineteen and never been kissed? Oh, you *are* precious — both of you!' She tossed a kiss to her parents on the hearth-rug and dragged Jack from the room. Jane watched their slim, young, khaki-clad figures romp down the lawn and dis-appear behind the clump of evergreens.

'Stephen,' said Jane, 'it's a very different generation. But what are we going to *do?*'

'I'm going to remember,' said Stephen, rising from his chair, 'how I felt when I wanted to marry Mumsy!' He took her hand in his. Dear old Stephen! His eyes were just a little moist behind his bone-rimmed spectacles. Jane kissed him very tenderly.

'Just the same,' said Jane, 'I wasn't a bit like Cicily.'

'You were just as sweet,' said Stephen, 'and nearly as young.'

'But I was different,' said Jane. 'I know I was different.' She sighed a little as she slipped from Stephen's embrace. 'Well — we'll see what Isabel has to say,' she said.

III

'I don't see why,' said Isabel, 'you object to Cicily's marrying Jack. Poor child, he's going to war next month. He may be killed ——' Her lip was trembling.

'Well,' said Muriel, 'I don't see why *you* object to Belle's marrying Albert. *He's* going to war next month and *he* may be killed.' Muriel's lip was not trembling. Her voice was as logical as her statement.

'Belle's younger,' said Isabel.

'Only a year,' said Jane.

'And Belle's different,' said Isabel. 'Cicily's always equal to any situation. She's so much more dominating. Cicily's one of the people you know will always come out on top. And Jack adores her. He's always adored her.'

'Well, Albert's one of the people you know will always come out on top,' said Muriel. 'I'm sure he's very dominating. And he's very much in love with Belle. I can't see why they shouldn't be very happy.'

'Of course,' said Isabel, producing her handkerchief, 'neither of them may ever come home from France.'

'But again they may,' said Jane a trifle cynically. 'If they don't, of course, I suppose a war marriage would not really hurt any one. But if they do, they'll have to live with each other for another fifty years or so.'

'It's very easy to see,' said Isabel reproachfully, from the depths of the handkerchief, 'that you haven't given a son to the nation.'

Jane felt a little ashamed of her cynical utterance. It was all wrong, however, to confuse the practical issues with sentimentality. They had been discussing the problem for hours in the Lakewood living-room. Robin and Isabel and Muriel had come out for dinner in order to discuss it, and now it was half-past ten and they were no nearer a solution than they had been at seven. Robin and Stephen had said very little all evening. Jane and Muriel and Isabel had said a great deal. But from the very beginning of the argument, Jane had been conscious of a fundamental difference between her point of view and that of the mothers of the prospective bridegrooms. Isabel and Muriel were staunchly united in wishing their sons to have everything — anything — before they went to the front.

'Those young lives,' said Isabel, now frankly sobbing, 'may end in another two months. We owe those boys all the fulfilment we can give them.'

Of course, however, she did not want Belle to marry Albert Lancaster. Logic had never been Isabel's strong point. She wanted Cicily to marry Jack and Belle to consent to an engagement. Albert would not be twenty until the first of August. And twenty was a preposterous age for a husband. Jane could easily understand, however, if Isabel couldn't, why pretty little pink-and-white Belle wanted to marry him.

Albert Lancaster was a very alluring young person. He seemed quite grown up. He seemed older than Jack, in fact, who was two years his senior. He had inherited his father's easy social charm and combined it with his mother's dark beauty. Not that Albert really looked like Muriel. He looked like her family, however, though not at all like a Jew. Rather like some young Greek of the Golden Age, with his pale, olive-coloured face, his dark eyes and hair, his aquiline nose, his short supercilious Greek lip, and his flat, low Greek brow

— a discus-thrower, perhaps, or runner — no, thought Jane, more like a youthful Bacchus. You felt that vine leaves would adorn his hair. They sometimes did, of course. That was probably one of the things that was troubling Isabel. Naturally she could not go into that in front of Muriel. Oh, yes — Jane could quite understand why Belle wanted to marry him.

Now Jack, on the other hand, Jack who looked just like Robin — Jack with his snub nose and pleasant friendly twinkle — Jack who had played with Cicily from her cradle — why did Cicily want to marry *him?* He was a sweet boy, of course. Clever and kindly and considerate. A much safer son-in-law than Albert Lancaster, with his looks and his inheritance and his vine leaves! But still — Jane really could not understand how Cicily could want to *marry* him.

'I don't see what either of you object to in either marriage,' said Muriel. 'We're all old friends. We've known all four children from the day of their birth. There's plenty of money. Cicily and Belle are charming girls and best friends. The boys have both been to Harvard and are going to war and are very attractive young men. My goodness! When you think what *some* people's children marry! I can't see why it's not all very suitable.'

'But Muriel, they're *children,*' put in Stephen from the depths of his armchair.

'Kids,' said Robin solemnly, from the corner of the sofa.

'I don't care,' said Muriel. 'I was only just twenty when I married, myself. And I've often thought,' she continued superbly, 'that life would have been quite a little easier for me if Bert hadn't been nineteen years older than I. I *believe* in early marriages. I think they keep a boy straight all those important years when his character is forming. And a girl has her babies early and gets through with all that sort of thing when she's still young enough to enjoy herself ——'

'But that's just what's *dangerous* about them!' wailed Isabel. Jane knew she had it on the tip of her tongue to say, 'Look at *you*, Muriel!' Time was when she would have said it. Isabel was growing discreet with age.

'I think you're very cynical,' said Muriel. 'I think it would be lovely — a double wedding, Jane, in your beautiful garden ——'

'In any case,' said Isabel, 'I think Belle should be married from her father's house. It's very sweet of you, Jane, to offer ——'

'I haven't offered!' cried Jane. 'I haven't done anything all evening but say we shouldn't let them. The boys will be sailing in six weeks ——' She saw, instantly, that she had not helped her cause at all. Isabel again buried her face in her handkerchief. Muriel returned to the charge.

'If little Steve were twenty, instead of fourteen, Jane, you wouldn't be so unfeeling!'

That was quite true, reflected Jane. If little Steve were the age to make suitable cannon fodder, she would want him to have everything, everything life had to give, before he went to France.

'I suppose,' said Isabel, wiping her eyes, 'I suppose we'll have to give in.'

'Of course we will,' said Muriel briskly. Then added piously, 'My greatest regret is that dear Bert isn't able to share in Albert's happiness.'

'How *is* he now, Muriel?' asked Isabel curiously. For a moment the war weddings were forgotten.

'Oh — quite helpless,' said Muriel. 'In bed, of course. He can't talk and I don't know how much he *does* understand. He has two very good nurses, however. Such pretty girls. I hope Bert can realize how pretty they are ——'

'But Isabel,' said Jane, returning to more important issues, 'you don't mean you think we've lost the fight? You don't mean you think we ought to *let* them?'

'How can we help it?' said Isabel. 'But about the double wedding ——'

'Oh, I think that would be *lovely!*' said Muriel again. 'Your apartment is so small, Isabel, and June's so pretty in the country. If Jane will take it off your hands ——'

'I *won't* take it off her hands,' said Jane. 'Anyway, I think we oughtn't to decide until we've talked it all over with Papa.'

'Oh — Papa!' said Isabel doubtfully. 'You know how Papa is, Jane. He's really quite — difficult, sometimes. The war has aged him awfully.'

'I don't think he's difficult,' said Jane. 'I think he's very wise. And I think we ought to talk with Mrs. Lester.'

'Well, Jane,' said Muriel, 'you know Mother's eighty. Of course she's wonderful and she adores Albert, but I often think she's a little out of sympathy with the modern generation. Rather critical, I mean.'

'Mamma's terribly critical,' said Isabel. 'Sometimes I think she just hates her grandchildren.'

'She doesn't understand them,' said Jane. 'But she loves them. And Papa adores them. He's always been so proud of Jack, Isabel — with the name and all.'

'Then he ought to want to see him happy,' said Isabel. She rose with a sigh as she spoke. 'Come on, Muriel, we must be getting back to town.'

'What do *you* think, Robin?' asked Jane. 'You haven't said a word all evening.'

'I think it's fierce,' said Robin solemnly. 'Like life.'

'But what can we *do?*' persisted Jane.

'Nothing, probably,' said Robin. 'Again like life.'

Jane slipped her arm through Stephen's. They walked slowly with their guests to the front door.

'Well — I'll talk to Belle again,' said Isabel. 'Perhaps she'll listen to reason. And I'll write to Jack at Rockford before I go to bed to-night.'

'I'm going to wire Albert,' said Muriel. 'A very hopeful wire. I think he needs cheering.'

'I'll take it up with Cicily,' said Jane. 'And Stephen wants to talk to her. But I know it won't do a bit of good.'

'Good-night,' said Isabel, from the depths of the motor. 'Button up your coat, Robin. It's a cold evening for June.'

'Good-night,' said Jane. The motor crunched slowly around the gravel curve of the driveway. Jane turned to Stephen. 'Stephen,' she said, 'what will we *do?*'

'Let nature take its course, I guess,' said Stephen grimly. 'You didn't get much help from Isabel.'

'Wasn't Muriel terrible?' said Jane. 'Did you hear what she said about Bert's trained nurses?'

'Yes,' said Stephen, turning back to the front door.

'I'm glad it's not Albert,' said Jane solemnly, as she entered the hall. 'I'm awfully sorry for Isabel. I couldn't bear it, Stephen, really, I couldn't bear it, if Cicily were going to marry Bert Lancaster's son.'

'It's pretty rough all right,' said Stephen. 'I'm sorry for Robin.'

'He's always adored Belle,' said Jane.

'*I've* always adored Cicily,' said Stephen.

'I know,' said Jane. 'But we like Jack.'

'He's a nice kid,' said Stephen. 'But as a husband for Cicily ——'

'I know,' said Jane. They stood for a moment, gazing rather helplessly into each other's eyes.

'Well,' said Stephen, turning to bolt the front door, 'we'd better go up to bed. I'll turn out the lights.'

He went back into the living-room. Jane started up the stairs. She was still overcome with a sense of inadequacy for not having foreseen this calamity. But who could have foreseen it? It was perfectly preposterous. What was the matter with the rising generation? What was the matter with her own? She thought again of herself and André. Of her father and mother. She felt she sympathized with them, as never before. But with Cicily, too, when she thought of André. First love — was there not a bloom about it that never came again? What would her life have been if she had married André? If she had married André would he seem now like Stephen? If she had married André she would never have loved Jimmy. She would never have known Jimmy. Jimmy would be alive now, married to Agnes, living in New York. Jane could not imagine her life without her love for Jimmy. Without her marriage to Stephen, for that matter. Yet when she thought of André and of her young self as she had been that last winter before she went to Bryn Mawr ——

Your inner life — how confusing it all was! A chaos of conflicting loyalties! You would like to think, of course, that you were the sort of woman who was capable of experiencing, once and forever, a central, dominating passion. But as far as the essential sense of emotional intimacy went, she might as well be André's wife, or Jimmy's, that moment, as Stephen's. Why had things turned out as they had? Predestination was probably the answer. Cause and effect. One thing leading to another. Free will was only a delusion. Why not turn fatalist, pure and simple, and not worry any longer? Not care.

But you *had* to care about your children. Worry about them, too. You had to and you ought to. When you thought of them all theories of predestination were completely shattered.

Jane turned to smile at Stephen, as he entered the blue

bedroom. He looked terribly tired and quite a little discouraged, but he gave her an answering smile.

IV

'The older I grow, Papa,' said Jane very seriously, 'the more I admire your technique as a parent.'

'That's very flattering of you, Kid,' said Mr. Ward with a twinkle.

'Why, Isabel and I *never* gave you and Mamma *any* trouble,' Jane went on, still very seriously.

'Oh, I don't know about that, Kid,' interrupted Mr. Ward. 'You went to Bryn Mawr over your mother's dead body ——'

'Oh — Bryn Mawr!' threw in Jane contemptuously.

'It seemed very important at the time,' said Mr. Ward. 'She thought it would damn you to eternal spinsterhood. And before that you had embarked at the age of seventeen on a clandestine engagement ——'

'It *wasn't* clandestine!' protested Jane. 'We told you right away!'

'Yes, you did,' admitted Mr. Ward, with his indulgent twinkle. 'You were very good children. Still — it was a bit disquieting ——'

They were sitting side by side on the old brown velvet sofa in the Pine Street library. The brilliant June sunshine was pouring in the west window, striking the glass bookcase doors and making them look a little dusty, just as it always had from time immemorial. The firelight was dancing on the shiny surfaces of polished walnut, here and there in the darker corners, and shining on the big brass humidor on the desk that held Mr. Ward's cigars. Mr. Ward always had a fire, now, even in summer. The room was hotter than it used to be and the big branching rubber tree in the west window was gone.

Otherwise everything about the Pine Street library was completely unchanged.

Everything, that is, but Mr. Ward himself. Jane, looking tenderly across the sofa at her father, was suddenly conscious of how old and frail he seemed. Isabel was right. The war had aged him. Or perhaps it was his retirement from business that had taken place two years before. Mr. Ward lived, now, in his little brown library. When Jane dropped in, she always found him there, settled comfortably in his leather armchair, reading biographies, or poring over the war news, or perhaps just smoking, reflectively, a solitary cigar.

The room was really very warm. Jane looked at the smouldering fire. Her glance, wandering casually over the familiar mantel-shelf, met the Bard of Avon's wise mahogany eye. The Bard of Avon always made her think of her wedding ceremony.

'Papa,' said Jane, 'how can you tell, how can you possibly tell, just whom your children ought to marry?'

'You can't,' said Mr. Ward promptly. 'But you can make a pretty good guess at whom they ought not to.'

'But how can you stop them?' said Jane.

'I don't know,' said Mr. Ward very seriously after a little pause.

'You stopped me,' said Jane. 'You stopped me because you made me feel, somehow or other, though I didn't agree with you, that you were inevitably right. Right, because you were my father. That's what's gone out of the family relationship since I was seventeen, Papa. Children don't think you are right any longer, just because you are a parent.'

'Well, you're not,' said Mr. Ward promptly. 'That's probably a step in the right direction, Kid. What's known as progress.'

'Well, it makes life terribly difficult for parents,' sighed Jane.

'And I can't help thinking it may make life terribly difficult for children.'

'Life's terribly difficult at times for every one,' said Mr. Ward. 'A little thing like filial obedience doesn't solve all the problems.'

'When I think of the *ex cathedra* pronouncements that Mamma used to make!' cried Jane. 'Why, I never thought of questioning them!'

'And were they always right?' asked Mr. Ward.

'They were usually wrong,' said Jane. 'But at least they stopped discussion and they decided the issue. Parents used to be just like umpires. All they had to do was to make a decision and stick to it!'

'It wasn't an ideal system,' was Mr. Ward's comment.

'You didn't question it when it was in fashion,' retorted Jane. 'You didn't have the slightest hesitation in forbidding me to marry André. But we loved each other. We truly did, Papa. You never really took that into consideration. I might have been very happy as André's wife.'

Mr. Ward's glance was just a little intent as he contemplated his younger daughter.

'You've been very happy as Stephen's wife, Kid,' he said gently.

'Yes,' said Jane uncertainly. Words were too crude to define the subtleties of emotion. 'Yes, I've been happy. But my marrying him was awfully irrelevant.' Suddenly that statement seemed terribly disloyal to Stephen. 'You know, Papa,' she said in extenuation, 'a war changed everything in my life.'

There was a pause, for a moment, in the sunlit room. Jane did not look at her father, but she knew, without looking, from his sudden, breathless silence that he had suffered a slight sense of shock. She realized then that her words were

open to misinterpretation. She glanced quickly up at him.
He *was* shocked. He looked at her a moment a little uncertainly. Then,

'Which war, Jane?' he asked steadily.

She was awfully glad that he had put the direct question.
In answering it she could answer all the unspoken questions
that had been worrying him for the last four years.

'The Spanish one,' she said gravely. 'The other didn't —
didn't really affect my action. I mean — I mean it was all
settled before ——' Her voice was failing her. She could not
bear to mention Jimmy's name.

'I'm glad to hear it, Kid,' said her father gently.

He understood. She would not have to mention it. Jane
drew a long breath and felt the emotional tension of the
moment snap as she did so. She could return now to the problems of the younger generation.

'All I mean is,' she went on brightly, 'you can't really tell,
can you, what will bring your children happiness? Perhaps
they *ought* to decide for themselves ——'

As she spoke, Mrs. Ward opened the library door. Isabel
followed her into the room. They had been talking together
in Mrs. Ward's bedroom.

'Well, I hope you've convinced Jane that she must put her
foot down,' said Mrs. Ward briskly. Her hand was on the
bell-rope to summon Minnie to bring in the tea.

'Mamma, you don't know what it's like to handle Belle
and Cicily,' said Isabel wearily.

'I handled you and Jane!' retorted Mrs. Ward. 'And very
foolish you often were! If it hadn't been for your father and
me ——'

Jane and her father burst simultaneously into irreverent
laughter. Mrs. Ward looked quite offended.

'You don't make it any easier, John, to control the grandchildren,' she said severely.

'I've retired,' said Mr. Ward, when he had subdued his laughter. 'From my family as from my business. At seventy-two I'm glad to be a spectator. I hand the controls over to Jane.'

v

'Jenny's really so homely,' said Cicily frankly, 'that I think we ought to feature it.'

'Feature it?' questioned Flora.

'Yes,' said Cicily, 'make her look quaint, you know; as if she were *meant* to be funny.'

'The first duty of a bridesmaid, in any case,' said Muriel, 'is to look less pretty than the bride.'

'No one could help looking less pretty than *these* brides,' said Flora, with a glance from Belle to Cicily.

Isabel looked pleased. Jane felt herself smiling. Jenny did not seem at all insulted by her sister's candour.

They were all sitting in Flora's hat shop. They had just decided on the model for the wedding veils and were now discussing the bridesmaid's hat.

Flora's hat shop was doing a booming business. It had been just about to die of inanition three years ago when the Belgian babies came along and gave it a new lease of life. Flora had been planning to close it when the idea came to her to change it into a war charity. 'Aux Armes des Alliés,' she had rechristened it, and pasted French war posters all over the cubistic designs of the coach-house. She had charged fantastic prices and had really made a great deal of money. She had photographs of all the Belgian babies she supported, on the walls of the fitting-rooms. In spite of the submarines she made semi-annual trips to Paris for the hats and the photographs. She was a member of several French relief committees and so managed to get a passport. When Mr. Furness died two years before, she had given large sums to the funds for war orphans. She had made a great many French friends and was talking, now, of going to live in Paris when the war was over — if it ever was. She would like a little apartment out near Passy. But now she was discussing the bridesmaid's hat.

'I think,' she said critically, backing away from Jenny and looking fixedly at her plain little face and straight, blonde, bobbed hair — 'I think — a poke bonnet. Yes, Jane! A pink poke bonnet — very pale. You're right, Cicily, she must be quaint! A hooped skirt, Isabel, a pink hooped skirt, with little garlands around it and a sweet, tight little bodice. Pale pink taffeta, don't you think, Muriel? And a little 1860 bouquet with ribbon streamers and a white lace frill. Oh, Jenny, my dear, you'll be charming! We'll emphasize your angles. You'll look like a cross-stitched design on a sampler! How old are you?'

'Sixteen,' said Jenny meekly.

'You don't look it,' said Flora. 'Do you think, Jane, that pantalettes would be going too far?'

Jane thought they would.

'I suppose you're right,' said Flora, 'though I always think a wedding should be primarily a pageant. This one will be lovely. The hot weather will bring out all the roses. What are you wearing, Jane?'

'What does the mother of the bride always wear?' said Jane ironically. 'Beige chiffon, of course. I didn't think I had any choice.'

'And Isabel, too?' said Flora critically.

'Well, no. Now that I think of it, Isabel is a mother of a bride and she's wearing grey.'

'Muriel's dress is lovely,' said Flora. 'I'm making her hat. Mauve. Let me make yours, Jane. For Heaven's sake, get a good one, for once!'

'All right,' said Jane indifferently. 'I'd be glad not to have to bother about it.'

'We've got to go,' said Cicily. 'We're going down to Crichton's with Aunt Isabel to pick out my tea-set.'

'I chose Belle's yesterday,' said Muriel as she rose.

'It's lovely,' said Isabel. 'It seems just a moment ago that you were choosing your own.'

'I know,' said Muriel. 'And Flora and Jane were trying on those blue bridesmaids' dresses. They *were* pretty.'

Jane thought of Flora's blue bridesmaid's dress lying crumpled on her bedroom chair the morning after her mother's death. She thought of herself hanging it up in Flora's closet, while Flora dressed in the little black frock that Mrs. Lester had brought over. She wondered if Flora were thinking of it, too. But Flora's face was very tranquil.

'Fittings for all of you, Wednesday morning,' she said. 'I'll have a beige model here, Jane, for you to look at.'

They all went out of the brown-stone stable and stood for a moment in the old carriage court. The Furnesses' back yard looked just as it always had. Flora had the playhouse painted every year. But the houses across Rush Street had all been rented to business firms. Dressmakers and milliners and decorators had signs over every door. The clean frilled lace curtains and evenly drawn shades in Flora's Victorian mansion seemed strangely out of place in their commercial environment. They recalled a vanished era. Flora's lace curtains looked just like her mother's — just as clean and just as frilly and just as Victorian. She kept the old place up beautifully. She even kept the orange tree blooming in the conservatory. But if she were going to live in Paris ——

Jane sighed. It did not seem to her just a moment ago that she had tried on Muriel's blue bridesmaid's dress.

VI

Jane stood at Isabel's side in the front row of the little congregation that had gathered in the rose garden. On her other hand, pressed close against the tightly drawn white satin ribbon, stood little Steve. Little Steve, at fourteen, was taller than his mother and looked exactly like his father. He was wearing his first long white flannel trousers, and Jane knew that he considered the occasion of the double wedding mainly important as his début into man's estate. Behind Jane stood Mr. and Mrs. Ward and Alden Carver, the only representative of the Carver family who had come West for the wedding. Mr. and Mrs. Carver no longer cared to undertake transcontinental travel. They were both over seventy. Silly had stayed at Gull Rocks to look after them.

Across the grassy aisle, Muriel, radiant under the new mauve hat, rested one graceful mauve arm on the back of Mrs. Lester's wheel-chair. Rosalie and Edith, once more imported from Cleveland for a family festival, supported their mother on the other side. Mrs. Lester, herself, colossal in shiny black taffeta, blinked like a wrinkled sibyl in the brilliant June sunshine. There was something a little sinister about her massive, motionless figure. Her aged face, under her mantilla cap of black lace, looked like a mask of tan wax. The wrinkles, the salient nose, the cascade of double chins might have been a clever sculptor's effigy of old age. Only the eyelids moved. Her bright dark eyes glittered behind them with a gleam of helpless intelligence that seemed imprisoned in the motionless mask. Mrs. Lester had deplored these marriages.

Behind the two families the garden was filled with guests. The orchestra beyond the clump of evergreens had just slipped from the riotous strains of 'Tipperary' into the first sentimental notes of the Barcarolle from the 'Tales of Hoffmann.' Muriel had requested it. It had been played at her wedding. Jane and Isabel had thought that the less this wedding was like Muriel's the better. Nevertheless, they had conceded the Barcarolle.

Jane stood motionless, her eyes on the arch of Dorothy Perkins roses under which the clergyman would soon appear. It was outlined against the pure blue of the June sky. High overhead one white cloud floated, a flying dome of alabaster, above the improvised altar. The clergyman was in ambush, behind the hedge with Jack and Albert and their attendant groomsmen, waiting for the bridal party to appear at the other end of the garden. Jane wondered why they did not come. She had kissed Cicily and arranged her train, just before walking up the aisle. She wished she could lean out, like Steve, over the white satin ribbons, and see whether anything had gone wrong.

As she was wondering, the orchestra, in response to some hidden signal, swelled into 'Lohengrin.' The clergyman, with the promptness of a marionette, swung out in white vestments under the arch of pink bloom. The four young men in khaki followed him. Jane heard Isabel catch her breath sharply at the sight of Jack. She saw Albert smile in self-conscious reassurance at Muriel across the aisle. Jack was staring straight down the grassy path, waiting for his first glimpse of Cicily. The first pair of khaki-clad ushers passed slowly by Jane. Then the second. Then the third. Then Jenny, successfully quaint, in her ridiculous hoopskirt. Her pale, plain little face was barely visible in the depths of Flora's poke bonnet. What Jane could see of it looked intensely serious. Her hands shook a little as they gripped the 1860 bouquet. Her knuckles were white. She turned to face the congregation just as Belle passed by, a cloud of floating tulle, on Robin's arm. Albert stepped out to meet her. Then

Jane saw Cicily, another cloud, her head held high, her feet spurning the earth, her hand on Stephen's elbow. She must have smiled at Jack. His funny snub-nosed face reflected the radiance of that smile. The 'Lohengrin' faded away into silence. The clergyman took up the ritual.

'Dearly beloved brethren, we are met together in the sight of God and this company ——'

In the sight of God. Was God really present, thought Jane, this sunny June afternoon, looking at them all, in her familiar Lakewood garden? Did God have time to take in all the weddings, or did He pick and choose? Did He sometimes withhold His blessing? Could God be summoned peremptorily to any altar? Did He never have another engagement? Was He not too busy this afternoon, for instance, on the battle-fields of France, to look in on this little ceremony in a Lakewood garden? The clergyman's voice droned on.

'—— the holy estate of matrimony, which is an honorable estate, instituted of God in the time of man's innocence ——'

In the time of man's innocence. That was, of course, the time for weddings. Jane thought fleetingly of André. Of herself in his arms. These four children were innocent enough. Too innocent. That was the difficulty. Too innocent to enter into that holy estate reverently, discreetly, advisedly, soberly, and in the fear of God. The modern generation was neither reverent, discreet, advised, nor sober. They were in fear of nothing. Certainly not of God. Certainly not of their parents. Robin and Stephen, standing side by side in that khaki-clad group of striplings, a little bald, a little grey, a little stooped, a little paunchy in their formal black broadcloth cutaways, waiting to give, reluctantly, these women to be married to these men, were the only reverent, discreet, advised, and sober individuals before that improvised altar. They were in fear of God. They were in fear of everything — for their children. But fear was foolish. Fear was, perhaps, hysterical. They were all good children. Isabel's sobs recalled Jane's attention to the ritual of betrothal.

'I, Cicily, take thee, John Ward, for my wedded husband ——'

John Ward. Her father's namesake. Isabel's first baby was marrying her own. Isabel's baby — only yesterday an armful of afghans — now a soldier in khaki, suitable cannon fodder, was marrying Cicily with her head like a dandelion. Marrying Cicily not twenty feet away from the site of the old sandpile where they had built their sand castles ——

'I, Albert, take thee, Isabel, for my wedded wife ——'

Albert Lancaster — the second Albert Lancaster — Muriel's beautiful little boy who had grown up to look like a youthful Bacchus and to act like one, too, sometimes — Cicily's laughing story of his behavior at the bachelors' dinner at the University Club the night before had been really outrageous — Albert Lancaster, who was his father's son — but only nineteen and heart-breakingly innocent in spite of the vine leaves — was marrying Belle — little Belle, with a face like an apple blossom.

When had she first thought that Belle looked like an apple blossom? Four years ago, at the foot of the stairs in the Lakewood hall, with Jimmy framed in the portières of the living-room door. Jimmy, watching her kiss little Belle. Jimmy, whose mocking, informal ghost had curiously no place at this ceremony in the Lakewood garden. It paled before Stephen's substantial presence. Stephen, who adored Cicily and had made the sandpile and had shared so consolingly in the worry and hurry and foreboding of the last hectic weeks. Weeks in which the sustaining sense of Jimmy's cheerful companionship had faded ever so imperceptibly, but irrevocably, out of the foreground of Jane's reveries. Lost in the bustle of prepa-

ration, the preoccupation of misgiving, Jane, for the first time
since Jimmy's death in France, had had no time for Jimmy.

'If I had gone away with him,' she reflected, 'if I had married him, I suppose we should both be here to-day, watching
Stephen give away Cicily. I should be feeling about Stephen
just as I do now' — for after all there was only one way to feel
about Stephen, standing helplessly by Cicily's side before that
improvised altar — 'and feeling about Jimmy the way I did
then ——'

A faint shiver of repulsion passed over Jane. She felt herself suddenly submerged in an ignoble sense of relief at the
realization of domestic decencies forever maintained, of vulgar complexities forever avoided. Were worlds well lost for
love? Jane did not know. Jane's love for Jimmy had presented in her life an absolutely insoluble problem. His death
had placed a question mark beyond it. If he had lived, perhaps she might have arrived at a solution. She only knew,
now, that she had acted in response to an inner instinct so
strong that love itself had stood vanquished before it. The
instinct was victorious, but the victory was barren. She had
tried to preserve the happiness of others. In reward she had
been left only with a feeble, futile feeling that, in any event,
her own happiness could never have been attained. A barren
victory. A victory that was essentially a defeat ——

Nevertheless, it was impossible to think of Jimmy standing
at her elbow, bound by the ties of wedlock at Cicily's marriage. He was a phantom lover. He had to be. No other kind
was possible for a Lakewood housewife — for Mrs. Stephen
Carver —— But should one sacrifice love to nothing more
than a sense of decorum?

The orchestra swelled joyously into the Mendelssohn wedding march. Jane had not heard the clergyman's last solemn
adjuration. The bridal couples turned from the altar. The

groomsmen and ushers drew their swords. Bright, virgin blades, flashing in the June sunshine. They made an arch of steel. Soon those swords would be spitting Germans. To-day they formed a nuptial canopy. Swords should be beaten into ploughshares. They should not spit Germans. Neither should they make an arch, a churchly, Gothic arch, a glamorous, romantic arch, under which young warriors — too young warriors — led their brides from glamour to reality.

Cicily, radiant on Jack's arm, threw her a sunshine smile. Belle, under shy eyelids, flashed a glance at Isabel. Jenny pranced down the grassy aisle to the rhythm of the Mendelssohn. Her nervousness was all gone. She was young and absurd and adorable. The ushers gallantly sheathed their swords and fell in to follow. Jane felt Stephen's hand upon her arm. She knew that she was looking at him stupidly. There were tears in his eyes. Robin was blowing his nose. Isabel was frankly weeping. Muriel, beyond the satin ribbons, was powdering her tear-stained cheeks. It was over. Jane realized that she had experienced no emotion whatever during the brief ceremony. It had been routed by thought. Confused, perplexing thought. Emotion would come, Jane knew, if she looked into Stephen's eyes. She would not look into them. She would take his arm and hold her head high and walk down that grassy aisle in the sight of that company — and God, if He were really there — as if she had approved of these weddings. Stephen read her heart. No one else should read it. Except her father — Jane caught his grave, anxious glance — and God, whose glance she could not catch.

The Mendelssohn had ceased. The congregation were nodding and whispering and smiling. The orchestra was playing 'Over There.' Jane slipped her fingers through the crook of Stephen's elbow. The ushers, already gathered around the punch-bowl under the apple tree, had begun to sing. The young male chorus swelled out joyously over the sunlit garden.

> 'Over there! Over there!
> Send the word — send the word over there!
> That the Yanks are coming, the Yanks are coming,
> With the drums rum-tumming everywhere!
> So prepare! Say a prayer! ——'

Jane moved with light step down the grassy aisle to the rollicking rhythm of the war song. If God were in that garden, He knew her misgivings. He knew that she was praying He had blessed those marriages. If there *was* a God. And if He was in that garden.

CHAPTER II

I

'MURIEL thinks,' said Isabel, 'that Belle should go into mourning.'

'I'm not surprised,' said Jane. 'The Lesters always had a lot of family feeling.'

'Just the same,' said Isabel, 'I've just bought all her maternity clothes. So soon after the trousseau. And they're so pretty. Modern clothes are really very concealing. When I think of the tight waists we had to wear — and all those pleats put in to let out! Don't you think it seems ridiculous to order another set?'

'Yes,' said Jane. 'But Muriel adored her mother. So did Edith and Rosalie.'

'Oh, I've no doubt,' said Isabel, 'that they'll all flap about like black crows for two years. But Belle's so young — she hardly knew Mrs. Lester — and the baby's coming in two months. She's worried about Albert. I hate to plunge her into black.'

Isabel was sitting on the window-seat in Jane's blue bedroom. They were discussing Mrs. Lester's death, which had occurred the night before, and Mrs. Lester's funeral, which would take place next day. Mrs. Lester had died in her sleep. She had been found dead by her maid coming in with her breakfast tray. Her death had been a great shock to Muriel.

'Belle hasn't heard from Albert?' asked Jane. 'Any plans, I mean?'

'He has no plans,' said Isabel resentfully. 'No more than Jack has. How can they plan, poor darlings? I think it's outrageous for the Government to keep them hanging around

France four months after the armistice! As far as I can see, it didn't do anybody a bit of good for them to go over. They might just as well have stayed in Rockford.'

That was quite true, reflected Jane. Jack had not even seen action. Albert had spent the last two days of the war sitting in a muddy trench. Neither boy had struck a blow at the Germans. Albert had not seen nearly as much fighting in France as Stephen had at San Juan Hill.

'Muriel's going to be a dreadful mother-in-law,' said Isabel irrelevantly.

Jane could not help smiling. She knew what Cicily thought of Isabel in that capacity. Belle and Cicily, in the absence of their young husbands, had seen a great deal of their mothers-in-law.

'You'd think,' Cicily had said, only last evening to Jane and Stephen, 'you'd think *she* was going to have the baby — not me!'

'You'd think,' said Isabel, while Jane was smiling, 'you'd think Muriel was going to have Belle's baby. She's bought her some lovely things, of course, but she's always interfering. And now she wants her to wear crêpe!'

'I'd like to wear crêpe myself,' said Jane. 'I loved Mrs. Lester.'

'She was a grand old matriarch,' said Isabel, rising with a sigh. 'Still, she was over eighty. Muriel knew she couldn't live forever. Queer, isn't it, that Bert should outlive her — in the state he's been in for the last five years?'

'How is Papa?' asked Jane, rising in her turn.

'Oh, much better. His cold is almost gone. Dr. Bancroft says he can go to the funeral.'

'Not up to Graceland?' said Jane, with a glance at the February sleet storm that was silvering the garden. 'In this weather?'

'I don't know about Graceland,' said Isabel, 'but, anyway, the church. They've asked him to be an honorary pall-bearer.'

'Of course,' said Jane. 'I suppose he was Mrs. Lester's oldest friend. He was awfully fond of her.'

'Well, every one was,' said Isabel. 'But I'm not going to let Belle go into mourning.'

'Black for the funeral,' urged Jane pacifically.

'Of course,' said Isabel. 'That's only decent.' She turned toward the door. 'How is Cicily feeling to-day?'

'Very well,' said Jane. 'She's in town at the concert.'

'They go everywhere, don't they?' said Isabel. 'They don't care how they look.'

'I think that's fine,' said Jane.

'But it's funny,' said Isabel. 'Last Friday night at the Casino I heard Cicily telling Billy Winter that she had engaged a room at the Lying-In Hospital. I spoke to her about that. I didn't quite like it.'

'They take it all as a matter of course,' said Jane.

'I know,' said Isabel. 'But to a young bachelor ——'

'I'm sure *he* didn't mind,' said Jane.

'He didn't,' said Isabel. 'But I thought he should have.'

'It's a different generation, old girl,' said Jane.

II

Last week it had been a bad cold. The morning after Mrs. Lester's funeral it had turned into bronchitis. Yesterday it was a touch of pneumonia. To-day ——

Jane stood in the doorway of Mr. Ward's library, holding a great sheaf of budding Ophelia roses, looking anxiously into Isabel's worried eyes.

'I'm glad you came in, Jane,' said Isabel soberly.

'Of course I came in,' said Jane. She walked quietly across

the room to her father's desk and put her flowers down on the two days' accumulation of mail that waited for him, propped up against the brass humidor. Then she turned again to face Isabel.

'I just can't realize it,' she said. 'Day before yesterday I was talking to him, here in this room.'

'I'm glad you came while Dr. Bancroft was here.' Isabel's voice was as worried as her eyes. 'He's upstairs with Mamma.'

'How's Mamma taking it?' asked Jane.

'Oh — she's fine,' said Isabel. 'She always is, you know, when there's anything *really* the matter. She didn't leave Papa's bedside all night. I don't think she got a wink of sleep. Minnie's been awful.'

'Awful?' questioned Jane.

'About the trained nurse. She just took one look at her and turned ugly. You know how Minnie is.'

'She's very capable,' said Jane. 'And she adores us all.'

'Yes,' said Isabel, 'but she likes to run the whole show herself. Mamma's been very silly about Minnie. She's let her think she was indispensable.'

'She pretty nearly is,' sighed Jane. 'She's not really acting up, is she?'

'Oh, no,' said Isabel. 'She's just terribly gloomy. Goes around, you know, with a tremendous chip on her shoulder. She does what the nurse tells her to, but she does it grudgingly. She looks as if she'd like to say, "Don't blame *me* if it rains!"'

'Does it bother Mamma?' asked Jane.

'Of course it does,' said Isabel. 'You know she always has Minnie's attitude on her mind.'

'It's ridiculous,' said Jane, 'at a time like this!'

'Of course it is,' said Isabel. Both women turned at the sound of a step in the hall.

'There's the doctor now,' said Jane, picking up her roses.

Mrs. Ward entered the room, followed by Dr. Bancroft. She had on her grey silk dinner dress. Jane realized that she could not have changed it since the night before. Her face looked terribly worn and weary and worried. She had taken off the black velvet ribbon she always wore about her throat in the evening. In the slight V-shaped décolletage of the grey silk dress the cords of her neck, freed from the restraining band, hung in slack, yellow furrows. There were great brown circles under her tired eyes. Dr. Bancroft, brisk and immaculate in his blue serge morning suit, looked extremely clean and clever and competent beside her.

'Jane!' said Mrs. Ward. 'I didn't know you'd come.' Her face quivered, a trifle emotionally, at the sight of the roses. She kissed her younger daughter.

'How is he?' Jane's eyes sought the doctor's.

'Fine!' said Dr. Bancroft briskly. 'In excellent shape, all things considered.'

'Is the second lung affected?' asked Jane.

'Just one tiny spot,' said Dr. Bancroft very cheerfully.

'Can I see him?' asked Jane. 'Can I take him these roses?'

'Certainly,' said Dr. Bancroft. 'But don't try to talk to him.'

'He's very drowsy,' said Mrs. Ward.

'He's tired,' said Dr. Bancroft. 'His system's been putting up a big fight all night. His vitality is amazing for a man of his age.' He smiled pleasantly at Mrs. Ward. 'Now, don't worry. What he needs is rest. Miss Coulter will order the oxygen. You'd better lie down yourself, this morning, Mrs. Ward. You look all in.' He turned from the doorway and met Minnie on the threshold. She glanced at him inimically. Minnie looked all in, too. But very gloomy.

'Get a nap, yourself, Minnie,' smiled Dr. Bancroft. 'There's nothing you can do.'

'I'll not nap,' said Minnie briefly.

'I'll drop in again after luncheon,' said the doctor casually. 'And, by the way, Mrs. Ward — I'm sending up a second nurse for the night work.'

'A second — nurse?' faltered Mrs. Ward.

Jane and Isabel looked into each other's eyes.

'Just to spare you,' said Dr. Bancroft. 'You must save your strength.' He smiled pleasantly at Jane and Isabel. 'Good-morning.' He brushed by Minnie's outraged figure and was gone.

Jane stood a moment in silence, fingering her roses. Her father had pneumonia — double pneumonia. And all because of the folly of going to Mrs. Lester's funeral. Standing beside an open grave for twenty minutes, bareheaded in the February breeze, ankle-deep in the February slush of a Graceland lot. Paying the last tribute, of course, to the friendship of a lifetime. But twenty minutes — by the grave of an old, old lady whose life was over—and now—double pneumonia.

'Well — I guess I'll go up,' said Jane. How long had they all been staring in silence at the door that had closed behind the doctor?

'I'll take you, Mrs. Carver,' said Minnie officiously.

Jane looked steadily into her eager, resentful face. Dear old Minnie, who had been with them all for more than thirty years! Jane slipped her arm around the plump waist above the white apron strings.

'Thank you, Minnie,' she said.

As she left the room, she saw her mother sink into her father's leather armchair. She walked slowly down the hall and up the stairs with Minnie. She had a queer dazed feeling

that this — this couldn't be happening. Not to her father.
Not to the Wards. Nothing — nothing — really serious had
ever happened to *them*. Jimmy's death, of course. But that
had only happened to *her*. It had not torn the fabric of family
life — it had not uprooted the associations of her earliest childhood. Cicily's marriage — worrying, perplexing, of course,
but not — not terrifying, like this sort of worry.

The house seemed quieter than usual. Hushed. Expectant.
Jane suddenly remembered the sinister silence of the upper
corridor of Flora's house that April morning twenty-two years
ago, when she had walked out under the budding elm trees
for her first encounter with death. The battered door — the
smell of gas — the feeling of little living Folly beneath her
feet — the incredulity — the finality — the horror. And
Stephen — hushed young Stephen — standing so gravely
between the green-and-gold portières in Flora's hall. The
terrible vividness of youthful impressions! But why did it all
come back to her now? Now — when she was trying to
fight off this senseless sense of impending tragedy — of
terror.

Jane tapped lightly on her father's door. It was opened by
Miss Coulter, in crisp, starched linen. Her smile, as she took
the roses, was just as brisk, just as cheerful as Dr. Bancroft's
had been. Jane entered her father's room. He was lying,
under meticulously folded sheets, in the big double black
walnut bedstead that he had shared with Jane's mother since
Jane's earliest memory. His eyes were closed and he was rest-
ing easily. His breath came curiously, however, in long, slow
gasps. His breast, beneath the meticulously folded sheets,
rose and fell, laboriously, with the effort of his breathing.

Nevertheless, at the sight of him, Jane felt a sudden flood
of reassurance. He did not look very ill. His face, beneath
his neatly combed white hair, was smoothly relaxed in sleep.

It looked unnatural only because Miss Coulter had removed his gold-framed spectacles.

The nurse came softly to the bedside, the roses in a glass vase in her hand. She placed them on the bed table.

'I'll tell him that you brought them, Mrs. Carver,' she murmured. 'I think you hadn't better stay just now.'

All sense of reassurance fell away from Jane at her hushed accents. Of course, he was terribly ill. He was seventy-three years old and he had double pneumonia. She would not kiss him — she would not touch him — she would not disturb him. He must have every chance. Jane turned from the bedside and joined Minnie on the threshold. With an air of crisp and kindly competence, Miss Coulter noiselessly closed the bedroom door.

When Jane reëntered the library, her mother was crying in her father's armchair. Isabel, standing on the hearthrug, was looking at her a little helplessly. She turned to stare at Jane's sober face. Jane realized, with a sudden sense of shock, that she had not seen her mother cry since her own wedding day.

'Mamma — don't,' she said brokenly, as she sank down on the arm of her father's chair. 'I think he looks *very* well ——'

Mrs. Ward only shook her grey head and went on silently crying. Isabel still stared helplessly from the hearthrug. A curious little flame of macabre excitement was flickering about the ashes of pity and grief and terror that choked Jane's heart. Her father had double pneumonia. Her father might be going to die. Something really serious had happened to the Wards.

III

Jane sat in a rocking-chair, drawn closely to her father's bedside. Beyond the bed, on a little walnut sofa, her mother and Isabel were sitting. At the farther end of the room, in two chairs by the fireside, Robin and Stephen were sharing their quiet vigil.

They were waiting in silence. They had been waiting in silence, just like that, for more than three hours. Dr. Bancroft and Miss Coulter had been in and out. They were talking to each other, now, in the dressing-room beyond the fireplace. Jane could hear their whispering voices very faintly in the silence of the sick-room. A silence otherwise unbroken, save for the occasional staccato whirr of a passing motor on the boulevard in front of the house, and by the slow rhythmic cadence of Mr. Ward's loud, laboured breathing. It was four o'clock in the morning and the motors passed very infrequently. The breathing went steadily on, however, with a dreadful, mechanical regularity. It assaulted the ear. It filled the quiet room like the roar of a bombardment. One shell fell. Then silence. Then another shell. Then silence. Then another shell.

The night-light was placed so that the bed lay in shadow, but Jane could see her father's figure very distinctly. His chest rose and fell, mechanically, in his rhythmic struggle for breath. The oxygen tank had been abandoned. It still stood on the floor beneath the bed table. Mr. Ward's face was white and pinched and drawn and completely weary — weary with the supreme exhaustion of approaching death. It showed no sign of consciousness. The eyes were closed and the mouth was slightly open. His hands lay relaxed on the meticulously ordered sheets.

Jane sat looking at those hands. Old hands, fragile and blue-veined, with a black seal ring upon one little finger. They were still her father's hands. The approach of death had not altered them as it had the drawn and weary face. The spark of life was in them. They were living hands. The face was terrifying. The face was relaxed, defenceless and beaten. It was no longer her father's living face. It had lost the spark.

But the breathing continued. The breathing continued in slow, even, raucous gasps. The gasps were terrifying, but not as terrifying as the intervals between them. The intervals seemed endless. Shaken by the dreadful deliberation of that laboured breathing, Jane wondered, terrified, in every interval, if the gasp would come again.

It did, however. It came with the impersonal regularity of a clock tick. Presently the clock would stop. Her father was dying. He would not live through the night. Three days ago he had sat in his leather armchair, in the library downstairs, lightly reassuring Jane on the state of his bronchitis. To-morrow he would be dead. The roses that Jane had brought to his bedside were still in the vase on the table. The buds had barely reached their prime. Only that morning her father had commented on their ephemeral, creamy bloom. Those roses would outlive him. Life would go on.

Life would go on for Jane without his sustaining presence. Without his tacit sympathy, his love, his watchfulness, his warning, worried glance. He had worried and warned and watched and loved and sympathized over Jane for forty-one years, and now he was dying. He was dying just at the time when Jane felt she could have rewarded his love and sympathy as never before. There was no longer any necessity for worrying and warning and watching over her personal drama. She had grown up. Soon she would grow old. She saw life, now, eye to eye with her father. She, too, had become a spectator. Her children had taken the stage.

Once she had worried him awfully. She had not heeded his warning. She had been swept by the intoxication of her love for Jimmy into indifference, into resentment even, toward that warning and that worry. She had given him a very bad time. Jane regretted that now. But she could not regret her love for Jimmy. With all his tenderness, with all his understanding, her father had not tried to understand that love. He had merely deplored it. 'Safety first' was always the parental slogan. Parents invariably deplored everything that threatened their children's security. Whatever their own experience had been, they desired for the younger generation only the most conventional, the most convenient, kind of happiness.

Her father's experience. Jane looked at the worn, white face that lay upon the pillow. It told no tales. The spirit was withdrawn from that face into some remote and impenetrable fastness, where it awaited in solitude the last adventure of life. It was oblivious of love, oblivious of care, oblivious of companionship. Stricken suddenly with a sense of the loneliness of death, Jane leaned forward to take her father's incredibly inert, intolerably touching hand. The fingers were cold. They returned no answering pressure. Jane softly withdrew her hand. She could not reach him.

But was death, as a matter of fact, any more lonely than life? What had Jane ever known about her father's actual earthly experience? Parents knew little enough of the emotional lives of their children, but children knew nothing of the emotional lives of their parents. The emotional life of a parent was a fantastic thought. In all the forty-one years that they had shared together, Jane had never achieved, she had never even sought to achieve, one single revealing glimpse of the secret stage on which the passionate personal drama of her father's life had been enacted.

What was that drama? Why had he loved her mother? Had he always loved her? Had there been no other girl before, no other woman after, he had met and married her?

What had her parents really been, when they shared the romance of their early youth? Jane knew how they had looked. She had always known that because of the pictures in the red plush family album downstairs in the rosewood cabinet in the yellow drawing-room. Glossy, matter-of-fact photographs of the early seventies. Her mother at nineteen, in her wedding dress, with its formal pleats and exaggerated bustle of thick white satin and its little frill of sheer white lace that stood up stiffly at the back of her slender neck and framed her young, round face and the preposterous waterfall of her blonde curly hair. Her graceful young figure was elegantly posed on a photographer's rustic bridge in the fashionable, back-breaking curve of the 'Grecian bend.' A charming, artificial figure. A pretty, grave little face. And her father framed in the oval of the opposite page. Her father in the middle twenties. A handsome young man with big dark eyes and a sensitive mouth and the faintest suspicion of a sideburn on his lean young cheeks. A serious young man, with hair just a little too long and a collar just a little too big, and black satin coat lapels that were cut a trifle queerly. How had those two young people made out with marriage? Jane could not really believe they were her parents. She had no sense of the continuity of their personality. They had died young — those two young people. They had not grown up into Mr. and Mrs. John Ward of Pine Street, who had always seemed to Jane, since her earliest memory, so staid, so settled, so more than middle-aged.

'All lives,' her father had said to her before Cicily's marriage, 'are difficult at times.' What had been his difficulties? Jane did not know. The difficulties of Victorian marriages had been mercifully concealed by Victorian reticence from the eyes and ears of Victorian children. But what, for that matter, did Cicily, Jenny, and Steve know of herself and Stephen?

Jane's eyes wandered from the white face on the pillow to her mother's dim figure sunk on the walnut sofa beyond the bed. Mrs. Ward was looking at her husband. Her eyes were dull with grief, her face expressionless with fatigue. What did her mother know, Jane wondered, that she and Isabel did not, of the passionate personal drama of her father's life? What *did* wives know of husbands, or husbands know of wives? Stephen had absolutely no conception of the thoughts that passed daily through her mind. No knowledge whatever of that vast accumulation of confused impressions and vague convictions and wistful desires that made up the world of revery in which she really lived. Stephen had his world of revery, too, of course. Every one had. In the first disarming experience of love you tried to share that world. You flung open the door. You offered the key. But somehow, in spite of love, with time and incident the door swung slowly shut again. You never noticed it until you found yourself locked securely in, with the key in your own pocket. You really wondered how it had come to be there. You could not remember just when or why you had stopped saying — everything. But at the end of twenty years of marriage it was astounding to consider the number of things, that somehow, you had never said —

Jane was roused from revery by Isabel's sudden movement, by her mother's sharp, stifled exclamation. She stared at her father's face. The mouth had dropped slightly more open. The chest was motionless. The slow raucous gasps were silenced. The bombardment had ceased.

'Dr. Bancroft! Dr. Bancroft!' cried Isabel shrilly. The doctor appeared instantly in the dressing-room door. He moved quickly to the bedside. Miss Coulter followed him. He took her father's hand and felt the wrist for a moment in silence. He looked at Mrs. Ward. Robin and Stephen had

crossed the room. They stood staring down at Mr. Ward
from the foot of the bed. Her mother was crying. Isabel's
arm was around her. They, too, were staring down at Mr.
Ward.

Her father was dead, thought Jane dully. Her father had
died, as she sat at his bedside thinking abstract thoughts of
life — of her own personal problems. How *could* she have
thought such thoughts at such a moment? Lost in the complications presented by her own drama, she had not seen
the curtain fall on the last act of her father's life. She had not
sensed the final approach of death. She had been totally un-
aware of that last, fearfully awaited gasp.

Her mother had risen. Isabel's arm was still around her.
Stephen's hand was on Jane's shoulder. She rose slowly from
her chair, staring down at the white, pinched face that lay
upon the pillow — the face that was not her father's.

'Come, dear,' said Stephen tenderly. At the sound of his
voice Jane felt her eyes fill suddenly with tears. Her father
was dead. Stephen's hand was on her elbow. His touch grew
firm and insistent.

'Come, dear,' he said again. He led her to the door. Robin
and Isabel were already there. Her mother was weeping in
their arms.

'Come, dear,' Robin was saying. Her father was dead, and
they were all running away from him. In response to some
strange, instinctive recoil, life was retreating from death.
They were leaving him to Dr. Bancroft and Miss Coulter.

'I — I want to stay!' cried Jane a little wildly.

'No, dear,' said Stephen protectively, 'come.' Somehow,
Jane found herself in the darkened hall. Her mother was at
her elbow.

'Come, Mamma, dear,' Isabel was saying.

'He's — dead,' said Mrs. Ward dully.

'Come, dear,' said Isabel insistently, through her tears.

'I've — no one — now,' said Mrs. Ward slowly.

Jane suddenly realized that Minnie had joined them. Her face was distorted with weeping.

'You've got me,' said Minnie. Competently she drew Mrs. Ward from Isabel's restraining arm. 'You come and lie down in the guest-room,' she said. Mrs. Ward permitted herself to be led away. Jane, in the darkened corridor, looked blankly, tearlessly, at Stephen, Isabel, and Robin. Her father was dead.

IV

Jane sat in the sunny corner of Cicily's room in the Lying-In Hospital, holding the week-old twins in her arms. How ridiculous, how adorable of them to *be* twins, she was thinking, as she gazed down at their absurdly red, absurdly wrinkled, absurdly tiny faces. Little John Ward and little Jane Ward Bridges! John and Jane — Cicily's son and daughter!

Jane had wondered, a trifle anxiously, if she would experience a pang at the sight of a grandchild — if grandmotherhood had birth pangs of its own. But no — she had produced her grand-twins, vicariously to be sure, without any spiritual travail. She loved being a grandmother. She loved little Jane, and especially little John Ward Bridges, little John Ward, who had come into the world to take up life and his name, just six weeks after his great-grandfather had left it. Life had gone on.

Jane wished, terribly, that her father might have lived to see this great-grandson. He so nearly had. Things happened so quickly as you grew older. Jane felt she had barely recovered from those three dreadful days when her father's life was hanging in the balance, from the shock of his death, from the pity and sorrow of the readjustment of her mother's life, when the hour arrived, at two o'clock one March morning, when, stealing out of bed and leaving a note for Stephen on her pincushion, she had rushed with Cicily in the motor from the Lakewood house to the Lying-In Hospital, where she had sat in a waiting-room, a beautifully furnished, green-walled waiting-room that looked exactly like the bleak parlour of an exceptionally good hotel, for six, eight, ten hours, waiting for Cicily's twins to come into the world.

Cicily had been born in the house on Pine Street. Jenny and Steve in the blue bedroom at Lakewood. Jane did not entirely hold with hospitals as a stage set for birth. In spite of surgeon's plaster labels stuck on newborn shoulder blades, in spite of scientific footprints taken in birth-rooms, Jane had been terribly afraid that the twins would be mixed up with some one else's babies. Cicily had laughed at her.

Cicily had laughed at her, consistently, throughout the whole terrible ordeal of birth. Laughed at her as they stole from the Lakewood house with the elaborate precaution not to waken Stephen. Laughed at her in the motor in that hurried drive through the nocturnal boulevards, laughed at the sight of that beautifully furnished waiting-room, laughed even between ether gasps in her breathless struggle, the last few minutes before the twins had arrived. Laughed most of all, in the tranquillity of her narrow, ordered bed, as she lay with the newborn babies in her arms, and said, twinkling up at Jane's joyful, relieved countenance:

'Well, if *this* is the curse of Eve, I don't think so much of it! What have women been howling about down the ages? Why, it's nothing — it's really *nothing* — to go through for two babies!'

Jane had stood astounded at her courage. Her courage and her common-sense — the two great virtues of the rising generation. Freedom from sentimentality. Freedom from the old taboos that had shackled humanity for generations. Bravery and bravado — they would take the rising generation far.

Cicily was lying, now, in the tranquillity of the ordered bed across the room from Jane. The room was a bower of flowers. Cicily was wearing a blue silk négligée that Muriel had sent her. Her lips were pale, but her eyes were bright and her dandelion head burned on the pillow like a yellow flame. She was holding a letter from Jack in her hands.

'I'm so happy, Mumsy,' she said. 'He'll be home in four weeks. Do you honestly think we can keep him from knowing it was twins until he gets here?'

'I honestly do,' smiled Jane.

'If Belle *didn't* write Albert. She *swears* she didn't.'

'I don't believe she did,' smiled Jane.

'Poor Belle!' laughed Cicily. 'She's so envious of me — with everything over.'

'It will be over for Belle next week,' smiled Jane.

'But it won't be twins!' said Cicily proudly. 'Not if there's anything in the law of chances!'

'It probably won't be twins,' smiled Jane.

'I've put it over Belle,' laughed Cicily, 'all along the line. Jack's twice as nice as Albert and my baby's twice as many as hers!'

'Nevertheless,' said Jane, 'I dare say Belle will continue to prefer her own husband and her own baby.'

'I suppose she will,' said Cicily, 'but I prefer mine. Give them to me, Mumsy, before Miss Billings comes in. It's almost time to nurse them.'

v

'Flora,' said Jane, 'they're the cutest things I ever saw! It was too dear of you to make them!'

'The last hats,' smiled Flora, 'that I'll ever make. I sold the good-will of the shop to-day.'

'And you're sailing Wednesday?' Jane passed the toast. She and Flora were having tea on the terrace. It was late in June. The first roses were beginning to bud. Flora had motored out for a farewell call. She had brought with her two little blue caps for the twins.

'Wednesday,' said Flora. 'It nearly killed me, Jane, to close the house.'

'I know it did,' said Jane.

'I'm staying at the Blackstone,' said Flora. 'The storage company took the furniture yesterday. I've sold the house to such a funny man — his name's Ed Brown. He's a bill-board king. He's going to turn it into studios for his commercial artists.'

'I don't see how you could do it,' said Jane.

'I wanted to do it,' said Flora. 'I wanted to keep myself from ever coming back. I would have, you know, as long as the house was there. And yet I was miserable in it. You don't know, Jane, how much I've missed Father.'

'Oh, yes, I do,' said Jane.

'At first, you know, I tried to keep busy with the hats and the war orphans. But I never *saw* the war orphans. And the hats — Jane, it was the hats that made me realize that I was growing old.'

'But you're not old!' cried Jane. Her protest was quite honest. Flora's slim, fashionable figure seemed to her as young as ever. Her face had lost the blank and weary expression it had worn for the first years after her father's death. In the sunlight of the terrace, the faint sheen of silver seemed only a high light on her red-gold hair.

'I'm forty-three,' sighed Flora, 'and I know I look it. I've known it from the moment I realized that I didn't want to try on the hats any longer. At first I couldn't wait to get them out of the boxes when they came from the customs-house. I used to put them all on and preen myself in front of the mirrors. But lately — lately, Jane — I didn't seem to want to. At first I just said to myself that the new styles were trying. But pretty soon I knew — I knew it was my face.'

'Flora!' cried Jane, in horror. 'Don't be ridiculous! You're lovely looking. You always were!'

'You don't understand, Jane,' said Flora accusingly. 'You don't care how you look. You never did.'

'I did, too!' cried Jane. 'Of course, I know I never looked like much of anything ——'

'But you're coming into your own, now, Jane,' said Flora, smiling. 'The fourth decade is your home field. You're going to spend the next ten years looking very happy and awfully amusing and pretty enough, while the beauties — the beauties fade and frizzle or grow red and blowsy, and finally rot — just rot and end up looking like exceptionally well-preserved corpses, fresh from the hand of a competent undertaker ——' Flora's voice was really trembling. 'So — I'm going to Paris, Jane, where the undertakers are exceedingly competent and there's some real life for middle-aged people. Here in Chicago what do I do but watch your children and Muriel's and Isabel's grow up and produce more children? It's terrible, Jane, it's really terrible ——' Again she broke off. 'What are you and Isabel going to do with your mother?'

'She's going on living in the old house with Minnie,' said Jane. 'Of course, it's dreadful there, now that the boulevard has gone through. Noisy and dirty and awfully commercial ——'

'And the elms all cut down,' said Flora sympathetically, 'when they widened the street.'

'But Mamma likes it,' said Jane. 'She likes the old house.

And Isabel's near her. She comes out here for the week-ends. I don't know *what* she'll do when we go to Gull Rocks.'

'You're going to Gull Rocks?' asked Flora.

'We have to,' said Jane. 'We really have to. Stephen's mother counts on it. And I've promised Cicily that she and Jack could have this house for the summer, while they're deciding what to do. Stephen's going to celebrate his fiftieth birthday by taking a two months' vacation.'

'Why don't you go abroad?' asked Flora.

'Stephen would rather sail that catboat,' smiled Jane.

'Jane, you've been a saint about Gull Rocks all these years,' said Flora earnestly. 'I couldn't stand it for a week.'

Yet Flora had stood Mr. Furness for twenty years, thought Jane. Stood that life, spent junketing about with a cribbage board in trains *de luxe*! Stood those expensive hotels in London and Paris and Rome and Madrid and Carlsbad and Biarritz and Dinard and Benares and Tokio!

'You've been the saint, Flora!' said Jane.

As she spoke Molly appeared, pushing the double perambulator around the clump of evergreens at the foot of the garden. She paused beneath the apple tree, put on the brake, and sat down on the green bench. Molly was Cicily's impeccable English nursemaid. She was infallible with the twins and very firm with Cicily. She liked Jane, however.

'Come and look at the babies,' said Jane.

The twins, very plump and pink and as alike as two pins, were blinking up at the June sunlight through the boughs of the apple tree. Molly had risen respectfully at Jane's approach. She had beautiful British manners.

'Aren't they funny?' said Flora. 'They look so clean. And somehow so — brand-new.'

'They *are* brand-new,' said Jane proudly. She stroked John Ward's velvety cheek with a proprietary finger. He responded immediately with a vague, toothless, infinitely touching smile and a spasmodic gesture of his small pink-sweatered arms.

'Sometimes he has a dimple,' said Jane.

'They're prettier than Belle's little girl,' said Flora. 'I hoped she was going to look like Muriel. But she doesn't.'

'She looks like Belle,' said Jane. 'Belle was a homely baby.'

'She's lovely now,' said Flora.

'Oh, lovely,' said Jane.

'Cicily's lovely, too,' said Flora.

'Yes,' said Jane.

'And so young,' said Flora wistfully.

'And so happy,' said Jane. 'They're both so happy since the boys came home.'

'Jane,' said Flora solemnly, as they turned to leave the garden, 'do you find that looking at the younger generation makes you think of your own life?'

'Yes,' said Jane, a bit uncertainly.

'It makes me think of lost opportunities,' said Flora — 'chances that will never come again.' They strolled across the lawn for a moment in silence. Then Flora spoke once more, this time a trifle tremulously: 'Do you know, Jane, that I've never been happy — happy like that, I mean — except for just the ten days that I was engaged to Inigo Fellowes.'

'I'm afraid,' said Jane slowly, as they ascended the terrace steps, 'that no one's ever happy like that for very long.'

'But for longer than ten days,' said Flora, still solemnly, 'and maybe more than once. Inigo's still very happy with his wife.'

'I didn't know he *had* a wife,' said Jane.

'Oh, yes,' said Flora. 'He's been married for twelve years. I met him in Paris during the war, you know. He'd lost a leg and was being shipped back to Australia. He lives there now. He showed me a picture of his two sons.'

Jane wondered why Inigo had felt he had to do that. It seemed a bit unnecessary. Though Flora, no doubt, had been wonderful about them.

'You've had such a — a normal life, Jane,' said Flora, as they ascended the terrace steps. 'You've always been so happy with Stephen.'

'Yes,' said Jane evenly, 'Stephen's a darling.'

'And now you have the children — to amuse you always.'

'Children,' said Jane doubtfully, 'don't always amuse you.'

'Don't they?' said Flora. 'I should think they would.'

'Well, they don't,' said Jane.

She kissed Flora good-bye very tenderly in the front hall. She stood on the doorstep and watched her motor recede down the gravel path. The passing of Flora meant a great deal to Jane. She would miss her frightfully. Her oldest friend. Except Muriel, who was, of course, so much less — less friendly. Not a friend like Agnes, of course. But Agnes was in New York. And now Flora would be in Paris. She might never see her again. With Stephen feeling the way he did about Gull Rocks, she might never go to Paris. Flora would meet André there. Flora would probably come to know André very well again ——

The striking of the clock in the hall behind her recalled Jane to a sense of the present. Six o'clock. Jenny ought to be home on the five-fifty. She was in town taking her College Entrance Board physics examination for Bryn Mawr. Jane was glad that she was going there. It had been hard to convince her that she should. Jenny cared very little for Bryn Mawr, but she cared even less for a social début. It was with the single idea of postponing that distressing event that Jenny had embraced the thought of a college education. Jenny was a girl's girl, pure and simple. So unlike Cicily, who had always had a crowd of boys about the house —— But where

was Cicily? She should be home that minute, nursing the
twins. She was probably out on the golf links. Stephen and
Jack would be back from the bank on the five-fifty. Jane had
tried in vain to impress on Cicily the elementary fact that she
ought to be home before Jack every evening. To precede your
husband to the conjugal hearth at nightfall had always
seemed to Jane the primary obligation of matrimony. But
Cicily had said she should worry! Suddenly she whirled
around the bushes at the entrance of the driveway in her
little Ford roadster. Her hat was off and her yellow bob was
blowing in the breeze.

'Just met Cousin Flora!' she called. She threw on her
brakes. The Ford stopped in a whirl of gravel. Cicily sprang
to the doorstep. 'Is Jack home?' she cried. 'Are the twins
howling?' She was unbuttoning her blouse as she rushed into
the hall. Jane followed her.

'Call Molly, will you, Mumsy? I've got to hurry! Gosh,
Jack should be here! We're dining in town, you know, this
evening!'

Jane turned toward the living-room in quest of Molly.

'Cousin Flora told me about the bonnets!' called Cicily
from the upper hall. 'Bring them up, will you? I'll look at
them while I nurse the babies!'

The impeccable Molly had heard the Ford. She met Jane
at the terrace doors. She had a twin tucked under each arm.

'I'm afraid Mrs. Bridges kept them waiting,' smiled Jane.

'Well — you know how young mothers are, ma'am,' said
Molly resignedly, and passed on through the living-room and
up the stairs.

Jane was not sure she *did* know, half as well as Molly did.
She closed the terrace doors to keep out the mosquitoes.
Molly always left them open. Young mothers were rather
perplexing to Jane. Cicily never worried about those babies

and never watched over them. She left them entirely to Molly's care. Molly did the watching and Jane did the worrying. Last week, for instance, when the supplementary bottle had not seemed to agree with little Jane, Molly had watched over formulas for hours and Jane had lain awake worrying for two whole nights. But Cicily had not been ruffled.

'It's up to the doctor, Mumsy,' she said. 'Babies always have their ups and downs. I can't invent a formula.'

Courage and common-sense, again, perhaps. Bravery and bravado. But it *did* seem a little heartless ——

The front door opened and Stephen and Jack and Jenny came in from the five-fifty.

'Jenny,' cried Jane, 'how did the exam go?'

'Oh, all right,' said Jenny calmly; 'but why should a girl know physics?'

Jack made a dive for the stairs.

'Golly!' he cried, 'I've got to step on it! Where's Cicily? Where are the kids?'

'In her room,' called Jane. She turned to smile at Stephen.

'That's boy's going to make a banker,' said Stephen proudly.

Jane slipped her arm around Jenny's thin young shoulders.

'Do you really think you passed?' she inquired.

'Oh, I guess so,' said Jenny. She tossed her felt hat on the hall table and ran her hand through her straight blonde bob. Her plain little face was twinkling at her mother in an indulgent smile. 'Don't fuss, Mumsy!'

Just then little Steve burst in at the front door. He looked flushed and excited and just a trifle mussy in grass-stained flannels. Tennis racket in hand he towered lankily over Jane.

'Mumsy, can we have dinner early? Can we have it at half-past six?'

'I don't think so,' said Jane, with a glance at the clock and a thought for the menu. Her eyes returned to her son. His blond, boyish beauty always made her heart beat a little faster. At fifteen he looked so much like Stephen — the young Stephen that Jane had met in Flora's ballroom. 'Why?'

'Well, because I promised Buzzy Barker that I'd take her to the seven-thirty movie. I said I'd be there in the car at seven-fifteen. I can't keep Buzzy waiting, Mumsy. I absolutely can't! If we can't have dinner early, I'll have to go without it, but I've been playing tennis all afternoon, and I think when a man comes home tired at night and says he'd like to have dinner early ——'

Jane, Stephen, and Jenny burst simultaneously into laughter.

'Go vamp the cook, Steve,' said Jenny unsympathetically. 'You're a devil with women!'

Steve vanished, with a contemptuous snort in the direction of the pantry.

'He's awful, Mumsy,' continued Jenny. 'And Buzzy Barker is the arch-petter of her generation.'

'You're all awful,' smiled Stephen, as he entered the living-room. 'I don't know how your mother puts up with you.'

Jane slipped her arm through his.

'Come out and look at the roses,' she said, 'they're lovely this time of day.'

Somehow it seemed to her at the moment that she put up with them all very easily. She *had* a normal life and children *did* amuse you! Arm in arm with Stephen she strolled across the terrace in the early evening air. A faint damp breeze was stealing in from the west — the very breath of the swamps. An amber sunset light was flooding the Skokie Valley. It turned the terrace turf a vivid yellow green. It intensified the kaleidoscopic colours of the flower border. The roses looked

redder and pinker than they did at high noon. Jane was
thinking of defrauded Flora. She was wondering why she,
herself, was ever discouraged about life. When she had
Stephen and three funny children and two ridiculous grand-
twins ——

'Do you remember the swamp this garden was sixteen years
ago?' said Stephen suddenly.

Jane nodded solemnly.

'It was under this apple tree,' she said, 'that I told you that
I knew Steve was going to be a boy. And you kissed me,
Stephen ——'

'I'll kiss you again,' said Stephen handsomely, suiting the
action to the words.

'Mumsy!' shrieked Steve from the pantry window. 'Stop
necking with Dad! Lena says we *can* have dinner at six-
thirty! I absolutely can't keep Buzzy waiting, Mumsy ——'

Jane slipped from Stephen's arms.

'Come in and eat and keep him quiet,' she said tranquilly.
Still arm in arm, they strolled back across the terrace. As
they entered the living-room, Cicily's voice was floating down
the stairs.

'Where *are* those bonnets of Cousin Flora's, Mumsy?'

'Jane,' said Stephen cheerfully, sinking into his armchair
and opening the 'Evening Post,' 'this house is Bedlam.'

'I like it Bedlam,' said Jane, smiling. She picked up Flora's
bonnets from the living-room table and started with them
toward the door. On the threshold she ran into Steve.

'Golly, Dad!' he was crying, aghast. 'Don't start to read
the paper before dinner! I absolutely can't keep Buzzy
waiting ——'

Jane walked slowly up the stairs, smoothing out the frilly
ruffles of Flora's little blue bonnets. She could still hear
Steve arguing incoherently with his father in the living-room.

On the first landing she caught the great guffaw of Jack's laughter as he played with the twins on Cicily's bed. Jenny was singing to the accompaniment of running water in the bathroom off her bedroom at the head of the stairs.

'Yes, sir, she's my baby!
Tra-la — I don't mean maybe!'

Ignoring her brother's views on early dinner, Jenny was obviously taking a tub. She had not bothered to close any doors.

There was nothing more satisfactory, thought Jane, as she knocked lightly at Cicily's threshold, than a large, quarrelsome, and united family.

'Mumsy!' shouted Steve from the lower hall. 'Dinner's served!'

'Come in!' called Cicily shrilly, over Jack's laughter.

'Jenny!' shouted Steve. 'Come on down! Dinner's ready!'

'Oh, shut up, Romeo!' shrieked Jenny affably, over the sound of running water.

Jane smiled indulgently as she opened Cicily's door. There was a comfortable domestic sense of reassurance about a house that was Bedlam. Bedlam was exactly the kind of a house she liked.

VI

Jane sat on the brick parapet of her little terrace, wondering if the soft October air was too cool for her mother. It was a lovely autumn afternoon. An Indian summer haze hung over the tanned stretch of the Skokie Valley. The leaves of the oak trees were wine-red. A few scattered clumps of marigolds and zinnias that had withstood the early frost still splashed the withered flower border with patches of orange and rose.

Isabel and Robin had motored Mrs. Ward out for Sunday

luncheon at Lakewood, and the sun was so warm and the terrace so sheltered and the last breath of summer so precious that Jane had suggested that they take their after-luncheon coffee in the open air. Mrs. Ward sat, her small black-garbed figure wrapped in the folds of a white Shetland shawl, sipping the hot liquid a shade gratefully. She was warming her thin, ringed hands on the outside of the little cup.

'Cold, Mamma?' asked Jane. 'That shawl's not very thick.'

'Certainly not,' said Mrs. Ward tartly. 'I'm never cold.'

Jane's eyes met Isabel's. They were always incredibly touched by their mother's perpetual, proud refusal to admit the infirmities of age. Infirmities that had seemed to creep insidiously upon her since her husband's death, eight months before. That death had vividly emphasized for Jane and Isabel the menace of the years.

Robin and Stephen were casually dressed in tan tweeds for a country week-end. The three women were still in mourning. Their crude, black figures stood out uncompromisingly against the soft russet background of the October garden. The sombre badge of grief seemed to draw them closer together, to emphasize the family unit and their common loss. Nevertheless, it was still impossible for Jane to realize that her father was dead. That he would never again make one of the little group that was gathered that sunny afternoon on her terrace. Never again meet her eyes with his indulgent twinkle, half-veiled in cigar smoke, as Isabel and her mother rattled off their brittle, shameless, incisive comment on life. Never again help solve a family problem, like the one now under discussion. Isabel was discussing it, very incisively.

'I hate,' she said, 'to have him give up his engineering.'

'He wants to give it up,' said Stephen eagerly.

'Not really,' said Isabel; 'he just thinks he ought to. I wish he could go to Tech this winter. Cicily could take a little flat in Boston.'

'My dear,' said Robin seriously, 'Jack ought to support his wife.'

'He's only twenty-three,' sighed Isabel.

'He oughtn't to *have* a wife,' put in Mrs. Ward, again rather tartly, 'at his age.'

'But he has,' said Robin, 'and he ought to support her.'

'He's planned on engineering since he was a little boy,' said Isabel plaintively. 'You know, Jane, I think it's really up to Cicily. If she told him she'd like to live in Boston ——'

'I know,' said Jane, 'but Cicily *wouldn't* like to live in Boston. She'd like to buy that four-acre lot and build a little French farmhouse and live here in Lakewood while Jack worked in Stephen's bank.'

'He's awfully good in the bank,' said Stephen.

Isabel rose impatiently from her chair and walked across the terrace. She stared a moment in silence at the tanned stretch of meadow.

'He's good at anything,' she said presently. Jane caught the sob that was trembling in her voice. 'But he ought to have his chance.'

'I think myself,' said Jane seriously, 'that Cicily's making a mistake. But you know how it is, Isabel. She likes Lakewood. She's made all her plans. She doesn't want to go into exile.'

'Boston isn't exile!' said Isabel, turning back to her chair.

'Thank you, Isabel!' threw in Stephen parenthetically.

'But Cicily thinks it is,' said Jane. 'She's never liked the Bostonians she met at Gull Rocks ——'

'I know how she feels,' said Robin generously. 'No woman wants a husband who's still in school. Besides, Isabel, *we* can't support them. I mean — we couldn't give Cicily the things she's accustomed to have. Jack made his decision when he married. He has a wife and two children. He can't settle back on his father-in-law for a meal ticket. Stephen's very generous to offer to build them that house and to give him such a good job in the bank.'

'I'm glad to have him there,' said Stephen warmly. 'He's a bright kid.'

'Just the same,' said Isabel, 'Jack's been building bridges since the age of ten. I can see him now with his first set of Meccano! He'll be awfully bored with banking! He'll never really like it.'

'Isabel,' said Mrs. Ward reprovingly, 'you shouldn't talk like that about banking.' Mrs. Ward had a solid Victorian respect for the source of her younger son-in-law's income. Her remark was ignored, however. In the heat of family discussion, Jane reflected, it was becoming increasingly customary to ignore Mrs. Ward.

'He'll like Cicily,' said Robin, 'and the twins and the little French farmhouse. He'll like the fun of starting out in life, on his own. He'll like himself if he's holding down an honest job.'

'Of course, I can understand,' said Isabel, 'that Jane would like to have Cicily near her, now Steve's at Milton and Jenny's in Bryn Mawr. I hate to give up Belle. But if it's for Albert's best good ——'

'How's Jenny getting on?' inquired Robin abruptly. He had always admired his plain little niece.

'She loves it,' smiled Jane. And Jenny really did. Her unexpected enthusiasm for the cloisters had made Jane very happy. 'She's rooming in Pembroke with Barbara Belmont — you know, the daughter of Stephen's friend.'

'Really?' said Isabel, a trifle incredulously. 'Belmont, the banker?' At heart, Jane knew, Isabel shared her mother's Victorian confidence in banks.

'Yes,' said Jane. 'He was in Stephen's class at Harvard.'

'Such nice girls go to college nowadays,' mused Isabel. The note of incredulity still lingered in her voice. 'Your friends were so queer, Jane.'

'They certainly were,' put in Mrs. Ward with a sigh.

A little flame of adolescent resentment flashed up in Jane's heart. She felt as if she were fourteen once more and had just bumped up against one of Isabel's and her mother's 'opinions.' At forty-two, however, resentment was articulate.

'I don't know what was queer about them,' she said indignantly, 'unless it was queer of them to be so very able. Agnes is one of the most successful dramatists on Broadway. Her new crime play's a wow. And Marion Park has just been appointed Dean of Radcliffe.'

'Well, I never knew Marion Park,' said Isabel doubtfully.

'But certainly no one would ever have expected Agnes Johnson to amount to anything,' said Mrs. Ward.

As she spoke, the door to the living-room opened and Cicily came out on the terrace. She was wearing a little green sport suit and carrying a roll of blue-prints in her hand. She shook her dandelion head and smiled charmingly at the assembled family.

'Oh, here you are!' she said pleasantly. 'Isn't it too cold for Granny? I want to show Uncle Robin the last plans for the house.' Unrolling a blue-print, she dropped down on her knees by his chair. Cicily still looked about fourteen years old, reflected Jane, tenderly. 'We want to get it started before the ground freezes ——' she began. Looking up, she met her mother-in-law's inimical eye. Something a little hard and indomitable glittered in Cicily's own. She did not look fourteen years old any longer. 'Oh, don't tell me you've been arguing about it all over again!' she cried mutinously.

'My dear,' said Jane, 'it's not a thing to be lightly decided.'

'Who's deciding it lightly?' cried Cicily hotly. 'Mumsy, you make me tired.'

'Don't talk like that, Cicily!' put in Mrs. Ward, and was again ignored.

'Aunt Isabel makes me tired!' continued Cicily. 'I get so sick of all this family discussion! You act exactly as if I didn't know what was good for Jack, myself! I'm his wife! I ought to know him by this time!'

'Cicily!' said Stephen warningly.

'Well, I *do* know him, Dad!' flashed Cicily, 'and I'm acting for his best good! Where would engineering get him? Three years at Tech and then building bridges and tunnels and railroad embankments at some jumping-off place all the rest of his life! Me, boarding in construction camps with Molly and the twins! Not even with Molly! She wouldn't go! What do we live for, anyway? He's much better off in your bank, leading a civilized life in a city where every one knows him!'

'Belle didn't talk like that,' said Isabel reprovingly, 'when Albert decided to go to Oxford.'

'Well, I shouldn't think she would!' flashed Cicily again. 'Oxford University isn't Boston Tech! Aunt Muriel's going to rent them a beautiful little house in that lovely country and Belle will meet a lot of distinguished people! I think Belle's life is going to be perfectly *grand!* If Albert really *does* go into the diplomatic service, Belle will have a *career!* She may end up in the Court of Saint James! I'd *love* to be an ambassador's lady ——'

'Albert's not an ambassador yet, Cicily,' twinkled Stephen;

'he's just succeeded with some difficulty in becoming an Oxford undergraduate.'

'It's a step in the right direction,' said Cicily. 'I wish to goodness Jack had his ambition.'

'Jack has his own ambitions,' said Stephen quietly.

'He certainly has!' retorted Cicily, 'and he ought to be protected from them! You can't tell me anything about Jack, Dad! I think he's just as sweet as you do. He's worth ten of Albert! But just the same he'll never get anywhere if I don't push him. I'm pushing him now, just as hard as I can, into your bank! It's a splendid opening!' She paused a trifle breathlessly, then smiled very sweetly at her father. 'You know you think so yourself, Dad, darling.'

Jane watched Stephen try to steel himself against that smile, then reluctantly succumb to it.

'I wouldn't offer Jack anything, Isabel,' he said slowly, 'that I didn't think was going to turn into a pretty good thing.'

'There!' cried Cicily in triumph, 'and our house is going to be perfectly ducky ——'

'Cicily ——' began Isabel portentously. Then even Isabel obviously saw that argument was a waste of breath. 'Let *me* see the blue-prints,' she said helplessly.

Cicily surrendered them with a forgiving smile. She rose and looked interestedly over her mother-in-law's shoulder.

'Do you think the linen closet is large enough?' she asked tactfully.

'No, I don't,' said Isabel judicially, 'and it ought to be nearer the clothes chute.'

'I'll have it changed,' said Cicily generously. It was the generosity of the victor.

Jane rose slowly from her seat on the parapet. She could not do anything about Cicily. She could, however, go into the house and bring out Stephen's overcoat to wrap around her mother. As she walked across the terrace, she could see Isabel bending interestedly over the blue-prints! Poor old Isabel! It was quite obvious that she had laid down her arms.

CHAPTER III

I

JANE stood by the piano in the Lakewood living-room, looking fixedly at the flowers that the children had sent her.
Fifty Killarney roses in a great glass bowl. Time was when
Jane had regarded a woman of fifty as standing with one foot
in the grave. Even now she was glad that Isabel was coming
out for tea. Isabel was fifty-five. Jane felt that it would be a
comfort to look at her. It had been a comfort that morning
to look at Stephen, who was fifty-eight. But men were different. To men, years brought distinction. To women, they
brought only grey hairs and crow's-feet, thick waistlines and
double chins.

Jane turned from the roses to glance at her reflection in the
gilt-framed mirror that hung over her Colonial mantelpiece.
Jane's waistline was nothing to be ashamed of. She had no
crow's-feet. When she remembered to hold her head high,
her chin, if slightly — well — mature, was certainly not
double. It could not be denied, however, that her hair was
very grey. Jane hated that. What had Jimmy once said? 'A
woman is young as long as she looks beguiling with mussy
hair.' Jane looked like the Witch of Endor, now, with mussy
hair. Still, she reflected courageously, she never allowed it
to be mussy. 'Well-groomed' — that was the adjective a well-
intentioned eulogist would have chosen with which to describe
Jane's hair at fifty. A barren adjective. An adjective devoid
of glamour and romance. Well-groomed hair, Jane reflected
sadly, would never have appealed to Jimmy.

Did it appeal to Stephen? Jane smiled a little fondly at the
thought. Stephen, she knew, had never even observed her

increasingly meticulous arrangement of hairnet and hairpins. To Stephen, Jane still looked like Jane, and, though she had ceased to be the phantom of delight that he had married, in Stephen's eyes Jane could never be fifty. And yet — she was. There were the smiling flowers to prove it.

Jane turned resolutely from the mirror. A woman of character on her fiftieth birthday, she told herself firmly, should not be staring despondently into a gilt-framed looking-glass regretting her vanished charms. A woman of character on her fiftieth birthday should have put vanity behind her. She should be competently and confidently taking stock of the more durable satisfactions of life.

There were plenty of them to take stock of, Jane reflected. Durable satisfactions were the kind she had gone in for. From her earliest girlhood some unerring instinct of emotional thrift had led her to select them at life's bargain counter. They had worn well. They had washed splendidly. They had not stretched nor shrunk nor faded. They were all nearly as good as new. They were, perhaps, Jane reminded herself, with a smile, a little out of fashion. Durable satisfactions were not in vogue any longer. Cicily professed to think nothing of them. But at fifty Jane could spread them all out before her and take solid Victorian comfort in the fact that there was not a shred of tarnished tinsel among them. No foolish purchases to regret. Only a very fortunate, a very happy woman could say that, Jane reflected wisely.

And yet — and yet — what wanton instinct whispered that a moment of divine extravagance would be rather glamorous to look back upon? That at fifty it would be cheering to remember having purchased — oh, long ago, of course — something superbly silly that you had loved and paid high for and —— But no, Jane's thoughts continued, if you had done that you would also have to remember that you had tired of it or worn it out or broken it in some deplorable revulsion of feeling. It was much better to have gone in for the satisfactions that endured. Satisfactions that endured like the familiar furniture of the Lakewood living-room. Jane's eyes surveyed the objects around her with a whimsical twinkle — the books, the Steinway, Stephen's armchair, her own sewing-table, tangible reminders of the solidity of her life. The very walls were eloquent of domesticity. The serenity of the pleasant, ordered room was very reassuring. It reminded her that she had nothing to worry about in her pleasant, ordered life.

The children, of course. You always worried about your children. Even about good children like Cicily, Jenny, and Steve. You worried about Cicily because she smoked too much and drank a little and played bridge for too high stakes and seemed a trifle moody — too reckless one day, too resigned the next. A curious mixture, at twenty-eight, of daring and domesticity. You worried about Jenny because she did not really like the life in Lakewood, because she did not care for dances and was not interested in any particular young man, and talked absurd nonsense about leaving home and taking a job and leading her own life. Jenny was twenty-five. She really should be falling in love with some one. You worried about Steve because — but of course that was only ridiculous! At twenty-three Steve was proving himself a chip of the old block. He was a most enthusiastic young banker. Stephen was delighted with him and Jane was delighted with Stephen's delight. She would not admit, even to herself, a certain perverse disappointment that her handsome young son, with the world at his feet and so full of a number of things, had embraced the prosaic career of a banker with such ardent abandon. It was nice, it was natural, she told herself firmly, that Steve should follow in his father's and his grandfather's footsteps. It was absurd of her to wish him a little more — adventurous. A little less conventional. A bit of a gypsy.

A gypsy. Jane had only known one gypsy. If she had run off with Jimmy and *they* had had a son — Jane pulled herself up abruptly. These were no thoughts for Mrs. Stephen Carver to be indulging herself in as she stood staring at the great glass bowl of Killarney roses that her three grown children had sent her on her fiftieth birthday. There was nothing in Steve to criticize, of course, save a certain youthful scorn for his Middle-Western environment, engendered by his education on the Atlantic seaboard. Three years at Milton and four at Harvard had transformed Steve into an ardent Bostonian. He had wanted to settle there and go into his grandfather's bank. His uncle Alden had encouraged the thought. But Stephen had felt that Chicago offered greater opportunities. Stephen had been for seven years the president of the Midland Loan and Trust Company. He had seated his only son, very firmly, on a high stool in his outer office.

Jane heard the doorbell. That would be Isabel. She turned from the roses as her sister entered. Isabel was well-groomed, too, Jane noticed with a sigh. Well-groomed and portly, with a stole of silver fox thrown around her substantial blue broadcloth shoulders and a smart little black hat pulled unbecomingly down over her worn round face, uncompromisingly concealing the soft waves of her silvery hair. Modern styles were made for the young, Jane reflected.

'Happy birthday!' said Isabel as she kissed her.

Jane acknowledged the ironic salute.

'You won't mind any other, you know,' smiled Isabel, 'until the sixtieth.'

'I don't mind this one,' said Jane stoutly.

'Tell that to the marines!' laughed Isabel. 'I'll never forget Muriel's! Wasn't she down?'

'She certainly was,' smiled Jane, 'in spite of the celebration.'

Muriel's fiftieth birthday had occurred last month. She had celebrated it by taking off her mourning for Bert. He had been dead two years.

'Muriel's gone off awfully,' sighed Isabel. It was rather a sigh of satisfaction, however. 'She's reverting to race as she gets older.'

'It was a mistake,' said Jane, 'for her to bob her hair.'

'It certainly was,' said Isabel. She threw off her fox fur and sank down in Stephen's armchair. 'Do you know that she's been seeing an awful lot of Ed Brown?'

'I know,' said Jane, 'and I can't understand it. I can't even understand how she came to know him. He's very unattractive.'

Isabel, as usual, could supply all required details.

'He gave her twenty-five thousand dollars in her campaign for the Crippled Children. She went to see him in Flora's old house. He's turned the gold parlour into his private office.'

A little shiver of repulsion passed over Jane.

'Don't, Isabel!' she cried. 'I can't bear to think of it!'

'Can you?' said Isabel. 'But he has. I suppose he was bowled over by the sight of Mrs. Albert Lancaster in the flesh! He's just the kind that would read all the society columns. Anyway, he drew out his check-book with a flourish and that gesture made a great hit with Muriel.'

'He must be as old as Bert Lancaster was,' mused Jane.

'Oh, no, dear,' said Isabel promptly. 'Bert was sixty-seven when he died. Ed Brown can't be a day over sixty.'

'Well, anyway,' said Jane, 'it won't come to anything.'

'Rosalie's not so sure,' said Isabel. 'He has millions. Bert's illness was awfully expensive, you know. And Muriel's been generous to Albert.'

'Oh, Isabel!' said Jane defensively. 'That won't make any difference! Whatever you may say against Muriel, she never cared about money. All Muriel ever wanted in life was excitement and admiration and ——'

'And love,' interrupted Isabel, with decision. 'Ed Brown could love her. Any man can do that. He could love her in an opera box and a Rolls-Royce town-car and a sable cape! I think Muriel would enjoy it immensely.'

'A bill-board king,' said Jane reflectively. 'I don't just see Muriel Lancaster as a bill-board queen.'

'He's the president of the Watseka Country Club,' said Isabel with a twinkle. 'But I think Muriel could be relied on to make him resign. He couldn't resign from his married daughters, however. I should think Pearl and Gertie would give Muriel pause for thought.'

Isabel's command of facts was really astounding.

'Are those their names?'

Isabel nodded solemnly.

'They're terrible, Jane. They play bridge in the afternoons in lace evening gowns and they wear white fox furs in street-cars! At home, I'm sure they have flats with sun parlours and sit in them in boudoir caps, reading the comic supplements of the Sunday papers ——'

'Isabel!' laughed Jane. 'You're simply morbid!'

'Merely clairvoyante,' smiled Isabel. 'But I tell you, Jane, since Bert died, curiously enough, Muriel's been rather lonely. She couldn't talk to him, of course. But as long as he lived she had to plan for him and quarrel with his nurses and argue with his doctors. It gave her something to do.'

Just then the maid entered the room, bearing the tea-tray. Isabel, pausing discreetly, glanced up at her, just as Mrs. Ward used to glance at Minnie.

'Where's Jenny?' she asked, on just her mother's note of hollow inquiry, as Jane poured the water on the tea leaves.

'Out walking with her dogs,' said Jane.

The maid left the room and Isabel promptly resumed.

'It's fun to flirt, you know, when you haven't much time for it. But you can't make a life out of philandering. Not even if you're Muriel. Especially at fifty.'

'Two lumps?' said Jane.

'Two lumps,' said Isabel. 'And lots of cream.' She rose to pick up her cup and stood silently on the hearthrug for a moment, absently stirring her tea. 'You know, Jane,' she resumed presently, 'it's a little difficult, from fifty on, to decide just what you *will* make a life out of. And speaking of that, old girl, what are we going to do about Mamma? She says she won't go away for the summer.'

'She must,' said Jane firmly, as she offered the toast.

'Well, she won't,' said Isabel, accepting a piece. 'She won't because of Minnie's asthma. Minnie has every kind of asthma there is — horse, rose, and goldenrod! Mamma says Minnie must stay in town. Or Minnie says Mamma must. It's too ridiculous, but I can't do a thing with her! We ought to have got rid of Minnie years ago, Jane. She rules Mamma with a rod of iron.'

'We're lucky to have her,' said Jane. 'Mamma adores her and she takes very good care of her.'

'We could take care of her,' said Isabel.

'Could we?' said Jane. 'I mean — you know, Isabel — *would* we? Mamma's awfully trying. Just as trying as Minnie, really. Minnie's the only person in the world who can manage her.'

'It's dreadful,' said Isabel, 'to think of Mamma being managed by a servant. When you remember how she used to be — so pretty and proud and decided.'

'She's a very old lady now,' said Jane. 'A very lonely old lady.'

'Jane,' said Isabel solemnly, 'when you see me getting like that, I hope you'll kill me.'

'We'll kill each other,' smiled Jane. 'Let's make a suicide pact.'

'I mean it,' said Isabel.

'So do I,' said Jane. 'We'll jump off the Michigan Boulevard Bridge together.' The thought had really caught Jane's fancy. 'Some early spring afternoon, I think, Isabel, when the ice is just out of the river and the first sea-gulls have come and the water's running very clear and green. We'll climb up on the parapet together — which will be difficult as we'll both be a little infirm — and take a last look down the boulevard, thinking of how it was once just Pine Street. We'll shut our eyes and remember the old square houses and the wide green yards and the elm trees, meeting over the cedar-block pavement. We'll remember the yellow ice wagons, Isabel, and the Furnesses' four-in-hand, and the bicycles and the hurdy-gurdies and our front steps on summer evenings. And then we'll take hands and say "Out, brief candle!" and jump! It would make a nine days' wonder and the front page of all the newspapers, but I think it would be worth it!'

'It would be worth it to Cicily and Belle and Jenny,' said Isabel cynically. 'They wouldn't have to cope with anything worse than a double funeral!'

'To Cicily and Jenny, perhaps,' assented Jane. 'Belle won't have to cope with much if Albert stays in the diplomatic service and keeps the ocean between you.'

'I hope he *won't* stay in it,' said Isabel. 'He's got as far up now as he can ever get without a great deal more money. You need *millions*, Jane, for even a second-rate embassy. Belle's awfully tired of being the wife of an under-secretary and having a different baby in a new city every third year. I hope to goodness if she ever has another it will be a son! Three daughters in nine years is enough for Belle to handle!'

'A boy in time saves nine!' smiled Jane. As she spoke she heard the doorbell. 'That's probably Cicily,' she said. 'She was going to bring over the children.'

In a moment, however, Muriel's voice was heard in the hall.

'Is Mrs. Carver at home?' She appeared in the doorway, holding a little package in her hands. Muriel hadn't gone off *much*, reflected Jane. She was looking very charming, that afternoon, in a new grey spring suit and a little red hat that matched the colour of her carmined lips. Her blue eyes were twinkling, as of old. There was a spirit of youth about Muriel that the frosts of fifty winters could not subdue. It triumphed over the ripe effulgence of her middle years. She looked well-groomed, however.

'How's the birthday girl?' she cried. 'Hello, Isabel!' Advancing to the hearthrug she kissed Jane warmly. 'Feeling rather low, old speed?'

'Not at all,' said Jane falsely. 'I like to be fifty.'

'I believe you,' said Muriel. 'It's a lovely age. "The last of life, for which the first was made!" How poets do lie! Never mind, darling, you'll feel better to-morrow. One gets used to everything!' She sank into an armchair and smiled up at Jane. 'Here's a present for you!'

Jane opened the little package. It contained a gold vanity case.

'Why, Muriel!' she cried. 'How — how magnificent!'

'*Use* that lipstick,' said Muriel firmly. 'Better and brighter lipsticks are the answer, Jane. No tea, darling! Such as it is, I'm trying to keep my figure! Do you see what I see, Jane? Is Isabel actually eating *chocolate cake?*'

'I certainly am,' said Isabel, a bit tartly.

'I can't have eaten a piece of chocolate cake,' said Muriel meditatively, 'for over fifteen years! But you eat it, Jane, and you don't get fat at all. Neither does Flora. I saw her in Paris last spring, just stuffing down *pâtisserie* at Rumpelmayer's, and she was a perfect thirty-six!'

'You're looking very pretty to-day, Muriel,' said Isabel suddenly. Her tone was not that of idle compliment. Rather of acute appraisal. She had been watching Muriel intently since her triumphal entrance.

Muriel glanced quickly up at her. Jane heard her catch her breath in a little excited gasp.

'I — I'm feeling rather pretty,' she said surprisingly. 'Do you know what I mean, girls — how you *do* sometimes feel pretty, from the inside out?'

Jane nodded solemnly. She understood. Though she herself had not *felt* pretty in just that way for years. Not since that last night when she had gone with Jimmy into the moonlit garden. It was such a happy, excited feeling. And it always told its story in your face. You only *felt* pretty, Jane reflected wisely, when you knew that some one else, whose opinion you cared about terribly, really thought you were.

'Muriel!' cried Isabel. 'What's the matter with you?'

Jane suddenly realized that Muriel was laughing. Laughing happily, excitedly, and yet a trifle shyly. There was something absurdly virginal about that happy, excited laughter. She clasped her gloved hands impulsively in a little confiding gesture that recalled to Jane's memory the Muriel of Miss Milgrim's School.

'Girls,' she said dramatically, 'I'm going to marry Ed Brown on the first of June!'

'M-Muriel!' stammered Jane. She rose to her feet. She did not dare to look at Isabel.

'I'm — terribly happy,' said Muriel faintly. She had

stopped laughing now. There were actually tears in her great blue eyes. Her carmined lips were trembling. The sudden display of emotion had curiously shattered the hard enamel of her brilliant, fading beauty. Jane took her in her arms. Muriel had never seemed more appealing. Jane felt terribly fond of her. She wanted to protect her from Isabel. From Isabel, who, quite unmoved, was still watching Muriel with that look of acute appraisal. Nevertheless, Jane, herself, could not suppress the thought that Muriel's ample, corseted figure felt very solid, very mature in her eager embrace. She despised herself for the thought.

'Muriel,' she said, 'I think it's lovely.'

'I know I'm ridiculous,' said Muriel, withdrawing from her arms and fumbling for a handkerchief in her little grey bag. 'But it's terribly cheering to be really ridiculous again. I — I was never very happy with Bert, you know. Ed really loves me. He — he's like a boy about me ——' Meeting Isabel's appraising eye she stopped abashed. 'I know you're thinking there's no fool like an old fool, Isabel!'

'I'm not!' protested Isabel. 'I'm not at all. I'm sure you'll be very happy ——' Her voice trailed off a trifle lamely.

'We're going around the world on our honeymoon,' said Muriel. 'We won't be back for a year.'

A honeymoon, thought Jane. A honeymoon for Muriel, who was her own contemporary. It was absurd, of course, but it was touching, too. It was touching to think that any one could have the courage to believe that life could begin over again at fifty. Love at fifty. It tired Jane to think of it. But perhaps it was possible. Autumn blossoming. A freak of nature, like the flowers of the witch-hazel, bursting weirdly into bloom in October when all the other bushes were bare. But — Ed Brown.

'Have you written Albert?' asked Isabel.

'I cabled him Saturday,' said Muriel. The familiar glint of shameless curiosity glittered in Isabel's eye. 'He was very much pleased,' said Muriel with dignity.

'Of course,' said Jane hastily. 'Why wouldn't he be?'

'Will he come back for the wedding?' asked Isabel suddenly. 'Will be bring Belle?'

'They're both coming,' said Muriel, smiling. 'And bringing the children.'

'You should have them for flower girls,' said Isabel wickedly.

'Ed has grandchildren, too,' said Muriel blandly. Jane felt the spectral presences of Pearl and Gertie hover for an instant in the circumambient air. But Isabel, thank Heaven, was obviously not going to refer to them. 'I'm going to have such fun, Jane,' went on Muriel, 'buying a trousseau. I'm going to be very foolish. I'm going in for black chiffon nightgowns and I saw a négligée last week at Castberg's ——'

A sudden shuffle, a sound of suppressed laughter, broke in upon their colloquy from the hall. Jane looked up quickly. She had not heard the doorbell ring. A tiny red-sweatered figure stood, tottering, in the doorway.

'Happy birfday, Granma!' it cried and staggering across the room fell tottering across Jane's knees. It was Robin Redbreast, her youngest grandchild.

'Magnificent!' cried Cicily's voice.

The twins appeared in the doorway. Tripping on rugs, slipping on the hardwood floor, they dashed across the living-room and cast themselves on Jane's neck.

'Happy birthday, Grandma!' they repeated.

Cicily stood on the threshold. She looked extremely pretty in a rose-coloured sport suit and immensely amused at her offspring's dramatic entrance.

'Hello, Mumsy!' she cried. 'Happy birthday again!

Hello, Aunt Isabel! I thought you'd be here. How do you do, Aunt Muriel?'

'Don't tell her,' whispered Muriel. 'Don't tell her until I've gone.' She rose as she spoke. Untangling herself from the arms of grandchildren, Jane walked with her to the door.

'I do feel a little silly,' confessed Muriel in the hall, 'in the presence of Albert's contemporaries.'

'Nonsense!' said Jane stoutly. Though she could not imagine what her own feelings would be if she had to announce her prospective marriage to Cicily. She kissed Muriel tenderly and returned to the living-room. Isabel had wasted no time. Cicily, standing on the hearthrug, was facing her mother-in-law in shocked, derisive incredulity.

'Oh, I don't believe it!' she was saying.

'It's true!' cried Isabel. 'It's perfectly true!'

'You're kidding me,' said Cicily.

'I'm not!' cried Isabel. 'Ask your mother!'

'It's true,' said Jane soberly.

'Aunt Muriel — is going to marry — Ed Brown?'

Jane nodded solemnly.

'My Gawd!' said Cicily profanely. Then, 'How absurd!'

'Why is it absurd?' inquired Jane a trifle sharply. She sat down again at the tea-table and removed Robin Redbreast's fingers from the sugar-bowl.

'It's so undignified,' said Cicily promptly. 'If Aunt Muriel wanted to marry again, why didn't she do it years ago?'

'My dear,' said Jane gently, 'her husband was living.'

'If you call it living,' said Cicily cheerfully. She had appropriated Robin Redbreast and was removing his scarlet sweater. Little Jane was already seated on Isabel's knee. Jane put her arm around John and drew him gently to her. She leaned her cheek against the embroidered chevron on the sleeve of his navy-blue reefer. The twins looked exactly alike, brown-eyed and solemn and very like their great-grandfather. Their souls were different, however. Matter-of-fact and matter-of-fancy, Jane always called them. John's soul was matter-of-fancy. He was a lovely, imaginative little boy. His big brown eyes looked up at her wistfully. There was nothing in the world more endearing, Jane reflected tenderly, than the freckles on an eight-year-old nose!

But Cicily was still intrigued with the problems of her Aunt Muriel.

'I should think she would have fallen in love with some one else long since,' she said.

Jane's eyes met Isabel's. She hoped her sister was going to restrain herself. The hope was vain, however.

'She's been falling in love with some one else every six months for the last thirty years,' said Isabel shortly.

'Why didn't she walk out on Uncle Bert, then?' asked Cicily lightly. 'Why didn't she get a divorce?'

Jane glanced uneasily at the twins. Eight-year-old children were very understanding. Cicily never seemed to care what she said in their hearing.

'The Lesters are a very conventional family,' she said gravely. 'I'm sure your Aunt Muriel never thought of divorce. Not even before Uncle Bert's stroke.'

'Why not?' asked Cicily again.

'She had Albert to consider,' said Isabel.

'Albert?' cried Cicily. Her voice was greatly astonished. 'What had Albert to do with it?'

'It would have broken up his home,' said Isabel, a trifle sententiously.

'Oh, I don't know,' said Cicily. 'He might have drawn a very good stepfather.'

'Men who love married women,' said Isabel with asperity, 'don't make very good stepfathers.'

Cicily looked up at her with interest. Robin Redbreast slid from her knees to the floor.

'Do you mean she really had lovers?'

Isabel did not reply. In her turn, she glanced a little uneasily at the twins. Her silence was very eloquent.

'How stupid of her!' said Cicily. 'A woman who takes a lover is always the underdog.'

'Your Aunt Muriel wasn't,' said Isabel. 'There was always a good deal of talk, of course, but she managed things very cleverly.'

'I don't believe in promiscuity,' said Cicily firmly.

'Cicily!' cried Isabel sharply. 'What words you use! At your age your mother and I wouldn't have ——'

'I can't see that it makes much difference what you *call* things, Aunt Isabel,' said Cicily cheerfully. 'You and Mother certainly didn't believe in it and I don't either. It isn't practical and it's terribly complicated. I believe in monogamy.'

'You reassure me, darling,' murmured Jane, with a smile.

'I believe,' continued Cicily stoutly, 'that when a married woman falls in love, she ought to march straight to the divorce court and make everything regular.'

'Oh,' said Jane, still with the smile, 'progressive monogamy.'

'Exactly,' said Cicily. Then added wisely, 'No woman is ever really happy trying to live with two men at once. And no woman is ever really happy without her marriage lines.'

'No woman is eventually happy,' said Jane rather solemnly, 'if she doesn't play the game with the cards that were dealt her.'

'Why?' said Cicily promptly. 'Not all games are like that. I think life's very like poker. You look over your hand and keep what you like, and what you don't, you discard. Throw away your Jack, you know, and hope for a king!'

Cicily was smiling a little over her play on words. It was an innocent little joke, of course, but Jane was very thankful that Isabel had not noticed it.

'And if you draw a deuce?' she said soberly.

'Have faith in the future,' said Cicily lightly, 'and keep your poker face. There's always a new deal.'

'You talk,' said Jane severely, 'as if a woman had nine lives like a cat.'

'She could have,' said Cicily, 'if she had vision and courage.'

'Vision!' cried Jane. 'What takes vision is to recognize the imperial qualities in the cards in your hand! What takes courage is to win the pot with a deuce spot!'

'I call that bluffing,' said Cicily, cheerfully. 'You fool the world, but you don't fool yourself. You may win the pot, but it's not worth the winning. What's fun is a game with a handful of face cards!'

For the last few minutes Isabel had not been listening to her argumentative daughter-in-law. Her next remark betrayed the fact that her thoughts had been wandering.

'Belle's coming back for the wedding,' she said.

'Really?' cried Cicily. Her face lit up at the thought. 'Oh, I'll love to see Belle again! Is she bringing the children?'

Isabel nodded cheerfully.

'What fun!' cried Cicily. 'What fun for all of us!'

It *would* be fun for all of them, Jane reflected, as she stood at the front door with Isabel an hour later and watched Cicily, attended by her cavalcade of children, disappear around the bushes at the entrance of the drive. The twins were trying to roller-skate, with a signal lack of success, on the gravel walk. The air resounded with their shrieks of triumph and emulation. Cicily was pushing an empty go-cart and guiding Robin Redbreast's faltering footsteps with a maternal hand. At the turn of the path she paused to wave gaily back at the two grandmothers.

'Cicily's a good mother,' said Isabel approvingly.

'She adores the children,' said Jane. 'You know, Isabel,' she added slowly, 'modern young people don't mean all they say.'

'I don't listen much to what Cicily says,' said Isabel. 'But what I catch sounds very wild.'

'Their talk is wild,' said Jane. 'But their lives are just as tame as ours were.'

'Except for the drink,' said Isabel.

'The drink, of course,' said Jane. 'But Cicily never takes too much.'

'I've seen her pretty gay at the Casino,' said Isabel. Then added honestly, 'But Jack was, too.'

'They all get pretty gay,' said Jane, 'but the nice ones don't get really tight. Not very tight, that is.'

'You don't have to get *very* tight to be pretty loose!' said Isabel. She beckoned for her car as she spoke. It was waiting by the service entrance. 'But I think you're right. They don't mean a thing by it.'

The motor drove slowly up to the front door. Isabel climbed into it.

'Good-bye, birthday child!' she cried, as it started into motion. She was waving cheerfully through the open window. 'I can't wait to tell Robin about Muriel.'

The car moved slowly down the drive. Jane lingered a moment on her doorstep looking after it in the pleasant May sunshine. Her thoughts were still busy with Cicily's wild talk. To Jane, Cicily seemed barely out of the nursery. She looked barely out of the nursery with her dandelion head and her short slim skirts and her silly silky little legs! She might have been pushing her doll's carriage down that drive! She

shouldn't be playing with thoughts like that, though. Edged
tools in the hands of a child.

Jane turned on her doorstep and walked slowly back into
the living-room to ring for the waitress to remove the ravaged
tea-tray. She sank down in Stephen's armchair. Of course
the silly child did not mean a word that she had been saying. Good women talked differently in different generations
but they always acted the same.

But did they? Women — good women — were getting divorced every day. Just as girls — good girls — were getting,
well — gay, every night. In Jane's mother's time a girl who
got drunk, a woman who was divorced, was an outcast, a public scandal, a skeleton in a family closet. In her time and
Isabel's she was a deplorable curiosity — more to be pitied
than censured, perhaps, but always to be deplored. Now
Cicily regarded intoxication as an incidental accident, de-
pendent on the quality of bootlegged liquor that was served at
a party. She regarded divorce as a practical aid to monoga-
mous living.

When Stephen and young Steve came in from the five-
fifty half an hour later, Jane was still sitting in the armchair.

'Jane?' called Stephen, from the front door. Before taking
off his overcoat he came into the living-room to give her another birthday kiss. 'What are you thinking about?' he inquired, 'all alone by the fire.'

'It's a godless age,' said Jane promptly.

Young Steve grinned pleasantly at her from the threshold.

'What have we done now?' he inquired cheerfully.

'It's what you *don't* do,' said Jane. 'Or rather what you
don't think — what you don't feel.'

'What's that got to do with God?' inquired Steve, as he,
too, kissed her.

'I don't know,' said Jane thoughtfully. 'I guess God's

here, all right, as much as He ever was. But you — you see Him differently.' Then suddenly it came to her just what sort of an age it was. 'It's a *graceless* age!' said Jane triumphantly.

'Not while you're in it,' said Stephen with gallantry.

'Bravo, Dad!' laughed Steve. 'That ought to cheer her!'

Jane looked tenderly up at her grey-haired, bald-headed Stephen. For a moment she saw him, slim, young, and debonair, standing by Mr. Bert Lancaster's side beneath the crystal chandelier of Flora's little third-floor ballroom. Almost as young as Steve, quite as care-free, just as good-looking. But yet an ardent supporter of the vanished dignities and decencies and decorums. Your husband's point of view was a refuge, thought Jane. It was a sanctuary to which you fled from the assaults of time and your own children. It was where you belonged. If your husband was fifty-eight, thought Jane, you wanted, yourself, to be fifty!

'I *am* cheered!' said Jane.

II

'I get awfully fed up with it,' said Cicily.

'With what?' asked Jane.

'With this,' said Cicily.

Jane's eyes followed her daughter's around the drawing-room of the little French farmhouse. It was a charming room. It was in perfect order. The May sunshine was streaming in over the yellow jonquils and white narcissus of the window-boxes. Streaming in over the pale, plain rug, lighting the ivory walls, glinting here and there on the gold frame of an antique mirror, the rim of a clear glass bowl, the smooth, polished surfaces of the few old pieces of French furniture with which the room was sparsely furnished. The abrupt dark eyes of a Marie Laurencin over the fireplace met Jane's enigmatically. That opal-tinted canvas was Cicily's most cherished possession. Jane, herself, thought it very queer. The enigma of those chocolate eyes set in that pale blank face always made her feel a trifle uncomfortable. The lips were cruel, she thought. Nevertheless, the room was charming.

'I don't know why you should,' she said slowly. 'It's all so nice.'

'It's nice enough,' said Cicily vaguely. Then added honestly, after a brief pause, 'It's just the way I like it, really. Only ——'

'Only what?' said Jane gently.

'Only nothing ever happens in it,' said Cicily with sudden emphasis. 'Do you know what I mean, Mumsy? Nothing ever happens to me. I sometimes feel as if these walls were just waiting to see something happen. Something *ought* to happen in a room as charming as this. I feel just that way about everything, Mumsy — about my clothes and the way I look and all the trouble I take about the maids and the meals and the children. I'm everlastingly setting the stage, but the drama never transpires. I'd like a little bit of drama, Mumsy. Something nice and unexpected and exciting. Something different. Before I'm too old to enjoy it.'

The last sentence dispelled Jane's sense of rising uneasiness with its touch of comic relief.

'You're twenty-eight, Cicily,' she said, smiling.

'I know,' said Cicily, 'but I've been married for nine years. I may be married for forty more. Am I just going to keep house in Lakewood for forty years? Keep house and play bridge and go in town to dinner and have people out for Sunday luncheon — the same people, Mumsy — until I grow old and grey-headed — too old even to *want* anything different ——' She broke off abruptly.

Jane considered her rather solemnly for a moment in silence. Then, 'Life's like that, Cicily,' she said.

'Not all lives,' said Cicily. 'There's Jenny — Jenny's only
three years younger than I am. She isn't really happy, I
think, Mumsy, but at least she's free. She could light out if
she wanted to — she will some day, if she doesn't marry —
and do almost anything. Make the world her oyster. But my
life's set. I signed on the dotted line before I was old enough
to know what I was doing. I don't mean that I really regret
it, Mumsy — Jack's always been sweet to me and I love my
children — I want to have more children — but just the
same ——' Cicily rose uneasily from her little French armchair and stood staring out into the afternoon sunshine over
the white and yellow heads of the jonquils and narcissus. 'Oh,
I don't know what I want! Just girlhood over again, I guess.
Just something else than this little front yard with the road to
the station going by beyond the privet hedge, and Jack coming home from the five-fifty with a quart of gin in his pocket
for a dinner-party full of people I wouldn't care if I never
saw again ——' She broke off once more and continued to
stare moodily out into the pleasant May sunshine.

Jane watched the aureole of her dandelion hair a moment
in silence. Then, 'Well, Jack brings home the gin — that's
something,' she ventured. She felt her attempt at the light
touch was a trifle strained, however.

Cicily turned to face her.

'Yes,' she said. 'He brings home the gin and he brings
home the bacon, and he brings home a toy for the children he
bought in the Northwestern Station. He adores the children
and he loves me, but honestly, Mumsy, it's years since he got
any kick out of marriage. He takes it as a matter of course.
He takes *me* as a matter of course. He never complains, but
he hates Dad's bank, and he's just as bored with suburban gin
as I am. I tell you, Mumsy, the excitement has gone out of
things for Jack, too. But he signed on the dotted line and he

sticks by his bargain. And he's only thirty-one — with forty years ahead of him! That's rather grim, isn't it? I don't know, of course, if he's ever realized just how grim it is ——' Again Cicily lapsed into silence. She threw herself despondently back in her armchair. 'Don't you think it's funny, Mumsy, the things you never discuss with your own husband?' Then, as Jane did not reply, 'Perhaps you did, though. I can't imagine any one having any inhibitions with Dad.'

Jane met her daughter's eyes for a moment in silence. She hoped her own were as enigmatic as those of the Marie Laurencin over the fireplace. She could not bring herself to discuss Stephen, even with Cicily.

'Don't worry about those inhibitions,' she said presently. 'For love creates them. Love and fear, which always go hand in hand. When you love people, you are always really afraid — afraid of hurting them, afraid of disillusioning them, afraid of the spoken word which may upset the apple cart. Respect for the spoken word, Cicily, is the greatest safeguard in life against catastrophe.'

Cicily's wide blue eyes were rather uncomprehending.

'Just the same I'd like to break down the barriers. I'd like to be with Jack the way I used to be — happy and free and wild. Not thinking, not considering. But I guess you can never feel that way twice — about the same person that is ——'

The sound of the front door closing broke in on Cicily's last perilous words. They were still trembling on the circumambient air when Jack, hat in hand, stood on the threshold.

'Hello, Aunt Jane!' he said. His friendly, pale blue eyes were twinkling cheerfully. 'I stopped at the garage in the village, Cicily, to see what was wrong with the Chrysler. They say you stripped those gears again. I wish ——'

A faint frown of irritation deepened on Cicily's white brow.

'Did you call up Field's about that bill?' she said. Then to Jane, 'Aunt Isabel always gets her account mixed up with ours.'

'I did,' said Jack. 'But it wasn't Mother this time. It was your return credits. On the last day of every month, Aunt Jane, Cicily has half the merchandise in the store waiting in our front hall to be called for.'

He advanced to the armchair as he spoke and kissed Cicily's pink cheek, a trifle absent-mindedly.

'Where are the kids?'

'Eating supper,' said Cicily. 'We're dining out.'

Jane rose. She felt incredibly depressed by this little conjugal colloquy. As she walked slowly home over the suburban sidewalks, past rows and rows of little brick and wood and stucco houses, temples of domesticity enshrined, this loveliest, leafy season of the year, in flowering lilacs and apple trees in bloom, she reflected stoically that marriage was, of course, like that. The first fine careless rapture was bound to go. Something else came — something else took its place — something you held as your most priceless possession by the time you were fifty. Nevertheless, it was disconcerting to have seen it so clearly happening to the next generation. It was disconcerting to know, without peradventure of a doubt, that, to cheerfully smiling, subconsciously philosophic Jack, Cicily had come to look only like Cicily.

III

'Muriel,' said Isabel, 'looked amazingly young.

'She certainly did,' said Jane.

'And wasn't she wonderful with Pearl and Gertie?'

'My heart rather warmed to Gertie,' said Jane. 'She was crying all through the ceremony.'

'It's enough to make anybody cry,' said Isabel, 'to see a sixty-year-old father making a fool of himself.'

They were sitting on the old brown sofa in the Pine Street library. An hour before they had seen Muriel depart in a shower of rice for her trip around the world with Ed Brown. The rice had been Albert's eleventh-hour inspiration. He had foraged for it in the kitchen and thrust it, hilariously, into the hands of the younger generation. His three little daughters had thrown it, delightedly, at their grandmother. The rice, Jane thought, had rather disconcerted Muriel.

The entire family were taking supper with Mrs. Ward. The children and grandchildren were making merry in the yellow drawing-room across the hall. Belle was strumming out Gershwin on the old Steinway upright. The throbbing notes of the jazz melody vibrated incongruously in the little brown library. The Bard of Avon looked a bit bewildered, Jane thought. His wide mahogany eyes stared blankly over the heads of the two sisters.

Mrs. Ward was in the dining-room with Minnie. It was a long time since Mrs. Ward had given so large a dinner-party — fifteen people, not counting Robin Redbreast and Belle's youngest daughter, who had had their puffed rice in the pantry and were now supposedly asleep in the guest-room upstairs. All family, of course. Still, Mrs. Ward had brought out the cut-glass goblets and the Royal Worcester china and her very best long damask tablecloth. She had had the silver loving-cup polished and had filled it with roses for the centre of the table. Jack had brought her some gin and vermouth and Isabel had lent her her cocktail glasses. Mrs. Ward was just making sure that the nut and candy dishes were placed straight with the candlesticks. Since Minnie had been promoted from the pantry to the rôle of companion, Mrs. Ward's confidence in a waitress's eye for symmetry had wavered.

'Albert was very funny,' said Isabel suddenly, 'with that rice.'

'Albert *is* funny,' said Jane. 'Funny and nice, too. He was sweet with Ed Brown, but yet you could see he didn't miss a trick. He was touched and amused and amusing, all at once. He treats his mother just like a contemporary.'

'Live and let live is always Albert's policy,' said Isabel. 'Belle finds it rather trying. Belle's like me — she always has an opinion. A completely tolerant husband can be very irritating.'

'I like him,' said Jane. 'I like him very much.' She hesitated for a moment toying with the thought of telling Isabel that she found Albert greatly improved, then abandoning it. You could not tell your sister that you found her son-in-law greatly improved, without tacitly implying that you had previously felt that there was room for great improvement.

Jane had never quite been able to overcome her prejudice against Albert because he was his father's son. Jane's distrustful dislike for Bert Lancaster was rooted deep in the hidden instincts of her childhood. She had subconsciously transferred it to his boy. That was unfair, Jane reflected honestly. Albert had sowed some wild oats in college. He had been a dangerously beautiful young man. Muriel had adored and spoiled him. But he had married Belle and gone to Oxford and entered the diplomatic service and had done very well for himself, until the lack of a great fortune had hampered his further advancement. He had given it up, temporarily, and come home to enter the aeroplane industry, to make, he had said laughingly, a million dollars. 'I've rented my soul to Mammon' had been his phrase.

'Here come the boys,' said Isabel suddenly. The robust sound of masculine laughter was heard in the hall. Robin and

Stephen entered the library, carrying Jack's cocktail and Isabel's glasses on Mrs. Ward's silver tray.

'Mamma!' called Jane.

'Children!' called Isabel.

The throb of the Gershwin stopped abruptly in the yellow drawing-room.

'Drinks!' rang out Cicily's voice above the talk and laughter.

Mrs. Ward entered the room. She looked a very pretty old lady in the new black silk dress she had bought for the wedding. Her cheeks were flushed with excitement over the nut and candy dishes.

'I hope that ice was cracked right for you, Robin,' she said anxiously. 'We don't know much about cocktails in this house. Your father never served them,' she added in superfluous explanation to Jane and Isabel. 'Just wine and a highball for the gentlemen. *Was* the ice right, Robin?'

'Perfect!' responded Robin with a twinkle. 'I never saw ice more expertly cracked!'

But Mrs. Ward did not smile.

'I'm very glad,' she said earnestly.

Just then the children trooped in from the hall. Jane looked up at them with a proud, proprietary smile. They were nice children. They made a pretty picture, in the modern manner, to be sure, as they clustered about the tray of cocktails. Jenny, slim, blonde, and boyish, in the tailor-made sport suit she affected at even a June wedding, sipping the amber liquid that was just the colour of her short, shining hair. Steve, a little flushed with nuptial champagne, singing a reminiscent fragment of the Gershwin as he shook the silver shaker. Belle and Cicily arm in arm on the hearthrug. Pretty Belle, who still looked like an apple blossom, a slightly paler, rather more full-blown apple blossom, clad in the flattering, fluttering pink panels of her French frock, and

Cicily smiling beside her, her flower-like head rising proudly from a sheaf of pale green chiffon. Pleasant, snub-nosed Jack coming up with a cocktail in either hand for his wife and his sister. Albert in the doorway, dark and distinguished, not very tall, lithe and slim-waisted, with something of the Greek athlete about him in spite of his cutaway, smiling, over the heads of the brown-eyed twins and his own two dark-haired daughters, at the young women on the hearthrug. Steve approached him with the silver shaker. Albert accepted his glass.

'I give you a toast,' he said suddenly. 'To Muriel and the reconstructed life!'

They all drank it riotously. Albert *was* sweet about his mother, thought Jane. So many sons would have resented that ridiculous *mésalliance*. Did Albert, in his heart? Isabel, of course, voiced the thought.

'How do you really feel about it, Albert?' she inquired curiously.

'Me?' said Albert innocently, extending his empty glass toward Steve. 'Why, I believe in reconstruction. Mother's had a pretty thin time the last fifteen years. It's never too late to mend. We all learned that in our copy-books. Another cocktail, Cicily?'

Cool and aloof and flower-like, Cicily accepted the glass. She flashed a brief, bright smile up into Albert's admiring eyes.

'I adore cocktails,' she said.

Suddenly across Jane's mind shot the picture of a very different Cicily. A mutinous, moody Cicily, turning in the sunshine of her little French window to declare, 'Jack's just as bored with suburban gin as I am!' This was Jack's gin, but the child did not look bored at all. Of course she was happy. She had not meant those perilous words that had troubled

Jane so profoundly. She was still smiling up at Albert Lancaster over the rim of her little crystal goblet.

'It's fire and ice,' she said, with a little thirsty gasp. 'Exciting. Like love and hate. Like life, as it ought to be.'

'Like you, as you are,' said Albert gallantly. His eyes were bent admiringly on her cool, blonde radiance. His gallantry, Jane thought, was a bit professional. A technique in handling women, very alien to Lakewood. But he had hit the nail on the head. 'Fire and ice' *was* rather like Cicily in her high moments. She did not seem at all impressed, however, with the accuracy of the description.

'He's irresistible, isn't he, Belle?' she was saying calmly.

The waitress appeared on the threshold. Jane caught a glimpse of Minnie's plump figure, hovering officiously in the hall beyond. Minnie was going to see that dinner, on this important occasion, was announced correctly.

'Come, children,' said Mrs. Ward.

Robin offered her his arm. Stephen appropriated Isabel. Steve turned up at Belle's elbow. Jenny clapped Jack familiarly on the shoulder.

'You're elected, old top!' she said.

Albert and Cicily were left alone on the hearthrug. She turned from him abruptly to place her empty glass on the mantel-shelf.

'Cicily,' smiled Albert, 'do you know what you've done while my back was turned? You've grown up into a damned dangerous woman!'

Cicily met his eyes with a frosty little twinkle of complete composure. Girls were wonderful, thought Jane. You would think, to look at her, that Cicily had been talked to like that for years.

'Then watch your step!' laughed Cicily. 'Don't get burned or frost-bitten.'

Jane followed them from the room, hand in hand with her grand-twins. Belle's dark-haired daughters trooped at her side. Their frizzy black curls recalled the Muriel of Miss Milgrim's School. It was fun, this reunion — it was lovely to have all this big family under one roof again.

Standing behind her chair, Jane looked down the long white damask expanse of the candlelit table, across the cut-glass goblets and the Royal Worcester china and the loving-cup of roses, to the frail little matriarch in a new black silk dress who was the head of the clan, then turned, instinctively, to her father's chair. Her brown-eyed grandson was going to occupy it — little John Ward Bridges, aged eight.

'I hope I live long enough,' she thought suddenly, 'to see *my* great-grandchildren.' Steve, on her other hand, was pulling out her chair. She sat down in the gay staccato confusion of talk and laughter. 'I hope I live long enough,' she thought solemnly, 'to see what happens to every one. To know they're safe ——'

Just then John Ward upset his glass of water in the nearest nut dish. In meeting the emergency of the moment, Jane forgot to be solemn. Later, she watched Cicily rather closely across the prattling queries and vast gastronomical silences of her grandson's table manners. Cicily never looked happier — never looked prettier—never seemed to take more trouble to be charming and gay. Jane felt she had been a very foolish mother. There was no need to be profoundly troubled.

CHAPTER IV

I

JANE sat at the wheel of her motor, absent-mindedly threading her way through the congested traffic of Sheridan Road. She had just returned to the West from her so-called holiday at Gull Rocks and was running into town to take tea with Isabel at her mother's.

Jane loved to drive a car and she loved the sense of relief, of escape, of expansion that she always experienced when she had left Gull Rocks behind her. The summer had been difficult. Jane was reviewing it in thought as she rolled down the boulevard. She was thinking of the old, old Carvers, now both over eighty; and of sacrificed Silly, who, a wiry sixty, never left home for an hour; and of Alden, who was *such* a stuffed shirt, a cartoon of a banker; and of the complications presented by the month in which Robin Redbreast and the twins had been with them, and of how Cicily had not realized when she sent them East with just Molly, the nurse, what it did to an old couple of eighty-odd to shelter three roistering great-grandchildren under their roof for thirty-one days; and of how Stephen still incredibly loved the place, and young Steve, too, and of how they had won seven races together and had been presented with a silver cup at the annual yacht club dinner, and of how delighted old Mr. Carver had been! Like a child, Mr. Carver was, and Stephen, too, and young Steve, over that silver cup! It was absurd of them, but it was very endearing. The summer *had* had its better moments. Nevertheless, Jane was glad to be home again.

It was a lovely late September afternoon. The lake still held its shade of summer blue. Its little curving waves, so unlike the ocean ones, were breaking and rippling along its yellow beaches. Jane could see them out of the corner of her eye, across the well-kept lawns of the squat, square brick and terra-cotta houses that lined the water-front. The geometric, skyscraping angles of the Edgewater Beach Hotel loomed up before her.

Curious to think that she had known this water-front when it was a waste of little yellow sand dunes and scrub-oak groves. Not a house in sight. Just stunted oaks and a few stone pines and sand — sandy roads along which you had to push your bicycle. Your bicycle — your Columbia Safety! It wasn't very far from here, just south of the old white lime-stone Marine Hospital, that she had picnicked with André and his father and mother the night that he had asked her to marry him. Asked her to marry him on the moonlit beach that had long since been gobbled up, filled in, and landscaped in the Lincoln Park extension. The very place had vanished, like the boy and girl, who had turned into Mrs. Stephen Carver of Lakewood and André Duroy, academician and distinguished sculptor.

There was a Diana of André's now in the Art Institute. Jane often dropped in to look at it. Often? Come, now, old girl, thought Jane, challenging with a smile her little mood of sentiment, *how* often? Twice a year, perhaps. She never found time for the Art Institute as often as she meant to. Still, she never went there without pausing for a moment before André's Diana.

Flora had never written much about him. More about his young wife, who seemed to be quite a girl. Quite a girl, in the discreet, sophisticated French manner that you read about in books and never quite believed in. Flora had a gift with the pen and Jane felt she knew a great deal about Cyprienne. Cyprienne was thirty-three. There was a lot of talk, Flora had said, about her and a young attaché in the British Embassy. His mother, a grand old dowager, was fearfully upset about it, for there was a name and a title and he was an only son. She was a Catholic, of course, and would never divorce. André was only fifty-two. It was hard on the young attaché. It was even harder, Jane thought, with Victorian simplicity, on André. Flora had never attempted to describe *his* reactions. Jane knew, however, just what kind of a husband André would be. There was enough of American upbringing in André, enough of Victorian Pine Street, to make him loathe a situation like that. And yet be kind — like all good American husbands who put up with their restless wives.

Restless wives — Cicily. A little unconscious smile played over Jane's lips as she paused for the traffic light at the entrance of the park and thought of how silly she had been to worry so much about Cicily last spring. The child had written her such happy letters all summer, and the moment she had seen her face, two days ago, at the gate of the Twentieth Century in the La Salle Street Station, she had known that the trouble, whatever it was, had blown over. It was nice for Cicily that Belle had taken that little house in Lakewood. She was full of plans for the early autumn parties. She had bought some pretty clothes.

They would all have a pleasant winter together, reflected Jane, as she rolled through the southern entrance of the park and out onto the stream-like bend of the Lake Shore Drive. It was a lovely street, she thought, edging that great, empty plane of blue and sparkling water. One of the loveliest city streets in the world. If it were in Paris, you would cross the ocean to see it. If it were in London, you would have heard of it all your life. If it were in Venice, the walls of the world's art galleries would be hung with oils and water-colours and etchings of its felicities of tint and line. But here, in Chicago, no one paid much attention to it. The decorous row of Victorian houses, withdrawn in their lawns, were discreetly curtained against that dazzling wash of light and colour. Only the new, bare, skyscraping apartments, rising here and there flush from the pavement, seemed aware of the view. They cheapened it, they commercialized it, they exploited it, but at least they knew it was there.

The Oak Street Beach, as Jane rolled past it, looked like a Sorolla canvas in the mellow afternoon sunshine. The golden sands were streaked and slashed and spotted with brilliant splashes of colour. Bathers, in suits of every conceivable hue, were sunning themselves on the beach. Men, incredibly brown, were breasting the blue waves. Girls were shrieking with delight in the nearer breakers. Children were paddling in the shallows. Jane had known the end of Oak Street before the beach had been there. The curve of filled-in land to the south had created it. Oak Street used to end in a row of waterlogged pilings, held in place by blocks of white limestone. Pilings on which ragged fishermen had sat, with tin cans of bait and strings of little silver fish at their side. It seemed just a year or two to Jane since she had seen the end of Oak Street looking just like that.

'Chicago,' thought Jane solemnly, 'makes you believe in Genesis. It makes you believe that in six days the Lord made heaven and earth.'

Jane loved Chicago. They would all have a pleasant winter together.

II

'I want to talk to you,' Isabel had whispered. 'Don't say anything in front of Mamma.'

She was handing Jane her teacup as she spoke, in the little

brown library. Mrs. Ward, preoccupied with misgivings on the consistency of the new cook's sponge cake, had not heard her. Jane had looked up, a little startled, into Isabel's plump, comfortable countenance. Her eyes looked rather worried.

'And how was Mrs. Carver's arthritis?' Mrs. Ward was inquiring of Jane. 'Poorly, I suppose, in that damp climate. We had a lovely summer in Chicago.'

Mrs. Ward always loved to talk about the infirmities of other old ladies, and she felt the need at the moment, to justify, in the minds of her daughters, her and Minnie's contested decision to spend the dog-days in town. Jane let the statement pass unchallenged. No one could do anything with Minnie, and her mother had borne the heat very well. If she *liked* to spend the summer one mile from Chicago's loop —— Isabel *did* look worried, thought Jane, as she commented favourably on the sponge cake. Probably Minnie was raising some kind of ruction again.

When she stood up to go an hour later, Isabel rose also.

'Run me home in your car, Jane,' she said.

The two sisters left the house together.

'Well, what is it?' asked Jane, as soon as they were seated in the motor.

'We can't talk here,' said Isabel. 'The traffic's too noisy. Run me out on the lake front. Isn't this street awful? We *ought* to make Mamma move.'

They certainly ought, thought Jane. Stripped of its elms, widened to twice its size, invaded by commerce and metamorphosed into North Michigan Boulevard, Pine Street bore no resemblance to the provincial thoroughfare of Jane's childhood. The wide yards had vanished, and many of the old red-brick and brown-stone houses had been pulled down to make way for the skyscrapers. Those that were left were defaced by bill-boards or disfigured with plate-glass show windows, in which gowns and cosmetics and lingerie were displayed for sale. Mrs. Ward was the only old resident, now living south of Chicago Avenue.

Jane turned down Superior Street in search of quiet. As they rolled past the dirty, decaying façade of a row of boarding-houses, she turned curiously to look at her sister. But Isabel was staring straight before her down the dusty street, her eyes on the flash of brilliant blue at the end of it that was the lake.

'Let's park on the curve,' she said, as Jane turned into the outer drive.

Jane drew up at the edge of the parkway. The curve commanded a view of the Oak Street Beach again, seen now across blue water, with a ragged fringe of skyscrapers beyond it, outlined against a sunset sky.

'What's on your mind, old girl?' said Jane.

'Can't you guess?' said Isabel.

Jane looked at her with increasing uneasiness. This curious reticence was very unlike Isabel. Isabel was usually delighted to break the bad news.

'No,' said Jane. 'I can't.'

'It's about Belle,' said Isabel.

'Isabel!' cried Jane. 'She's not having another baby?'

'No,' said Isabel. 'I almost wish she were. It might help matters. But then, again, it might only make them worse.'

'What *are* you talking about?' cried Jane.

Isabel looked at her for a moment in silence.

'Cicily and Albert,' she said.

Jane really felt her heart turn over. She stared, dumbfounded, at Isabel.

'Cicily and — Albert?' she stammered.

'It's making Belle awfully unhappy,' said Isabel. Then,

almost angrily, 'Jane, you don't mean to say you haven't
noticed it?'

'How could I have noticed it?' cried Jane, almost angrily in
her turn. 'I've been away all summer. I don't believe it,
anyway. Cicily wouldn't — Cicily couldn't ——'

'Well, Cicily *has*,' said Isabel grimly.

'I don't believe it,' said Jane again.

'You'll have to believe it,' said Isabel sharply. 'She was with
him every minute all summer. She sent the children to Gull
Rocks to get them out of the way. She used to motor out with
him to that damned airport and fly with him all day and then
motor in town at night and dine with him at the night clubs.
Of course I don't say there was any real *harm* in it, Jane, but it
made Belle perfectly miserable. She felt so humiliated — and
bewildered. Why, Cicily was her best friend.'

'What — what does Jack think?' asked Jane slowly.

'I don't know what he thinks,' said Isabel. 'He'd be the
last, of course, to criticize Cicily. He acts — he acts exactly
as if it weren't happening.' Her voice was trembling a little.
'I wouldn't speak to him about it for worlds.'

'Of course not,' said Jane quickly. 'It — it's not a thing to
talk about. But I know you're exaggerating it, Isabel. You
know Cicily ——'

'Yes, I know Cicily,' put in Isabel ironically.

'She's pretty and gay and only twenty-eight. She's been
married nine years and she never really had her fling. I — I
suppose Albert turned her head. I think it's outrageous of
him to take advantage of her ——'

'Take advantage of her!' cried Isabel.

'Take advantage of her inexperience ——'

'Jane! You know as well as I do that such affairs are always
the woman's fault! The idea of Cicily, the mother of three
children ——'

'It's just a harmless flirtation!' cried Jane. She was conscious of blind prejudice as she spoke. She knew nothing about it.

'It's not a very pretty flirtation,' said Isabel.

'I agree with you,' said Jane soberly.

'And it's made a different woman of Cicily. Surely, Jane, you saw ——'

'I saw she looked very happy,' said Jane.

'A woman's always happy,' said Isabel, 'when she's falling in love.'

'She's *not* falling in love,' said Jane decidedly. She saw it all clearly now, in a flash of revelation. 'She's just falling for Albert. She's falling for excitement and admiration and fun. She'll snap out of it, Isabel.'

'Will you speak to her?' asked Isabel.

'I — don't — know,' said Jane slowly. 'I don't know if it would do any good. Don't you remember how you felt yourself, Isabel, about — about parents — speaking? It only irritated you.'

'I certainly don't!' cried Isabel sharply. 'There was never any occasion for parents to speak about a thing like that to me. Or to you, either, Jane.'

Jane sat a moment in silence, staring across the deep blue water at the glowing embers in the Western sky.

'I can remember — I can remember,' she said slowly, 'how I felt about parents — mixing in and — and spoiling things that were really lovely ——'

'What things?' pursued Isabel hotly. 'You never had a beau in your life, Jane, after you married Stephen — unless you count little Jimmy Trent! But this — this is serious.'

'Perhaps,' said Jane. 'I'll think it over. But somehow I don't believe much in parental influence. It's something inside *yourself* that makes you behave, you know. Matthew

Arnold knew — "the enduring power not ourselves which makes for righteousness." I don't believe that Cicily would ever really be unkind — would ever knowingly hurt others.'

'But she *is* hurting them!' cried Isabel. 'She's hurting Belle, this minute!'

'Well, she'll stop,' said Jane stoutly. 'She'll stop when she realizes.'

Isabel opened the door of the motor.

'I'm going to walk home,' she said. She stood a moment hesitatingly by the side of the car. 'It — it upsets me so to talk about it, Jane.' Her lips were trembling again. 'I'm going to walk home and — and think of something else. I don't want to worry Robin. We've never talked about it. I suppose that seems funny to you, Jane, but ——' She broke off a little helplessly.

'No. No, it doesn't,' said Jane. 'I'm glad you haven't. I never worry Stephen. So many things blow over, you know, and if you haven't *said* anything ——'

'Exactly,' said Isabel.

Jane stared a moment in silence, down into her troubled eyes.

'Children can just *wreck* you,' said Isabel.

Jane nodded.

'Give my love to Robin,' she said. She set the gears in motion and moved slowly off down the boulevard. 'Little Jimmy Trent,' she was thinking. So *that* was all that Isabel had ever realized. She felt a sudden flood of sympathy for Cicily. Cicily, intoxicated with the wine of admiration. Cicily succumbing to the transcendent temptation to quicken a passion, to love and be loved. It was all very wrong, however. And very dangerous. Such temptations must be overcome. The wine of admiration could be forsworn. Cicily would, of course, forswear it. She *could* not speak to her. But she could watch. She could worry. That was what parents were for.

III

It was one o'clock on a late November morning and the first Assembly ball was in full swing in the ballroom of the Blackstone Hotel. The room was brilliantly lighted. Its gilded walls were hung with smilax and banked with palms and chrysanthemums. The floor was filled with dancers. A few elderly ladies, in full evening dress, were clustered in little groups on a row of gilt chairs, under the palms. A great crowd of young men were massed near the door. From that crowd, black broadcloth figures continually detached themselves, dashed into the revolving throng, tapped young women cavalierly on naked shoulders, drew them from their partners' embrace and stalked solemnly off with them.

Modern dances always seemed stalking and solemn to Jane. She was sitting in the balcony that ran round the room, her arms on the smilax-hung railing gazing down at the kaleidoscope of light and movement and colour on the floor. She was wearing a new black velvet evening gown — every one wore a new gown to the first Assembly — and she was vaguely wondering if the cane seat of her gilt chair was creasing the skirt. The balcony was crowded with other middle-aged women in other new evening gowns, sparsely attended by a sprinkling of middle-aged men.

Twenty feet away down the line of spectators sat Isabel, with Stephen, resigned and somnolent, standing behind her chair. Robin sat at Jane's elbow. Jane knew every one present and was tired of seeing them. She had seen them at an endless succession of first Assembly balls. To-night they looked just as they always had. At the other balls they had worn other new evening gowns. That was the only difference. On an Oriental rug at the ballroom door a row of Jane's contemporaries stood in line to receive the guests as they entered the room. Jane could remember when the hostesses at an Assembly ball had looked to her like a group of bedizened old ladies, pathetically tricked out in the garb of folly. Now the dancers seemed to her incredibly young.

Jane was watching Jenny, revolving on the floor beneath in the arms of what looked to Jane like an extremely Bacchic young man. She was wishing that Steve would cut in on her and take her away from him. Steve was a bit Bacchic, too, however. Too Bacchic to notice his sister's predicament. He was standing by the receiving line, rallying Cora Delafield. Cora Delafield was at least five years Jane's senior, but she rather specialized in Bacchic young men. Steve thought her very entertaining. Jane wished that Cicily would come. Her dinner-party was late. Jane wanted, ridiculously, to look just once at Cicily in her new white velvet, before taking Stephen home to bed.

Robin said something, but Jane could not hear it. She could not hear anything above the clash of the jazz orchestra at the end of the balcony. Modern balls were frightfully noisy. And there were always two orchestras, so you never had one single intermittent moment of peace. Stephen looked dog-tired. It was mean of her to keep him up a moment longer. It was mean of her to have brought him at all. Absurd to go to balls when you were fifty! You danced three times, perhaps, lumbering around the room with the more courteous men of your dinner-party, and then you retired to the balcony and talked to your brother-in-law, while you watched your own children.

Good gracious! Jenny's young man had almost fallen down in negotiating a turn. He had torn the flounce of her blue chiffon gown. Steve had disappeared, taking Cora Delafield with him. Cora's young men would do anything in

reason, but they would not lead her out on the dancing floor.
She tipped the scales at two hundred pounds.

Cora had the right idea, however. If you were going to go
to balls in your fifth decade, it was much better to go in for
Bacchic young men, on any terms, than to sit in the balcony,
watching your own children and straining your ears to catch
the amiable conversation of your brother-in-law, over the din
of those infernal saxophones.

Why, there was Jack! Jack cutting in on Jenny, the darling! Jack could always be relied on. Jenny was talking and
they were both laughing uproariously, casting discreet
glances back at the Bacchic young man, left standing be-
fuddled in the centre of the ballroom floor. Jenny was undoubtedly repeating some alcoholic anecdote! Girls did not
care nowadays what they said, or what was said to them.
Jane tried to imagine what would have happened to a Bacchic
young man at a dance in Chicago in the middle nineties.
Social ostracism — nothing less. Prohibition had turned ball-
rooms into barrooms.

But where was Cicily? There was Belle, lovely-looking, too,
in that silver gauze gown. Could Isabel be right? Was she
worried, was she really worried, over Cicily and Albert? She
did not look as if she had a care in the world, one-stepping
mystically, with sweet raised face and half-closed eyes, in the
arms of Billy Winter. *He* was a nice young man. Why didn't
Jenny fancy *him?* Why didn't Jenny fancy any one? She was
twenty-six years old. It was nonsense — it was utter nonsense — her talk of wanting to leave home and live in New
York and run dog kennels in Westchester County with Barbara Belmont.

But where *was* Cicily? If Jack and Belle were here, Cicily
and Albert must be somewhere in the offing. They had
come up in a taxi together, perhaps, from some young mar-

ried dinner. Stopped, possibly, at a night club. Jane suddenly realized how tired she was. And how tired of wondering, as she had wondered for two months, just what was happening to Cicily in taxis and in night clubs.

The lights were dimming. The lights were going out. The orchestra was silenced. A spotlight shone brilliantly down on the centre of the ballroom floor. A young man indistinguishable in the darkness, his shirt-front picked out startlingly in the silver radiance, was shouting that Miss Ivy Montgomery, from the company of 'Hot Chocolates' now playing at the Selwyn, would offer a dance. A slender quadroon in a spangled evening gown slipped suddenly into the spotlight. Her sleek oiled hair was shining. She smiled hugely, good-humouredly, her white teeth gleaming in the brutal orifice of her thick rouged lips. The orchestra crashed into a barbaric orgy of sound.

Where *was* Cicily, thought Jane, as she watched the contorted evolutions of Miss Montgomery's Charleston — or was it a Black Bottom? — as she listened to the applause that broke from the apparently spellbound audience at the end of the dance. Where *was* Cicily, she thought, as two darky comedians followed Miss Montgomery into the spotlight, and tapped their flapping shoes and cracked their age-old jokes, to the accompaniment of throbbing saxophones and bursts of appreciative laughter.

The lights flashed up. The darkies had vanished. The dancers, in twos and fours and sixes, took possession once more of the ballroom floor. Jane glanced at her wrist watch. It was almost two o'clock. But there *was* Cicily! Cicily, slim and slinky in the folds of the new white velvet, passing down the receiving line, bending her dandelion head in charming deference before the dowager hostesses. And Albert was behind her. Well — Jane had known he would be. He *was* good-looking. He stood waiting, tranquilly, under a palm, for Cicily to complete her amenities. Belle floated by, with Billy Winter again, her gauze flounces brushing her husband's knee. She nodded serenely at him. Cicily abandoned the last dowager with a final radiant smile. There was a faint shadow of inattention in that radiance, however. It sprang from some inner joy. Jane shrewdly suspected that Cicily had not heard one word that the dowager had been saying. Albert stepped out to meet her. His fine young face was absolutely impassive. As Cicily moved into his arms, her glance swept the balcony. Meeting her mother's eye, she smiled so innocently, so gaily, that no one but Jane herself would ever have sensed that there was something a bit unnatural in the innocence, in the gaiety, of that smile.

'She wishes that I weren't watching her,' thought Jane, as she smiled and nodded brightly in response.

IV

Jane was walking briskly down the main street of Lakewood, enjoying the first winter snowfall. The air was damply mild. Great feathery flakes were drifting all around her. The ground was covered with a thin, wet blanket of snow. The roofs of the village stores, the bare boughs of the oak trees, were frosted with soft, white icing. The whiteness of the world contrasted vividly with the yellow grey of the December sky.

Jane was on her way to the Woman's Club, to watch her grandchildren's dancing class. She often dropped in, on Tuesday afternoons, to look at it. In the midst of the uncertainties and perplexities engendered by the sight of her own children, Jane always found a glimpse of her grandchildren very comforting. Moreover, in a world of shifting values, of mental hazards and moral doubts, there was something absurdly reassuring in the sight of anything that remained so exactly the same as dancing school.

This afternoon, for instance, as soon as she entered the vestibule of the Woman's Club, the reassuring notes of the 'Blue Danube' fell caressingly on her ears. Mr. Bournique was still teaching children to waltz. Teaching the twins to waltz, as he had taught Cicily and Jenny and Steve, as his father had taught Jane herself. Jane could distinctly recall her sensations when *she* had waltzed to the strains of the 'Blue Danube,' not with a partner, but standing with Flora and Muriel in a long line of little girls, with a long line of little boys behind them, her eyes conscientiously fixed on old Mr. Bournique's striped trouser legs and black patent-leather shoes. She remembered her white organdie dress, with pink ribbons run through it, and the fat pink satin bows on her thin pigtails. That was before she was old enough to be ashamed of her pigtails, to long for curls — before she had met André. The Bourniques were an institution in Chicago, as old as the aristocracy of the Western city.

Jane entered the ballroom. And there was Mr. Bournique, grey-haired and slender, dominating the scene, gliding and bending to the thin, tinkling strains of the Woman's Club piano. And there was the line of little girls and the line of little boys, gliding and bending behind him, their eyes conscientiously fixed on his striped trouser legs and black patent-leather shoes. Slick-haired little boys in blue serge suits and fairy-like little girls in light thin dresses. One fat little boy who could not keep time and one fat little girl who would never get partners. Every dancing class, reflected Jane, as she sat down at the end of the row of indifferent governesses in the far corner of the room, every dancing class had one fat little girl who was always reduced to dancing with Mr. Bournique, who could not aspire to even the fat little boy who could not keep time for a partner.

Her grandson noticed her immediately. He waved and grinned and lost his step in welcome. His sister was an excellent dancer. She had inherited Jane's straight hair, however. But straight hair was not the curse of woman that it had been forty years ago. Belle's little daughters' wiry black curls bobbed up and down like shavings, just as Muriel's had done in the late eighties. Mr. Bournique's castanets clapped sharply in his gloved hands. The music stopped abruptly in the middle of a bar.

'Take partners!' he said.

The little girls sat down promptly on the benches that lined the room. The little boys walked deliberately over to them. They scanned the little girls' indifferent faces indifferently. They bowed profoundly before their chosen partners. The little girls rose and curtsied. Mr. Bournique's castanets clapped sharply in his gloved hands. The music started abruptly. The children began waltzing falteringly, their heads bent, their eyes on their own feet. All but the fat little girl, who, clasped in the firm gloved hands of Mr. Bournique, was moving about the room with the grace of a fairy.

This was much more fun, thought Jane, than watching a first Assembly ball. And it *was* reassuring to see so much Deportment — deportment with a capital D! It might be the late eighties all over again! Just then Jane heard Cicily's low laugh ring out happily in the hall without.

'Oh, yes, you do!' she was saying. 'They're utterly darling!'

Jane's startled eyes were on the doorway when Cicily and Albert entered the room. Her first impression was that never, never, had she seen the child looking so pretty. Her dark fox fur, her little black hat, were silvered with melting snowflakes. Her cheeks were pink and her eyes were bright and her lips were parted in a little possessive smile of provocative mockery. She was glancing over her shoulder at Albert

— Albert, who was obviously entering the ballroom under protest, who would much rather have prolonged his walk with Cicily in the privacy of the first December snowstorm without. She sank into a chair near the entrance, laughed up at him, and then, with a little gesture of confiding intimacy, reached up to touch his sleeve and motion him down into the seat at her side. He covered her hand with his own and sat down, saying something straight into her sparkling eyes. Cicily did not reply. She withdrew her hand and turned away and sat looking at the waltzing children, her eyes bright with happiness, her lips still parted in a little involuntary smile. Albert sat motionless, his eyes upon her profile.

Jane turned away her glance. She felt suddenly guilty. This — this was just like eavesdropping, listening at doors, peeking through keyholes. She would not look at Cicily again.

Jane never knew how long she had remained, her unseeing eyes fixed rigidly on the little faltering dancers, wondering, helplessly, what ought to be done. When next she noticed him, Mr. Bournique, arm in arm with a decorous little lady who had to stand on tiptoe to reach his elbow, was leading the final grand march around the room. He paused at the door, to bow meticulously to each tiny couple as they made their ultimate exit. Over his grey head Jane could see that Cicily's chair was empty. So they had seen her and, thinking themselves unseen, had slipped away together into the December snowstorm. Where were they now? What were they saying? Into what perilous indiscretion was Cicily falling? Little John Ward was pulling at her elbow.

'Did you see Mother, Grandma, here with Uncle Albert?'

Jane stared a moment in silence down into his wide brown eyes.

'Was she here, darling?'

'Yes. But she didn't wait. How'll we get home? Jane's putting on her overshoes.'

In the tangle of perplexities confronting her, Jane recognized with relief that her first practical obligation was clear. She would walk home in the dark with the twins.

v

Jane sat in a corner of Cicily's French drawing-room, waiting for Cicily to come home. Walking with the twins through the snowy streets of Lakewood, withdrawn from their artless prattle in the sanctuary of thought, Jane had finally arrived at a decision. Something must be done — and done quickly. She would speak to Cicily. She would not procrastinate. She would not falter. She would go in with the twins and talk with Cicily that very afternoon. Perhaps she would find Albert in the little French drawing-room. If so, she would wait, stonily, tactlessly, until he had withdrawn.

She had not found Albert. The maid at the door had informed her that Mrs. Bridges had not yet come in. The girl had thrown a concerned glance at Jane's snow-powdered coat and saturated shoes. She had turned on one drawing-room lamp and lit the fire under the Marie Laurencin and had brought Jane a little pot of tea on a painted tray.

Jane had consumed the reviving liquid very gratefully. The twins were upstairs in the playroom, doing their home work. Robin Redbreast was eating his supper in the dining-room across the hall. When she had first come in, Jane had not felt equal to sustaining a conversation with even Robin Redbreast. She had finished her tea and was gazing, somewhat like a rabbit fascinated by a snake, at the blank chocolate-coloured eyes and thin, cruel lips of the Marie Laurencin, thinking that the opal-tinted lady had rather the air of passing an ironical comment on her own agitated state of mind.

The mood of the Marie Laurencin was the modern one of
detached cynicism. 'Well, what of it?' she seemed to be
saying. 'Why carry on like this about it? Surely you're not
surprised!'

Jane tried to think that she was *not* surprised, feeling an
absurd obligation to justify her Victorian point of view to the
opal-tinted lady. At least she admitted that she should not be
surprised. This was only the sort of thing that happened, unhappily, now and then in every age. However, when it concerned your own daughter —— But Albert Lancaster was
merely running true to form. He was his father's son. He
had dragged Cicily into this mess. He would soon tire of
her. And then — what a hell of readjustment awaited the
poor child.

Jane was roused from revery by the sound of the front door
opening and closing. Cicily's light step was heard in the hall.
She was alone. Albert had not come in with her. Her voice,
very practical and pleasant, was addressing the waitress at
the door.

'Send the car to the Woman's Club for the twins at once,
Ella. I forgot to stop in at their dancing school. They must
be waiting.'

Jane heard the waitress start to speak, but Cicily did not
pause for a reply. She appeared, abruptly, in the door of the
little French drawing-room. The shoulders of her coat, her
dark fox fur, her little black hat were all thickly frosted with
soft wet snow. She must have been walking in the storm ever
since she had left the Woman's Club. She did not see Jane.
She walked quickly over to the antique mirror that hung between the windows. Standing directly in front of it she
stared, wide-eyed, at her own reflection in the glass. Jane
stared, too, a startled, involuntary stare, at the face in the
mirror. The cheeks were rose-red, the eyes were starry

bright, the lips were parted in a reminiscent smile. Suddenly
Cicily gave a little gasp.

'Oh!' she said softly, and pressing her dark-gloved hands
to her rose-red cheeks, continued to stare, wide-eyed at the
face in the mirror.

'Cicily,' said Jane gently.

The child started, terrifically. Then faced about, her lips
no longer smiling, her eyes no longer starry. Slowly, like a
curtain, a veil of controlled indifference dropped over her
features.

'Mumsy!' she said. 'I didn't know you were there. You
frightened me.'

Jane rose slowly from her chair in the corner.

'Cicily,' she said, 'I've come to talk to you.'

Behind the veil of indifference, Cicily's young face hardened
defensively.

'What about?' she said.

Jane drew a long breath.

'About yourself — and Albert.'

There was a brief pause. Cicily moved to the fireplace
and, stripping off her gloves, stood with her back to the room,
holding her hands out to the warmth of the crackling flames.

'I wouldn't, Mumsy,' she said finally.

'I have to,' said Jane. She was conscious that her knees
were wobbling disconcertingly. She sat down rather suddenly
in the armchair near the fire. There was another pause.
Cicily continued to gaze down at the burning logs. She
moved her thin, white hands a trifle nervously. The firelight
sparkled on the diamond in her engagement ring. Jane
looked steadily at those thin white hands.

'Well,' said Cicily, finally, 'all right. Shoot. I suppose you
have to get it off your chest.' She turned abruptly as she
spoke and flung herself moodily down on the hearthrug. She

tossed off her little black hat and dark fox fur. The snow on them was melting rapidly in the heat from the fire. There was quite a little puddle on the light grey rug before Jane spoke again.

'Cicily,' she began slowly, 'I don't — I don't know quite what's happening, but I know it's dangerous. I know you're not behaving — just the way you ought to behave. Don't think I don't sympathize with you, because I do ——' She stopped, checked by the sight of the little scornful smile that was flickering on Cicily's lips, then continued lamely, 'I *do* sympathize with you, Cicily, but ——'

'But you believe in the Ten Commandments,' said Cicily brightly. 'Especially the seventh. Well — so do I, Mumsy, and I haven't broken it. There. Will that satisfy you?'

'Cicily,' said Jane reproachfully, 'I'm not joking.'

'Neither am I,' said Cicily promptly. 'I don't think adultery's a joke. And I shouldn't dream of committing it. Some do, of course, but I've always thought they were fools. I'm keeping my head, Mumsy, I'm keeping it like anything. But I haven't made up my mind. Until I do, I don't see what's the use of discussion.'

'You don't see — what's the use of discussion?' faltered Jane.

'No, I don't,' said Cicily bluntly. 'It's my affair. Mine and Albert's. And, in a secondary capacity, of course, Jack's and Belle's. It's a very difficult situation, and it all depends on me. I don't want to make any mistake!'

'But Cicily!' — Jane's protest was almost shrill — 'you *are* making a mistake! You're making one this minute! It's a terrible mistake for you to sit there and talk as if there were anything but one thing to do!'

'And what's that?' said Cicily ironically.

'Put Albert Lancaster out of your life immediately,' said

Jane firmly. 'And forget him as soon as you can.' She regretted her sharp words as soon as they were spoken. They seemed absurdly melodramatic, punctured by Cicily's light monosyllable.

'Why?'

'Why?' echoed Jane. 'Why, because you're a married woman with three dear children and Albert's a married man with three children of his own. Because Belle was your best friend and Jack's always been a good and loyal husband ——'
Jane stopped for breath.

'Yes,' said Cicily slowly. 'Jack's always been a good and loyal husband and I've always been a good and loyal wife. We've been married nearly ten years and I'm horribly bored with him. He's really bored with me, though, of course, he won't admit it. It would be perfectly impossible for either of us to recapture the emotion that brought us together. It's gone forever. The same thing is perfectly true of Belle and Albert. I've fallen in love with Albert. He's fallen in love with me. I can't see why that situation has anything to do with a dead past. I'm not robbing Jack if I give my love to Albert. Jack hasn't had my love for years. I'm not robbing Belle if Albert gives his love to me. Belle had her innings ten years ago. I don't grudge them to her. But it's my turn now.'

'Cicily!' cried Jane in horror. 'You mustn't *talk* like that! You mustn't *think* like that!'

'Why not?' said Cicily. 'What **are** your brains given you for, except to think with? I believe in being practical. That's why I haven't made up my mind. There are a great many practical difficulties to consider. If I should divorce Jack ——'

'*Divorce Jack?*' cried Jane.

'And Belle should divorce Albert,' continued Cicily imperturbably, 'there would still be a lot of adjustments to be made. There are the children for one thing ——'

'I'm glad you give them a passing thought,' said Jane ironically.

'Don't be sarcastic, Mumsy,' smiled Cicily cheerfully. 'It's not your line. You know I adore my children. And Albert's are sweet. The children *do* present complications. But perhaps we could solve them. They're all awfully young. They'd soon get used to it. I like the lovely picture of a sweet, united home, just as much as you do, Mumsy. But our homes *aren't* sweet and united. There's no use kidding yourself that they are. But' — Cicily's young face clouded thoughtfully as she spoke — 'you see there's the money.'

'The *what?*' cried Jane. This conversation was really taking on the horror of a nightmare.

'The money,' said Cicily. 'You see we haven't got any. Not any to speak of. Aunt Muriel made ducks and drakes of all she had during Uncle Bert's illness. She gave a lot to Albert during those years abroad. Albert really can't afford to run two households. Six children and two wives are no joke! He'd want to give Belle a whacking big alimony. I'd want her to have one. On the other hand, I really couldn't take money from Jack — now, could I? — not even for the support of his children, if I were living with Albert. Perhaps that seems Quixotic to you, Mumsy, but ——'

'Quixotic!' cried Jane. This *must* be a nightmare.

'But that's the way I feel,' ended Cicily tranquilly. Then added abruptly, 'Has it ever occurred to you, Mumsy, that Dad only gives me three thousand a year?'

In the midst of the horror a ridiculous impulse to vindicate Stephen rose hotly in Jane's heart.

'He gave you this house and lot. He gave Jack his job in the bank!'

'They wouldn't do *me* much good,' said Cicily calmly, 'in

the present crisis. I'd ruin Albert. I really would. He wants
to get back into the diplomatic service. He's trying to save a
fortune. Of course, there's Ed Brown — but Albert says he
really couldn't bring himself to come down on him to pay a
brand-new stepson's wife a princely alimony! And I don't
blame him. Ed Brown *does* seem a trifle remote. Of course, if
Dad would settle about three hundred thousand on me ——'

Jane rose from her chair.

'Cicily,' she said solemnly, 'I wouldn't have believed — I
really — would — not — have — believed — that you could
really shock me ——'

'You think he wouldn't?' said Cicily anxiously.

Jane did not stoop to reply. She walked in silence to the
door. She could hear Cicily scrambling to her feet behind her.

'It would fix up everything,' said Cicily, 'if he would. I
know lots of girls would just take that alimony and think
nothing of it, but I couldn't do it. And Albert feels just that
way. We wouldn't want Belle to give up anything. I couldn't
bear it if she had to go back with the children and live with
Aunt Isabel ——' Strolling down the hall, she slipped her
hand confidingly through Jane's elbow.

'Cicily,' said Jane with dignity, 'I'm not going to discuss
it. If you don't *see* that this talk is shocking ——'

'All right, Mumsy,' said Cicily cheerfully. 'I told you you
hadn't better. But you would and you did and I've been
perfectly frank with you.' Jane opened the front door. 'See
here, darling, you can't walk home in this weather. I'll order
the car.'

'I don't want the car,' said Jane pettishly. 'I prefer to
walk.' Her pettishness was that of an irritated old lady. It
reminded her of her own mother. The storm had turned
into a blizzard. Small, icy flakes were driving horizontally
across the darkness in the shaft of light that shone from the

front door. She could not walk, of course. Cicily had already rung for Ella. She gave her order tranquilly. Then turned to smile mischievously at Jane's sombre face.

'It's a compliment, Mumsy,' she said, 'when your children are perfectly frank with you. But you won't face facts. Your generation believes in fairies!' The hall was growing cold. Cicily closed the door. 'I'm going to talk to Dad, myself, I think,' she said slowly.

Jane did not reply. She still had the sense of nightmare. This — this would devastate Stephen. She would have to tell him. Tell Stephen — who adored Cicily. Mother and daughter stood in silence until the headlights of the motor, wheeling in the darkness, were visible through the glass panel of the door.

'Good-night,' said Cicily. Jane, still, did not reply. 'Mumsy, don't be an *ass!*' cried Cicily brightly. She kissed Jane very warmly. Jane clung to her for a moment in silence. 'Button up your coat, dear! Don't slip on the steps!'

Jane did not look back. She did not dare to, on the icy path. The wind was very strong. But Cicily's voice floated out to her in the darkness.

'Don't worry, Mumsy!'

The friendly chauffeur met her halfway to the car. He took her arm to steady her. Jane was suddenly reminded again of her mother. She *was* an old lady. Or about to become one. Useless to try to understand the younger generation. But she would have to tell Stephen. She would have to tell Stephen that night.

VI

Jane did not tell Stephen that night, however. When she rang her front doorbell, Stephen, himself, opened the door. His face looked strangely shocked and very, very serious.

'I've been waiting for you,' he said simply.

'Stephen!' cried Jane. 'Stephen, what's happened?'

'I've had a wire from Alden,' he answered. 'Father died of heart failure at his desk in the bank, at half-past three this afternoon.'

CHAPTER V

I

JANE sat, relaxed and weary, in the arms of a wing chair in the front parlour of the Carvers' house on Beacon Street, thinking soberly of the perfect end of her father-in-law's life. Sudden death, at eighty-eight, in his office chair. No pain, no partings, no illness nor foreboding. It was hard on the family, however. It had been a great shock to Stephen. It had been a shock to the children, curiously enough, for they had never seemed to care much for their grandfather. In latter years he had been a very irascible old gentleman.

Across the room, uncomfortably erect, Cicily and Jenny were perched on the slippery black horsehair upholstery of a mahogany sofa. Their bright young blondness was accentuated by their sombre mourning. They looked subdued and preternaturally grave, however. Stephen, who seemed, Jane thought, unspeakably tired, was sitting in a stiff-backed Sheraton chair in the middle of the room, absently staring over his daughters' heads at a large steel engraving, 'The Return of the Mayflower,' that hung over the mahogany sofa. Young Steve was standing by the white marble mantelpiece. His eyes were wandering, with a faint twinkle of amusement, from the glass dome of wax flowers on top of it to the great jar of dried grasses, combined with peacock feathers, that adorned the hearth at his feet. Mrs. Carver never had a fire in the front parlour. Jane knew he was longing for a cigarette and hoped he would refrain from lighting one. Old Mr. Carver had never held with cigarettes — 'coffin nails,' he had called them — and Mrs. Carver only allowed Alden to smoke his in the big brown library that overlooked the river.

Alden himself was pacing up and down the room, skirting
the old mahogany rockers and marble-topped tables and
plush-covered footstools with care. The furniture in the
Carvers' front parlour was oddly assorted. The Colonial
period rubbed elbows with the Victorian age. There were
several good eighteenth-century pieces that had been in the
family for generations and, mingled with them, were the
rosewood 'parlour suite' that Mrs. Carver had bought in the
first year of her marriage, and a triple-tiered black walnut
whatnot that had been left to Mr. Carver in the will of a
favourite sister, and an old cerise plush armchair, with a
fringe of braided tassels, where Mr. Carver always used to
sit, and a large glass cabinet of Chinese Chippendale design,
in which were displayed a collection of curios assembled by
long-dead Carvers in the course of their voyages on the whale-
ships and merchantmen that had carried them over the seven
seas — ivory pie-cutters and paper-knives and bodkins, a set
of Chinese beads which included a jade necklace that Cicily
had always coveted, a tiny model of a clipper ship, miraculously erect in a small-necked rum bottle, tortoise-shell snuff-
boxes, ebony chessmen, sandalwood fans, a bronze Javanese
gong of intricate pattern, and a small marble replica of the
Leaning Tower of Pisa. Also a first edition of Oliver Wendell
Holmes's 'The School Boy,' personally autographed and in-
scribed to Mr. Carver by Mr. Holmes.

Jane liked the funny cluttered room, however. She liked
the old incongruous furniture and the silly curios and 'The
Return of the Mayflower.' She liked the sense of the past that
curiously consecrated this ridiculous collection of inanimate
objects that people had cared for and loved. No modern
decorator could catch it, she thought, no matter how passionate his preoccupation with antiquity.

'Where *is* Mother?' said Alden suddenly.

Alden seemed a trifle out of humour. Tired, of course.
Fearfully tired. They had all just returned from the service
in the cemetery and Mrs. Carver had gone upstairs with Silly
to take off her bonnet, in preparation for the Reading of the
Will, in the front parlour. The Reading of the Will was a
ceremony that all proper Carvers felt should follow a burial
as day follows dawn. Jane had thought, considering how exhausted they all were and how long that Unitarian minister
had prayed his impromptu prayers, that it would be just as
well to defer it until the next morning. But Alden, as head of
the family, had been adamant. And Mrs. Carver had thought
it would be only correct. And Stephen had said that they
might as well get it over. And Silly had murmured that it did
not seem quite respectful to wait.

As Alden spoke, Mrs. Carver and Silly came into the parlour. Her mother-in-law, at eighty-four, Jane thought, was a
very miraculous old lady. What a strain she had been under,
what a shock she had sustained — the tragic termination of
sixty-three years of marriage! Yet Mrs. Carver, as she entered the room, looked just as she *had* looked for the last ten
years. She wore her familiar house gown of loose black silk.
Mrs. Carver thought extremes were very foolish. She had
not gone in for widow's weeds. Her little white collar was
fastened by a mourning pin of black jet. It was the only con-
cession she had made to the solemnity of the day. She had
told Jane, before setting out for the cemetery, that she had
worn that pin to the funeral of her mother in eighteen-
seventy-nine. Beneath the straight parting of her thin white
hair, her face looked only a little tired and rather worried
than sad. Jane soon saw what was worrying her. She walked
straight across the room and pulled down one window shade
until it was even with the other. A grief-stricken parlour
maid, Jane thought with a smile, in raising them after the

family had left the house for the funeral, had had no thought for the critical eyes across Beacon Street. Mrs. Carver turned and faced her family.

'Alden,' she said, 'you look tired. Would you like a glass of port?'

Alden shook his head. He produced an imposing-looking document from the inside pocket of his cutaway.

'Stephen,' continued Mrs. Carver, 'you're not comfortable in that stiff chair. You'd better take your father's. Sit down, Steve, and don't fidget about.' She had seated herself, as she spoke, in the seat that Stephen had abandoned. Jane rose, with a gesture toward her own armchair. 'No, Jane, I like a straight back. Now, Alden, find a nice place for yourself with a good light. Silly! Turn on the lamp for Alden. Can you see, dear? Then I think we're quite ready.'

As Alden unfolded his imposing document, Silly sank down on a footstool beside his chair, her lank figure relaxed in lines of complete fatigue. In the folds of her new mourning Silly really looked as old as Mrs. Carver, thought Jane. Her hair was just as white and her face infinitely more weary. Two old ladies — mother and daughter! It was a shame about Silly. She had never had a life. She had never even achieved one care-free summer with Susan Frothingham, one trip abroad alone, one spree, one careless burst of freedom to enjoy and remember. Susan Frothingham had been dead for seven years, carried off by a gust of pneumonia in the flu epidemic of nineteen-twenty. It *was* a shame about Silly. But Alden was clearing his throat. He was looking at them all very solemnly through his *pince-nez* eye-glasses over the top of the imposing document.

The assembled Carvers stirred a trifle uneasily. A faint, tense thrill seemed to run around the room. The best, the most grief-stricken of families, Jane thought with a smile, were not quite impervious to the dramatic suspense of the moment in which a will is read. But Alden was speaking.

'I was made the executor of this will,' he was saying, and surely there was a hint of irritation in his voice, 'but I never knew anything about its contents until yesterday morning, when I found it in Father's safety-deposit box. He made it twelve years ago, just after Uncle Stephen's death.'

Alden paused to adjust his eye-glasses, and again the assembled Carvers stirred a trifle uneasily. A dreadful phrase from the pen of John Galsworthy flashed through Jane's mind. 'Old Soames Forsyte would cut up a very warm man.' Old Mr. Carver would cut up a very warm man, also. But Jane felt curiously detached from the provisions of his testament. Stephen had more money, now, than Jane could spend the income on. And a Carver would always leave his fortune to Carvers. Soon Stephen would have too much money. Too much money to leave, in his turn, to his children. But that day, fortunately, thought Jane with a glance at Cicily, would not come soon. But Alden had resumed.

'The first provision, I am happy to say and you will all be happy to hear' — Alden's voice had brightened a trifle — 'is the foundation of a trust fund of one hundred thousand dollars for Aunt Marie, the interest on which is to continue the allowance that Father had been making her since the death of Uncle Stephen, the principal to go, on her death, to Harvard College, to form the nucleus of a Stephen Carver Memorial Fund, the purpose of which will be to purchase books and manuscripts for the Department of Reformation Drama, of which Uncle Stephen so long held the chair.'

Why, Alden was making a speech, thought Jane irreverently, as the Carvers about her moved and murmured their gratified approbation. But that *was* nice for Aunt Marie. She was a bedridden old lady, now, in a Cambridge flat.

'I *must* remember,' thought Jane to herself, 'to go to see her to-morrow.' But Alden was again speaking.

Jane listened, absently, to the elaborate phrases that rolled from his lips. He was reading from the document, now, and it was all frightfully legal. Jane caught the gist of it, however. It was quite as she had thought. A Carver would always leave his fortune to Carvers. The estate was large, but no larger than Jane had expected. It was a simple will. Jane automatically checked off the bequests in her mind as they were read.

One million dollars outright to Alden and one million dollars outright to Stephen. One million dollars left in trust with Alden and Stephen, the income of which was to be expended on Mrs. Carver for her lifetime and to be expended on Silly after her death. Poor old Silly! How like Mr. Carver to leave sixty-year-old Silly — not a nickel outright, but a deferred million in trust! Alden's voice was rolling on.

It was the wish of the testator that Mrs. Carver should keep up the Beacon Street house and the place at Gull Rocks just as they had been kept in the testator's lifetime, and that Silly should keep them up after her death. On the death of Silly, Alden, and Stephen, both houses were to go to young Steve, 'the last perpetuator of the Carver name.' When all debts were paid and some minor bequests to the servants attended to, the residue of the estate, if any, was to be divided between Mr. Carver's three grandchildren, Cicily, Jenny, and Steve.

A proper Carver will, thought Jane. And exactly like her father-in-law. One hundred thousand dollars to Harvard College and three million to Carvers. All debts paid, poor relations pensioned, old servants remembered, and Silly ignored. Exactly like her father-in-law. Jane hoped that Silly would come into the income of that million before she was seventy. She hoped she would make ducks and drakes of it when she did. But no — she would undoubtedly save it for Stephen's children. For Silly was a Carver.

At all events, the will did not affect *her* life, thought Jane. She felt curiously indifferent to the possession of that added million. There was a little awkward pause when Alden had finished speaking. It was broken by Mrs. Carver.

'Thank you, Alden,' she said simply.

'I never realized,' said Silly — and her voice was slightly shaken — 'I never realized that Father had so much money.'

'Why should you have realized it?' said Mrs. Carver sharply. 'Money is not to be spoken of.' Mrs. Carver still talked to Silly as if she were a child. Her dignified reproof put a sudden quietus on further discussion of the will.

'I'm going to take a walk,' declared Steve abruptly.

Cicily's and Jenny's eyes met his. Cicily, Jane thought, looked a trifle downcast. The three children rose simultaneously to their feet.

'We'll go with you,' said Jenny.

'Don't be late for supper,' said Mrs. Carver. She smiled very kindly up at Silly, who had risen from the footstool and was standing patiently by her chair. 'I think I'll lie down now, but I don't feel like sleeping. I wish you'd come up and read the "Transcript" to me, Silly.'

Mother and daughter left the room. The children turned toward the door.

'It's all right for them to go, isn't it, Stephen?' asked Jane. 'I mean — it won't create a scandal if any one sees them carousing up Beacon Street?'

'Well — I shouldn't advise them to carouse,' smiled Stephen.

'I should hope not!' put in Alden.

'We won't carouse!' twinkled Jenny. 'We'll walk *very* discreetly.'

'We'll walk lugubriously,' said Steve cheerfully, 'if Uncle Alden things we'd better.'

Alden did not stoop to reply.

'Get along with you!' said Stephen, still smiling. When they had left the room, however, and he had turned to Alden, his face was very grave. Alden was folding up the document and putting it back into the inside pocket of his cutaway. Stephen walked over to him and stood for a moment at his side in silence. Then, 'I'm sorry, Alden,' he said.

Caught by the gravity of his tone, Jane looked quickly up at him. Alden did not speak for a moment. When he did, his voice was thickened with emotion.

'Father — Father wasn't quite himself these last years. If he had been he would have realized.'

'Of course he would,' said Stephen warmly.

'He would have changed it,' said Alden, still in that thickened voice.

'What *are* you talking about?' cried Jane sharply. She rose from her chair as she spoke and walked to Stephen's side.

'We — we've rather walked off with the lion's share, Jane,' said Stephen quietly. 'We and ours.'

'I don't understand,' said Jane.

Alden turned on her almost belligerently.

'Don't you know what bank stocks have been doing in the last ten years?' he inquired angrily. 'Since Father made that will the estate's doubled. In nineteen-fifteen the residue was worth about fifty thousand dollars. And now your children are going to come into a cool three million — or nearly that ——' He stopped abruptly. He stared, astonished, at Jane's horrified face.

'Stephen,' she said faintly, 'Stephen — that's not true, is it?'

Stephen nodded gravely.

'It's rather rough on Alden — and on Silly, too, of course
——' Then he, too, stopped, for Jane had suddenly begun to
cry.

'Oh, Stephen — Stephen — can't anything be done?'

'I'm afraid not, darling.' His arms were around her. She
was sobbing rather wildly.

'Don't take it like that, Jane,' said Alden kindly. He pulled
himself together. 'It — it's not so very important.'

'You don't know!' cried Jane. 'You don't know — anything about it!'

Alden let that insult pass unchallenged. He was rapidly
revising his opinion of his sister-in-law. She had never seemed
to him an hysterical woman. But this stroke of luck had quite
unbalanced her.

'You don't know anything!' she kept repeating. 'You don't
know anything, either of you! You don't know anything at
all!'

II

On looking back on the first few weeks that followed her
father-in-law's death, Jane was always most impressed by the
astounding efficiency of her children. The explosive efficiency
of her children. Jane felt as if the dead hand of Mr. Carver
had pulled the corks from the three bottles of extremely
effervescent champagne. Event followed event with cata-
strophic rapidity.

It was young Steve who threw the first bomb. He threw it
in Boston the day after his grandfather's funeral, just two
hours after he had heard of his legacy. He walked in abruptly
on Alden and Stephen and Jane, who were discussing the
questions of inheritance tax and probate in the old brown
library that overlooked the river.

'The contents of both houses must be appraised immediately,' Alden was saying, when his nephew entered the room.

'Am I interrupting?' said Steve amiably. 'I want to ask Uncle Alden a question.'

'I've told you everything I know about that bequest already,' said Alden, with that faint hint of irritation in his tone.

'This isn't about the bequest,' said Steve cheerfully. 'And it's a very simple question. Have you got a job for me?'

'A job for you?' echoed Alden.

'Yes. In the Bay State Trust Company. I want to live here.'

'Here?' echoed Jane.

'Well, not in this house,' said Steve calmly. 'Though I like that view of the river. But in Boston. I've always loved Boston. I think it's the place for Carvers to live.'

'You're right there, my boy,' put in Alden approvingly.

'I've just been taking,' said Steve — and his eye brightened — 'a walk around Beacon Hill. You don't know what it does to me, Mumsy. I simply love it. It's the call of the blood or something. I'm going to buy a little old red-brick house on Chestnut or Mount Vernon Street — a little old red-brick house with a white front door and a bright brass knocker and lavender-tinted panes of old glass in its front window. I'm going to buy the best old stuff I can get to furnish it with. It's going to be — well — if not an American Wing, at least an American Lean-to! The Metropolitan is going to envy me some of my pieces. I'm going to have a good cook and a better cellar and give delightful little parties. I'm going to be Boston's Most Desirable Bachelor. But I'm not going to end up like Uncle Alden!' Steve paused to smile engagingly at his astounded relatives. 'On my twenty-ninth birthday, I'm going to marry the season's most eligible débutante — and her name will be Cabot or Lodge or Lowell — and replenish the dwindling Carver stock. I'm going to have ten children in the good old New England tradition, and marry them all off to the best Back Bay connections. There! That's a brief résumé of my earthly plans and ambitions. But in the mean time, I need a job. I'd rather be in Grandfather's bank than in any other. So I thought if Uncle Alden had a high stool vacant, I'd just put in a bid for it. If not ——'

But Alden's face was shining with approbation.

'Of course I have, Steve!' he said warmly. 'And I must say this would have delighted your grandfather! Wouldn't it have delighted him, Stephen?'

Jane looked quickly at Stephen's face. Her own sense of defeat was clearly written there.

'I suppose it would have,' he said slowly. 'But, just the same, Steve's really a Westerner. Partly by blood and wholly by upbringing ——'

Jane loved him for his words. Alden looked pained.

'Do you call an education at Milton and Harvard a Western upbringing?' he inquired with acerbity.

Stephen laughed shortly.

'I suppose we should have sent him to the high school in Lakewood,' he said a trifle bitterly.

'And to some fresh-water college?' inquired Alden. 'Don't be absurd, Stephen!'

'You don't need me, Dad, in the Midland Loan and Trust Company,' said Steve persuasively. 'You've got Jack.'

'I want you, nevertheless,' said Stephen soberly.

'But I want this, Dad,' said Steve. He walked to the window as he spoke and gazed out over the back yards of Beacon Street and the sparkling blue river toward the grey domes and cornices of the Tech buildings across the basin. 'I — want — this. I want to live forever in sight of that little gold dome that tops Beacon Hill. I know what I want, Dad ——'

'In that case,' said Stephen dryly, 'you'll probably get it. Carvers usually do. Male Carvers, that is ——'

Jane knew he was thinking of wasted Silly.

'I'm sorry for your wife, Steve,' she commented tartly.

'Oh — she'll like it,' said Steve easily. 'I'll pick one that will.'

It was all arranged with Alden in the next half-hour.

'Darling,' said Jane, as she left the room with Stephen, 'perhaps he'll tire of it. Perhaps he'll come home.' She tried to make her weary voice ring clear with conviction. But she knew he wouldn't. Stephen knew it, too. He had nothing to add to the arguments he had been vainly propounding for the last half-hour.

'Jane — you're a trump!' was all he said.

III

It was on the Twentieth Century, three days later, that Jenny issued her ultimatum. The female Carvers in the rising generation yielded nothing in determination to the male. Jane and Stephen were sitting in their compartment, looking out at the bleak midwinter landscape of the Berkshire Hills, when she thrust her blonde head around their door.

'They've had a lot of snow,' Stephen was just saying absently. He had been saying things like that, very absently and at long intervals, ever since the train had pulled out of the Back Bay Station. Jane was terribly sorry for him.

'What are you two doing?' cried Jenny very gaily. 'Holding hands, as I live and breathe! You look like a coloured lithograph of "The Golden Wedding"! Something that comes out with the Sunday Supplement!' She perched lightly on the arm of the Pullman seat and dropped a casual kiss on Jane's hair. 'Now, listen, darlings,' she continued brightly. 'I've got something to tell you. I don't know if you'll like it but it has to be told.'

Jane looked up in alarm at Jenny's cheerful countenance.

'Jenny,' she said quickly, 'if it's anything unpleasant ——'

'It's not really unpleasant, Mumsy,' said Jenny reassuringly. Then with a shrug of resignation, 'But I rather think you'll hate it. Last night in Boston I wrote Barbara Belmont.'

'About what?' said Jane sharply.

'About my legacy,' returned Jenny calmly. 'I told her to look around for those kennels in Westchester County. I told her that, if she could square *her* family, I'd take a little apartment with her this spring in New York. Then we could buy the dogs and fix over the house — I hope we can find an old one — and move out the end of June. I thought we could spend the summer in Westchester and get to know our business and move back into the New York apartment in November —— What's the matter, Mumsy?' She stopped to stare in astonishment down into Jane's agitated face.

'*What's the matter?*' roared Stephen. His tone was really a roar. 'Don't talk nonsense, Jenny! You two girls can't go off on your own and live by yourselves in a shack in the country and a flat in New York! Bill Belmont will never listen to you! It's perfectly preposterous! It isn't safe! Kids like you ——'

'I'm twenty-six years old, Dad,' said Jenny evenly. 'And I've just come into eight hundred and fifty thousand dollars ——'

'Jenny!' said Jane warningly.

'But I have, Mumsy,' said Jenny reasonably. 'And it makes all the difference. You're just like Grandma Carver! You think it's vulgar to talk of money. Well — I'm *not* talking of money. I'm talking of freedom. Sometimes I think they are one and the same thing. Look at Aunt Silly! Just *look* at Aunt Silly! What tied her hands, I want to know, but the purse-strings?' Jenny paused to glare triumphantly at her parents. Then went on truculently: 'If you think I'm going to grow old into *that* kind of a spinster, you're very much mistaken! Not with eight hundred and fifty thousand dollars! If you think I'm vulgar ——'

'Jenny,' said Jane gently, 'I don't think you're vulgar.' She paused for a moment, trying helplessly to define just what she thought Jenny was. It was very difficult, however. That reference to Silly had taken the wind out of Jane's sails. Jenny immediately took advantage of her pause.

'Barbara and I have wanted to do this thing together ever since we left Bryn Mawr! We've waited five years. Five years ought to convince you and the Belmonts that we know what we're talking about. We're not marrying women — at least we never have been — we're not interested in husbands — we're interested in *ourselves* ——'

'Jenny,' said Jane very seriously, 'that sort of mutually inclusive and exclusive friendship with another girl is not very wise. It doesn't lead to anything. It ——' She paused again, as Stephen pressed her fingers. He was right, of course. Better not say too much. But ——

'Oh, for Heaven's sake!' Jenny was exclaiming disgustedly. 'You make me tired! There's nothing mutually inclusive and exclusive about Barbara and me! Do you think we're going to dig a little Well of Loneliness? We're not! We're going to *raise dogs!* We're going to get out from under our families! We don't want to marry until we meet a man we fancy! In the mean time we want to be independent. If we were sons, you'd think it was all right for us to run dog kennels.'

'*I* shouldn't,' put in Stephen abruptly. 'If a son of mine wanted to run dog kennels, I'd think he was a damn fool!'

'Well, that's a matter of opinion,' said Jenny very sweetly. 'I like dogs. I like them, on the whole, rather better than people. I'm never going to go to another dance. I'm never

going to go to another Lakewood dinner-party. I'm going to
mess around in dirty tweeds in that heavenly country for
eight months of the year and live very smartly in New York
for the other four. I'm going to *enjoy* myself, as I haven't
since I left the Bryn Mawr campus. I ——'

'Jenny,' said Jane, 'I think we've had about enough of this
Emancipation Proclamation. Your father and I are very
tired. We've had a bad week.'

'Of course you have!' Jenny's young face was suddenly
alight with sympathy. 'You know, Mumsy, it's awfully hard
to realize that your grandfather is your father's father. It's
hard to realize, I mean, that Dad is just as cut up as I should
be if he — if he had dropped dead at his office desk. That
would *kill* me, Dad, it really would ——' Jenny paused to
look across Jane very fondly at Stephen. Jane, in her turn,
promptly took advantage of the pause.

'Yet you want to live in Westchester?'

'Dad wanted to live in Chicago,' said Jenny.

'That was different,' said Jane.

'Why was it different?' flashed Jenny. She rose to her feet
as she spoke.

Jane had not thought of the answer to her question before
Jenny stood at the door of the compartment.

'Why was it different, Stephen?' she asked, when they were
once more alone.

'Because she is a girl,' said Stephen promptly.

That was not the answer, thought Jane dumbly, her heart
vaguely stirred, perhaps, by the old doctrines of President M.
Carey Thomas. That was not the answer. Was the answer
that now Stephen was a parent and that then he had been a
child? Was that where all the difference lay? But no — this
generation was something else again — it was rude — it was
ruthless — it was completely self-confident. But self-con-

fidence was a virtue. Not entirely an attractive virtue, however. More than the purse-strings had tied poor Silly's hands.
Intangible scruples. The bonds of affection. Some inner
grace. Jane sat a long time in silence, her fingers once more
slipped comfortingly into Stephen's hand. A silence that was
eventually broken by her husband.

'The Hudson's frozen over,' said Stephen absently.

His voice recalled Jane from the little hell of worry in
which she had been blindly revolving. Stephen did not yet
know about Cicily. She would *have* to tell him. But not
now. Stephen had had enough.

'Why, so it is!' said Jane.

IV

Jane sat in the window of the Lakewood living-room, cross-
stitching little brown and scarlet robins on a bib that she was
making for Robin Redbreast's fourth Christmas. The Skokie
Valley was a plain of spotless white. The sun was high and
the sky was blue and the bare boughs of the oak trees were
outlined with a crust of silvery snow that was melting, a little,
in the heat of the December noon. Jenny was stretched on
the sofa, intent on the pages of 'The American Kennels
Gazette.' She was investigating the state of the market on
Russian wolf hounds.

It was Saturday and Stephen would soon be home for
luncheon. Young Steve was staying late at the bank. He was
winding up his affairs there very conscientiously, preparatory
to his departure for Boston on the New Year.

'Mumsy,' said Jenny presently.

'Yes,' said Jane.

'Has it occurred to you that Dad's looking rather off his
feed? Since we came home from Boston, I mean?'

'Yes,' said Jane soberly, 'it has.'

'Why don't you go off together somewhere — take a trip to Egypt or a Mediterranean cruise?'

'Dad couldn't leave the bank,' said Jane shortly. 'And I wouldn't want to leave you children.'

'It seems to me,' said Jenny cheerfully, 'that we children are leaving you.'

'Cicily isn't,' said Jane with equal cheerfulness. 'And we have the grandchildren.'

'Mumsy,' said Jenny earnestly, 'do you know I think parents make a mistake to count so much on their children? I think you and Dad ought to have more fun on your own. When you were young, Mumsy, weren't you ever bored with Lakewood? Didn't you want to see the world?'

'Yes, I was,' said Jane honestly. 'I wanted to see the world.'

'Well, then, why don't you?' said Jenny eagerly. 'Why don't you, now you can?'

'But I can't,' said Jane.

'Why not?' said Jenny.

'Because I'm needed here,' said Jane a trifle tartly.

'That's just nonsense,' said Jenny very reasonably. 'What do you do here that couldn't be left undone?'

On that outrageous question Jane heard Stephen's latch-key. He opened the front door and walked across the hall to hang up his hat and coat. His step, Jane thought, was just a little heavy. He smiled a trifle absently at his wife and daughter, from the living-room door.

'Am I late?' he asked.

'No. Just in time,' said Jane. She rose to touch the bell as she spoke.

Stephen *did* look off his feed. He looked as if something were worrying him. Something more than Jenny and Steve. He had looked just that way for the last ten days — ever since their return from his father's funeral. He had had almost nothing to say on the further chimerical development of Jenny's and Steve's plans for emancipation. Jane, sensing his preoccupation, had said nothing about Cicily. And Cicily, amazingly, had said nothing about herself. She had accepted the news of her legacy in Boston with incredulous joy. But she had made no comment on her domestic situation. She had returned to the little French farmhouse in silence. She had brought her children three times to see Jane. In their presence, of course, discussion of her predicament — if wilful wrongdoing could be *called* a predicament — was impossible. Jane had almost begun to hope, against hope, that Cicily had recognized the error of her ways. That financial freedom had brought emotional enlightenment. That as soon as the door was opened, Cicily had realized that she did not want to leave home. Perhaps she would never have to tell Stephen. Or tell him, at least, only of an evil that had been avoided, a peril that had been escaped, a sin that had been atoned.

'Luncheon is served, madam,' said the waitress.

Jenny chatted pleasantly of the charms of Russian wolf hounds while they sat at table. Stephen toyed with his chop, picked at his salad, and ignored his soufflé.

'I want to talk to your mother,' he said abruptly, when they had reëntered the living-room.

'About me?' smiled Jenny. 'What have I done?'

But Stephen did not smile.

'Run along, dear,' said Jane.

Jenny picked up 'The American Kennels Gazette' and left the room. Jane turned inquiringly toward Stephen. He had seated himself in his armchair near the fire. He sat for some time in silence, gazing abstractedly at the blazing logs.

'Well, dear?' ventured Jane presently.

'I don't know how to begin,' said Stephen soberly. He had not raised his eyes from the fire.

'Stephen!' cried Jane in alarm. She sat down on the arm of his chair. 'Stephen, what is it?'

'It's going to be a shock to you,' said Stephen. 'It was a great shock to me. I've known it for ten days and I haven't known how to tell you. Cicily is going to divorce Jack.'

'Stephen!' cried Jane, aghast. Then, 'Who told you?'

'Cicily,' said Stephen. 'She came down to my office in the bank the day after we came home from Boston. I hope I handled her right, Jane ——' Stephen's face was terribly troubled.

'What did you do?' asked Jane.

'I lost my temper,' said Stephen simply. 'I hit the ceiling. She said she wanted to marry Albert Lancaster and I said we would never allow it — that she was disgraceful — that ——'

'And what did *she* do?' asked Jane.

'She went away,' said Stephen. 'She kissed me and went away. This morning she came back again.'

'Yes?' said Jane breathlessly.

'She came back,' said Stephen slowly, 'to say that everything was settled. Belle and Jack have consented. Albert talked to Robin this morning. Belle's going to Reno in January ——'

'Oh, Stephen!' cried Jane.

'And Cicily's sailing for Paris next week.'

'Next week!' cried Jane.

'Next week,' said Stephen. 'She says she wants to spend Christmas Day on the boat — because of the children, you know. She does — she *does* think of the children, Jane ——' Stephen's voice was faltering.

'Stephen,' said Jane very solemnly, 'this just can't be. We've got to stop her.'

'You try,' said Stephen grimly.

Just then Jane heard the doorbell.

'I don't want to see any one, Irma!' she called to the waitress.

But when the front door opened, Jane heard Isabel's voice. Her sister's quick step crossed the hall.

'Jane!' she called sharply. 'Jane! Stephen!'

Jane exchanged one long look with Stephen.

'This is going to be perfectly terrible,' she said. Then, 'Here we are, Isabel!'

Isabel appeared in the living-room door. Her eyes were red and her worn, round face was swollen. She must have been crying all the way out from town in her car. She still held a damp little handkerchief, twisted into a tight, round ball in her hand.

'What did I tell you, Jane?' was the first thing she said.

'Isabel, darling,' said Jane, 'come in and sit down and help us. We're trying to decide what we must do.'

'What you must do!' cried Isabel. 'You must stop Cicily!'

'How?' said Jane.

'I don't care,' said Isabel, 'as long as you stop her!' She sank down on a sofa near the fire. She looked accusingly up at Jane. 'You know I saw what was coming, Jane. I warned you. But of course I never really knew — I never even imagined anything like this could happen until Belle came in this morning and told me all about it. It was dreadful, Jane, for Mamma was there. Belle never thought of her — of how, I mean, we'd have to break it to her. Belle's like me — she speaks right out. And Mamma was *awful*, Jane. It was a terrible shock to her and she went all to pieces.'

'What do you mean?' asked Jane anxiously. 'What did she do?'

'Talked,' said Isabel briefly. 'She rather sought refuge in

the old-time religion. She thinks Cicily's damned — utterly damned. And she told Belle she was worse than Cicily for condoning sin, in cold blood. For letting Albert off, I mean. For going to Reno. And that knocked Belle up. She'd been very calm and controlled before. And she began to cry — she just cried her heart out, Jane! I had to send for Minnie to take Mamma away, so I could talk to Belle. And then Robin came home. He was utterly shattered. He'd just had the most awful, heartless interview with Albert in his office. About settlements, I mean, and horrible, final things like that. I'd just got Belle quiet, but that set her off again. She's simply distracted, Jane — and we tried to get hold of Jack, but he wasn't at the bank and he wasn't out here in Lakewood. And I didn't want any lunch, so I just left Belle with Robin and came straight to talk to you and Stephen. You must stop Cicily!' Isabel paused for breath.

'Poor — little — Belle,' said Stephen, slowly. 'Poor young kid!'

'Isabel ——' said Jane impulsively, then paused. After a moment she went on, however. 'I think that's very fine of Belle — to let Albert go, I mean. Do you know — does she — does she really love him?'

'Does she *love* him?' cried Isabel indignantly. 'Of course she loves him! She married him, didn't she?'

'Yes,' said Jane slowly. 'She married him. But ——'

'And she's got three lovely children. Of course she loves him. And Jack loves Cicily. He really does, Jane, though I don't see how he can. He loves her and he adores his babies and ——'

'I know,' said Jane. 'I know. I'd always count on Jack.'

'I just can't realize it,' said Isabel. 'A double scandal like this in our family! In *our* family, Jane. I feel as if it weren't possible — as if I must be dreaming. When will you see Cicily?'

'Now,' said Jane. She rose decisively to her feet as she spoke. 'Will you come, Stephen?'

Stephen shook his head very soberly.

'You'd get on better without me, Jane. I said my say to Cicily this morning. I don't know that she'll ever want to see me again. Not this afternoon, at any rate.'

Bending over the back of his armchair, Jane kissed his grey hair very tenderly.

'Then you stay here with Isabel,' she said.

v

'But Cicily,' said Jane, half an hour later, 'have you never heard of *conduct?*' She was sitting hand in hand with her daughter on the sofa in the little French drawing-room.

'I have,' said Cicily firmly, 'and I think I'm conducting myself very well!' The child's young voice rang true with conviction.

'How can you think that, Cicily?' said Jane sadly. 'I'm not asking you to consider your father or me, or your grandmother, or your Aunt Isabel, or your Uncle Robin. But leaving us all out of it, you're wrecking ten lives.'

'Meaning Albert's and Belle's and Jack's and mine and the lives of all six children?' smiled Cicily. 'Mumsy, don't be hysterical!'

'But you are, Cicily,' said Jane. 'You're wrecking them all for your own individual pleasure. You're utterly selfish. You don't care what havoc you make ——'

'I'm *not* making havoc!' cried Cicily indignantly. 'I'm not making havoc, any more than a surgeon is who performs a necessary operation. No one likes operations. They're very unpleasant. But they save lives. People cry and carry on, but later they're glad they had them. It takes time, of course, to get over a major incision. But you wait, Mumsy. In two years' time we'll all be a great deal happier. A great deal happier than we've been for years.'

'You will, perhaps,' said Jane. 'And possibly Albert. But what about Jack and Belle?'

'Don't talk about Belle!' cried Cicily contemptuously.

'I have to talk about her,' said Jane very seriously. 'You have to think of her. You're doing her a great wrong.'

'Mumsy,' cried Cicily, 'you are not civilized. You have the morals of the Stone Age! You really have! I'm not wronging Belle! She doesn't love Albert. She just wants to hang on to him because she doesn't love any one else! If she did, she'd be all smiles. No one likes to be left, Mumsy, but if Belle were doing the leaving ——'

'But she's not,' said Jane firmly. 'Facts are facts. Belle says she loves her husband.'

'Well, she's never said that to me,' said Cicily. 'And she's never had the nerve to say it to Albert either. Do you know what she said to Albert?' Cicily's voice was rising excitedly. 'She told Albert to take me for his mistress. She told Albert she didn't care *what* he did, if he wouldn't ask for divorce!'

'She was thinking of the children,' said Jane defensively.

'Bunk!' said Cicily succinctly. She rose, as she spoke, from the little French sofa. 'It would be fine for *my* children, wouldn't it? A situation like that? Jack's been great about it, Mumsy. He really has. He didn't talk like that.'

'Where is he?' said Jane. 'I'd like to speak to him.'

'He moved out yesterday,' said Cicily calmly. 'He's living at the University Club.'

'Oh, Cicily!' said Jane pitifully.

For the first time in this distressing interview, Cicily herself seemed slightly shaken. She walked across the room and stood with her back to Jane, fingering the white and yellow heads of the jonquils and narcissus in the window-boxes. Her hands were trembling a little.

'I won't say, Mumsy,' she said — and her voice was slightly tremulous — 'I won't say that it wasn't a bad moment when he left this house. But it's always a bad moment when you go up to the operating room. And for divorce they can't give you ether. I wish they could. I wish we could all just go to sleep and wake up when it was safely over.' She turned from the window-boxes to face her mother. 'It *will* be safely over, Mumsy. I'm not going to weaken. I'm not going to be sentimental.' She took her stand on the hearthrug and looked firmly at Jane. 'It's utter nonsense to think that if you love one man you can be happy living with another. You don't understand that, Mumsy, because you've always loved Dad. There never was any one else. If there had been ——' Cicily's voice trailed suddenly off into silence. She was staring at Jane. 'Mumsy!' she cried quickly. 'Don't tell me there ever *was* any one else? Mumsy! *was* there?'

'Yes,' said Jane soberly. Suddenly she felt very near to Cicily. It seemed important to tell her the whole truth. 'Yes. There was.'

Cicily's face was alight with sympathy. 'Before Dad, Mumsy — or after?'

Jane suddenly felt that the whole truth could not be told. 'B-before,' she said.

Cicily looked at her. 'And after, Mumsy? Never after?'

Jane's eyes fell before her daughter's. 'Once,' she said.

'Mumsy!' cried Cicily. '*Tell* me! I never ——'

'I don't want to tell you,' said Jane.

'Did you tell Dad?'

'No,' said Jane.

'Mumsy!' cried Cicily. 'Did you really deceive him?'

'I deceived him,' said Jane soberly.

'My God!' said Cicily. 'When and how?'

'Oh, long ago,' said Jane. 'And just as every one else does, I suppose. I loved a man who loved me. And when he told me, I told him. And I — I said I'd go away with him. But I didn't.'

'What next?' said Cicily.

'Nothing next,' said Jane.

'Was that *all?*' said Cicily.

'Yes,' said Jane.

'You didn't go away with him, nor — nor — you know, Mumsy — you didn't — *without* going away?'

'I didn't.'

'You just loved him, and didn't?'

'Yes.'

'And you call that deception?'

'I call that deception,' said Jane.

Cicily's eyes were unbelievably twinkling. 'Mumsy,' she said, 'is that all the story?'

'That's all the story,' said Jane.

Cicily drew a long breath. 'Well, I believe you,' she said. 'But I don't know why I do. Resisted temptations become lost opportunities, Mumsy. Haven't you always regretted it?'

'I've never regretted it,' said Jane.

'Not the loving, of course,' said Cicily, 'but the not going away.'

'Not that either,' said Jane.

'Mumsy,' said Cicily, 'you are simply incredible. You are *not* civilized. You *have* the morals of the Stone Age! I should think an experience like that would make you see how wise I am to take my happiness ——'

'You don't achieve happiness,' said Jane very seriously, 'by *taking* it.'

'How do you know?' said Cicily promptly. 'You never tried!'

'I've always been happy,' said Jane with dignity, 'with your father.'

'I can't believe that, Mumsy. Not after what you've told me.'

'Well, I'm happy now,' said Jane. 'Much happier now than if ——'

'But that's what you don't know, Mumsy!' said Cicily, smiling. 'And what I'll never know either. You have to choose in life!'

Jane rose slowly from the little French sofa. 'Cicily,' she said, 'how can I stop you?'

'You can't,' said Cicily.

It was terribly true.

'But you can love me,' said Cicily. She walked quickly across the room and took Jane in her arms. 'You can love me always. You *will* love me, won't you, Mumsy — whatever happens?'

Jane felt the hot tears running down her cheeks.

'Cicily!' she cried. 'I love you — terribly. I want to help you — I want to save you! I want you to be happy, but I know you won't be!'

'I shall be for a while,' said Cicily cheerfully. 'And after that we'll see.'

It was on that philosophic utterance that Jane left her. When she reached her living-room again, she found Jack standing on the hearthrug. He was facing Isabel and Stephen a trifle belligerently. He looked tired and worn and worried. He had no smile for Jane.

'I know you think, sir,' he was saying wearily, 'that I ought to be able to keep her — that I ought to refuse to let her go. But how can I? You can't insist on living with a woman who doesn't want to live with you — if you love her, you can't.'

'Well, Jane?' said Isabel. 'Did you make any headway?'

Jane shook her head.

'Jack,' she said slowly, 'I'm ashamed of my daughter.'

Jack threw her a little twisted smile. 'Don't say that, Aunt Jane. I'm proud of my wife. I always have been and I can't break the habit. Cicily's all right. She'll pull through. We'll all pull through, somehow.'

'But what will you *do*, Jack?' wailed Isabel.

'I haven't thought it out,' said Jack. 'But you can always do something. The world is wide, you know.' He looked, rather hesitatingly, at Stephen. 'I thought I'd leave the bank, sir, for a time, at any rate.' That would be hard on Stephen, thought Jane swiftly. 'I'd like to take up my engineering. I want to leave Lakewood, and I thought if I began to fool around with those old problems again — go back to school, perhaps ——'

'Atta boy!' It was Jenny's cheerful voice. She was standing in the doorway, smiling in at them all very tranquilly.

'Jenny, come in,' said Stephen soberly. 'We have something to tell you.'

'I've known about it for weeks, Dad,' said Jenny affably. She advanced to the hearthrug and thrust her arm through Jack's. 'Cicily's a fool, but she must run through her folly. It's a great shame that the world was organized with two sexes. It makes for a lot of trouble. I'm all on Jack's side. I have been from the start. I'm thinking of marrying him myself, if he'll turn that old bean of his to the raising of Russian wolf hounds!'

Jack met his sister-in-law's levity with rather an uncertain smile. She grinned cheerfully at him.

'Want a drink, Jacky?'

'Jenny!' cried Isabel, in shocked accents.

'Of course he does!' persisted Jenny coolly. 'I'll ring for a cocktail.' As she walked toward the bell, her clear young eyes wandered brightly over the ravaged faces of the older generation. 'Do you know, you're all taking this a great deal too seriously? It's not the end of the world. It's not even the end of Cicily and Jack and Albert and Belle. They're all going to live to make you a great deal more trouble. Save your strength, boys and girls, for future crises!' She turned to meet the maid. 'A whiskey sour, Irma, and some anchovy sandwiches. You'll all feel better when you've had a drink.'

It was, Jane was reflecting, an incredible generation. They took nothing seriously. Unless, perhaps, the preservation of the light touch. But Jack looked distinctly cheered. And very grateful to Jenny. Yet Jack loved Cicily —— When the whiskey arrived, Jane was very much surprised to find herself drinking it. She drank two cocktails. Isabel did, too, and ate four anchovy sandwiches as well.

'I had no lunch,' she remarked in melancholy explanation. Then, 'I'll run you in town, Jack,' she said, putting down her glass.

'No, I'm going over to call on the kids,' said Jack very surprisingly. 'They leave in three days.' He turned toward the door.

'I'll see you at the Winters' musicale to-night,' said Jenny.

'I'm not — quite sure,' said Jack slowly.

'Nonsense!' said Jenny. 'Of course I will. The Casino, at nine. You must make Belle go, Aunt Isabel. You must make her wear her prettiest frock!'

'Belle wouldn't *dream* of going,' said Isabel with dignity.

'I bet she does,' said Jenny. 'And rightly so!'

'Jenny,' said Jane gently, 'don't.'

'Cicily and Albert won't be there, Mumsy. He'll be out

here with her, as she's going in three days. And if they were, what of it? *What of it?* Why carry on so about it? It's all in the day's work. Can't you take divorce a little more calmly?'

No, she couldn't, thought Jane, when Jack and Isabel had gone and Jenny had returned to her room and 'The American Kennels Gazette' and she was left alone with Stephen before the living-room fire. She really couldn't and she did not want to. What was the world coming to? What had gone out of life? What was missing in the moral fibre of the rising generation? Did decency mean nothing to them? Did loyalty? Did love? Did love mean too much, perhaps? One kind of love. It was a sex-ridden age. For the last twenty years the writers and doctors, the scientists and philosophers, had been preaching sex — illuminating its urges, justifying its demands, prophesying its victory. But the province of writers and doctors, of scientists and philosophers, was preaching, not practice. Could it be possible that ordinary men and women, like Jack and Cicily, like Albert and Belle, on whom the work of the world and the future of children depended, had been naïve enough to take this nonsense about sex-fulfilment seriously? Did they really believe it to be predominantly important? Sex-fulfilment, Jane thought hotly, was predominantly important only in the monkey house. Elsewhere character counted.

But these children had character. They had managed this appalling affair with extraordinary ability and restraint. They had a code, Jane dimly perceived, a code that was based — on what? Bravado and barbarism or courage and common-sense? It was very perplexing. It was very complicated. It was wrecking the older generation. But it was not a clear-cut issue, Jane admitted with a sigh, between the apes and the angels.

CHAPTER VI

I

NEW YORK was shining and shimmering in the first summer heat. Jane stood at her window in the Plaza Hotel, looking out over the feathery green tree-tops of Central Park at the long grey line of skyscrapers that reared their incredible towers against the serene background of the blue June sky. A black river of traffic streamed up and down Fifth Avenue. Here and there, like high lights on the water, Jane could catch the glint of a yellow taxi, the sheen of a green bus, the flash of sunlight from a moving windshield. New York looked cleaner and smarter and gayer than Chicago. It looked brand-new. Chicago, Jane thought, had a curious quality of antiquity. Like London. Looking down Adams Street, for instance, toward the smoke-stained portico of the Art Institute, with the old grey lions on guard. It was probably merely a question of the soot-smirched façades. New York, however, could boast a blue sky and a bright sun, just like the country. But it was much hotter than Lakewood. In spite of their unholy errand, Jane was glad that she and Stephen were going to sail in the morning.

The room behind her was crowded with luggage, neatly ticketed for the steamer. Stephen was seated in a plush arm-chair, perusing the columns of the 'New York Times.' Jenny had met them at the Century, two hours before, looking very *chic* and New-Yorky, Jane had thought, in a new grey covert-cloth suit and a little black skull cap, pulled smartly back from her round forehead. She had come up with them to the Plaza and had perched on top of a trunk, swinging her heels and talking of her kennels in Bedford Hills. She had bought

forty dogs and found a good man to take charge of them, but
the repairs on the farmhouse had been rather delayed. She
and Barbara could not move out until the first of July.
It was just as well, Jenny had said, for now Jane and Stephen
could see their penthouse on East Seventy-Ninth Street.
They were to dine there that evening with Steve, who was
coming from Boston on a late afternoon train to wave his
parents off from the dock the next morning.

Jenny had talked for two hours, Jane was just realizing,
and had run off for a luncheon engagement, without men-
tioning Cicily's name. Without referring to the unholy errand. No one would have gleaned, from Jenny's cheerful
conversation, that her parents were not bound on a casual
summer spree, a sight-seeing tour, a light-hearted holiday.
No one could have gathered that they had embarked on a
monstrous pilgrimage to the divorce courts of France, that in
three short weeks they would see one marriage of Cicily's
outrageously dissolved and another outrageously consecrated.

They would not have embarked on it, Jane thought with a
sigh, if it had not been for the grandchildren. Albert was
already in Paris. Muriel and Ed Brown, completing their
circuit of the globe, were to meet him there for the wedding.
Stephen would have washed his hands of the whole affair,
would have left his daughter to the tender ministrations of
Flora and Muriel, would have let her be given away at the
altar by even Ed Brown, if it had not been so pathetically
obvious that no one but Molly, the nurse, was going to look
after the twins and Robin Redbreast.

Cicily was going to Russia for her honeymoon. To Russia
and across Siberia and over the Gobi Desert to Pekin, where
Albert's new job awaited him in the legation. The twins and
Robin Redbreast were to summer at Gull Rocks. At Gull
Rocks and Lakewood, where Cicily was to join them in

October and 'see all the family,' she had cheerily written, before carrying her children off to begin life in Pekin. Cicily had thought the impeccable Molly, who had been, after all, nine years with the twins, was quite capable of taking the children from Paris to Gull Rocks. Muriel had agreed with her, while regretting that she and Ed Brown were to summer in England. But Jane had been outraged at the suggestion. 'She just thinks of the physical care,' she had said to Stephen. 'She doesn't consider what it will do to those babies to see her marry again.' And she had offered to make the monstrous pilgrimage alone.

Stephen, of course, had scouted that suggestion. 'I guess it's a leading from the Lord,' he had said heavily. 'I guess we both belong there.'

But this pleasant June morning, as Jane stood looking out over the feathery green tree-tops of Central Park, she had a guilty feeling that she was going to enjoy the pilgrimage, in spite of its monstrosity. Enjoy it more than Stephen would, at any rate. No woman was quite proof against the excitement of a trip to Paris. Jane had not seen Paris for twenty-three years. She had not seen New York for five. Every mother wanted to be with her daughter on her wedding day — on *all* her wedding days, thought Jane, with a little rueful smile. And — she would see André again.

She would certainly see André — unless by ill luck he were out of Paris. Flora would arrange it. André himself would arrange it. She and André would meet — it would be almost like meeting on the other side of the Jordan — after thirty-four years of separation. They would meet and talk about life and she would feel again that old sense of intimacy, of identity, almost, with the boy that —— After all, there had never been any one quite like André. They had seen life eye to eye. They had experienced together that first tremulous intimacy of passion. Not with Stephen, not with Jimmy, had she ever felt just that unity of interest and emotion. With Stephen there had been questioning — did she love him, should she marry him? With Jimmy there had been conflict — she *should* not love him, she *should* not marry him. With André it had all been as simple as the Garden of Eden. First love, Jane supposed, was always like that.

'Well, I've got to go,' said Stephen. He was lunching on Wall Street with Bill Belmont.

'Take a taxi, dear,' said Jane. 'It's very warm. Don't experiment with the subway.'

'Don't worry,' said Stephen. 'My subway days are over. They were over when I turned sixty. Take a taxi, yourself.'

'I will,' said Jane. She was lunching with Agnes. It was funny how young she felt, just because she was going to see Agnes again. She glanced in the mirror before leaving the room. A sedate, grey-haired, much more than middle-aged lady glanced back at her. A lady discreetly attired in a black-and-white foulard dress and sensible kid walking-shoes and a black straw hat, perched just a little too high for fashion on a head with too much hair! But Jane only laughed. She laughed out loud alone in her hotel bedroom. Agnes would look like that, too. But it was only a joke. She and Agnes would know that the sedate, grey-haired, much more than middle-aged ladies were incredible changelings. When she and Agnes were together they were sitting on a Bryn Mawr window-seat. When she and Agnes were together they defied time and eternity. They laughed at the joke.

II

Agnes lived on Beekman Place in an old brown-stone front house that she had bought twelve years ago. She had spent the proceeds of her third play upon it, figuring that it would be as good an investment as any other for little Agnes. It was very tall and narrow, with two rooms on each floor, and it had a garden, about as big as a postage stamp, overlooking the East River. There was not much in the garden but a privet hedge and a flagged path and one small poplar tree that was shining and shivering, that bright June day, in frail, pale bloom.

Agnes's writing-room overlooked the garden. It had walnut panelling and book-lined walls and a large eighteenth-century table desk, with a typewriter on it, in a corner near the fireplace. Agnes and Jane spent most of the afternoon on the window-seat, looking out at the view. Jane liked the view. The grey-green river, glittering under smoke and sun, eddied swiftly past the parapet at the foot of the garden. City tugs and excursion boats plied up and down the stream, the grey towers of the Queensborough Bridge were etched against the enamelled sky, and the grass on Blackwell's Island was the brilliant emerald green of city parks in June. Kept grass, thought Jane, that grows behind iron palings, man-made like the skyscrapers, but very tranquil and pleasant to look upon in the wilderness of brick and stone that was New York.

They talked of Cicily and her coming marriage. They talked of Jenny and her Seventy-Ninth Street penthouse. They talked of Steve and his house on Beacon Hill. They talked of Agnes's work and of Agnes's daughter.

Agnes turned out a play a year now. She had written twelve and had disposed of all of them, and only three had failed. One, to be sure, had had only a *succès d'estime*. It had been fun to work on it, but Agnes was never going to write a play like *that* again. Agnes was never going to finish her novel or write any more short stories, unless her luck failed her on Broadway. Agnes had banked two hundred and fifty thousand dollars in the course of the last fourteen years and bought the house on Beekman Place and educated little Agnes.

Little Agnes was a Bryn Mawr junior. She had been prepared at the Brearley School and had gone in with a lot of nice girls whom she knew very well and was majoring in biology and physics. Little Agnes wanted to be a doctor, and was planning to enter the College of Physicians and Surgeons at Columbia, just as soon as she graduated. She was off on a house party now in the Berkshire Hills.

Marion Park had been kind to little Agnes and thought the child had ability. Though Agnes had often been back to the college and had seen Marion standing in Miss Thomas's rostrum in a black silk Ph.D. gown with blue stripes on its flowing sleeves and a little black mortar board on her still brown hair, it seemed just as strange to her as it did to Jane to think that Marion Park was now President of Bryn Mawr. Agnes's plump, authoritative person was a familiar figure on Broadway. Her grey head was crowned with authentic dramatic laurels. Jane was a grandmother three times over. Yet it seemed incredible to both of them that a contemporary of theirs could be a college president. Incredible to think that Marion, with whom they had so often sat upon a Bryn Mawr window-seat, could have become a privileged person like Miss Thomas — Miss Thomas, who had always seemed to them not quite of this world of every day.

'Does little Agnes feel that way about Marion?' asked Jane.

'The rising generation,' said Agnes with a smile, 'doesn't feel that way about any one on God's green earth.'

'Do you remember what Papa said about her,' said Jane, 'that first night in Pembroke, when he sat next to her at supper? "I bet that girl will amount to something some day."'

'Your father was always right about people,' said Agnes.

That, of course, made Jane think instantly of Jimmy. Had

her father been right about Jimmy or had he been blinded by parental fears? Jane knew more now about parental fears than she had in the days when Jimmy had aroused them in the breast of her father. She knew they were very blinding.

'What's the matter, Jane?' asked Agnes. 'You look so sober.'

'I was thinking of Jimmy,' said Jane quietly. 'I was thinking of how proud he would have been of you, Agnes, and of how he would have loved all this.' Her glance wandered over the cheerful, luxurious room, then came to rest on the restless river rolling past the window.

'Yes. He would have loved it,' said Agnes gently. 'For a time. Jimmy loved success and comfort. But if he never worked for them, Jane, it was only because he loved other things more. He wasn't like me. I'm a money-maker, pure and simple. But Jimmy was a gypsy. Jimmy loved success for the fun of it and comfort for the ease of it, but they would soon have bored him. Jimmy could never have sat on this window-seat and looked at all those boats without wanting to charter a tug for Shanghai or Singapore. Jimmy would never have locked up his money in banks or sunk it in bricks and mortar. He wouldn't have been any happier, really, on Beekman Place than he was on Charlton Street. Jimmy's happiness was always just around the corner.'

Jane listened in silence. *She* had been around the corner, of course. Was that why she had represented happiness to Jimmy? If so, how lucky, how very, very lucky, that she had never let him discover that her street was no different from any other thoroughfare!

Agnes was very wise. Agnes was wonderful. Agnes knew everything — except one thing. In all the years of their common experience, thought Jane, nothing bound her to

Agnes as closely as the secret that Agnes would never share. She rose to leave her a little sadly.

'I hate to think of what's before you, Jane,' said Agnes. 'But remember one thing — there *can't* be understanding between two generations. I'm convinced of that. Love, Jane, and sympathy, but never understanding. We must take our children's ideas on faith. We can never make them our own. Remember that and save yourself unhappiness.'

III

Jane tried to remember it that very evening, as she sat by Stephen's side on a black-and-silver divan in the shrimp-pink drawing-room of Jenny's East Seventy-Ninth Street penthouse. The penthouse was small and very, very modern. Jane could not understand its scheme of decoration. From the Euclid designs of the geometric silver furniture to the tank of living goldfish set in the marble walls of Jenny's black bathroom, it all looked very queer to Jane. It looked queerer than queer to Stephen. His face had been a study when he had seen the goldfish. Young Steve had thought nothing of it.

'I don't like this arty stuff,' he had said with brotherly candour. 'I'd change this entire roomful of modern truck for one genuine Duncan Phyfe table!'

Jenny had laughed at him and so had Barbara and so had the young interior decorator who had designed the room. Rather to Jane's surprise, Jenny and Barbara had invited three of their friends to meet Jane and Stephen — three young men, who, at the first glance, seemed almost as queer to Jane as the tiny modern penthouse.

One was the interior decorator, of course, a clever-looking young Jew in London evening clothes. He painted, Barbara had murmured, and had done some tremendous things, and condescended to run his shop on Madison Avenue, only because one must live. One must, thought Jane, and presumably in London evening clothes. Looking at a canvas of his that hung over the silver fireplace, Jane was not surprised that he found it practical to sell chintzes on the side. It looked like a broken kaleidoscope of green and pink and yellow glass. Jane wondered if it were a sunset or a woman, then realized that her ideas of painting were outdated. It was obviously a reaction, or, at the most concrete, a passion or a mood. Jane knew she was benighted about modern art. But honest, at least. She admitted frankly that she could not speak its language.

The second friend was a volatile young Englishman, the musical comedy star who had just finished playing the lead in 'Laugh, Lady, Laugh,' a show that had been 'packing them in,' so Jenny had informed Jane, for the last eighteen months on Broadway. Jane thought his crisp blond hair just a ripple too curly and the strength of his clear-cut jaw line a trifle weak. Nothing made a man look weaker, Jane reflected with a twinkle, than a strong chin. He was very nice and friendly, however. His name was Eric Arthur and he had a *penchant* for Russian wolf hounds. He had two with him on tour, with which he walked in Central Park every day at noon. They had formed his first bond with Jenny. She had met him at a party at Pierre's and they had talked of the wolf hounds immediately.

The third friend looked more to Jane like some one whom you would conceivably ask to dinner in Lakewood. That was her first impression and she immediately despised herself for it. A thought like that was distinctly unworthy. It was just like her mother and Isabel. Jane was determined to like Jenny's friends. This third young man was only a little anæmic-looking. He came from Hartford, Connecticut, and he had gone to Yale University and he was the youthful curator of prints at the Metropolitan. He had struck up an argument with Steve immediately on the question of the eternal merit of Currier and Ives.

All three of them, at any rate, seemed to be on the most intimate terms with Jenny and with Barbara. The curator of prints was their amateur bootlegger, the interior decorator was furnishing the farmhouse at Bedford Hills, the musical comedy star was full of wise thoughts on English kennels where they could buy a few better bitches. He was sailing for Liverpool next week and would take the matter up for them.

Jane learned all this before they had finished with the cocktails. They did not finish with the cocktails for some time. Champagne was served with the perfect little dinner, and chartreuse afterward, and, later in the evening, a highball for the men.

By nine o'clock the curator of prints and the musical comedy star were both a little flushed and loquacious. By ten they were distinctly hilarious. The young Jew did not drink, and Steve, Jane was thankful to note, was behaving himself, though he rated his sister's taste in liquor much higher than her taste in decoration. By eleven all the young people were shouting the lyrics from 'Laugh, Lady, Laugh,' around the grand piano, while Eric Arthur pounded out the melody on the keys. Stephen looked fearfully tired. Jane knew she ought to take him back to the Plaza, but she did not like to leave the girls alone at a party that was going just like this. Ridiculous, of course. Jenny and Barbara were left alone at all their other parties. They looked completely in command of themselves and the situation. Too young and too pretty, however, to ——

They *did* look ridiculously young. And rather as if preposterously masquerading in this little modern penthouse of their own. Barbara wore a black lace smoking-jacket over a gown of trailing black chiffon. Her curly red hair was cropped close, like a prize-fighter's, on her aristocratic little head. She wore her cigarette — that was the verb that came to Jane's mind — in a long green jade holder. She was standing at Eric Arthur's shoulder, highball in hand, her arm thrust casually through the curator's elbow, singing the jazz melodies with mock emotion. Jenny was hanging over the end of the grand piano, singing, too. She was, Jane thought, rather amazingly dressed in black velvet pajamas, with a long loose coat of cherry-coloured silk. Her shiny pale hair was brushed straight off her forehead and cut short like a boy's at the white nape of her neck. Two long paste earrings glittered at her ears. Between them her plain, distinguished little face looked out at Jane with exactly the same expression as her poor Aunt Silly's. But Jenny had been born in the right period. There was a premium set now on distinguished plainness. Jenny's lank figure in its bizarre costume, Jenny's homely face with the hair strained off her high forehead, was the essence of smartness. She looked like a cover design for 'Vanity Fair.'

It *was* the period, of course, Jane reflected soberly. It was not the children. Young people had always sung cheerily around grand pianos. It was prohibition and the emancipation of women and the new freedom of the sexes. There was no real harm in it. But was this just Jenny's idea of 'living smartly in New York'? It was not Jane's. It was not Stephen's. It was not Bill Belmont's. In his brown-stone residence on East Sixty-First Street, Bill Belmont, Jane knew, was as mystified as she and Stephen were at the charms of the penthouse.

Eric Arthur had run through the score of 'Laugh, Lady, Laugh,' but his nimble fingers were still rattling over the keys. A shout of applause burst from his little audience.

'Sing it, Eric!' they cried.

'It's the new song hit from "Sunny Side Up"!' Jenny tossed in explanation to her parents. Eric Arthur's tender young tenor dominated the uproar. He was singing *appassionata*, uplifted by highballs.

> 'Turn on the heat! Start in to strut!
> Wiggle and wobble and warm up the hut!
> Oh! Oh! It's thirty below!
> Turn on the heat, fifty degrees!
> Get hot for papa, or papa will freeze!
> Oh! Oh! Start melting the snow!
> If you are good, my little radiator ——'

This was *not* living smartly in New York, thought Jane firmly. Young people had always sung cheerily around grand pianos. But not — not drunk. Not — not songs like that. She rose to leave the party.

'Jenny,' she whispered, 'you ought to send them home.'

Jenny's eyes met hers with a little indulgent twinkle.

'I mean it, Jenny,' said Jane.

'All right,' said Jenny calmly. 'I will.' She moved to Barbara's side and whispered in her ear. Barbara laughed a little, then glanced at Jane and Stephen. Jenny clapped her hands, then clapped them again, more vehemently, until the clamour about the piano ceased.

'You've got to go home, boys,' she said in the sudden silence. 'It's twelve o'clock and Mother's a blue-ribbon girl. She thinks we've all had enough!'

The blunt statement was met with a burst of good-humoured laughter. Eric rose from the piano bench and drained the last of his highball. They were no drunker, Jane reflected, than she had seen many young men at perfectly respectable parties at home. The young Jewish decorator said good-night to her very politely. He was really a nice boy, thought Jane. He got the two inebriates out of the room much quicker than Jane would have thought possible. Jane heard Barbara make a date with the curator of prints for luncheon next day. She wondered if he would remember it. When they had finally taken themselves off, Jenny turned to her parents.

'You didn't like them, did you, Mumsy?' she said. 'But you *know* Eric's funny when he's tight.'

'They say, Mr. Carver,' said Barbara conversationally to Stephen, 'that the tighter he is, the funnier he is in the show. He keeps putting in lines — I don't suppose he knows what he's saying — but they always bring down the house ——'

'It's a gift!' laughed Jenny. She was placing Jane's evening wrap around Jane's shoulders. 'I'll meet you at the dock,' she said. She kissed Jane tenderly and threw her arms around Stephen. She looked absurd and adorable, Jane thought, as she smiled up into his weary face — like some fragile, fantastic clown, in those loose black velvet trousers and that cherry-coloured sack. Barbara was rallying Steve at the door. No one, Jane thought suddenly, had yet mentioned Cicily's name.

'I wish I were going with you,' smiled Jenny. 'But we're going to have a fearfully busy month at the kennels.'

'I wish I were going with them,' said Steve, 'but I'm just getting into my stride at the bank.'

'You'll have a lovely time,' said Barbara.

'Won't they?' smiled Jenny.

'You bet they will!' said Steve.

It was a conspiracy, Jane decided, as she plunged earthward in the elevator. It was a friendly conspiracy of silence, to keep two foolish old people from worrying over something they could not control — something that was none of their business, really. Steve chatted pleasantly all the way back to the Plaza in the taxi about modern decoration *versus*

Duncan Phyfe tables. Jane did not listen. They did not know what they had lost in life, these kindly, capable, clever young people who did not believe in worry. Stephen looked terribly tired in the bright, white light of the Plaza lobby. She should have taken him away from that party at ten o'clock. They did not know that they had lost *any-thing*, she thought, as she plunged skyward in the Plaza elevator. But Stephen knew. And she knew. Though it was difficult to define it.

IV

Paris, thought Jane — the city of joy! She glanced across the railway carriage at Stephen's face. It looked rather grim. Stephen was rested, however. The six days at sea had been good for him. Stephen was a sailor and, in spite of parental anxieties, he had responded immediately to the tang of the briny breeze and the roll of the deep-sea swell. While still in the Ambrose Channel, he had seemed perceptibly more cheerful. He had landed at Cherbourg that morning, looking tanned and healthy and braced for his ordeal. The grimness had returned to his face rather slowly, as he had sat silently all day, staring out through the window of the railway carriage at the pleasant midsummer French landscape.

The train was pulling slowly into the Gare Saint-Lazare. A group of porters were assailing the door of the carriage. The air rang with their staccato utterance. Jane caught a whiff of garlic and was suddenly exalted with a feeling of adventure. It was a real breath from a foreign land. The train had stopped. The porters stormed the luggage rack. Jane and Stephen descended to the platform.

'Je veux un taxi,' said Jane.

The porters responded with a flood of eloquence. Jane and Stephen following their blue smocked figures through the crowd. Steamer acquaintances waved and smiled. Jane caught other whiffs of garlic. She could not subdue that sense of adventure. Ten days in Paris! She was smiling a little excitedly, when she first caught sight of Cicily—Cicily standing with the three children and Molly at the gate of the train.

'*Look* at Robin Redbreast!' she cried gaily to Stephen. '*Isn't* he *huge?*'

It was then that she saw Albert. She suffered a quick sense of shock. Why hadn't she expected to see him? Of course he would be there. Nevertheless, his presence seemed vaguely indecent in that little family gathering. The pleasant, snubnosed, twinkle-eyed ghost of Jack loomed at his side. He lifted Robin Redbreast to his shoulder. They were all laughing and waving. Cicily looked radiant. The twins dashed into Jane's arms.

'Mumsy!' cried Cicily. She kissed Jane warmly. Then turned to greet her father. Albert thrust Robin Redbreast into Jane's embrace. Over the child's yellow head, surprisingly, he kissed her.

'Aunt Jane,' he was saying affectionately, 'it was great of you to come!'

Cicily's arm was thrust through Stephen's. She was talking excitedly as she led him through the crowded concourse.

'I reserved your rooms at the Chatham. Why do you go there? Aunt Muriel's at the Ritz. I wish I had room for you in my flat, but it's perfectly tiny. Molly hates it. Just one bathroom and we froze all winter. But it's sweet now. You can sit on the balcony and see the Arc de Triomphe.'

Albert was hailing two taxis.

'I suppose you want to go straight to the hotel, sir, and rest,' he was saying. 'Did you have a smooth passage? We're going to have a gay week.'

'Cousin Flora's simply wild to see you, Mumsy,' interrupted Cicily. 'She's been awfully nice to me. She knows the smartest people — real frogs, you know — and she asked me to all her parties. I've simply loved it. I don't want to go to Pekin at all. I'd like to live here all my life — if it weren't so far from Lakewood.'

Stephen was succumbing, with a faintly constrained smile, to Cicily's gay garrulity. She broke off suddenly to squeeze his elbow and kiss his cheek. Albert took up the burden of her song.

'We're all dining to-night at L'Escargot. Do you like snails, Aunt Jane? We're going to pick up Mother and my esteemed stepfather at the Ritz — my esteemed stepfather is really all right, you know. He's a good sort. We'll all get a drink at the Ritz bar. The Ritz bar's quite a sight, sir ——'

'Let's send the children home with Molly,' said Cicily gaily, 'and go up to the Chatham with Mumsy and Dad. I've got so much to say to you, darlings, that I don't know where to begin. We're going to be married in Cousin Flora's apartment. Just the families, you know. I know you'll like my dress, Mumsy. I won't let Albert see it ——'

This was another conspiracy, thought Jane, as she climbed into the waiting taxi. A conspiracy, this time, not of silence, but of chatter. A friendly conspiracy to keep two foolish old people from worrying over something that they could not control. A conspiracy to prove that this was a very usual situation, a very gay situation, a very happy situation — a situation that called for frivolity and celebration. A party, in fact. A purely social occasion.

But did not Cicily, Jane wondered, as their taxi dodged and tooted through chaotic traffic of the old grey streets, did not Cicily, beneath the gay garrulity of her light and laughing chatter, feel at all disturbed by her equivocal position as Albert's fiancée and Jack's wife? Jane, herself, felt profoundly disturbed by it. Belle's divorce had been granted in Reno the end of March. Albert had been — could you call him a bachelor? — for three months. Yet Jane could not really consider the engagement as a *fait accompli* until next Wednesday morning, when Cicily's decree would be made final and Cicily, herself, would be — hateful word — free. She would be married three days later in Flora's apartment. But not until Wednesday noon, Jane told herself, firmly, would she recognize the engagement. If she did not recognize it, however, what was Albert's status in the crowded little taxi? It was terribly complicated. It was terribly sordid. Glancing from Cicily's bright, smiling countenance to Stephen's grim, constrained one, Jane could not agree with Albert's initial statement. They would not have a gay week.

v

Jane and Flora were sitting side by side on the Empire sofa of Jane's little green sitting-room in the Chatham Hotel. The sitting-room was rather small and rather over-upholstered. It was extremely Empire and extremely green. The green carpet, the green curtains, the green wall-paper, and the green furniture were all emblazoned with Napoleonic emblems. Gold crowns and laurel wreaths and bees met the eye at every turn. Jane thought it looked rather sweet and stuffy and French, but 'I can't think in this room for the buzzing' had been Stephen's laconic comment, when Cicily and Albert had finally left them alone in it, yesterday afternoon.

It was ten o'clock in the morning and Flora had just come in. She had brought a big box of roses and she was terribly glad to see Jane. Stephen was downtairs in the dining-room eating what he termed 'a Christian breakfast.' Jane's tray of coffee and rolls and honey was still on the sitting-room table.

'Jane,' said Flora, 'you're incredibly the same.'

'Am I?' said Jane a little wistfully. She had not seen Flora for nine years. Flora, she thought, looked subtly subdued and sophisticated. Silver-haired and slender in her grey French frock she no longer suggested anything as bright and gay and concrete as a Dresden-china shepherdess. Frail and faded, well-dressed and weary, there was something just a little shadowy about Flora. She looked like a Sargent portrait of herself, Jane decided. There was nothing shadowy, however, in her enthusiasm over this reunion.

'Of course I don't mean you *look* the same, Jane,' she continued honestly. 'But you look as if you *were* the same! And that's even nicer.'

'We're all the same,' said Jane stoutly. 'That's one of the things you learn by growing old. Nobody ever changes.'

'Children do,' smiled Flora. 'I was surprised at Cicily. She was a pretty child, but she's grown up into much more than that. You must be very proud of her.'

Jane's eyes met Flora's for a moment in silence.

'Well, Flora,' said Jane slowly, 'I can't say that I am.'

Flora took Jane's hand and squeezed it before she spoke.

'Jane,' she said gently, 'the war changed everything. Even over here, it's all quite different. People don't act as they used to do — they don't think as they used to do. Cicily's a sweet child. It was a pleasure to have her here in Paris. She has lived so discreetly and charmingly in that little flat up near the Étoile — every one likes her — her children are adorable and Albert's a delightful young man. I think they'll be very happy.'

'They don't deserve to be very happy,' said Jane.

'But you want them to be,' said Flora brightly. Flora seemed almost a member of the friendly conspiracy. 'And speaking of happiness,' she went on gaily, 'isn't Muriel *funny* with Ed Brown? She's a perfect wife.'

'He's a perfect husband,' smiled Jane.

'Well, Jane!' laughed Flora, 'I think that statement's a trifle exaggerated. He's really awful — pretty awful, I mean. He's been in Paris three weeks and he hasn't talked of anything but prohibition. With disfavour, my dear — don't misunderstand me! — with distinct disfavour! But he makes Muriel sublimely happy!' She paused to twinkle, brightly, for a moment at Jane's non-committal countenance. 'Jane,' she said, 'you're no gossip. You never were. You're holding out on me. I wish Isabel were here.'

'Well, I don't,' said Jane, with emphasis.

Flora stopped in confusion. 'No, I suppose you don't,' she said. 'It — it must have been *terrible*, Jane. All in the family, I mean.'

'It *was* terrible,' said Jane.

'Muriel's very happy about it. She loves Cicily.'

'Muriel,' said Jane deliberately, 'has no moral sense. She never had. She's always been frivolous about falling in love. About *any* one's falling in love ——'

'Jane,' said Flora suddenly, 'André Duroy's not in Paris.'

The simple statement fell in a little pool of silence.

'Oh,' said Jane, after a moment. 'Well, I thought perhaps he wouldn't be.' She tried to make her voice sound very casual. 'People *aren't* in cities much, you know, in the month of July. I thought he'd be off with his wife in the country.'

'He's not with his wife,' said Flora meaningly. 'His wife's at Cowes. She has a lot of English friends, you know.' Flora's voice had lost nothing of its meaning.

'Yes, I know,' said Jane hastily. Letters were one thing, she thought, and talk was another. Jane did not want to sit gossiping with Flora about André's wife. It seemed vaguely indecent. But it did not take two to make a gossip.

'She has their boy with her. She's very discreet. He's a

nice child. Thirteen years old and he looks *just* like André.
André's in the French Alps, I think. He has a studio up there
somewhere. I sent him a letter.'

'You sent him a letter?' said Jane.

'Yes. To say you were coming. I asked him to the wedding.'

'Oh — he won't come down for it,' said Jane defensively.

She was conscious of wishing, rather wildly, that Flora had
not written. He would not come, of course. And yet — and
yet — Jane felt curiously hurt, in advance, to know he was
not coming. It would have been much nicer if André had
never known that she was in Paris. If André had not had
forced on him that faintly ungracious gesture of declining to
cross France to see the girl who —— Ridiculously, Jane was
thinking of that letter he had written her when he had received the Prix de Rome. Of how she had read it in her little
room on Pine Street, at the window that overlooked the
willow tree. If André had not written that letter, she might
not have married Stephen. What nonsense! Of course she
would have married Stephen. On what other basis than that
of marriage with Stephen were the last thirty years imagin-
able?

'I think he will,' said Flora. 'He quite fell for Cicily ——'

Just then Stephen entered the room. Flora greeted him
with enthusiasm. They sat down together on the Empire sofa
and began to talk about Chicago. Jane did not listen. She
was thinking of how very odd it was to think that Cicily knew
André. That Cicily might know him quite well. That she
might know him, absurdly, much better than Jane herself did.
Cicily was only five years younger than Cyprienne. Jane was
seventeen years older. Oh, well — of course he would not
cross France to come to the wedding.

VI

Jane and Stephen and Cicily and Albert were strolling down the rue Vaugirard on their way to the Luxembourg Museum. They had just lunched at Foyot's on a perfect sole and *fraises à la crême*. Five of Jane's ten days in Paris had passed. They had passed very quickly, she had just been thinking, and mainly in the consumption of food and drink. Cocktails at the Ritz bar, snails at L'Escargot, *blinis* at the Russian Maisonnette, *cointreau* at the Café de la Rotonde, fish food at Prunier's, absinthe at the Dome, Muriel's magnificent little dinner at Le Pré Catelan, Flora's smart one in her apartment, champagne and sparkling Burgundy and Rhine wine in brown, long-necked bottles — curious memories to blend with the sense of perplexity and despair that the sight of Cicily and Albert and the three grandchildren had engendered.

The three grandchildren had been very endearing and Cicily and Albert had devoted themselves to the entertainment of the older generation. Between their engagements at restaurants they had crowded in two trips to the Louvre and one to Notre Dame, a visit to the Cluny Museum, a drive through the midsummer Bois, a motor ride to Versailles, a jaunt by boat down the Seine to Saint-Cloud, a wild evening on Montmartre and a mild one at the Comédie-Française. That night they were taking the twins to the Cirque Madrano, to watch the Fratellinis. The Fratellinis, Albert had explained to Jane, were the funniest clowns in the world. At the moment, between lunch at Foyot's and tea with Flora, they had just time to take in the Luxembourg Gallery. There was not much in it, Cicily had said.

The friendly conspiracy of chatter, Jane thought as they crossed the sun-washed court, had never faltered. The illusion of the 'party' had been consistently sustained. The two foolish old people, she reflected, as they climbed the grey stone steps of the museum, had not been left alone for an hour to think or to worry. The children had been kind and capable and very, very clever. There had been no emotional moments, no awkward discussions, no embarrassing *contretemps*. They were carrying it all off beautifully. They would carry it all off beautifully until the end.

Nevertheless, Jane had felt during the last five days that she would have been glad of an hour in which to think or not think, worry or not worry, as she chose. An hour, perhaps, in which to look at Paris, without the tinkling accompaniment of the friendly conspiracy of chatter.

They entered the main gallery.

'We've got to hurry,' said Cicily.

Jane thought how much she wished that she were entering the main gallery alone. It looked just as she remembered it. The walls were hung with the same fine Gobelin tapestries. The familiar bronze and marble figures stood on their pedestals. Jane had not seen them for twenty years, but she remembered them well. Stephen and Albert were conscientiously buying catalogues. Cicily had paused before a case of Sèvres china. A rough-hewn Rodin arrested Jane's attention. But Jane had not come to the Luxembourg to look at the Rodins. Jane had come to the Luxembourg for quite another purpose. She moved away from Cicily and strolled casually to the corner where André's Eve awaited her. Jane stared up at her. She stood smiling provocatively over her yet untasted apple — an Eve still innocent, yet subtly provocative. Jane gazed in silence at her rounded cheeks, at the fresh virginal curves of her parted lips. Could it be possible, Jane was thinking, that she had ever looked like that? That she had ever smiled like that? Could it be possible that she had ever been anything so fresh and young and fair and inexperienced? Stephen and Cicily turned up at her elbow. Jane was conscious of a quick fear that Cicily would recognize that smile, that Stephen would comment on it. But Stephen was glancing up at the Eve with a look of complete indifference. Jane suddenly realized that Stephen had quite forgotten that it was a Duroy. But Cicily had opened her catalogue.

'It's awfully *vieux jeu*, isn't it?' she was saying calmly. 'He's nice, though. I met him at Cousin Flora's.'

Albert slipped his arm through Jane's. 'There are some good paintings,' he was saying, 'but most of them have been moved to the Louvre.'

Jane passed at his side from the entrance hall to the farther galleries. She wandered, blindly, past a succession of canvases. Cicily's light prattle fell unheeded on her ears. An hour later, when they stood once more in the entrance hall, Jane could not remember one single painting that she had seen in the Luxembourg.

'Come look at the gardens,' Albert was saying. 'They're really charming.'

'You go without me,' said Jane. 'I'm a little tired.'

'It won't take a minute,' said Albert brightly.

'I'll wait here,' said Jane.

Stephen and Cicily and Albert moved toward the door. From the grey light of the entrance hall, Jane watched them descend the stone steps in the dazzling sunlight of the Paris afternoon. She walked slowly back to the Eve. 'There is something of you in all my nymphs and Eves and saints and Madonnas,' she was thinking. 'Something you brought into my life. Romance, I guess. Nothing more tangible.'

She *had* been young once, thought Jane, as she stood staring up at the Eve. She had been fresh and fair and inexperienced. She had smiled like that. Twenty-three years ago, Stephen himself had recognized that smile. Absurd, ridiculous, however, that fleeting fear that Cicily would recognize it now!

Jane wondered vaguely what Eve had looked like after thirty years with Adam. After Cain and Abel had disappointed her. Why had no one ever thought of doing Eve at the age of fifty-one? Cicily's light voice broke in upon her revery. Jane turned with a start.

'I wonder who she is, Mumsy?' said Cicily.

'Who — she is?' faltered Jane.

'Yes,' said Cicily brightly. 'They say that all those rather saccharine ladies of his are some one, Mumsy. They're a record of his sentimental journey. His wife's the Venus in the Metropolitan. He did it the year he was married. I think' — Cicily's blue eyes gleamed experimentally — 'I think it would be rather nice to be loved by an artist who would re-create you and preserve you forever in words or paint or marble. Though I suppose you'd grow up and beyond his idea of you and then you'd want to throw a brick at what he'd done. It must give lots of André Duroy's old girls a pain to look at what he once thought they were. You'd wonder, you know, if you ever *had* been anything so silly. And you'd fear you had. One's always silly, Mumsy, when one's in love. Which is quite as it should be. But the silliness should be ephemeral. It shouldn't be perpetuated in words or paint or marble, any more than it is in life. Don't you think so, Mumsy?'

Jane's eyes were still on the Eve. 'I don't know,' she said. 'There's Keats — and the "Grecian Urn" — "Forever wilt thou love and she be fair." '

'It doesn't sound so good,' said Cicily, 'if you read it "Forever wilt thou love and she be silly"!' She tucked her arm under Jane's elbow. 'Come on, Mumsy, Albert and Dad are waiting.'

VII

'I think,' said Stephen, 'I'll try to take a nap.'

'Why don't you, dear?' said Jane.

Jane herself was far from feeling sleepy. She had been sitting in silence for the last half-hour on the Empire sofa in the little green sitting room, watching Stephen turn over the pages of the Paris 'Herald' and the London 'Times.' She rose, now, and followed him into their bedroom. It was rather a relief, she was thinking, to have something definite to do, even if that something was only pulling down three window-shades and raising one window and tucking a light steamer rug over Stephen's recumbent form. Stephen was looking very grim and tired. They had had a hard day, though nothing much had happened in it. At eleven in the morning Cicily had telephoned. She had telephoned to announce that her lawyer had just called her up from the courtroom to inform her that her decree had been made final. There had been no complications and the last requirement had been complied with. That was all there had been to the formal proceedings that Jane and Stephen had tragically prepared themselves to witness. Two months ago two foreign lawyers had spoken in an alien tongue. Cicily had murmured a few French words of acquiescence. A judge had entered an interlocutory judgment. To-day that judgment had been entered on the records of the Bureau of Vital Statistics. And a marriage had been dissolved.

Cicily had planned to have a little lunch with Albert. She had arranged for Jane and Stephen, however, to join Muriel and Ed Brown at the Ritz. That luncheon with Muriel, Jane reflected, had been rather like the first meal after a family funeral. Though, of course, you did not usually have to take the first meal after a family funeral in a public restaurant and you did not usually have to talk through it about prohibition

with Ed Brown. Jane and Stephen had returned very early in
the afternoon to their rooms at the Chatham.

Jane closed the bedroom door and reëntered the green
sitting-room. She sat down on the Empire sofa. From behind
the heavy green curtains of the long French windows the
sharp, staccato uproar of the traffic on the rue Daunou rang
in her ears. The shrill, toy-like toots of the French taxis
punctuated the sound. Cities had voices, thought Jane.
Chicago rumbled and New York hummed and Paris tooted.
Jane glanced at the London 'Times' and the Paris 'Herald.'
She felt curiously empty-handed, but she did not seem to
want to read the papers. Reading the papers, Jane reflected,
was the eternal resource of men. It offered no distraction to
women. She had at last her hour alone in Paris and she did
not know what to do with it. She wondered what Cicily and
Albert were doing. She thought of the Bureau of Vital Statistics. The Catholics were right. Metaphysically speaking,
there was no such thing as divorce. Marriage was a mystical
union of body and spirit. It was a state of being. It could not
be dissolved by legal procedure. The past could not be denied. The present was its consequence. The future — but as
far as the future went, though Cicily seemed to Jane as much
Jack's wife as she had ever been, she was going to marry Albert Lancaster in Flora's apartment in three days' time. After
that, Jane reflected hopelessly, she would be *two* men's wife!
It was frightfully complicated, metaphysically speaking.

Just then Jane heard a knock on the door.

'Entrez!' she cried, with a curious sense of relief. But it was
only a bell-boy. He had a letter on a little silver tray. 'Merci,'
said Jane and fumbled for a franc. The letter was from
Isabel.

Jane opened it before the bell-boy had left the room. Isabel's letters were always good reading. This one contained a

surprise, and Jane felt, as she read it, exactly as if Isabel were sitting beside her on the little Empire sofa. Her sister's very accents clung to the sixteen closely written pages.

'DEAREST JANE,

'I haven't written, but I've been awfully busy. I've been thinking of you, of course, and of Stephen, too. I sometimes feel that all this has been harder on Robin and Stephen than on you and me. In a way, I think, fathers care more than mothers what happens to daughters.

'I care most about Jack. But, Jane, I'm beginning to feel much happier about him. He loved his work at Tech, and as soon as he left there this June, he took a summer job with the telephone company down near Mexico City. I've just had his first letter. He's stringing wires and building bridges, just as Cicily said he would. He misses the children fearfully, of course, but he could not have taken them to Mexico, in any case. Nevertheless, they are the insuperable problem.

'At any rate, work is the thing for Jack to tie to, just now. It can't betray him, as a woman might. It's so much safer to love things than people.

'This brings me to Belle's news. It's what I've been so busy over these last two weeks. It's still a great secret, but I know it will make you and Stephen happier to know it. She's engaged to Billy Winter. She's not going to announce it, but just marry him quietly here in the apartment some afternoon and slip off to Murray Bay for her honeymoon. Robin and I are going to keep the babies while she's gone. Billy's rented a Palmer House on Ritchie Court for the winter.

'Belle has no misgivings about anything and almost no regrets. And to hear Billy talk, you'd think every one was divorced and remarried. Of course, in a way, I hate it and so does Robin. But we like Billy and he's sweet with Belle's children. She's so glad, now, they're all girls. She's going to give them Billy's name. She's really in love again, I think, and if she's happy, perhaps it will all work out for the best. But I can't get used to this modern idea that you can scrap the past and wipe the slate clean and begin life over again.

'I haven't told Mamma anything about it and shan't, until after the wedding. She keeps right on saying she doesn't want to see Cicily or Albert ever again. But she'll get over that, of course.

'Her blood pressure has been flaring up and she's had some dizzy spells that have worried me. She fusses a lot about the house, and Minnie quarrels with all the other servants. She just made Mamma dismiss an excellent waitress I got her — such a nice girl who didn't want her Sundays out — because she thought the pantry cupboards weren't very clean.

Of course they *aren't* as clean as they were when Minnie used to keep them. But the neighbourhood's so dirty now. That factory on Erie Street always burns soft coal. I don't blame the waitress — and, anyway, Jane, you know what I mean, what *difference* does it make? The main thing is to keep Mamma tranquil, and she'd never know about the pantry cupboards if Minnie didn't tell her.

'She ought to move, of course, into some nice apartment that would be easy to live in, but she won't hear of it. They're going to pull down the house across the yard and put up a skyscraper. It will take away all the south sun and the blank north wall will be hideous to look at. I hate to think what Minnie will say when the wreckers begin. The plaster dust will sift in all the windows and the noise will be frightful. After that steel riveting, I suppose, all summer and fall.

'If you were here, I'd really advise trying to move them at once, but I honestly don't feel up to all the argument alone.

And, after all, perhaps it wouldn't be worth while. Mamma's seventy-seven and she'd never really feel at home anywhere else. She doesn't *do* anything any more. She never goes out. Just walks around that empty house, rummaging in bureau drawers and boxes, going over her possessions and trying to throw things away. You know Mamma always kept everything, and the closets are all full of perfectly worthless objects. She doesn't accomplish a thing, of course, and it tires her fearfully. But she won't stay quiet.

'She's always very sweet with me when I drop in, and I think she's quite happy. But Minnie says she talks a lot about how she wants to leave things. She mentions that to me, sometimes, and I just hate to hear her. It's queer — you'd think it would make her feel so sad, but she seems rather to enjoy it. I think it makes her feel important again — you know, something to be reckoned with. Perhaps at seventy-seven that's the only way you *can* feel important — by disposing of your property. That would account for lots of startling wills, wouldn't it, Jane?

'She told me last week that you were to have the seed-pearl set and I was to have the amethyst necklace. It really made me cry. She says she wants that opal pin that she always said was Cicily's to go to Belle, now, along with the cameos. But she'll change her mind about that, of course, when she hears of Billy Winter.

'Minnie reads the paper to her every night in the library. They're always sitting there together when Robin and I drop in. Reading the paper or talking over old times. In a way it seems awful — Mamma talking like that with Minnie — But Minnie's really the only one, now, who remembers the things that Mamma likes to talk about. She always stands up very nicely when Robin and I are there, but I know when we've gone she just settles down in Papa's armchair, and she doesn't wear her apron any longer. I think I ought to try to make her, but Robin says to let her alone.

'I wouldn't write Mamma much about the wedding if I were you. Not even about the children. It would only upset her. Her great-grandchildren don't seem to mean much to her any more. They're just things that make the general situation worse. I dread telling her about Belle. She keeps saying she's glad that Papa was spared all this. And Mrs. Lester. She always speaks as if they had died just last week. And, after all, it's nine years now.

'Of course, Jane, I think we really feel just as badly about it as Mamma does. But we have to carry it off. Old people are just like children. They have no mercy on you. I get so sick of trying to defend the situation to Mamma and Minnie, when I think, in my heart, there's *no* defence for it.

'Well — when Jack's a full-fledged engineer and Belle and Billy have settled down in Ritchie Court and Cicily and Albert are living in Pekin, I suppose we'll all shake down in some dreadful modern way and accept the situation and not even feel awkward about it. Cicily's children are still my grandchildren and Belle's children are Muriel's grandchildren as well as mine. We're all held together by the hands of babies, which, I suppose, are the strongest links in the world. Nevertheless, Cicily and Albert won't live in Pekin forever, and I just can't bear to think of the Christmas dinners and Thanksgiving luncheons that are ahead of us! It all seems so terribly confused and sordid.

'But I'm fifty-six, old dear, and you're fifty-one and Stephen's turned sixty and Robin's sixty-three. The children will all have to live with the messes they've made a great deal longer than we will. So I suppose it's none of our business — how they work out their own salvation. I wish I could really think so.

'ISABEL

'P.S. Write me all about the wedding — what Cicily wore and how Muriel looked, and *all* about Flora and what she had to say about Ed Brown. It's funny to think of him in a front pew at one of *our* family weddings!

'I wish you could see Belle. She looks so young and happy again.

'ISABEL'

Jane read the letter through three times and then sat staring at it in silence. She was thinking of Cicily. Of Cicily, sitting at her side on the sofa of her little French drawing-room in Lakewood and saying courageously, 'In two years' time we'll all be a great deal happier. A great deal happier than we've been for years.' It was, however, 'a dreadful modern way' to find your happiness. Jane had no sympathy with it. She did not even feel sure that Belle's engagement made matters any better. It made them worse, perhaps. More trivial, more meaningless, more like the monkey house. She would not tell Cicily, she reflected firmly, about Belle's engagement. She would not give her that satisfaction.

VIII

Three days later, when Jane entered Flora's drawing-room with Stephen, she had no particular sense that she was going to witness the consecration of a marriage. The civil rites of France that they had all subscribed to that morning had made Cicily, she conceded, Albert's lawful wife. This blessing of the Church seemed but an irrelevant afterthought. Cicily had set her heart on it, however. It was part of the party. It all went to prove that this was a very usual situation, a very gay situation, a very happy situation. It was the consummation of the friendly conspiracy of chatter.

Flora's beautiful formal room was swept and garnished for

the ceremony. It was always a little bare. The polished floor
was sparsely adorned with three small rugs. The furniture
was clustered in little social groups of chairs and sofas and
small convenient tables. A Renoir hung over the fireplace —
it was the only picture in the room — the portrait of a plump
dark lady in a red velvet gown with a shirred bustle and a
fair-haired child in a white muslin frock with a blue sash.
The room was filled with vases of white lilies and curtained
against the crude glare of the July sunshine. The perfume of
the flowers, the subdued light, the faint gleam, here and there,
of glass and gilt and parquet, the tranquillity of the Victorian
lady over the fireplace, all subtly contributed to the sense of
space and serenity that was the room's distinguishing charac-
teristic. The windows were open, their silken hangings moving a little in the gentle July breeze. The uproar of the Paris
traffic was hushed in Flora's neighbourhood. The tiny, rippling plash of some fountain in an outer court could be distinctly heard above the voices of Flora's guests.

Flora's guests were very few in number. Jane's eyes found
Cicily at once. She was at Albert's side, smiling up into the
face of a rather more than middle-aged gentleman, who was
standing, when Jane entered the drawing-room, with his back
to the door. Her gown *was* charming — a daffodil yellow
chiffon. A great straw shade hat hid her golden hair. She was
carrying a sheaf of yellow calla lilies. The three children were
being restrained by Molly in a distant corner of the room.
Robin Redbreast was scuffling on the shiny floor. To judge
by their rosy, excited faces they had no sense of the solemnity
of the occasion. Flora, in a frock of pale grey taffeta, was
talking to Ed Brown on the hearth beneath the Renoir. Ed
Brown looked very cheerful. He had a gardenia in the buttonhole of his cutaway. Muriel, in a striking new costume of
black-and-white satin, was chatting very pleasantly with the

Church of England clergyman. He was a very callow young clergyman, and he did not look entirely at his ease with Muriel. She was doing her best for him, however. She had turned the full battery of her deeply shaded, bright blue eyes upon his embarrassed countenance. Her carmined lips were smiling.

'Here you are, Jane!' cried Flora.

Cicily waved her yellow lilies. The more than middle-aged gentleman at whom she had been smiling turned as she did so. Across the slippery expanse of polished floor, Jane stared at him, astounded. She suffered a distinct sense of shock. She was back, instantly, in Chicago in the early nineties. She was back in the Duroys' little crowded living-room in the Saint James Apartments. She had two thin pigtails and a sense of social inadequacy and she was staring at Mr. Duroy! He had come! It was André! But how exactly like his father! The greying beard, the beribboned eyeglasses, the shred of scarlet silk run through the buttonhole! The wise, sophisticated gleam in the shrewd brown eyes!

The eyes were not sufficiently sophisticated, however, to veil their expression of complete astonishment. André stared at Jane. She saw the glint of amazement fade quickly from his face. A broad smile of pleasure supplanted it. It had struck her like lightning, however. She knew what it meant. She was fifty-one years old. Then André was holding both her hands in his own.

'Jane!' he was crying. 'It is really you!' Looking up at the bearded face, meeting the wise, sophisticated gleam behind the beribboned eye-glasses, Jane was desperately trying to realize that it was really André.

'And this is Stephen,' she said confusedly.

The men shook hands.. Cicily kissed her prettily over the yellow lilies. Albert tore his eyes from his bride to smile happily, reassuringly at Jane. The clergyman slipped away to get into his vestments. Cicily was taking command of the situation.

'I'll stand here near the windows,' she was saying gaily. 'I want the children near me, Molly! And you, too, Mumsy!'

André was staring at Jane. She still felt he must be Mr. Duroy. Cicily slipped her arm around her waist.

'Have you heard from Aunt Isabel?' she asked. 'Albert had a cable from Belle this noon. She was married yesterday to Billy Winter.' Her blue eyes, meeting Jane's, were twinkling with tranquil amusement. 'She wouldn't let me get ahead of her! But isn't it nice?'

The clergyman had returned. His vested figure looked strangely out of place in Flora's drawing-room.

'Come, Dad!' cried Cicily. 'You know your place by this time!'

The little company had gathered in an informal semi-circle. Stephen looked very grim as he took his stand by Cicily. Ed Brown was beaming, in step-paternal solicitude, at the ardent young face of Albert. Robin Redbreast was clinging to Molly's hand. Jane moved to put her arms around the twins. Little John Ward smiled happily up at her. André was covertly watching her, all the time, from his stand between Flora and Muriel. The Church of England clergyman opened his prayer book.

'Dearly beloved brethren,' he said, 'we are met together in the sight of God and this company to join together this man and this woman —— '

Jane turned her eyes from the flushed and radiant face of her recalcitrant daughter. She would not look at it. She could not look at it. This was worse than *any* wedding. This was worse than all the weddings. The measured tones of the clergyman's voice recalled with frightful vividness the ceremony in her little Lakewood garden. Was she the only wedding guest, Jane wondered dumbly, that saw so plainly the pleasant, snub-nosed, twinkle-eyed ghost of Jack, standing at Cicily's side?

IX

'I didn't think you'd come,' said Jane.

'Of course I came,' said André.

They were sitting side by side in a taxi that was rolling down the Avenue des Champs Élysées. Half an hour before Jane had seen Cicily depart for her honeymoon with Albert Lancaster. The parting with the children had been painfully emotional. Cicily herself had been very much moved. Little Jane had wept, and John had clung to his mother, and Robin Redbreast had tried to run after her as she paused on Albert's arm, in the doorway of Flora's apartment, to toss one last tremulous kiss to Jane.

'Well — that's over!' Stephen had said, when she had vanished. Personally Jane felt that it had just begun. The summer stretched before her with the children to watch over — the autumn with its inevitable parting—the years ahead with their adjustments and compromises. Then André had spoken.

'Are you really going to-morrow?' he had asked.

Jane had nodded.

'Then won't you come back with me, now, to my studio? I want to talk to you.'

'Oh, go, Jane!' Flora had cried. 'André's studio is awfully interesting.'

'I think,' Jane had said rather slowly, 'I'd better go back to the Chatham with Stephen. The children are dining with us, so Molly can pack.'

'Won't Stephen come, too?' said André, a little hesitantly.

'No,' said Stephen abruptly. 'I — I think I'd like to be
with the kids. But why don't *you* go, Jane?'

And André had picked up his hat. That was how Jane had
come to be with him in the taxi. She was still trying to realize
that he was really himself. It was a great waste of André, she
reflected, to have to meet him after thirty-four years at Cicily's
wedding. Her thoughts were with the grandchildren. It was
hard to concentrate on André, after all she had just been
through. Perhaps at fifty-one, however, it would always be
hard to concentrate on *any* man. At fifty-one, you were per-
petually torn by conflicting preoccupations. Meeting André's
gaze with a smile, Jane observed, a trifle whimsically, that he,
at least, had achieved concentration. His wise, sophisticated
brown eyes were bent earnestly upon her.

'You didn't *really* think I wouldn't come, did you?' said
André.

'I didn't know,' said Jane. Then added honestly, 'I didn't
want to hope too much that you would.'

'Why not?' smiled André.

'For fear of being disappointed,' said Jane promptly. 'I like
to keep my illusions.'

'Am I one of your illusions, Jane?' asked André, with a
twinkle.

'You always have been,' said Jane soberly.

André laughed at that. 'The same honest Jane!' he said, as
the taxi drew up at the curbing.

As André paid the cabman, Jane stood on the sidewalk and
wondered where she was. She stared up at the grey stone
façade of the building before her. She had not noticed where
the taxi was going. It had crossed the Seine. That was all she
knew. She felt a pleasing little sense of adventure as she followed André through some iron gates, across the corner of
a crumbling courtyard, and in a tall carved doorway that

opened on the court. A curved stone stairway stretched before her, leading up into comparative darkness. Jane's sense of adventure deepened.

'It's three flights up,' said André, 'and there is no lift.'

Jane tried not to catch her breath too audibly as she plodded up the stairs, her hand on the iron rail. Her sense of adventure had faded a little. How ignominious, she was thinking, how fifty-one, to have to puff and pant on a staircase at André's side! On the third landing he unlocked a door.

'Come in,' he said.

Jane found herself in a large light white-washed room, the walls of which were hung with charcoal sketches and lined with bronze and plaster and marble figures. A frame platform occupied the centre of the floor. On it were placed a high stool, a box of sculptor's tools, and a tall ambiguous form that was draped in a white cloth. A grand piano stood in one corner. Near it were clustered a divan, two comfortable armchairs, and a tea-table. Above them a great square window looked out over the rounded tops of an avenue of horsechestnuts, down a curving vista of narrow grey street to the Gothic portico of a little hunchbacked church. One of the tourist-free, nameless old churches, Jane thought, that you always meant to visit in Paris and never did!

'Well, how do you like it?' asked André.

'I love it,' said Jane.

She sat down in an armchair and smiled up at André. She was beginning to feel that this bearded gentleman was really the boy that she had loved. The grandchildren seemed very far away. She felt a tremulous little sense of intimacy at the thought that this was André's very own studio and that they were alone in it together.

'I do all my work here,' said André.

Jane gazed about her. The place looked very business-like.

The armchairs were worn and the divan was covered with a frayed Indian rug and a heterogeneous collection of cushions that had seen better days. The tea-set was a little dusty. Jane felt, absurdly, that she would like to wash that tea-set for André!

'Would you like some tea?' he asked.

Jane shook her head.

'I can get it,' said André. 'I live here, you know, a great deal of the time. I've a bedroom and a kitchen on the court.'

'I thought,' said Jane, 'you had a house in Paris.'

'I have,' said André, 'but my wife's not often in it. I live there, usually, when she's in town.'

His words made Jane think instantly of the older Duroys. Of Mr. Duroy, looking just like André, riding that tandem bicycle with his wife!

'André,' she said, 'where is your mother?'

'She lives in England,' said André soberly. 'Father died twenty years ago in Prague. Mother went back to my grandfather's house in Bath.'

'The one you told me about,' smiled Jane, 'in the Royal Crescent?'

'The same,' said André, answering her smile. 'Mother's seventy-three, you know. She's very active. She breezes in here every few months and washes up those teacups!' He broke off abruptly. 'Are you interested in sculpture?'

'I'm interested in yours,' said Jane.

Her eyes were wandering over the bronze and plaster and marble figures. They were charming, Jane thought. It was absurd of Cicily to call that Eve *vieux jeu!* It was absurd of Cicily to say —— Jane rose suddenly from her chair. Her gaze on the bronze and plaster and marble figures had grown a little more intent. She walked the length of the room in silence. André's nymphs and Eves and saints and Madonnas drooped on every pedestal. Soft limbs and clinging draperies met the eye at every turn. The charcoal sketches on the walls vaguely revealed the grace of feminine curves. There *was* a certain harem-like quality to André's studio! Would she have noticed it, Jane wondered, if it had not been for Cicily's cynical words in the Luxembourg Gallery? Why — it was an absolutely Adamless Eden! Except for André, of course.

'I must show you what I'm doing now,' he said suddenly. He turned toward the frame platform. 'It's a war memorial,' he explained, as he removed the cloth from the ambiguous form. 'Isn't she charming?'

She *was* charming. She was just that. Jane stared in silence at the unfinished figure — a lovely girlish angel, sheathing a broken sword over a young dead warrior. Angels should be sexless, thought Jane quickly. Over young dead warriors their wings should droop in pity, not in love.

'Isn't she charming?' repeated André. 'My angel?'

Who was she? Jane could not help thinking. It was one of those thoughts that you despised yourself for, of course.

'Yes,' she said doubtfully. 'Yes, but ——'

'But what?' smiled André.

'Not awfully — angelic.' Jane wondered, as she spoke, just why she felt that she must make her criticism articulate. It was part of the old fourteen-year-old feeling of intimacy, perhaps. The feeling that she always owed André the truth. He was smiling again a trifle ironically.

'A little earthy, you think, my angel?'

Jane nodded soberly.

'Perhaps you're right,' said André cheerfully. 'Some of my angels *have* been a little earthy, you know.'

Jane looked at André. She still had that funny feeling that she owed him the truth.

'That's too bad,' she said.

'Oh, I don't know,' said André. 'I've liked them earthy.'
Jane could not quite respond to his comical smile.

'Wasn't that — rather foolish of you?' she said slowly. She
was beginning to feel a terrible prig! André was looking at
her with a very amused twinkle in his shrewd brown eyes.

'*Qui vit sans folie n'est pas si sage qu'il croît,*' he said. 'La
Rochefoucauld said that, Jane. He was a very wise old boy.'

Jane's glance had dropped before André's twinkle.

'Yes,' she said slowly, 'but ——'

'But what?' said André again.

Jane's eyes were on his hands. She had felt a little shock of
recognition when she looked at them. Hands did not change
as faces did, she thought. André's were still the strong sculptor's hands of his boyhood. Prig or no prig, Jane felt an inexplicable impulse to give André good advice.

'André,' she said solemnly, 'you ought to snap out of all this.
Leave Paris. Go out to the provinces and forget the earthy
angels. You've still got twenty years ahead of you.' André
was smiling at her very amusedly, but Jane was not abashed.
'You ought to come back to the corn belt, André. I know that
seems ridiculous, but it's true. Come back to the corn belt
and do a bronze of Lincoln. Spend a winter in Springfield,
Illinois, and get to know the rail-splitter. It would do you
good.'

He shook his head. 'It's not in my line,' he said. 'I tried a
bronze of Foch last year. I had a good commission, but I
couldn't get interested.'

'You *would* get interested,' urged Jane, 'if you really worked
at it. You get interested in anything you actually experience.'

Again André's smile was very much amused. But rather
tender.

'It's thirty-four years since I last saw you, Jane,' he said.
'What have *you* experienced?'

He had dismissed the subject. He spoke as if to a child. Jane suddenly felt very young and virginal, but just a little irritated.

'I've experienced Stephen,' she said briefly.

'That all, Jane?' asked André. Under his ironic eye Jane felt far from confidential. She succumbed to an impulse to dismiss a subject herself.

'Of course,' she said.

'I wonder,' said André gallantly. But the gallantry was not very convincing. He did not seem incredulous. Jane was not surprised. She knew, of course, that she did not look any longer like the kind of woman who had ever experienced anything very much.

'But if it's true,' continued André lightly, 'don't let it trouble you. *L'amour fait passer le temps, le temps fait passer l'amour.* It all comes to the same thing in the end, Jane, whatever we experience.'

Jane stared at him, appalled. He was pulling the cloth back over his earthy angel. He seemed quite unconscious of the significance of his utterance. Of the significance of the lesson that he had learned from life. Jane did not feel young and virginal and irritated any longer. She felt fifty-one years old and quite stripped of illusion. But very sorry for André.

'I must go,' she said. 'I must go back to Stephen.' The grandchildren seemed much nearer than they had twenty minutes before. André smiled pleasantly at her as she preceded him out of the studio.

'I loved seeing your angel,' said Jane politely.

They descended the stairs together in silence. They crossed the crumbling courtyard and went out through the iron gates. André whistled for a taxi. Jane could not think of anything more to say to him. She was thinking of the faith that she had kept with the lover of her girlhood. *'L'amour fait passer le*

temps, le temps fait passer l'amour.' Jane wished very sincerely
that André had stayed in the French Alps. She wished that
she had never come to his studio. The taxi rolled up to the
curb. André handed her into it.

'Good-bye,' said Jane.

'*Au revoir*,' said André. He *did* look exactly like his father —
in spite of the earthy angels! 'It's been great to see you, Jane!'

'Good-bye,' said Jane again. She smiled and nodded gaily.
The taxi rolled off down the curving vista of the narrow grey
street. It tooted its horn and turned abruptly at the Gothic
portico of the little hunchbacked church. The quai, the
Seine, the Isle Saint-Louis and the towers of Notre Dame
swung quickly into view. The day was fading into a sunset
haze. But Jane was not thinking of the view. She was thinking of how things turned out. Of the inevitable disillusion of
life.

'It all comes to the same thing in the end, Jane, whatever
we experience.' But that was not true. That was a very falla-
cious philosophy! For, obviously, you did not come to the
same thing in the end, yourself. You were, eventually, the
product of your experience.

Jane's mind returned to the problems of her children. If
she had had Cicily's courage of conviction, she reflected with
a dawning twinkle, she might have married André and remarried Stephen and run away with Jimmy. Her life might
have been the more interesting for those forbidden experi-
ments. But she would not have been the same Jane at fifty-
one. Not that Jane thought so much of the Jane she was. Or
did she? Did you not always, Jane asked herself honestly,
think a little too tenderly of the kind of person that you had
turned out to be?

Cicily had been right about one thing. You had to choose
in life. And perhaps you never gave up anything except what

some secret self-knowledge whispered that you did not really care to possess. But no, thought Jane! She had made her sacrifices in agony of spirit. She had made them in simplicity and sincerity and because of that curious inner scruple that Matthew Arnold had defined — that 'enduring power, not ourselves, which makes for righteousness.' But to what end?

For Cicily had been right about another thing. You did not know — you could not ever tell — just where the path you had not taken would have led you. Cicily and Albert, on their way to Russia, were very happy. Belle and Billy were happy in Murray Bay. Jack, stringing his telephone wires and building his bridges down near Mexico City, was well on the road, perhaps, to a more enduring happiness than he had ever known before. The six children, Jane was prepared to admit, would probably fare quite as well at the hands of five affectionate parents as they had at the hands of four. Jane could not conscientiously claim that the world was any the worse for Cicily's bad behaviour.

To what end, then, did you struggle to live with dignity and decency and decorum? To play the game with the cards that were dealt you? Was it only to cultivate in your own character that intangible quality that Jane, for want of a better word, had defined as grace? Was it only to feel self-respectful on your deathbed? That seemed a barren reward.

'I have lived and accomplished the task that Destiny gave me, and now I shall pass beneath the earth no common shade.' Dido had said that. Across the years Dido had said that to Jane and Agnes on the Johnsons' little front porch 'west of Clark Street.' Jane could remember thinking it was 'nice and proud.' Dido's niceness and her pride had illumined the difficult hexameters of Virgil's 'Æneid.' They had burned with a brighter light than the flames of her funeral pyre.

The reward, however, still seemed a trifle barren. To pass

beneath the earth no common shade. That romantic prospect was not as inviting to Jane at fifty-one as it had been at sixteen. A place in the hierarchy of heaven seemed rather unimportant. Jane felt a little weary, facing an immortality that would prove in the end only one more social adventure. She would prefer oblivion.

But André had not been right about experience. If André had married Jane and settled down in Lakewood, he would not have been the bearded cynic he was at fifty-three. Wives had a lot to do with it. It was Cyprienne — and the earthy angels, of course — Jane thought indulgently, who had made André what he was to-day. '*L'amour fait passer le temps, le temps fait passer l'amour!*' What words to hear from the lips of the man whose romantic memory you had been tenderly cherishing for thirty-four years! From the lips of the boy who had walked so bravely, so proudly out of your youth down Victorian Pine Street! Jane was thinking again of the inevitable disillusion of life. Was it inevitable, she wondered? If Jimmy had lived, would he be as dead as André?

x

But Stephen had lived and he was still very much alive. That consoling thought struck Jane the moment that she entered the little green sitting-room in the Chatham Hotel, and she felt distinctly cheered by it. Stephen was sitting between the twins on the Empire sofa, with Robin Redbreast on his knees. He looked cheerfully up at Jane over the book he was reading. Jane recognized it at once. It was the familiar copy of the King Arthur Stories, from their library at home. Stephen must have taken it from the shelf, Jane thought swiftly, and packed it in his trunk for the grandchildren without saying anything to her about it. Stephen *was* a darling! Husbands had a lot to do with it, too, of course. Stephen had

had a lot to do with the sort of Jane Jane found herself at fifty-one. Facing Stephen and the grandchildren she felt a little ashamed of her recent preoccupation with André and with Jimmy.

'Go on,' she said. 'Don't stop reading.' She sank into a chair. The children wriggled their approval.

Stephen's eyes returned to the book. 'We're just finishing,' he said.

Jane knew the story well. It was the first adventure of Sir Percival in the Forest of Arroy. The boyish Sir Percival — Jane's favourite knight. She had heard Stephen read it innumerable times to Cicily, Jenny, and Steve. Years ago now, of course, though it seemed only yesterday. When she closed her eyes, Jane lost all sense of time. She lost all sense of the grandchildren. When Jane closed her eyes, she was no longer in Paris. But she was not in the Forest of Arroy. She was back once more in the Lakewood living-room, and Stephen was sitting in his armchair with the children around him, and Cicily's hair was long and crinkly, and Jenny's round forehead was topped with her Alice in Wonderland comb, and Steve was wearing his first sailor suit.

How odd it was, thought Jane, that children grew up so unexpectedly. On looking back down the years, you could not see just what you had done — just what you had let them do that —— And once they had escaped you, what was there to say to them? But Stephen was finishing the story of Sir Percival.

'"And as it was with Sir Percival in that first adventure, so may you meet with a like success when you ride forth upon your first undertakings after you have entered into the glory of your knighthood, with your life lying before you and a whole world whereinto you may freely enter to do your devoirs to the glory of God and your own honour."'

There it was in a nutshell. That was all there was for parents to say to children. You could bring them up according to your lights, but in the end you could only watch them ride forth and wish them well. And parents should remember, Jane admitted with a sigh, that the whole world should be freely entered, and that the idea of devoirs was apt to differ in successive generations.

Stephen closed the book. Robin Redbreast wriggled off his knee. Little John Ward's eyes were shining. His sister's face, however, looked a trifle wistful. Perhaps she had not been listening so very attentively.

'I wonder,' she said slowly, 'I wonder where Mother is now.'

Stephen's eyes met Jane's. 'I was thinking,' he said, 'we might all go out to the theatre this evening.'

'*All* of us?' cried little Jane. Her eyes were shining now like John Ward's.

'All of us,' said Stephen solemnly.

'Not Robin Redbreast?' said John Ward.

'Yes, Robin Redbreast,' said Stephen.

The twins began jumping up and down in ecstasy. Robin Redbreast's four-year-old countenance was stupefied with delight. It was fun to please children. You could please them so easily. Nevertheless, Jane looked inquiringly at Stephen.

'There's a company reviving the Gilbert and Sullivan operas at the Comédie des Champs Élysées,' said Stephen. 'I found it in the Paris "Herald." To-night they're playing "The Mikado."'

The twins' jumps had accelerated into a spirited game of tag. They were chasing Robin Redbreast around the Empire sofa. Stephen, King Arthur stories in hand, had risen to his feet. He was looking indulgently at his grandchildren and humming a little tune. He did not know the words, of course.

Stephen never knew the words of anything! But Jane knew them. She walked over to Stephen and put her arm through his.

Robin Redbreast had collided with the centre table. He promptly fell down, and little Jane fell over him and John Ward triumphantly tagged her on an uplifted ankle. Stephen was still looking indulgently at his grandchildren and he was still humming his tune. The grimness, Jane realized suddenly, had quite faded from his face. Jane's eyes returned to the twins and Robin Redbreast. The unspoken words of Stephen's tune were ringing in her ears:

> 'Everything is a source of fun,
>   Nobody's safe, for we care for none,
>   Life is a joke that's just begun —— '

When you looked at a child, Jane reflected solemnly, you could never believe that it would grow up to disappoint you.

THE END

CPSIA information can be obtained at www.ICGtesting.com
Printed in the USA
241964LV00001B/8/A